The Daughters of Ironbridge

Mollie Walton has always been fascinated by history and on a trip to Shropshire, while gazing down from the iron bridge, found the inspiration for her debut saga novel, *The Daughters of Ironbridge*.

Also by Mollie Walton:
The Secrets of Ironbridge
The Orphan of Ironbridge

The Daughters of Ironbridge

MOLLIE WALTON

ZAFFRE

First published in Great Britain in 2019 by
ZAFFRE
An imprint of Bonnier Books UK
4th Floor, Victoria House,
Bloomsbury Square,
London WC1B 4DA
Owned by Bonnier Books
Sveavägen 56, Stockholm, Sweden

A CIP catalogue record for this book is available from the British Library.

PAPERBACK ISBN: 978-1-78576-763-0

Also available as an ebook

7 9 10 8

Typeset by IDSUK (Data Connection) Ltd
Printed and bound in Great Britain by Clays Ltd, Elcograf S.p.A.

MIX
Paper from responsible sources
FSC® C018072

Zaffre is an imprint of Bonnier Books UK
www.bonnierbooks.co.uk

To my lovely Mam, my compass in fair weather or foul.

Prologue

The iron bridge glimmered in the moonlight. A woman trudged across it, carrying a precious package. She could barely walk, one foot dragging as she struggled to place it before the other, dry leaves crisping underfoot, her pale face wincing with every step. She peered up at the full moon, took some distant hope from it and looked down at the face of her child, asleep in her arms, wrapped in rags. She tucked the cloth tighter around her tiny baby, trying to protect it as best she could from the autumn chill. She could feel its bones. It was thin, too thin and too quiet. She had given her child every ounce of milk she could but it had dried up. She was too hungry herself to nourish her child. Weak and exhausted, she knew she could not go much further. With all of her will, she reached the centre of the bridge. The centrepiece stated the date it was built: 1779. Fifty-five years ago, just over a half century, since the town itself began to bloom alongside its namesake. Her master had been a boy then, a spoilt boy no doubt; that family always spoiled their children. It was why they all turned out that way, all turned out bad. She looked down at her babe in arms again.

'Not you, little'un,' she whispered, her throat hoarse from thirst. 'You'll be different. You'll be sunlight, not moonlight.'

She kissed her child's head and looked up at the imposing mansion, built on iron money, that loomed above the town, above the bridge, above them all. If only she could keep going. But her legs were now as heavy and immovable as stone. She had come to the limit of her endurance, the final shred of her strength gone. She heard footsteps. She looked up to see a man in a broad hat walking purposefully across the bridge. He was coming towards her and he was talking to her.

'Good woman,' he was saying, 'can I assist 'ee?'

Good woman, she thought. *I was a good girl, once.* Her thighs were shaking. She felt her knees buckle. 'Will you help me, sir?' she croaked. 'Please, hold my baby as I canna stand no longer.'

The man, who she now saw wore the simple, curious clothes of a Quaker, came to her quickly and took the child. The moment the weight of her warm bundle was lifted from her, it was as if her body knew before her mind did that it was time to rest. She felt her legs give way and the bridge came up quickly, the ground smacking her face with a hard, iron slap. She heard her child whimper in the kind man's arms. It was the last sound she heard.

Chapter 1

Fire and smoke, suffocating and infernal, reached up into the sky, staining it red and black for miles around. A traveller approaching Ironbridge and Coalbrookdale would be met with the wonder of it and stop to stare. The blast furnace belched with heat and life all day and all night, the whole year round. Men fed its mouth with fuel, men like John Woodvine, furnace fillers who nourished the monster to try and meet its hunger, but it was never satisfied. Always, the furnace wanted more. They filled the barrows with coke, iron ore and limestone, pushed them out along a gangway and tipped the charge into the boiling throat of the furnace. Inside, the heat did its magical work and out came molten iron in the cast-house below. Around them, the fire, smoke and gas billowed and blinded them.

A shift at the furnace was twelve hours of hard labour and in the heat of this summer, it was hard indeed. John Woodvine thought to himself, and not for the first time, *It'll be summat like this in Hell.* John would come home filthy with smut and ash and so exhausted of limb and heart, his wife Rachel and his daughter Anny barely had a word from him before he collapsed on their hard bed. Rachel would wake him to eat before he fell back into a dead sleep again till the birds about their cottage sang and day had come, then he would have to start it all again. Excepting Sundays, his one day of rest, when he could talk to Rachel and watch Anny grow and giggle, sweet child that she was.

'Woodvine!' shouted the foreman. 'Stop your dreaming, mon!'

John shook his head to rid it of his daydreams. A moment of distraction in this awful, dangerous place could be fatal. Men were injured here; blinded, lost fingers, lost arms, received dreadful burns from fire, steam or hot metal, suffocated, bruised and battered, limbs crushed. Some never recovered to work again; some died. You had to have your wits about you. He looked about him, focused his eyes and forced himself to concentrate. But he had a bad feeling that something was amiss.

'Look out, there!' someone shouted and John whipped around, terrified of what terrible thing was coming this time.

Anny looked at her fingers. They were red raw from scrubbing clothes. They had welts from carrying the buckets back from the water pump, a third of a mile away. They were not even her clothes, or her parents' clothes either. Her mother took in washing to make ends meet. Anny did not go to school. She had been working for three years now, since she was nine years old. She looked up at her mother, careworn and sweating in the heat of a hot June day, as she pushed a shirt through the mangle, huffing and puffing.

'Let me do that for you, Mother,' Anny said and went to her, but her mother shook her head.

'I worry about your fingers,' she said, and shooed her daughter away. 'I canna have you losing your fingers.'

'Dunna be daft, I'm turned twelve. I anna got little fingers anymore.'

Her mother looked up at her and smiled. 'You're right. I always think of you as my babby. But you're a young lady now.'

Anny smiled then saw her mother's face fall. What was she thinking about, that made her sad? 'What is it?'

'Just thinking that I wish I could give you more, Anny.'

'But you give me everything. You give me all your love, every day. And you feed me and keep me warm.' She wiped the sweat from her brow. 'Leastways, too warm, sometimes!'

They laughed. But her mother was still frowning. 'And you taught me to read and write when everyone said what's the point of it, for a lass like me? But you did it anyway.'

'Yes, well, maybe they were right. What can you do with your book learning here? I was learnt to do it by my mother. But what could I ever do with mine, in this house, with these piles of washing ever biding for me and never seeming to lessen?'

'It's good we have plenty of washing. Because washing means money and that means we'll be all right.'

Her mother smiled proudly at her. 'Always the sharp one. Oh, but I wish you could be a lady, Anny. A proper lady like that Margaret King. You were born in the same month, in the same year. I wish I coulda given you everything she had.'

Anny wrinkled her nose in disgust. 'Oh, I wouldna want her life. Not all that curtseying and how-do-you-do. I wanna be here with you and Father.'

'Oh, your father! Your father's bait!' cried her mother. 'His slice of pie is there on the side. He forgot it this morning. Run and take it to him. He'll be clemmed without it.'

Anny grabbed the cloth-wrapped slice of fidget pie, his favourite. Her mother lovingly made a portable dinner for her father six days a week. It might be a slab of rabbit or pigeon pie, or if times were hard it would be filled with crow or sparrow. Or it might only be a Dawley doorstep, simply a hunk of bread spread with butter or sometimes cheese. Or if a pig they had shares in had been butchered, it might be his favourite: a thick wedge of the gammon, apple, tatties and onion pie he loved so much.

'You'd best hurry, lass!' cried her mother, but Anny wanted to do one thing before she went. She grabbed a stubby pencil from the stool beside the hearth where she would sit and write stories and poems of an evening. Taking a scrap of paper her parents saved up to purchase for her, she scribbled a quick note: *I love you more than anything, even more than cake!* She slipped the note inside the cloth and sped from the room.

Anny was thrilled to be away from the endless washing and the heat inside their tiny house. She ran across the dusty yard, their home flanked by six other dwellings shoved up against each other. She thought, *It's as if those builders wanted us poor folk to take up as little room in the world as we can*. Some of the neighbourhood wives outside their tiny houses looked up and saw her whisk by. One neighbour, Mary Malone, taking the scraps out for the pig, called to her, 'Lucky littl'un!' ribbing her for escaping work. 'Where are you heading, lass?'

'There and back to see how far it is!' cried Anny, and ran off. It was a bit bold, but folk didn't seem to mind her kind of cheek. They liked her clever replies. And people liked to smile at her. Her father always said she was a laughing lass, a kind one and sweet-natured. She knew she was not overly pretty, but she had an open, friendly face dotted with freckles. Her beauty was all in her thick red hair, as her mother would say, the colour of a fox's coat. She was clever like a fox too, though never sly. Some said that Woodvine girl was too clever for her own good.

Her mother had taught her to read and write. She had some ambition for Anny, but often said she could not see how any of them could escape the narrow confines of their situation as poor ironworkers. Her parents told Anny she was a ray of sunshine in that dark world of iron ore and coal dust and endless toil. Despite the hard work at home, Anny was always cheerful and took her greatest pleasure in anything that used her mind.

'Dear heart,' her mother would call her sometimes. 'One day you'll escape this place for good.' But Anny didn't want to escape it. Despite everything, she loved her life here by the river. As she moved through the trees towards the water, the air buzzed with summer heat and insect life. Butterflies fluttered along the banks of yellow and pink weeds blooming haphazardly along the riverbanks. On the river itself, a variety of craft passed by, barges, trows and wherries carrying people and produce and the odd circular coracle paddled by a fisherman apiece. The shouts of watermen and the clangour of the forges downstream rang along the banks, muffled only slightly in the thicker parts of the wood. The water flowed smugly along, lazy and warm that day. It seemed proud of itself, how it made life here possible for every living thing – water voles, rats, otters, ducks, moorhen, snipe, chub, shad and elvers – as well as the people who needed it to survive. For the mighty River Severn provided folk with water to drink and wash with, also transporting the goods and materials that industry swallowed and vomited out into the world from this leafy, deep-wooded part of Shropshire.

Anny trotted along the river path, enjoying her burst of freedom from the toil of washing. But her fun was short-lived, for the air grew thicker as she approached the furnace, filled with heat and the stink of industry. Soon she saw the blast furnace, set up above the riverbank, belching out cruel fire into the already sticky warmth of the summer afternoon, and the racket of the ironworks was roaring over her.

Anny climbed up the bank to gasp at the furnace. It never ceased to amaze her. She thought it awful, in the true sense of the word: a thing of awe. She was proud her father worked there. His seemed an important job, a vital one, sending iron out into the world to make pots and pans, railings and boot scrapers, hearths and grates, benches and balusters, window frames and sills, eaves and gutters, even bridges and boats. She clutched her father's lunch and stared at the crimson flames, felt the blast of heat in her face, before looking down to scan the figures around and about, searching for her father. But there was a big group of men all bent over something in the yard before the furnace, some shaking their heads, some waving their hands in distress, calling out to others who came running. Something was wrong. Something had happened.

Her pride in her father's work replaced with terror, she ran across to the huddle of ironworkers and tried to peer through the gaps between their backs. Someone was on the ground. She could see a man's legs poking out. They were still, very still.

'Who is it?' she said, but nobody could hear her little, high voice behind them. So there was nothing for it but to thump on the backs of the men closest to her. She simply had to get through this wall of men to see who was on the ground. Her fists pummelled them as she cried out, 'Let me through!' The bodies parted and she heard gruff shouts of 'What's this?' and 'Oi!' but she didn't care. She simply must know. She saw the man's naked chest, slicked with sweat, smut and matted hair and then, with a horrible shock, saw the bloody mess of his arm, burned and crushed. His arm was destroyed. But she had no time to be horrified, no time to feel sick or look away. She peered at his face, turned away from her, covered with black. They often joked that all ironworkers looked the same, their features disguised by filth when they worked. She bent over the man's face and felt her heart leap into her mouth. *Was it him? Was it Father?*

Chapter 2

Slap! Hard and swift, right across Margaret's cheek, catching a tooth against her lip, so she knew it would bleed afterwards.

'You will go to Grandfather's wake, you little wretch. And if you tell Papa I hit you, I will deny it and you know he always believes me over you.'

Margaret dabbed her fingers against her mouth and there it was: blood. She looked at her elder brother Cyril who saw the blood too and smirked proudly. He took pride in his ability to maim and wound, to hurt others in any way he saw fit.

'Now clean yourself up and present yourself downstairs forthwith. You're an embarrassment to this family.'

Cyril turned on his heel and left the room, leaving the door open, as even door-shutting was beneath him. Margaret stood up from her bed and closed the door, catching a glimpse of a maid, Lucy, who gave her a quick, sad but understanding smile. She wanted to run to Lucy, even though she did not really know the girl. Lucy had a nice face and she felt Lucy would understand her and sympathise with her. Margaret had seen Cyril shout at Lucy, too, so she knew the girl must feel the same. But it was forbidden by her father to converse beyond what was strictly necessary with the servants. As an iron-master, Mr King would not countenance fraternisation between his daughter and that other breed of person, a lowly servant. Even the ironworkers were beneath him. He conducted all his business with them through his estate manager, Mr Brotherton, a chatty man with red cheeks whose booming voice frightened Margaret a little, though he was friendly. Lots of things frightened her. Margaret knew what a bitter disappointment she was to her father, knew she had caused great harm to the family, killing her mother in childbirth and thus was born cursed. She carried the weight of that daily.

'Now then,' she tried to comfort herself, inspecting her cheek in the dressing table mirror. She could powder it to cover the red mark. The bloody lip would be impossible to hide. She'd have to invent another clumsy fall, all too easily believed by her father. Her face powdered, she said aloud, 'That'll have to do.' She talked to herself from time to time, mostly because there was nobody else to talk to.

She left her bedroom and crept down the stairs, the hubbub of her grandfather's wake drifting up to her, filling her with her usual dread of social occasions. She liked gentle people, talking quietly to quiet folk. But her family's gatherings were always noisy, full of loud-mouthed relatives, sharp-faced and unforgiving. She knew she wasn't like them and she knew she was a disappointment. As she approached the door to the drawing room, she steeled herself and turned the handle. As usual, nobody noted her entrance and she was able to slink over to a chair in the corner without incident. The room was populated by a crowd of relatives all dressed in black, holding cups and saucers or tiny plates of cucumber sandwiches and thin slices of fruit cake. Her father – Mr Ralph King – was holding forth about his father – Mr Ralph King senior – who had been buried that morning. Margaret had not loved her grandfather. He was a bullying man. A few months ago he had had a funny turn and since then had been bedbound and wordless, with staring, accusing green eyes that disturbed her. Her father was saying what a great man he was, a pillar of the community. 'Beloved of nobleman and commoner alike,' said Mr King.

'Beloved? Stuff and nonsense. Not even I liked him. And I was his wife!'

An embarrassed silence fell over the room and Margaret stared at her grandmother, Alice King, the matriarch of the family and now its oldest member.

'After all, I only told him yesterday that he was a cold man, an iceberg of a man. He had no feelings. Like stone. Like ice. I told him that. Only yesterday.'

Nobody spoke. Awkward glances were swapped. Her husband had died over a week before. Grandmother could be sharp and cutting. But Margaret admired her for her straight-talking, no-nonsense approach to life. She wished so much that she was more like her. They said that when she married into the King family, she ruled it so imperiously that she earned the nickname Queenie, and it had stayed with her ever since. Margaret was a little afraid of her grandmother's moods, but Queenie was the only member of her family she could talk to. Their conversations were often brief, but at least her grandmother made time for her every now and then. At least Queenie did not seem so very disappointed in her shyness – she did not indulge it – but she seemed content to let Margaret be watchful and quiet, without punishing her for it, as her father and brother did.

'Mother . . .' Mr King began. When he pleaded with his mother, Margaret noticed that her father's voice was high and whining, which made her smile to herself. Only Queenie could bully Ralph King. This gave Margaret pleasure. She liked her grandmother, though she was somewhat odd, it had to be said.

'Mother nothing. He was a nasty old goat. Everybody knew it. Everybody is thinking it, but nobody has the nerve to say it. I'm glad he's dead. And so are you, Ralph. We all are. Good riddance to him. Now then, where are my meringues? I specifically asked Cook for some little hazelnut meringues.'

Queenie's latest rant over, the guests resumed their hushed discussions, now peppered with smirks at the way the great Mr King could never control his mother. Margaret watched them – utterly ignored and content to be so – wondering how people performed this magical feat called conversation. If she could master it, perhaps she could find a friend. But, schooled at home and with only a cruel brother for company, kept closeted away from the world and its ruffians and blackguards – as her father described it – there wasn't much chance of that.

Once the guests had departed, Margaret watched her father standing proudly before the fireplace, his shoulders back, his chest puffed out and his stomach sticking out the furthest before him. He was pleased with himself. The wake had largely been a success. The Mayor of the borough and his wife had attended, as well as a clutch of other local dignitaries. The service had been suitably sombre and the weather had held. She imagined Father would be most pleased that no summer rain had caused his new shoes to become muddied. He glanced over at his mother and his gaze narrowed. He would be annoyed at her, for embarrassing him. Margaret guessed her father had been hoping Queenie would have retired from a fit of fatigue, yet she had chosen to stay – nobody could tell Queenie what to do – but only because there were some hazelnut meringues left. 'She could eat and eat and never get fat,' he would say of his mother, with envy.

Then she saw her father pass his hand over his own rounded stomach and glance at his pretty young wife, Benjamina. This was the woman he had married two years ago, twenty years his junior. She was only nineteen years of age now, only seven years older than Margaret and five years older than Cyril. The Mayor had not been able to take his eyes off her. Her father smiled smugly, then breathed out quite sharply. Margaret wondered if he felt his trousers pinch under his bloated stomach.

Her father turned to look upon his beloved son. *My little prince*, her father would fondly call him. Cyril gazed up at him, awaiting his father's next words. Cyril's blond, unruly curls framed his permanently red, round cheeks. He was short of stature for fourteen, and Father sometimes told him he was 'a bit of a runt'. Cyril was slim and lithe, yet Father once said, 'I shall have to watch your treats. I can't have a fat hog of a son.' But despite his critical remarks from time to time, the boy seemed to fawn over him.

Then her father turned to look straight at her and grimaced. Whenever he noticed her, he made a face like that. She lowered her eyes, staring at her hands in her lap. She knew she was not unpleasant to look at. She could never be as handsome as Benjamina, of course, but she was considered quite pretty. She had the same blonde curls as her brother, yet much larger eyes. But she knew her lack of social graces was a bitter disappointment to her father. He said to her once, 'When you are a bit older, you'll have plenty of suitors. You are rich, after all. But will you be able to speak a word to them? Nobody wants a wife as silent as the grave. A quiet one, yes. That is agreeable. Nobody wants a scold. But not one who couldn't say boo to a goose. What am I going to do with you?'

Sometimes she wondered if he might prefer it if she never married. That way, she could wait upon him and Benjamina as they got older. She would stay in this house for the rest of his life, a useful nursemaid. Best of all, being family, there was no need to pay her a wage. The thought of such a fate sickened her. If only her mother had survived. Her poor mother, who had died bringing her into the world.

Her mother was a shadowy figure in her life, as her father never spoke of her. All she'd heard from him was that she was a 'weak, yellow-haired girl'. What a cruel description for the person who had been the centre of his world, who haunted Margaret with her loss. She thought she might cry then, as she considered her real mother, dying in childbed, lost forever. She wanted to slip away and go to her room, and weep quietly, alone.

But her father was clearing his throat, ready to make a pronouncement. Her grandfather used to stand just there and make those regularly. Now it was her father's turn, and how gratifying it must be for him, to step into his dead father's place and be the man of the family at long last.

'My children,' he began, closing his eyes for a moment to savour their attention. 'There is undoubted sadness at my father's passing, which I am sure you both feel keenly too. But I must say that this is also a new beginning for us all. For myself, it is an opportunity to honour his memory, to prove myself worthy and take his place in society, that of one of the original and most powerful ironmasters in Shropshire.'

'Oh yes, Papa,' said Cyril. 'And I will take your place in years to come. Three proud generations of great and mighty gentlemen.'

'That is the right and true way of things,' simpered Benjamina, a picture in the latest fashions, lolling on the chaise longue. She could always be relied upon to agree with him. Margaret watched her stepmother pet her horrid little dog, a hot-tempered King Charles Spaniel called Chloe. She'd tried so hard to like her stepmother, as Benjamina was the only mother she had ever known. But this child-woman was as much like a doll as any woman who ever lived. She was in love with her lapdog and adored it more than anything else, apart from dresses and ribbons, and little cakes and sweets. Perhaps the worst thing about Benjamina was that she was another voice in the house that echoed Mr King's every whim. Margaret knew that wives must obey their husbands, but Benjamina's simpering ways seemed somehow false. She wondered what really went on in that empty head of hers. They rarely spoke to each other, because they had not a word in common. Margaret despised her. In fact, as she looked about her close family, she realised with a pang how much she hated all of them – excepting

Queenie – and then she felt guilty about such thoughts. But the truth remained: her family was dreadful and it made her ache with loneliness.

'Hmph!' began Queenie. Margaret turned to her with interest, eager to see what her disreputable grandmother would come out with next. "There was nothing great about him. He was a sneak and a liar. Just ask the baby on the bridge. See what the baby on the bridge would have to say about this 'great' man, eh?'

'Enough, Mother!' shouted Mr King, then checked himself. 'Perhaps it is time for an afternoon nap.'

'I do not nap!' said Queenie, with disgust. Everybody knew she did have unofficial naps all the time, but never admitted it as she seemed to see it as a sign of weakness.

'Then perhaps you have consumed too much sugar and it has addled your brain. The things you come up with, I really don't know. Some might say they were the ramblings of an eccentric woman. You'll have to be careful, or others would say you need to be put away.'

Queenie turned her head sharply and narrowed her eyes at her son. 'Whatever you think of yourself, you will never do that to me. I control the money in this house. This house itself and everything in it belong to me, not you. And I have the controlling interest in the iron business, too. Never forget that. That was the meat of your father's will and well you know it. Despite being a weak and selfish man, he never liked you, and he trusted me. He knew I had a mind for business. So watch your step, my son. You and everything you think you own belong to me.'

Queenie's eyes were full of fire. But in a moment, she sighed and suddenly did look very tired. Lately she had that way, of being feisty and defiant, then losing interest in it all and changing her mind. Maybe she was a little touched after all, thought Margaret. But then she thought of this 'baby on the bridge'. Margaret had heard Queenie speak of this before in recent months, only ever a brief mention and a hint of something bad. Her father always reacted angrily, then twisted the subject. Margaret had once plucked up the courage to ask her grandmother, who was the baby on the bridge? But Queenie had just smiled, tapped her nose with one long, bony finger and said, 'That's for the squirrels to know.'

Margaret watched Queenie leave the room, accompanied by her lady's maid, Jenkins. Now was the time for her to slip out, too, but she knew her father would tell her off if she didn't formally ask permission. She noticed Cyril had already left a few minutes before, bored of his elders and free to come and go as he pleased.

'May I leave now, Papa? I am suffering from one of my headaches,' she said quietly.

'If you must, Margaret. You let me down again today. You did not even attempt to converse with our visitors. You really must improve yourself, or people will say you are indeed the weakling strain of the family.'

Her stepmother tittered.

'May I go?' Margaret whispered, desperate to escape.

'Yes, yes.' Her father dismissed her with a wave of his hand.

She left the room, crossed the hall and slipped outside into the courtyard. Her split lip was throbbing. Nobody had even noticed her injury, or at least no one had commented upon it. She was thankful for this, as she was not a confident liar and if she told the truth about Cyril, he would only make her pay for it later. But it left her feeling hollow, too, that nobody cared enough to ask after her. She tried to be a good girl, to do the things her father demanded of her. She did not defy him or anyone in the household for that matter. She was polite and helpful at all times. She tried not to get in anyone's way, even the servants. But she never received any credit for these virtues. They were silent graces, she supposed. Not so easy to hear as fawning and flattery. It was as if her true self were invisible, a ghost of a girl in her own home, her own life. Time for a walk. Anything to get away from that house, that family. To find a moment's peace.

She was permitted to take a turn about the gardens. She was not permitted to stray any further than that. Her father had expressly forbidden her from entering the woods 'where the common people go'. She had walked about the grounds so often these past years, she knew every bush, every flower, every blade of grass in the place. Beyond the boundaries lay the woods, the river below. How she longed to wander there, free of the pull of the house, of her family. But she never had.

What was stopping her, really? Would anyone notice if she strayed from the grounds for a half hour? She looked behind her at the windows of Southover, blank like blind eyes. Nobody was there. It wouldn't hurt, would it, just to have a quick look? There was no wall to climb over, no door to unlock. Just a quick step across the deep borders and around the boundary trees and she would be into the woods, deep, dark and unknown, as mysterious as an enchanted forest to Margaret. Many times she had thought of it, many times she had been too nervous to defy her father. But today, her hatred of her home and everyone in it was strong and the pull of the wilderness beyond equally so. Margaret decided to allow herself this small act of defiance. Today she would go into the forest. And explore.

Chapter 3

'Anny!'

She whipped round and looked up.

'Anny, get away from there!'

'Oh, Father!' she cried and threw herself at him, felt his strong arms wrap around her like they always had, ever since she was tiny and he could toss her into the air like straw. She was too big for that now – tall, lanky and a bit clumsy, as the other children often reminded her. But her father was tall, too, and he lifted her up off the ground and took her away from that place, that huddle of workers and the man with the ruined arm on the ground. He put her down away from the scene, nearer the river in a quieter place where they could talk.

'What're you doing here? You shouldna be seeing this, wench.'

'I thought it was you, Father. Oh, I'm so glad it inna you!'

She hugged him again, then added, 'That sounds wrong. That poor man. Is he . . . dead?'

Her father nodded, his eyes straying to the body on the ground. 'He was from Broseley. Three chillun at home. He was only young.'

Neither spoke. Anny thought about the children, who would never know their father. And what would happen to their mother now? *I'm still glad it inna my father,* she thought, then wondered if she were wicked, thinking like that.

'Here,' she said, and passed him the lunch she had brought, almost forgotten about in the drama. 'Open it.'

'I've lost my appetite,' he said, grimly.

'Just open it up, please?'

He did so and out slipped the note. He smiled, despite himself and the gravity of the scene.

'Oh, Anny, you silly wench. What does it say? You know I canna read a word of it.'

A man in a hat approached them. It was the foreman, Mr Pritchard. He was a nice man, despite being over her father. He never had airs and graces and he was fair with the men. Today he looked rather grim.

'Drodsome business,' said Father.

'Yes, bad business. We'll need to let the master know. He'll want an inquiry. But it's Mr King senior's funeral today. He won't want to be bothered with this. But he'll have to be. Oh, hell.' Pritchard drew his hand across his sweaty face, smudging the dirt, sighing all the while. Then he looked down at Anny and smiled. People always smiled at Anny. But then his face changed, when he remembered where he was and what he had to do.

'Hello there, Anny. You shouldn't be here, not now.'

'I just brought Father's bait. And a note.'

Pritchard looked to Woodvine's hands and saw the note there. 'A note, eh? You can read and write, can you, Anny?'

'Oh yes,' she beamed proudly. 'My mother taught me.'

'Well, no offence to your father, but it wouldn't be him that taught you, eh, Woodvine? Not the brightest! But, by God, the strongest and the hardest worker I ever saw. Strong in the arm, thick in the head, so they say.'

Anny was not pleased with the slight to her father's intellect. He wasn't stupid, not by a long chalk. But Father didn't seem to mind. The ironworkers always engaged in plenty of banter and never seemed to take themselves too seriously.

'We're mightily proud of her,' he said and squeezed his daughter's shoulder.

Pritchard said, 'You seem like a clever'un then, lass. Can you do a job for me?'

'Yes,' answered the girl, curious and willing, but she looked to her father for some reassurance, and he gave a little nod.

'I need someone to go straight up to the big house and give a message to the estate manager, tell him to tell the master about this poor man here. The estate manager's office is behind the big house in a little brick dwelling. He's called Mr Brotherton and his secretary is his wife, Mrs Brotherton. One or both of them is usually there this time of day. The name of the dead man is Lakelin. Can you remember all of that?'

'Course she can,' said Father.

'Of course I can,' she replied and again her father nodded, his eyes keen.

And off she went. A mission, a job for the foreman. She thought of the poor dead man and of his wife and children. But she was gladdened, too, that she could be of use and she was proud that the foreman had trusted her with such an important role. To carry a message to the estate manager, Mr Brotherton, that would be relayed to Mr King himself. She felt important. *If I'd never written that note to Father*, she thought, *Mr Pritchard wouldna have seen how clever I am and I wouldna be on my way to the big house.* Book learning does that, she realised. It was a ticket to the world of men.

Anny took the walk up the riverside towards the imposing King house – named Southover due to its aspect – situated high on the hillside frowning down upon the iron bridge. She thought of Mr King the iron-master, who had a reputation for being stern and cold. She thought of King's daughter Margaret, whom she glimpsed once from a carriage window; she looked beautiful and had ringlets in her golden hair. Anny felt a poke of envy for Margaret, remembering that she was born the same month as her. She wondered what might have happened if the babies had been swapped, and how different her life might have been. She'd have those ringlets now! But Anny knew that she'd rather have her poor old father than horrid Mr King any day of the week, for all his riches. The huge, dark King house loomed up before her, and as she went around the back to find the estate office, she swallowed her nerves and knocked confidently on the door.

Mr Brotherton looked confused to find a young village girl appearing at his door.

'I carry an important message from Mr Pritchard. A man called Lakelin has been injured at the furnace. Very seriously injured. In fact, he has passed away from the serious nature of his injuries.'

'Oh Lord,' said Brotherton, his gaze shifting to consider all the things that must be done.

Anny went on, 'He leaves his wife a widow and his children fatherless. They live in Broseley. He was only young. It is a drodsome business.'

Anny waited and eventually he recalled her presence and eyed her curiously.

'You're good with words,' he said.

'So my mother tells me,' said Anny. 'And father. He's Mr John Woodvine. He works at the furnace.'

'Good man, Woodvine,' he replied.

Anny replied, 'Would you like me to write a note down for you to take back to Mr Pritchard?'

'You can read and write, child?'

'I can. My mother taught me.'

'No need to write it down on this occasion. You clearly have a good memory. Go and tell Mr Pritchard that he must send a man into town to arrange a cart to be sent for the . . . for Lakelin. Tell him that I will inform the master, and I'll send Mrs Brotherton to Broseley to tell the family. Then I shall come down to the furnace directly. Are you sure you can you remember all of that?'

'I am certain,' she said firmly and looked him straight in the eye.

'I believe you, child.' He thought for a moment, then added, 'You can run for me again, if you wish. Come back here each morning, if your mother can spare you. I have plenty of errands for a reliable runner. Can you read a clock? Get here for eight every morning and I'll have jobs for you to do until lunchtime, shall we say till twelve?' He fished in his pocket and gave her a penny.

'Oh yes, Mr Brotherton! Thank you, Mr Brotherton!' beamed Anny, clutching the coin in her hot hand. She'd have to talk to Mother first, of course, but the time she'd miss helping her mother would be more than made up by the coins she'd earn. A real job! At the big house, no less!

As Anny crossed the courtyard, heading for the path to the woods, she caught sight of Master Cyril, standing near to the stable block, half hidden around the corner.

As she moved forward, she saw he was not alone. He was holding fast to the arm of a servant girl, his other hand raised, pointing viciously towards her face. She could not hear his words, but it looked as if the girl had committed some terrible crime, the way he was jabbing at her, his face distorted as he spat words at her. *No need to twist her arm like that*, thought Anny. The boy's face was ugly in its rage. Anny shuddered. Her new post at the big house felt tarnished already. *As long as I avoid him*, she thought, *it'll be all right.*

She raced off into the woods to take the path back down to the furnace. A few steps in and her eager ears picked up a sound. She glanced round, but saw nothing. She went on with less haste, her ears pricked. There it was again. She stopped and peered into the woods. She thought with a slight air of panic, *It inna that awful boy?* Then she saw the bounce of blonde curls as someone turned their head. It was a girl.

'Who's there?' called Anny. 'Come out, you sneaky beggar. I'm not frit of you.'

A figure stepped out from behind a tree. Anny was shocked to see it was the daughter of the big house, Miss Margaret King. Anny muttered under her breath, 'What's she doing here?' as she curtseyed awkwardly while the girl, also very awkward, attempted to step lightly through the woods towards her. Not an outdoor kind of a girl, Anny noted. What on earth could she want, out here in the woodland?

'Afternoon, miss,' said Anny, watching the girl, who looked pale and nervous. Anny was anxious to rush off and deliver her message, but didn't feel she could ignore the young miss. As she came closer, Anny saw that she had a split lip. She wondered how that had come about.

'Hello there,' said Miss King.

'I am very sorry for addressing you so, just now, Miss King. I heard a noise and didna know – I mean, I *did not* know it was the young lady of the house. Please accept my being sorry, for I did not mean any offence.' Anny knew she was rambling, but she was mindful of her new position with Mr Brotherton. She didn't want this getting back to him and for her to lose her position before she'd even started. *I'll have to start stopping my tongue*, she thought.

'Not . . .' began Miss King, but her voice cracked a little and she stopped. It was as if her voice wasn't used to talking and it came out wrong. She swallowed and tried again. 'Not at all. I didn't mean to startle you. It was my fault for being secretive.'

'That's true,' said Anny, without thinking.

'I'm not supposed to be out here,' said Miss King, wide-eyed.

'Out where?' said Anny.

'In the woods.'

'Why not?'

'My father says it's where the . . .' Miss King stopped and bit her lip again, then winced. That split lip must be bothering her.

'Where the what?'

'Nothing. But it's forbidden anyway. I decided to . . . to defy my father.'

Anny had no idea what to say to this, but Miss King seemed pleased with herself, so Anny replied, 'Good for you.'

'Thank you,' said Miss King, and smiled. She winced again, as it must have hurt her lip. What a nervy thing she was. She was very pale and looked a little poorly, but her hair was in lovely ringlets and she had a pretty face, but a sadness about the eyes. An awkward silence followed.

'Did you just come from Southover?' asked Miss King.

'Yes, miss. From today I work for Mr Brotherton. I'm a kind of messenger for him.'

'I'm . . . I'm a little afraid of Mr Brotherton.'

'Really?' said Anny, shocked that any King could be afraid of anything, with all their money to bolster them against the world. 'He's all right.'

'It's just his voice. It sort of booms. I don't like loud voices. My father's is loud and he shouts at me sometimes. Is your father like that?'

'No, not even a little bit. He's proper jam, me father. I mean, he's a good person, miss.'

Miss King looked disappointed. Or was it envious?

'That's nice. My name is Margaret. What's your name?'

'Anny, miss.'

'Please call me Margaret.'

Miss King's eyes were so big and wide. She looked a little lost.

'I dunna think I can do that, miss. Not with . . . you know. Me working for your father. And our . . . different stations in life.'

'How did you come by the post, Anny? I've never heard of a girl messenger before. It's always been boys. I was always jealous of them. Running here and there, out in the world, something useful to do.'

Anny felt proud to relate it. 'It's because me mother – *my* mother – taught me to read and write. And the foreman at the blast furnace saw I could, and he sent me with a message and Mr Brotherton liked me, so there you are.'

'You can read and write?' Miss King looked and sounded quite amazed. Anny bridled against it.

'Why, yes. Not all of us poor folk are daft, you know.'

But Anny immediately regretted her rash words, because the girl looked crestfallen. Anny felt bad.

'I am sorry,' said Anny, and took a step towards Miss King. 'That was hard of me. You didn't mean anything by it. It is strange, a lass like me learning her letters. I know that. Please forgive me, Miss King.'

'Margaret,' she replied, and smiled. It was a lovely smile and it made Anny smile too. 'I think it's marvellous you've learnt to read and write. I love reading . . .'

The quiet confession touched Anny. Then she remembered her errand, the crucial message for Mr Pritchard. She scolded herself inwardly, but then again, she was not used to being important.

'I am terribly sorry, but I must go. There has been a death at the furnace and I'm taking a message back from Mr Brotherton to Mr Pritchard.'

'A death?' said Margaret.

'Yes. A young man. With a wife and children.'

'Oh, how terrible!' cried Margaret and covered her mouth with her hand, her eyes shining with tears. It warmed Anny to see how it affected the young girl. Did the poor matter that much to the rich?

'It is, miss. But I really must go.'

'Can I see you again, Anny?'

'I'm sure you will, about the place.'

'No, I mean, can we arrange to meet, like this? In a quiet place? I'm not very good around other people. But I think I could talk to you. I would like to, I mean. Talk to you, that is.'

Anny felt quite pleased at the request. Truthfully, she was also curious to see what the young lady of the house might have to say to a village wench like herself.

'Mr Brotherton said I would be finished at twelve.'

'Then can we meet hereabouts, soon after twelve, tomorrow?'

'Yes, miss,' said Anny and turned to go. She had been delayed and was worried Mr Brotherton would get down there before her and then she would have failed in her duty.

'Please call me Margaret,' she heard the girl shout to her as she ran away.

'Yes, miss,' she called back and raced through the trees.

Back at home that afternoon, her mother was thrilled at the news of her new post, and did not seem to mind at all that Anny would be absent from the washing work each morning.

'I shall come back home as soon as ever I can afterwards,' said Anny.

'Dunna fret,' said her mother. 'You stay as long as you're needed. Mr Brotherton might need you past twelve, and that's fine by me. This is a great chance for you, Anny. Working for the King family! You make yourself available to them at all times, whatever they're wanting. You wanna make a good impression.'

Anny almost mentioned her plans to meet Miss King, but somehow it didn't seem right to tell Mother.

The next morning she arrived early at Mr Brotherton's door. He had three errands for her that morning: a trip to the stationers in town to collect some ink; a message for the undertaker about arrangements for Lakelin and a note to be taken to the doctor's house on Tontine Hill about something, Anny didn't know what. None of her business, of course. She stood at the door to the office once she'd finished. It was quiet there at the office. The little brick building stood beside the woods and the big house loomed across the way. There was no hustle and bustle of people like in the town, and there was not the roar of industry her father had to work with every day. When Mr Brotherton came outside to give her direction, she took a peek past him into the office itself and saw Mrs Brotherton working with a pen at her desk. She looked up and gave Anny a small but friendly smile, which Anny returned. Mrs Brotherton's desk was busy yet tidy, furnished with all manner of stationery that Anny could only dream of. Oh, to have pens and bottles of ink and a blotter and fine paper, rather than a stubby pencil and scraps to write upon! To have a desk to work at, instead of her own lap. Anny had always enjoyed writing, adored it. But it always seemed a pointless extravagance, like wearing a lace apron. Now she had a glimpse of something a person could do with writing, a woman even.

When Mr Brotherton was done with her, she ran down the woodland path, racing to meet her new friend. She felt her legs weaken at the effort. She had not eaten since dawn and was ravenous. As she rounded a bend she spotted Miss King standing on the path and beside her on the ground a small wicker basket, its contents covered with a chequered cloth.

'I am sorry if the hour is late,' puffed Anny.

'It is not. I arrived early. I thought you would be hungry having worked all morning, and so I have brought us a picnic, if that is acceptable?'

'Oh, miss!' cried Anny, delighted, then checked herself. 'You did not have to do that. I can eat at home later.'

Miss King looked forlorn. 'But I asked Cook to pack all the things I liked, and I did so want to share them with you.' She knelt down and removed the cloth to reveal a dazzling selection of goodies. Anny spied a pie, sandwiches of some sort, boiled eggs, strawberries and slices of cake layered with purple jam.

Anny licked her lips. 'If you're sure, then if I may say so, I'd love to, miss!'

They sat down on the forest floor, Anny cross-legged and Miss King with her legs tucked neatly under her skirts. At first, they talked a bit about their families, then ate together in companionable silence. Anny was intent on the food. It was so good. Her mother cooked hearty dishes from the ingredients they could afford and what they could grow or find. Anny had never had cause to complain about her meals. But this was something else. The sandwiches were filled with roast beef, succulent and chewy. The pie was some sort of game bird – rich and spicy – encased in a savoury jelly and crisp pastry.

The cake was light and very sugary, the jam inside thick with juicy pieces of plum.

She looked up from her obsessive focus on the food to see Miss King watching her, nibbling on a strawberry and smiling. Anny smiled back.

'Thank you, miss. For all this.'

'Please don't thank me. It is my pleasure. I used to picnic with my governess from time to time. But she left us and I have not eaten out of doors for many months. I'm so glad you were kind enough to share it with me.'

'Dunna you have any friends?' said Anny and immediately regretted it. 'I am sorry, I didna mean . . .'

'No, it's fine. The answer to your question is no. I don't have a friend in the world. It's rather pathetic, isn't it?'

Anny looked away. 'Here,' she said and held out a piece of cake to Miss King. 'You need to eat more or I'll polish off the whole lot.'

Miss King's face lit up and she took a big mouthful of it, so big that Anny laughed, and she snorted and they giggled helplessly, morsels of cake spraying onto the forest floor. Once Miss King's mouth was clear, she had wiped her face on the chequered cloth and they had stopped laughing, she said again to Anny, 'Please will you call me Margaret?'

'I'll consider it,' said Anny with a cheeky smile and they laughed again. They began to talk then, Margaret querying Anny about her family and her village. The conversation was mostly one way, as Margaret was full of questions and Anny did not feel able to ask the same kinds of things, not after putting her foot in it about friends. It was also tricky because of Margaret's position; Anny did not feel it was her place to quiz the girl. And anyway, it was nice to gabble on about herself for once. Nobody else was interested in the everyday particulars of Anny Woodvine's life.

The food all gone and the sun long past midday, Anny knew it was time to go, though she could easily have curled up there and had a nap to digest this marvellous meal. They stood up and brushed themselves off. There was an awkward moment where neither knew quite what to say next.

'Ta-ta for now, Miss King.'

'Margaret?'

'No, I'm Anny.'

'Oh, Anny, you are a one! Will you meet me again tomorrow? And the day after that?'

Anny was tempted, especially if food like this was in the offing. But there was something about it that did not feel quite right. Her mother would not approve, she knew that, especially not of taking food without repaying the favour. She also knew she wouldn't be telling her mother about this, about any of it.

'It inna that easy for me, miss. I have to work for my mother at home in the afternoons. I ought to be back there now.'

'Yes, of course.'

Miss King's face was so sad, Anny felt a pang. 'But I could meet you here next week, same day, same time? That should be all right.'

'That would be lovely. I'll bring another picnic.'

'No, miss, it'll be my turn then. I'll bring something, dunna fret.' As she said the words, she felt her stomach twist into a knot at what she could possibly offer Miss King from her humble table. Well, she would just have to manage it. It was the right thing to do.

They were both true to their word and met the following week. They were easier with each other this time. It felt less like a curious encounter and more like companionship. It was the beginning of a friendship, one that grew as they met each week throughout the long, baking summer.

It was also the beginning of Anny lying to her mother, something that left a bad taste in her mouth. She'd told her white lies before, of course she had, like every child. But it was the first time she had set out deliberately to deceive her parents. She did not like it, but it excited her, too. It made her cheeks go hot. She kept telling herself that she was doing nothing wrong. And each time she saw Margaret she convinced herself further that there was nothing to feel bad about. They were just being sensible about it, that was all. After all, they both knew their families – and society itself – would disapprove heartily of the rich girl and the poor girl picnicking together in the woods. But families weren't right about everything, and society could be stupid. When the two girls met now, they did not feel that they were so very different anymore. They were not employer and employee; they were not even rich and poor. When they were together, chatting and laughing, they were simply Anny and Margaret.

But as the weeks went on, her work for Mr Brotherton increased and she was kept later each time. He always found so many things for her to do and tutted when she had to leave to go home to her mother. She had already had to miss one meeting with Margaret. She felt bad about it, but what could she do? Particularly as it looked as if Mr Brotherton was going to need her more and more at the office and she would not be able to meet Margaret so often. Even today she was running late, and her first words to Margaret had been an apology.

'Really, Anny, please do not apologise,' Margaret was quick to reply. 'It is not of your making. You are only doing your job. But it did give me an idea . . .'

'What's that, then?'

'Since you can read and write so well, I was wondering . . .' She bit her lip in thought. 'Maybe you and I . . . perhaps we could . . . write to each other?'

'I've heard that people do write letters to friends. But I never had a friend who could write.'

'And,' continued Margaret, 'whenever I leave a letter for you, I'll leave some paper and a pencil for you to write back. Then you don't have to worry about the . . . well, the cost to yourself. If that's agreeable.' Anny did not like charity, not directed at herself or her family, anyway. But she could see that Margaret was being kind, not hoity-toity. Besides, she really could do with a more reliable source of writing materials.

'But how could we deliver them? They can't come to the house, then everyone'll know about us.'

Margaret considered this. 'Well, perhaps we could leave the letters somewhere safe, somewhere only we knew about. And then nobody would need to know.'

'I know the very place!' cried Anny. 'Not far from here, down by the riverside. There's an old lime tree with a hollow in the trunk. I used to hide flowers in there for the fairies. I'll show you.'

It wasn't far and was back towards the big house. Anny knew these woods like the back of her hand and she pointed out to Margaret a few natural landmarks on the way, so that Margaret could find the right tree again when she was alone. They were peering inside the hollow and laughing about Anny's flower fairy offerings, when they heard a shout nearby. Both girls turned, but Margaret's face was full of fear.

'That's Cyril's voice. That's my brother.'

Anny watched Margaret, who was now shaking, her hands and bottom lip trembling. Her friend so rarely talked about her family; sometimes it seemed they talked about everything else, but the mere mention of her family seemed to steal Margaret's voice.

'Is he calling you?' said Anny in a hoarse whisper.

They stood and listened, then heard more sounds, followed by movement through the undergrowth. They instinctively hid behind the tree with the hollow. Through the trees, they saw Cyril pass by. He was not alone. He was pulling behind him the servant girl Anny had seen him bullying once.

'It's Lucy,' whispered Margaret.

They both watched as the two passed by, the servant girl saying things quietly to Cyril. Anny caught the odd word, mostly 'please' and 'Master'. But his grip on her wrist was strong and she could not get away. Then he stopped. Anny and Margaret froze. He pulled Lucy towards him, then shoved her up against the nearest tree. His face was very close to hers and he was saying something in her ear. She was twisting away from him. He held her against the tree with his left arm, as his right hand went down, found the bottom of her hem and thrust up under her skirts. He was fumbling around for something. Margaret turned away and sobbed, then covered her mouth with terror that he might hear her.

Anny turned to Margaret. She whispered, 'We mun help her.'

'No!' replied Margaret, full of panic. 'We cannot. We must pretend we never saw a thing.'

'That inna right.'

'You don't know my brother like I do. He will find a way to punish us, you more than me. He has a hatred of . . . others less . . .'

'Poor folk,' said Anny.

'Yes. He will punish you. You'll lose your post. And he'll beat me.'

The two girls stared at each other, then turned back to gaze upon the scene unfolding before them. The boy's hand reaching up under the servant girl's dress, the sobs of the girl, his cruel sneer, his coarse whisperings of who knows what in her ear.

Anny said, 'This is wrong. All wrong.' She turned away and looked about on the forest floor.

'What are you doing?' whispered Margaret.

'Something. Something is better than nothing.' Anny found what she was looking for. A sizeable stone. She picked it up.

Margaret gasped. 'What on earth are you going to do with that?'

Anny aimed and threw it at a tree ten feet or so away from the struggling pair. It hit the trunk full square and bounced into the bracken. Cyril turned at the sound. The moment he was distracted, Lucy seemed to find a hidden strength and shoved Cyril hard. He stumbled back and cried out. Lucy dashed away through the woods towards the house.

'Anny, you are marvellous!' whispered Margaret.

'You'd have done the same, if you'd thought of it.'

'No, I would not. I'm not like you, Anny. I wish I were.'

They both turned and crouched lower as they heard Cyril swearing. Puffed and red-faced, he dusted himself down, then began to walk back in a leisurely way. Anny guessed he knew he could do this whenever he chose. There was no rush. It was all part of some horrible game. Once he was gone, the girls looked at each other nervously.

'I have to go,' said Margaret. 'I am so sorry about . . . all this.' Anny could sense shame in Margaret.

'It inna your fault. He inna your fault.' Anny thought, *He's a proper monster.* She looked at her friend Margaret, for that is what she had become. 'You're not like your family, you're good and kind . . .'

'Oh, Anny, there are times I wish I weren't a King. That I could be someone else, anybody else.'

'It'll be all right, Margaret. You inna just a King, you're my best friend. With me you can be just Margaret. Even better, you can be Peggy. Yes, that'd be perfect. To me you'll be Peggy, not Miss King or even Margaret.'

Margaret grinned from ear to ear. 'I've never had a pet name! Oh, yes please, Anny! Thank you!'

'Ta-ta for now, Peggy.'

'Good day, Anny.'

The two girls solemnly shook hands, then laughed. They turned in opposite directions and both went off, making their way home.

Dusk was approaching and an evening wind whistled through the forest. Anny pulled her shawl about her as she walked thoughtfully, thinking of her friend, her job and interesting times ahead. Yet slicing through the warm glow of a friendship with Peggy was the cold fact of Cyril. Above, the sky seemed to mirror her thoughts, as a rash of dark clouds swept in and the woodland ahead was cast in deep shadow as she moved through it, homewards.

Chapter 4

Dear Anny,

I am so heartened to have found a true friend such as yourself, and I find in writing that I can tell you things I somehow could never say aloud. My life to this point has been a struggle. My family are difficult people. My father is hard and unyielding. I believe he sees me as a disappointment because I find it difficult to talk to people in social situations such as balls and even tea parties and so forth. My stepmother is a silly woman who is only a few years older than I and adores her nasty little lapdog more than life itself. She thinks she is beautiful because she has big eyes and thick hair but her mouth is always in a turned-down position above a pointed chin, which gives her a most disagreeable and witching air always and, I believe, is the revelation of her true nature. My brother is a fiend. I do not need to explain more to you of this, as you have witnessed it yourself with your own eyes. I could not believe how brave you were when you threw that rock. I wish I were more like you!

My grandmother is the nicest of all my close family, in that I do not believe she hates me. She does talk to me at times. However, she does say odd things from time to time and I wonder if she is a little touched.

Thus, my home is not a place one might call particularly happy. I am fortunate that I have fine clothes, a warm bed and good food to eat. My family is rich, after all. But if my family were judged on its good company alone, I might well be the poorest girl in Shropshire.

Please tell me about your family, Anny, and how they are with you.

Fondest regards,
Margaret (Peggy)

Post Scriptum: please be aware that if my family ever saw these words I have written about them, or if this letter were ever to fall into public hands, I would be in the direst of straits. Perhaps I am foolish to write these thoughts down. However, this is the first time in my life I have had a true confidante, and I am emboldened by this to speak the truth. It is a great weight lifted from me that I can speak openly to a friend of my woes. Thank you for being that friend, Anny. I believe I can trust you, as you seem to have a kind, open nature. So please keep my letters very safe and secret. Thank you again.

Anny found Margaret's letter the very next day, in the hollow in the tree which they had agreed would be their postmaster. There were some parts of the letter she had to read again – despite being a good little reader – as she was not accustomed to reading such high-flown sentiments. It was a thrill to receive a letter, as this was Anny's very first. She decided she'd have to try her best to write in 'proper' English. She was delighted to have a confidante, but was ashamed that a worm of annoyance was wriggling inside her about some of the contents of Peggy's letter. This girl had everything a person could wish for, while so many people she knew had nothing, and still she was not happy. Anny had always thought if she had all the King's wealth, she'd never complain again. But even as she thought it, Anny knew she was wrong about that. She wouldn't trade her family for a room full of nice dresses, if it meant Mr King were her father and Cyril were her brother. She shuddered at the thought. *Who'd ha' thought that you could pity a rich girl?*

Dear Peggy,

Course I will keep your letters secret. I will keep all your secrets safe. That is what friends do. We should make a solemn pact never to tell our secrets to any living soul. What do you say to that? I think it is a sure way of friendship. Also I am thinking that we should make another pact and that is against boys. I know lots of boys round here where I live and I can tell you that they are not to trust. With secrets or any other important matters. It sounds to me that your brother is another like this. We should make a pact that boys never come between us. You have asked about my family and I could write all night about how good they are to me, as they surely, surely are. There is only one of me which is not usual as much of our neighbours have bundles of children but my mother had me and nearly died and something went wrong inside after and then she could not bring any more children into the world. I used to weep for this, as I wanted a sister for many years but now I am thinking it is a blessing as there are not many mouths to feed in our home and I can get some peace for my reading and writing which is my true joy. God is mysterious in his ways.

In your next letter, tell me what you eat for your meals. In every particular detail.

Yours sincerely,
Anny Woodvine

Post Scriptum: please explain what Post Scriptum means.

Also you are right about your brother. I do not like to speak ill of others but he is a nasty piece of work. I was at Mr Brotherton's office this morning and saw Master Cyril kick a dog. Only because it was there. And because he could. Mr Brotherton sighed and shook his *head. The dog crawled away under a tree and Master Cyril laughed his fill at this. I do wonder what makes a person lungeous like this. If you do not know that word, it is proper useful. It means spiteful.*

Anny read over her last paragraph and nearly struck it out. Should she be more cautious? What if her letter were found and read by the Kings? She would lose her new position at the estate office for certain. It might even endanger her father's position at the furnace. But something in Peggy's honesty was infectious and she wanted to match it. She wanted a friend to have secrets with, someone clever like herself, who she could share her deep thoughts with in a way no local girl had ever been able to match. And there was something thrilling about being friends with Miss King, the daughter of the big house, the daughter of not only her own boss but her father's boss. It was lucky and golden, somehow. Maybe it might even come in useful one day. As excited as she was by the prospect, something told her that she must continue to keep the whole fact of it secret. She mustn't tell her mother or her father. She knew they would not approve and they would warn her against it. She could not clearly work out their reasons for it, but she just knew they would. Something obscure stirred in her that it could mean strife, somewhere along the twisting path of time. But she was a girl, a child entering young adulthood, and whisperings of trouble served only to make the whole thing more thrilling still. She folded up the letter and, evading her mother's keen eye, slipped out unnoticed to the woods and made her way to the fairy tree, whistling as she went.

With nothing to do that day beyond terrorising dogs and servants, Cyril King decided to walk the circuit of his family's dominion. He wanted to see everything that the Kings owned. He strolled down through the woods towards the ironworks, his face beginning to prickle with heat. He wished he could remove his cap and so-called summer coat, though it was still infernally hot. He wished at times he had the life of a river waif, running about barefoot and shirtless. Only in the summer, though. He muttered to himself grumpily as he approached the furnace, great wafts of heat assaulting him the closer he came. Industry produced heat and heat transformed into money, he realised. He did not think of the manpower slaving away to create that heat in the first place. He thought only of his place astride it all.

All this will one day be mine, Cyril thought. This puffed his chest with pride, but he was also plagued with doubt. Was he up to the job? All these massive piles of matter to be dug from the ground, melted, moulded, refined, rolled, flattened, transported and sold. It was daunting, to say the least. And something he would never admit to his father, he hated industry. He hated the filth and the stink of it, the noise and intrusion of it. Luckily, an ironmaster could afford to hire help to deal with the worst of it and stay behind the scenes in a much more civilised situation of an office or up at Southover. Mr Brotherton came to see Papa daily in his study to speak of business matters. Other fellows – probably some sort of lowly manager – from the furnace, the forge and the mill would sometimes appear, cap in hand, at the estate office yet rarely, if ever, managed an audience with his father. It was the men that worried Cyril most. How did one talk to such rascals? Even Mr Brotherton unsettled him, with his twinkling eyes, something knowing behind them, as if he knew Cyril's secret doubts of his own worth. Mr Brotherton always spoke to him in that way too, that half-mocking way, overly polite but somehow undermined by wry humour. *You're not up to this*, his voice and those eyes seemed to say. *Neither is your father, just as your grandmother and grandfather knew. We run this place. You lot are not needed. Just your money. Run along.*

Cyril hawked up a good load of phlegm and spat on the ground in a fit of pique. The more he thought about it, the more he was determined to prove himself to these damned fellows. How dare Brotherton and the like mock him? A small part of him knew that there was no evidence whatsoever that any of his father's men mocked him, spoke of him or even registered his existence in their busy, difficult lives. But it was a small part, easily silenced. He marched down to the yard in front of the furnace and spotted a group of men drinking from large tankards, in what must have been a few minutes out of their back-breaking shift. But it riled him, these people guzzling his father's ale. He knew it was their daily ration, but at this moment Cyril did not care to acknowledge that fact.

'You there,' he called, waving his hand dismissively. Nobody turned. Nobody heard him. This annoyed him further. He stomped harder towards the men. 'I said, *you there*, damn you!'

This got their attention. The wall of backs broke and a row of black-smudged faces turned sharply, their white eyes alarmed, their red mouths open. Then their faces changed as they saw whose voice it was and yes, *there*, a smirk, he was sure of it. That blackguard was laughing at him, wasn't he?

'What do you think you are doing?' Cyril shouted and stood his ground, arms folded, as he'd seen his father do when telling him off for his own laziness or stupidity. But the men just stood there, gawping at him. 'What the devil is wrong with you? Answer me, damn you!'

Others had turned to watch, all frozen in place, yet one or two now were taking draughts from their beer again, which seemed the height of rudeness. One of the men stepped forward, a large man, built like a Shire horse, with arms as thick as thighs and hands like hams.

Cyril shuddered at the size of him and steeled himself. He wouldn't be intimidated by such a thundering idiot as this mountain of a man.

'Can I be of help to you, Master King?' said the man. This took Cyril aback, who was expecting some garbled labourer's nonsense to come from his wide mouth.

Cyril cleared his throat and squared up to him. 'I said, what do you think you are doing?'

The men shuffled awkwardly, one holding up his beer and looking at it, as if to answer. Why wouldn't they speak? They must be fools. He turned back to the big man.

'Will you not answer your betters?'

Some of the men shuffled and looked to the ground. One even shook his head, Cyril was sure of it.

'You there. How dare you shake your head at me! I am your superior.'

The big man took another step towards him and Cyril took a stumbling half-step backwards and someone sniggered.

'Master King, what can we do for you?' said the big man. 'We are supping our beer that your father provides for us. It is only for a short time, and then we mun be back at our work again, no danger.'

Cyril looked up at the man's eyes. The man's daughter and wife would have seen kindness and goodness there; the foreman Pritchard would have seen his hardest-working, strongest and most loyal man at the furnace.

But Cyril King saw only his own smallness and pathetic misplaced anger reflected back at him.

'How dare you speak to me,' he uttered low and guttural, clearing his throat.

'But you addressed us, young sir,' continued the man. The downright bloody cheek of these lower orders!

'How dare you presume to speak to me!' shouted Cyril, but it came out as a kind of squawk, like a parakeet he'd seen at the fairground once. 'What . . . what is your name?'

The man glanced sidelong, unwilling to respond.

'Answer me, damn you!'

Then another man came forward. He was less dirty than the rest, perhaps less of an idiot than the others.

'I'm the furnace clerk, Master King. My name's Pritchard. I'm the foreman and I'm in charge here. What can I do for you?'

'What is this man's name? He was insolent.'

The man and Pritchard looked at each other. Something passed between them in their look, something too adult for Cyril to grasp, which annoyed him further.

'Tell me your name, or you shall hang for it, by God!' shrieked Cyril. That shut them up. He knew he did not have such power, but it gave him the feel of it, just to say it. He realised he could say anything he liked to these people. Anything at all. It gave him a thrill.

Pritchard was about to speak but the big man interrupted him. 'My name is John Woodvine, sir. I have worked at your father's furnace these past score years, man and boy. If I have offended you, I am sorely sorry for it. Please accept my apology, most sincere like.'

Woodvine looked at the ground, Pritchard looked at him and the men stood with their chins up staring at Cyril.

Cyril had no idea what to say.

'Is our business concluded, Master King?' said Pritchard. 'I would like these men to get back to their duties now, if agreeable.'

Cyril turned and marched away, his face roasting hot from the furnace and his own self-hatred. But as much as he hated himself, he hated those working men more. Their sense of purpose, their camaraderie and loyalty. But most of all the swagger of having a useful job to do in this world. How he hated them all for that. Now he had a new name to add to his list of fools who had wronged him and must pay: John Woodvine.

Chapter 5

August passed in a haze of heat and letter-writing. Margaret sat in her room, her eye on the door, her pillow on her lap, propped up to hide the latest letter from Anny. She finished reading it and swiftly hid it away in a wooden music box she kept at the bottom of her handkerchief drawer. If Cyril found these letters . . . well, it did not bear thinking about. He would have no cause to ever want a handkerchief – as a child he always was snot-nosed, but he had no interest in girlish items, so she hoped he'd never look in there. She had secured a pink ribbon around the growing stack of letters which she tied and untied fondly each time, smiling at her good fortune to have found such a correspondent and such a friend.

She had tried to explain to Anny that she had never had friends. No friends at all. The person she spent most time with was her maid, Royce, who did her hair every day and tended to her physical needs. But Royce was stiff, cold and quite old. Margaret could not talk to her. They barely spoke. Their relationship was purely functional. She'd asked her father if she could have the young, nice one, Lucy, as her maid, but she was informed that Lucy was only a tweenie maid and not at all the right class for a lady's maid for the daughter of a King. So, Margaret could not even make a friend in her own house.

But Anny, full of sunshine and fun, surrounded by close neighbours – sometimes too close for comfort, Anny once wrote – had had plenty of friends in her life, had never been without them. Margaret, educated at home – only in writing, embroidery, French and piano-playing from a half-hearted Parisian governess who had disappeared without warning the summer before – and never permitted to speak to local children, let alone play with them, had grown to the age of twelve a lonely girl. Tormented by her brother and bullied by her father, she had become accustomed to her own company. Now Anny had appeared in her life, she was beginning to understand the magic of friendship. It was new and exciting. It was easy to allow it to become an obsession.

She tried to stop herself from gushing too much in her letters. But she found it almost impossible to play-act nonchalance and instead poured out all her feelings to Anny. Her friend did not reciprocate in kind; Anny's letters rarely spoke of her feelings, instead they were always friendly and full of fascinating detail about her daily life. Reading about the lives of the working class was as exotic to Margaret as if she were reading about the wildlife of Africa. Anny seemed to enjoy similar details about Margaret's life, yet Margaret felt a little ashamed every time she described the ease with which she passed her days. She sometimes invented minor troubles to make her day sound more vexing than it was, but worried this would make her sound as if she were trying to make something out of nothing. So she filled her letters with her feelings, her loneliness and her overwhelming regard for Anny. She wondered if it would help if she gave Anny presents, but would Anny take this as an insult? Margaret agonised now over that possibility. She had never had a friend before – let alone one from a different social class – and did not know how to be a friend herself.

She was a worrier, and worried about this. Still seated on her bed, staring at the drawer in which her precious letters were hidden, she thought, *What if I drive her away?* The thought terrified her. She wanted help; she needed someone to tell her how to be a friend, before she did the wrong thing and lost this one through some dreadful *faux pas*. If only there was someone she could talk to about it. Only one person sprang to mind, as there was only one person other than Anny that Margaret would ever have a hope of confiding in. 'Grandmother,' she said aloud. Could she talk to her about such things? There was only one way to find out.

She found Queenie seated on a high-back wing chair in the drawing room, snoring noisily. It was Mr King's chair usually and Margaret smiled to see she'd used it to have a quick snooze, thinking herself hidden from prying servants' eyes, yet her lusty snoring gave the game away to all and sundry.

Since her grandfather's death three months ago, Margaret had noticed that Queenie had changed. She used to be up and about from dawn till dusk and beyond, involved in the business and socialising with local worthies and clients. Since her husband had gone, she had taken to her bed more and more. She had withdrawn from the family. And her odd comments had popped into everyday conversation. Margaret could see that her grandparents had not been particularly fond of one another, but perhaps her grandfather's death had upset her grandmother more than anyone realised. She felt sad for her grandmother and vowed to try to spend more time in her company from now on. Perhaps they could take up a pastime together, such as playing cards or something similar, where conversation was unnecessary. Anny might enjoy her conversation, but Margaret knew none in her family, not even Queenie, felt that way.

Luckily, Benjamina was taking her afternoon rest in her own room, her father was out on business and Cyril was off roaming who knows where. Margaret came in quietly, so as not to wake her grandmother, determined to sit and wait for her to awake and for herself to build up the courage to talk to her. She had to come up with a plausible story for the friendship.

The visiting cousin of some local dignitary's daughter, perhaps; they could have met at a tea party and become correspondents. Yes, that sounded all right. That might happen. But Queenie knew that Margaret never spoke to a soul. Maybe Margaret could convince her that she had developed some confidence recently, that the girl was shy. She began to invent more and more elaborate flights of fancy about this fictional friend until she thought to herself, *Why not tell her the truth? Why not try, at least?* Then Queenie awoke with a start and let out a piercing cry.

Margaret leapt to her feet and went to her.

'Are you well, Grandmother?'

'The baby!' cried Queenie.

Her hands rose up and were flapping about, her eyes still filmy with sleep.

'What baby?' asked Margaret, alarmed.

Queenie sat bolt upright and said in a low, knowing tone, 'The baby on the bridge. That poor girl died, right there.'

Then Queenie put her hands over her face. Margaret reached out to touch her grandmother's hands, so forlorn did she look. But Queenie awoke from her half-waking, half-dreaming moment and registered her granddaughter's presence.

'What's this?' she muttered. 'What are you about?'

Margaret withdrew her hands and looked down, to give Queenie a moment to recover herself.

'You were dreaming, Grandmother,' she said quietly.

'No, I was not,' asserted Queenie. 'I wasn't even asleep.'

Margaret looked up at Queenie and their eyes met; a flicker of a smile passed on their lips, a shared, rare moment of connection between them. Minutes ago, Margaret would have taken the opportunity to ask her grandmother's advice about her friendship with Anny. But now, something else had taken its place, something more compelling still.

'Won't you tell me who the baby on the bridge is, please, Grandmother?'

For a moment, Margaret thought she might answer, but all Queenie said was, 'It's a fortunate child that escapes the King family.'

Margaret's feelings about her family chimed with her grandmother's sentiment and this gave her a little courage to speak of it. 'I feel that way, too, Grandmother.'

'Feel?' Queenie snapped. Queenie never did seem to have much time for feelings or talk of such things.

'About the King family. I find it . . . difficult sometimes.'

'You have everything you need, child.'

'I do and I am grateful. But it's just that . . . I do feel very alone.'

'That is the woman's lot. We must suffer alone.'

Margaret swallowed nervously, but was determined to go on.

'But if I had a friend, it would help me.'

'Friend? What friend?'

'I've met someone, Grandmother. And she could be a great friend to me. But I've never . . .'

'Where? What? Who?' quizzed Queenie, leaning forward and scrutinising Margaret's face.

'It is a girl who . . .' Margaret hesitated. Whatever she said, however she dressed it up, she knew her grandmother's fierce gaze would reduce it to ashes. Perhaps this was a mistake. But she had started it now and may as well finish it. Maybe her grandmother would surprise her and understand. She wouldn't know if she didn't try. 'She is a local girl, a girl from the village along the river. She is employed by Mr Brotherton in the office. She can . . .'

'What's this? A worker? A friendship with a worker?'

'She can read and write, Grandmother.'

'Out of the question, child. How could you even consider such a thing? We do not mix with such people.'

'But if you could only meet her, you would see. She is so clever and bright and . . .'

Queenie held up her hand, her palm facing outwards, as steady and rigid as a stone wall. 'It is not so very long until you will come out into society and make acquaintances of your own class, after which you will make a good marriage and produce children. You will be too busy running a household to have time for friendship.'

Margaret saw her life stretching ahead of her into a desert of tedious yet fretful social events, ending with an arranged union of some approved male of her family's choosing. And it terrified her. Her fear made her bold and she spoke again to her grandmother.

'But if I could have one friend to see me through the years before that day. I am so lonely, Grandmother. Sometimes I fear I may die of loneliness.'

'Pish-tosh! Nobody ever died of unhap . . .' But something stopped Queenie and she did not finish her sentence. A moment of memory seemed to sweep over her features. She looked down, rearranged her hands in her lap and composed herself. 'We are the Kings. We did not attain our position today by fraternising with the lower orders. You are your father's daughter – a King – and you have our family name to uphold at all times. Let there be no more talk of friendships with the labouring class.'

Queenie told the child to run along. *That little wallflower*, Queenie thought. Harmless enough and a heart full of secrets, no doubt. But the child was too young to be trusted with the truth as yet, if ever. One day, perhaps, if she proved herself a bit more spirited, showed she had a bit of backbone. Queenie despised weakness. She inwardly scolded herself. She really mustn't fall asleep during the day like that. It left her at a disadvantage. This never would have happened when her husband was alive. For all his faults, he was a marvel at organising their lives. Everything was arranged with military precision and fixed timings, every minute of the day accounted for. It gave her life a comforting structure, which she missed. The moment he died, she had watched the life rattle from his body and was surprised to find she had felt a tidal wave of relief. This man was gone from her life. Now she could begin again, regain her former self, her former life before marrying so young and disappearing into an existence for which nothing in her girlhood had prepared her. She did not have to brook his company for one moment more on this earth, and as the head of the King family she could marshal them in the right direction.

But in the days following, she began to feel inordinately tired. She could not stay awake or concentrate on things for long. She took to her bed most days, when before, a scheduled bed nap had been something she'd mocked, something that the elderly required and she did not consider herself elderly by any means, being only in her late fifties. The day after he passed away, she handed over the operations of the ironworks almost completely to her son, despite her fears that he was not up to the job. She hoped the responsibility would be the making of him. Ralph's death had aged her, overnight it seemed. She had taken to sleeping in the day and waking all night. Everything was out of kilter. She felt adrift in her life.

She'd hated Ralph King senior by the end, of that there was no doubt. But in some ways he was a useful husband. How she had desired him once! She scoffed to think of it. But she had been young and foolish, a pretty little flibbertigibbet; she'd danced with all the local young men, and could have snapped her fingers and they would all have come running. Ralph was older, less keen. Still waters run deep, she had thought of him. She wanted to break through that cool exterior and explore his depths. But it was all a facade. Once married, she soon realised there was nothing hidden beneath. Only a frozen emptiness. He made love like he was avenging something, cold, thrusting and heartless. Bed soon became a place to be dreaded. Her girlish days were long gone, too soon. Then came the babies.

Queenie thought of her twin daughters, both dead before six months had passed: tuberculosis. Her eyes filled and she brutally slapped away the tears. *No, one mustn't give in to grief.* It was forty-odd years ago, indeed. She had her son after that. And then, no more. Her husband did not visit her bed from then on. He had tired of her. He had developed a taste for virgins.

But her one child who survived, her son, had been her great hope and joy, at first. It was after his birth she'd found her strength and earned her nickname, Queenie. He was a bonny baby, plump and chuckling. But his true character soon revealed itself. Whatever differences she had with her husband, they certainly saw eye to eye on the failings of their son Ralph. *Look at him now*, she thought, with disgust. A great disappointment: lazy, proud and selfish. *Look at the grandson, the same.*

But the granddaughter . . . she might prove interesting, one day. There was something behind those shy blue eyes that made one wonder what she was thinking. Those eyes, just like Queenie's sister, Selina. The very picture of her sister's face – same eyes, same nose, same mouth. But the girl had none of Selina's spirit. And there was another key difference: Margaret's eyes were clear and open, not a shade of oddness in them. *Not clouded by trouble*, she thought with relief. *Nothing like my dear sister.*

As grateful as she was for that difference, she couldn't help but be reminded of Selina each time she saw Margaret. She thought back to a time before she was Queenie, when she'd been just Alice and Selina had been with her every day. To have lived with her dear sister Selina forever, perhaps in a simple cottage, covered in wisteria and surrounded by pea plants, like the home of her old piano teacher. No husbands, no fathers, no children, no grandchildren – that would have been the best life she could imagine. Thinking of it now brought a tear to her eye – how happy they would have been! Alice and Selina, alone in perfect companionship. If only her life had been that way. But it had been Alice's duty to marry well. By the time Alice was sixteen Selina was already beginning to show signs of oddness, forcing her parents to expedite Alice's marriage. Selina had always been a curious child, creating a world filled with fairy tales, some read from delicately illustrated books but mostly weaved from her imagination. Their parents began to keep her away from visitors and the servants whispered about her below stairs. Everyone thought Selina was ill, but Alice alone knew how brilliant and bright her sister was. But difference threatens those who want to be normal and her sister was talked about in increasingly worried tones.

While Alice blossomed into an eligible young woman, her older sister retreated further into the nursery. Soon, Alice was married. It all seemed like a great adventure, until she realised that she would have to live with this man, share his bed and be subject to his every desire and whim. Alice's absence drove her sister to worse excesses and Ralph restricted her visits with Selina to once a month. He said they had an unnatural attachment. Each visit brought a further degradation. Selina would pluck at her cheeks, cry out as if a spectre or spider had appeared above Alice's head, talk in strings of words about people she'd never met. They took her away.

Some months later, news came that Selina had died. Years later, she discovered Selina had hanged herself from her door.

With Selina gone, Alice was alone in the world, and Ralph had the ammunition to keep her in line. What befell one sister could befall the other.

She did the only thing she could think of to survive: she made that life her own. She became the perfect wife, the perfect mother, the perfect hostess. She learnt the family business and drove it forward, making the King name the greatest in the neighbourhood, in the county and beyond. She felt she had truly earned the name of Queenie.

But at what cost? It was always the females who seemed to pay the price. It was a hard fact but it was true, and her granddaughter needed to learn that now, the sooner the better. Life was hard for everyone but hardest for the weak. The way through life was littered with the corpses of those who could not stay the journey. Only the strong survived.

She thought of the night before, when she had looked from her bedroom window, sleepless as ever, and watched the family tombstones glow whitely in the bright moonlight. How she wished she could have seen her sister's spirit there, flitting between the graves, her long, pale hair catching the moonbeams, silvery and spectral. She did not believe in ghosts. It was all stuff and nonsense the common people spoke of in their uneducated ignorance. But how good it would be to see her sister again, even as a spirit. And how curious it would be, that her spectre should appear in this graveyard, when her body was buried long ago, not here, but in that dreadful place, the place where strangers would pay pennies to view the inmates, a kind of zoo of human misery. *How cruel people are.* She thought of the ghosts of her dead daughters, how dearly she would love to see them playing amongst the gravestones. They would laugh and chase each other, their skirts and beribboned hair fluttering in some spectral breeze. They had died as babies, so they would not come to her as proper little girls, but she could dream, couldn't she? She would call to them and they would turn and smile at her, then continue their frolics. She thought then of the baby on the bridge, crying out in the night, its mother dead and cold in the grave. She recalled the day Jenkins had told her, that the maid she'd dismissed had been found dead on the bridge. But there was more: gossip had spread that the girl had been holding a baby, which someone had taken in. She thought of her husband's icy heart, dead too now. Queenie shuddered, then shook her head to rid it of all maudlin thoughts.

'Enough of this,' she said and made the great effort it took to raise herself from the chair. She needed a walk, to blow away the cobwebs. She would take a turn down by the lake and return past the pet cemetery. What fun it would be to see the ghosts of her old dogs frolicking there today! But no: she must stop with these foolish thoughts. She would be firm with herself. She should turn her attention to worldly matters and ensure that the King family continued to prosper.

Chapter 6

'You're doing a fine job there, Anny,' said Mrs Brotherton. She had kind, grey eyes that were always smiling, even when her mouth was set. 'One day, you might work in a bigger office somewhere. Maybe even Shrewsbury, who knows!' Anny looked up from her work and smiled back, then continued copying out the long list of ironworkers and their pay for that month. A job in Shrewsbury. Imagine that, actually living in the county town of Shrewsbury, looking out from your office window and seeing the town folk going to and fro, the coaches clattering over the cobbles, the bells of the churches chiming – that's how she pictured it, anyhow. How marvellous that would be! That could never happen, not to an ironworker's girl like her. Or could it?

Anny felt gratified. She was so glad that within only a few months she had moved up from a messenger and general runabout to a clerical assistant, and her pay had moved up too. She often thought of that first time she was invited in to the office itself. Mrs Brotherton had been ill and Mr Brotherton was huffing and puffing about the work that needed to be done. He had asked her to come in to the office so he could test her handwriting. She had never written with a pen before, so he gave her a pencil and asked her to copy out some lists of figures and names. She had sat at a small desk, focusing on forming her shapes beautifully on the page. Mr Brotherton had been delighted with her neat work and later that day had shown her how to use a pen. She took to it like a foal to standing, wobbly at first but determined and soon an expert. With Mrs Brotherton sick, Anny found herself buried in paper, ink and neatly copied-out ledgers, and within days Mr Brotherton wrote to her mother and requested that Anny be permitted to work for them full-time, and that her pay would increase to match her working hours, of course. Everyone was delighted with the arrangement.

Since then, Mr and Mrs Brotherton had taken Anny under their wing. They had no children of their own – 'It was God's manner of making us useful to other young'uns,' said Mrs Brotherton – and they had adopted Anny, in a way. They even let her call them Mr B and Mrs B; as Mr B said, their name was a bit of a mouthful. They were teaching her the skills needed to administer an office such as this one: the papers and ink and pens and pencils and blotters and bills that were required to keep it all running smoothly. She wrote out letters and lists and requests and so forth for them. Her parents were proud as punch, of course, and sorely glad of the extra money coming in. It saved Anny from the drudgery of washing at home and also from a life in service, or worse, which might have been coming.

Her other option had been pit girl, full of back-breaking hours of picking out the ironstone from the clay on a waste tip and carrying it in a basket on her head to pile onto another great heap. The tedium of it, the endless, mindless nothingness. Worse still were the jobs that girls did down the mines, where rats and goblins lived. Those girls rarely saw the light of day and so many died young. Plenty of her friends did these jobs, and Anny wanted nothing to do with that. She loved her friends; she had grown up with them. But there was a difference between them now. Anny's hands were softer and her face less ravaged by wind and weather and work, though her eyes and fingers often ached from the strain of too much writing in the dim light of the approaching winter. Her childhood playmates did not speak to her as much as they used to, sitting in huddles in their rare free moments and flirting with the local boys. That Peter Malone – her neighbour's son who worked at the forge – was always giving her the eye, but most of the other boys and girls ignored her. She found Peter's attention flattering and he was a nice-looking lad and easy to get along with. She liked the way he spoke, as he was quite clever with words sometimes, usually when he was teasing her. But she found that the things her local friends talked about did not interest her much these days and they seemed to sense it. She was still attached to them, for comfort mostly. Anny began to feel left out, even a little shunned.

She was contemplating this one cold night, warming herself by the hearth with her father, the room dimly lit by a single oil lamp.

'Ow bist, my wench?' he said.

'I'm thinking on the young'uns hereabouts. It's as if *they* think that *I* think that *I* am better than *them*, but I dunna think that at all.'

'It's the price you pay for being a clever'un,' he replied. 'It separates the wheat from the chaff. You just need to get used to it. You are better'an them now. Simple as that.'

'No, I'm not. I just do a different job, that's all. Folk who do finer jobs than me are no better than me, are they?'

John Woodvine gazed into the fire, a slight smile about his tired eyes, tapping his clay pipe on his bottom lip thoughtfully. 'You're too clever by half for me, my lass,' he said.

'No, Father,' she went on, a terrier with every argument. 'You must agree. The Kings are no better than us, are they? For all their money and learning, they are . . .' She thought of Margaret. 'They are our equals.' Then she thought of the brother. 'Or indeed our inferiors, if you count Master Cyril.'

Her father looked up, frowning.

'What do you know of him? Of Master Cyril?'

An image of Cyril's hand thrusting up that poor servant girl's skirts leapt into her mind. She felt queasy. She hated to think on it, but she did think on it often. It disturbed her and fascinated her in equal measure. Questions filled her mind: what was he doing up there? What did he want up there? She knew something of how babies came into the world, but didn't think hands and fingers had much to do with it. Or violence. Or throwing someone up against a tree and whispering nasty things in their ear. She didn't understand it, didn't understand him, that boy who kicks dogs. He was rather handsome, for sure, those pretty blond curls. But his mouth was cruel and his eyes were frightening. She did not like to think of him at all.

'Enough to know he is a bad'un.'

Her father sat upright and looked directly at her. 'You're right, my lass. You stay away from him. He is a bad'un, a rotten'un if truth be known. He made trouble for me at the furnace for no good reason.'

'What trouble?' asked Anny, worried.

'It's naught for you to worry about. It's just I think he took against me that day, Anny. And I wouldna want you to be caught up in that, not with your prize post at the King office. Just do your best to stay clear of him. There's a good wench.'

'Oh, I will, Father. Dunna you fret about that.' She stood up, stepped over to her father and put her arms around his neck, kissing his rough cheek. 'I can look after myself, no danger.'

It played on her mind though. Sometimes, from her desk in the office, she could hear Cyril shouting at the stable men or the yelp of dogs in his path. She would lift her head and listen intently, but he would always pass on, to some mischief or other. Luckily, he had no interest in the estate office or anything clerical, and never appeared there. She felt safe from him in its wood-panelled interior, cosseted and looked after by her kindly bosses.

Until one October morning. Anny was at her desk, copying out a letter to an iron merchant from Birmingham. It gave her much pleasure that her words would be transported far and away to such exotic places as these great cities of the Midlands and beyond. One day she wondered if a letter by her hand might reach as far as London. Mr B was going through a pile of receipts, while Mrs B was out on an errand. The office had an air of quiet industry, just the rustle of Mr B's papers and the scratch of her pen on paper, the tap of her nib on the glass rim of the inkpot. Outside, it was a blustery day where the wind swept up clouds of autumn leaves in the courtyard and threw them around like fiery confetti, some blowing in at the office door as it opened abruptly, and there stood Master Cyril.

Anny glanced at her boss, who lowered his eyebrows at the sight. Cyril looked both impatient and bored.

'Brotherton,' he said. 'My father tells me I must get to know the business. He's sent me here to start. You are to show me around, apprise me of certain particulars. It won't take long. It all looks dull and easy for any man of letters.'

Cyril glanced about the office with disdain, until he noticed Anny, who immediately fell to writing again, afraid to look up, afraid to meet those cruel eyes and be any sort of object of curiosity for them.

'Indeed, Master King. I'd be delighted to. Let me start with the accounts. We can go into my office and leave others to their business.' He opened out his arms, gesturing defferentially towards his room, where the safe and the accounts were kept, where Mr Brotherton did much of his wages work and Anny rarely entered.

But Cyril was not moving and instead stood quite still. Anny felt as if the top of her head were burning. But she would not look up. If she stared long enough at the nib of her pen, at the ink that issued in loops and lines from it, then perhaps this intruder would vanish into thin air and order would be restored.

'And who is this? Look at me, girl. You should get up when I enter and wish me good morning.'

She placed her pen in its stand, lifted her head and looked straight at him. She held his gaze while she stood up and performed a slow, slight dip of a curtsey.

Mr Brotherton cleared his throat and said, 'This is Anny Woodvine, our clerical assistant.'

Anny said, 'Good morning, sir.' Cyril's eyes had watched every movement, had peered about her body as if scrutinising an iron bar for flaws. Then he looked away. His cheeks were pink and he looked perturbed. Anny lowered her eyes and stared at the floor.

'Well, come on then, man. For heaven's sake, I can't stand around here all day waiting for the likes of you.' Cyril marched past Anny's desk and into Mr B's room. Anny wanted to glance at Mr B, see what he made of all this. But she kept her gaze low, not wanting to look at Cyril again. Mr B walked by her and said quietly, 'You may carry on, Anny.'

The door was shut behind them and she sat, picked up her pen and dipped it in the ink, blotted it carefully, then went to write. But she could not concentrate, listening to the barking voice next door and Mr B's conciliatory tone. She heard Cyril say, 'Show me the safe. I want to see all the money my father earns. I want to see it piled up.'

'Huh,' Anny quietly scoffed to herself. *It's not your father earns all that money*, she thought. *It's men like my father. And the Brothertons. And me!*

Then Cyril was shouting. 'How dare you! I am my father's heir and will be your master one day. Open the safe this instant. And don't forget to lock it afterwards. Any one of these workers on this estate would steal it as soon as look at it. That girl out there, for instance.'

What? The cheek of it! She heard Mr B say something about her, but his kind voice could not be clearly discerned through the door.

'I'm sure you do,' Cyril retorted. There was no problem hearing his strident tones. 'Because you are soft on the lower classes, Brotherton, being so close to that station yourself. The thought that an office girl like that is trusted to open and close the safe is outrageous.'

He really was such a nasty piece of work. And how dare he suggest she was not to be trusted! She remembered the first time Mr B had shown her how to unlock the safe. There were two keys, one kept in a hidden drawer in a bureau in his office and the other in a similar secret drawer in Mrs B's desk. She had felt a thrill, not because of the money, but because of the trust with which she felt imbued. She had experienced a true connection with the Messrs B that day and now Cyril King wanted to taint that. Mr B came out to fetch the other key from his wife's desk, letting out a long, vexed sigh.

He collected the key and went back into his office and shut the door. It went very quiet in there. She assumed they were looking at the money. She imagined Cyril fingering it, worshipping it. Herself, she knew its value, how it meant the difference between surviving and dying for her people. But she did not love it for its sake alone. It was only a means to an end for her. But these rich, they coveted it, hoarded it. How the upper classes disgusted her. Except Peggy, of course. Peggy was different. Somehow she had come through the mill of her revolting family and emerged untarnished, pure somehow. A kind and loving person. A true friend. Nothing would ever come between them. But her brother was barking orders again and a chill went down her back, as if Jack Frost ran his fingers down her spine.

Her nib hovered above the page, as if stuck in time. Then a drop of ink splashed onto her neat letter and ruined it. She scolded herself and screwed up the paper, shoving it into her pocket, afraid of admitting the waste of it to her employer. She wanted to get out of the office and away from Cyril. Luckily she recalled that Mrs B had asked her to pop down to the village to collect some green ink. Mrs B always wrote out the work rota in different colours for the different parts of the ironworks. At a glance, one could see exactly which part of the business the paperwork pertained to. Anny loved learning these little tricks of the trade, though Mrs B said it was not a cost-effective way of doing things, but it was how Mrs King senior always did things, and she'd insisted on it continuing. Anny jumped up and grabbed her shawl and bonnet, opening and closing the door as soundlessly as she could, to evade being heard. Only once she had a mile between her and Cyril King did she feel she could relax once more. She hoped against hope that his visit had been a singular event and that he'd soon tire of his father's directives. *If I never see him again*, she thought as she entered the stationer's – her favourite shop in the town, full of delights, better than a sweet shop to her – *it won't be a minute too soon.*

However, Anny was to hope in vain. Cyril made a point of attending the office regularly after that. Mostly, he would ignore her and bark a few things at Mr or Mrs B before disappearing again, but always she felt his eyes on her.

It wasn't until some weeks later, when Mrs B was out of the office and Mr B was shut in his room with Mr Pritchard, that Anny found herself facing Cyril. She was sitting quietly at her desk when the door opened and Anny looked up to see Cyril step in. He gave a quick glance to the empty desk to one side and the closed door opposite, then smiled smugly and shut the door slowly behind him.

He turned and said brusquely, 'Miss Woodvine.'

'Yes, sir,' she said and then remembered to stand up and curtsey. He motioned to her to sit down, then looked at his hands as if he had no idea what to do with them. He clasped them and said once more, softer this time, 'Miss Woodvine.'

Anny stared at him. Should she speak again?

He stepped over to her and hesitated, then awkwardly seated himself on the corner of her desk. Anny looked down from embarrassment, the sight of his thigh bulging towards her papers being just too much.

'Tell me about your work. What is it you do all day?'

'Clerical duties,' she answered, her eyes on her desk.

'I see, I see.' She glanced up to see him stroking his chin, as if she had spoken of some matter of great import. 'And you work with a pen and ink?'

She looked down again. 'Yes, sir.'

'Different coloured inks, I see.'

'Yes, sir.'

'And you assist Brotherton and his wife in . . . matters related to . . . clerical duties?'

'Yes, sir.'

'And you have worked here for some months, Miss Woodvine.'

'Yes, sir.'

'Woodvine. Are you related? To the Woodvine at the furnace?'

Anny had felt the heat of discomfort from the nearness of Cyril on her desk. Now, she felt his fingers prying into her life and it sickened her. What was he about?

'That is my father, sir.'

'Is he, indeed?'

Anny did not respond.

'Look at me when I'm addressing you, girl,' he snapped and she had to look up at those cruel blue eyes, hypnotic and revolting all at once. But he did not look at her with a mocking sneer, as she had seen him give others. When she looked up at him, his face softened and he seemed to be searching for something in hers. The intensity of that searching blue gaze was deeply disturbing to her and she could not bear it. She looked down again.

'I did not mean . . .' began Cyril, but then he paused and stuttered as he continued, 'A pretty girl. You are. A very pretty girl. But you must, in your position, you see . . . You are . . . different from the other girls. I've never met a girl remotely like you. I am growing fond of you, Anny. Very fond.'

Anny could not believe her ears. The young master speaking so frankly to her, so softly. She had assumed he only wanted one thing from her, as with any other female subordinate he took a fancy to. But now? 'Anyway,' he went on swiftly, ignoring her lack of response to his declaration, 'perhaps you would come and sit with me one time and talk to me? Or we could go for a walk together? In the woods.'

At that moment, Mr B and Pritchard appeared from the inner office and both stopped nervously at the sight of Cyril. He hopped up from Anny's desk and bid good afternoon to all, swiftly leaving and slamming the door behind him. Mr B looked at Anny. She wanted to smile at him, but her eyes were wide with alarm. She'd not forgotten what happened to the last girl Cyril had taken into the woods. Whatever he said, Cyril King had a bad way with girls and it was always more force than fondness.

From that day forward, Anny did all she could to avoid the young master, but somehow he always contrived some way to be near her.

It was just a few days later when she saw Cyril hanging around outside the office at home time. Shaking at the thought of her long walk alone through the forest, she asked Mr B if she could stay behind to do some extra paperwork.

'But you've done more than your fair share today, my dear,' said Mr B. 'You run along home.'

She turned and eyed the courtyard nervously, hoping his figure had gone, but there he was, kicking about a stone, hands in pockets, waiting, waiting for something. Or someone. Mr B joined her at the door and then said, 'I see.'

He pulled the door to and said to Anny, 'Wait here for a moment, then you will see that you can go home soon, unmolested.'

'Thank you, sir,' said Anny, so grateful she wanted to cry.

Mr B smiled and a glance was exchanged between him and his wife, who came to Anny and asked after her mother and father. Anny answered politely, yet her attention was on Mr B, who had gone outside and was talking to Cyril. The boy looked annoyed as he looked in her direction. Anny flinched at the expression on his face, as if burned by it. But Cyril did leave, and soon he and Mr B were gone behind the line of trees that led up to the big house.

'Off you go now, Anny. Don't dilly-dally on the way. Quick march home,' said Mrs B, a knowing look in her eye.

'I will. Thank you, ma'am,' said Anny and Mrs B looked down at her kindly, yet her eyes were worried.

Anny ran home that evening, a stray twig scratching her face as she rushed through the woods to the safety of home. All the way, her mind twisted in knots. She must work out a way to escape this creature, this fly in the ointment. Her job at the office had been like a gift from heaven, so happy and fulfilled she felt. But then there was Cyril. She sensed he could ruin her happiness, every last drop of it. She wished he were an insect she could squash beneath the heel of her boot. If only. She knew there was no way to avoid him. He was a gatekeeper for the next stage of her life and she had to work out how to charm him, evade him or destroy him. Surely there must be a way.

She could not eat much that night, and felt sick all evening. She said she had a bad belly and went to bed early. She wanted to tell her mother and father about Cyril, about his strange looks and his declaration, but how could she frame it? She did not know how to explain it to them. It shamed her. And anyway, what could they do about it? What could anyone do?

She kept her candle alight to write a letter to Peggy. It always cheered her to write to her friend. Peggy, dear Peggy. So nice and caring, so interesting and interested. So different from her elder brother; how could they be siblings and turn out so opposing, like sun and moon? She knew Peggy hated Cyril. Perhaps she could write to her about Cyril's unwanted attentions, see if his sister could reason with him. But she knew it was hopeless. Peggy feared Cyril even more than she did. She put her pencil down, the letter unwritten.

But if Peggy knew her friend was in danger from Cyril, the kind of danger that the poor maid Lucy had suffered in the woods, surely she would do something? Anny decided that a letter was not the place to approach this. It must be explained to Peggy face to face. It needed to be somewhere away from the office, away from the big house or even the woods, in case Cyril found them on one of his roaming walks. She decided on a plan and began to write, new hope fuelling her tired fingers.

Chapter 7

Dearest Peggy,

I am considering that it is high time we meet up again as friends do. I also wish to speak to you of a private matter that would be best away from your home or even the woods. I cannot explain by letter but all will become clear when I see you. I am wondering if you would like to try a small adventure. If I meet you by our fairy tree, I could bring for you some clothing such as an ordinary working girl of my circle may wear, and you could use this to dress in. As you never come to the village, no one will recognise you. Then we could go to my house and I would introduce you to all as another girl who works at Mr B's office. They would not know the difference and would be accepting of it if I explained it right. I think this would be fun, and would allow us to talk freely away from the big house and my work, and away from other prying ears. It could be such fun, and I imagine it would amuse you to dress up and to see where I live and my neighbours. You are always so nosy about such things in your letters, which I find most curious as I cannot imagine what a young lady like yourself could possibly find interesting in my way of life, but indeed your many questions on the subject convince me of this.

What do you say to my plan, Peggy? Are you game for such a thing?

Yours sincerely and with great friendship always,
Anny

Margaret's delight could barely be contained. A 'small adventure', Anny had called it. Nothing could be further from the truth for Margaret. It was the greatest adventure of her life so far, bar none! To not only escape her home and environs, to dress up in the costume of another class, to meet new people and pretend to be another. Another name, another girl, another life. It was the most thrilling idea she could imagine. At breakfast on the Saturday morning, she almost gave herself away by laughing aloud when spooning out her eggs. She could barely eat, but knew she had to keep up appearances. Nobody cared where she was most of the time or what she was doing. Cyril was busy with their father and Queenie had a bad chest and was staying in bed, ringing her bell commandingly for Jenkins to bring warm compresses and hot lemon drinks at regular intervals. Everything was perfect. She passed the morning in a frenzy of anticipation. Margaret found her least fussy dress and smallest bonnet with the least number of ribbons to tie to keep it in place. At lunch-time she asked for lunch in her room, tied it up in a cloth and left the house by the back stairs.

It was November and unseasonably warm outside. She was glad of this, as the thought of shedding her coat and dress and putting on Anny's clothes – whatever on earth Anny had found for her to wear – would be a chilly business in the woods on a normal November day. In the shade it felt brisk, yet the sun was out and the feel of it on her face was good and warm. She loved the creaking of the tree boughs and the slow splash of heavy fish in the river beyond, the bird calls of alarm as she passed by and then the unmistakable sound of her friend, calling her name, the name only her dear friend reserved for her.

'Peggy! Over here!' Anny stood, a bundle in her arms, in the midst of a circle of trees just beyond their fairy oak. She had chosen her spot well, as it afforded a little cover from the elements and any passing strangers, though they rarely saw walkers here.

'Anny!' called Margaret, beside herself with excitement, breaking into a run and nearly tripping over some tree roots in her rush to see her friend.

Anny placed the bundle on the ground as Margaret approached, then the girls threw their arms around each other, laughing and laughing. It was so good to see each other!

'Those ringlets,' Anny said and tutted. 'They shall never pass for a working lass. What were you thinking, putting those in today?'

Margaret's hand went to feel one of her sausage curls defensively. 'Royce does this with my hair every day. One cannot arouse suspicion by changing one's routine for no good reason.'

'Who's Royce again?'

'My maid, of course.'

Anny laughed, a rich, throaty laugh like a boy. 'Well, of course, it was *my* maid's day off, hence *my* locks resemble a fox dragged through a hedge backwards! One canna get a reliable maid these days, can one?'

'You are mocking me!' cried Margaret, good-naturedly, though she was a little affronted.

'I am, I am. It is my job to laugh at the rich and your job to take it. It is the way of things. Now then, let's get those fine clothes off and here's my cousin's dress. She is away with family and I borrowed it from her closet. Here, let's dress your hair too. I'll pin it back up and hide those ringlets. Dunna fuss now. Dear to goodness, these ribbons take an age to undo.'

'Oh, you are a scold!' cried Margaret, laughing, poking Anny in the side to make her laugh, as they pulled off her clothes. The cousin's dress was of a rough brown checked material but was a decent enough fit. There was a shawl of beige and dark green, so soft to the touch that Margaret held it to her cheek. There were stout boots and a plain bonnet, Anny re-dressing Margaret's hair to take some of the lady out of it. Bonnet on, boots on and Anny stood looking her up and down.

'We'll have to hope nobody eyes your fine stockings. But other than that, you'll do. Oh, but we need a name for you. Something ordinary.'

'Mary?'

'Yes, Mary will do. Mary . . . Brown. That's the dullest name I ever heard.'

'Mary Brown it is,' said Margaret, thoughtfully. 'I wonder what Mary Brown's life is like.'

'Oh, awful,' said Anny. 'She's beaten every day at noon by her father, a terrible drinker. Her mother is on the streets of Shoosby and thrown in prison for doing terrible things with rich gentlemen. She has five younger sisters who all rely on her weekly pennies from Mr B's office to survive, and Mary Brown cooks them cabbage soup every night of the week so they all have stomach cramps and fart themselves to sleep.'

They fell about laughing at that, so much so that Margaret got a stitch.

They stashed Margaret's rich girl clothes beneath a bush in the little copse she'd changed in, then linked arms and walked on through the woods towards the tiny hamlet that Anny called home. All the way they talked and talked, a rushing river of words. As Margaret talked, she glanced at her friend and saw she was frowning at her.

'What is it, Anny?'

'That voice of yours, the words you use. Too much governess talk for this lot. You'll have to curb it. Use a bit of local talk. Now then, instead of *How are you?* you say *Ow bist?*'

'How be-ist?' attempted Margaret.

'Well, just say it quicker. And when you wanna say *going to* you wanna say *gunna,* and when you wanna say *want to,* you wanna say *wanna*. Like, you might say, *I'm gunna wanna do that after*. You try it.'

Margaret looked at her friend's eager face and wanted so very much to please her. 'I'm gur-ner wur-ner do that arrfter.'

Anny's face was a complete blank. 'I think it's best all round if you just keep your mouth shut!'

At that, Margaret laughed and agreed, 'You know best, Anny.'

They went on their way. Margaret did not want to let her friend down. She decided to play the shy card – she could do that. She knew it well.

'Here we are!' cried Anny, as they quickened their step down an incline. Ahead of them was a shambling collection of huts and small houses along the riverbank, mostly housing ironworkers and some miners, some brickmakers and a few random others. Anny's neighbours were hanging clothes out to dry, feeding pigs, collecting eggs, smoking pipes, talking, shouting at the children. A girl saw the two of them coming and shouted out to Anny, asking who the stranger was. Anny said simply, 'From the office.'

'Another'un who never uses her hands, is it?' shouted the girl.

Anny turned to Margaret and said, 'They think I reckon I'm big-sorted because I dunna do hard labour anymore.' Then Anny turned back to her friends and called out, 'Try writing a letter without using your hands!'

Margaret marvelled at Anny's bravery, shouting at her friends like that. There were a few retorts and shakings of the head and hand gestures. It was all good-natured banter but something that Margaret had never experienced. She may as well have been on the moon. This was a world where people shouted at each other for fun. The only shouting in her house was in anger and usually preceded violence: a slap across the mouth, a verbal insult. *You're a great disappointment. You're an embarrassment to this family. You killed your mother.* And so forth. She really would rather be Mary Brown, for all her flatulent sisters.

'Day off from pushing a pen, is it, Anny?' said a boy behind them. The girls turned to see a tall blond lad, hands in pockets, smiling at Anny. 'What terrible hard work it must be.'

'Oh, it is, Peter Malone. Those pens are awful heavy.'

'I'm sure. I warrant those hands are nice and soft, with no washing done or ironstone picking. I warrant they're soft as kitten ears.'

'You'll never know!' laughed Anny. 'I wouldn't touch you with a barge pole!'

Peter Malone glanced in Margaret's direction, then stepped closer to Anny and whispered to her, loud enough for Margaret to catch it, 'A kiss is out of the question, then?'

'Get off with you, hobbety-hoy!' cried a good-natured voice close by and Margaret turned to see a woman with flushed cheeks and broad, strong forearms, hands on her hips. Meanwhile, Peter Malone slunk off in response, grinning all the while. The cheek! The way these people spoke to one another! It was shocking. It was also thrilling.

Anny said, 'This is my mother. This is Mary Brown, who works at Mr B's office.'

Margaret was about to bob down in a curtsey when she remembered Mary Brown and said quietly, 'Pleased to meet you.' Is that something a lower-class girl would say?

'What's for tea, Mother?' said Anny. Margaret sensed she was changing the subject to distract her mother's curious gaze.

'Why, it's two jumps to the pantry door, Anny. Now run along, you lasses.'

Margaret felt she had evaded capture, thanking providence that Mr Woodvine was doing his Saturday shift at the furnace and was not due home until teatime. If anyone might recognise her as the young lady of the big house, it might be him, though she doubted it. How much attention was paid by everyone to her on her rare trips out of the house, she imagined it was little if any.

Anny chatted merrily to Margaret for a while about the different families who lived in her row of houses and what they were like, what jobs they did, tittle-tattle and gossip. Then they spent some time watching the little ones play a game of jacks that they'd fashioned from old animal bones found in the woods. Then, a man came from one of the little houses, an older man, dressed in plain clothes, the telltale flat-brimmed hat of a Quaker bobbing past them. Margaret saw that behind him toddled a very young child, maybe a year old, its arms outstretched, its hands opening and closing and its face upturned in delight towards the Quaker man. The child called out and he turned around, picked the child up and whispered in its ear, carrying it back to the cottage as it squirmed and giggled in his embrace. At the door stood a woman around the same advanced age. They were perhaps in their sixties, both white-haired. He gave the child to the woman and went on his way.

Margaret thought of Queenie and wondered if she'd ever carried her granddaughter in her arms. Again, that sense of deflation, that she would rather have Mary Brown's life any day of the week than her own. 'What nice grandparents,' she observed to Anny.

'Oh, not grandparents but parents,' said Anny.

'Indeed?' questioned Margaret, intrigued. 'But, their age?'

'Well, they adopted her. The baby came in recent months to live here. The Quaker family have taken it in. They have a grown-up son, a miner. Nobody knows who the baby belongs to and tongues do wag about it. But they are such good, caring people that nobody really minds, and so the villagers have taken the child to heart as one of us.'

Margaret thought, *It must be their son's child, surely, born out of wedlock and brought from the mother.* She watched the old woman take up the child. Ah, it was pretty, golden-haired with a laughing face.

'Anny, wonna you help with this a minute?' called Mrs Woodvine and Anny trotted off to her mother, who was doing something with a knife to a heap of turnips. Margaret had not the first clue how to deal with a turnip, and anyway, she did not want to engage in conversation with Mrs Woodvine too much, lest she give herself away. Also, she found herself drawn to the Quaker family and wanted to continue watching them. She wandered towards their house, listening to the child's sweet laughter. The woman was chucking her under the chin and talking gently to her.

'Come 'ere, little'un. Weer'st thee bin, eh? What's thee bin doin'? Me little ducky egg.'

Did anyone ever speak so lovingly to me? she wondered. The woman looked up as Margaret approached.

Margaret stopped, unaware that she had even walked over there, so lost in the reverie was she.

'Good day,' said the woman.

'Erm . . .' Margaret cleared her throat. 'Good afternoon.'

'A friend of the Woodvines, I see.'

'Yes, of Anny's. We work together.'

The toddler was staring at Margaret now, an uncertain hand grasping at her adoptive mother's apron for reassurance.

'What is her name?' asked Margaret.

'This be Martha,' said the woman. 'And I be Hannah Beddoes.'

'I'm Margaret,' said Margaret. 'No! I am not. I am Mary! Mary Brown.'

Hannah Beddoes looked amused, then replied, 'An easy error to make. The names are similar. Margaret and Mary. And Martha.'

'Yes,' muttered Margaret, keenly aware of her flaming-hot cheeks. What a terrible liar she was.

'Ma-ma-ma-ma-ma,' babbled the child, her eyes firmly fixed on Margaret, who crouched down and held out her hand to the child. One swift glance at Hannah gave her the courage she needed and she took some wobbly steps over to Margaret. Her speed increased, but the momentum was too much for her newly acquired walking and she tripped, falling into Margaret's arms. She was a brave little thing and did not cry. Up close,

Margaret stared at the girl's upturned face, now able to see what bright, large green eyes the child had. Extraordinary eyes.

'You are so pretty,' murmured Margaret, transfixed by the eyes. It was as if she had seen those eyes before somewhere, in another face, so familiar were they to her. 'Such a pretty one, she could be a fairy child. A changeling.'

Hannah Beddoes sniffed, and one look showed she did not approve of the comment.

'Oh, I am sorry, I did not mean . . . I mean . . .' Margaret stuttered, mortified.

'Think naught on it, my dear. She is a curious chicken, in her looks, indeed she is. And the babby did come from off, but not so very far away. She had a tragic story, you see. But it was God's will that my husband should be the one to find the babby and keep her safe.'

Margaret touched the little girl's face, who shrank from her and tottered back to Hannah. 'I cannot think of a luckier child, I really cannot,' said Margaret, looking about her at the ramshackle line of cottages and their disrepair, the poverty ingrained in the muddy boots and grimy faces of all who lived there. Yet she knew she'd trade her life with this green-eyed child in a moment.

'Time to go, Mary Brown!' called Anny as she approached.

Margaret wished the Quaker woman a good day and hurried to join Anny.

On their walk back to the fairy tree, Anny fell quiet. It seemed that her mind was heavy with something. Margaret suddenly recalled what Anny had said in her letter, that she had something to discuss with her. In all this excitement, she had forgotten it.

'You said in your letter that you wanted to talk to me about a private matter?'

'Yes,' said Anny and stopped walking. 'I do need to talk to you about summat.'

'Anything,' said Margaret, and meant it.

'It's about Cyril.'

'Cyril? What about him?'

'He's been bothering me at work.'

'Bothering? How?' A churning began in Margaret's stomach.

'He wants to talk with me, or sit with me, or go arm-in-crook with me. Mr B is very good and heads him off, distracting him and such, while I slip away. But I canna keep it up forever, and one day he will find me alone and . . .'

A flash of imagery jumped into Margaret's mind – Cyril pushing Lucy against a tree. Oh, the thought of it, the very idea of it for Anny.

'But Anny, didn't you know? He's going away.'

'Eh?'

'Yes, Father is sending him away to boarding school. He's always had a tutor, but I overheard Father say he was lazy and needed taking in hand, that going out into the world would be good for him. He's starting in the new year, when he turns fifteen. I've seen his uniform and kit, so I know it will surely happen. It was decided only recently and we have not written this week, seeing as we were about to meet up again. And I was so excited with the visit, it went completely out of my mind today to tell you.'

Anny fell to her knees. Margaret, shocked, crouched beside her friend, whose face was in her hands and she was sobbing, really sobbing.

'Oh Anny, oh Anny, my dear, dear friend. You should've told me. I wish you'd have told me sooner.'

Anny rested her head on her friend's shoulder as they hugged.

'Well, I am telling you now. And you dunna know how happy your news has made me. I could skip and dance and sing!'

The girls stood up and Anny wiped away her tears on her shawl.

'I do know how happy, as I am the same! It's as if a great stone were lifted from my chest. No more slaps for me, no more bullying. Until he returns in the holidays, that is.'

Anny's expression clouded. 'When will that be?'

'Well, not as often as all that. I heard Father and Queenie discussing it and they said that they were sending him away to make a man out of him and that meant no mollycoddling, and that he must not come home at weekends or half-terms. So he must stay until Christmas and thereafter only be allowed home three times a year, in April, August and December. And he's going there for three years, at least!'

'All my Christmases have come at once!' squealed Anny and, hitching her skirt up from her boots, did that little skip and dance of which she'd spoken. Then she stopped suddenly and said, 'Let us hope he inna expelled for bad behaviour.'

'Oh yes, let's pray to God to keep him good! He's a terrible coward though, Anny, so I think it's more likely that, never having been a regular schoolboy, he is the one who will be bullied and kept in line. I would like to see that happen with my own eyes. I would take great pleasure in it!'

'Me too,' said Anny. 'Though I'd rather never lay eyes on him again. No offence.'

'None taken!' laughed Margaret.

The friends linked arms and went on merrily to the fairy tree, gossiping about the locals Margaret had just met.

'You're so lucky to have so many friends, Anny. I do envy you.'

Anny sighed and said, 'I used to have lots of friends. Too many. All bothering me and making noise when I wanted to be peaceful. But now, since I started working at the office, they don't come to me so much anymore. I've changed, I suppose, and they can see it. Now they mostly just tease me about it. They dunna understand me.'

'I do,' said Margaret, squeezing her friend's arm. 'You are simply trying to make a better life for yourself. There is nothing wrong in that.'

'Exactly!' said Anny. 'You see that. But they only think I'm getting above myself. Especially that Peter Malone. He's always on at me about it. Laughing at me. Well, I dunna find it funny anymore.'

'Is Peter Malone in love with you?' Margaret asked.

'Oh, I dunna know and I dunna care! I'm not interested in him or any boys. I'm far too busy.'

'He seemed to like you very much.'

Seeming embarrassed at the turn of conversation, Anny became dismissive. 'He's nothing and nobody. Dunna waste any more of your thoughts on the likes of him.'

They walked on in silence, Margaret wondering what it was like to be wanted like the Malone boy obviously wanted Anny. It must be the most marvellous feeling. She envied Anny that. She envied Peter Malone, his easy way of talking. She envied Anny's neighbours, their simple, happy lives, as she pictured it.

'I have a question about your neighbours,' she said, as they reached the tree and she began to shed her working clothes. 'The Quaker baby. Where did it come from? Does anybody know?'

'Nobody really knows,' said Anny nonchalantly. 'But I heard my mother say they found the baby on the iron bridge.'

As Margaret changed back into her rich girl's clothes, a phrase echoed over and over in her mind. *The baby on the bridge, the baby on the bridge.* It must be the same one her grandmother mentioned, mustn't it? But what could Queenie have to do with this green-eyed foundling? Then she knew where she'd seen those eyes before. Her grandfather had those same large, bright green eyes.

Once home, Margaret sought out Queenie in bed, surrounded by the clutter of illness: used handkerchiefs and hot compresses gone cold scattered amongst the sheets.

'How are you, Grandmother? Are you improving?'

'So, you've deigned to see me, child,' said Queenie testily. Then, more softly, seeming to recall that she was meant to be at death's door, 'Where can you have been all afternoon?'

'By the river, walking. That's all.'

'It does look a pleasant day, from what I can see from my sickbed.'

'It is. Quite warm. Grandmother, I wanted to ask you about something.'

'What is it now?'

Margaret had to frame it carefully. She must ensure it sounded casual, something overheard.

'Out walking, there were some local children playing in the woods. They were gossiping and one of them said about a baby that had been found on the bridge.'

Queenie looked at Margaret sharply, then turned away and closed her eyes.

'Leave me now, child.'

'But Grandmother, why is it that you talk of this baby, of it escaping the King family?' Margaret wanted to say it had green eyes, but she realised that would give her away, that she had seen the child itself. Questions would come thick and fast from Queenie about where she had really been that afternoon.

'I told you to leave. Your prattling on about nothing has exhausted me.'

'But it is not nothing, is it, Grandmother? Please tell me.'

'There is nothing to tell! Ridiculous child.'

'I will keep it secret. I am good at keeping secrets.'

'Oh, I am sure you are. Butter wouldn't melt. Those huge, innocent blue eyes of yours.'

'The baby on the bridge—'

Queenie pushed herself upright in bed and fixed her granddaughter with a harsh eye. 'Never ask me about that again. Never even mention it again in my hearing. Never, do you hear me?'

'But why?' cried Margaret.

'How dare you quiz me! You, a mere child. A mere girl! The King men act however they please. There was nothing I could ever do about it and nothing you can either. The men of this family are cruel.'

'I know this to be true,' said Margaret. She struggled to form the words, unaccustomed as she was to having anything other than small talk with her family. But she knew this was an important moment, that something crucial was hovering just beyond her reach. 'But I admire you, Grandmother, for the way you stand up to them and speak the truth.'

'Well, that is all very well, but it is sound and fury, signifying nothing. A woman can say what she likes, but the fact of her life remains. We can fashion a life from the scraps our men leave us, but that is all a woman's life is made of. The leavings of cruel men. You would do well to learn that now, before you are courted and wed. Now, where is Jenkins? I am ill and you have upset me. Fetch Jenkins this instant. And then, do go away.'

Chapter 8

Three years passed slowly for Cyril. The daily torture of boarding school: running and fighting, shouting and crying, writing and arithmetic, kings and queens, Latin and Greek, cricket and rowing, beatings and fear – the brutal camaraderie and casual violence of boys cooped up together in an upmarket prison paid for handsomely by their willing parents. Whatever little pockets of softness he had in him were gone by the age of eighteen. He had made some friends for life – fierce friendships forged in combat – and enemies, mostly amongst the masters for whom he dreamt up elaborate revenge fantasies he planned to carry out when he was older, a free man and out from under their dictatorship. The school had done its job admirably. The boy he had once been was gone; the man he was becoming had been hacked out of stone and stood proudly at the edge of adulthood, sturdy and jagged. His hunger to dominate females had matured into a cleverer, sneakier power play of sweet talk and mind games. He knew that some girls would not put up with violence, but wanted to hear and believe certain falsehoods in order to spread their legs. There were no girls in his environment to practise upon, but he made sure that trips into the local town were peppered with flirtations with local shop girls and other passing riff-raff of a certain class, higher than maids and lower than ladies. He sometimes found himself behind a bush in a park for a bout of sexual fumbling with one or other of these hussies. But all of them were simply passing through his affections, waiting for the day when he'd leave this cursed gaol of a school and go back home, ready to take up his position on his father's estate and declare his love to Anny. He loved her, or believed he did. What did he want from her? To bed her, every night and every morning too if possible, but also to be improved by her; he admired her. Mostly, he looked forward to the day when he would gloriously take her, the thought of her thick red hair flung across his face making him stiff with eager sexual anticipation.

Three years passed peacefully for Margaret, who had found her portion of contentment after a miserable childhood. Her daily round began with practising the piano, from which she derived huge pleasure, as she had a natural ability for it, a good ear and quick fingers. She played from the heart and found new pieces a welcome challenge that gave her the feeling of meeting new friends. She read many books from her father's largely untouched and undusted library. Her favourites were historical romances and any French literature. She spent much of her small allowance on ordering books written in French and tore open the deliveries when each arrived. How she loved to read aloud in French, in her bedroom, of course, as her father was as anti-French as the next roast beef Englishman. She wrote long letters to Anny. She spent her afternoons taking walks, sometimes 'happening by chance' on Anny at lunchtime to gossip on the path down from the office. The two houses knew that the girls were acquainted by now, though they acted in a restrained and civil manner to each other when others were about, and in private like the close, bosom friends they really were. At teatime every day, Margaret spent an hour with Queenie, not talking much, but playing Old Maid, their new obsession. They would gamble with dried peas, or seeds, or conkers, whatever the season provided. The only blot on her landscape were the thrice-yearly home visits from Cyril, where she mostly made herself very scarce or posted herself at the library window, which had a view across the courtyard to Mr Brotherton's office; if she saw Cyril heading in that direction, she would call to him and try to distract him – Queenie wanted him, Father wanted him, Cook wanted him – to give Anny time to escape from the office temporarily. Her only other problem was her father and his child-wife's continued efforts to match her up with the sons of landed gentry. She found she could not speak to any of them of anything that actually mattered to her. Indeed, she cultivated her reputation for shyness by appearing deliberately boring. Her friendship with Anny had taught her how to speak her true feelings, but with these ill-chosen suitors she clammed up, on purpose. Awkward walks were characterised by long silences, that these young men might have found appealing at first in the demure, pretty blonde, but soon became tiresome for a young man eager to make his way in the world. What a blessed release it was for her when each one fell by the wayside and stopped calling, and she could go back to her books and music. She secretly delighted in thwarting her parents' plans for her future. She was proud of her lovely hair and large eyes, her pale face and long limbs; she dreamt of a dashing romantic hero with flashing, French eyes that would come to her room at night, unannounced and undone by passion for her and her alone. She woke up damp and restless, yearning for something she did not understand yet could not resist. She wanted a different life than the one her father had planned for her.

Three years passed feverishly for Anny, a whirlwind of ambition and optimism. Her father was doing well and there was talk of promotion for him. For years he had been a furnace filler, tipping the charge relentlessly into the furnace mouth. Now he had a chance of becoming a founder, descending from the mouth of hell into the cast-house, where the molten metal ran into sand-sculpted troughs. The founders would guide the surge of iron into the channels and sub-channels, called the sow and pigs, as they resembled piglets feeding at their mother's belly. It was work that required more skill, and Pritchard had put her father's name forward. She was forming a deep conviction that hard work and belief in oneself led to success. All one needed was to do it and then good things would happen. Her work at the office went from strength to strength, learning side by side with the Brothertons, who grew as fond of her as kin. Her language changed, improved as far as she was concerned, as she moved further away from the local words and sayings of her family, friends and neighbours and grew more alike with her betters, as she saw them. It pleased her more and more to listen to herself talk. She excelled at problem-solving, her mind quick-thinking and logical. Her handwriting continued to develop beautifully, yet she tired of clerical work. She joined Mr B more in his office, discussing labour troubles and matters of commerce with him, learning from him always yet surprising him often with her insight into how to get the best out of people, whether workers or merchants; how to make them feel appreciated yet also get their best deal for the estate. Everyone winning was always her goal. She, too, wrote long letters to her friend, Peggy. She, too, did all she could to avoid Cyril when he visited three times a year. Sometimes she was not able to give him the slip and was forced to engage in conversation. He was not as arrogant, impatient and utterly objectionable as he had been in his earlier youth, but she did not like him or trust him. The hint of cruelty remained in his eyes and she did not like to look at them, as they made her insides twist and jerk, a most unpleasant and confusing sensation. Romance was a stranger to her, as the inept attempts of local lads to steal a kiss or more were always spurned forthrightly. They had no ambition, no get-up-and-go, no prospects. She stared at herself in the looking glass and hated her freckles, cursed her red hair. She had creamy skin and elegant narrow feet, which she admired, but wondered if anyone would ever notice such things, strapped up in her boots, or stuck in a dim, wood-panelled office. She longed for a young man like her, a good man, a moral man, with a burning ambition to change the world. Hand in hand, they would stride forward into the future. They would be masters of their own destinies. They would brush aside with ease any obstacles, which would disperse like wispy dandelion seeds on a warm breeze. She believed in this future utterly and saw no earthly reason why it would not all come to pass one day soon. All she needed was to find him.

Anny was writing when she first saw Jake Ashford. People came in and out of the office all day, and with Cyril still away at school she did not flinch when the office door opened. Mr B was in his room with the door closed, in conference with Pritchard. Mrs B was poorly and taking the day in bed. Anny was going to pop over to the cottage to see her and make her a little broth. She just wanted to get this letter finished. The door opened and she did not want to interrupt her work, so finished the sentence she was on, then looked up impatiently.

'Good morning,' said the young man standing before her. 'Or is it afternoon?'

Anny stared at him. He was an outsider to these parts. She had lived near Ironbridge all her life and worked at that office day in, day out for three years, and she knew everyone who was likely to come in. This one was new. He was far too well dressed for an ironworker, too fashionable for a merchant or salesman and not well dressed enough for a friend of the Kings. He fitted into no category she had experience of and was therefore a mystery. His enigmatic air was complemented by dark eyes and a tall, broad-shouldered frame curving into a narrow waist, clothed in a smart frock coat and he was holding a large leather wallet secured with a strap. He removed a tall hat to reveal a luxuriant mop of black hair, parted at the side and curly about the ears. *Who could this magnificent stranger be?*

Anny glanced downwards, struggling to contain her obvious curiosity and managed to utter, 'Can I be of assistance?'

'I do hope so. My name is Jake Ashford and I am an artist.'

'A what?' said Anny, before she could stop herself, then cursed her big mouth. Of course she knew what an artist was. Well, she had an inkling. But she had made herself look ignorant, she felt. 'I should say, an artist? How interesting.'

Jake Ashford's face broke into a smile and Anny could not help but smile too. Perhaps she had not made such a fool of herself. 'Thank you. I have come here to paint the wonders of industry.'

The what of what? she nearly blurted, but checked herself. *What could he want here?* 'I see,' she said, though she didn't.

'I wish to paint the developments happening here, in your area, to help show the world how extraordinary it is.'

'Is it? Extraordinary, I mean?' Anny couldn't see how her home town could be of interest to anyone. It's true she was proud of her father and his work, making iron that was shipped across the country, even abroad. But it was hard to see why anyone would want to come and see the processes by which it was made, let alone paint it. It was like painting the swan's feet and not the swan.

'Oh, yes!' he enthused. 'This is the centre of a revolution that is being felt all over the world. It must be recorded for posterity. Other artists have visited areas of industry to record the great rate of change taking place. Painters, poets and writers flock to them.'

'Do they?' she asked, amazed. *Here? Our little town?*

'Oh, indeed. The world's first iron bridge built here was a mighty advertisement to visitors to say, *Look, see what we have created here!* We come to marvel at the wonders of technology, improving year on year, the rate of change astonishing. And that is why I am here now. I wish to ask permission to visit the King ironworks and its workers and make sketches. I will then turn these into paintings, works of art for all to see the beauty and majesty of what is happening here.'

Anny was completely wrapped up in his words now. 'Beauty? What is beautiful about an ironworks? I've been around it all my days and never seen much beauty in it.'

Jake Ashford took a step closer, placed his hat on Anny's desk and raised his hands in the air. 'The night sky above the furnace here turns blood red and scarlet, fiery orange and burnt umber. It is spectacular! Have you not seen it?'

'Of course I've seen it!' she cried. 'I live here! My father works there.'

'He does?'

'Yes, he's worked at the furnace for years.'

'Can you not see its beauty? The hellish colours? The power of it?'

Anny pictured it in her mind's eye and thought about how impressive it was. He was right. She was simply accustomed to it.

'I suppose it is. I cannot, imagine a painting of it though. But I think you could make it beautiful.'

Her mouth moving faster than her thoughts, as usual. She was really thinking that *he* was beautiful, all fired up like that; she could almost see the flames reflected in those deep, dark eyes. She looked away and noted again the leather folder he held and wondered if his drawings were in there. She was about to ask to see them when the door behind her opened and out came Mr B and Pritchard, who were talking away until they saw the young man in their midst. Both stopped, and Mr B said, 'And who's this? May we help you, young sir?'

'This is Mr Ashford,' said Anny. 'He's here to paint.'

The older men's faces were as blank as her own at first. Once it had all been explained, Mr B was soon drawn into Jake's vision, too. He talked with Jake for some time and Anny listened intently, not able to add much to the conversation but watching Jake Ashford the whole time. Mr B agreed to take him up to the big house to speak with the master.

'I'll go and see Mrs B afterwards, Anny. You have your lunch in peace, go where you will. Don't forget to lock up.'

As Mr B left the office, he held the door open for the artist, who paused before he left. 'It was a pleasure to meet you, Miss . . . ?'

'Woodvine. But you can call me Anny.'

'And you must call me Jake,' he said with a smile, and bowed to her, flourishing his hat before him and walking out, the door shut firmly behind him by Mr B.

Anny did not eat her lunch that day. She had not the stomach for it. She did not even leave the office. She hoped Jake Ashford would return with Mr B. But he did not. She sat at her desk all afternoon, distracted from her beloved work for the first time since Cyril's unwanted visits. She wondered what Mr King would say to this young artist. Would he be flattered by the attention or see the young man as beneath him? Anny willed him to accept. If Jake were granted permission, he would be about quite a bit. He would paint her father's workplace and maybe even her father, who knew? Could she show him around? Could she be his guide? What would Father think of this? Her mind was filling with questions. But the uppermost one was this: when would she see Jake Ashford again?

Whenever Margaret heard people in the house, it was usually either business associates of her father or fatuous friends of her stepmother, and neither were of any interest to her. She found both sets of people intimidating and usually slunk off to her room and stayed there. These days her parents had more or less given up on the idea of her being any sort of social animal and left her alone. She heard the door open that let in business visitors and heard Mr B's booming voice first. Well aware from Anny's accounts of how nice Mr B really was, she had no fear of him anymore, but anyone loud always set her on edge. She was seated in the library reading a French novel when she heard him and did not have time to get past him up the stairs to her room, so hoped that they would not come in here. Mr B was with someone, that was clear, as he was talking away and a voice was answering, quietly at first, so she had to strain to hear. What were they talking about? Something about the business, about the furnace? She went back to her book. But the other voice was louder now and talking about colour. Lots of colours. He was listing colours and applying them to the things he had seen. His voice was quick, eager and intelligent. She heard the maid say that her father had stepped out briefly and would they like to wait for him in the library? Before she had time to gather herself, the door was opening and the visitors were inside.

'Ah, Miss King!' cried Mr B, his voice as piercing as ever. Beside him stood a dark-eyed young man, but before she had time to fully register him, Mr B went on, 'Studious, as ever. Always a nose in a book. There never was such a child for quiet contemplation as Miss King. Never wants to talk, eh? Except to our Anny, the only one who ever was able to draw a conversation from you, Miss King.'

Margaret bowed her head, perceiving a slight criticism. She had no idea what to say to that; she never did in these moments of social chit-chat. It was always better for everyone if she just disappeared upstairs. Then, another voice spoke.

'But I see we are disturbing you, miss. My humblest apologies. I should wait outside, in the grounds perhaps.'

Margaret looked up. The young man was handsome, decidedly so. And his politeness to her made him seem even more so. Mr B was wittering on about her and her books and how her father wouldn't be long, yet she had lost all sense of what he was saying. Only those eyes held her. Intent, direct and as black as coals. She was compelled to do something she never did: she interrupted Mr B in full flight.

'Won't you introduce me?' she asked, never taking her gaze from the young man.

'Why, of course,' said Mr B. 'Mr Ashford, this is Miss King, the daughter of the household. Miss King, this is Mr Jake Ashford, an artist and painter who wishes to paint your father's ironworks and seeks his permission. A most interesting project, I must say.'

Margaret knew it was not etiquette to shake hands with a young man who was not of her acquaintance. She politely nodded her head and Jake Ashford did the same. Then, he spoke to her.

'I see you are reading in French, Miss King. When I was in Paris, the French shook hands with the left, as they deemed the left hand to be nearer the heart.'

Margaret stared at him. How she wished that when introduced she had extended her hand and felt his own. She was sure it would not be that worst of things – a clammy handshake – but instead imagined it warm and dry, firm and lingering. Her hands tingled at the thought. There was a moment of stillness between them, broken by the sound of her father returning in the hall beyond the library door.

'What?' she heard him say. 'There is a what in the library?' Margaret looked down at her lap. It was the instant effect her father had on her. She wished to look up again at Jake Ashford, but the heaviness of her head in her father's imminent presence prevented her from doing so.

The door opened and her father entered, saying curtly, 'What is this all about, Brotherton?'

Margaret listened to the introductions and explanations with her head still lowered, her eyes burning a hole in the French words on the page before her. Jake Ashford had been in Paris. What was he doing there? Painting, perhaps? How she longed to speak to him of it. She had never been given leave to visit France, her father being such a hater of the people, but she desired to utterly. A vision of walking in the gardens of the Palace of Versailles with Jake Ashford leapt to mind and she started at it, so ridiculous was it. But oh, what a lovely vision! She listened and willed her father to do the right thing, the best thing, for her, that is. Invite this young man to paint his stupid ironworks, but then to stay and become an acquaintance of the family. But her father was taking some convincing.

'But why on earth would an artist want to come here of all places? Shropshire is pretty enough, I suppose, but there are finer places to paint, surely.'

Jake held up his hands towards the window and made the shape of a frame in the air. All eyes turned to his hands and waited for his next pronouncement. 'Ironbridge and Coalbrookdale,' he declared. Names so familiar to Margaret were transformed into something epic in Jake Ashford's tones. 'Surrounded by thick forest yet smothered in coal dust, lit by the constant burning of the fires from the ironworks. Due to the complex geology of this area, a range of vital industries have sprung up along the majestic River Severn. The hills and banks are clustered with steam engines, limestone mines, brick kilns and tar ovens. Wagons loaded with ironstone and coal trundle on iron railways down the inclined plane from the pits to be delivered to the works that will transform them into vital products. Their fruits include pig iron, cast iron and wrought iron; chinaware and fine porcelain; pipes and ceramic tiles – these riches then sent out across the world. What finer subject could a modern artist find than this?'

Brotherton nodded proudly, as if he himself were solely responsible for the marvels the young man described.

Her father looked impressed, too, but was not quite won over as yet.

'Let us peruse your work, then,' he said. 'I cannot possibly agree until I have seen your calibre for myself. I assume you have some in that receptacle by your feet?'

Jake picked up the wallet and opened it on the table at which Margaret was sitting. She closed her book and pushed it to one side. Out came sketch after sketch of charcoal on creamy white paper. Beautiful buildings with elaborate architecture that she could only imagine might have been French or Italian or who knew what, as her education had been so limited and mostly self-administered. There were pictures of birds too and people, large crowd scenes or vignettes of individuals, great bridges that spanned mighty rivers and detailed studies of statues she imagined he must have seen in lofty museums. The beauty of the lines and curves that spilled across the table thrilled her, as if Jake Ashford's very mind had been poured forth before her. What a fascinating person he was, and very clearly talented. She thought the drawings were marvellous. She stole glimpses of him when she could and saw how he stared at her father, so keen was he to impress, it seemed. She wished the decision had been hers and that he had been looking at her so keenly.

Her father was quiet for some time, leafing through the sketches, his mouth tight and his expression giving nothing away. At long last, he spoke. 'These are good,

Ashford. You can draw, I'll give you that. But look here. These European flounces are all very well. But you must be aware that industry is a place of danger and you will be responsible for yourself at all times. I do not have the manpower to chaperone you when molten iron is about. You must be sensible and exhibit . . . common sense.'

'I quite understand,' said Jake. 'I have travelled in Europe alone these past months, and believe I have developed a keen sense of self-preservation.'

'Well then, I cannot see any harm in it. You may become our resident artist. I will pay a small stipend to assist you in your endeavours, if you agree to paint my wife too. I desire a painting of her. Can you do that? Can you manage portraits?'

'I certainly can, sir. I would be honoured to paint anyone for you, sir. Anyone in your household.'

Margaret's heart leapt. Just imagine it, sitting for a painting for him, spending hours with him. Oh, it was too much to bear!

'Yes, well, we shall see about that. Now then, I am a busy man. Brotherton will attend to you and arrange suitable accommodation. See to it, Brotherton.' With that, Mr King left the room and Mr B instantly began to prattle on about the project.

Margaret carefully placed her chair back and stood. Jake was tidying away his sketches and Margaret wanted to help. She picked up one and passed it to him, which he took with a kind smile directed straight at her. She picked up another, a lovely sketch of a formal flower garden, perhaps in Paris, perhaps in Rome, somewhere beautiful. Her eyes lingered on it. The country around here was handsome, nobody could deny it; the Severn was banked by rich, dense woodland and rolling hills beyond. But that was wild and this was tamed nature, rows of hedging and swirls of what looked like tulips, making a stunning pattern of perfect symmetry.

'If you like it, you may keep that,' said Jake.

Margaret shook her head and went to hand it back – unable to agree to a gift from an unknown young man – but she wanted badly to keep it, and worried too that it would look ungrateful. She drew it to her, looked at it again and raised her eyes to his.

'Thank you,' she whispered, and clutched the picture tenderly.

'It is nothing, but you are welcome, Miss King. Most welcome.'

When he had gone, she stared and stared at his drawing. Her drawing, now. She looked up and out of the window, without thinking, clutching the picture tenderly against her chest. When she came to, she saw that the charcoal had imprinted itself onto her yellow dress, leaving a black mark across her breast. She ran her fingers over it, leaving a smudge of darkness on her hand.

Chapter 9

It was noon and Anny had escaped from the office, walked hurriedly down to Ironbridge and sought out a bench upon which to eat her lunch. She was just finishing off the Dawley doorstep spread with butter she had brought with her, when she saw Jake Ashford walking in a leisurely fashion up the street towards her. It was just as she had hoped. As she hurriedly brushed crumbs from her mouth and skirts, he saw her, smiled and increased his pace. They had spoken with each other several times now, either in the office or by chance, in town or near the ironworks. They had talked about his art and her work and more. She had never had such conversations in her life. She picked over the substance of their discussions after each one, rehearsing the arguments she would offer if the subject arose between them again. She was keen to impress him with her thinking, afraid that if she did not keep up with him, he would tire of their meetings. And these meetings had become the bright centre of her life. He seemed to have sought her out at the same bench she had been sitting on the last time they met – or was it merely a coincidence?

'I find you here again, Anny. A welcome escape from the rigours of work?'

'Ah, but I love my work. You know that.'

'True, true. Although, you are one of the few, perhaps. May I?' He motioned to the empty space beside her and she nodded keenly. He took his seat, placing his bag and wallet down on either side.

'Perhaps you're right,' said Anny. 'I know how lucky I am to find my work valuable and enjoyable, when to many it is a chore or a curse.'

'It is not luck in your case, though. Your mother taught you for a purpose and you made the most of that. There was design in it and you grasped it and let your ambition guide you.'

'But you are the same, Mr Ashford. You love your work and you are driven by it. Did you always know you wanted to be an artist?'

'Not until I travelled and saw the old masters. And please, call me Jake.'

Could she? They were friends now, she supposed. But who were these old masters he spoke of? She wondered if she should pretend to understand. But she knew that she'd never get anywhere in life by fakery. She knew nothing of art, and dearly longed for an education like his, even like Peggy's, as limited as that was. But she was not ashamed of this fact, particularly with Jake, who she felt understood that her lack of education was beyond her control, not a part of her but a fact of circumstance.

'What are the old masters?'

He gave her a potted history of Western art, which she tried to follow, but eventually gave up and contented herself with listening to his voice. Then he came to the point.

'These men painted scenes from the Bible, from ancient mythology. What relevance has that to me today? To you, or to any of us? It also seemed like the province of the rich, the classically educated. I knew this was not what I wanted to paint, definitely not. I want to get to the centre of things, to the core of mankind, not its luckiest, its richest, its most dominant. I want to answer the great unanswered questions. On my return, I determined that I would go out into the real world, into the everyday lives of the working people of our great country and discover for myself the substance of what really matters in this day and age.'

To listen to him speak of such things was a thrill like no other. She watched his mouth move with the passion of his thoughts, memorised the tiny details in the nuances of his face: the way he looked far ahead as he spoke, as if his inner eye had travelled forward in time and had already arrived in the future; the way his neck would flush pink when he spoke with fervour, and the way he would listen to her speak. She especially loved the way one eyebrow went up and the other down when she let slip something gushing about him or his ideas, as if to say, *I am not worthy of your fine words*. His modesty made him all the more attractive.

'I am quite sure I never heard a soul speak about the workers the way you do,' said Anny.

'I am not the only one who feels this way. There are writers all over Europe who see the world as I do, the artificial boundaries that exist between the wealthy and the poor. I want to change the way the rich see the working classes. I want my art to show them the dignity in a hard day's work, the wonder of the changes taking place in industry right here on your home ground – not from the scientist's or industrialist's point of view – but from the ordinary folk, how each man and woman is contributing towards this great movement. People like your father. I have sketched him at work, Anny. There is more honour in that man's muscle and sinew than in a thousand Greek heroes. For our modern times, your father is the hero!'

Anny laughed delightedly. If Father could hear himself called a hero, he would laugh his fill, too. But Jake's vision of him rang true for her and touched her heart.

'I am so very proud of my father and the job he does. His work has never been easy, even now he's been promoted. Not only the sweat of it, but the business side of it – the ironmasters and the way they treat the workers. It's not a new thing, been going on like this for years. Why, when he was a young man he stood witness to strikes and uprisings. He often tells us the story, at the fireside of an evening, of when his father's coal-mining friends gathered in protest at the cinder heaps, and the yeomanry were called and opened fire. Two colliers were killed. Others were arrested and one ringleader was hanged. They called it the Battle of Cinderloo. It sounds like a name heroes might choose. But it came to nothing, and still the workers are suffering at the whim of their masters. The working man is stamped on and crushed like an earywig.'

To say these things aloud, and to this handsome young man who listened intently to her every word, was like gulping down wine. Heady and dangerous.

'Seditious talk, Anny,' said Jake, with an approving smile. She did not know the meaning of this, but it sounded good to her.

'Truth, that's all.'

'I know it. I hope my art can help to bridge that gap between the classes. That is my aim. To create a clearer understanding between the masters and the workers. The honour would be mine, to attempt this necessary feat, to use my art for good purpose. It may be folly but I would rather try and fail than live a life of regret.'

Anny listened intently and marvelled at his resolve. Everything she felt was wrong with the world was found here in its polar opposite: this optimistic, heartfelt young man. He was talented, which was appealing enough, but he was also earnest – an irresistible mixture.

Jake went on. 'But I fear it may be a fool's errand. What bridge could ever span that gap, when the rich and the poor are separated as utterly as fish from birds? They live in different worlds. That the rich and poor could ever understand each other seems impossible.'

'Not impossible,' said Anny.

'How so?'

Anny glanced at him, his earnest face. Should she go on?

'I have a friend . . . a rich friend. We understand each other.'

'And how has this come about?'

Anny paused again. Surely he could be trusted. She believed it.

'My best friend is Miss King. Miss Margaret King, up at the big house. It's a secret we share. Most people know we are acquaintances, that we make polite talk with each other if we happen to meet. But what they do not know is that we have been friends for years, have written letters to each other for years.'

'Extraordinary!'

'And she is rich and I am poor, but we understand each other all right. Always have. Why, we are like sisters. Secret sisters.'

Jake clapped his hands and laughed. 'You are full of surprises!'

Anny grinned at this. It delighted her to delight him. The world went on behind them, around and beyond them, but her world consisted only of Jake's words and Jake's eyes.

He said, 'I have met Miss King. She is an intelligent, thoughtful young woman, I can see that. But other than that, she seemed entirely typical of her class. Accomplished, no doubt, yet uninspiring I'd thought, however pretty she may be.'

Pretty. The word sliced through her intimacy with Jake like a knife through butter. The day after both she and Margaret had first met Jake, they had contrived to find each other almost at the same moment, and had let the words tumble out simultaneously, talking under and over each other about all of his attributes. They giggled and blushed, enjoying the opportunity to talk to another who clearly felt the same way. There was a comradeship in it that nobody else but these two girls could understand, the complete wonderfulness of Jake Ashford. Yet, there was a moment, in that very first talk, when both girls had paused and were clearly, obviously, lost in their own private thoughts of him. Then they both glanced up and caught the other at it, a look passed between them, a knowledge of connection in their joint regard for him, yet it left an aftertaste of rivalry, of jealousy, of division. Anny tasted it again at this moment, at Jake's mention of Peggy.

Jake continued, oblivious to the upset he had caused, 'And to hear that you two are friends is quite delicious.

I am going up to the King house later, to fulfil my first appointment to paint Mrs King. I shall give your warm regards to Miss King, wink at her and see if she keeps your secret better than you have, Anny!'

Anny frowned and replied, 'Oh please, no! It was a confidence. I did not mean . . .'

Jake tipped his head back and laughed. 'Oh, but you are too easy to tease! Far too easy!'

Anny relaxed and found herself disarmed by a laugh, his own being infectious.

He lowered his voice and looked straight at her: 'I would never share your confidences, Anny. I wouldn't dream of it. After all, if you could not trust me, then I would lose my chance forever to . . . to become better acquainted with you. If that is something that you wish for also. Do you? Do you wish to see me again and talk this way, another time? Many more times? Do you, Anny?'

'I do,' Anny whispered, as if the words came from deep inside her and had lost their sound by the time they reached her lips. She said again, much more clearly, 'I do.'

'Now that you are home for good, Cyril my boy, you will take up your rightful place at my side. In your sojourns at home, you have accompanied me these past years in all aspects of the business and you have been educated to the correct . . . height – or is it depth? – to have developed your intellect and your sense of duty. I hope you realise how expensive your education was, and how grateful you ought to be for the opportunity?'

Cyril bowed his head suitably and replied, 'Yes, Father, of course. It has been the most enlightening education a boy could wish for.'

He thought of the way old Cadman would bring down his great leather shoe onto any boy's arse he was beating. He was an exceedingly tall man, so his shoes were enormous.

'A man, Cyril. You are a young man now.'

Then why do you call me 'my boy', you idiot? Cyril thought. He thought then of Bostock, the older boy who had also beaten him regularly, with even more viciousness than the masters. '*We shall beat the boy out of you yet, King*,' Bostock used to explain to him, as if each attack were doing him a favour, arming him for the journey into manhood. Oh yes, he had certainly become a man now. He had seen everything. He wondered if his father had been similarly treated in his own time. He supposed not, as if so, why would any father put his own son through that? He would never forgive his father for sending him to that place. Cyril was not the forgiving type. But Ralph King was useful to him – held his future in his hands – so he would play the game and continue to flatter the stupid old duffer.

'Yes, Father. I am ready and willing to serve. I was thinking that I would like to assist Brotherton in his office. There are some nuances of the selling part of the business that I feel I need somewhat more acquaintance with.'

And there is a flame-haired beauty I feel I need far more acquaintance with, thought Cyril. He was working his way up to proposing to Anny. But, as little as she seemed to care for him now, he put this down to her fear for her position. If he could persuade his father that he wanted this girl, then he could reassure Anny that his intentions were honourable – well, some of them – and that her life would be changed forever; she would become the lady of the house. After all, his father had married some jumped-up adolescent strumpet whose parentage was decidedly suspect. Why couldn't his son do the same? But deep down he knew his father would probably never agree to it, yet Anny didn't know that. And maybe he could keep her in a little house, a secret mistress. He was sure his grandfather used to bed the maids. Why couldn't he have his own little worker to bed? He thought, *Why can't I have what I want? I've always had what I want.*

'I cannot see there is much depth to what Brotherton and his ilk do. But if you feel it necessary, for a short time, you may. When you see Brotherton, ask him when this artist fellow is coming to the house. We made an arrangement for him to begin Benjamina's portrait, but I cannot recall when.'

'What artist fellow would that be, Father? What portrait?'

'Oh, some young fellow, a sketcher, who has been recording scenes around these parts. Quite talented, yes. Fired up with the enthusiasm of his craft. These artist types are all passion, you know. He has a Romany air. Ashford, his name. Well, he will do a good job of the portrait. I want him to get started on it.'

Cyril thanked his father. He didn't like the sound of this artist fellow, this Ashford or whatever he called himself, not one bit. You could never trust the artistic types; he knew this from school. There was always something queer about them. And smug, too. He would soon put him in his place, if he saw him about. This fellow was a servant, like any below-stairs washerwoman, and he must remember his place.

It was lunchtime when Cyril marched outside towards the office. *Oh, dash it*, he thought. Anny would probably be having her food somewhere. Margaret was not at home today, visiting some musical concert with Queenie, so Anny wouldn't be chatting with her. Those two were too chatty all round. He didn't like it. He wanted Anny to be his, not his sister's. Although, once he gathered enough courage to talk to his father about marrying Anny, perhaps Margaret could be a useful ally. Yes, that could work in his favour. Perhaps he should talk to the little wretch about it. He'd do that later. He opened the office door to find no Anny. On her lunch, Brotherton informed him. He knew he was supposed to be staying in the office to learn things, but he made his excuses and left. *Where would she be?* He walked down the lane towards Ironbridge. Perhaps she had gone into the town.

Ironbridge had only been in existence as a town these past few decades since the bridge itself was built. Now it was a bustling collection of a weekly market, coaching inns and boarding houses, a bank, post office, printers, grocers and drapers, lawyers and doctors, ironmongers and watchmakers, a meeting house, a school and a newly built church on the hill, and so on and so forth. All human life was here. Cyril thought of the ant nests he used to drown with buckets of water as a boy, only to find another spring up on a nearby patch of ground. Crawling things always found a space to crawl in, even under slimy rocks. You could never escape them. In his younger days, he had loved to bolt from the house and wander through town, jostling with people and looking for girls. These days, the locals mostly disgusted him. Their petty little lives. Each one of them thought they were useful and important. He hated them for that. He knew that many of them were truly necessary, to those around them. He felt he had more in common with the beggars than the workers or the merchants, the shopkeepers and the professionals. He had no place in life, no role. Anny had that. She worked hard and was valued. He wanted to take that away from her, make her his to own and mould in his arms, in his house. His value would be increased by subsuming everything Anny was.

Then, he saw her. It was her red hair he saw first. He could always spot it a mile away; a glorious beacon. She was not wearing her bonnet. She was seated on a bench looking down. Perhaps her lunch was in her lap. What good fortune, to find her away from the office, where they could talk properly. But what was this? A dark-haired man beside her was in conversation with her and she was smiling at him, smiling broadly, veritably beaming at him. The man took off his hat and ran his fingers through his black hair. He had the look of a gypsy about him. Was this the artist fellow? He had a bag on one side – to carry his damned brushes and paraphernalia, he supposed – and a wallet on the other, full of scribbles, no doubt. Cyril stood across the road and watched the two of them. The man opened up his wallet and produced some scraps of paper, in which Anny showed great interest, nodding and talking, looking up to this man, listening intently to every word he spoke.

What had this blasted artist fellow got that he hadn't? He had money and position, a safe future ahead of him. How dare this stranger fraternise with the local girls! The man cupped his hand over his mouth and leant towards Anny, whose head then fell back with laughter. Cyril's eyes narrowed. If this artist fellow was on the scene, well then, it was time to do something about it. In a moment, he would dodge the carts and horse dung on the road and go over there, tell this upstart a thing or two. Any moment now, he would do it. But the man was standing up, taking his leave of Anny with an affected flourish of his hat and a ridiculous bow. Anny watched him go, and Cyril watched Anny watching him. Cyril's blood was up. He straightened his cravat and prepared to cross the busy road. Into his mind came an image of Anny's laughing face tipped backwards in joy, but she was in bed and the man beneath her was not himself, but the damnable gypsy. *This will not be borne*, he told himself. *I will show her who her true master is.* But Anny was up and walking off towards the office at quite a pace. Cyril considered running after her. But what King had ever run after anybody for anything? No, he could wait. He would let his blood boil all afternoon and then, in a secluded place, he would find her, mark her and bag her.

Chapter 10

Margaret waited in the hall, listening to the silence behind the door in the sitting room. She imagined she could hear his brushes dabbing the canvas or the scrape of a knife on the palette mixing the correct hue of gold for Benjamina's silk dress. But in truth, he was most likely doing some preliminary sketches. She could hear nothing and had not the bravery to enter and see for herself Jake's progress with the portrait. She hovered uncertainly, picturing herself turning that brass doorknob and breezing in, asking him if he required any refreshment. She could do that. But she knew she never would. Instead she sat down on a chair in the hallway and waited. It was his first appointment painting her stepmother, so she didn't know how long they would be. If she retired upstairs, she might miss his exit, but if she stayed out here and he came upon her, sitting in her hallway alone, he would surely know she had been waiting for him. *Oh, what to do?*

Then, the door opened and there he was, her decision taken out of her hands. He smiled at her and closed the door gently behind him. He walked towards her with a confidential air, came quite close and – to her alarm and delight – bent his mouth to her ear and whispered, 'Your mother is fast asleep. With her mouth wide open!'

Margaret felt her cheeks burning. She felt quite faint at his nearness. 'She is not my mother,' was all she could think of to say.

Jake stood upright and smiled again, this time lowering his head in deference. 'Of course. Your stepmother. Please forgive me.'

Margaret stood and said, 'Not at all. Well, I must say it is time for her daily nap. Was her dog asleep too? It usually sleeps at this hour.'

'Yes, and it does exhibit a wide range of bodily functions when it sleeps,' he said with a wry smile, again bending closer to whisper, 'particularly of the windy variety.'

Margaret could not help but laugh. He went on, 'One wonders what exertions the lady of the house engages in to require a daily nap. She tells me she does not ride, walk or even leave home if she can help it. It's a wonder how such indolence can be so exhausting.'

Margaret was shocked by Jake's cheek but also rather thrilled by it. 'Mr Ashford, be careful. If my father were to hear you talk in such a way, you would be out on your ear in a trice!'

'But will you tell on me, Miss King?'

She said quietly, 'Of course not.' This confidence between them gave her a different kind of confidence to add, 'Shall we take a turn about the grounds, if you have the time?'

'I would be delighted,' he said and bowed slightly with his arm out, for her to lead the way.

As they crossed the hallway to the front door, she wondered what Anny would make of her asking Jake Ashford to walk with her. At once, she knew that she would not be telling Anny. She wished she could share this with her friend, but she knew she would not. She did not wish to analyse why this was, and instead pushed it to the back of her mind. She did not have time to consider that now, as Jake Ashford was asking her about botany. He wanted to know the names of certain shrubs they were passing and of the trees that circled the formal garden to the side of the house. She was pleased, as it was a subject about which she was quite knowledgeable, having read of them and spent much time in her childhood in the library or out of doors, both excellent for avoiding company. He revealed his ignorance of plants and flowers and the world of nature, having been brought up exclusively in a town house with no garden, front or back.

'I come from a middling sort of background that has recently moved up in the world. My father was a wine merchant in Birmingham, who then expanded into coffee houses, and thereby has made a pretty penny. I was given a good education and even a special tutor in art, which has always been my passion. My father kindly paid for me to take a trip to the near continent – a kind of truncated version of the grand tour – visiting Florence, Rome and Paris to see the great artworks there.'

'I would dearly love to visit Paris,' said Margaret.

'Ah, Paris. Such beauty all around you, everywhere one looks in that city. So unlike London. And certainly Birmingham. Yet there is beauty here in Ironbridge, true beauty, sometimes in the most unexpected of places.'

He smiled at her knowingly and she flushed hopelessly, unable to control her blushes. She changed the subject. 'Which was your favourite city that you visited?'

'Paris, indeed. The architecture and gardens are marvellous. I visited the Palace of Versailles. Have you heard of it?'

'Oh, yes! I have read of it.'

'Picture it. You walk into the central courtyard and you are surrounded by stone the colour of sun-baked sand, punctuated by row upon row of windows gazing glassily down upon you. The slate roof is topped with golden decoration. Indeed, there is gold everywhere to be seen. Particularly in the long gallery – they call it *La Galerie des Glaces* – the Hall of Mirrors – oh, but of course, you would know that, being a French speaker.'

As he spoke, the images he painted with his words flowered in her mind. 'Yes, the Hall of Mirrors. I cannot imagine anything so beautiful.'

'It is a stunning sight. The sun streams through the windows and is dazzled in return by its reflection in the mirrors that line the wall, surrounded by a profusion of fleur-de-lis and chubby, golden babies. One cannot help but be overwhelmed by such richness. But outside is where I felt most delight, in the formal gardens. I imagine that you might feel more at home there too, Miss King, with your knowledge of botany?'

'Perhaps,' she uttered. She loved to listen to him. She had never travelled further than Shrewsbury, and felt how provincial she was. She dearly wished she had something to say that would interest him but could think of nothing but more questions. 'How were the gardens?'

'They are extraordinary, constructed like a painting or even, one could say, like the finest, hand-painted wallpaper. Great swathes of patterned grass and path combine to produce a design best seen from the air, I'd imagine. Only the birds could truly appreciate the gardens at Versailles!'

'It sounds . . . wonderful,' she gasped.

'Oh, Miss King, you would be in heaven there, I am certain.'

A vision came to her for a second time, of Parisian walks with Jake. Just the thought of it made her blush again. She watched him as he walked, carefully, out of the corner of her eye. Then, he stopped.

'Miss King, may I speak freely?'

'Yes,' she said, alive with anticipation.

'I do hope I am not boring you. I worry that I am.'

'Oh, no, indeed. Quite the opposite, I assure you!'

'Ah, thank you, Miss King. I feel I am talking and talking away and you must be quite sick of me, because I have noticed that you do not speak very much.'

There came her blushes again, but this time, they signalled a flush of humiliation. Her old anxiety, her social awkwardness, was here again. And now it threatened to ruin this new delight, her relationship with this extraordinary young man.

'Mr Ashford,' she began, but faltered. She did not know how to explain herself to him. She felt that she had failed him, that it was in fact she who bored him. She was about to make her excuses and leave, when he stopped walking. She looked up at him.

'Miss King, I am afraid that I have insulted you, and that was strictly not my intention. It is so unusual in our class to find someone who does not prattle on in incessant and tedious small talk. It revolts me, this obsession the upper classes have with chattering about nothing, spending hours and days and weeks of their pointless lives on such mediocrity! That is one reason, of the many reasons, why I value talking to our mutual friend Miss Woodvine so much, as she seems to have no capacity for small talk whatsoever and always straightway cuts to the chase in all our conversations. Don't you find this is true of Anny Woodvine, Miss King? So easy to converse with, she is quite a joy.'

This sudden mention of Anny caught Margaret wholly by surprise. Of course, she knew they had met, but did not know they were on such good terms. *Quite a joy . . .* She looked down at her feet as they walked. She suddenly felt quite floored and had no idea what to say. But he was going on, filling the void for her.

'But also, how refreshing it is to find a person from the more refined classes such as yourself, who is careful and considered in her speech, who speaks only of those things that truly matter. It is like an oasis after a desert of trivialities. Please forgive me if you felt I was criticising your quietude. It is quite the opposite, I assure you. I admire it hugely.'

Now she found she could not speak, because she was quite overcome. But she wanted to speak, she wanted to say so much to him. She managed only a muffled 'thank you'.

'You are sure I have not upset you in any way?'

'Oh no, indeed. As you say, quite the opposite. Quite the opposite.'

'I am relieved. So, could I ask that, each time I come to paint your stepmother, we could walk like this and converse?'

'I would like that very much.' Margaret felt a sharp breathlessness building in her chest.

'To think that I have that time with you to look forward to . . . Well, it has cheered me so. My visits to you will be the high point of my week!'

'And mine! I will live for it!' she replied, before she had a chance to be shy. She was so unaccustomed to speaking her feelings to a man – indeed, she had never done so in her life.

Yet he smiled so kindly at her, that she relaxed and found herself smiling too. A little chuckle escaped his lips and she laughed too. How natural it was to be with him, how much easier than anyone in her family, those people who she was supposed to feel at ease with.

They fell silent for a while and walked on, past the vegetables growing lustily in the walled garden, strung round with twine and labels; past the beehive buzzing with life yet contained in their white, wooden home, their honey stolen at intervals; past the fuchsias and chrysanthemums beaming brilliantly in the afternoon sun, yet penned in by canes and perfect alignment in fixed patterns.

Jake broke their comfortable silence. 'It is a beautiful garden you have here. But so restrained, so trussed up and ordered. Nature is tamed here, I see,' he said and she looked at him. There was a look in his eye, something she could not place, but it made her feel weak at the knees. He went on, 'Wouldn't it be satisfying to see it run wild?'

She felt out of her depth and yet ready to dive deeper into a sea of impulsiveness. A wave of tingles ran over her whole body as she looked into his eyes. It was something she associated with certain passages in certain French novels she had read. It was something that alarmed her, and yet she wanted it more than anything. She could not put a name to it but it was the most powerful thing she had ever felt and it seemed to emanate from Jake Ashford's eyes.

Overcome by her feelings, she mumbled something about feeling unwell, unable to say a proper goodbye, mortified at her inability to speak. She rushed across the gardens, around the corner of the house, nearly colliding with Cyril, who was marching from the direction of the woods, a look of thunder on his face.

'Watch out, you bloody fool!' he spat at her, as he pushed her aside and leapt up the steps to the front door, taking them two at a time. She did not have time to wonder what had angered him in particular that day, as she was intent on her own escape from public view. She ran up to her room and shut the door. She curled up on her bed, closed her eyes and breathed deeply to calm herself. It was her first true experience of lust. It frightened her and it thrilled her. It was more exciting than any of her novels.

That evening, Anny left the office after work with a head full of daydreams. She walked down the woodland path towards home with slow, languorous steps. Lately, she had been distracted at work and this was unlike her. Work was everything, closely followed by her family and her friendship with Peggy. But now there was Jake. She found herself often wanting to arrange time alone specifically to think about him. She looked for opportunities to be on her own so that she could devote the proper thinking time to the exclusive contemplation of Jake Ashford.

She marvelled how her life had been proceeding very nicely in one direction, more than a girl like her could have hoped for, with all its promise. And then this new element had suddenly dropped into her path, this young man, this artist. How strange life was, with its surprises and chance encounters, always when one least expected it! One could pray for things and they would never come, but then one day, when you were looking the other way, life served you up something delicious. Oh, and he was delicious! No, she mustn't characterise him that way. He was a serious person, a creative person, not a fancy piece of baggage. And his ambition, his artistic aims, all of this about him was so admirable. But those eyes. The way he looked at her, in a manner no local boy had ever done. When her eyes met with Jake's, there was a deep connection she had never experienced, like a series of small explosions happening in her mind. Surely the only name that she could give it was love.

But there was a stone in her path to true love. She tried not to think of it that way, but there it was, all the same: Peggy. Anny wondered if Peggy was sweet on Jake too. At first, it had been fun to share their impressions of the new arrival. After that, neither had mentioned Jake again; it became the elephant in the room. Anny did not tell her best friend of the meetings she'd had with him, of their long discussions, of her burgeoning feelings. And she did not ask Peggy if she had seen him either. The truth was that Anny did not want to hear about Jake from Peggy's mouth. She wanted to block out the wider world when it came to Jake; she wanted to pretend that he only spoke with her and that, along with his art, these were his only preoccupations.

Anny put it out of mind. She only wanted happy thoughts this day. Her dear friend Peggy, her true love Jake, her work with the Brothertons, her dear parents happy to see her so settled – and who knows what else the bright future held? She saw a simple white bindweed flower on its vine encircling a tree and plucked it, to feel the soft petals in her hand, to hold it to her breast and sigh with languid pleasure at her thoughts. The warm summer breeze whispered through the woods and teased her hair, free from the bonnet she carried, too hot for this glorious July day, brimming with birdsong and the buzzing of bees and the scent of earth and bracken.

'Anny! Ahoy there, Anny!'

The voice assaulted her. It shattered her thoughts as surely as a brick through a hothouse roof. She whipped round, hoping against hope she had mistaken its owner. She had not.

'Why, fancy coming across you here. Are you not late leaving work?'

Cyril's face was red and puffed, as he lumbered up the incline beneath her. A quick survey of her surroundings showed her they were out of sight of both the road and the office, and she was still far from her home. She turned and quickened her step onwards, tying her bonnet back on as if for protection.

'Indeed not,' she said, avoiding looking at him.

'Ah, then,' he said, out of breath and reaching her side, struggling to keep pace with her now. 'You will have a little time to speak with me then.'

'I fear not. I must be getting on, as I have so much to do at home.'

'Ah, but I must insist, Anny. I simply must speak with you on a matter of great importance.'

Anny strode onwards, her breaths short and ragged. 'Perhaps in the office another day, sir,' she managed to say, despite the panic rising in her throat now. His hand was on her arm and she stiffened and stopped dead.

'How can you call me that, Anny? How can you call me "sir", after all these years?'

Anny would not look at him. She stared ahead, her eyes fixed on the path home, its safety well out of reach. 'It is the correct name for your position, sir. And my own, as your father's employee. Now if . . .'

His voice came closer. 'But I would like that to change. I would like us to form an alternative kind of relationship.'

'That will not be possible. Our stations in life are too different.'

'But you are friends with my sister. You have overcome the difference in your stations to become close friends, I see.'

She stared at the ground now, at her feet. Her mind raced; how to escape this, how to run without seeming to run. But it was impossible. The only thing to do was block his every verbal attempt and thereby shut down the conversation, as a handful of sand on a flame.

'We are not close friends, only acquaintances.'

Cyril laughed gently, a knowing laugh. 'But that is not true, is it, Anny? You are speaking falsehoods to me now. I know about the letters and the secret meetings. I'm not a fool, you know. But don't worry, I will keep your secret.'

She looked at him now. His expression was a sneer but it softened when their eyes met. 'Oh Anny,' he sighed, his hand still on her arm, squeezing it joltingly, no softness or rhythm in his touch. 'Let us not worry about such things, about who your father is, or my father. None of this matters, when two people are . . . when they could be . . . when we should be . . .'

He does not know how to speak of love, she thought, *he doesn't have it in him*. 'Oh Anny,' he said again. 'Such a lovely face, such red, red hair.' Without releasing his grip, his other hand reached up to touch her head and she jerked back suddenly, causing him to stumble.

'Now then!' he said, his face changing, annoyance and hurt pride in his eyes.

'I am promised to another,' she blurted out.

His eyes narrowed. 'What other?'

'Never you mind. That is my business.' Her fear made her bold.

'That blasted artist fellow?'

What did Cyril know of Jake? She instantly regretted her confession. It was not true, not by any understanding with Jake. But it was true in her heart and it was the only thing she could think of to fend him off.

Cyril's hands were on her again, grasping her upper arms. His face was transfiguring into anger. 'Is it? That Ashford? I saw you with him in town. I was watching you, the way you stare at him. It is not seemly.'

The thought of Cyril spying on them made bile rise in her throat. But her immediate danger was at hand and she must think straight.

'Release me,' she said steadily and looked directly at him. '*This* is not seemly.'

His face altered again, as changeable as spring weather. Now he implored her, still gripping her arms. 'Will you not satisfy me, Anny? A kiss? I have waited so long for a kiss from those rosy lips,' and he lurched towards her. With a great effort, she wrenched herself away from him and began to walk hurriedly away. He caught up with her and took hold of her again, saying her name over and over, trying to put his mouth to her neck. His embrace was incredibly strong, iron and solid against her resolve to escape.

Her mouth was close to his ear, so she used her voice, the only weapon she had left: 'Are you gunna shove yer hand up my skirts, like you do with the other servants? Is that what this is, eh? You gunna rape and ravish me, you forsaken bastard?'

It stopped him. It worked. He still held her tightly but he had stopped. He held her before him, so he could look in her eyes. Now his face was all hearts and flowers. 'How can you say such words to me, Anny? Don't you know how I adore you? How I've always, always adored you?'

She changed tack too. 'Well then, this is not the action of a man who adores me. Unhand me and give me my dignity again, if you truly do adore me.'

He did so. She thought briefly of running but he was too fast and too strong for her. She had the advantage now, and must build upon it.

'This is not the way to woo a girl,' she said gently. But it was the wrong thing to say. It angered him.

'And I suppose that silver-tongued counterfeit fop knows how to woo you, eh, with his ridiculous bowing and stupid drawings. Don't you see, he's not good enough for you. He will never earn enough money from his scribblings to provide for you.'

'We will save our money. We will earn it by honest labour and save it until we have enough. That's what our kind do. We don't have things handed to us on a silver platter. We earn our way through life, with dignity.' She was ranting now and had no idea why. Why argue with this monster? Why pretend that she and Jake had a plan? But perhaps saying it aloud would make it so.

'You are right. You do have dignity, Anny. It is in you. You were born for better things. And I can give you those things. Marry me, Anny. Become the lady of Southover, take your rightful place above your natural station. I don't care where you come from, how poor you are, who your family is. It is no matter to me that Woodvine is your father, that he is a low employee of my father's, that your mother takes in dirty clothes. You are not like them, Anny. You are a queen amongst them. Take my hand, and you can rise above all this mean ignorance. Oh, the fine things I could give you! You would be in heaven! Don't you want that? Don't you want to leave all that filthy squalor behind?'

Anny listened, incredulous. Her body was still primed for flight but a rage had risen in her now. 'We are not filthy. We do not live in squalor. We are not mean or ignorant. We are proud and hard-working people. Jake Ashford understands that, even your sister understands that. But you will never know it, because you are the one who is ignorant and mean. You strut and preen and stamp on small things beneath your feet. You pass through your pointless life blind to anything but getting what you want, when you want it. You will never be half the man my father is, if you laboured all your days, you would never. It is not in your nature. You are cruel and selfish, in love with yourself and your kind. You disgust me. I would not marry you if my freedom depended on it, if my very life depended on it. I would rather die!'

Her words had cut to the quick, she could see that. His face was white with shock. But his eyes were black with hate. He had no words left. She took the moment it gave her and ran. She ran down the woodland path, tripping over roots, her arms flailing, her throat rasping with dry fear. She could not hear him pursue her, but she did not dare stop. At last, she saw the edge of her village, there in all its dependability. Salvation. But everything seemed at sea, the ground rippling like water, her head swimming with confusion. She stopped and glanced behind her. Nothing there. She put her hands to her head to steady herself. She had escaped him. She was safe. But everything had changed. Somehow, she knew that. Something irreversible had happened, and she feared it.

Chapter 11

Anny did not tell her mother or father about Cyril. She was too ashamed, too disturbed. Also, she felt she did not need to tell her parents, despite her fear. She would handle it herself. She could handle Cyril King. But then, the fear crept back in. What would Cyril do next? She knew him well enough to know how damned proud he was, how he would detest any suggestion of humiliation. And what could her parents do, anyway? Nothing, precisely nothing. They would tell her to leave Mr King's employ, that's what they would do. They would say it wasn't safe. Well, damn that course of action. Why should Cyril King chase her out of her job? She had worked so hard for it, and it would lead on to wonderful things – a post in Shrewsbury, as Mrs B had once mentioned. Or beyond, if certain other circumstances developed, maybe in Birmingham, who knew? Yes, that was it. Jake was the answer. It was the perfect time. If she went to Jake now, confessed the horrible scene with Cyril, it would be sure to gain his sympathy. Then, to tell him of her true feelings. How could he refuse to love her? She was sure it was on the tip of his tongue anyway. Then, they could announce their engagement straightaway and stop Cyril in his tracks. He could have no designs, no revenge, once her relationship with Jake was above board and out in the world. Yes, the time was now. And what a relief it would be, to tell Jake how she really felt and to hear his feelings for her, to lock eyes, to kiss . . .

The day after Cyril's assault, she spoke to Mr B and managed to free up an extra hour that afternoon after lunch. She did not like lying to him – she said her mother was poorly – but needs must. She left the office in search of Jake. He had in the past sought her out at the office a couple of times at lunchtime, but she could not wait to see if he would today. She was on a mission. She asked Lucy if Mr Ashford were in the house today, but he was not. Perhaps he was in one of his other haunts, the furnace where he drew detailed line drawings of the men guiding molten iron into the moulds, the riverside sketching the curves and struts of the iron bridge; or perhaps he was further afield, and she would not find him. She was hungry and tired, rushing about from place to place, but she felt too nervous to eat. Then, with a wash of relief and excitement, she saw him, coming out of the baker's, cramming a pie into his mouth messily. It surprised her a little, as he always had perfect manners, but it amused her too and she thought of all his little ways she would get to know once they had an understanding between them and they could truly be themselves together.

She looked both ways at the busy lunchtime traffic on the High Street before crossing and calling to him. He turned, looking alarmed, then his face altered as he saw her. He smiled broadly and wiped his face and waistcoat down, the crumbs flying this way and that into the mud beneath his boots. She could not help but beam at him, as he held her happiness in his hands and each view of him released it from her face. But as she approached, her fears must have crept back into her eyes, for he looked concerned and frowned upon her as she reached him.

'What is it, Anny?'

She loved the way they were on first-name terms. She loved the way he said her name, the vowels clipped and precise, his accent speaking of city life and education.

'I must speak with you. Can we walk? I have much to tell you.'

'Of course. Let us cross the bridge, then go down the steps underneath it and walk along the path upstream, away from the furnace. We can find some peace there.'

The sound of the ironworks nearby receded as they descended to the path and walked onwards, past a coracle hut on stilts, where a man came out hoisting his circular boat onto his back to carry it down to the water's edge. They passed along the path bordered by woods of oak and birch, dotted here and there with pretty cottages, gardens and orchards. They could hear the roaring of the forge pools in the distance, emptying themselves into each other in cascades, a sound like remote thunder.

'What's wrong, Anny? Please tell me.'

'It is a shameful thing to tell. But not shaming of me, but of him. I've never done any small thing to encourage him or such behaviour.'

'Anny, do start at the beginning. You do have this habit of rambling so. You could take a leaf out of Miss King's book and cull your words a little, you know.'

The mention of Peggy caught her short. Why was he talking about her? 'Well, Margaret could talk a bit more, if you ask me. She is too shy for her own good.'

'I am only teasing you, Anny. Now, who are we talking of? Who is he? And what did he do?'

'Master King. Cyril King. He followed me in the woods. He accosted me. Took hold of me.'

Jake stopped walking and stared at her. 'Did he hurt you? Are you . . . intact? Are you well?'

The look in his eyes, of deep concern, was encouraging. She hesitated to speak, to hold onto his gaze for a moment longer and drink it in. 'I am quite well, thank you. He did not . . . interfere with me, except he manhandled me and tried to kiss me. But I fought him off.'

'But that is outrageous! How dare he! This is another example of the upper classes taking advantage of those they perceive as beneath them. I would guess he does this to all his father's employees.'

'No, it was more than that. He told me he loved me, that he wanted to marry me. Me! Become the lady at the big house!'

'And what did you say to him? I hope you said no. He's a pigeon-livered idiot, that one. Not right for you, not at all.'

'Well, I told him no, of course.'

'That must have been tricky, to turn down the master's son. What reason did you give?'

'I told him I was promised to another.'

'That was clever! Did he believe you?'

'Yes, and he guessed who it was.'

'And who is it, Anny? Someone from your father's ironworks? Or a handsome coal miner? You are too good for all of them, Anny. But you'll find someone in Shrewsbury, when you go to work there. You'll see. Someone worthy of you, of your intellect. You're wasted on the dolts around these parts.'

Every twist and turn of this conversation took her by surprise. She had to keep her wits about her to negotiate it and keep on track. 'No, Jake. He did not guess any of the local boys. You see, he was spying on *us*. He saw us talking on the bench and he followed me from there. He is jealous of *you*, Jake. You must watch yourself. He is vengeful, I feel it. You must protect yourself.'

'Me?' said Jake, incredulous. 'Why would he suspect me? How ridiculous!'

This was not the reaction Anny was hoping for. She stopped walking and yet Jake did not immediately notice, carrying on a few paces until he turned and frowned at her.

'It is not ridiculous, Jake. Not to me.'

He came closer. 'My dear girl . . .' He trailed off, seemed torn somehow, glanced across the river and frowned again. She held her breath. 'I like you very much indeed, you must know that.'

'I have hoped it,' she said.

'Yes, but it is not so simple as that. Life is not so simple.'

'It can be. Love is simple. We love or we do not love.'

He laughed, a gentle scoff. 'Love is perhaps the most complex part of life. But no, in this case – in *our* case – there are other complications at play. You see, I am not here to find love. I am here to pursue my art. Whatever else arises, this is my sole purpose. It is a stronger bond I have with my art than any other. It is hard for others to comprehend, those who do not have ambition. But I believe, of all people, you can understand it. You have that drive, too, that burning ambition, to change yourself, to change your environment, to change the world even. I saw this in you from the very first and knew we felt the same, that we were kindred spirits that way.'

'Yes!' she gasped. 'We are kindred spirits. And that is why . . .'

'No, Anny. I am sorry to rudely interrupt you, but no. I am guessing where you might be leading in your words, but I cannot follow. I am wedded to my art. It comes first for me in everything. Why, when I am painting, I do not eat, I do not sleep, I am obsessed. It means more to me than anything, more than the commonplace necessities of life that dull people worship. More than my health, more indeed than the fairer sex. I have no ambitions when it comes to love or marriage. I never have. I am a complete novice in the art of love. Only the art of drawing and painting has been my passion. Any woman in my life will find herself playing second fiddle, and that would be most unfair. Besides, even if I were to love another, I could not promise myself. I am not earning a living from my art. I am not established. Even if I wanted to . . . to marry . . . I could not.'

The weight of disappointment was too great to bear. But she had not given up yet. 'But I know all of this, Jake. I understand this about you. As you say, we are kindred that way. And I will wait. I will wait as long as it takes for you to become established in society.'

'I could not ask that of you, Anny. It might be years.'

'I don't care!' she cried. There was some hope rising in her now. 'I would wait a lifetime! Find your place in the art world, find your success, which I know in my heart will be coming for you, when your paintings of these scenes, this place, are seen. I feel it, Jake. I know it. I believe in you.'

'You are too kind, Anny.'

'No. No, it is not kindness.'

'It is, and you have too much of it to give. I cannot let you wait for me. It might be years. And I may never become successful. I do not have the blind faith in myself that you do.'

'It is not blind faith. It is knowledge. And it is love. I love you, Jake.'

She wanted to reach up and kiss him now, now as he looked into her eyes, listening to her passionate regard for him. But she was unsure of him, so unsure that she waited for him to be the one. She wanted a sign, a movement from him, that he wanted her. He was moving towards her; she closed her eyes. She felt his arms go about her; but his face moved to the left and went over her shoulder. He was patting her on the back.

'There, there,' he was saying. 'You're a good girl, Anny.'

This was not what she wanted to hear. The feel of his arms about her, even in this brotherly way, was overwhelming and she felt herself press into him. The heat of their closeness was heady and bitter, as she felt he was holding back from her. She had to make him feel what she felt. Surely he would, if she breathed on his neck like this, if she sighed like this, if she pushed her fingers into the hair at the nape of his neck, like this, like this.

She moved her mouth to his and pressed her lips to his. He did not resist. The kiss was chaste, lips to lips, gentle and tender.

She opened her eyes to see his closed.

'Anny,' he whispered, and they kissed again. 'You are so lovely.'

'You are everything to me,' she whispered back, then looked up at him.

'Should I ask you to wait for me, Anny? Is that wrong of me?'

Her heart leapt. 'How can it be wrong when we love each other?'

'Will you, then? Will you wait for me and come to me when I have made my fortune?'

'I will, I will!'

He kissed her again, and this time their mouths opened. She felt her whole body turn molten, fired by the burning heat in her heart.

Good, heavy breasts, this one, thought Jake as he walked along the path. *Not skinny, like the other*. He'd left Anny by the riverside, sure in his love and full of foolish happiness.

Jake's past was something he had become adept at rewriting. He selected only the information to reveal to others which could be of use to him. Of course, neither Anny nor Margaret knew how many women he had bedded. Neither did Jake, as he had lost count of the females long ago. Neither Anny nor Margaret knew how heavily he was in debt. Neither did Jake, as he had lost count of the debtors, too, long ago. He had also never availed them of the fact that he had been disowned by his father.

As he strolled along, he replayed the circumstances in his life that had brought him to this moment. His parents had a disposable income and spoilt their two daughters and their youngest, a son. Jake's father was besotted with his son and yet at the same time hard on him. Having come from lowly parentage and worked himself up 'from nothing', as he termed it, Mr Ashford was determined his children would be swathed in as much luxury as he could afford. Yet his keen work ethic conflicted with this and he took it out on his only son, alternately fond and rough, chucking the boy under the chin one minute, then slapping him hard for insubordination the next. Rather than training his son up in the business, Ashford senior indulged the boy's one passion: art. However, on his return from the continent, he was called to his father's study and instructed to demonstrate what he had achieved on this expensive trip. Mr Ashford liked to indulge his son to a point, but beyond this he knew that only talent and skill would make any return in this world. He perused his son's work carefully, frowning. Then he had turned and said the words that still haunted Jake: 'It's not good enough, Jake. Not good enough by half. You're not a painter, and never will be. I've done my best for you, boy, and I have to admit that it was in error. You need to knock this idea of art on the head now and come into the business with me. No sense wasting any more time.'

Jake had been humiliated. He had compared his own skills with other artists he'd met on the continent. He knew he was not one of the best. But he was not one of the worst either. He had some skill, and surely this would improve with time. He told his father that nobody started off perfect, it'd take time to mature, like a good wine. He said how much his trip had changed him, how he wanted to change the world. He explained that he believed they were living through the most extraordinary era, one never before seen and never to be repeated, of such rapid and impressive change as to addle one's brain. Yet, at the age of twenty and full of energy, he felt ready for anything, eager to grasp this new era with both hands and let it speed him into the future. He had a great ambition to get to the heart of society and see what burned there. But his words had left his father cold.

'What a load of claptrap,' his father had scoffed. 'Fine words butter no parsnips. I'll not have a lazy, self-serving son. Put those ideas out of your head once and for all. Your talent is paltry and it will not serve those big ideas of yours.'

Jake had stomped out of the room, out of the house, and went off to get roaring drunk at a local tavern, after which he awoke with his face on the sagging breast of a much older prostitute, and he hoped he didn't have the clap. He'd slunk home to find his father raging, who, at the sight of him, grabbed him by the collar and pulled him close, spitting in his ear, 'You stink of booze and quim, lad. How dare you dirty my home and the home of your sisters and mother with your debauchery.' His father had thrown him to the floor, upon which Jake's head smashed into the hall table and broke his mother's china plate reserved for visiting cards from the great and the good. This was the final straw.

'Get out there in the world, boy, and don't come back until you've found yourself a living or a wealthy bride. Don't bother to darken my doorstep again until you've found one or the other. Be gone with you.'

One out of two will do, thought Jake, as he remembered Margaret's blue eyes sultry with desire every time she looked at him. In the meantime, he could amuse himself with this lovely redhead. And she was so very willing, he thought, she had allowed him to run his fingers up and down her back, her pelvis pressing against his in her need for him. Her passion for him would serve to make the rich one jealous. If he played his cards right, he could be married to a rich bride before the month's end and return home to his father in style. With his wife's money and his father's inheritance, he would never have to scrape a living again and could paint for his own gratification, not money. He could open a gallery in Ironbridge or Shrewsbury and display his industrial paintings for a fee, make a few more pennies and show his father who was the true artist around here, with paying customers eager to see his work.

'I will wait for you, until the end of time,' Anny had said, her voice hoarse with emotion.

Maybe he would bed the redhead on the sly after the wedding celebrations were done. He suspected the blonde was too prim to let him in as much as he needed. He had healthy, natural appetites, for sex and for money. These two would serve nicely to satisfy them.

Chapter 12

Cyril left the house by the back door and crossed the lawn. It was still wet with dew, his brown shoes were soaked black with it, and he shivered in the early chill. He was heading for a tall oak tree, one he had identified days before as being close enough to the office to watch the comings and goings, yet broad enough to hide behind and not be seen. He stood and waited. Anny appeared from the forest path, humming to herself, her work bag that held her lunch and other female sundries swinging to and fro. She was happy. He hesitated. He felt a surge of something for her, not only desire, but something else he did not understand. He felt it for no one else. Something like fondness. But the old knowledge crept in like a thief, that she did not care for him. She hated him. And what right had she to be so happy this day? He watched her retrieve the key from her skirts and open the door. He thought, *So, Anny has her own key to the office. That is most useful to know*. Now he waited further, but not for long, as minutes later, Brotherton was seen coming up the hill. No Mrs Brotherton today. That was fortunate.

Ill again, no doubt. A malingerer. He would deal with that later.

He turned and went around the house, skirting the gravel pathway his facile stepmother regularly minced down with her yappy little dog. He did not want anyone to hear his step. He reached the stable yard. The stink of horse dung and sweat emanated from the stables, while the fragrance of damp leaves and bracken drifted from the woodland that surrounded them. All of this was cut through with the tang of industry, of coal fire and metal, leaking from the works down the hill and upriver. He saw the stable lad gently brushing down a horse, which nickered and shook its head.

'You there,' he called and the boy looked up, startled. Everyone around here looked at him like that. A mixture of fear and . . . something else. Repulsion, was it? No, respect. Yes, that was it: respect. 'You. Come here. Take a message for me. Go and see Anny Woodvine in the estate office and tell her my father requires her attendance in the library immediately. And tell her that she must wait in the library until my father comes. Do you understand?'

The boy carefully placed his horse brushes upon their hangings on the stable wall. Cyril shouted, 'Hurry up, damn you!' at which the boy bolted from the stable like a colt, the horse whinnying with fright.

'Stop!' he called, and the boy skidded to a halt. 'I said, do you understand?'

'Yessir. I do. Go tell Anny to wait upon the master o'er in the library.'

'Not wait *upon*, you imbecile. Wait *for*. And she must be told to wait in the library until my father comes for her. Do you get it now?'

'Yessir.'

'And mind, do not mention my name at all. I am not in the habit of playing the part of messenger boy and do not wish to start a career as one. Do not say my name, do you hear? Well, hurry up, then.'

Cyril watched him go, then turned and walked back to the house the other way. He came round to the kitchen door. The smell of bacon wafted out and piqued his nose, causing his unfed stomach to grumble. He would eat once he had finished this business. The cook was in the pantry, shouting orders through at the help. Right by the door, he looked down upon an indeterminate maid on her knees, sweeping up a pile of grit with a small brush – he never could remember all their pointless names, especially the plain ones, like this one – and barked at her, 'Where is Lucy?'

That same look, except this one was tinged with horror. His reputation preceded him amongst the maids, he thought with some pride. 'Doin' the fireplace, sir, in the drawing room.'

'Fetch her immediately and bring her here.'

'Yessir,' muttered the ugly thing and clattered off, stupidly carrying her dustpan with her. He waited impatiently, thinking of the time it would take Anny to get to the library. His father was out all day, visiting friends in Oswestry, leaving at dawn. With a start, he realised that the stable boy would know this, would have attended or at least seen his father leave in the barouche. Well, what of it? The boy would follow orders, he would not speak out of turn. He would not question the young master of the house; would not, could not, as he did not have the wit for it.

Lucy arrived, her eyes wide and white. Cyril took some pleasure from the fear he generated in his past victim. This one was special – he liked her milky-white skin, the scent of soap in her hair. She kept herself very clean, this one. But she had been replaced in his affections by Anny and he had not bothered with her in a while. Still she would not meet his look and came to the door, staring down at her boots.

'Lucy, take a message to the estate office from my grandmother, Mrs King senior. Tell Mr Brotherton that she requires two bottles of green ink to be collected from the stationer's on Madeley Road. He must be the one to fetch it and he must take it back to the office and keep it on his desk to be collected later. Have you got that? Repeat it back to me.'

'I mun take . . .'

'Speak up, girl!'

She cleared her throat, never once looking up from her feet, then began again. She gave a good account of it and the most crucial part was there, that Mr B must not take the ink to the big house, but go back to the office.

Then he leant close to her and whispered in her ear, as he was wont to do in previous times, 'And I do not want my name mentioned to anyone regarding this. It was not me who passed this message on. If anyone ever asks, you are to say that Mrs King senior herself gave it to you. Do you comprehend me, girl?'

'Yessir,' she muttered, utterly still but breathing quickly.

'Get on with you then.'

He watched her go. He went into the house through the garden room and went into his father's study. He thought he knew which drawer the keys were kept in but he was wrong. He opened and shut all the drawers he could see until he finally found them in a single drawer in an occasional table by the door. He left the study and crossed the entrance hall. He thought he heard a door click – he'd been jangling the keys in his hand as he walked and abruptly stopped – but there was no one there. Back out across the garden room and through the glass door. Then he crossed the lawn again, this time in the direction of the woods. He went in deep, hearing the alarm calls of birds announcing his trespass. He needed to come from a place of cover to approach the office. He crept up to the window as quietly as he could and peered in. Anny's chair was unoccupied. He stepped around the neat brick building and looked in through Brotherton's window. Nobody there either. From his pocket, he retrieved the office key. He must remember to replace it later, or all might be lost. Looking behind him at the house, then at the path down to town, he satisfied himself that nobody was around and he turned the key in the lock. He knew Brotherton would lock up behind himself, good worker that he was. Once inside, he retrieved the two safe keys from the secret drawers. Then he approached the safe.

There was around a hundred pounds or so in there. He had to make a quick decision. How much should he take? How much would look correct? He decided upon thirty pounds. More would be too readily noticed, less would be a waste of the risk expended to take it.

He relocked the safe and replaced the keys, before going to Anny's desk. Where was her bag? She always had it with her, every morning. It was not hanging on the coat stand, or on the back of her chair. His eyes scoured the walls for pegs, but there was none. He started to sweat. He thought he heard the sound of feet approaching and rushed to the door, but there was no one. He thought feverishly, where could it be? She was a sensible girl and a neat one. Where would she put it? He eyed her desk and saw it had three drawers, two small and one large at the base. He pulled it open and there it was, stashed neatly in the bottom drawer. It had a clasp that was shaped like two halves of one heart. He paused. He was assaulted by a wave of nausea. His face was slick with sweat now. He did not have to do this. He could abort the whole scheme. But a memory came to him of her face, cursing him, hating him, and that artist rogue making her laugh. How dare such a girl spurn him! They were too proud by half, those Woodvines. The daughter must have learnt her pride from her insolent father, like that time at the furnace, all those years ago, when Woodvine had made a fool of him before the men. Well, now they would pay for their insolence. He forced open the clasp to Anny's bag and dropped in the cash, shoving it to the bottom of the bag, underneath the lunch wrapped carefully in a cloth. He clasped the bag and pushed the drawer shut.

But her lunch. She would get her lunch out of her bag long before counting up at the end of the day and she would see the money and know. He opened the drawer again and took out her bag, placing it on the desk. He nearly upset an inkpot and watched in a moment of horror as it tipped to one side a fraction, then fell back to its place, the red ink sloshing. His grandmother's damned stupid idea of all that coloured ink. It could have been the end of this, if blood-red ink had flooded across the desk. He opened the bag and looked inside. What he wanted was an inner pocket, something he could place the money inside that she would not necessarily look in between now and the end of the day. He took out her lunch, a handkerchief, a coin purse and a small notebook. These things of Anny's touched him and he paused. But his hand felt a button. He peered inside the bag's recesses and saw the pocket. He fumbled with the button and opened it, relieved to see there was nothing already inside; Anny clearly had no secrets. It was just large enough to stash the money inside. He put all her belongings back in just the way she had left them. He fastened the button, closed the bag and put it away in the drawer, then lurched to the door and slammed it shut, locking it clumsily, almost dropping the key. He rushed back to the garden room and went in through the glass door. Nobody about, thankfully. Straight to his father's study to replace the key, then across the hallway to the stairs. He threw a quick glance at the library, where Anny would be seated, waiting nervously for his father, who would never come. He turned from her and stumbled up the staircase and across the landing to his room. He shut the door, went straight to his wash bowl and vomited into it, retching for minutes after, the yellowish slime of his bile smeared across the back of his hand. There, it was done. Now he needed to deal with Anny.

Anny stood stiffly by the library window. She did not dare sit down. She could not fathom why Mr King would want to see her, unless she was in some kind of bother. Heat prickled around her collar and her stomach churned. But she knew she had been working as well as usual, had met all of Mr B's requests, though they had had a little quarrel that morning. No, not a quarrel as such, but a disagreement. She had asked him if he would be so kind as to write her a reference if she were to start applying for jobs in Shrewsbury. They had talked about it in the past and the Brothertons had always been so supportive. But he had seemed flustered by the request and made excuses for her not leaving presently and giving it some time before making such a rash move, as he put it. She was frustrated with his negative response, but supposed it was to do with Mrs B being ill again and so much work to be done. He was being a bit unreasonable and the uncomfortable look on his face told her he knew that, but he insisted that she was needed far too much in the office to leave them at present. He had gone into his room and shut the door, which he rarely did when they were working alone in the office together and she felt shut out. She decided she would talk to his wife when she was back, see if she could soften her and then Mrs B might be able to work on her husband's resolve a little.

But why had she been summoned here, to talk to Mr King? Mr B had said only today how invaluable she was, and she had never arrived late or mislaid anything or given anyone any cheek or . . . Could it possibly have anything to do with Cyril? Surely not. It couldn't be. She put her hands to her hot cheeks and felt a little faint. Then, the door opened.

'Anny!'

It was Peggy. To see her friend's open, smiling face here in this worrisome place was like a cooling breeze.

'Oh, Peggy! I'm that happy it's you.' Peggy came over to her, a look of concern clouding her features and her face looked pale. 'Are you well, Peggy? You look white as a sheet.'

'It is only I feel a little washed out. A good night's sleep will cure it. But what of you, my dear? I can see something is wrong, and I cannot imagine for the life of me why you are here in the library alone. Is there an emergency? Are you awaiting someone?'

'I was told to come and wait for your father, but I have no clue why.'

Peggy frowned. 'My father? But he is not at home.'

'He has stepped out?'

'No, he left very early this morning. I believe he is in Oswestry for the day and will return by teatime.'

'Oh, I am glad to hear that!' cried Anny. It must have been a mistake then. But what a strange one. Anny's relief swept across her face so clearly that Margaret smiled at her and reached out a hand to touch her shoulder.

'Is anything amiss, dear Anny? It is so long since we've spoken and I . . . I have missed you. I have missed . . . our confidences.'

Anny felt a brief flash of guilt. Things had moved so quickly with Jake, and then there was the trouble with Cyril . . . There had been no time to tell Peggy about either.

'Oh, Peggy, I have so much to share with you. Good news and bad news.'

'I have news, too!' Margaret's face lit up and Anny wondered what on earth it could be. 'But you first. What is your news? Bad first, to get it over with.'

The library door opened. Cyril strode in and turned his head in an exaggerated double take, whereupon he smirked at both of them. 'Now then, what have we here? Not so secret meetings anymore, eh? Flaunting your mismatched friendship before the whole household, is it now? I don't know. I come in to fetch a book and find the help seated in the library with the young lady of the house. Whatever next?'

Margaret stood up and faced her brother. 'As if you ever read a book, Cyril King. Are you spying on us?'

Anny nearly burst out laughing to hear Peggy stand up to her brother so. That was a first!

'Shut up, you little worm,' spat Cyril. 'And get back to the office, girl. How dare you sit here like an esteemed visitor.'

Anny stood and dusted non-existent dust from her skirt. 'I was told to wait in here for your father.'

Cyril scoffed. 'That's not possible. My father is out all day. Who on earth told you that?'

‘The stable boy, Paddy. He said that I was to wait for Mr King in the library. No, he said, I must wait upon Mr King. And I said, Upon? And he said, No, I must wait *for* Mr King in the library.’

‘That halfwit. He was dropped on his head as a baby. Everyone knows that. Now, get back to work. Hurry up, damn you.’

Anny quickly nodded to her friend as she walked past her. The conversation with Peggy would have to wait.

Anny left the room in a hurry and was worried to hear Cyril was walking right behind her. She did not turn. She did not give him that pleasure. She walked steadily and with dignity out of the servants’ entrance and around the house to the office. All the while, Cyril’s footsteps haunted hers. She stopped at the office door and turned the handle to discover it was locked. Now, where could Mr B be? She retrieved the key from her skirts and put it in the door. As she opened it, she turned to confront Cyril. She could not allow him to come into the office and be alone with her in there. As she turned, she was surprised to see he was walking away, down the lane towards the town. She shuddered. His whims were disturbing. Oh, for the day when she and Jake could escape this place! As she went in and shut the office door, she looked about her at the office that had housed her day in, day out for four years, had taught her so much, had raised her from washer girl to office junior. Despite Mr B’s reluctance, she knew it was time to strike out now, to apply for jobs in Shrewsbury. Indeed, if she secured a better job, with a higher wage, then she and Jake would be one step closer to marriage. She pictured herself moving to Shrewsbury, her parents saying a fond goodbye as she climbed onto the coach, her trunk deposited on the top and the coach rattling along the roads to their grand county town, a place of dreams she had never been, where they said the jolly old river ran through topped by arching stone bridges, flanked by beautiful houses and churches full of history and pots overflowing with flowers on every street.

She sat at her desk and began her first task of the day. She worked alone for some time, over a half hour. Where could Mr B be? At least Cyril had not returned. That was something to be thankful for. Then she heard footsteps approaching and looked up. In came Mr B, puffed and looking annoyed.

'Well, I must say, what a to-do.'

'Can I help, sir?' said Anny.

'No, my dear. It is simply that I am so behind now. What with you being called away, I then received a message from Mrs King senior to fetch ink from town.'

'I could have done that for you.'

'Indeed! But you had to see Mr King. Is everything well?'

'Well, that is the curious thing. He is away from home all day. Went at dawn, apparently. I cannot think what got into Paddy, telling me that.'

But with no answers to be found they both got back to work.

The day passed slowly, with reams of figures to record, accounts to settle, sums to be done and papers to sort. Anny spent much of it thinking of Jake and their future, and worrying over the threat from Cyril. Near the end of the day, she heard the carriage arrive. Anny felt the same nerves from that morning, now that the master had returned. What if the message for her to see him had been correct, but delivered late, and he had wanted to see her? What if he still wanted to see her? What if he turned up now, at the door? She still could not imagine what on earth it could be about, if that did happen. She was distracted by the racing of her thoughts and did not notice Mr B come through and stand thoughtfully before her. She looked up.

'There is money missing from the safe.'

The statement shocked Anny. 'Shall we count it again?'

'I have counted it twice,' said Mr B, his face a picture of worry.

'Let us count it again together.'

They went through and she looked at the ledger on his desk, checked the amount that should be there and then set to counting the money with him, speaking the amounts aloud and jotting down each denomination on his blotter. Then she added up all of the amounts and wrote a total. It matched Mr B's twice-done calculations and was exactly thirty pounds off what the total should have been.

'But how can there be?' she said. 'It isn't possible. The count was all correct last night. Where could it have gone in the space of a day?'

Mr B was running his hand through his thinning hair and suddenly looked so much older than he had only minutes before.

'Oh, my word,' he breathed out raggedly, his hand on his forehead. 'Did I leave the office unlocked when I went to town?'

'No, you didn't,' said Anny. 'When I came back from the house, it was locked. I distinctly remember taking the key from my pocket and unlocking it. And the office was locked this morning too, when I arrived.'

'Oh, thank heavens,' said Mr B and slumped onto the corner of his wife's empty desk. He was thinking now; frowning. Then he looked up at her.

'When I returned from town, you were here alone, Anny. Did you leave the office for a moment during that time? Did you leave it unlocked? I'm sorry, my dear, but I have to ask.'

'No, I did not, sir. I assure you of that. I did not leave this office for a moment after I returned from the library. I came in. Master Cyril followed me from the house and saw me enter. Then I sat at my desk and worked until you came back. I was here the whole time.'

'Are you sure?'

'I am absolutely certain of it. I was here alone the whole time. And the door was locked when I came back from the house. No question about it.'

Mr B's eyes darkened, then he stood and went to the door, saying, 'There's nothing else for it. I have to inform Mr King.'

And out he went. She listened to his footsteps receding towards the house. Her mind was racing. How could this be? Where could the money be? She knew neither of them were to blame, but someone would have to be held responsible. Surely it could not be her, as Mr B was her senior. He was in the position of responsibility. She felt bad about wishing that on him, but if it came to it, better him than her. His years working for the Kings might stand him in good stead, whereas she was convinced that they would dismiss her in an instant if it was deemed to be her fault. There was that period of time when she was alone in the office. Would they hold her responsible, because of that? And what of the strange requests that morning, for both of them to leave the office? A creeping fear began to squeeze her lungs. There was something rotten hidden here and it was beginning to stink.

Footsteps approached. Mr King appeared first, stepping rather awkwardly into the office he had probably not set foot in for years. Mr B hovered behind him, wringing his hands like the very definition of anxiety. Then the door darkened again and in came Cyril. What was he doing there? Anny's chest tightened and she stood up and made a quick bob of a curtsey to Mr King.

'Your name again?' spoke Mr King, haughtily.

'Anny Woodvine, sir.'

'You comprehend the seriousness of this situation?'

'I do, sir.'

'Money has been found to have gone missing from this office. Mr Brotherton informs me that the office was not left unlocked at any time. Do you concur with this, Woodvine?'

'I do, sir.'

'Are you certain of it?'

'I am, sir. The office was locked last night when we left, it was locked this morning when I arrived. When I came back from the house, it was locked. It was not left open and unoccupied at any time.'

'From the house, you say? What do you mean, from the house?'

Anny looked at Mr B, expecting him to take over the explanation. But he said nothing.

'I was called to the house this morning, sir, to wait upon you, in the library. I mean to say, to wait for you in the library.'

'Me?' said Mr King, observing her incredulously. '*You* were called to wait for *me*?'

Anny looked at Mr B, who would not meet her eye. But he did at last speak up. 'Yes, it is the case that the stable boy came with a message, that Miss Woodvine should go to the house to wait for you in the library. That is the case.'

'What on earth could the boy be thinking?' scoffed Mr King.

'The boy is an imbecile,' interjected Cyril, staring at Anny yet speaking to his father. 'Or else easily led.'

'What do you mean by that, my boy?'

'Nothing. Just stating the facts as I see them.'

'But why would this stable boy say such a thing, when it was patently not true?'

Mr B cleared his throat, then said, 'May I just add that I did not actually hear him give the message to Miss Woodvine. I heard only the door open and Anny speaking with him. Then she popped her head into my room and told me what the boy had said. I did not hear it with my own ears.'

Anny turned to stare at him, but he avoided returning her gaze. Was he covering his own back and shoving the blame onto her? She couldn't believe he'd do such a thing. She expected more loyalty from Mr B.

Mr King frowned and looked back at Anny. 'Mr Brotherton tells me that he went to town to fetch some ink for my mother. And that when he returned, you were here in the office, alone. Is that the case?'

'Yes,' said Anny, her voice small. She did not like the way this conversation was proceeding. She did not like it at all. She knew she had done nothing wrong. But there were hints and suggestions buzzing in the thick air of that room and she feared them.

'How long were you alone in the office?' asked Mr King. A slight movement from Cyril, a leaning in, listening.

'A matter of . . . less than an hour?'

'As much as that?' said Cyril.

Mr King sighed and placed his hands into his pockets. Mr B was staring ahead, intensely. Anny did not know what Cyril's expression was, as she would not look at him.

'Woodvine, you were the only person alone in this office on a day that money has gone missing from the safe. You will have to be searched. Your person and your belongings.'

At last, Mr B spoke up, quietly. 'This girl is a very good worker, Mr King. I cannot see that she would have any shadow upon her in this case. Is this really necessary?'

Then, Cyril's voice: 'The girl knows how to open the safe. Brotherton told me himself.'

'Is this true?' Mr King asked Mr B, who looked exasperated but had to reply, 'Yes it is, but . . .'

'Then the girl must be searched. Stand here, girl. Do you have a bag? A cloak?'

Anny came out from beside her desk, where she had been standing, using it as a kind of protection.

'Brotherton, do it.'

Mr B came forward reluctantly and could not meet her eye. She raised her arms and stared straight ahead, inspecting the grain of the wood panelling on the office wall, every knot, every blemish. Mr B patted her hips, then withdrew again, his hands shaking. 'I can feel nothing untoward, sir.'

'Girl, pull out any pockets you have in your apparel.'

'I have none, sir.'

Cyril had fetched her cloak and held it up to the light. 'Nothing here, Father.'

'You have a bag, then?'

'I do, in the bottom drawer.'

She went to step towards the desk, but Mr King said, 'No, Brotherton will do it.'

Mr B approached and took the bag out. Anny thought, *What of it? They will find nothing and then they will leave me be.*

'On the desk,' said Mr King. 'Remove all of its contents.'

Mr B took everything out and placed Anny's things gingerly beside the bag.

'Too slowly, man,' said King impatiently. 'Here, hand it over.'

He took the empty bag and ferreted around inside it. Then, he stopped. He fiddled with something. Anny stared at him. He looked up at her, the first time Mr King had looked clearly at her and registered her as a human being. He looked inside the bag.

'A button,' he said. 'A pocket. Something is inside it.'

'There is nothing inside it,' said Anny. 'I keep nothing in there.'

But there was a rustling sound and Mr King withdrew his hand and in his fist were banknotes.

Mr B gasped. 'Oh, Anny,' he muttered.

'The rat is in the trap,' said King.

'I didn't do this!' cried Anny.

'Be quiet, girl,' said Mr King.

'I did not do this,' replied Anny, her voice lower, stronger and more powerful than she had ever heard herself speak before.

'Silence! How dare you deny the evidence before our very eyes! You have been caught in the act of robbery. Brotherton, go and fetch the constable from Ironbridge to secure this offender and take her into custody. If one is not available, we may need to send to Jackfield or Broseley and if so, we shall secure her here.'

Mr B did not even glance at Anny, but left quickly.

'But Mr King,' she began again. 'I had no reason to steal this money. I have always served you well. I have always valued this post. Why would I steal from my employer? Why would I bite the hand that feeds me?'

Cyril piped up, 'I know why she stole the money, Father. She is seeing that artist fellow, Ashford. Secret meetings. Kissing on the towpath. Everybody is talking of it. I've seen them. She is planning to run away with him. She stole the money to pay for their elopement.'

Oh, the tommy rotter! Such lies he had brewed up, but stirred in with a few facts to give the flavour of truth to it.

'Is this true?'

Anny hesitated. 'No, I mean, yes, it is about Jake . . . Mr Ashford . . . but not what you are saying or the way you are . . .'

Mr King interrupted. 'There is the motive, here is the evidence. You have been caught out in your crime. I shall immediately take this evidence to my friend, Mr Cribb, the magistrate. I have no doubt he will make the charge of theft and you will be committed to Shrewsbury Prison to await trial.'

'But Mr King!' cried Anny. 'Please listen to me!'

'How dare you speak to me thus! Do not make things worse for yourself. I will not listen to one more word from your dishonest mouth. And to think, we gave you a chance in life, a step up from the gutter. And this is how you repay us. Look on, my boy, look on at the result of kindness to the lower classes. This is how the scum answers it. With felony. With theft. With treachery.'

Anny looked now at Cyril, who was glaring at her and grinning in triumph. But his face was sliding away, melting and running into his neck, the walls tilting sideways at crazy angles, the room turning topsy-turvy and she was falling, falling. Her whole world was capsizing and she reached out for something to grab hold of, seeing her hands looming huge before her eyes. Then came darkness.

Chapter 13

John Woodvine was on his break, swilling beer, when he saw Brotherton coming down the path to the furnace. His first thought was trouble. It was always trouble when management came. But he did not think it was trouble for himself. He had done nothing to concern himself about, other than work like an ox, as usual. He turned away to put down his tankard and turned back to see Brotherton looking straight at him, his face wearing an expression that could only be described as shameful.

'What's this now?' he heard Pritchard say, who walked past him towards Brotherton.

Brotherton nodded at John and said something inaudible to Pritchard, who gestured for John to come. They walked away from the furnace to a quieter spot along the path, John's mind whirling like falling sycamore seeds. What had he done? What new trouble was this?

Brotherton cleared his throat and spoke to a spot on John's chest, just below his shoulder. He could not look him in the eye.

'Your daughter has been arrested for theft.'

John did not respond. The words made no sense to him. He stared at Brotherton, his mind like an old man considering the great effort of standing up from a chair. He was waiting for the words to mean something.

'What? Anny?' said Pritchard, similarly incredulous.

'Money was missing from the safe at the end of the day and it was found in her bag.'

'This is daft,' said Pritchard, shaking his head. John still could not speak. Why was the man speaking these lies, as stupid as saying the sky were green?

'I want you to know that I don't believe she could have done it,' Brotherton said.

'Of course she bloody didn't,' replied Pritchard.

But John only wanted to know one thing.

'Where is she?'

'She has been taken to the lock-up in town by the constable.'

With that John turned to Pritchard to tell him he was off to the lock-up. He was already walking away before Pritchard could respond.

When he got there, he banged on the door and the constable came out, a younger man he knew a little from the village, called Finch.

'Move along. No visitors.'

He heard a desperate sound from within.

'Father!' It was Anny.

He shouted back to her, 'I am here!'

'I said, move along.'

John eyed the man. He'd known his father, died of strong drink. He'd never liked this one. A sneak, everyone said. Nobody was surprised when he joined the law.

'Finch, it's me. You know me. It's John Woodvine. I knew your father.'

'I have my instructions,' said Finch and crossed his arms over his narrow chest.

'You know my Anny. You know she's a good'un. It's all rot this business. Let me in to see her.'

But Finch planted his feet firmly astride the doorway and stiffened his lip.

John stared at Finch's weaselly little face. He leant closer to it and was struck by the stink of bad breath. He spoke, low and slow. 'Let me in, Finch.'

'You threatening me, Woodvine? Is that what you're about?'

'I'm not threatenin', I'm tellin'. You dunna step aside, I shall make you, mon.'

Finch's eyes widened, but still he would not budge. It seemed the weasel was made of iron.

'Dunna hit him, Father!' shouted Anny.

John stared at Finch.

'It'll make things worse for me a hundredfold if you do,' she added. She was right. Always the clever one. John unclenched his fists and took a step backwards.

Finch cleared his throat and said, 'The magistrate has already been seen at his home to peruse the evidence and he immediately charged the felon with theft. The felon will thus be taken to Shrewsbury Prison on the morrow. And I'll do you the kindness of informing you that visiting day's the day after, on Saturday. Not that you deserve such kindness, with your idle threats.'

'Come see me on Saturday, then, Father,' called Anny. Her voice was clear and strong, but he knew her so well; only he could discern the quavering note in it. When she was a little one, she had the same tone after she'd fall and scrape a knee, hopping right up, brushing herself off, trying to be brave. Any fuss would set her off weeping. He knew now that she was about to cry and he didn't want to upset her further.

'I will be there.'

'All right, Father!'

'Dunna you worry, Anny. We'll get this sorted out.'

'I know you will, Father.'

He glared again at Finch. He had called Anny a 'felon'. The word had sickened him. How he wanted to douse him in the chops. Instead, he kicked the wall of the lock-up. Finch leant in and sneered at John, adding, 'Like fadder, like darter,' and shut the door in his face.

He could have beaten it down with his bare hands. But it would not have helped her. The vision of her in there, friendless and afraid, tore at his heart as he stared at the walls that stood between them. He marched off, not giving the door the satisfaction of seeing him loiter there, impotent.

On the walk home from the lock-up, he knew he should rush to give his wife the news, but instead his legs felt like lead. He dreaded telling Rachel. She never took bad news well. She worked so hard without tiring, but a hint of bad luck could send her into a swoon. She was sensitive that way, and superstitious, always fearing the worst. He was generally the cheerful one, willing to see the goodness in the world. And the world had treated him quite well, thus far. But how quickly a man's life can turn. He had been at work that afternoon, struggling on against exhaustion, thinking his biggest problem was how to get enough sleep before his next shift. Work had filled his life for more years than he cared to remember. It had seemed to have a purpose, to support his parents' family, then to provide for his own, to give his wife and daughter a home, food on the table and a future for Anny. All that work, all that sweat, all the noise and the heat and the danger. What was it all for? A man works himself nearly to death and then, out of the blue, comes this, landing in his path with no way past it, no way round it or over it or through it. He did not often have poetic thoughts, but he thought then, *You walk through your life and the way is long, the way is hard. But you keep on going. Then summat happens and the land slips down upon you – all the rubble and the trees and the rocks and the earth – all slides down and buries you. You couldna see it coming and you couldna run in time.*

Rachel called him her rock. Well, now he had to prove it. He had to protect Anny from this, he had to protect Rachel from this. He had to solve it. Brotherton said the money had been found in her bag. Then, someone must have put it there. Who would put it there? Why? It made no sense. He knew in his bones that Anny would never steal, would never lie, would never cheat. She did not have it in her. She had no secrets from him or from Rachel, he was sure of that. And if it was money she needed, she would have known to just come to them, tell them. They'd help her, whatever it was. And anyway, she was earning it herself, earning it very well and she was saving. She had cash in a box under the floorboards in her room. She'd been saving it for months, to set her up when she got to Shrewsbury. They'd discussed it all. Why would she need to steal? Questions, questions and no answers.

He'd have to talk to someone educated, someone in the know, who would tell him what he could do. Would he have to hire counsel? They'd have no money to pay it. He could use Anny's savings. But that was her money, for her new life. Well, she'd have no life if she was found guilty of this crime, so her savings it would be. How would he find reliable counsel? He knew no one in Shrewsbury, knew nothing of the city at all. He'd lived his whole life in Ironbridge and never travelled further up than Oakengates, further down than Bridgnorth. He'd had no need to. His father had worked for the ironmasters and so had he. Their world was work and home. There was no need of anything further afield. His trips away had been family events, nothing more: weddings and funerals, the bookends of life. Some people did a good deal of toing and froing about the place and what was it all for? People were the same everywhere, he was sure of that. It might be interesting to some to see other places. But the woodland and the river running through it around his home was all he needed, all he wanted. The walk to Shrewsbury would be the furthest he'd ever been from home. And it was for the most terrible reason he could imagine, other than the death of a loved one; yes, that was the only thing that would be worse than this, if Anny was gravely ill or gone forever.

He thought back to the night Anny came into the world. Rachel had bled and bled and they all said she'd die, but she didn't. No more babies after that, and just as well. In the hours he thought he'd lose his wife, he blamed himself for bringing her to this pass, for giving her a baby to bear and that bearing would kill her. When she recovered and the baby thrived, he thanked God for saving them both and wished to never have another child. They did not have relations for a year or more after. He missed it, he mourned it, but he was determined that she wouldn't be put in danger again, ever again, his beloved Rachel. He thanked God again, for giving him Anny, for keeping Rachel alive. He would have liked a big brood, as he loved little children, babies most of all, their absolute innocence and complete reliance on him. He liked nothing more than to be relied upon. It was his lifeblood. He'd see an old man who lived alone in the town or a widower or a bachelor and shudder; to be alone, to be unwanted, unnecessary, unloved. He'd rather die. But one child it was to be and he was content. More than content! His girl, his Anny, was the sun and moon to him. He loved to watch her sleep when she was a baby, not that she slept much as she was always up and about wanting to learn the next new thing. These days he would sit by the fire of an evening and watch her writing away at the table, see the pencil she held moving in mysterious shapes across the paper, shapes that were beyond his mind and always would be. He liked nothing more than to listen to her talk, the way he could sense her mind racing and see her trip over her words to catch up with it. Rachel was much brighter than him, he'd always known that, but to think that they had created this little wonder, this clever girl with her words and her thoughts. And that hair, that deep red hair like leaves on the turn. His own had been pale and orangey when he was younger, deepening to a reddish-brown scored with grey nowadays, while his wife's hair was the colour of tree bark. Together they had made this miracle, this beautiful, sparky girl, this child of his heart. His one child. He had only this one, singular vessel to pour all his fatherly affection into and it brimmed over with his love.

Now his one child was in danger, mortal danger. His wife would be floored by it, he was certain of that. It was his job to protect them both. What other point was there in a husband and father than that? His walk was coming to an end and his cottage was just along the way from here. How he wished he could slow down time and never reach it, never step over its threshold, never stand before his wife and tell her this darksome thing.

Chapter 14

Anny had dreamt of this. She had dreamt of entering the city of Shrewsbury, drinking it all in for the first time, seeing the pale stone of the walls and the coloured windows of the churches. She had imagined herself coming into the city by coach, gazing at the majestic buildings. The wheels of the coach barrelling along the streets, she would arrive at a busy square and the archway to the yard of a coaching inn, where she would alight and find her way to her lodgings; and recently, she had pictured an addition; later that day, after she had received her trunk and unpacked, there would come someone knocking upon the outer door and her landlady would call her down to greet her gentleman caller and there would be Jake, come to take her out to supper. She had pictured this, all of it, many times.

Now, she really was entering Shrewsbury for the first time, not in her imagination, but in full wakefulness, and nothing could have been further from her dreams. She was sitting on the back of a farmer's cart pulled by a leisurely old nag, shoved up beside three other women, reeking of the lock-up they'd all been in for the night, where the walls seeped with mildew and the room stank of damp and piss and the odour of unwashed, desperate bodies. The constable sat opposite them on the cart, silent and stoic but watchful, not speaking a word to any of them. The other women had not spoken to her either. Two of these were very poor, filthy and dishevelled. One had been drunk in the lock-up the night before and was now moaning and groaning at every bump in the road. The other had been rouged like a Frenchwoman and slept almost the whole time, seeming unsurprised by the whole business. The third was a nursing mother, dressed more respectably, who cooed at her baby and nursed it or else wept silently, tears running down her face and snot pouring from her nose, which she wiped away from time to time, but who never talked, except whisperings to her child. Anny could not bring herself to speak to them either. She had existed in a state of pure terror since the moment she had awoken at the lock-up in Ironbridge the day before. She had fainted in the office and had not come round until she was incarcerated. She knew nothing of what had occurred in between. The thought of being out cold, her body not her own, was horrible.

She had not slept at all that night and rued it now, as sleeping had proven impossible on the bumpy cart that had taken the best part of a day to travel the fifteen or so miles from Ironbridge to Shrewsbury. At least it was summer and at least it was not raining, though at some points on the road the sun had beaten down upon her face so harshly, she felt as if her skin was beginning to sizzle like bacon. She had pulled her cloak over her face but then felt suffocated by it. Walkers on the road and others in carts passing by had stared at her, some laughing, shaking their heads. One child threw a couple of stones in her direction and some men shouted at her and her fellow female felons, calling them hedge-creepers, then laughed raucously.

She watched all of this occur in a kind of stupefied horror, unable to process the nightmare that was truly happening to her. Her life of only a day before was gone, replaced by an existence in places and in company she had never considered, let alone imagined herself inhabiting. It was as if her tongue had seized up at the shock, that her brain had no frame of reference to compare this madness to and so had simply given up trying to respond to it. She was in shock, and could not fathom what had happened to ruin her life so quickly, so completely.

The cart passed over the sparkling Severn on a stately stone bridge, the river high, with here and there a tree emerging from it, the lower trunk submerged. They meandered on through a maze of streets, then climbed a long, slow hill past ancient, timber-framed buildings on each side. Anny looked up and saw the castle walls looming above them, rough-hewn and reddish, topped by grey battlements stark against the blue skies. The cart turned off the main roadway and took a track upwards further, the castle on her right, her constant stony companion until the cart came to a sudden halt. There before them was a gatehouse, a large, imposing structure of sandy-coloured stone, two bulging circular buildings on each side and an archway in the middle. The constable motioned at them to get down, still not deigning to speak actual words to them. The cart driver lit up a pipe and ignored them too. Anny looked around at him, unspeakably jealous that this man would be returning along the road to her home town, a place she wondered if she would ever set eyes on again. The constable was arguing with him about the fee, so many pence a mile from Ironbridge to bring the felons.

Then he grunted at the women to follow him. After no food or drink since a cup of water and a hunk of old bread in the lock-up that morning, Anny was unsteady on her feet and feared she might pass out. They were led towards the archway. The constable had words with the gatekeeper, who used two keys to unlock the tall, iron gates. She wondered if the gates had been produced with local iron. Had her grandfather's hands fashioned the iron rails that would soon stand between her and the freedom of the streets? Above the gates sat an alcove inside which had been placed a bodiless statue, the grey face of a stern man looking downwards upon them as they passed under it. Despite the heat, the stone eyes frowning at her gave her a chill and she drew her cloak around her. The woman's baby had awoken and was starting to fuss. Its small sobs soon reached a crescendo of wailing. This desperate sound accompanied them as they passed into the courtyard of Shrewsbury Prison. The gates were locked behind them.

The constable said to the gatekeeper, 'This'un a vagrant. This'un assisting a murder. This'un theft. This'un with the nipper is debt. Here y'are.'

He handed over some papers from inside his coat and continued conversing gruffly with the gatekeeper. Anny stared at the woman who had been wearing rouge the night before, which had since rubbed off. She was accused of assisting a murder. A murder! Anny had spent all night in a cell and all day on a cart with a woman who had assisted a murderer. Her mind raced with scenarios of who this woman might have helped in murdering and the murderer she had helped. She did not look like a violent woman. She just looked very tired and very bored.

Her attention was drawn away by the rising voice of the gatekeeper, 'Nay, she canna and you had no business bringing it here,' the gatekeeper was saying, pointing at the mother. 'It needs taking back to its own parish.'

'She's nursing it, you fool. If you think I'm taking a starving waif back on a day's journey by cart, you're half-soaked,' said the constable, and with that, he demanded the gate be opened and he be allowed to leave.

Two men approached them and the gatekeeper said, 'Go with the turnkeys, then,' and motioned them to walk through another archway into a courtyard. It was surrounded by two high walls on either side and before them the frontispiece to a long building, with arched windows along the breadth of it, all barred. She could hear shouts and calls from people behind the bars, the deeper voices of men coming from the left, the higher voices of women from the right. One turnkey took the murderer's assistant, while the rest of them, including Anny, followed the other turnkey through a door, past an office with a brass plaque screwed to the closed door entitled 'Keeper'.

'You've missed supper,' said the turnkey, not looking round at them. 'Straight to the cell.'

They followed him round to the right, walking on through a maze of corridors, alive with the stink of many bodies and the grumblings, mutterings, chatter and yelling of women. Some shouted at them as they went past: 'What did you bring us?' and suchlike. One bright spark with a throaty voice called out, 'Abandon hope all ye who enter here!' They walked on past small groups of cells arranged around a central area. Each group also had an open room that the guard pointed at and said, 'Cells there, court there and that's the day room.' He hacked up a good load of phlegm and spat it out in a grey, jellied lump onto the ground and then said, 'In the morning, follow the others. Wash outside, then breakfast. Surgeon'll see you, give you the once-o'er. Matron'll see you and give you your uniform. Set you to work. Your court is yours to keep tidy.'

They stopped at one of the courts and the turnkey said, 'Debtors. You with young'un. You're in there. Visitors you can have daily except Sundays. Regular visitors in the Visitor's Room or your husband, if you have'un, in your cell. You'll get a half-pint of wine. Not now. Tomorrow.'

The woman bowed her head onto her baby's and went into her cell alone. The turnkey locked the door. Some cells were single, like that; others had three beds in. Anny prayed for a single. They walked on and stopped again. The turnkey said, 'Here we are. Female Felons for Trial.' He opened a cell door and inside were three beds and two women, who looked around. 'You. Theft. In there.'

Anny walked in and the door clanked shut behind her. The sound of the key turning screwed her insides. She stood awkwardly on a grubby rag rug in the centre of the small space between the beds. The women were seated together on one bed, knees close together as if caught sharing secrets. They stared at her and Anny took a quick look around. There was a chamber pot in the corner filled to overflowing. Apart from that, the cell held only its beds and its inhabitants. And a high, small window, its view out of sight and reach; barred, of course.

'Now then, Theft. What's your real name?'

Anny looked at the women. Both wore the plain grey shapeless dress of the prison uniform. This one looked to be the same age as her mother, the other much younger, more like her age.

'Anny.'

'I'm Ellen, this is Jane. First time inside? You look like it is. You look as frightened as a mouse in cat country.'

Jane tittered at this.

'Yes, first time.'

'Sit down then. That's your bed over there.'

Anny stepped over to the spare cot. It had a thin mattress on it, which as she sat down made the rustling sound of straw stuffing. She could feel the bedstead through it, hard and bony against her behind. Where had these iron bedframes been forged? She thought of her father and wanted to weep. Folded up at the end of the bed were two sheets and two blankets.

'You look like a good wench,' said Ellen. 'But you're mucky. You'll need to scrub yourself right in the morning, or you won't get your breakfast, mind.'

'She has purty hair,' said Jane in a small, high voice. Jane's hand was resting on Ellen's knee, like fond sisters. 'Bonny colour.'

'Thank you,' said Anny. Jane smiled at her, a crooked, unsettling smile. Her hair was such a light yellow, it was almost white. Her pale eyes wandered a bit. Perhaps her thoughts, too.

'Not married, lass?' said Ellen. Her brown hair had grey streaks in it and there were dark pouches under her eyes and her cheeks and chin sagged. She looked directly at Anny without blinking. Anny was afraid of her but couldn't explain why, as Ellen was talking kindly to her.

Anny shook her head. 'I live with my parents in Ironbridge.' She could not stop thinking of her father. Her mother too. What would they be thinking? They would be beside themselves. 'They'll likely visit tomorrow. See how I'm faring.' Somehow she wanted to prove that she had support, she had others outside this hell who cared about her. That she was not alone in this place. But even one night's wait here sickened her with fear. She thought she might start sobbing again, so bit her lip. She would not cry in front of these two.

'What did you steal?' said Ellen, those blank eyes unblinking.

'I didn't. I didn't do it.'

Jane tittered again.

'Of course you didna, lass. I didna write any threatening letters either, did I, Janey, eh?'

'No, Nelly. No, you never did,' said Jane, shaking her head violently from side to side, whereupon they both laughed and held onto each other, rocking back and forth. *If they touch me*, thought Anny, *I shall scream*.

Ellen stopped laughing and peered at Anny, looked her up and down. 'Give me your hands.'

Anny did not want to. She hesitated.

'Give me your hands, for God's sake, girl. I dunna bite.'

'Not hands, anyway,' said Jane, mysteriously.

Anny could see no way round it. She held out her hands slowly, watching Ellen warily. Ellen took them roughly and rubbed them, turned them this way and that, then dropped them.

'Office worker,' she said, triumphantly.

'Yes,' said Anny.

'I knew it. Not rough enough for hard work. Ink under your nails. We've got an educated miss here, not unlike myself, Jane. You mun mind your manners round this'un. I suppose you'll be wanting a glass of wine, my lady.'

Anny remembered what the turnkey had said to the nursing mother. 'Will we get ours tomorrow?'

'Your what?' said Ellen.

'Our wine?'

Ellen and Jane looked round at each other and fell about laughing again. 'Ooh, Lady Ann of Ironbridge is wanting her wine!'

Anny waited for the mockery to subside. 'But the woman with the baby, he said to her . . .'

'That's just for debtors,' snapped Ellen. 'You're a felon. You dunna get the same privileges.'

Jane piped up, 'She's a fine'un, like the last. They'll make her monitor, now the other'un's been sent yonder.'

Anny frowned and Ellen said, 'Yes, they will, no doubt. She looks like the type who'd suck up to the turnkeys, this'un. Just like the last'un. Well, it did her no good, let me tell you, Lady Ann. She was Theft like you and she herself got transported for seven years, she did. Being the keeper's pet did her no good at all, wunna do her no good either, out in Australia.'

Anny felt her head would explode. The effort was enormous, of remaining vigilant of these two, of keeping her mouth closed on a scream, of stopping herself from running to the door and pounding upon it. Her head felt so heavy, so heavy. She let it drop into her hands and screwed her eyes shut. She would not cry, must not cry.

She heard Ellen sigh heavily. 'Lie down and sleep,' she said in a kinder voice.

Anny did so. Too exhausted to make the bed up with the sheets and blankets, she rested her head upon them and was out in less than a minute.

She woke in full darkness. It was a hot night, stifling in the tiny cell. She felt suffocated by the heat and the stench of the chamber pot and her two companions' bodily emissions. Her mouth was so dry she thought she would gag. Oh, for a cup of cool water. She would give her life for it. She could not think of any other thing for several minutes, just water, water, water, a drink, a drink, a drink. To think of how busy her mind had been only a day and a half before, filled with girlish notions of love and kissing and a happy future. And now she would die for a sip of water. She listened to the other women breathing. The tears came then. She could not stop them. They flowed out of her eyes like the gush from a waterwheel, unstoppable, unending. She let them run into her mouth. At least they moistened her tongue a little, despite their saltiness. She pursed her lips to stop a sound escaping, but that betrayed her too and let out one small sob.

Jane suddenly sat bolt upright. She stared over at Anny, who stopped whimpering immediately. Jane stood and stepped over to her. Anny looked up and Jane brought her hand down very fast, whacking her hard on the ear. Anny cried out, then bit her lip and cupped her hands over her poor ear. Her ear throbbed with sharp pain. Jane bent down very close and delivered her words in a breathy yet vicious whisper: 'Hush your noise! I'm in here for assault, see? I know how to handle meself with a chit like you. You wake me up again and I shall thrash you. I shall murder you.'

Chapter 15

Margaret had found out that morning. She had gone to sleep early the night before with bad pains from the monthly curse. She had slept late and was breakfasting in bed when the news came. It was the maid, Lucy, that had gently knocked on her door, come in and told her: 'I thought you'd want to know, miss. Your friend, Miss Woodvine. They say she took money from the safe. They found it in her bag.'

The news had almost shocked Margaret into silence. It was so preposterous. 'Lucy, what are you talking about?'

'Anny, miss. They're saying she stole from the master.'

'It is a mistake,' said Margaret. 'Anny would never do that.'

'Yes, miss,' said Lucy.

'But, what is happening? Where is she now?'

'The constable Finch came and they locked her up last night. It's said she'll go to the Dana today to wait for trial.'

'The what?'

'The prison in Shrewsbury. They call it the Dana there.'

'What do her parents say? They must be distraught.'

'Her father goes to visit her tomorrow, I heard. At the prison.'

'Forgive me, Lucy, but I must go and speak with my father.'

Margaret had not known what to do. She was frightened of her father, more so of Cyril. But she had to do something. She called for her maid Royce, who dressed her. Then she gathered her nerve and went straight to her father's study, knocking meekly on the door. But he was not at home. He had gone out for the day. Cyril too. Queenie was in bed and not to be disturbed. Her father did not return all day. She sat in her room and thought it all through. It filled her with fear, the thought of acting beyond the narrow confines of her existence, but her friend's peril spurred her on.

She swallowed her nerves and walked to the stables. She spoke quietly with the coach driver and instructed him to take her to Shrewsbury first thing in the morning. The driver looked askance, momentarily seeming to doubt her authority. She had cleared her throat and spoken louder, telling him to be ready at dawn. She knew that all of her family were slugabeds, unless a trip out beckoned them from their abandoned sleep. She could leave early and face her father's wrath when she returned. Then, once she understood the situation better, having heard the details from Anny herself, she would speak to her father. She would insist, she would make him listen. Seeing Anny would give her the strength to do it, to face him and tell him: this simply must be wrong. This was not possible. Anny would never do this. Her father must believe her.

The ride to Shrewsbury the next morning was long, hot and uncomfortable. She tried to imagine the inside of a prison, tried to picture her friend there, but all that came were scenes from French novels of convicts chained in dungeons with long white beards. She scolded herself for being so unworldly, so sheltered and foolish. When she arrived, she must face it with fortitude, for her friend, for Anny.

The coach wound its way through the city that she had visited before, for trips to the theatre and to buy clothes with Benjamina. She had seen the castle on the hill and glimpsed the prison beyond it, but had never given it a second thought. The coach jolted to a stop and the driver opened the door for her. She gathered her embroidered purse and hitched up her stiff skirts as she descended the step onto the street. Then, someone said her name.

She looked up. Before her stood a very tall, very broad man, dishevelled, his boots grey with dust, his hair thick with it, his face grimed by it. She had not heard what he'd said and was about to ask what on earth he wanted, when she recognised something in his face. He spoke again: 'I am Anny's father, come to see her. Are you come to see her too, miss?'

'Indeed, Mr Woodvine,' she said kindly. 'One moment, please.' She turned to the driver and told him to wait for her there, for as long as it took. The driver nodded and prepared to move along to find a more permanent spot to rest in. She looked back at Anny's father and glanced behind him. 'Is your wife here with you?'

'She is at home. She . . . took it badly. She collapsed.'

Margaret thought of the strong-armed, vital woman she had met and could not imagine her fainting. Only news as bad as this could fell such a woman.

'Oh, I am so sorry to hear of it. Is she being looked after?'

'She is. We have good neighbours. She is not strong enough to travel, so I have come alone, bringing things for Anny that her mother packed for her last night.'

'Mr Woodvine, how did you travel here today?'

'Walked through the night,' he said, fingering his hat nervously.

'Please forgive me,' she said. 'I have been so thoughtless. I should have arranged to take you myself.'

'Very kind of you, miss. But I think we both know, that wouldna do.'

Perhaps he is right, she thought. But she felt it was the right thing to say. 'Yes, I have come to see Anny.

You may not know, sir, that your daughter and I are dear friends. I'm sorry to say we have hidden this fact for some years now. We felt it would be better to be . . . discreet about such a close friendship. But I assure you, that Anny is the best friend I have in the whole world.'

Woodvine seemed abashed by this. He looked down, sidelong, up. Then he said, 'I didna know of that. But I'm hoping now it'll be something that'll help my girl. Can you help her, miss? Can you?'

'I will do anything in my power,' she said earnestly. 'Anything a friend can do, I shall do.' But she had nothing for him, no plans and no information. She saw his expectant face and wanted to answer it, to give him the hope he clearly wanted, but she had only her position, her money, her friendship to offer. What good it would do, she knew not. She smiled at him wanly, pityingly, and his face changed. It fell and hardened. He shoved his hat back on his head.

'You'd better not go in there, miss,' he said gruffly. 'Not a place for young ladies.'

'Oh, but Mr Woodvine, I am determined. I must see Anny. Shall we not go in together? It would be my honour if you accompanied me.' Something in his face and manner made him comfortable to talk to. She had not been this at ease talking to someone since Jake. She saw Anny's features in this man's face and it made her feel at home.

'Mr Woodvine, I assure you that once I have heard Anny's side of the story, I will be going directly to talk to my father. I am convinced that this must surely be a miscarriage of justice.'

'That's what I think,' said Woodvine, his face lit with possibility now. 'My lass would never do this.'

'I know that, sir. I do. Anny is the most honest, upright person I know. Your family are well respected in my father's works and in the neighbourhood. I am sure we can settle this, once we have the facts.'

She had no idea where this resolve had come from, never in her life being sure of herself in any single thing. But there was a first time for everything, and this was hers. How would she persuade her father? What could ever move a weak-minded, selfish fool such as Ralph King to help a girl like Anny? Now, standing with Anny's father, she saw he was everything that Mr King was not. In his shabby working clothes he had more dignity in his fingernail than her father would ever have in his whole person. She felt that envy again, that pang of wanting to have another family, another life. The wish to be a changeling. But then she caught herself, her stupid self, wishing her lucky life away while her poor friend sat in the hellish place before them. And Anny's father stood and looked to her, the rich friend, for some crumb of help.

'Come,' she went on. 'Let us go and see her now.'

Woodvine nodded and they approached the gate. Once inside, the gatekeeper searched through Woodvine's package, scattering the contents. Three bread rolls fell onto the filthy floor and Margaret cried out as they were soiled. The silly man, ruining Anny's precious food like that. She helped Woodvine pick them up.

'Should we throw these away?' she said quietly to Woodvine.

'No, miss. She'll be in need of them.'

She noted that the gatekeeper did not ask to see inside her purse. They waited in silence for some time, the gatekeeper having taken Anny's name and told them someone would come soon. She glanced at Woodvine, who stood as solid as oak, patient, unreadable. Then a man in uniform approached and gestured at them to follow. What came next was as a nightmare, the kind of dream that wakes you in dreaded wonder at how your mind could dream up such a thing, yet this was real. The sounds that came from the women, the screams and yelps and sobs. The stink that flowed through the fetid air, so thick and rank that Margaret feared she would faint. Woodvine kept an eye on her, at one stage putting a hesitant arm about her shoulder to steer her away from arms reaching out from bars, streaked with filth and what looked like dried blood and their owner screeching at the rich girl passing, calling her words that Margaret had never heard but sounded like the names that demons would dream up in hell for the torture of its inhabitants.

Not soon enough, they arrived at a room set out with tables and chairs at which sat women in grey dresses and opposite them an assortment of people, mostly poor, one or two more well-to-do. There was a woman nursing her baby, and the thought of babies existing in this dreadful place sickened Margaret more than anything. And then she saw Anny.

Woodvine was already there. He had stridden across the room before Margaret had had a chance to register her friend, so different did she look at first glance, an impression that increased with every step towards her. It had only been three days, but already Anny looked like a shadow of the feisty young woman she knew and loved. Her face was pasty, marked only with dark shadows beneath her eyes. Her glorious copper tresses were mostly hidden under an off-white cap, the strands that escaped messily were lank and greasy, the hair dirty-red, as if the colour had leaked out of it. She sat upright though, her back straight, her face uplifted. They had not broken her yet. She stood as her father approached, her face crumpling into distress and joy intermixed, an expression Margaret had never seen in a person until that moment and it broke her heart. Margaret's eyes filled with tears and she caught a sob in her handkerchief, raised to her nose to try in vain to block out the smell. She watched as Anny's father threw his arms about her, his huge frame enveloping her utterly so that she temporarily disappeared, but a guard by the wall shouted at them 'No touching!' and they pulled apart reluctantly, Woodvine shooting a look of hatred at the man, as if he would kill him with a flick of his hand. Anny was whispering to him, beckoning him to sit down, her eyes wary of trouble. Then she looked over and spotted Margaret. Her face changed again, this time showing surprise, then a smile and a frown at once, her hand raised towards her. Margaret came quickly, grasping it, and then remembering the guard's order, letting go quickly and taking the seat that Woodvine held ready for her, trying to dust it off. Margaret had worn her plainest, dullest gown but still felt a perfect idiot in that place, like a peacock in a coal mine.

'Ow bist, my wench? How be it here?' Woodvine was gabbling. 'I brought things from home. Here, food, clothes. Your mother packed them. She's ill or she woulda come. No, dunna fret. Dunna fret, little'un. Dunna cry. She'll be right. Just upset with all this business. I'm here. I'm here, now. Dunna cry, my sweet lass.'

Woodvine's commentary ran on desperately as Anny wept and wept. She had not spoken properly yet; neither had Margaret. She was crying too; her eyes blurred, she wiped them with her lace handkerchief which soon crumpled into a useless wet rag. She had another one in her sleeve and passed it instead to Anny, who did not see it, blinded by tears as she was. Woodvine took it and used it to wipe his daughter's face tenderly, so tenderly, the huge hands capable of such sensitivity.

After a time, Anny calmed down and composed herself. She looked up at her father, then at Peggy, and forced a feeble smile.

'Thank you for coming,' she said in a small voice.

'Anny,' said Margaret, determined to be of some use now. 'I intend to speak to my father about this tonight. I need to know everything you can tell me of what happened. I need all of the facts, so that we can try to fathom what happened here. So we can solve it.'

Anny nodded solemnly, then began to tell it all: how Paddy had come and called her away to the library, which of course Margaret remembered, how strange that was; how she'd gone back, followed by Cyril, and unlocked the office, found it empty, Brotherton away somewhere; how she'd worked for a while then he'd come back, complaining of an errand to town for Mrs King senior, to fetch some ink, usually Anny's job, so that was strange, too; then they'd worked all day and only discovered the money missing at the end of the day; how Mr King had found it in her bag.

Margaret had listened keenly to each turn of events. 'So, the office was left locked and unoccupied for a time, between Mr B being sent to town and you returning from the house.'

'Yes, that's right.'

'That's when it happened,' said Margaret.

'Yes, that's what I think,' said Anny, her tired eyes brightening.

‘Think what?’ said Woodvine, slow to catch on.

Margaret answered, ‘Someone went into the office when it was unoccupied, took the money from the safe and put it in Anny’s bag.’

‘Yes!’ cried Anny.

Woodvine said, ‘But who? Who would do such a thing? Why wouldna they just take it for themselves? And how would they get in? It was locked. Who could do that and how? Why?’

So many questions. But Margaret knew. She looked at Anny and saw that Anny knew too. She wondered if Anny did not want to speak of this before her father, but saw also that they must be allies now, the three of them, if they were to save her.

‘Anny,’ she said and leant forward, speaking low. ‘That day, in the library, you were going to tell me something but we were interrupted. What was it?’

Anny glanced at her father.

‘What is it, lass?’ he said gently.

‘Cyril – Master King – he found me in the woods the day before and he asked me to be his wife.’

‘What?’ gasped Woodvine, turning to Margaret for some enlightenment, but did not wait for further explanation, his mind clearly running onwards. ‘Well, if he’s sweet on you then this problem is solved. He can vouch for you. He will speak to his father, surely.’

‘No,’ said Margaret firmly. ‘Anny, what did you say to Cyril when he asked you?’

Anny looked down at her lap, pain flitting across her eyes. 'I refused him.'

'Well, I'm not surprised,' began Woodvine, then, remembering the company they kept, gave a sidelong look at Margaret and muttered, 'No offence to you, miss.'

'None taken,' said Margaret. 'How did it proceed, Anny? How did Cyril take it?'

'Not well,' said Anny, grimly. 'He . . .' Another glance at her father.

'Please, Anny,' said Margaret. 'We must know it all.'

'He attacked me, tried to kiss me. I fought him off. I told him I hated him. I ran away.'

'I'll get him,' said Woodvine, in a guttural tone. 'I'll get him and I'll lamp him.'

'No, you won't!' said Anny. 'Mother needs you. Don't get yourself in here, for assault.'

'It's more serious than that,' said Margaret, and they both looked at her. 'From what you've told me, Anny, I am convinced of it. Cyril put that money in your bag, as revenge for turning him down.'

'Yes,' said Anny. 'I'm certain of it.'

Woodvine erupted, standing up, his puny chair careering backwards as if made of matchsticks. 'I'll murder 'im!' He stood, puffing like a bull, clenching his fists. Two guards hopped to it and were beside him in a second, shouting at him to clear out. There was a scuffle and Anny called out to her father to calm down, and to the guards to leave him be. Thus, Woodvine was manhandled from the room, calling behind him to Anny, saying sorry, how sorry he was. Margaret called to him, told him to wait for her outside, that she would come presently. One of the guards stayed and told her she'd have to go too.

'If I may, a further few minutes is all I require to speak to Miss Woodvine here. I would be most grateful.' She smiled at the sour-faced oik who stank of spirits and sweat. He grinned as she raised her purse a notch, catching his eye. She removed a couple of coins from it and handed them to him.

'Long as you want, miss! Well, until visiting time is up, anyhow,' he said, taking the coins and performing a twisted kind of bow, taking his place again in the corner, watching her closely as she sat down once more with Anny.

'Dear Anny,' said Margaret, risking the guard's wrath by taking her friend's hand and enfolding it.

'I'm so glad you came. I'm so glad you're here,' said Anny. It was the kind of thing someone would say and smile, but there was no smile. It was as if her face had been newly made, only for sadness.

'I will talk to my father tonight. But it will have to be handled carefully. I will have to think on it, how it is to be done best. He adores my brother and will not hear him badly spoken of by others, so I need to be clever in the way I do it, the way I say it to him.'

'Thank you,' said Anny, staring desperately at her now, squeezing her hand. 'And I hope to God it works. I cannot stand it here much longer.'

'Visiting time is nearly up,' called the guard and people began to busy themselves to leave. Anny said, 'There's no time, Peggy. Listen, does Jake Ashford know I'm here? Does he know about this?'

The mention of Jake's name was a shock to Margaret. What was this? She frowned at it.

'Well, I don't know, Anny. I've not seen Mr Ashford these past few days.'

'Will you take him a message for me, Peggy? Please? I know he comes to the big house. Will you please tell him something from me?'

Margaret fought to control her expression. 'Of course I will. What is it?'

'Tell him I didn't do it. Tell him you're going to help me. Tell him . . . to wait.'

'Wait . . . for what?' said Margaret.

'Visiting time is over now. Out you go. Out you all go,' called the guard, who was joined by a turnkey, ready to take the prisoners back.

'And Peggy,' said Anny, standing, grasping her friend's hand now so tightly, so desperately it crushed her fingers, 'tell him to visit me. Please! Tell him to come to me, as soon as he can, Peggy. Please!'

The visitors were leaving and the guard was approaching. Anny released her friend's hand and turned from her, a turnkey standing between them, ushering the prisoners out.

'I will speak to my father,' called Margaret, as Anny gathered up her package and left the room by a back door. Anny looked back once, eyes pleading, then disappeared into a gloomy corridor beyond. Despite the weight of this terrible place upon her, Anny's bearing was ramrod straight. So, was there an understanding between Anny and Jake Ashford? Margaret's heart twisted with it. It couldn't be. Jake had asked to spend more time with her. There must be some mistake. How she wanted her friend to possess this happiness, and yet at the same time how she smarted with envy. Could it be true? Whatever the case was, she had to drive it from her mind. The only thing that mattered now was helping Anny to get out of this hellish place. Margaret inhaled deeply, breathing in the stink of the prison, which only minutes before had sent her coughing into her lace handkerchief. But she was determined to overcome her previous sensibilities. As she left the room and followed the turnkey out into the corridors and beyond, she felt she was changing inside. For the first time in her sheltered life, she had been shaken to the core by the reality of what other people had to endure in this world. How stupid she'd been, how pathetic and scared and shy – and of what? These were real problems, solid, unavoidable problems as heavy as iron, and as immovable. And now her dear friend was in mortal danger and she was the only one on earth who could do anything about it. She felt herself grown an inch by the time she reached the prison gates, and as she left the prison behind and entered into the sunshiny afternoon, she emerged as a new creature.

Chapter 16

Ralph King sat at his study desk, looking down gloomily at his mound of a belly that pushed up against the drawer handle. Where did it all come from, this flesh? As a younger man, he had been able to eat like a pig and never put on an ounce. He hunted, walked, rode and even swam without a second thought. Nowadays he broke into a sweat climbing the stairs. He thought about going up there to look at himself in the mirror, to turn sideways and see if his profile was worse than the last time he looked. But Benjamina was up there, taking her customary nap. What on earth did she do to warrant a sleep every afternoon? Weakness, that was it. Women were weak. But she ate bonbons and cake and other delicacies and all of it disappeared without blemish into her slim frame. Her breasts and hips and buttocks were womanly and ample, he thought with a minor jolt, but everywhere else was lean and firm. How did she do it? How he envied her that. It must be born in her. Or perhaps it was age. She was so very young, at twenty-three. And he felt so very old, though surely forty-three was not ancient. He felt somehow he was ageing more quickly than her. She was receding from him, growing distant. With a looming sense of doom, he wondered why his pretty wife did not want to bed him anymore. She had been voracious when they first married and now had cooled off considerably, always complaining of headaches and so forth. Even when they did, she would just lie there and stare off into the distance, waiting for it to be over. And why did she always ask him to leave her alone straight afterward? She said she didn't want a child yet, as she was too young. He could understand that. He didn't want one either in particular, but surely this was unnatural for a woman. His first wife had had two, long before she was twenty-three. But look what happened to her. Celia, lovely, loving Celia. She had been so innocent, so giving, so sweet. Benjamina's lasciviousness had been stimulating to begin with, but it didn't last and now it seemed tarnished, when he thought of Celia. It nearly broke him, when she bled and died like that in their bed. How he hated Margaret after that; couldn't hold his baby daughter in his arms without cursing her. That was wrong, he knew that. But can a man help how he feels, really feels? No, he cannot. And no man loved a woman more than he had loved Celia. His love for Benjamina – well, that was lust. And necessity. Mostly lust. Her body, soft here, tight there, open to him. Or had been, once upon a time. Maybe he should tell her he wanted a child and then she'd be duty bound to perform. Yes, he'd try that. And stop eating so much.

He realised that he was lonely. Yes, the great Ralph King. Did his wife love him? His daughter? His mother, even? Anyone? Cyril. His beloved son. Did the boy love him, though? Could he love anyone, that boy? The doubts came thick and fast, like flies to fresh manure. The boy had that cruelty in him, just like Ralph King senior, his own father. He knew they'd both had their way violently with maids about the place. He'd heard his father grunting away with them at night, seen his son manhandling them. He'd had words with Cyril, only one time, when he was caught almost in the act, ravishing that pretty one, Lucy. It would cause such a scandal if word got out. Didn't the boy know to keep his activities private? He'd never had the urge, himself. He never wanted to touch the lower classes, if he could help it. Couldn't understand it.

And then there was Margaret. Only today she had taken the barouche without asking and kept it out all day and was still not back. He was furious with her. So out of character and so damnably selfish. Cyril had wanted to take it out this morning, and he himself had required it this afternoon. They had to make do with the curricle. What in heaven's name was the girl thinking, sneaking off like that at first light? How dare she! He'd have a word or two to say about that when she returned.

And Benjamina. He'd have a word or two with her as well, this evening.

A knock on the door dragged him from his musing and he called whoever it was to enter. It was Brunt, his faithful butler of over thirty years, around when he was a boy and his father was young and vital. That should be the way of things, servants committing themselves to one family. So many of these younger ones hopped from job to job, never sticking at anything. Times were changing and he did not like it. He did not like it at all. Brunt was waiting for him.

'What is it, Brunt?'

'Messrs Brotherton and Pritchard are here, with their daily report. Shall I show them in, sir?'

'Indeed, indeed,' said King, forcing himself to appear businesslike. Oh hell, these meetings were tedious. And, if he admitted it fully to himself, they were confusing. They often tried to explain things to him of the nature of the business, and he so often failed to grasp the gist of what they were banging on about and ended up bluffing his way through it and hoping nobody noticed. He was sure, actually, that nobody did notice. He was very good at bluffing.

The two men came in, caps in hand. Ralph would usually stand up and address them from in front of the fireplace but today he was weary and quite comfortable in his position at his desk. He remained seated and said, 'Proceed, gentlemen.'

Brotherton began with some figures about labour and materials, then something about breakage in the machinery at the rolling mill that would need fixing – something about the screws of the pillars of the rolls that would need re-cutting – and Ralph just said affirmative things on occasion and hoped Brotherton would shut up soon, which he did. Then Pritchard started up about the illness of some key workman which delayed production, and then about working hours and Ralph lost interest. Why did they bother him with such things? So far, no questions had been asked, so he felt unencumbered by having to do anything more than nod sagely and agree with all of their conclusions, unless it involved the spending of more money, in which case his ears always pricked up and he weeded out such revolutionary ideas and crushed them.

Just then, the sound of a coach and horses coming up the drive alerted him to the return of his daughter. He must get rid of these fools and take her to task for her behaviour. Surely they had finished by now. He attuned his mind to the string of words that came from Brotherton's mouth and nodded twice. But then Pritchard piped up and was talking about materials, and how the cost would be increased but that it would surely be a worthy investment, and so forth.

'What's this?' said Ralph, and the two men stopped and stared in embarrassed silence. 'Pritchard, do go over what you just said, as I can hardly believe my ears.'

'Uh . . . well, sir, the problem is occurring with the raw materials. The coke and the limestone we are supplied with needs a more uniform preparation, if slips are to be avoided.'

What were slips again? Oh, the processes that went on in these blast furnaces were so complicated, one needed to concentrate damnably hard to understand them.

'Slips?'

More staring. 'Yes, sir, slips,' said Pritchard.

'And your argument again is . . . what? About slipping?'

'Slips, not slipping, sir. You see, at times the materials stick to the inside wall of the furnace and cause a blockage. That's your slip. If it builds all the way across, that's a scaffold. That's very dangerous, sir, and could cause an explosion. The coke and limestone we're presently receiving are of a poorer quality. The pieces are so uneven as to cause blockages, as they burn at different rates. We need to increase the checks on the production of our materials to ensure a more uniform size and . . .'

'It sounds expensive, Pritchard.'

Brotherton piped up. 'Not really, sir. It might be only further instructions needed to the bridgestocker in the proper preparation of the materials and may only require a small increase in expenditure, due to the . . .'

'No,' said Ralph and decided to clench his fist and place it commandingly on his desk for effect. 'No, no, no. This business is already spending far too much money on labour and materials. We will not be adopting anything that drives the cost up further.'

Pritchard started up again: 'But, sir, the safety of the furnace and therefore the men themselves . . .'

'Are well taken care of,' Ralph interrupted.

'With respect, sir,' Pritchard began. Well, he didn't like the sound of that. If he had respect, he wouldn't need to declare it in such a presumptuous manner.

'Now then, Pritchard, this won't do. This really will not do. You come in here and make these demands like a common highwayman. Yes, it needed saying. My furnace runs very well and has done these past years. I trust in the ability of you and your workers to keep an eye on these things and do your best with the materials you are given. Why, if we spent all the money in the world on perfect materials and perfect labourers, I dare say we'd have a perfect ironworks. But we would not make a profit, would we now, hmm? And you would not earn a wage and neither would any of your men and I would be a beggar on the streets alongside you.'

He would have liked to add, *And what do you say to that, eh, Pritchard?* But he restrained himself. He had made his point, brilliantly. He didn't need to rub their noses in it, though it was tempting. But he had had quite enough of these two for now and was itching to launch his wrath at his daughter.

He rang the bell for Brunt and when he came, told him to escort them out and bring Margaret to him forthwith. When Brotherton and Pritchard had finally gone, he breathed a sigh of relief. Another problem dealt with in an excellent manner, and any possible humiliations due to muddles had been swiftly side-stepped. He got up from his chair, which took more effort than he'd like and took up his favourite spot by the fireplace, sucked in his stomach and waited. There was a knock on the door.

'Enter.'

In came his daughter, and her appearance surprised him. Somehow, she looked older than she had only the day before. Her bearing was more upright and her gaze more direct. She suddenly seemed the very image of her dead mother, the same large mouth, swan-like neck and graceful hands. He really must remember to be nicer to her in general terms, but not at this moment. Now what was needed was a hard lesson.

Chapter 17

At the sight of her father, Margaret quailed. She had never willingly approached him to converse about anything. But she knew that the moment had come to steel herself and act, for justice, but most of all, for her friend.

'Father, I must speak with you,' she said and approached quickly, placing her purse on his desk with a confident gesture that seemed to unsettle him.

'Indeed you must. What is the meaning of this, Margaret? How dare you take the barouche today without my permission! What makes you think that a girl of your tender years can go gallivanting about the countryside without a chaperone, without . . . my permission, as I have just said. I demand an explanation.'

'Never mind about that, Father. It is something else I need to discuss with you.'

Her hands were trembling and she clasped them together to steady herself.

'What in God's name is this? What has happened to my shy, retiring daughter of only yesterday? Who is this arch young woman accosting me with demands? I say again, Margaret . . .'

'No, Father, really. We don't have time for that now. We must discuss Anny Woodvine.'

'What is this, now? Woodvine? What the devil . . .'

'I've been to see her in Shrewsbury. She's innocent, Father.' Margaret walked over to the fireplace and stood at the other end of it, directly opposite him.

'You've been *where*? To *Shrewsbury*?'

'Yes, I visited her in prison. I saw her father there. We spoke to her. She told us everything that happened. And I must say . . . it is my duty to inform you . . .'

'You? You went to Shrewsbury Prison? With an iron-worker? A *prison*?'

She took a step towards him. She was within striking distance now. She felt her knees weakening but she forced herself to stay upright. She would not allow him to win this one. Everything was at stake now.

'Yes, Father, but that is of no consequence. You really must listen to me, Father. I have to . . .'

He hit her very hard across her right cheek. She did not fall to the ground. Instead, she bent right over, but her knees did not give way. She cradled her cheek in one hand, but stood her ground and looked up at him.

'I will be heard,' she said, quietly but firmly.

'Must I strike you again?' he said, his voice low.

'Cyril put that money in Anny Woodvine's bag. He did it out of revenge.'

'What witchcraft is this? What lies are you cooking up? This is madness!'

He went to hit her again, but she was wise to it now and dodged out of the way, causing him to stumble forward. He caught his balance with one hand on the mantelpiece. She hopped behind his leather armchair, the bulk of it between them.

'It's the truth, Father, and you must hear it. Cyril is no good. He's rotten to the core.'

Margaret was still stationed behind the chair, her eyes alert, her stance ready to flit away again. He was looking at her with narrowed eyes, as if trying to fathom her. Perhaps he was realising that his old ways were not working now. She would not be cowed by the back of his hand. She could see him changing tack. What would he say next?

'I am sorry I struck you, Margaret,' he said carefully. 'I lost my temper there for a moment and it is regrettable. It won't happen again. Let us discuss this like civilised people. Here, come sit beside me and we shall reason this out, together.'

He put his hand out to her. She hesitated. She did not take his hand but she did come out from behind the chair. He sat in his leather chair and motioned to her to sit on the matching footstool, but she declined and stood on the hearthrug. She did not trust him. She knew at that moment that she truly hated him. But she needed him to save Anny. And so she must listen and deal with him. It was heartening to see him acting more reasonably.

She began, 'You may well be unaware of this, but Cyril has been after Anny Woodvine for years.'

'It is his way with the servant girls. An unfortunate weakness, but one I am preparing to take in hand.'

'No, Father. It is more than that with Anny. He asked her to marry him.'

'He did *what*?'

Margaret thought her father might explode. 'He told her he wanted her to be his wife. But she refused him.'

'Has he told you of this himself?'

'No, but Anny told me. And I trust Anny with my life. I never knew a more honest person than Anny Woodvine. Mr Brotherton would concur with this, I am sure. And he can confirm that Cyril was always bothering Anny at the office and trying to get her alone. Just ask him.'

Her father was pinching at his lower lip, staring at the floor.

Margaret went on, 'Father, you know what Cyril is like, how proud he is. It would have humiliated him, to be refused by a girl like Anny. He would have wanted revenge. He must have come up with this plan to ruin her. But she is innocent of this crime. Cyril orchestrated the whole thing. We must force Cyril to admit it and you must tell the court to let her go.'

She was standing over him, her arms crossed in an unfeminine stance which would probably infuriate him.

Speaking the truth had given her courage. Also, he had not shouted at her again and he had not tried to deny what she said. This gave her hope that, finally, her father might just take her side, for the first time in her life. It felt extraordinary to talk to him in such an open, direct way. To be on equal terms, almost. She felt a great shift in power was occurring. Her father took a breath and she prepared herself for his next pronouncement.

'My dear, I have listened to your accusations. There is no question of your brother being involved in any such plot. And there is no question of doubt in Woodvine's guilt of theft, as charged. If you choose to speak your ridiculous theories about this elaborate plot that my son is supposed to have been involved in, I will disown you as my daughter. Not only that, I will personally see to it that our family doctor pronounces that you are feeble of mind, just as your grandmother is, and just as her sister was, who, as you know, though we never speak of it, killed herself in a lunatic asylum, the family shame. So, you see there is in the female side of this family a weakness, a propensity to madness . . . of invention and imaginings. Any such story bandied about by you concerning any male member of this family will be met with your own incarceration. You will be as surely locked up as your friend Woodvine. But there is one difference. In her case, she will go to trial and may be fortunate; she may be transported to Australia for seven years and not serve her time in a prison here. You, on the other hand, would be sent to an institution for the rest of your life. Mark my words, my girl, for I will make sure of it. So, the choice is yours. It will be your freedom or hers.'

The child came into the room, her face white with shock, a scalding red mark on her cheek and a bluish bloom beside her eye. Queenie glanced at Jenkins, who shot her a knowing look back. Queenie nodded and Jenkins went to the girl, made a bit of a fuss about her and steered her to sit down on the end of the bed.

'Oh, Grandmother!' cried Margaret and sobbed, covering her face, which made the girl flinch at the touch.

'Stop that now!' Queenie heard herself cry. She did not intend it to sound so harsh, but she could not abide tears, she really could not. 'Crying never did a person one shred of good,' she continued in a softer voice. It seemed to do the trick as Margaret calmed a little and wiped her face, wincing from the tenderness around her left eye. 'I am not one to condone your father's violence, but you must admit that it is your own doing on this occasion, disappearing like that without permission.'

Margaret looked up at her. Those blue eyes, just like Selina's, her poor lost sister. 'It wasn't that, Grandmother. It was about Anny.'

'Who on earth is Anny?'

'Anny is my friend. Anny Woodvine. She works at the office with Mr Brotherton.'

'The thief?'

Margaret shuffled closer along the bed, her tears gone now, a look of activated energy in her eyes. Queenie felt alarmed. What could the girl have to do with this person? She had heard of it from Jenkins, the shame of it, the degradation of having a thief in their midst, a cuckoo in the nest, whose sex and lowly station in life had been overlooked and who had been given a chance at a plum job, only to betray them all and take their cash, like a common pickpocket.

'Grandmother, I must tell you the truth. I tried to tell Father but he would not listen. Anny is not a thief. She is innocent. Cyril wanted to marry her and she said no, so he put the money in her bag. It's all a lie. She is in prison now and we must help her. We simply must help her, Grandmother.'

The words of the girl had tumbled out at such a pace that Queenie's sense of it was muddled. There was something about this thief and her grandson and marriage and prison. It all sounded like a romance novel and not at all what Margaret ought to be reading. She would have a word with Ralph about that, about curbing his daughter's reading habits, which were tending to the dangerous by the sounds of it. But then she remembered they were talking of something real, that Margaret had been struck by her father and that something bad had occurred. Could it be real? Cyril and a common office girl?

'I do not believe a word of it,' said Queenie, finally, and looked at Jenkins, who nodded her head, her mouth set in a hard, straight line. If Jenkins agreed, it was sure to be right. She took comfort from that. But Margaret was standing up, taking a step closer to her, looking down upon her and talking again. What could the child be thinking?

'It is the truth, Grandmother. Cyril is rotten, through and through. He attacked Anny in the woods. He has been doing it to the maids for years. Surely you're aware of this.'

A quick glance at Jenkins, who raised her eyebrows and looked askance. So Cyril was about the same business as his grandfather, was he? As her husband? Yes, she could believe that.

Margaret went on. 'Anny is a good person, Grandmother. A wonderful person. She works hard and has ambition. She has no reason to lie or steal. She was planning to apply for better jobs in Shrewsbury.'

Queenie was now focused on what the child was saying. Sometimes her mind fogged over, like the stealthy arrival of the mist that hung about the river in autumn. It would linger a while and her thoughts would be confused and lost. But then a meaningful word, a look, a deed by others about her could bring her back instantly to herself; the mist of her mind would be burned away and she would find herself as clear and sharp as she ever was in her youth. She sat up straighter in her bed and said, 'Perhaps she stole the money to help set herself up in Shrewsbury. Have you thought of that, hmm?'

'Why would she risk it, though? She would ruin her chances. She is intelligent, far cleverer than I. She had no necessity to steal, with her good job and the promise of a career to come.'

'You are young and do not know people. People are stupid. People act in a stupid manner, a nonsensical manner. If you try to fathom every act that people do and why they have done it, why, that would be a futile exercise.'

'This one is not stupid. I *know* her.'

'Sit down, child, will you? You are hurting my neck, making me gawp up at you like this.' Margaret seated herself and continued to stare unsettlingly at her, her back straight and her hands folded in her lap. *She is blossoming*, thought Queenie. 'Now, how could you possibly know an office girl like that well enough to make these pronouncements about her character?'

'She and I have been friends for years, secret friends and correspondents. We began writing to each other as children and have met up many times since. She is the person I know best in the world. She is my dearest friend.'

'How did I not know of this?' said Queenie. How could such shenanigans have been occurring in her household without her knowledge?

'I did tell you, Grandmother. When I first met Anny years ago, I told you I wanted to be friends with her.'

'And I advised you then that it was a preposterous idea. But you defied me! How can this have come to pass, in our family? Friendships with servants?'

The child was protesting about it, saying something about an office, but Queenie was not listening. She was scolding herself inwardly. It was because she spent too much time in bed these days. Yes, that was it. Well, this would not do. She would have to insist that Jenkins got her up and about more. She had become indolent and this was the outcome. The child needed taking in hand. 'Well, I must say, any such friendship is wholly ill-advised and should never have been allowed to prosper in the first place. The poor are an unknown quantity, my dear. We can as little understand the workings of their minds as that of Benjamina's dog. They are simply another species.'

'You would say that of Jenkins, would you?' said Margaret, not looking round at the subject of her sentence.

The very thought! Queenie saw Jenkins puff up with consternation. Jenkins, her mainstay, her friend, her everything! 'What a ridiculous notion!' she spluttered at Margaret. 'Jenkins is not poor. She has a job for good here. Well, until I pass on, but I have ensured she will be looked after when I am gone. The idea that Jenkins is poor or could ever be poor is insulting and you must apologise immediately, girl.'

Jenkins had folded her arms and was looking pointedly above Margaret's head, with an air of disgruntled forbearance that Queenie loved about her.

'Please, Grandmother, we digress. I am merely saying that Anny is not poor and is not another species. She is a wholly dependable, intelligent person who has been cruelly wronged. Cyril – your grandson – has committed a crime. He is the one who has stolen money and has then tried to blame it on an innocent person. He is the criminal.'

Another moment of lucidity came to Queenie. Her grandson, a criminal? Whatever the boy had done, this must never be permitted to come to pass. The family name would be in tatters. She alone knew what she had suffered and sacrificed all these years to bolster the King family name. Her dear sister had died for it. Selina, her darling Selina . . .

To think of all that had been lost to make the King name what it was, all that Queenie had suffered to build this family into the tower of strength it was today. And now this girl, this office girl, was going to bring it all crashing down? With nasty accusations of attacks and theft and whatnot? An ironworker's daughter at that? A nobody? Never!

'Grandmother!' cried the girl and Queenie was snapped back into the present moment. What was it they were doing again? Margaret's voice was shrill and harsh. 'What do you have to say about Cyril? What are we to do?'

'Why,' said Queenie, recovering her senses and sitting up straighter, 'nothing. Absolutely nothing. It is out of the family's hands and there is nothing to be done. If the girl is innocent, then the truth will out in court. The family cannot be seen to bring disgrace upon itself. As the elder of this clan, I will never allow the King name to be brought into disrepute by accusations against any member of this family. Now, go away, child. Never let me hear you speak of it again.'

There. Another crisis averted. The girl was still wittering on, something about her father threatening her but Queenie had stopped listening and waved her hands to shoo the noise and fuss away, which Jenkins did with swift economy. When the girl had gone, she said to Jenkins, 'I'm still queen of this castle.'

Jenkins winked at her and plumped her pillows. Queenie soon drifted into a dreamless sleep. When she awoke, it was dark. Jenkins must be next door, asleep. She turned her head towards the drawn curtains and saw a slit of light emanating from outside. Not daylight, but a shifting, curious sort of a light that was bright then dimmer, bright again. She stared at it for some time, her eyes adjusting to the pulse of it. She felt compelled to leave her bed and seek it out. She drew back the curtain and looked down upon her family graveyard.

An apparition stood before the grave of Ralph senior, pulsing with light. Queenie blinked and looked again. It was still there, gazing across the graveyard into the distance. Its hair and skin were the hue of moonshine. Its eyes emanated the bluish flare of a city street gas lamp. Queenie pinched herself, hard, and cried out. But still the vision was there and had not moved. Could it be real? Was she losing her mind? She had hoped to see spirits before, those of the ones she had loved the most and lost. But this was not her sister and it was not her daughters. It was some other entity and it stood below her, as real as herself. And it was beautiful.

Queenie gazed at its splendour, then shuddered when she recognised that exquisite face. It was Blaize. The servant girl, Betsy Blaize. It was the maid she and her husband had dismissed five years before. It looked up, directly at her. It stretched out its arms and opened out its palms, showing her how empty its embrace was with no baby to fill it. It spoke to her, though not with its mouth. She heard the voice of Betsy Blaize in her mind. It said four words only, but those four little words terrified Queenie so greatly, she turned abruptly from the window and cried out, losing her footing and falling to the floor. Jenkins arrived from the next room, in a flurry of white nightdress and unpinned hair, rescued her from her collapse and got her back into bed. Jenkins scolded her for being out of bed at the witching hour. Queenie grasped Jenkins's arm and glared at her. 'Yes, it is the hour of the witch. She visited me. She told me. She cursed us.'

Jenkins tried to soothe her and lay her down but Queenie was having none of it. She must tell Jenkins what the ghost had said.

'This house will fall.'

Chapter 18

The following morning, Margaret arose early. She breakfasted alone, glad to be by herself. She felt so lost and powerless. Her family was beyond redemption, even Queenie. She wondered what rock they had found to crawl under and hoped they were hiding in shame. She knew Queenie and Benjamina usually breakfasted in bed but the absence of her father and brother was odd. They did not materialise for church either, which was highly irregular. When she, her grandmother and stepmother returned from church, she made her excuses and went upstairs. Her every movement felt mechanical, like a repetitive steam hammer along the river that marked time. But all the while she was screaming on the inside. Desperate for some way to save Anny, she changed into walking boots and a warmer cloak. It was a drizzly day, misty and muggy after the yellow heat of the day before. She left the house, unnoticed, made her way down to the riverside and walked through the woodland fringe towards the Woodvines' cottage, her tread slow and a little clumsy.

She was tired. She had wept a lot the night before. Her eye ached where her father had walloped her. Memories of Anny's imprisonment and visions of her own possible incarceration haunted her through the night, whether her eyes were open or closed. She feared for Anny, feared her father's threat. She did not know much of what had happened to her grandmother's sister, Selina, as it was a tale that had been silenced long ago. There were whisperings in the family and Cyril had mentioned it once or twice, about their lunatic great-aunt. As bad as Anny's prison was, she could only imagine that a madhouse was worse. It was too terrifying to contemplate. She tried not to think of it, but then her mind filled with the anguish of not being able to help her friend, of the promises she'd made to Anny and Mr Woodvine. Stupid, reckless promises. But she had been so sure of herself yesterday. So sure that truth would win the day, that all one had to do was state the facts and the world would listen, and change.

Too soon, she arrived at the cosy gathering of houses where the Woodvines lived. She dreaded this visit, of what she had to report to Anny's parents. She had not seen John Woodvine again the day before. He had not waited for her outside the prison and she had instructed her driver to look out for him on the road home, but he hadn't been seen. She hoped he had found his way home all right. As she approached the house, the neighbourhood children looked up from their games as she passed.

Mr Woodvine appeared at the door as she neared it, his face lit up with expectation. Oh, how cruel it was to bring bad news to these good people! His wife could be seen behind him and they both came outside and nodded to Margaret, smiling uncertainly and both of them wiping their hands, as if she deserved it. But she did not deserve it, any of their politeness or kindness. She had failed.

'Miss King,' said John Woodvine. 'Please come in. We are glad to see you.'

She stepped over the threshold into Anny's house. She had glimpsed it before, during her fancy dress ruse as Anny's workmate, all those years ago. But she hadn't seen much of it, as she'd been too shy to speak to Mrs Woodvine and had stayed outside, so sure was she that her hopeless attempts at blending in would be scuppered if she opened her mouth. What she wouldn't do to turn back the clock to that day.

Once inside, there came to her a delicious aroma of dough. She saw it placed on the windowsill in earthenware pans to rise. It was small inside the house, very small. It was a one-storey dwelling, the front room a neat square with three chairs arranged about a fireplace. One took a few steps and reached the kitchen area, a large table and every other surface and piece of furniture swathed in the products of Mrs Woodvine's washing work. Beyond the kitchen were two doors, to each of the bedrooms. All of the walls lacked plaster and thus the lumps and bumps of the stone that built the cottage jutted out into the room on all sides. But instead of feeling hemmed in by this, it gave the rooms a cosy, comforting appearance, as if the walls themselves were part of the family, gathering it in and keeping it safe. Such a tiny dwelling, so little room. But so filled with love all these years, replete with happiness. Until now.

'May I fetch you any . . . refreshments, Miss King?' asked Mrs Woodvine, her eyes ringed by deep shadows. How little she must have slept these past few nights.

'No, please. I require nothing. Thank you. I must speak with you both.' Margaret faltered here, as she had no idea how to continue, how to explain what had occurred. There was much she could not say to them, to anyone, so that anything she said would only be a fraction of the truth. With that in mind, it was so difficult to know how to convey her sympathy for them, how to explain how hard she had tried. If they only knew how much she had wept for Anny. But there she went again, feeling sorry for herself. She wanted to slap her own face.

'Please sit,' said Mr Woodvine. She glanced at him and his face was dark. He had such an expressive face, as if one could read the weather of it changing moment to moment. Then, it was overcast. He knew it was not good news. Margaret sat down on a chair and the others did so too. There was no more putting it off. Now she must speak.

'I am sorry to say . . .'

Immediately Mrs Woodvine began weeping. Oh heavens, oh God. What could she say to make this better? Nothing. Nothing. Mr Woodvine was shushing his wife gently and patting her shoulder, staring into the bare grate of an empty fireplace as he did so. The muggy day had turned it stuffy in that little house, almost unbearably so, and Margaret could feel wet patches blooming under her arms and behind her knees. She forced herself to go on. 'I have spoken to both my father and my grandmother. They were both . . . unwilling to change their positions on the matter. My father will not withdraw the charges against Anny.'

At the mention of her daughter's name, Mrs Woodvine sobbed loudly and hid her face. Mr Woodvine turned his towards Margaret – he was not able to look at her directly – and said, 'It might be best if you go now, miss.'

Margaret stood up quickly, the speed of it and the heat in there making her unsteady. There was so much more she wanted to say but she knew she was no longer welcome. Yesterday, she had been a friend. Now she was just another King. She made it to the door without speaking and out into the day, the heavy air cooler out here and most welcome. She breathed deeply and was about to flee the scene when Mr Woodvine appeared beside her.

'I ought to say . . .' he began, wiping a hand over his eyes, 'I mean . . . I mean to say that I am grateful . . . that we are grateful to you, miss. For trying. For visiting Anny. There's many that wouldna done that, that would've done naught for her, for our kind. It was good of you.'

Now Margaret wanted to sob. But she was so impressed by Mr Woodvine's dignity, she forced herself to keep her emotions at bay. 'I wish I could do more. I do have one last attempt, and that is to speak with my brother. He is a . . . difficult person. But I am determined to confront him at least. I will be doing this upon my return to the house. I will be honest and say that I doubt anything will come of it. But I must try. For Anny.'

Mr Woodvine listened to her speak with such intensity, she almost looked away. Then she saw he was looking at the side of her face where she had been struck. Even in this moment of desolation, his expression showed he still reserved some pity for her. She put her hand up without thinking, to shield it. She had forgotten the bruise since arriving. There were more important things to consider.

'I'd better . . .' Woodvine trailed off, a gesture towards the cottage sufficed.

'Yes, of course. Thank you. And, I'm sorry.'

He shook his head and looked about, as if searching for the right words. But there were no right words.

Margaret turned and started the trudge homewards. She saw the Quaker cottage and out in front of it were the old couple and the child. She had not seen them for years. The child must now be – how old? Four or five? – and was more lovely than ever. The girl had such a healthful bloom about her cheeks, she seemed formed from milk and red roses, like an enchanted child from a fairy tale. Margaret watched her as she slowly passed by. *The baby on the bridge*. She thought of Queenie's mysterious words, that this was a lucky child to have escaped the King family. She recalled how the child had the same green eyes as her dead grandfather. It all pointed to the old story, the rich master and the poor maid. But Margaret could not prove it. And she didn't care to. Queenie had been right: for all their wealth, it was still the lucky child that escaped the King family. Her dear friend's life was about to be ruined by the very same family, her family. It sickened her. Her own family was like poison in her veins.

At the very least, she would confront Cyril and attempt to force him to admit his guilt. When she arrived home, she went to look for him. She knocked on his door to no answer, but this was not unusual. Cyril rarely followed convention when it came to basic manners. She could hear him moving around in there, though, so she opened the door and stepped inside.

'What the devil do you want?' he scowled at her. He was standing at his wardrobe, choosing cravats, several draped over his arm already. Behind him stood a trunk, the lid open to show it had been fully packed by his manservant already, and Cyril was finishing off with his own crucial choices of which neckwear he most desired.

'Where are you going?' said Margaret.

'To Germany, if you must know.'

'What for?'

He finished with the cravats and threw them onto the trunk, knowing his servant would sort them out later.

'Cyril, what for? Why are you going to Germany?'

'To an ironworks there. To learn the business, from the continental perspective.'

Margaret recognised her father's words in Cyril's mocking tone. To spirit him away, she realised. Across the sea and out of reach. He would have no part in the trial and no case to answer. She had always thought of her father as a bit dim. Now she saw he could be rather clever, when it served him, or was it Queenie's hand in this? Cyril was getting away with it, scot-free and out of harm's way, while Anny would languish in prison. The world protected men like that, she realised. The world was unfair.

'I must speak with you before you go.'

'I am about to leave, so there is no time,' he said with finality.

'This is important, Cyril. It is about Anny.'

He shot a glance at her, his eyes widened with – what was it? Worry? Concern? Guilt? Then he looked away to hide it and went to stand at the window, looking out. 'I have nothing to say on that matter. Some office girl caught thieving is far beneath my notice.'

'But I know differently.' Margaret never knew what tack to take with her brother, but she decided that a bullying approach would never work on him, as he could out-bully just about anyone, except their father. But perhaps she could appeal to something else in him. 'I know you had feelings for Anny.'

For once, Cyril did not speak. Margaret used the moment to go on.

'She is in a terrible place. A terrible state.'

'What has that to do with us?' he said, strangely quiet for him. Was she getting through to him?

'Could we not help her, Cyril?'

'She has made her own bed.'

She knew this utterance was fraught with meaning. She could hear Cyril's jealousy in it. He must have found out something about Anny's feelings for Jake. Margaret had tasted that bitter disappointment, as much as she hated herself for it. The thought of Anny and Jake was torture to her. Perhaps she and her brother had something in common, at long last.

'This is true,' she said, choosing her words with the utmost care. 'It is hard to see others make choices that . . . we do not like, that hurt us.'

Cyril made a scoffing sound and turned to her. 'What do you know about such things?'

She almost told him. She heard the words in her mind: *I am in love with Jake Ashford*. But she could not speak it, not to this viper – she did not trust him an inch with that precious cargo – but also these were words she did not wish to reveal to anyone. Anyone but Jake. It shamed her that she still hoped for a future with Jake when it was becoming clear to her that Anny still hoped for the same.

She must do whatever it took to help Anny. That was her role now, to save her friend. 'All I know is that Anny Woodvine is innocent. She did not steal that money. She does not deserve this fate.'

'You know nothing of the sort,' Cyril spat and strode back to his trunk, fiddling with the cravats, looking busy.

'I do and so do you. Because you are the one who took the money, Cyril.'

He glared at her. 'Say that again,' he said in a low, threatening voice. 'I dare you.'

'I am not afraid of you, Cyril King. Not anymore.'

'You should be.' She saw his right fist clench slowly, deliberately.

'But I have the truth on my side. I know you loved Anny once. I think you still do. Come with me to Father and tell him what happened, explain about Jake Ashford. Father might even understand. He has loved and lost our mother, after all. All it would take is a word from you and Father could withdraw the charges and Anny would be free.'

'Lies! Lies, all of it. I had nothing to do with it!' Cyril's voice broke, his face contorted.

'And who knows,' she went on, fired up with momentum now. 'If Anny knew you had set her free, perhaps she might forgive you. Perhaps she would come to you to thank you. Perhaps . . .' A horrible thought came to her and her mind was racing so fast she had no time to stop and look at it closely, so she blurted it aloud: 'Perhaps she would drop Jake Ashford in favour of you, and he would be . . .'

Cyril's face changed. His eyes lit with a cruel sneer. 'He would be *what*? What would he be, sister? Yours?'

'No, I meant he would be spurned and you . . . that you . . . you could turn Anny to love you.'

Cyril laughed and stared at her, nodding. 'Dear sister. We are more alike than I ever thought possible. So, you want the artist?'

'I never . . .'

'Oh no, it is too late for that. You have revealed yourself. It does you credit that you fight for your friend when it would suit you far better if she rotted in prison forever or was sent across the world never to be seen again. Yet if she is to be free, you argue that she might come to me, that she would be grateful, that she would forsake her jumped-up little scribbler for me. How convenient that would be for you!'

'No, you have twisted everything! This is not . . .'

Cyril was shaking his head and smiling smugly. 'The fact is that you have nothing to taint me. There is no evidence against me, no proof I had anything to do with it. I will go to Germany today and think no more on this trifling little drama. You, I suspect, will go to your room and twist your sheets about you in passionate contemplation of Jake Ashford and his lead-smudged fingers . . .'

Margaret clenched and unclenched her own fists, furious at herself yet also wanting very much to smash that smug look from Cyril's face. How could she have let this conversation veer so far off track? It was all her fault.

'I am busy now, preparing for my journey. Leave me. And if you ever find proof of my crime, be sure to march straight to Father with it, won't you?'

And he lifted his hands and gestured her away, as if shooing a fly. She knew she was beaten. But she had found her voice. She would not go silently.

'You think you have won. But you are the one who will be alone for all of your days and nights. For you do not have the capacity to love. And so you are cursed, Cyril King, to live alone and die alone.'

With that, she turned and left. He did not shout after her. She heard the door slam behind her. She felt some satisfaction at this, at least. But beneath it was the dull ache of having failed, again.

How could she help Anny now? She thought she might offer to testify in court to Anny's good character, even tell them of her suspicions of her brother, but Cyril was quite right – she had no evidence, no proof. Who would believe her? It all seemed hopeless. Nobody would support her in this endeavour and her father would send her away to a fate worse than death. Suddenly, she felt utterly alone in the world. Her family were against her and she had lost her only friend. She had no one, not a soul that cared for her, no one she could talk to.

But there was someone. Jake. Oh, Jake! Of course – she must take Anny's message to him. This comforting thought was spiked with conflicted feelings as she found she was jealous of the message, which appalled her. She would deliver the message. At the very least, it meant it was some small thing she could do for Anny and now she had a reason to see him, to talk to him alone. Another feeling assaulted her: remorse. How could she feel excitement at seeing him, at this time of all times? What a terrible person she was. But she reminded herself that she had no one, and that the small grain of hope at seeing someone who seemed to like her was not so unforgivable, was it?

An idea rose in her mind, as innocently as thistledown on a breeze. She would go to his lodgings and see him. She might be seen; there might be a scandal. She realised that she did not give a damn. She had kept on her boots and cloak and took up her purse from the bed. She quietly descended the stairs, keeping a lookout for her father bustling about, and managed to get to the front door without being seen.

Jake had mentioned once where he was lodging, or at least, the house he was in, to the left of the Tontine Hotel, immediately opposite the iron bridge. She wasn't used to walking the streets without a chaperone. But now, here she was. Alone, walking along the road to town. No family, no restraints. There was a marvellous kind of freedom in it, walking along a path on your own. The air around her body and head gave her a giddiness. Imagine it, to walk away from this family and never go back. This thought gave her a jolt.

She was coming down Lincoln Hill, past the rows of low, neat brick houses with cellar windows peeping out below street level. She glanced back up the hill and could see the King house from here, her family home. It was perched above the town, looking down upon it, literally and figuratively. The people surrounding her, busy in their own lives, all believed themselves to be the masters of their own existences, the protagonists of their own stories. None of them cared a hoot about the Kings, about her father or her brother or herself. Quite rightly. What was it about class that set one above another? The thought of never returning to that house felt like the longest, coolest draught of water after a hot day. As she rounded the bottom of the hill and turned into the High Street, where the Tontine Hotel was situated, it occurred to her that, more than anything she had ever wanted, she would sell her soul to escape from her own story and walk right out of it.

She thought of the baby on the bridge she had seen that morning, frolicking in front of its humble home. She felt inspired by the baby's example: how happy its life was, how simple and sweet. Of course, there would be hardships, living the life they did, down there amongst the struggling poor. Look what happened to a family like the Woodvines, when the forces of the rich were drawn against them. But the Quaker child was raised by kind and loving people and no amount of money can buy you that kind of comfort and love. Margaret knew that more than most.

As she passed the Tontine and looked for the building beside it, she thought of Jake Ashford. Whatever her mission was that day, whatever her love for Anny, her need to support her friend, she knew that underneath all of this beat her heart and it beat for him alone. She loved him. And amidst the ruin of her family life, her love rose like a phoenix and gave her a burning strength within her. Everything in her life had been thrown into question, and now she felt sure that Jake Ashford was the answer.

The house had only one door. She knocked upon it and waited. The door opened and there stood a middle-aged woman with a pinched face bordered by greasy ringlets. Margaret was given a quick look up and down and then the woman put on a simpering smile.

'How may I help you, miss?' said the woman.

'I am Miss King, from the big house.'

'Of course y'are, of course y'are!' said the woman delightedly. 'What assistance or service can I be of to you, Miss King?'

'I have a message for a Mr Ashford. He has been painting a portrait up at the house and I need to convey a message to him from my father.' The woman was starting to frown a little. 'Would it be at all possible to discover if Mr Ashford were at home? So that I could deliver the message to him? In person?'

She knew it was unorthodox. Why had the family not sent a messenger? But she braved it out and smiled at the woman, who seemed eager to please. Perhaps a coin would be in order, if she was veering towards being unhelpful.

'I can deliver the message for you, miss, unless . . .'

The woman eyed the purse that Margaret was clutching.

'Is Mr Ashford at home?'

'He is, miss. I believe he is sleeping.'

'At lunchtime?' queried Margaret.

'Oh yes, miss. He often does that. He's been home late every night this week. Out . . . painting, I should think. Such a dedicated artist.'

'Indeed,' said Margaret, uncertainly. She looked down at her purse, snapped it open and reached inside. One coin, two . . . how many would it take? She wanted to glance behind her, to see who was looking at the King girl bargaining with a landlady of a gentleman's residence, in full view of the whole town. The scandal was unthinkable. But she felt as if the ropes that had tethered her to the ground had been freed and she was floating up, up above her class, her reputation and all the weights and restrictions it brought with it. She was beyond the pale and she did not care one jot for it anymore. Even pretence seemed pointless.

'I will give you this, if you will take me to him,' she said, looking the woman straight in the eye.

'Come in then,' said the woman throatily and shut the door. She pocketed the money swiftly and pointed up the stairs. 'Top floor. The attic room.' And with that, she went off down the corridor to her own rooms, not giving Miss King a second look. Their business was concluded.

Margaret looked up the stairs and felt light-headed. They seemed incredibly steep and her head was swimming. Her stomach lurched. She began to climb, her breath quickening. The top room had a tiny landing and she stood on it, before the door, the only thing that stood between her and him. She listened at it, to see if she could hear him inside. She felt dizzy and steadied herself with a hand upon his door. She gathered her courage and made a fist, then knocked. No reply, no movement. She knocked again. Had the woman lied, to get her money for nothing? But then there was a shuffling inside. She held her breath. Footsteps. The door opened.

There he stood, black glossy hair on end, squinting at her through his sleep-addled eyes, which soon snapped open when he saw who it was. He was dressed, that is, he had on his trousers and a shirt, untucked. No waistcoat or socks, she noticed, glancing at his naked feet with a shock.

'My dear Miss King!' he cried. 'Is there an emergency?'

'No, Mr Ashford. I am sorry . . . to awaken you from your slumber.'

'Not at all,' he said, running his fingers through his hair in a vain attempt to control it. It delighted her to see him so ruffled, so normal, so unprepared. His real self, beyond all pretence and manners. 'Please tell me how I can assist you. I am worried for you, Miss King.'

'I came to bring you a message of the utmost importance and I could not wait upon . . . the more . . . accustomed channels. I simply had to come. Can you forgive me?'

Jake listened to this with a serious face, but now he smiled. 'There is nothing to forgive. I am only apologetic to receive you in a state of such dishevelment. But please, I am unforgivable, allowing you to stand there and not invite you in. It is very humble, if you will forgive me.' He began hurriedly tucking in his shirt and stepping back.

'Not at all,' she said and entered. It had a smell of things new to her, a heady mixture of maleness she had perceived emanating from her brother's room at times, and perhaps wine and pipe smoke, or something similar. It made her head spin. Luckily, the windows were open and a breeze came in and brought with it a breath of fresh air badly needed and she felt a little recovered.

'I have water, if you would like a glass.'

'Yes, please,' she said and sat upon a wooden chair that stood beside a table covered in papers and pencils. An easel was beside the window, surrounded on the wooden floorboards by a mess of paints, brushes and a palette. Against the other wall was a narrow bed, its covers awry. Beside it were a pair of shoes, kicked off, one on its side on top of a fallen pile of books, some splayed open, others shut. Suits and shirts hung on the picture rail and hats hung on nails on the wall. A cabinet held other secrets, topped with a basin and jug. His whole existence in one room. It was the most wonderful room she had ever visited in her life.

He fetched her a glass from a cupboard and poured out water from another jug that stood on a little table beside his bed. He drew up another mismatched chair and sat opposite her. He looked down at his feet and saw he had no socks. There was a moment of awkwardness where he seemed to consider whether or not to fetch his socks, and then he glanced up at her.

'Your feet do not offend me, Mr Ashford,' she said. She smiled and he smiled. Then they laughed. It broke the ice, and now they could sit more comfortably together.

'Please, Miss King, I am quite alarmed by the news that you bring. What can it be?'

'It is about Miss Woodvine. Anny. I do not know if you are aware of what has befallen her.'

'I am not. I have been busy with my paintings these past few days. I have been inspired. I have barely left my room.'

That is not what his landlady said, Margaret thought. But perhaps she was a liar. She dismissed this thought and proceeded to tell him all about Anny. She left no detail out. She trusted Jake. She knew implicitly that he would understand. He listened attentively, shaking his head at each new awful turn of events. But he did not comment on anything she said, not even a 'How terrible!' or 'Poor Anny!' Perhaps it was a characteristic of male speech, that men said only what was necessary. Now she came to the difficult part.

'When I saw her in that place, she asked something of me. Well, it was something she asked of you, Mr Ashford.'

'Please, please call me Jake. I believe, sitting here together in my shabby lodgings, we may be permitted to use our Christian names, may we not?'

'Of course,' she said, but was a little perturbed at him smiling at this, at a moment when she had told him the most dreadful news. Perhaps he was nervous. 'Anny asked something of you, Jake. She said to tell you that she didn't do it. I tried to help her . . . You've heard that part of the tale at least, including my own failure.'

'You are too hard on yourself, Margaret,' he said and leant forward, his elbows on his knees, his hands clasped beneath his chin, his eyes dark and full of sympathy.

'Not hard enough, I fear,' she said quietly, as she looked down, away from his captivating gaze. 'There is more. She asked that you wait.'

'Wait?'

'Yes. She said, "Tell him to wait". And also that you must come to visit her, as soon as you are able.'

Jake stood up quite suddenly. He stepped over to the window and looked out of it. She could not see his face. She turned in her chair and watched the back of his head as he talked.

'I do not think that I am able to do that.'

'I could send our carriage to transport you, if that is what you require to travel to Shrewsbury.'

'No, it is not that. I do not think it is a good idea for me to visit Anny.'

'Why ever not?'

'Anny and I spoke of . . . a future. A possible future. She wanted me to promise. But I could not.'

Margaret had guessed at this, of course, as Anny had asked her to tell Jake to come to her in prison. But to hear it from Jake's mouth was hard. It felt like a slap in the face, yet she cursed herself for wanting to help her friend and yet at the same time . . . at the same time, she wanted something else entirely.

'I had to explain to her that it was not that simple. I could not promise her. I tried to let her down gently. But you see, I am an artist. I am wedded to my art.'

'Of course,' said Margaret. 'I quite understand,' though indeed she did not really understand. What a complicated person he was, how deeply his feelings ran. It was the artist in him that made him so profound.

'I knew you would,' he said and turned to her, looking down at her.

Margaret heard herself ask him a question, before she had time to regret it. 'Do you love Anny?'

'I am fond of her. But I find myself caught between two mistresses.'

She held her breath. She stared at him. 'Which two?' she said and it came out as a whisper.

'My art and my fondness for Anny.'

'Indeed,' she said and looked away.

'She would make a good wife and she does love me, I'm sure of that. But there is a further obstacle.'

'What is that?'

'There is another.'

'Another what?'

'I love another.'

Margaret felt she might be sick. She could not speak a word.

He went on, 'But I believe the match is impossible. I am unworthy of her. I am so very glad I can confide in you of this. You are such a very good listener.'

He smiled at her and she forced her mouth to turn upwards just a touch. 'Who is it, this other match?' she managed to say, though she wished to rush from the room.

'Why, it is you, of course.'

'Me?'

'Yes, dear Margaret. But I suspect your father would never allow it, and so I have repressed my feelings for you and instead have allowed Anny's feelings to rule my own. It may be wrong of me, but I do not know how I must act for the best.'

'You have feelings for me?'

'I do, I do, my dear. How could I not? You are divine.'

He looked searchingly at her, then he fell to his knees and took her hands.

'Could it be,' he began and kissed her hand so gently, 'that you feel the same for me? Can you tell me your feelings for me, dear Margaret?'

'Why, I love you, Jake.'

'You do? Oh, my dear!'

He leant in and kissed her lightly on the lips. She leant in further and kissed him again, softer, longer. But suddenly he withdrew and stood up. She stood up too, not wanting to be further apart than the breadth of their kisses. But Jake had let go of her hands and was running his fingers madly through his hair.

'But what of Anny? And your father? Oh, I am overwrought. I cannot think straight with you here, so close to me. I am intoxicated by your presence. I need time to think it all through. There must be some way we can be together. Can I come to see you tomorrow? Not here. Let us meet in the woods, away from prying eyes.'

'Of course. Do you know the place where the two paths meet in the woods, just beyond the coracle sheds?'

'I do, I have passed it on my walks.'

'Shall we meet there at noon, tomorrow?'

'At noon.'

They stood and watched each other.

They kissed again. This time his tongue was in her mouth. It was so wet, such a queer taste of tobacco and sleep, a sour taste that startled her, but her desire for it was so overwhelming that she welcomed the bitterness and fed from it. Kissing this way was a kind of devouring and she had a hunger for it.

Desire in her rose like a wave and she pressed herself against him with such force, their teeth clashed. She felt mortified with her own clumsiness but he was kind about it and stroked her cheek, held her and shushed her. Then, he let go and took a step back.

'My dear girl, please. There is nothing I would like more than to kiss you again, a hundred times. A thousand times more! But we must be sensible. There is much to consider. I will meet you tomorrow, as planned. And we shall talk it all through. Do not fret. Sleep well tonight, my love, and I will see you on the morrow.'

It was hard to leave him, so hard. It was only when she came down the stairs and saw the landlady standing in the hall, smirking at her, that she recalled the shame of what she had done. And as she stepped outside into the street and looked up at the iron bridge, she recognised the forlorn figure of Mrs Woodvine crossing over it, laden down with linen, delivering her work to the households of the town. Margaret turned in an instant and rushed away up the street, fairly breaking into a run to get up onto the hill and away from that woman, that kind, sweet woman. Anny's mother. She had started the day with a visit to Anny's parents and ended it by smashing the fragile hopes of their daughter because of her own selfish desires. But he loved her. *Jake Ashford loves me*, she told herself. And Anny loved him, waited for him, in that hellish place. Oh God in heaven, what had she done? Was there ever a betrayal lower and more cowardly than this? Anny's pale face in the prison floated before her in her mind's eye. *How could you, Peggy? How could you?*

Chapter 19

'Ow bist thee faring, Anny?'

'Fair to middling, Mother.'

There was so much that Anny could not tell her mother. It was her first visit, and when Mother came into the room and gave her the seed cake, bread, ham and apples she'd brought from home, Anny fell to eating it like something feral. Ham first. Meat! The smell of it drove her mad, and she saw the other prisoners in there waiting for their visitors sniffing the air like dogs. She had not said much yet, only one word that she mouthed as she came in, 'Mother!' But then the smell of food took her and she could think of nothing more until she had it in her hands. Her mother watched her devour the meat, then move on to the bread, but put a firm hand on Anny's and said, 'Slow down. You'll make yourself heave. Save it for later.'

She shook her head hurriedly. 'They'll take it from me.'

'Who? The guards?'

She shook her head again, now working on the cake. 'The others.' She had no time to explain. She had to eat all of this before they sent her back. Her mother waited for her to eat, wiping her eyes with the tips of her fingers from time to time. Her mother couldn't stop the tears coming, but was doing her best to hide them.

When she'd finished eating, she came back to herself and remembered that her dear mother was there. She wanted ever so much to feel her mother's arms around her, but she didn't want to risk a beating from that one over there. He was one of the worst turnkeys, mean and petty. Her cellmate Jane had gone off with him three times these past days and come back sore and achy, but also with crumbs and wine stains down her front, so it was worth it, Jane said. Was it worth it? Anny had been considering it. She'd had some offers but never spoke to the turnkeys if she could help it, and always avoided their gazes and whisperings. But the hunger had been getting to her, gnawing at her and she'd nearly succumbed yesterday when they gave her no breakfast gruel, saying she was not tidy and clean enough. But now she'd had her mother's food, she'd be able to hold out for a while longer.

'What do they feed you, lass?'

'Gruel for breakfast. Potatoes or soup for dinner. Gruel or soup for supper. Some bread each day. Not enough of it. Never enough.'

It was good to talk, to hear her own voice. She spoke to nobody here. It was banned in her cell. Ellen had banned it. 'I dunna wanna hear a peep out of you again.

Not a sound. If you cry, we'll leather you. If you snore, we'll leather you. And no talking, not ever.'

She went on, getting a feel for it now, remembering how she'd loved to talk in her other life, in the time before this. That time seemed to have never happened. Everything was this now. 'Soup sounds good, doesn't it? You would think it was good. Nourishing.' That was a nice word. 'But it's not. It's lukewarm, greasy water with bits of who-knows-what floating in it.'

'Anny, I wanna say I'm that sorry I couldna come sooner. It took me very bad like, all this. And you know how weak I get when I hear bad news. It is a terrible failing of mine and I curse myself for it and I am sorry for it. I shoulda been there with your father that first time he came but the shock had me laid up for days. I wish I were stronger for you.'

'Please don't fret,' said Anny and reached out to touch her mother's cheek, withdrawing her hand quickly as she glanced at the guards, knowing they would shout at her for touching. Mother followed her gaze and frowned at the man who lolled against the wall.

'Do they treat you well, the guards?'

What could she say to that? Mother did not need to know the truth. If she had a bruise here or there her mother might notice. There was a big one on her arm, yet luckily her sleeve covered it. Everyone knew the turnkeys would beat you as soon as look at you, but they showed a little care to keep it off the face.

'I don't speak to them,' she said, eyeing the one at the door.

'Do you have to work? You look tired.'

She was exhausted. But mostly that was because she could not sleep at night. There were comings and goings from the cells, sad women crying, mad women screaming and her own cellmates plotting and whispering before they fell into a deep, guttural sleep. She would rather listen to the cacophony of the blast furnace all night, every night instead of the random, terrifying sounds that emitted from these cells, all cloaked in a heavy silence between them that smothered you and mocked you, an emptiness that reminded you of everything you had lost. Sometimes she wondered if she were going mad herself.

'Anny, do you have to work? Do they make you work?'

'I'm the monitor of our court. Our group of rooms. Every morning, I have to make sure the rooms and arcades are swept and washed down. That windows and doors are opened on dry days and all the beds are turned down to air. If I do that right, I'm supposed to get fourpence a week. In credit, like. Not in my hand. On Mondays, they put a table out in the courtyard and you can buy things, like cheese or stockings. But only if you've done your job as monitor. But the others don't do as I say, so I've not received anything yet. During the day, I work in the wash house. Just like back at home with you, Mother.'

They both smiled grimly. Simpler days. Happy days. She never thought she'd miss it. Now she believed she'd give her right arm to be a washerwoman with her mother again at home. If she had, none of this would ever have happened.

"This is what happens when you get above your station,' she said, thinking aloud. She hadn't intended to actually say it.

'What can you mean, Anny? This inna your fault. Never your fault. Dunna tell yourself that ever.'

'If I'd never worked for the Kings, this would never have happened. I should've stayed with you. Why didn't I stay with you?'

This was the kind of thing that tortured her in those silences at night. That, and why she didn't simply lie back and let Cyril King do what he wanted with her. If he'd bedded her, he'd have probably grown tired of her and not even pursued the marriage. She could've played that smarter.

Her mother was weeping openly now. She couldn't keep it in anymore.

'Hush now, Mother.'

'I'm sorry, lass. Look at you. I'm the one who should be comforting you. Oh, dear heart. You're so strong.'

Anny scoffed then checked herself. She did not want to upset her mother further. 'Yes, I am coping. Is there any news of when the hearing shall be?'

'No news to us.'

'To me neither. They tell us nothing here.' She had lain awake at night obsessing over the possibilities of her punishment, if found guilty, which she would surely be. It could be imprisonment, probably with hard labour, which would mean years of breaking stones. At least you'd get more food each day. It could be transportation to Australia. Never to see your family again and banished to a foreign isle, if the ship journey didn't kill you first. Then, there was hanging. It was unusual, for a woman to be hanged for theft. But it could happen. She imagined the rope around her neck, the moments before. Would she scream? Would she weep? Would she face it with dignity?

'Tell me more about your days. Is there no one you can talk to? What's the keeper like? Is he a good man? Can you talk to him about more food?'

Some of this she could speak about. It was generally a safe topic for her mother to hear. 'He seems a good enough man. He visits the cells once a day but just gives us a quick look, nothing more than that. It is said we are allowed to make complaint to him but he never gives us the time to do so and all the women are afraid of him.'

'I've heard there are male prisoners here too,' said Mother, looking worried. 'Do you ever see them?'

'No, we are separate at all times,' said Anny, glad of this, yet knowing that the turnkeys were worse than any prisoner she could imagine.

'What else do you do here? Do they give you time to stretch your legs?'

'We have time in the exercise yard daily.' A place of bullying, taunts and being thrust up against the brick wall by a turnkey, maybe clouted on your body somewhere for looking at them the wrong way. But yes, you could stretch your legs. She did not say any of this to her mother, of course.

'And do they let you read and write at all? I know how you must miss it.'

'We have Bible class every morning. We listen to the chaplain read. And as monitor, I am responsible for the prayer book in our day room.' She did not go on to say that, as monitor, she was also responsible for telling tales on other prisoners. She would never do it, under threat of various methods of subtle torture from her cellmates, but then she incurred the wrath of the turnkeys, who would grab her and twist her arm to make her say something about the others and the tricks they got up to, but she never did. A quick whack on the leg or back with a turnkey stick would be her reward for that. 'There is a schoolmaster, but when they heard I could already read and write, they said I had no need of lessons.'

'Could you ask to be his assistant?'

'I have already asked. They said no.'

'It would get you away from all that washing. I worry about your soft hands going hard again.' Her mother took Anny's hands and began to inspect them. Anny knew she could get a clout from the guard for it, but the feel of her mother's beloved hands around her own was so overwhelmingly comforting, she had to force herself not to sob with relief. She knew the shape and texture of her mother's hands better than almost any other thing she could think of and they meant home, they meant safety and love. 'No ink stains anymore. I miss those,' Mother said, sadly. Tears ran silently from Anny and dripped onto her arms. Her mother squeezed her hands and muttered, 'I meant to be more help. And I've been no help at all.'

'No touching,' called out the guard and Anny snatched her hands away. She did not wish to get on that one's bad side. She leant a little closer and whispered, 'Just by coming you have helped. Just to see a friendly face makes such a difference here in this . . . place.'

Her mother looked up at her, fearful. 'How bad is it? Are you suffering badly? I mun know, Anny. I need to know.'

Oh, the things she wished she could tell her. More than anything, she longed to describe the horrible scene only the day before, where she stood in the yard and listened to the sound of death. The yard was usually filled with the mutterings of inmates and the harsh shouts of guards. But that day, all the inhabitants were silenced by the sound of a great crowd of people arriving all morning outside the gates, their hubbub floating over the walls, bringing the flavour of freedom. The crowd was silenced by a stern voice that read out a long list of information, too indistinct to hear the details, with only the pious tone discernible from beyond the high yard walls. Then, two other male voices spoke their turn but again, no words could be heard clearly. After this, there were some shouts from the crowd, replied to with some unkind laughter, some heckling and more laughter. Then, there was a long silence. A snapping sound of rope pulled taut and a cheer went up. So ended the lives of two Irish thieves, she heard later. Two men hanged atop the prison gates, for theft. The sound of the laughing crowd haunted her, that so many should come to witness death and that they should find it worthy of amusement. The world was cruel and full of bad'uns. The good people were as teardrops in an ocean. The ones who cared a jot for you were fewer still and the ones who loved you, numbered on the fingers of one hand. Love. What was it good for now? It could bring only temporary comfort but it could not fetch her out of here, and it could not save her from this hell or from the gallows. But the comfort of it was better than nothing.

'Mother, before you go, and it will be that time soon, I must tell you that I have a sweetheart. I have an understanding with the artist Jake Ashford. I asked Margaret to tell him to please come and visit me. Will you find him and tell him too? Please?'

'A young mon? An understanding?'

The turnkey called time and everyone stood up sharpish. She never kept them waiting. Her mother's face was confused and frightened. She wished she'd asked this earlier, so she'd have time to explain the understanding between Jake and herself and how much she desired to see him. But there, it was done now and she was leaving the room, looking back at her mother, whose hands were over her face now, her tears freely flowing. Anny called back to her, 'Tell him?' and Mother nodded quickly and lifted a hand, calling her name and saying farewell, till next time.

In the corridor, the turnkey shoved her hard, so that she fell against the wall and felt the cold stone bite into her soft cheek. She wouldn't give him the satisfaction of a look, let alone a complaint. Now that her mother had gone, she would speak to nobody until another visitor came. She missed talking so much; she spoke to herself in her mind often, great long monologues commenting on all the madness surrounding her and telling herself stories of her past, of the people she loved. It was a kind of prayer, it was offered up to the god of her mind to keep her from losing it. She prayed for deliverance, for help to come from Margaret, for her mother to stay well and her father to be safe at the ironworks and, most of all, for Jake to visit her.

Chapter 20

John Woodvine listened obsessively to every detail Rachel gave of her visit to their daughter. As she spoke, the rage that built up inside him, fit to blow, every time he thought of Anny in that place, was like nothing he had ever experienced. To be fifteen miles from his beloved girl, to be able to walk there, to be able to see her even, in a room across a table, and speak to her; to be able to do all these things and yet not scoop her up in his arms and take her from that place. These were the things that could drive a man to madness.

'There was one more thing she told me, John,' said Rachel. 'She said she has a young mon. She wants him to visit her. Did you know? I didna know she had someone sweet on her.'

'What young mon?' said John. He had heard nothing about this. He'd been relieved, actually, that Anny had never seemed interested in that sort of thing. She'd always given the boys round their house short shrift. She was devoted to her work and her family and long may that continue, he used to tell himself. Now this, a sweetheart? It made him feel a bit queasy but at the same time, a seed of expectancy was planted in him and he wondered for a moment if something helpful might come of it.

'She said he was an artist called Jake Ashford. You know him?'

That scribbler? Could him and Anny . . . really? 'Yes, I've seen him. He comes to the furnace sometimes and sketches what's occurring around and about. He keeps himself to himself, mostly. Some of the men ribbed him a bit when he first came, but they soon got bored of it and left him to his own devices after that.'

'Is he a good man?' said Rachel, looking at him hopefully.

'He's no great shakes, is my impression. I dunna know. But I'm gunna find out. He's certainly better off than us. Good clothes. Not wealthy, like the Kings. But good clothes, you know. Smart.' John thought more about him and an uneasy memory of his general impression that the lad was a bit of a fop, maybe even one who liked boys rather than girls, was the sort of whisperings that went round. And what kind of living could be made from scribbling?

'Well,' said Rachel, 'if he has a well-to-do family and if he's promised to our Anny, perhaps his family could help her. Perhaps they could go to the Kings and speak for her.'

'Are they promised?'

'She didna say. She only said something about an understanding.'

'Well, why didna you ask her? Why didna you get more out of her, for God's sake?' John's voice grew much louder. He was on edge all the time these days and found it increasingly hard to control his temper. But the hurt look in his wife's eyes toned him down and he dropped his head, ashamed of raising his voice to her.

'She only mentioned it in the last moments, before they took her away,' said Rachel, and put her hand on his arm. She understood. She never held it against him. Oh, this woman. What a fine wife she was. What a lucky man he'd been, in this at least.

'I will certainly look him out. If he inna at work today, I'll ask around and find out where he's lodging. I'll find him, dunna worry, dear.'

He reached over and put his arms around his wife, drew her to him and kissed her tenderly. After all these years, the feel of her was home and all things good. She had always been too good for him, a good wench like she was with her book learning. But she chose him. The warm roundness of her woman's body was everything he ever wanted. It was obvious to think it, that a man loved his wife, but then so many men he knew didn't seem to feel it, not anymore. They complained bitterly about theirs, and some of them sought comfort elsewhere. Not him. Not ever. But these days, the sadness that he and Rachel both bore like a cross on their backs tainted all comfort he felt with her. He felt he had let her down, by allowing this terrible thing to happen to their child. He would fight till the end of his days to get her out of there. He kissed Rachel again, this time a peck on the cheek and a big squeeze, before he pulled back and looked at her.

'I'm thinking of leaving a bit early for my shift. I'm thinking of going up to the big house and asking to talk to Mr King.'

'Oh, my dear, are you sure? If his own daughter . . .'

'I know, I know what we said. I know he hit her, and why would he listen to me if he didna listen to her? But I'm thinking we mighta got all this around the wrong way. Think on it. She's his daughter and he might have a hundred reasons we're ignorant of to give his daughter a slap. Maybe she's been playing away from home, maybe she's a real handful, who knows? Nobody knows what goes on inside a family, behind closed doors, except them people themselves. Maybe he wouldna listen to her because he still thinks of her as a nipper. Dunna take her serious, like. I know I'm the same sometimes with Anny, despite all her learning. Maybe if I presented the case to him very civil, very serious, very polite like, he might listen. It's worth a try, inna it? I know it is. And I'm gunna do it.'

It was Rachel's turn to put her arms around him now and kiss her husband. 'You're a good man, John

Woodvine. How would I manage without you? Like a frog without a pond.'

'Like a mole without a hole.'

They both laughed. It was a small laugh but the only one they'd shared in days. He was beginning to feel something like hope kindling inside him. He took up his lunch and his work gloves and stashed them in the ragged bag he stowed across his chest. He left, striding with new purpose along the river then up the path to the big house. He went to the servants' entrance. He knew he couldn't march up to the front door. There was a girl there, cleaning the step. He told her his business and she said she'd ask the butler. The butler came – a wizened old'un with a mistrustful eye – and said the master wasn't available. John told the man who he was and told him something of his tale of woe. He asked only for a minute of the master's time. The butler went away for quite a bit – John began to wonder if he'd be late for his shift – but then the old bloke came back.

'One minute,' he said. 'But you're too dirty for the house. You'll be seen outside the estate office. Go and wait there.'

John went over to Anny's old workplace and scowled at it. It brought back bitter memories and he wished he'd not had to see it. The rage was rising in him again and he had to swallow it. He must be respectful and respectable for Mr King. His stomach lurched and he cleared his throat several times, a bile rising there that he could not cough out. Then, footsteps were coming along the gravel and there was King, his stomach preceding him and John felt he might stride right up to the bastard and give him a bunch of fives in his face. He clenched his fists and stood up straighter. King was not looking at him and stopped near to the door of the office, as if he were about to go in but instead turned, folded his arms sedately across his chest, his elbows resting on his girth. He said, 'You have your minute, Woodvine.' King looked pompously into the air to the left of John's shoulder. John tried not to let this put him off. He cleared his throat one last time and began.

'Mr King, you may know I am Anny Woodvine's father.'

'Obviously, obviously. Don't waste your one minute on pleasantries, man. Time is ticking.'

John rushed on, rattled now. 'I mean to say that she is my daughter and I would do anything to help her. I am sorry for calling on you unannounced but I canna stand to see her suffer anymore in that prison, and so here I am. I wish to tell you, sir, that I heartily believe in my daughter's innocence. She never had no reason before to steal and has never been that kind of a girl or person. She had been saving money for her advancement and was proud of her job here. She had no reason to steal and no need to. She knew we would help her too, as much as we were able. She has never lied to me, never hidden things from us. To think of her as a thief is very much not in her way, not in the way of what she is, in her character, in her . . . well, the good girl and person that she finds herself . . . that we find herself to be. To be of.'

'Good God, man, don't tie yourself in knots.'

John took a breath. He wanted to throttle this pig. But he must control his feelings, to help Anny.

'I am not a well-spoken man, I know that, sir.'

'Indeed not.'

Another breath, deeper this time. 'But I am honest and true, sir. And I beg of you to reconsider this case and this charge.'

Now King focused his eyes on John, his head tipped back as he wasn't a tall man and John was huge. King now deigned to speak directly to him. 'Woodvine, I agreed to see you today as I could not fathom what would possess you to approach my house with such impudence, and so I came out of mere curiosity. I thought you must have some compelling new evidence to put before me of your daughter's innocence. Was there a mysterious man in black cape and mask who tiptoed up the driveway and planted the money in your daughter's bag? Or was it a fairy queen who stole through the window glass by magic and put it there?'

Jesus Christ, the mon is mocking me, thought John. How he wanted to kill him, actually murder him, right there and then, watch the life pour out of him onto the gravel. 'No, sir,' he said, his blood as cold as ice now.

'I dunna believe it was a mysterious man or the fairies that did it. I believe it was someone else, sir. But not my daughter, sir. Someone else.'

King narrowed his eyes. 'And who did you think it might be, Woodvine? Do tell.'

'Someone with a grudge against her.'

'Do you have the name of such a person?'

John looked at King. The master actually looked interested. Maybe he knew it was his son that did it, maybe he knew and didn't care. Or maybe he genuinely didn't know and maybe he was genuinely asking.

'I dunna have a name, but . . .'

'Well, then,' said King, with a dismissive wave of his hand.

'No, sir, please, sir. I mean to say, there are many who are envious of my daughter, sir. That may seem strange to one like . . . to one of your . . .' The struggle to be eloquent was hard, but he knew this was his chance and he must dredge up every word he could to fight this battle. '. . . *station* in life, sir. But my daughter is clever and pretty and hard-working. She has all the boys after her and all the girls jealous of her and her success. She is never proud, though. I meant to say, she has pride in her post and her work. But she never acts proud or . . . in *conceited* ways. She is very humble about herself. But there are those in this world that when they see such a person as her . . . as *she* . . . they dunna like it. They wanna smash it. They might even want to take it and make it . . . make her their own. And if that person canna have it, they might . . . do bad things, sir. In their revengeful thoughts, they might do a bad thing. But any man can understand that. Show me a man who's never had a revengeful thought. It can be . . . forgiven. If . . . things are put right . . . by a person.'

Halfway through that speech, John had begun to feel as if King were turning. His narrow gaze had gone and he was listening, really listening to his words. But by the end, John had begun to realise that King knew only too well what his son had done, that he understood only too well what John's meaning was. Now was the crucial moment. Which way would King turn?

'You seem to lean towards some hidden meaning, Woodvine. Is that so?'

'I only wish to save my daughter. My innocent daughter. I swear that she is innocent, on my very life.'

'Life is cheap,' muttered King.

'If it were my death that could save her from this, I would gladly give it.'

'Nobody is asking for that, Woodvine. Please resist melodrama.'

John was lost now. What was the man saying? What else could he say himself? 'Please, sir. Will you give me your verdict? What say you, sir?'

'What say I? Who do you think you are talking to, man?'

John clenched his fists and screwed his eyes shut. *God, give me strength with this bastard!* his mind shouted, but he managed to contain it and instead opened his eyes and said, 'Please, sir, I humbly beg of you, show my daughter mercy and leastways, please, investigate this further. Please, I beg you. I am begging you, sir.' He had run out of words. He thought about getting down upon his knees on the gravel.

'Woodvine, you have had more than your minute. You have presented no new evidence, no compelling arguments and no facts to back up your position. You have verged on harassment, a most inadvisable position to take with your master. And I am your master, Woodvine, do not forget that. If you continue with these claims against me and against my son—'

John gasped. King stopped, his mouth open. He actually said it. He actually came out and said it. John leapt on it. 'I never said a word about your son, sir.'

'Yes, well. No. You did not and neither . . .' King was blustering now, waving his hands about, his face colouring into the hue of a ripe Victoria plum. 'Well, God save us, what on earth am I doing conferring with a giant dolt in my back yard about legal matters? I cannot imagine what possessed me. I am too kind, that is it. I am too kind for my own good. Now, listen here. You've had your hearing and that's the end of it. If you continue with this, I'll have no choice but to dismiss you. I've half a mind to in any case. The cheek of it! But I am not a cruel man. So you will escape with your wages docked for a month. You will work at half pay for four weeks and be glad you have kept your job. Now, get off my land and get back to work.'

King stomped off, the gravel flicking from his heels and tip-tapping his retreat.

It was over. John stood with his shoulders hunched, all of his fight draining out of him. There was nothing to do but go. He walked straight into the woods and forged on through the bracken, his legs whipped by low branches and spikily caressed by banks of nettles. He did not look where he was going, just knew it was downhill, down to the furnace, along the river here somewhere. He had not the heart to stop walking, for if he did, he thought he would surely scream or tear his hair out or dash his head against a tree trunk.

If he'd been a cleverer man, he might have used words better. He might have outwitted that fat idiot and made him admit it was his son that did it. Well, he almost did. But it was not enough. King would never give up his own or at the very least, would never allow his son to be called into question. And even if King did admit it to him, it would only be a working man's word against the ironmaster. Everybody knew how that one would work out: in the master's favour, of course. The way of the world. John felt it was a fool's errand, and he'd only made things worse. Now his pay was docked and they'd struggle with the loss of money. He was lucky he hadn't been demoted from his new position in the cast-house or even dismissed.

He walked on, hurriedly, worried that Pritchard might dock his pay further if he turned up very late. He began to jog through the trees, getting faster, the speed taking away his breath and his memories, the ground rushing at him as he leapt forward down the incline. He tripped over a tree root and fell forward heavily, his huge frame crashing into ferns and jolting every bone as he skidded to a halt. He turned onto his back and groaned, staring up into the meeting of the treetops that sheltered him overhead. He did not move, could not move. He despised King, but he hated himself more. He had failed Anny.

Then, he heard voices. A high one, a low one. He lay very still and listened. They were close by, the sound of the undergrowth signalling they were walking away from the path, as he had been. They were talking as they walked, in serious tones, question and answer, sounding earnest and concerned. If he stood up now, they'd probably see him and be shocked by a man looming out at them. If they stumbled across him, they'd be more shocked still. He'd have a hard time explaining why he was hidden away in the woods, and the last thing he needed was to draw further notice. The voices were close enough to hear now. They had stopped.

'Here?' said the female. She sounded young. 'Is it here you wish us to stop? The wood is thick here, that is certain. Thick and full of secrets.'

'To think, you were the quiet one,' said the male. 'Now you're full of poetry.'

'It is love that has done it. It gives me the words to sing.'

'Enough of that now. I will have to stop that mouth of yours.'

Next came silence, then as John strained his ears to listen beyond the birdsong and the breeze that ruffled the thousands of leaves about him, he heard the girl moaning, high and reedy. They must be kissing. He listened on, miserable, frozen. They were quiet for a long while. Then she spoke again.

'Will you give me your promise?'

'I will, I will. Oh, my sweet, sweet girl. I want to be with you. But I fear your father will never approve the match. What are we to do? Oh, Margaret.'

John sat bolt upright. He looked around, in the direction of the voices. They were a little downhill and were up against a tree, not turned in his direction. It was Margaret King all right. Who was the man? They were kissing again and John could not see his face. Then the man came up for air. It was him. The scribbler. It was Anny's sweetheart, Jake Ashford.

'I don't care, I don't care!' cried Margaret, as she ran her fingers ardently through Ashford's hair. 'I will be with you come hell or high water! Kiss me again!'

John could not look away. He moved slowly. He did not have the vitality left in him to murder these two, as his hands might have wished any other time. He barely had the vigour to stand. He got to his feet stealthily and managed to reach the broad trunk of a nearby oak and stand behind it for a moment, hidden from their view. They were talking again, then kissing. In their passion, they did not seem to notice a giant of a man sidling through the trees away from them.

The sounds of industry were soon upon him. How many more shocks can a person stand? How much disappointment? He felt like a man in the stocks, humiliated and pummelled with the mockery of life and circumstance. Nothing he did came right. And those Kings. Those Kings were all alike. That girl who had simpered and smiled and looked the part of pity and kindness and was now whoring herself in the woods with Anny's sweetheart. Those Kings. They were poison, every last one of them.

When he arrived at the furnace, he glanced at Pritchard, who must have seen the look of thunder on his face and did not say a word, not a word about his lateness or his dishevelled appearance. John realised there were bits of bracken stuck to his clothes and his face was aching where he must have struck his head in the fall. He went straight to the cast-house, where the metal had just been declared fit to run and so the men were rushing to action. He worked in a rage, throwing things down and whacking things about. One of his workmates shouted at him, 'What the bloody 'ell's up with you, mon?'

'Bloody well leave me be,' he shouted in return and looked up with a slaying expression that made his mate slink away. John stopped for a moment to catch his breath, going over to the door of the cast-house to calm down. Looking outside, he saw at the edge of the river, leaning on a trunk and watching the scene, the figure of a young man. He was holding a pencil and sketching energetically across a page clipped to a board. John's eyesight was not good, he had to squint to make out the face, but there was no mistaking the action. It was Ashford. The little bastard had left off kissing the King girl and come down here to practise his wretched hobby, while Anny festered in prison desperately awaiting his visit that would never come. And it would be him who had to tell his girl of Jake and Margaret. How much more could she take?

'There will be blood today,' said John, and threw down his gloves and made a beeline for Ashford. He cared for nothing anymore, only that someone would pay. Someone had to pay for all this.

There came shouting from nearby. Men around him pointed up at the top of the furnace. Clouds of dust were issuing from the top. Pritchard was running past him, waving his arms and shouting, 'More burden! More burden!'

As an ex-furnace filler, John knew what was happening. He had seen it before. Blockages in the furnace built up and had to be cleared by a swift increase in the amount of materials tipped into the opening at the top. He turned and ran up the incline to help shift the loads. Another great cloud of dust spewed forth from the furnace's blazing mouth, filled with fiery embers. Men at the very top fell backwards and twisted away, trying to escape from it, stumbling and tripping over each other in their haste. All in a moment, there was a great roaring sound from deep within the furnace, like the din of a thousand cattle stampeding down a hill. Seconds later, the top of the furnace exploded in a riot of fire, stone, brick, lime, coke, liquefied iron and luminescent dust. There were no more sounds, no more sights to see. He had no time to think of his daughter, of his wife or of his life upon this cruel earth.

Chapter 21

Margaret was in her room when the blast came. Her shelves rattled and a troop of prancing porcelain ponies wobbled violently and fell, smashing into shards on the floor. Margaret had been lying on her bed, replaying every moment with Jake. She thought the world was coming to an end. She had read once of an earthquake in a novel and wondered for a second if these ever occurred in Shropshire. When the sound and the vibrations passed, she came to and ran out of the room. Her father was downstairs shouting at Brunt, as if all this were his doing.

'From the direction of the works,' Brunt was saying.

'Good God,' said her father and issued instructions about collecting his coat and hat.

Benjamina came out onto the landing, sleepy-eyed and squinting at the harsh light of day interrupting her afternoon nap. Queenie was calling from her room: 'Jenkins! Jenkins!' Margaret heard the lady's maid's footsteps running from the adjoining room, then her voice soothing her grandmother. It was as if time had slowed almost to a halt, and yet Margaret's perceptions were screwed up to the highest notch. She ignored her step-mother's sleepy questioning and went down the stairs quickly. She could hear running on the gravel outside. She went out of the sitting room garden door to see Cook telling the maids not to go, but Lucy – Margaret's favourite maid – was running ahead of the others and not stopping for Cook or anyone. For a moment, she wondered why they were all running down there. What could maids and a stable boy do? But then she scolded herself as she realised that, of course, all of these local girls and lads had family that were ironworkers – uncles and cousins, brothers and fathers. Fathers. Anny. John Woodvine!

'Lucy!' she called out and ran to the woodland path that everyone was heading down. 'Lucy, stop!' She saw the girl turn, about to run on, so she called again. 'Lucy, please, it's Miss Margaret. Please!'

Lucy spotted her from the edge of the wood and hesitated. Margaret could see she wanted to run on with the others. She went towards Lucy and called to her. 'I'm sorry, Lucy. Do you have family down there?'

'Course, miss. My uncles. Four of 'em.'

Margaret caught up with her. 'I'm sorry. You must go. But please, will you find out if John Woodvine is well? Anny's father?'

‘I surely will, miss,’ said Lucy and did not wait to be dismissed, tearing down the hill, fleetly winding her way through the trees till Margaret lost sight of her.

She turned to see her father and Brotherton coming from the office and running down the path. She had never seen her father run. Mrs Brotherton was standing at the door to the office, wringing her hands. Margaret rushed over to her.

‘What do you think it is, Mrs Brotherton?’ She saw that the woman was already crying.

‘Oh, my dear. You should not be here. You must go back to your room. Your father will be angry if he sees you are not safe.’

‘Please, do tell me what has happened exactly.’

‘There was an explosion at the blast furnace. Sounds like the whole thing blew. It’ll be a miracle if there aren’t a dozen or more dead. Oh my, it is a terrible day for all of us. Terrible. I must go and fetch the surgeon.’

‘I do hope you don’t have family there, do you?’

‘Oh, miss, do go back in the house, do,’ said Mrs Brotherton peevishly. ‘This is no place for you.’ With that, she pulled the office door to behind her and locked it with a key she kept on a cord around her waist. She bustled off down the path and Margaret felt herself well and truly discharged. She wandered back to the house and went up the stairs. No sign of Benjamina. She’d probably gone straight back to her nap. She knocked on Queenie’s door. Jenkins answered it, looking harassed.

'Not now, miss,' she said and shut the door in her face.

Margaret waited in her room for a while. She sat by the window that gave out on to the driveway, looking out for her father returning. Then, she went downstairs and sat in the library, watching the opening to the woodland path and the edge of the office for any comings and goings. But there were none. She wanted to leave the house, sneak down through the woods and see for herself. She nearly did it once or twice, nearly got up the courage. But she was afraid. She was too afraid, of what she might see, of the horrors that awaited an observer at the aftermath of an explosion. She had once seen a painting in a book that depicted hell and it was full of tiny people in various stages of torment in dark caves, fire blooming all around. That was the image in her mind now. She knew she was not strong enough to bear it. So she prayed instead, that there were not too many dead, that most had escaped miraculously with their lives, perhaps just some injuries. And most of all, that Anny's father, that good, good man John Woodvine, had not been by the furnace when it blew, that he had been at home, or by the riverside, or anywhere else but there. Was there a chance? Of course there was. And she was sure he'd be all right, she had a good feeling. Surely, two appalling things could not happen to one family?

But, of course, they could. Life could be cruel. Woodvine could have been miles away or inches. He could be alive or dead. Dead. Jake! Suddenly, she remembered that Jake said he was going to do some sketching. He had his bag with him. He had walked away from her, leaving her panting from his kisses, in the direction of the furnace. He had not said where he was going precisely, but it could have been there. Would he have been close enough to be hurt? Killed even? She ran from the room. She crossed the lawn and headed for the woods. Then she heard someone running up the path and turned to see her father approaching the house, in a state of exertion, puffed out and grubby-faced. She went to him and saw that all of his clothes were smeared with dirt. He was pulling off his cravat.

'Father, please, tell me. How many hurt?'

'Not now, Margaret,' he said and stormed past her, calling, 'Get back in the house, for God's sake!'

'Father, please!' she cried and followed him. 'I must know. Is Jake Ashford killed? And John Woodvine?'

'We don't know names. Nobody knows names. It's just butchery everywhere. Lord knows what effect it'll have on profits. The break in production will cost us a fortune. Now, get away with you, girl!'

He took the stairs two at a time and disappeared into his room. Margaret felt faint. She went back out into the garden. She could not bear to face it, the scene of carnage that must be down there. But she could not wait either. She went to her room and took her purse, collected her cloak and bonnet and walked away down the path to town. She would go to Jake's lodgings, see if he were there. That was something she could do. As she walked down the hill, she realised that everyone she passed was rushing past her, all heading towards the river or the woods, all in the direction of the blast. The town was emptying and she was in the course of the flood. She fought her way through it, hearing all manner of voices concerned, worried, shocked, shouting and some sobbing.

She reached Jake's lodgings and banged on the door. No answer. She tried again, and still no answer. Nobody at home. Now, she felt nauseous. She decided she would not go home again and wait. She grimly set her mind to follow the crowd. Jostling along with so many others, her progress was slow. She began to feel queasy, the smell and heat, the clamour of horrified voices. Then she heard her name, her surname. King this and King that. People were talking about her father. She managed to catch a snippet here and there and all of it was bad. There were curse words, followed by her family name. There was such anger and disgust. They blamed her father for this. She felt her cheeks glow hot with shame and pulled her bonnet forwards to shield her face. Yet why would they blame him? Surely it was an accident. But there were whispers of delayed repairs, faulty equipment, inferior materials . . . Should she turn round and go back? She was not far from the furnace site now, and the crowd was so thick here. She kept her head down and her feet shuffling forward.

The crowd slowed and she could hear cries, women weeping and being comforted. She looked up and was surrounded by heads, shaking and gasping. As she came past the last clump of riverside trees and the furnace loomed into view, the sight froze her.

The brick structure of the furnace was gone, only the rubble of its foundations remaining, jagged like broken teeth. Broad grey puddles of solidified iron splattered the scene, as if a giant's paint pot had been kicked over. There were huge lumps of wall punctuating the churned ground down to the riverside, some still glowing with embers. Everything was veiled in dust, patches of white, brown, reddish and black dust cloaked the ruins, the earth and the surrounding vegetation. There were men everywhere, standing in groups, walking amongst the ruins, muttering to each other. There were a couple of blankets on the ground, here and there, lumpy, unmoving forms beneath them, feet stuck out of the end, some with boots on, some bootless, naked feet. Elsewhere, there were bodies with only a coat thrown over to cover the faces. A large cart was arriving along the riverside road from downstream, trundling along the rutty way, drawn by oxen. Some of the men moved towards the bodies and began to lift them into the cart. The crowd's noise changed, its voices slowing and deepening into moans of sympathy and thence to a kind of shuffling silence, as if nobody wanted to utter a sound in the presence of the moving of the dead. Margaret looked away, unable to bear the sight of the bodies, having been cradled by the firm ground, now hanging limp and loose between the men who carried them. She turned her gaze towards the furnace itself, her father's moneymaker, now just wreckage. She saw a man fish for something in the piles of scattered bricks and lift it up. It was a boot, with half a leg attached to it, blown off at the knee, its stump bloody and glistening through the lime dust. But there was no sign of Jake or of John Woodvine.

'Miss,' said a voice to her left.

Margaret flinched as if slapped. Had someone recognised her? She turned her head away, terrified to show her face. A hand touched her arm.

'Miss, you shouldna be here.'

Margaret had to turn and look. It was her maid, Lucy. To see her face there in that ghastly place was like balm.

'Oh, Lucy,' she said and felt her face crumpling.

'You shouldna be seeing all this, miss.'

'Please,' Margaret whispered and glanced about, hoping that Lucy would cotton on that nobody must know who she was.

Lucy nodded and said, 'I shall walk back with you.'

'But your family . . .'

'No sign of them yet.'

She fought to calm herself and fall into step with the sad, slow gait of the returning crowd, aware of Lucy's presence beside her. After what felt like hours yet was just a matter of minutes, she found herself ascending the steps to the road by the iron bridge. They were met with a logjam of people, some coming, some going, in a melee of confusion, like a gathering of boiling wreckage in the path of a flood.

She felt Lucy's hand on her arm, steering her onto the bridge, away from the worst of the throng.

'We can wait here a moment,' said Lucy. 'Catch your breath. Then you ought to get yourself home.'

'Thank you,' said Margaret in a small voice. 'You are so kind.'

'I am that surprised to see you here, miss.'

'I felt I should come,' said Margaret, 'Mr Woodvine, Jake Ashford. Have you seen them?'

'No, miss.'

'Oh, Lucy. This is beyond bearing . . . and all the fault of the Kings. What must you think of us? What must everyone here think? I know what they are saying, about . . . my father, the family. I know they say it is his fault. He should be there, he should be down there, helping. Instead he came home. I saw him retreat to his room. He ran upstairs, I tell you.'

Lucy did not speak. Her face betrayed no opinion. But she was listening and this gave Margaret the confidence to go on. 'But I want you to know that I am not like him, or my brother. I am not one of them. I never have been. I know my family is rotten and I cannot imagine why anyone would want to work for them, especially a kind and good person like you, Lucy. I cannot understand it.'

Lucy looked down, a grim smile played about her lips and she answered, 'We must work, miss. We have no choice as to our masters. And all masters are the same.'

Margaret was shamed by her forgetting of this hard truth.

'You are right. I am sorry, Lucy.'

'Dunna fret yourself, miss. It is the way of the world.'

'But it doesn't have to be so, does it? Cannot we strive for change?'

'Change is for the rich, not for the likes of me and mine.'

Margaret stared at Lucy's face. She was an attractive girl, pale skin and pink cheeks, black hair tucked neatly under her cap and pretty dark eyes. It was the first time Margaret had observed her closely, the first time she had ever looked carefully at one of the servants' faces, looked into their eyes to see the person they were, not simply the role they played in her father's house.

'I am powerless, too, in my own way,' Margaret said to Lucy, whose eyebrows rose just a touch, enough to show her derision of such a statement, yet sufficient to remain respectful. 'I know you don't believe that, but it is true. Yet, there are ways. There are ways we can break free of our bonds. One of them is friendship. It can break down the barriers between us.'

She expected another world-weary retort from Lucy, but the girl was quiet, regarding her steadily for a moment with those small, intelligent eyes. Then she glanced about her. 'I should get back now, miss. But, in all this muddle, I still have no word on my uncles. I've been down there and back and all over town looking for word, and none yet. Will you give me leave to keep looking, leave from my post at the house?'

'Of course, Lucy. Will you bring me news of John Woodvine and Jake Ashford?'

'I will if I can, miss,' she said and turned away, slotting into the crowd and moving as one with them, her drab servant's clothes mingling her into obscurity amongst her people.

Margaret stood on the bridge and looked through the iron rails, the river flowing peacefully beneath her, oblivious to the human drama enacted upon its banks. She watched those coming from the direction of the blast, shaking their heads, some of the women crying, others covering their eyes with their hands.

She wanted to run, run home and never leave it. She raised her head to catch a glimpse of her house on the hill, presiding over the town. Despite the rot that she knew grew daily within that house, it was the only home she knew. She turned her eyes to the road, summoning the courage to enter the fray.

Then, she saw him.

'Jake!' she screamed. 'Jake Ashford!' Some looked around but she was not alone in calling out, as here at the bridge there was a loud hubbub of voices, of similar reunions and shouts and cries. Jake had not heard her and was pushing his way through the throng to get across the road to his lodgings. She rushed to him and reached him at his door.

'Jake!' she cried again and grasped his arm. He turned to her.

'Oh, Margaret!' he gasped and let her throw her arms about him.

'Are you hurt?' she said.

'I am well, quite well. I was there. I was there, Margaret!' His eyes were lit up and his face was grubby.

'You are not hurt? Are you sure?'

'Quite sure. I was along the river a way and was sketching a scene of the workers framed by trees when it went off. I was thrown to the ground by the blast, but I was not injured. I was very lucky.'

'Oh, thank heavens!' she cried and began to sob, resting her head on this chest. He patted her on the back then stood her upright.

'There, there, dear girl. I am well. But many others are not. It is the most incredible scene down there.

I simply cannot describe it. But I must not, for you will never sleep again if I do.'

'I was just there myself, Jake. It was terrible. The worst thing I have seen in my life.'

'What on earth possessed you to go down there?'

'I came to find you and Anny's father. I did not see you there. A maid of ours took me away from it.'

'Well, she did right. These are not sights for eyes as beautiful as yours. Now then, I lost my bag in the blast. I must go upstairs and fetch more materials. I must record it.'

'You are going back there? To *sketch*?'

'I must! This is an extraordinary event. I must record it for posterity.'

Margaret stared at him. 'Please do not go back there. Please stay with me.'

'Ah, my little mouse,' he said and took her hands, squeezing them. 'There is no danger now. I am fine. You must go home and stay safe. I will come to you soon. Then, we will talk. We will make plans. But for now, I must go. You do understand, don't you?'

She thought of what he'd said about his mistress, art, who now had put fire in his belly; he would not be turned.

'Of course. Please be careful there, Jake. And if you can, please can you ask about Mr Woodvine, Anny's father? And come to the house to tell me if you hear news of him? Will you do that for me, Jake?'

'I will do what I can.'

'And you will send me word, of when and where we can meet next?'

'Of course I will, my sweet. Now, go. Go home. I will see you anon.'

With that, he turned and went into his lodging house and shut the door in her face.

She walked home and waited in her room for hours. Cook prepared a plate of cold meats and had them sent up to her in her room. In the late evening, she heard sounds downstairs of doors closing and the voices of servants. She went out onto the landing and made her way across to the servants' staircase. She heard weary feet coming up them, and there was Lucy.

'Lucy, I am glad to see you,' she said. Lucy stopped on the stairs and lifted her face. It was grimy like the others who'd come from the site, but Lucy's eyes were ghostly, haunted by what they had seen, no doubt. 'Is your family safe?'

'Yes, miss. All my uncles are safe.'

'What good fortune, Lucy. I am so glad to hear that. How did they escape it?'

'They was in a different part of the works. Luckily none of them near the blast.'

'Lucy, did you hear any news of the Woodvines? Of Anny's father?'

Lucy did not speak. She looked down at her feet. She shook her head.

'Do you mean, you have no news? Or that it is bad news?'

'It is bad news, miss. The worst. John Woodvine is dead.'

Chapter 22

Anny did not open her eyes. She knew she was awake, she knew that the touch of Jake's hand on her face had been a dream, she knew she was in the worst room she had ever been in her life. She had thought the cell must be the worst, until she fell ill with fever and they brought her here, to the prison infirmary. After days of fever, of a boiling heat in her body that left her wordless and limp, she had begun to cool down and slowly crawl back to the land of the living. At her lowest moments, she did not know if she wished to recover or not. She wanted to escape the infirmary but the cell was nowhere she ever wanted to be again. The only thing that kept her going was the thought of what her death would do to those who loved her. Her father and mother mostly, but also, Peggy. And Jake? How she longed for him. Her dreams were plagued by soft, sweet memories of his touch. But she was haunted by doubt. Did he love her? Why had he not come to her? There was something about him that made her doubt herself, her own judgement. She wanted him, indeed she did, but his love was not for her alone – she had to share it with his art. It was not how she pictured love would be: simple, warm and good. Jake's love was like fire, but cold too, like a mirror on a winter's morning.

On waking in the infirmary, the smell hit her first. The only thing close to it was the butcher's stall in Ironbridge mixed with the stench of the stale sweat of the men coming back from the furnace, including her father. Bless him, but he did stink after a shift. There was another smell in there, something sickly and sweet she couldn't place. Something to do with death.

She lay listening to the sounds of the sick. Some were coughing, others moaning, one snored. She could hear her heart beating, as it echoed dully deep inside her ears. She thought about how nobody else in the world could hear that sound but her. She was the only person allowed inside her own mind. This thought had comforted her these past weeks in prison. Whatever was happening outside of her body, or to her body, nobody could get inside her head. It was her refuge.

She heard voices in the corridor beyond the infirmary. Her eyes opened and she looked towards the door but could not see anyone. She scanned the room, to see if anyone else had passed in the night. Two had perished since she'd been in there, carted away, staring, dead eyes still open, no sheet to cover them, taken with no ceremony. She wondered where they were buried, if anyone informed their families. It was a gloomy room lit only by candles, with eight beds arranged in two rows along each opposite wall, three of them occupied with sleeping prisoners, two men and one other woman. It was very hot and airless in there. She craved water but they were only given a small cup once a day. This was not a place where the sick were tended. This was a place where most came to die.

There were those voices again. She saw a silhouette appear in the doorway, joined by another. She couldn't make out the faces. But then she heard her surname and she saw the matron turn and look at her. She pulled herself upright. Was it Jake? Oh, let it be Jake! She squinted at the figures in the doorway, one of whom stepped into the room, where the candlelight caught her face.

'Peggy!' said Anny, her voice cracking as her throat was so dry.

Peggy looked at her and smiled, then turned to the figure behind her, who Anny saw was Brotherton. Mr B! Come to see her with Peggy? She still held his disloyalty against him but maybe he was making amends now. Could it be . . . good news? Why else would both of them come? Was she to be released? Oh, happy day, if it were true!

'I fear this was a mistake,' said Brotherton and looked about to turn around and leave.

'Wait outside if you must,' said Margaret. 'I am going to talk to Anny.'

Margaret walked over to Anny's bed and sat down at the end of it, smiling wanly. Anny saw Mr B wait at the door, then he stepped outside into the corridor. Anny thought, *Why is he not coming to me?* Anny looked back at Peggy, whose face showed the shock she knew came from her own pale and drawn appearance. She guessed she must look so much worse than the last time Margaret had seen her. She imagined she must look years older.

'It's me, Anny. It's Peggy. I am here. I came to tell you—'

'Is Jake with you? Is he here?' she asked weakly.

'Jake is not here, no. I am sorry, Anny. I do not think he will be coming. But I am here.'

'Why? Did you talk to him? What did he say?'

'Only that he must serve his art. I think he is too committed to his vocation. He isn't deserving of you, Anny. You need a man who will devote himself to you.'

Anny's head dropped and she covered her face with her hands. *I knew it*, she thought. *I knew he was not a good man. Deep down, I knew it. He is selfish and untrustworthy.*

'Oh, Anny, please don't take it so. *Please.*'

Anny looked up and set her face straight. 'I am glad you told me the truth and that I won't have to waste my time thinking of him any longer.'

Oh, but it sustained me, she thought. *It kept me going in this awful place. How I have missed him. How I will miss the thought of him.*

She could not keep up the brave face. She broke down and sobbed. Peggy handed her a clean handkerchief, pure white, embroidered fancily with the letters M and K. Then Peggy reached over and put her arms about her and held her as she cried.

'He's not the one for you,' Peggy went on. 'Not this one, not him. Forget him. Better to cry for him now and forget him. Better for everyone,' said Peggy.

Through her tears, Anny wondered, *What does she mean, better for everyone?*

'I am so sorry, Anny,' said a voice behind them. It was Mr B. Anny looked up.

'Mr B,' she managed, wiping her eyes and composing herself.

'Yes, Anny. Oh, I don't know what to say. I doubt I can add anything to what Miss King must have said so eloquently.'

'No, Mr Brotherton! Not yet!' said Margaret urgently.

'We will all miss your father,' Brotherton went on. 'A good man. The best. Such a worker he was, like no other.'

Anny looked at Peggy. 'What's this?'

'Oh, Anny,' said Margaret and brought her fist to her mouth.

Nausea rose in Anny's throat. Her head felt like it was draining of blood. 'What is this about my father?'

'But Miss King, have you not . . . ?' began Mr B incredulously.

'Your father . . .' said Peggy, looking at her with wide, fearful eyes. 'There was an accident. At the furnace. There was an explosion. Your father, Anny . . .' She reached over and took Anny's hands in her own.

'No.' Anny's voice was low at first. 'No,' she said again, louder and higher.

'It was an accident,' said Brotherton. 'Fifteen dead, Anny. Your father was one of them.'

'No, no, no.' Anny was shaking her head now, her eyes moving erratically with each phrase, each new thought. Not Father, not dear old Father. Not him, never him. He was in the cast-house these days, much safer than the furnace top.

'There is a mistake. It cannot be Father.'

Mr B shook his head. 'There is no error, Anny. It is definitely your father. They say he ran towards the furnace top just before it was about to blow, to help the others, but got caught in the blast himself. He died a hero, Anny.'

'And my mother?'

'She's taken the news badly and isn't well enough to come, but she will recover.'

Anny's mind had been racing, but now it stopped dead, as if hit by a heavy object and trapped beneath it. There was no point in struggling. That would only cause more pain.

'No,' she whispered, the truth dawning on her now. 'No.'

'It is a tragedy,' said Mr B in a soothing tone. 'A terrible, awful tragedy. A terrible, awful accident.'

'No,' said Anny again and looked up at Mr B. Something new was brewing in her now. It was not grief or pity. It was not misery. It was anger, pure, white-hot rage. 'This was not an accident. Father used to tell me about the furnace. About the danger. There were blockages, poor materials. King could have stopped this. It's his fault. Not an accident. It's King's doing.'

Peggy was staring at her, shaking her head. 'You,' said Anny and looked upon her, as if seeing her clearly for the first time. 'You are a King. It's your fault. It's all your fault.'

'No, Anny!' said Mr B, attempting to soothe her. 'Miss King is here to . . .'

'No!' It came out as a screech. Anny thrust Peggy's hands away. 'The Kings are behind this. They are behind everything. How could I have trusted you? You, just another King!'

'Anny, please!' Peggy was sobbing now.

'You're the worst of the lot! You pretend to be good, but you're just like them. What have you ever done for me? You desperate . . . little *bitch*! You had no friends of your own, so you picked on me. Made me think I could aspire to something, a better life. But look at you. Why should I want anything that you have, anything that you are? You're pathetic. You disgust me. You're all the same. We were never friends.'

'We were, Anny, please! I've always loved you. If you only knew how I've tried to help you.'

'Oh, poor you! Poor little rich girl!' Anny spat out the words like poison on her tongue. 'Do you want me to pity you now? We were always different. You'll always have a pillow to lay your pretty little head on. Below the poor, there is no pillow. There is only a hole, a bloody great hole with the workhouse, poverty, disease and death at the bottom of it. Rich and poor can never be friends.'

Mr B tried to intervene. 'Oh, Anny, you don't know what you're saying.'

'Shut up, you snivelling bastard!' Anny cried. 'You're as bad as the Kings. When did you ever speak up for me? When did you ever risk a moment of your comfortable little life to speak for me? You knew I'd never steal, you knew that and so did your wife. But here I am. And where is Cyril? Off scot-free, no doubt. And you knew about the furnace, too, about the danger. And yet here you are. And where is my father? Dead. Dead! Murdered by the likes of you – and you!'

Mr B patted Peggy on the shoulder and muttered, 'She's not herself. We must go.' Peggy stood up reluctantly and followed Mr B to the door. The other prisoners in their sickbeds were all wide awake and upright now, enjoying the show, one man grinning at Peggy as she passed. They could do that, Peggy and Mr B, they could walk out of here and never come back. But she was left here, in this hell, with the knowledge of her lost father haunting her forever. *Oh, Father! There could never be a daughter who loved a father more than me. My lovely father, my dear father. Gone. Ruined. Dead.* The rage boiled in her like the furnace that killed her father. Now, it was about to blow.

Anny shouted after them: 'That's it. Run away, you bloody cowards. That's right. Canna stand the truth? Run away, back to your wife who I tended when she was sick I dunna know how many times. Where is she, eh? And you, run back to Jake Ashford. Oh yes, dunna think I dunna know what your game is. *He's not the one for you, Anny.* Oh yes, we all know why that is. Because you're after him for yourself!'

At this, Peggy turned to Anny, her face betraying her. 'I knew it!' cried Anny, with bitter triumph. She guessed it the moment Peggy had said 'Better for everyone'. But she did not know if it were true, not until this moment, when Peggy's guilt-ridden eyes gave it all away. She looked at the face of this young woman who had been her closest friend, her ally in a difficult world. She felt ice water run through her veins. Hate had replaced love in every fibre of her being. She spoke again to Peggy, in a low, unearthly voice, 'You traitorous whore.'

Peggy flinched. A stab in the heart. Good! Anny felt she could kill her just by looking at her. Anny was panting with exertion, her skin shining with sweat, her eyes bright with hate.

Peggy muttered, 'I shall come again soon, when you are better.'

'No, you will not!' shouted Anny, mustering energy for one last blow. 'I never want to see you again. I curse you, Peggy, and I curse Jake Ashford. I curse you to lose everything you have and to a miserable life and a lonely death. I curse you, Margaret King!'

Chapter 23

Margaret sat on her bed and stared at the walls of her room. She knew she was tired but were her eyes deceiving her? She could swear that the walls were closing in on all sides, all four slowly but steadily moving towards her, to crush her. She closed her eyes to escape it and pictured instead her best friend's face, twisted with hate, screaming at her. She jumped up from the bed and left the room. She had only been back from Shrewsbury for a quarter hour or so, yet she was rushing out of the door again. She could not bear to stay in that house. She could not bear her own memories. She walked hurriedly along the path to town, the summer sun beating down on her like a judgement and making her sweat. She wanted to rip off her bonnet and cloak and throw them down, feel the sun on her bare skin and the breeze in her hair. But not only was it unseemly, it would be drawing attention to herself and she could not risk that. It was several days since the blast, yet the town would not forget the accident so quickly, would never forget it, she guessed. She must remain incognito and calm herself down. She slowed her pace and caught her breath, trying to regulate her step with her breathing, two long steps for every breath: one, two, one, two.

I am behaving like a mad person, she thought. *Is it in our family, this madness, as Father said?* She thought of the walls closing in, of Queenie's oddness, of what happened to her great-aunt Selina. Perhaps it was. Perhaps all the women of the family had this feebleness of mind. But then it occurred to her that whatever weakness ran in their female blood, it was corroded further by the acid of the King males. They destroyed things, by design or by carelessness. As she walked she decided that they would not destroy her. There was only one way to escape them and that was by leaving that place, for good. She knew where she was heading now, to Jake.

The very thought of him twisted her insides, not merely from her desire for him, but from the remembrance of Anny. She shook her head to clear her thoughts. Yes, she could crucify herself for the rest of her life about Anny or she could buck up and realise she had done all she could. She had begged her father and her grandmother to withdraw the charges, she had confronted her brother to force him to confess and she had not stolen Jake from Anny: he had made that choice himself.

In the aftermath of the blast, Margaret had tracked down Mrs Woodvine, hired her a doctor. She'd gone to Mr Brotherton to ensure Anny was told, and when no family could be found to take Anny the news, she had gone herself. True, she'd made a mess of it, and it seemed little enough in the face of Anny's pain, but it was all that was within Margaret's power. Even if she sacrificed everything and walked away from Jake, what would that win Anny?

She thought of Jake. He had not contacted her since the day of the blast and she did not want to bother him, but she was restless and ached to see him. She wanted to make their plans, to escape before further tragedy could strike.

There was no escape for her friend. Anny's father was dead, her mother ill and her imprisonment seemed certain, with nobody to speak for her and no other comfort for her. She did not blame her friend for her anger. But because Anny's life was over, did Margaret's need to end? Anny's curse . . . Margaret's eyes welled up and blurred her path ahead, the bridge on her left, the Tontine Hotel to her right. And then she was there, standing before the door to Jake's lodgings. He was everything to her now, he was all she had left.

She knocked on the door. After a wait and the sound of heavy footsteps, it opened. There was his landlady, an obsequious smile on her face, which vanished.

'What do you want?' she said in a hard-edged tone.

Margaret's shock made her pause. They had spoken before. Could the landlady not remember her? 'Uh, good afternoon. I would like . . . is Mr Ashford at home?'

'The cheek of yer! Showing yer face round here.'

Then it dawned on her. The landlady had recollected her very well. She knew exactly who she was.

'I would be most obliged if you could tell me if Mr Ashford is at home. I have an important communication for him.' Margaret lifted up her purse and snapped it open, just as she had done the previous occasion she was here.

The woman snarled, 'You Kings think your money can solve everything. I've got friends round here lost family because of you and yours. It's blood money now.'

Margaret felt as if she had been slapped in the face. But she also believed she could not be blamed for her father's mismanagement. That was simply unfair and, quite frankly, bullying. And she had had enough of being bullied. She jutted out her chin and said, 'If you will not tell me if he is here, then I shall go and look for myself.'

'Oh, will you now, missy?' began the landlady, squaring up to Margaret, yet they were distracted by the sound of footsteps coming down the stairs. Then Jake appeared and saw Margaret, his face showing surprise.

'Miss King!' he said and smiled. 'Do come in.'

The landlady said, 'Not in here. I run a respectable house, me.'

Jake glanced at Margaret, then replied, 'I was just about to go out in any case. Will you take a walk with me, Miss King?'

She nodded and Jake came out onto the pavement. His landlady slammed the door behind him. At the nearness of Jake and the horrid treatment of that woman, Margaret wanted to burst out crying but she controlled herself. Jake's expression showed concern for her. 'We shall find a quiet place to talk,' he said and she nodded. Taking her arm, he led her over the street. Jake paid the toll for them both to cross the bridge. They went down onto the river path, walking away from town until they reached a secluded spot, then stopped. Margaret glanced about to see if anyone was around and then threw her arms round him and began to weep.

'There, there. My darling, sweet girl.'

'Oh Jake, I cannot bear it any longer.'

'Surely not, my darling. You have so much to be happy about. You have me, for one.'

'I know, but everything else is hopeless. The accident. The town blames my family. And rightly so! I saw Anny, and she too blames me. She also knows about you and me. She guessed it. Oh, she screamed at me, cursed me. She hates me. She was my only friend.'

He kissed her tenderly and it stopped her tears. Her desire for him was greater than her grief, in that moment.

'We must leave,' she said. 'We must get away, before it's too late.'

'I wish I could make it all better,' he whispered to her.

'You could. You can, Jake. Let us run away together.'

'Run away? Where?'

'Paris. We could be together, walk the gardens, read poetry . . . and be far from the curse of the King family.'

Jake took her hands in his own and said, 'Do you mean . . . could you mean, to elope, my love?'

'Are you asking me to marry you?' she whispered and held her breath.

Jake sighed and squeezed her hands. 'There is nothing I want more. But I have few funds and my father would not sanction us running away together. He would expect a dowry from your father. I cannot rely on him to fund this trip for the sake of elopement. He would never agree. I do not have enough money, my love, and I know of no way to put my hands on such an amount as we would need for the journey.'

'I do.'

'Do what, my love?'

'I know a way of finding the money. I can do it tonight. I can take it from my father's office.'

'That sounds like a terrible risk,' he said, looking worried.

'I would do it, for us. I know exactly how. Cyril's crime and Anny's descriptions have taught me where my father's keys are and how to open the safe. I will do it for us.'

Jake smiled widely and kissed her again, this time with passion. 'Then we shall go! Tonight, my love?'

She hesitated a moment. This night? Could she do it? Could she turn her life on its head this very night? What had she to stay for? 'Tonight!' she said.

'Will it give you enough time? To pack a bag? To take the money?'

'Yes. I intend to travel light.'

'I shall meet you on the bridge then, by moonlight. What time?'

'Midnight,' she said and he kissed her again, so long and so slow, she thought she would melt.

It was the most romantic moment of her life. Nobody could feel this way and be wrong. It must be right.

They collected themselves and walked back, he to his lodgings to pack and she to Southover.

Margaret rushed up the stairs to her room and began packing feverishly. She looked around at all her precious possessions. She was surprised at how easy it was to leave much of it behind. She quietly selected the most valuable items from her collection. Anything small, easy to carry and valuable. They would need as much as she could take to start their new life. With each step she felt empowered and trembled with excitement. Taking one last look at the room that had been home all her life, Margaret said goodbye to it and found she had never felt so free. Lifting her bag she turned to leave, only to find herself facing Lucy. Her heart stuttered as she realised how quickly her new life could end.

'Lucy!'

'Miss . . . What . . . ?'

Margaret lunged forward and gripped Lucy's hand and pleaded with her, 'Oh, Lucy, you must not say a word. I'm eloping, escaping this cursed family and starting a new life.'

'But, miss, I—'

'Lucy, I'm begging you. I cannot stay here. It is this family, this house. I believe it is rotten to the core. This family is poison.'

Lucy stared at her again, that unblinking, direct stare.

'I believe you understand what I mean by that, Lucy. Is that true?'

Lucy continued to look and say nothing. Then, almost imperceptibly, she nodded.

'I thought you would. I know you have had some . . . trouble from my brother. Anny Woodvine and I were in the woods once, years ago. We saw him with you. We threw a rock to distract him. You got away.'

'You did that, miss?'

Margaret considered embroidering the truth, to show herself in a better light. But she said, 'No. It was not I. It was Anny. She was always like that. Always thinking of others . . . Oh, Lucy. Anny is in a terrible state. In that hellish place, the prison. And she has been so ill. When I went to her, to tell her about her father, she screamed at me. She cursed me.'

Margaret wanted to sob, but knew it was self-indulgence. It was Anny who had the right to weep, not her.

'It inna your fault, miss. What your father did. What your brother did. None of it is your fault.'

'That's kind of you, Lucy. But, you see, that's why I must go, before I end up like Anny, or worse, like my family. My only regret in leaving is that I cannot save Anny. Anny Woodvine never did a bad thing in her life. She is goodness itself. So brave and honest and true.'

'She is, right enough. Good people, the Woodvines.'

'Yes, good people. The opposite of my people. Mine are heartless. And cruel. I am sorry that I did not help you more. With Cyril. I am so sorry for that.'

Lucy looked at her feet. 'There was nothing you coulda done, miss. I know he hits you. We all live in fear of him.'

'But what he was doing to you that day, in the forest. It was unforgivable.'

Lucy still stared at her feet. She let out a long, heart-felt sigh, so affecting was it, that Margaret felt she must ask her, 'What is it, Lucy? Is there something you wish to tell me?'

'Oh, miss,' whispered Lucy.

'What is it, Lucy?'

'It was worse, much worse than that.'

'What is it?'

'My shame and my disgrace.'

Margaret felt a chill run up her spine. 'I am sure that is not true. Please, Lucy, sit beside me on the bed. Please, tell me.'

Lucy looked at the bed, as if considering the idea of sitting beside her mistress. But she did not. She did not lift her head but began to speak.

'When I was a young'un, I decided I was going to save myself for marriage, not even kiss a boy till I met the right one at church. And then I pictured he'd treat me right and we'd step out together. One day, he'd ask me very polite like and very respectful, if I'd be his wife. That was my dream. But that will never happen now. Not now Master Cyril has stuck his filthy thing in me all those times and then one time, he gave me a life growing inside of me.'

Margaret covered her mouth and shook her head.

Lucy went on. 'But the child died inside me. I lay in my attic room that winter night and it bled out all over the bed. Jenkins dealt with it and nobody was told. I had to wash out my own sheets. I could hardly stand up from the loss of it. The pain was summat terrible, both in my insides and in my heart. For I hated the child that grew inside me, put there without my saying so, without me wanting it. By that . . . that *monster* Cyril King.'

'Oh, Lucy,' Margaret whispered, tears coming now. 'I am . . .' But Lucy interrupted her. Lucy's story, that had started as a trickle of words, gushed out like a flood.

'But I loved it too, that child, for it was mine and part of me, and it was innocent, surely, as are all babes. And I would have loved it, if it had grown and come naturally, instead of weeping through like a bad monthly. Jenkins fished it out from the mess and took it away. I've always wanted to ask Jenkins what she did with the little thing. It would have been very tiny, as it was only a few weeks in. It might've been the size of a plum. Would it have had fingers and toes yet? Would it have had feelings or thinkings or memories? I sang to it as it bled out of me. I sang it the songs my mother had crooned to me when I was little, after we'd lost my father and the dark days began. The job here at the King house had come as a blessing, to help us survive in those difficult times. But I hadna been here long before I caught the whiff of evil in this house. I was only eleven when Cyril first grabbed me, sticking his tongue in my mouth on the servants' staircase. I didna know what was happening to me. I never told a soul. I had to keep this job. How I hated him, how I hated all of you, I'm sorry to say, miss. But I had to keep this job, for my mother. I had no choice.'

Lucy fell silent. Margaret tried to think of the right words to say next. But what could she possibly say, to this girl who had been so cruelly used by Margaret's own family? Nothing could make it better. Nothing could make it right. She could only stare at her own hands, wringing uselessly in her lap. Guilt-ridden hands, King hands, with the stain of Lucy's sacrifice all over them.

'I am so, so sorry, Lucy. I don't know how to . . . I don't know what . . .'

'Dunna fret, miss,' said Lucy, and though she still stared at the floor, she moved her hand and put it over Margaret's own. 'It never were your doing. It's that Master Cyril. It is his crime.'

'And not his only one.'

'That's right. Not his only one.'

Margaret looked at Lucy. 'I know something else he did, Lucy. Another crime. I told my father and my grandmother, but they have done nothing about it. I confronted him, but he did not care. My father threatened to send me to the asylum if I ever told a soul.' But she wanted to tell Lucy, very much. What harm would it do now, now she was running away to Paris?

'I know what it is, miss.'

'I don't think you do, Lucy. This is about Anny.'

'I know all about it. Everyone knew he was after Anny. When I found out, I was grateful at first, that he'd moved on from me to another girl. But I liked Anny, we all did. I thought she would escape him, though. She was cleverer than me. Then, that morning he came to the kitchen door, and he gave these orders to me and to Paddy, about her waiting in the library and suchlike. It was all very queer. I knew that look in his eye, when he was up to mischief. Like he enjoys cruel thoughts and cruel deeds. So I fetched Paddy and we followed him. Very quiet like. We followed him to the office and we hid in the woods. Then we saw him go in. So we crept up to the window of Mr B's room and we watched him.

He took the money out of the safe. We crept around the office, ever so light-footed. We looked in the other window. We saw him messing about in Anny's drawer. He took her bag out. He put the money in.'

Margaret's eyes fairly popped. 'You saw the whole thing? Why did you not come forward?'

Lucy glared at Margaret. 'Do you think I am a fool because I am not your equal?'

Margaret hurriedly shook her head. 'Oh no, no. I would never think that.'

'Then you mun know, miss, that it would do no good. Who would believe us, a maid and a stable boy? Who would even listen? And we would lose our jobs.'

'Yes, of course. You are right. I am sorry, Lucy.'

'It was awful, though. To see Anny taken away and locked up. And then her father gone. I know what it is like to lose a father and I feel sorrowful for Anny in a heartfelt way for that. I admired her, too. To come from that low place in life and work her way up like that. I feel dreadful about it all. Anny dunna deserve that, nobody good does. Master Cyril mun pay for what he did. But he never will. And Anny will be sent away across the ocean. Or hanged. It is the way of things. When my baby perished, I knew it was his fault, but I felt bad for it too, that it was *my* fault it died, by letting it slip out of me. It's like being careless, to lose hold of a child so easy, though I fought to save it, praying all the night through, that terrible night. Did it go to Heaven, my tiny babby's soul?

Surely it would, surely the Lord could not turn away such a small, innocent thing, despite the sins of the father and even those of the mother, myself. I felt a part of the fault, by working for this family, by staying on after Cyril's ruin of me, for swallowing up my guilt and pretending nothing had happened. But I told you afore, miss, these are the hard choices of the poor. I did my best to save my babby but it died anyway. I did my best for it. That will have to be enough on Judgement Day.'

Oh, the courage of this young woman. She was looking at Margaret that way again, that clear-eyed, honest stare. No tears now. They had all been shed many moons ago, she guessed. Lucy Arnett's fortitude shamed Margaret. Listening to her story, hearing those words of pain and survival changed Margaret forever. Something clicked in her head, a cog slotting into place, set in motion. 'No,' she said. 'No. We will not allow this.'

'We dunna have no choice.'

'Yes, yes, we do.' Her mind was moving fast now, possibility rushing like water over the wheel. 'Lucy, listen to me. You've said this to me before, that there is no chance for change, that this is the way the world works. Well, what if it didn't have to be that way? What if we could try, just one time, to change things? To make things better for everyone who counts? For Anny and for you. What would you say to that?'

'I would say they'd have me guts for garters.'

'Have faith, Lucy. If it fails, I shall give you money anyway. I shall leave it for you here, secretly, hidden in my room.'

'If what fails? What money? Are you mad, miss?'

Margaret lifted her head up. 'No. I am not. Now, listen carefully. For we are going to fix this. I have nothing to lose, as I am away this very night. And whatever happens, I promise that you will be free of this place. We are going to make that change and make things right. Do you believe me, Lucy? Do you trust me?'

Lucy narrowed her eyes at Margaret. 'Dunna go all round the Wrekin. Stop blethering and tell me. What's yer plan?'

Chapter 24

Queenie sat in her favourite chair in the drawing room. Her son Ralph sat opposite her, reading an illustrated paper of some sort, something cheap and thrilling, no doubt. He had not the wit to read books. Every so often, he would snort with amusement. Queenie watched him with her usual distaste. What a lonely thing it was to dislike your own child. Nobody understood, nobody except Jenkins. Ah, Jenkins. Her only confidante. If Jenkins ever left her . . . The thought was too much to bear! But Queenie was worried. There was talk in the house, gossip amongst the servants of how the Kings were responsible for the explosion. Queenie felt the danger of a great scandal unfolding and she smarted at this. She knew there would be plenty around these parts who would love to see the Kings in disarray. It was satisfying to the envious poor. The poor around these parts had suffered, indeed they had. But didn't the poor always suffer? Now the rich were getting some of it too. And nobody deserved to suffer more than this family, some may be saying. She knew her useless son would mismanage it, as always. She needed to keep her wits about her and step in. Something needed to be done, and soon. Reparation must be made, swiftly, to the affected families, the ones with dead and injured men and boys. There must be some sort of grand gathering, a service to honour the lives lost. She should meet with Brotherton and Pritchard on the morrow, to arrange these things and to talk about the future of the iron-works, now production at the furnace had been halted. The accounts must be scrutinised, money rerouted to other parts of the operation, new revenues of cash flow must be sought out. She had seen her son running about like a headless chicken, trying to solve the mess, but nothing had been decided, nothing achieved. It was her turn now. This could bring them down, destroy not only their reputation but the business itself.

The stark, bright image of Blaize's ghost appeared in her mind and gave her a chill. The curse would come true, if they weren't careful. This was just the kind of thing that destroyed good families. Well, not on her watch. Nothing must be allowed to threaten the King family reputation. Everything from then on must be about the limitation of the damage, stemming the flow and rebuilding their defences. The fortress of the Kings must not fall.

The drawing room door opened. Queenie did not look round, as she assumed it was Benjamina joining them – that indolent, lazy strumpet. But there was not the whiff of Benjamina's sickly perfume. Instead, two sets of footsteps came across the hard floor and onto the rug before her. There stood Margaret and another figure, one of the maids. Queenie had heard that Margaret had been to Shrewsbury again that day. The last time she took the barouche without asking, all hell broke loose, but her son was so preoccupied with his own troubles these days, he barely noticed what the girl was up to. Queenie had noticed, though, and had made her mind up to call her granddaughter in the following day and discuss these reckless trips to Shrewsbury to see the Woodvine girl. All right, the girl's father had been killed and that couldn't be helped. But it was not seemly for the King daughter to be involved any more than was necessary. That was something else on her list: take Margaret in hand. The child needed a husband, and soon.

Ralph looked up, peeved to be interrupted. 'What is this?'

Margaret spoke first, the servant girl standing with her hands clasped behind her back, eyes down. Queenie felt unsettled. Something was not right here.

'Grandmother, Father, I must speak with you both.'

'Arnett, is it?' said Queenie, fixing her eye on the servant girl. She was always good with servants' names, prided herself on it.

The girl looked up, not wide-eyed and fearful as Queenie expected, but she looked straight at her, direct and steady. 'Yes, ma'am.'

'What is the meaning of this?' spluttered Ralph.

'It concerns Cyril,' said Margaret. 'I have approached you both before to voice my concerns about my brother's behaviour. I have told you both that I was convinced of Cyril's guilt in the matter of the theft of money from the safe. But my concerns were dismissed and Anny Woodvine remains imprisoned for a crime she did not commit.'

'This again,' said Ralph in a low, threatening voice. Queenie saw her son's hackles rise. Would he strike the girl? Possibly not in front of a servant. This was something the King men liked to imagine was done in private, though word always got around. But whatever Margaret had suffered from her father in the past, it did not stop her now. Queenie saw her turn her gaze on her father, unintimidated and determined.

'Yes, this again, Father. But now we have a witness. Lucy Arnett, a maidservant of this household who has served us faithfully for many years. She has something to impart to you both. And I urge you to listen to what she has to say.'

'Get out,' said Ralph simply, placing his reading material on the settee beside him, looking about ready to leap up and box both their ears.

'No,' said Queenie. Ralph glared at her. 'Let them speak. I am curious.'

'The very idea . . .' began Ralph.

'They will be heard. In these trying times, the whole community in mourning, never let it be said that the

Kings do not listen to reason, that we are too far above the common fray to at least let them be heard. Proceed, Arnett. Tell us what you wish to say.'

Ralph puffed and shuffled in his seat, his anger barely contained. But Queenie could see that he was caught in the trap of having to appease the neighbourhood, and this servant girl was one of theirs, so he had to resist, for appearances' sake. 'Arnett, go on. Say your piece.'

The girl had her wary eye on Ralph, her body stiff with tension. She turned to Queenie, and there came that clear look again. She began to speak, no hint of a wobble in her voice. Queenie was convinced in that moment that anything this girl had to say was the truth, no doubt whatsoever.

'On the day that Anny Woodvine was arrested, Master Cyril sent for me. This was first thing in the morning. He told me to take a message to Mr Brotherton, that he should go to town for ink. He said the message had come from Mrs King senior. From yourself, ma'am.'

'Did he now?' said Queenie. What a fool Cyril was, involving her. Anyone in the household would know she would never send Cyril to do such a thing. Why would she need that idiot boy, when she had Jenkins?

'Yes, he did, ma'am. He surely did. He said to make sure that Mr Brotherton himself was sent to town to fetch the ink, green ink, for you, ma'am. Then he said, very certain like, that I was not to tell anyone that it was him that gave me the message. That if I was ever asked about it, I shouldna mention his name and I should say that Mrs – that is, you, ma'am – were the one that gave me the message for Mr Brotherton. Well, I did as I was asked and delivered the message. Then, the stable boy, Paddy, came to see me soon after. He was worried about summat. He said Master Cyril had been to see him earlier, had told him to take a message to the office, that Anny Woodvine must go to the library and wait on you, sir.'

Queenie was even more impressed with Arnett, now that she had had the nerve to address Ralph directly, despite his barely contained rage. She liked this girl. She liked any girl with spirit.

Arnett continued, 'Paddy was worried because he knew you were out all that day, sir, because he'd seen you go himself, up before the larks. He liked Anny, did Paddy, and he didna want to think of her alone in the library waiting for you, sir, when you were never going to come. Well, not till hours away, leastways. I told him not to interfere with family business and get on with his job. But after, I went back into the house and I saw Master Cyril go into your study, sir, and he came out holding your keys, sir, and he went off towards the office. Why would Master Cyril do all this? Why did he send those messages from you, ma'am, and from you, sir, that were not true? And why would he take the keys to the office from your room, sir? Why would he do all that?'

'You were spying on my grandson, then?' said Queenie.

'Servants dunna need to spy, when things are done before their very eyes. Servants are invisible to gentlefolk sometimes, so they say. But we do see things, ma'am, sir. We see things and we know things.'

This last statement hung heavy in the air like cigar smoke. Arnett waited. King, red-faced, looked at Queenie.

Margaret said, 'Go on, Lucy. Tell them what happened next.'

'So, Paddy and I, we were worried about what it all meant. We were suspicious. You must forgive us our cheek but we thought we should follow him, follow Master Cyril and see what he was about. So we did. We crept behind and saw him. He went into the office. We peeked through the windows. He took the money from the safe and he put it in Anny Woodvine's bag. Paddy and I saw him do it, clear as day.'

Queenie said, 'And why did you not speak up before now? If this were true, you should have said something before the Woodvine girl was taken away. Why have you waited so long for the truth to be shared, if it is indeed the truth and not some tale of your own devising?'

Queenie was bluffing. She had not one shred of doubt that the girl was speaking plainly. Margaret answered for her: 'I have encouraged her to speak out now but I'm sure we all know that, without my support in this matter, it is a universal truth that servants are not listened to. That they fear being dismissed over any hint of disloyalty to their masters. Lucy did not say anything about this before as she feared losing her job. She cannot afford to do so, as she has a widowed mother to support.'

Ralph spluttered, 'The perfect excuse for blackmail then, this sob story about her poor mother! Throwing false accusations of theft at my son!'

'It is not false. And he has done worse than theft,' said Arnett. The courage of the girl! Queenie was eager to hear more from her, but a creeping sense of unease caused her to shiver. What more was there? What else had she to tell of Cyril King?

Margaret placed her hand tenderly on Arnett's arm. 'Shall I . . . ?' Margaret began. For the first time, Arnett appeared to falter. She blinked rapidly and looked down at her shoes. She nodded.

Margaret said bluntly, 'Cyril raped Lucy. Many times. He gave her a child. The child died . . . before birth . . . and the whole thing was covered up by Jenkins.'

Jenkins? What had Jenkins to do with this? Queenie was certain Jenkins would have told her of such a thing. But now she regarded this girl, who had raised her head and was looking now at Margaret, her eyes steady again, her back straight. She knew it was true. She knew that Jenkins had hidden it from her to protect her. Queenie felt sickened. Another girl's life ruined. Another hateful crime perpetrated by the King men.

'This is slander of the worst . . .'

'Shut up, Ralph.'

'There is no proof of this!' he cried. 'Just the word of a common slut below stairs!'

Margaret stepped forward towards her father and pointed at him. 'You are wrong. There are many in this house that know this to be true. Paddy the stable boy saw Cyril take the money. And Jenkins, Grandmother's own trusted lady's maid cleared up the bloody remains of this girl's dead child, of your son's dead child. When will you stop protecting him, when you know him to be rotten to the core?'

Ralph cried, 'Never! I will never stop protecting my only son!'

Queenie saw the situation getting out of hand. 'Now then, we must remain calm.' But Margaret was not listening.

'And that is your greatest failing. Cyril is rotten through and through. But even if you cannot see that, know this: if word of this gets out, this family's name will be mud. The explosion at the furnace already has our reputation in tatters. The careless death of our men is already a disaster for investors and clients. And I know you were responsible. You knowingly used materials that were inferior and were sure to lead to an accident. It was only a matter of time. And if the truth comes out of Cyril as a thief, a liar and a rapist, our name will be destroyed. Cyril King is this family's heir. He must make a good marriage and produce his own heir. What decent family in their right mind would willingly offer a large dowry and wed their daughter to Cyril King, with stories like this on everyone's lips? Bad blood, they will say. Those Kings have bad blood. We all know this family has a history of abusing young women, and it is only a matter of time before more secrets come out. And the name of King will always be spat out, like a bitter taste on the tongue. If you do nothing to remedy this, you, Father and you, Grandmother, then you leave us with no choice. We will speak the truth, far and wide. And make no mistake. This house will fall!'

Those four words shocked Queenie rigid. She felt her body seize up, pinning her to her seat. How did Margaret know of this? Had the ghost visited her too? But she could see that the child was not looking knowingly at her. She was incensed with a hatred of her father, her brother, of all the Kings. Margaret had turned. She would not care if her name were ruined, if indeed the house and everything in it fell to the ground. She would never give up on this and her determination alone would ruin their name, if the truth did not do it by itself. If Queenie dismissed these children and their threats, the curse of Betsy Blaize would come to pass.

'I never thought I'd . . .' began Ralph, too stupid even now to see how close they all were to ruin.

'Silence!' Queenie cried, her strength mustered and returning admirably, now, when she needed it. Her son stopped. He might make a noise about being the master, but everyone knew it was Queenie who ruled this roost. 'There will be no more argument. It is clear now how things proceeded. You, Arnett. I suspect you do not want to stay in this house, but of course you will be in need of employment. I will write you an excellent reference, but it will be best for all if you leave our employ as soon as you are able. I will give you three months' wages and a bonus, if you will leave tonight and never mention any detail of this again.'

The maid looked her in the eye and nodded. 'Agreed.'

'Good,' said Queenie and turned away.

'On one condition,' said Arnett.

'You are in no position . . .' began Queenie.

But the maid interrupted her. 'That they let Anny Woodvine go. You can do that, sir, ma'am. I know if you drop those charges against her, they'll set her free. That's my condition.'

'And mine, too,' added Margaret. 'Anny must be released. If you drop the charges, Father, and Anny is freed, with no stain about her name, and if Lucy is given a good reference and the wages you suggest, Grandmother, then and only then will we keep our silence about these crimes of Cyril. We shall never speak of them more.'

Queenie smiled at Margaret with begrudging admiration. Despite her distasteful threats, Queenie was pleased her granddaughter was coming into her own, at last. She wondered what the girl would do with this new-found confidence. Ralph clearly did not feel the same way about his daughter. He huffed, threw his hands up in the air, then folded his arms tightly. He had lost his voice all of a sudden, but let out a kind of frustrated whine. What a wretched man he was. But no matter. It was the old sow who would make this decision, not the squealing piglet.

'It shall be done,' said Queenie. 'You are dismissed, both of you.'

Her granddaughter was grinning at Arnett. Was this all a game to her? True, she was proud of Margaret for finding her backbone, but the girl had turned traitor to her own family. God knows Queenie had hated the Kings at times over the years, but never had she been a turncoat. There were rules about such things. These young ones these days had no sense of duty or honour. But these two had the Kings in a pickle and a deal had to be done. Margaret and Arnett left the room. She heard them talk excitedly outside. She never thought she'd live to see the day when servants and family plotted together and crowed about it. All except her and Jenkins, of course. They had their own rules.

'Mother, this is a travesty. How can you support such lies?'

'So, now you speak. Once the children are gone.'

'I would not deign to argue like fishwives before them. But now you and I will have this out. What can you be thinking, giving in to their demands? It's a disgrace! Never in all his years would Father have accepted such a thing.'

Queenie looked at her son and heard his wheedling voice, as she might watch a fly buzzing against a window, aware of its struggle but having no pity for it, just annoyance at its noise.

She said simply, 'We will agree to it. They are not lies, as well you know.'

'We do not know that.'

Queenie sighed. She had no time for nonsense. 'Cyril is capable of all this and far worse. Let us not pretend, not to each other. And the girl is right. The scandal of it all coming out would ruin us, coming after the monumental mess you made at the furnace.'

'That was an accident! How many times do I . . .'

'Do not pretend with me, my son. It is your mother who listens to your pathetic protestations. All of this is your fault. Penny-pinching and lack of forethought. Spoiling that wretched boy and not attending to his rotten behaviour earlier. Yet the fault lies not only at your door. I blame myself, too. I should have been more vigilant. I have not been myself these past years. But all that will change now. I am taking control again.'

Ralph stood up and loomed over her. But even this physical show of strength had no impact on her. She saw him only as he once was, red-faced in short trousers, throwing himself on the floor in a tantrum. 'You are not yourself!' he spat at her. 'You are quite right. You have lost your mind. And if you insist on allowing those two little sluts to blackmail us, I'll send you away. I will denounce you, you and your traitorous granddaughter. You're all the same. Just like your crazy sister.'

Queenie had heard such threats before. But she had her own plan now for how to waylay that one. 'Oh, you could try, Ralph King. You could try. But first, consider this. Not only would your mother and daughter be denouncing your lying, thieving, raping son. They would then be tainted with the poison of madness. Who would marry into the King family then?'

'I don't need you or them, any of you! I have a new, young wife who adores me!'

'Ha!' crowed Queenie. 'Your weakest strike yet. Everyone knows Benjamina does not allow you to bed her these days. Even if you did manage to breed, it would still have tainted blood if this all comes out.'

Queenie thought her son might strike her then. His cheeks, always a little purplish due to his debauched state of health, seemed to darken further, as did his hateful eyes. But he said nothing. He had nothing to say. Everything she said was true.

'And furthermore, if you threaten me again with the asylum, never forget that I have the controlling interest in the business and of this house. And I will sell. I will sell my percentage of the ironworks and I will even sell Southover if I have to. I will do so and go to live abroad, alone.'

Ralph's chin actually dropped. He hadn't seen that one coming. 'And you know how useless you are at managing this business. You would never manage with a new partner, who would see through your incompetence in a flash. And the thought of you trailing behind me and coming to live abroad is ridiculous. You are not an adventurous man, Ralph. You never have been. Always lazy, always useless. A life of indolence and luxury is all you are fit for.'

He was staring at the floor now, his eyes dazed. He muttered, 'Because of you. If I am a useless son, then it is your fault. You are the mother. You should have loved me more.'

Was there a tear in his eye? This gave Queenie pause, but only momentarily. Ralph King senior had taught her the value of a heart of stone. 'Love did not make us rich. Love did not raise the Kings above all others in Ironbridge and its environs. Your father knew that. I know it. And so do you. Look at your children. They hate you. Everyone does. But it is no matter. The business remains, the money remains and the name of King remains. You cannot manage without me. You never have. This latest disaster is proof of it. You can't pass it on to your son either, as he is as bad as you – worse, if that's possible.

No, you need me to run this for you, or you will drive this business into the ground. My mourning period for your father is done. I am coming back to take over the business. I am stronger than ever. I will not require anything of you other than to behave yourself and spend our money, when I give it to you. Cyril must be left in Germany until all whispers of this scandal have passed. Margaret must be taken in hand and married off as soon as we are able. Now, all you need to do is inform the magistrate that you wish to withdraw the charge of theft against Anny Woodvine. Do it immediately and insist it be acted upon with haste. Now go.'

Ralph had nothing left to fight with, no words to use as weapons. He was a fool at times, but he knew when he was beaten. He summoned as much dignity as he could to stand and then said pompously, 'I shall inform the magistrate that I wish to withdraw the charge of theft against Anny Woodvine,' as if it were his own idea, all along. With that, he walked sedately from the room.

Queenie's head fell forward. She felt utterly shattered. She would call for dear Jenkins in a minute, but not yet. She did not want her son to see her in need. She had to appear fearless now. But she was not fearless. She looked at her hands to see them trembling. She thought, *Is it enough?* Would paying off Cyril's victim and saving this poor girl from prison be enough? From now on, every act must serve to save the name of King and to atone for their past sins. She congratulated herself for taking control of this latest drama. Every decision she made must serve the aim to prevent the fall of the house of King. But still Queenie wondered. The image of the white-haired spirit beside her husband's grave sprang up in her weary mind. *Would it be enough to appease the ghost of Betsy Blaize?*

Chapter 25

Margaret and Jake were married a day after they had arrived in Paris, in a shabby little church with strangers for witnesses. Their honeymoon was a stay in a mangy hotel for a few nights. He quickly found them an apartment owned by a musician friend of his who was off travelling: two rooms, above a butcher's. They had so little, but Margaret had never been happier. And Paris, beautiful Paris, its thronging streets alive with liberty, did not disappoint. Their early days were spent together, in and out of cafés and bistros, sipping bowls of coffee and chocolate, feasting on sweet, sticky pastries and crusty bread spread thickly with apricot jam or honey. They ate tiny sardines in oil mashed onto toasted bread, chicken in a rich red sauce or beef with tiny onions and whole cloves of the stinking yet succulent garlic. The Kings kept a good table, but the food of Paris was a riot of taste and colour like nothing she'd ever consumed before. Her days were spent walking and kissing and eating, her evenings spent in more feasting and drinking with his artist friends, she sipping the local wine, careful with the quantity, as she was not used to it. But Jake and his friends guzzled it down nightly, until they could barely walk. To trip along a dark Paris street long after midnight and giggle herself hoarse at the antics of Jake and his drunken friends – what larks! Never had she laughed so much in her life!

Those who were still not too far gone would come back to their little room, or they would go to friends' apartments and chat and read till the dawn chorus brought her to the window to see the pink light of day seeping into the dark skies. One of Jake's friends loved to read and Margaret scoured his bookshelves, taking down favourite French novels she had read and discussing them with him. Sometimes she spoke in French, soon realising her language was a little bookish and rusty. They laughed at her, but good-naturedly, as at least she tried. Jake's French was hopeless and they appreciated her making the effort. She quickly learnt some of the new street lingo and felt more at home in the language as the days and nights passed. Another friend had a piano in his room and Margaret delighted them with Mozart and Beethoven, as much as her fingers could remember through the fog of memory and wine. She was a good player and many said so, that she should perform, that she should teach them, or their sisters, or their children, or the children of friends and family. It occurred to her that this could be a way for her to support Jake, to give lessons and charge for it. To earn her own money would be quite something – utter freedom! As she played, she became lost in the music and delighted with her talent, now properly appreciated. They applauded her and asked for more; they laughed with her and talked to her. For the first time in her life, she felt at home in society. There was no small talk, only discussions of literature, art and music. She was a small-town girl come to the big city, yet still she held her own in these talks, citing books she had read and music she loved. She listened to their knowledge of painting and sculpture, drinking it all in, learning new ideas from them as a child gulps milk. At Southover, she had grown up in an icy, loveless existence consisting of confinement and bullying. Now she was bathing in the warmth of Paris, her whims indulged and satisfied, her voice heard and answered, her thoughts echoed and delighted in. She had found a place where she belonged.

Jake and Margaret were quite the couple, celebrated as the romantic duo who had escaped their families' old-fashioned expectations and eloped to Paris. They were welcomed everywhere and kissed on both cheeks, hugged and sang to, spoken about and spoken to, every day and night. The Margaret of her childhood would have run in horror from such extremes of companionship, but she revelled in it. And then there was Jake. Kissing had seemed the height of glory, until she had felt him inside her, truly inside her and the feeling of completeness was so overwhelming, she often cried real tears during their lovemaking. She felt life would be like this forever, an endless whirl of bed and parties, wine and laughter. It was intoxicating, unsettling and sometimes scarily out of control, but it was so utterly different from her previous life as to be as addictive as opium.

But the months passed, and sex, parties and wine couldn't make up for the increasing hollowness in the rest of their life together. There was no purpose or direction to their existence. Only chaos prevailed. And she felt Jake was drawing away from her. He began to go out alone much of the time, armed with his sketching book and pencils. She found herself walking the streets looking for greenery, a park or a stream, or even a tree, but there was precious little of it in this part of the city. He would come back hours later, often drunk, often denying it, saying how the muse had left him, shouting about it and throwing himself down in despair. She tried to comfort him, but he was inconsolable. He said the muse had abandoned him, ever since . . . but he wouldn't finish those sentences and she knew he meant ever since the elopement. It racked her with remorse, that through her desire to possess him, she was robbing him of his gift. To assuage her guilt, she would give him money from the roll of cash she had in a stocking hidden in a drawer, and he would disappear again for hours. The night she ran away from Ironbridge, she had stolen the money from her father's safe. It seemed a vast amount – and appeared to double in size when it was changed into French currency – and she was certain it would last them for years, that they would live the high life until Jake's undoubted talent would catch the eye of a Parisian gallery owner and his artistic career would be made. But he seemed to be spending most of it on drink. And the money was running out so quickly, too quickly. She knew he was taking from it when she wasn't looking. She knew he was spending it on drinking, and who knew what else.

In the long evenings she spent alone, when he had not come home at all since lunchtime, she would think of the library back home – why had she not brought any English books with her? She missed the sight of her own language on the page. She would think of the woods and the River Severn – why did the city feel like death to her, when home had been so full of life, of living things all around her? She even missed the sound of the steam hammer, booming through the trees, marking out time, to be replaced here by the clattering of coaches and hooves, the shouts of street sellers and arguing couples – exotic and exciting at first, harsh and jangling now.

When he did take her out with his friends, she tired of the constant drinking and began to stop after a glass. But Jake showed no signs of abatement and, if anything, drank more than before. And Jake was not a jovial drunk. His artist friends – who she now began to see in a new light, a ramshackle lot, all come to France to waste away their talent through strong drink and carousing – began to warn her about him. Night after night, one or other would come to her laughing, saying colourful and unsettling things about him, such as, 'You've bagged yourself a blackguard there, Miss Margaret', and 'Don't try to cage him like an animal. He'll tear your throat out.'

Then, only three months after their arrival, she had stopped bleeding. She was vomiting each morning and felt drained all day. It was Jake who explained it to her. She was with child. She felt so woefully uneducated and unprepared. She stopped drinking wine as it made her feel worse. Suddenly, without the drink to fog her mind, she saw her life for what it was. And she did not like it.

Chapter 26

Anny's father had walked these miles between Shrewsbury and Ironbridge in one morning. But he had been strong as an ox and tall as a tree. Anny was weakened by her months inside and the minimal rations. The gaol fever that had floored her for weeks was gone, but that had taken a lot out of her too. She used to bound up the forest paths with an innate knowledge of how strong her young legs were, how far they'd take her. She remembered feeling invincible, that she would never tire, never falter, never die even. The folly of youth, that they think they shall live forever. One bad turn of circumstance and the body crumbles. It was frightening how quickly that could happen. She had been a little plump once, a curve to her hips and limbs that was pleasing to the male eye, though she'd sometimes wished to be more svelte and slim like some girls. Now the flesh had dropped from her body and she was skin and bone. It was November, and it was cold. Her body gave her no comfort and she shivered as she walked.

Leaving the prison had been nothing like Anny had imagined. No family to greet her, no friends to ferry her home. The prison warden hadn't let her leave till the afternoon and her progress on the road to Ironbridge was slow. She had little natural sense of direction and had to wait around for passers-by to ask at various junctions of roads if she were on the right path. She had a vision of wandering around in circles for the rest of her life, until she dropped in exhaustion. It was good to be outside, though. She'd rather die on the road than in that vermin-infested hospital. A man died in there one night and the surgeon didn't come till morning and the rats were already on him by the time they came to take the body away. The smell was still in her nostrils, the rich and heady variety of prison stench. She wondered if she'd ever lose it. As she walked, slowly, she breathed deeply, taking in the scents of fresh, new air, winter greenery and earth.

People used to delight her. She had once loved to be in crowded places, like the fair at Christmastime or the May Day dancing, surrounded by the excitement of new faces and the buzz of humanity. Now, people disgusted her. She had seen bodies and minds at their most degraded. Peggy had told her once of a book about a man who travelled to foreign lands and met giants and midgets and also intelligent horses who had people as beasts roaming around on all fours. That writer must have been inside a gaol. Thoughts of Peggy. Yes, well, she did not wish to think of Peggy.

She'd had no word from home since that day. She'd not heard from Peggy or Brotherton – not surprising, but still. Nothing from Jake, of course. Most worryingly, nothing from Mother. It had been four months since her father's death. Two months since she had been called into the warden's office and informed that the charges had been dropped and she would soon leave. She had told no one. She'd heard of prisoners bragging about release and then being beaten or even murdered by inmates or guards, as a kind of revenge and punishment, as if to say, *You're not getting away that lightly; you must suffer, as we do.* She kept it quiet. Instead she lived as much inside her own head as she could, in a time before all pain, where she washed clothes with her mother and ran to take her father's lunch. That was when it all started, with Mr Lakelin's death. If she'd not written a note to her father, Pritchard would not have noticed how clever she was. She should have refused Pritchard's request, should have said no to Brotherton, should have stayed at home with Mother. Everything would have been different, everything would have been better, if she hadn't got ideas above her station. It was all her fault. Well, she'd learnt her lesson. As she trudged along the road home, she knew her life would not aspire to be anything more than it was. That way pain and madness lay.

She had to sleep on the roadside that night. She had no food, no money. She asked the guard at the gate about her earnings while she'd been in prison, her promised earnings of a penny a week for this or that duty, more for her washing work and her role as monitor. He laughed at her. She was packed off in someone else's shabby dress, too short, halfway up the leg and too tight under the arms. No bonnet. A tatty shawl with holes in it. She looked like a ragamuffin. Her smart work clothes she'd been brought in wearing had gone, probably sold on by the guards. Her boots pinched and by nightfall she had red raw skin where her heels should have been. She found a quiet road with woodland running along it on one side, fields on the other. She went behind a little copse of trees, so that she could not be seen from the road. She didn't want any unwelcome attention from travellers. It was a bitter night. She did not sleep. Her body was racked with quaking.

When dawn came thinly, she pulled her boots back on and cried out at the blisters. The sky above was luminous, a bright yellow-grey that promised snow. The wind whipped up. There were few people on the roads. All sensible folk were inside. Carriages rumbled past and she barely looked up. She had to keep going, keep going, keep going. She had to get home. Snow began falling; bright flecks of ice lashed by the wind into her face, hair, eyelashes, sticky and wet. She was afraid, very afraid her body would not hold out and she would collapse there, in the deepening snow and simply die, a few miles from home. To come so far, to be so near. No, no, that would not be her fate. She willed herself onwards and banished all thought but the movement forward, onwards, home. One foot before the other. Her whole existence was reduced to her feet.

It was the afternoon of the second day when she saw the iron bridge. She did not turn and look up at the King house. She went down the slippery steps to the riverside and stumbled, nearly falling into the high, broad river. It had not frozen over yet, though it might if this cold grew and lasted the winter through. The water was churning beneath the roiling blizzard, confusing her eye with its complex movement. She felt she might faint, but she closed her eyes and recovered herself. Then she forced herself onwards. So close now, so close. Her collection of houses came into view and she saw her parents' cottage and cried out with relief, sobbing and muttering as she approached. The door was shut against the cold and she fell against it, banging with her fist.

'Mother,' she cried. 'Mother, Mother!'

Anny had slumped to the ground and fell inwards as the door opened.

'Mother,' she whispered, but when she looked up, there was a man with a big black moustache staring at her.

'Get away with yer!' he said.

'Mother,' she whispered again. She heard voices from inside the house. They were asking who it was.

'Some vagabond. There's nothing for you here. Get away with yer, I say,' said the man and began to shove her from the door.

'Anny?' A different voice came from behind her, away from the house. 'Is that you, Anny?'

Her name. She had not heard her name spoken in so long. At the prison, they called her Woodvine or Theft or worse, much worse. The door to her parents' house was shoved shut against her and she turned deliriously in the direction of the voice.

'Bless my soul, it's Anny Woodvine,' it said. It was a woman's voice. 'Peter, Peter! Come quickly! It's Rachel's daughter.'

There were arms about her, strong male arms and the whiff of coal dust. She was lifted from the ground and felt her head falling backwards over an arm, the snowflakes rushing into her face, into her mouth and landing on her tongue. The rest was a blur that melted into sleep, a restless sleep filled with nightmares of falling through ice into the river, being swept along by the current and banging her fists in vain upon its frozen ceiling, watching the white sky looking down upon her as she drowned.

She awoke in a bed, tucked up in sheets and blankets. Her eyes were crusted with the sleep of many days. Her feet were bound with bandages. Her filthy dress was gone and she was clothed in a cosy, long-sleeved nightdress of soft material. Her hair was clean and smelled of soap. Was this heaven? It felt like heaven. Warmth and comfort. It was evening or night-time, the room flickering with candlelight. She had a dim memory of being sat up and liquid being spooned into her mouth. Was that a dream?

'Anny,' came a voice, the same voice she'd heard at her mother's door.

'Where is my mother?' she said, her voice croaky through disuse.

A face came into view, an older face, about the same age as her mother, but not her mother.

'Dunna fret, lass,' said the woman and smiled. She sat down on the bed and passed her cool, dry hand over Anny's forehead.

'Is my mother dead?' said Anny. The moment she said it, she realised that had been her greatest fear, lying beneath the surface as she slept.

'No, lass! No, she's all right. But she dunna live here no more.'

Anny focused her eyes on the woman's face. 'I know you,' she said.

'I know you do, lass. I'm your neighbour. You remember my son, dunna you?'

Another face appeared, standing tall above the bed. It was a local lad who'd tried to woo her once, many moons ago. He smiled at her. It was a kind face. Two kind faces.

'Mrs Mary Malone,' said Anny. 'And Peter Malone.'

Anny did not have the strength to say more. Seeing the faces of their old neighbours had the most peculiar effect on her; she felt as if she were tumbling down a hole, a dark, earthy descent into her childhood. When she landed, she curled up in a hollow, snug and warm and content. Her eyes glazed over and closed. She drifted into a deep sleep. Safe, at last.

Chapter 27

They called it the quickening, that odd fluttering sensation when the unborn child could first be felt inside the mother. Margaret had read that in a novel once and loved the term. The idea that the woman was quick with child, that it was making its presence known. It began for her on a quiet Sunday morning. She was lying on the hard, rough cot they slept in below the small, high window, the only window in the room. If she stood up on the bed and peeked out of the window, she could look out across the grey roofs, chimneys, skylights and domes of Paris, stretching out as a jumbled vista that seemed romantic at first, oppressive now. Jake was sprawled out on the floor, not having made it to the bed the night before. She looked across at him. Even snoring open-mouthed, his hair greasy with sweat and plastered across his face, she still felt the old desire lift in her. But something else was there, deep down inside and it wasn't calling for him. It was the quickening.

'Oh, my life!' she said aloud, then checked herself, as she did not wish to wake her husband.

They'd had a fearful row the night before. It wasn't the first.

Looking back on the past few months, she realised the cracks had begun to show from the earliest days, though she had chosen to ignore them. On the journey across the channel he thought of his own comfort before hers in every regard and she allowed him to, feeling comfort in comforting him. She overlooked his selfishness in a hundred tiny ways every day, but once she was with child, her feelings on this changed. Jake was still her world, but there was a newcomer there. And as the life grew inside her, her thoughts were filled with her baby and not with her husband. He was annoyed that she was not obsessing over him anymore. He would pout and say she did not love him. She would throw her arms about him and kiss him and kiss him, asking how could he say such things, when she waited for him every day impatient for his company. This he would take offence at, saying she was trying to trap him and must he stay there every day to hear her nonsense and not be off living life, painting life, as he ought to be? She would caress his hair and try to calm him, tell him how talented and clever he was, and he would be assuaged, sometimes. But there was truly no pleasing him.

So it went on, these endless squabbles about how hard his life was, how little she understood him, how selfish she was. He began to shrink in stature before her very eyes. The morning she felt the quickening, she lay and watched him sleep for hours. The night before had been their worst row yet. Some horrible home truths had come out. She had accused him of taking her money too much, too often and what were they to do when it ran out? What about things for the baby, and what about their future?

The conversation was still fresh in her mind, the wounds it inflicted still felt in her heart.

'Our future is taken care of,' said Jake dismissively, taking another gulp of wine.

Did he mean his art? She had not seen him do a painting since they'd arrived, and his sketches were few and far between these days. He had never sold a picture, in all the time she'd known him.

'In what way?' she asked, carefully, not wishing to anger him.

'We will return to your father's house, of course. With a child in your belly, all will be forgiven and we shall live in style in Shropshire. I have in mind a little gallery in the town. I met a fellow in Ironbridge who loved the idea. We'll need your father's capital to set it up. I'm just waiting for you to get a bit fatter and then we'll go.'

'But . . . I stole from my father. All that money. He'll never forgive me.'

'Oh, yes he will. He just needs to see with his own eyes the condition you're in. What with the marriage certificate and my gift of the gab and your poor little victim act, that'll sway him. Then once your family are in the bag, I shall present you – ripe belly and King fortune – to my father and he shall welcome me as the prodigal son. We shall have his blessing and money, too. It'll all work out, you'll see.'

Margaret was horrified. 'But I do not wish to return to my family. I hate my family. I thought you understood that.'

'Oh, what rot! Did you think we'd live in this hole forever, little mouse? This is a holiday for us. But we must go back. We have to get what's rightly ours.'

'I would welcome the idea of visiting your family. But I never want to see mine again. Can we not do that, and just avoid my old life altogether?'

It seemed perfectly reasonable to her and she quite liked the idea of meeting his parents and seeing his family home in Birmingham, enjoying a hot drink in one of his father's coffee houses. It must be better than this miserable life, at any rate.

'Don't be a bloody fool,' he said. 'I can't go home empty-handed.'

'But you won't be. You shall have me. And our child.'

'That's not enough! I can't go back without a rich wife, he told me so, in no uncertain terms. A rich wife or to make my fortune by my art. Well, the latter will never happen, that's clear to me now. So, a rich wife it must be. And you are rich. You just need to bend the knee to your dear papa and grandmamma and all will be well. And all manner of things will be well!'

He was swigging back the wine now, his speech slurring, his cheeks red and his forehead shining with sweat.

'I won't do it,' she said quietly.

He turned a cold eye on her. 'Oh, yes, you will, mouse.'

'You can't make me,' she said, feeling she sounded like a recalcitrant child. But she meant it all the same.

He stood up swiftly and staggered, the speed making him dizzy. Margaret didn't know what he would do next. She eyed the door and thought of how she could get to it and evade his reach. He recovered himself and lurched towards her. She made a break for it, but he grabbed her and fell on her, his dead weight pinning her to the wooden floorboards.

'The child!' she cried.

'Shut up! Shut up!' he was spitting in her ear. 'I never wanted you, you simpering little bitch. I wanted the redhead more. She had something about her. By God, I wanted the local whores more than I ever wanted you. Even your stepmother, that brainless slut, was better in bed than you.'

He heaved himself up and slapped her hard across the face, the effort of it making him fall sideways and bang his head on the floor with an almighty crack. All was quiet. As she struggled away, sobbing and holding her belly protectively, she heard him moaning. Not dead, then. He muttered a few incomprehensible sounds then turned on his side and slept like an infant. Heartsick, she put her hand to her cheek. Whores? Anny? Benjamina? What a fool she'd been. She thought of all the times a man had hit her: her brother, her father and now her husband. And she decided, enough was enough. She made herself a promise: never again would a man strike her.

That was last night. Now, she felt her baby's fluttering movements inside her and it seemed like a clarion call. She looked again at her husband. So, he had bedded Benjamina. He had wanted to bed Anny. He had been with prostitutes. He had never wanted her, never loved her. He was a drunk and a failure. Despite everything, she could not hate him. He was her first love. Or rather, she could not hate the man she had fallen in love with. But the man lying down there was not that man. He had never existed and was a fiction of her own making. It was astonishing, how completely one could invent a life and believe it to be true.

This life was over, she knew that now. As quiet as the mouse he named her, she stood. She dressed. She found her money and packed a few essentials into a carpet bag. She left her husband sleeping on the floor. Descending the spiral staircase, the smell of dead animals growing stronger with every step, she marvelled at how stupid she had been, how naive and reckless. She thought, *A bigger fool there never was upon this earth.* She resigned herself to making the best of her disappointing and difficult life ahead, her growing babe inside her at least being a source of joy.

But as she thought of her unborn child, she recalled how her father and brother had always called her the weakling strain of the family. She wanted at that moment to prove them wrong, to never live down to the King family's low expectations of poor little Margaret, the poor little mouse. She thought for a moment of her pointless education, how she could play the piano well and could speak French. Perhaps it wasn't so pointless after all. She could try teaching English and piano to French children, just as their artist friends had suggested. It was a tall order, for an Englishwoman on her own to make her way in a foreign country. Margaret felt her baby quickening inside her again and it spurred her on, out into the street. She was encouraged too by her memories of Anny's strength and bravery. She still blamed herself for Anny's ruin. And she realised that their friendship might have been Anny's downfall, but it was the very making of herself. Fuelled by her determination to prove her family wrong and her admiration for the strength of her lost friend, she walked away from her husband and into the Paris morning, full of hope and the resolve to make a life for herself, without the Kings, without Jake, without anyone but herself and her child. She would do it; she would be strong and she would survive. Anny had taught her how.

Chapter 28

In the time after her salvation, Anny was feverish. She was aware only of sips of water and the gentle touch of a cool cloth about her face. Days or weeks passed; she had no way of telling. A day came when she felt brighter and wanted to say something. She watched her saviours pottering about their tiny house and she said, 'Thank you.'

They turned round to look at her and came to her, smiling at each other.

'Do you know your own name?' said the woman.

'Anny.'

'And mine?' said the young man.

'Dunna fuss the wench, son!'

'Peter,' said Anny. 'And Mary.'

'That's right,' said Mary.

'Malone. Mary and Peter Malone,' added Anny.

'Nothing wrong with your memory then,' said Mary. 'Glad to see it. You were in a terrible state when we found you. But I'm glad to see you're still all there. I'll get you some soup and Peter will sit and talk with you, wonna you, Peter?'

She went off to the kitchen table. Peter drew up a stool and sat down beside the bed. He looked awkward but willing. His arms were ingrained with coal dust. A miner, then.

'You used to work at the forge,' said Anny.

'I did, but I didna wanna stay there after . . .' He trailed off.

'After what?'

Peter looked round at his mother. He was tall and strapping, his arms muscular, his neck thick and his face well formed with high cheekbones. They were around the same age, him and herself, yet she'd not mixed much with the neighbours since she'd started working at the big house. What a fool she'd been. What fine friendships she could have had. He'd grown into a man since the last time she'd seen him, kicking about with the other kids. But he looked like a child again when he turned his worried face to Mary.

'The blast?' said Anny. 'Do you mean the blast?'

'Yes, the accident at the furnace.'

'That was no accident,' said Anny. 'That was King's fault.'

'Well, no. I mean, yes. That's what they say. That's what I say. That's why I left King's employ.'

'Really?'

'I couldna stand to line the man's pockets after that. I'm a collier now. Different master.'

'What's it like, down the mine?'

'Oh, you dunna wanna know about that,' said Peter.

'I do,' said Anny.

Mary appeared, carrying over a tray with a steaming bowl. 'Here's your soup. Come now, Peter. You'll tire Anny out with all this chit-chat. Let me feed her now. Fetch that extra pillow, will you, lad?'

Mary helped her sit up a little and spooned the soup into her mouth. It was good to taste good food. Life came down to simple things like this. Simple, good things.

'Thank you,' she said to Mary, when they were done.

'You're very welcome,' she replied, standing up to return the bowl to the table. Peter was sitting by the fire, reading a book. Mary pottered around the table. Anny closed her eyes and listened to the comforting sound of a mother's tasks at day's end.

'Mrs Malone,' she said and opened her eyes. 'Where is my mother?'

Rachel was sent for and came the next day, a Sunday. There were many tears and kisses and hugs and hand-holding, much of which had been banned by the prison, of course. Anny noticed Peter watching them with shining eyes, an emotional young man. Mother looked like an angel to Anny, but after talking with her for a while, she could see that her mother's face was drawn and she had black shadows of exhaustion beneath her eyes.

'I shall come home with you today, Mother. I shall help you at home. I'm never leaving you again. I want to stay with you always, just the two of us.'

'Oh, my dear lass. Dunna say such things. You have had a bad time. But you will rally and then you will make your own life.'

'No,' said Anny strongly, hauling herself to sit up. 'No, I won't. I don't want any part of it. Any of it. I just want to be with you.'

'Dunna upset yourself, Anny, please,' said her mother and soothed her, stroking her hand and easing her back down on the pillows. 'You mun rest. You mun get well. Mary wants to nurse you back to health and I will visit when I can.'

Anny glanced over at Mary, who was whipping up cake batter with a wooden spoon, wafts of sweetness filling the little house. Anny whispered, 'They are very kind and I am so grateful. But I should come home with you, to my own home.'

Mother looked down and shook her head. 'It is not what you think, Anny. It is a bad place, in a bad part of town. I lost our home after Father died, as I couldna pay the rent. They say King will pay compensation to the families but it's not come yet and it was too late for me. I had to find any place I could afford on my earnings and it inna good. I'm working all hours, washing at home and I do a bit of picking at the pit too. I canna look after you, lass. You are much better off here, until you are strong.'

Anny saw the shame in her mother's eyes. The old rage swelled in her at the mention of King. But she had not the strength or appetite for railing against her foe. She only wanted to comfort her mother. 'If that's what you think is best, then that's what we shall do. I shall be strong again, you'll see. And then there'll be two wages coming in and we'll get you out of there and into a good home again. Don't you fret, Mother. We shall do it together, you and I.'

Her mother left. She wouldn't stay for cake, as she had to get back to work. Anny was despondent after. She turned on her side and stared at the wall for a long time. Peter brought her a slice of seed cake, warm from baking. He sat with her and they ate their cake in silence. She felt comfortable sitting there, not talking. It was curious how awkward that felt with some people. But Mary and Peter were comfortable people and they didn't seem to expect anything from her.

'Could you tell me about the mine?' she asked him.

'If it would entertain you,' he said with a small smile. 'Though heaven knows why it should.'

'It would.' She wanted to hear about something completely different, something that was not about iron, or prison, or family, or love. Something safe to listen to.

'The pay is all right. There are worser jobs. I like the work very well. There are old lads and young chappers and plenty of chunnering on about life.'

'Tell me what it's like, underground. So I can picture it.'

'It's a rum old world down there,' he began. She watched him stare into space as he conjured it in his mind. 'When we descend the shaft, we're lowered down on chains and each hold a candle, a bunch of us like a catch of fish. The chain has broken in many a pit and sometimes a man can fall down the shaft and be killed. We strip off to work and put our clothes back on before we come up. The shadows flicker across the black walls and can haunt you a little at first. You think of all the weight of the world above you and what if it comes crashing down upon your head? But you have to have faith that it wonna or you'd lose your mind down there. Once you get used to it, there is a peace to be had in the dark, a kind of understanding between you and the deep earth.'

He's a born storyteller, Anny thought. It must come from the books he read by the fire or maybe it was just him, a natural talent. 'You're wasted down there,' she said.

He looked up and stared at her, his cheeks colouring. 'Oh, I dunna think so. I'm strong and I work hard for them.'

'I mean, you speak so well. You ought to be . . .' She trailed off and thought of all the things that Peter Malone could do in the world, with his gift for speaking, his turn of phrase, his reading. Another reader, like her. His mother must have had hopes for him, to teach him that. But Anny realised she was doing it again, aspiring. And she knew what came of that.

'Ought to be what?' he said and leant forward, his eyes intense with interest.

'Exactly what you are,' said Anny, and smiled at him. He beamed at her. She liked him very much already. How had she not noticed what a nice lad he was, when he was living on her very doorstep all those years? He was everything that Jake Ashford was not – honest, hard-working and humble. And a poet too, in his way.

'Anny, I'd like to say that your father . . . well, he was a good mon, a rare mon, decent through and through. Everybody thought it, everybody said it. It was a terrible day when he left the earth, when all of them did. But he was the best of them, the best of men.'

Anny looked at Peter, moved and grateful. She had been so alone in her grieving, so alone. She let her tears come and he waited for her to cry it out. He didn't try to stop her and he didn't try to comfort her. His quiet, patient presence there was comfort enough and somehow he knew that.

They talked into the evening, Mary scolding her son for not letting Anny rest. And in the days that followed, when he came back from the mine, Anny would insist on wrapping her shawl about her and going outside to throw scraps for the pig, to give him the privacy to have his tin bath by the fire. She thought of him there, scrubbing the black dust from his skin, only to suffer it all again the following day. She was getting stronger by the day and it wouldn't be long before she could join her mother. Yet Mary and Peter seemed in no hurry to shift her and told her to stay as long as she needed. It was company for Mary during the day and Peter said earnestly that she should stay as long as she ever wanted. Anny believed them. They were truly good people and they were fond of her, very fond. And she felt the same for them, increasingly so. But Mother needed her, and one day she would need to leave this comfortable house and go back out into the world, face whatever it might throw at her and begin again.

She carried inside her the shame of gaol, despite her innocence of the crime. It had tainted her through and through; like contagion seeping into a lake, it spread through her and reached every part of her. From a practical viewpoint, it had ruined her chance of a clerical job and a better life.

She thought of the day Peggy came to her house, dressed up in her cousin's clothes. She realised she had done the same all those years working at the office. None of it had been real, though she had heartily believed in it at the time. The forces of society did not want the poor girl to rise above her origins – it smashed that nonsense down with an iron fist. She thought of her father, his years of toil. And for what? To line King's pockets? No, it was more than that. It was for her and her mother. That's what it was for. And it was worth it, to provide a home and put food on the table. It was noble, it was good and it was enough.

As her health returned and her hair shone red again, she could feel the life coursing through her. She was luminous with it; she knew that as Peter Malone could not take his eyes from her, or she from him. When Mother visited, she looked as tired as ever, but her spirit was buoyed by her daughter's rejuvenation and she always left smiling. She told Anny, 'Each new day is a gift.' Anny thought about this, about her darkest days these past months. She told Peter all about it, when Mary was asleep, in their long winter evenings by the fire, discussing books and thoughts and their lives to this point. Things about prison that she knew she would never tell her mother; but she felt she could tell him anything. They even spoke of the future, of what it might hold for them. They began to talk of a shared future, hinting at it, knowing yet shy looks across the dancing light of the hearth.

Her shame of her prison time was receding with each footstep she took towards her recovery, replaced by a growing pride that she had survived it. She hated the Kings, to be sure, and that would never leave her. But the best revenge was to survive, to live and to love. To stay with her people and work hard with them and for them. Her people were the best in the world, hands down. The upper classes could keep their fancy clothes and their silly lives. Never again would she aspire to be like them. Never again would she try to play their game. There was release to be had when you let go of those tethers, of aspiration, of wanting and of envy. She had been bound by it, and worse: she had known true imprisonment. Now, she had been handed her freedom, the raw material out of which a life could be crafted. What would she make of it? Despite everything that had been lost, her future was in her own hands and that was good enough for Anny Woodvine.

Epilogue

Queenie sat alone in the library. She placed her hands on the table and brushed her fingers across the cover of a French novel that Margaret had left there months before and nobody had thought to tidy away. *She will miss her books*, thought Queenie. She wondered how her granddaughter was faring. There had been no word. For such a quiet girl, it was curious how empty the house seemed without her presence. The house felt haunted by too much absence now. Cyril was still away in Germany. Some of the younger servants had left the King employ after the explosion. With no young people around, the house felt empty. It was like Hamelin, after the piper had exacted his revenge.

Queenie shuddered. The curse on the house. It was coming true, she was sure of it. First the blast, and now Margaret gone. But these things were not random occurrences, unlucky events. These things had reasons, they had fault. The men of this house were to blame. Her grandson interfered with that Woodvine girl, which set off a chain reaction of events that led to Margaret running away and ruining her life. Her son scrimped on the furnace expenses and caused an appalling tragedy, that left a seething hostility towards the King name in the town and far beyond. Son and grandson acted entirely through their own stupid selfishness. These men carelessly smashed their way through people's lives like a beater on a pheasant shoot. They'd destroyed the lives of these two women, and who knew how many more? Her husband had been their model, his own vicious nature leaving victims strewn in its wake. How many more vengeful spirits like Betsy Blaize would turn up at the graveyard seeking recompense? This time, the Woodvines had paid the dearest price, but the Kings would pay too. She feared now a feud would grow from this, a hatred that could last years, generations even. She would not blame them. The men of this house were like a canker that would one day fell the family tree.

But not if she could help it. She sat upright and steeled herself. She'd said she would take back the reins, yet Margaret's loss had taken the wind from her sails. But, no more. This simply would not do, sitting here feeling sorry for herself, feeling powerless. Yes, it was the King men that had brought things to this pass, but she herself had allowed them to happen, through her own weakness and lack of vigilance. She stood up and resolved to walk that day, to walk every day. She vowed to regain her strength through vigorous daily exercise and to regain her mind through clarity of purpose and thought. She left the library and passed across the hall. If Jenkins had seen her, she would have instructed her to put on her fur-lined cloak, hat and leather gloves. But she did not wish to cosset herself. She wished to feel the cold sharpen up her bones and wake her from this years-long stupor she had allowed herself to fall into like an enchantment, like a drug. Well, now she was awake and no handsome prince's tender kiss had been needed. She'd kicked herself awake, and now she was going to kick this forsaken family into shape. She ignored the closet with her outdoor garb in it and crossed the garden room, leaving the house through the glass door. She would take a turn about the grounds and work out a plan of action.

The February air was bitter. The hour was later than she had realised and a grey gloaming was falling, the sky darkening. Queenie watched her breath blow puffs like a chilly steam engine and walked onwards, skirting the house and heading for the herb garden, her favourite part of the grounds. The beds were largely bare, the twiggy remnants of summer lushness stark and dead around her. She marched onwards and with each ten steps forward she listed her recent triumphs to warm herself. The day after Margaret had left, she had met with Brotherton and Pritchard. They agreed to write off the furnace part of the ironworks for good. There had been talk of rebuilding, but it was hopeless. The furnace was already inefficient before it blew and the town would not send its men to work at a King furnace again. The forge, however, was doing well and so were the rolling mill and the foundry. Yet there was talk that iron in this area was on its way out. So she would diversify – buy up other businesses, perhaps a brickworks or shares in a mine. That was where the future lay. She made Brotherton and Pritchard into partners and met with them daily to secure the recovery of the King fortunes. Soon, they would pay some reparation to the families of the dead and injured, but only a small amount, enough not to be insulting and not too much to damage the ironworks' profits. In the spring, once the business was back on its feet, she would send for Cyril and instruct the partners to train him up properly in the business. This would circumvent her useless son completely. There, that was that sorted.

As to Margaret, she thought about ways to find her and bring her back into the fold. She thought of hiring men who could follow her trail and track her down, a constable or suchlike who could do with the extra cash. But the more she plotted this, the more she disliked the idea. Yes, her granddaughter should be here to take up her rightful place in the King family. But what if she were happy? Did happiness matter? She realised that the first emotion she'd felt when told of her granddaughter's elopement was envy. Actually, she was glad that Margaret has escaped. She wished she'd had the nerve to do the same all those years ago when they married her off so young. Margaret had escaped the King family. Others had, too. The Woodvine girl, despite her terrible losses along the way, had been lucky to escape its grip and was free now. That servant Arnett had escaped, with a good settlement and reference and no more interference from the Kings. Even that innocent child – the baby on the bridge – she imagined had been blessed by escaping from the Kings. Yes, it was a lucky child that escaped the King family.

She stopped walking. She had walked right through the herb garden and, without noticing, had turned back towards the graveyard, so caught up in her plans she had been. She was penetratingly cold now, her teeth chattering, her bones aching. It was nearly dark and the fog of confusion began to descend in her mind. She fought to clear it.

'No,' she said aloud. 'No, I will not allow it. I am Alice King and I am the queen of this castle.'

'Your castle walls will fall,' said a voice.

Queenie gasped and looked up. There, beside her husband's grave, stood again the ghost of Betsy Blaize, the maid her husband had raped from the age of twelve till she fell pregnant with his baseborn child at fifteen and who had died on the iron bridge at the tender age of sixteen. Her eyes burned bluer than ever and her long, luxurious white hair flowed over her shoulders like an avalanche.

'Blaize!' she gasped, her hands shaking from fear and the cold. 'I am sorry. I should have stopped it. I should have done more. Forgive me, Betsy. Oh, I beg you to forgive me.'

The spirit spoke again. 'Dark times are ahead. The crucible will purify. The house will fall.'

Queenie dropped to her knees and sobbed. She could not feel her fingers now or the skin on her face, so numbed were they with nightfall and haunting.

'I have done good deeds. I have helped others more lowly than ourselves. I have made reparation. Is this not enough? What can I do? Tell me what I can do to save ourselves.'

Then, she felt a curious sensation in that frigid place: a hot waft of air enveloped her. She looked up and the ghost was leaning down towards her, breathing warmth across her face and hands, which tingled now with life. The ghost was smiling curiously at her, then spoke once morc.

'After the fire, I will come again. A baby will bridge the divide.'

Queenie hid her face in her hands to escape the spirit's gaze. She felt the cold deep in her bones and wondered how long she had been sitting by the graveside. Time seemed to have lost its meaning, as frozen as the hard ground beneath her. At the crunching sound of footsteps, she slowly turned her head to see Jenkins approaching. The ghost was nowhere to be seen.

Jenkins helped her to her feet and they began the slow trudge back to the house.

'The baby, the baby on the bridge,' Queenie was muttering.

'What are you doing, you mad old bat?' said Jenkins. 'It's black as your grandfather's hat out here.'

Queenie peered at her maid, right in the eye. 'Jenkins, where have you been? I could have died for all you care!'

'Hush your noise, woman. You'll outlive us all.'

Then there came a sound, a breathy whisper behind that made Queenie turn and look back. The ghost was still there, watching her with accusing eyes. Then it turned, took one long look at the resting place of Ralph King senior and faded from the night, leaving Queenie shivering in the gathering gloom.

Acknowledgements

The Royal Literary Fund, whose award of a grant and fellowship has saved me and means I can write these books in peace. I will be forever grateful. A particular thanks to Eileen Gunn and Steve Cook of the RLF, for coming to see me and supporting my applications throughout.

Shroppiemon, founder and administrator of the hugely popular Facebook group Memories of Shropshire, dialect master and number one research support of this book during its writing. He has always been on hand for questions concerning dialect and local history, as well as reading in detail the final draft and offering reams of helpful advice. Couldn't have done it without you, mon.

Stephen Dewhirst, of the Broseley Local History Society, for essential information on ironworks in the 1830s. Also, huge thanks for reading the final draft and offering such useful advice on a range of issues.

Pete Jackson, for all things pertaining to Cinderloo.

Geoff Fletcher, for detailed and fascinating help on a range of Shropshire issues, such as providing photos, information on an 1801 walking tour of the area, family history and dialect.

All the members and administrators of the various Shropshire Facebook groups who kindly let me join, for generously giving great advice on dialect and local history, as well as recommending resources:

- Memories of Shropshire
- Shropshire Tales, History and Memories
- Telford Memories
- Ironbridge and Coalbrookdale pictures
- Ironbridge ♥ through the Dale Yesteryear

Nicholas Feeney, for information on local history.

Sarah Davis of the Shropshire archives, for particular help about Shrewsbury Prison rules.

Toby Neal of the Shropshire Star, for dialect help.

Rita Rich-Mulcahy, for helpful advice on the local accent and dialect for the audiobook.

Staff at the range of Ironbridge Gorge Museums, for invaluable information on the area and its history, who do a fantastic job of keeping that history alive.

Joanne Smith, Museum Registrar at the Ironbridge Gorge Museum Trust, for book recommendations and useful contacts.

Kerry Hadley, for advice on Black Country matters and a variety of other matters, professional and personal, including making me snort with laughter on a regular basis.

Early readers – Lucy Adams, Lynn Downing, Kathy Kendall, Pauline Lancaster, Louisa Treger and Sue White – for reading with such speed and enthusiasm, giving me confidence to carry on with my first foray into saga.

My dear brother Jon Chadwick and his lovely wife Pauline, for hosting and looking after Poppy and me during our many research visits to the Ironbridge area.

My agent Laura Macdougall, for the brilliant idea of suggesting saga in the first place and for always being there for me; the best agent this novelist can imagine. Also gratitude to all at United Agents for support and help.

My editor Tara Loder, for believing in this story from day one, for coming all the way to my kitchen table to discuss character arcs and for superlative editing, honing this tale into the novel it is today.

Everyone at Bonnier – special mentions to Sarah Bauer, Katie Lumsden, Eleanor Dryden, Sahina Bibi, Imogen Sebba, Felice McKeown, Ellen Turner and Kate Parkin – for making me so welcome and providing brilliant support throughout the writing, editing and publicity process.

Book bloggers, readers, reviewers and booksellers, for continued support in my writing career, sticking with me through the transition from Mascull to Walton and championing anything I write. I am so grateful to you all.

Tim Marchant, web designer, for creating wonderful Mollie Walton and Rebecca Mascull websites, which are even more gorgeous than I envisioned.

Sasha Drennan and Gill Hart at Lindum Books in Lincoln, for supporting this writer in everything she writes – whatever my name or genre! – and providing friendship and chats. And always stocking my books on your lovely shelves.

My author friends, those in and out of various collectives, such as my dear and original Prime Writers, and newer groups to me like the Savvies, the Loungers, the Romantic Novelists' Association and the Saga Girls – you have kept me sane, educated me and kept me smiling. Special thanks to Kerry Drewery, as ever.

All my Facebook mates, for indulging my penchant for cat videos and edgy humour.

My friends and family, for keeping me going with advice, hugs, childcare and other invaluable resources during the writing of this book.

Vanessa Lafaye, who cheered with me when I got this book contract, yet left us too soon to read it. You were my beta reader extraordinaire and my beloved friend. I miss you, darling.

Colin Miles, for loitering, laughs and love.

Poppy, my darling daughter, for making it so easy, every day, in every way, to be your mother.

MEMORY LANE

Welcome to the world of Mollie Walton!

Keep reading for more from Mollie Walton, to discover a recipe that features in this novel and for an extract from the next book in the series . . .

We'd also like to welcome you to Memory Lane, a place to discuss the very best saga stories from authors you know and love with other readers, plus get recommendations for new books we think you'll enjoy. Read on and join our club!

MEMORY LANE

www.MemoryLane.Club

/MemoryLaneClub

MEMORY LANE

Dear Readers,

In the summer of 2016, I took my daughter to visit my brother and his wife in Shropshire. I'd never been to the county and knew nothing about it. All I remembered was an old friend of mine from university days saying she'd been to Ironbridge, how it was the first iron bridge ever built and that the area was the cradle of the industrial revolution. She also said it was beautiful there. I recalled thinking, how can something be industrial *and* beautiful? We arrived in Ironbridge and took a walk up to its main attraction, the glorious iron bridge itself, spanning the River Severn. We walked to the centre of the bridge and I looked down through the iron bars at the slow-moving river below. And then it happened.

It's what I like to call the 'history shivers'. This isn't a phrase I created; I've heard writers and history enthusiasts use it when you experience something that really takes you back to a past age. I felt it when I saw the Brontë sisters' writing table at their home in Haworth. And I felt it that day, standing on the iron bridge. I suddenly had a vision of how the river must have looked two hundred years before, flanked by all manner of burning, smoking industry, fed by the workers and masters who fuelled it, sending goods out into the rest of the world along the river and roads, the canals and railways. All that was gone now, but the remnants remained, overgrown by the beauty of nature. My friend had been right.

Just weeks before, my literary agent Laura had brilliantly suggested a brand new idea to me: writing a saga trilogy. She wanted me to come up with an idea for a story – families, industry, a beautiful yet industrial setting, conflict and drama. Standing on the bridge, I knew this was the place. Looking at both sides of the river, I realised I had my two families: one of poor workers, the other of rich masters. I had my setting, my characters, my conflict and drama all built in, just by gazing down from the bridge. I was itching to start writing! We visited some of the many museums of the area and everything I looked at took on a new meaning: this was where my two families lived and worked; this is what they ate and how they dressed and where they travelled to and so on. I took dozens of photos, bought a lot of books and postcards and started filling a notebook with ideas. The two families sprang almost fully formed into my head: the masters lived in a house on the top of the hill, looking down on everybody below. The workers lived in the ramshackle cottages that grew along the river when industry took hold.

MEMORY LANE

When I got home, I sketched out a family tree, then, by researching common names of Shropshire, I was able to fill in the blanks. I had my Woodvines and my Kings, my two daughters, their secret friendship and the troubles that awaited them. I planned out their lives over forty years, over three generations and three books, all mysteriously linked by a baby found on the bridge . . .

I went back to the area several times, visiting other important sites, such as the ruins of the Bedlam Furnaces, the Coalbrookdale Museum of Iron and the Dana, otherwise known as Shrewsbury Prison. I fell in love with the area and with my characters, Anny and Margaret. My agent was delighted with the whole project too. When my publisher took on the saga trilogy, I found my editor Tara, who loved these girls and their story as much as I did. We talked about them always as if they were real people! We cared deeply what happened to them; we felt bad when we put them through hard times and cheered them on when they battled against adversity. Such is the stuff of saga! I hope you love them as much as we do.

Best wishes,
Mollie

MEMORY LANE

Glossary of Shropshire Dialect Terms

Definitions have been collated from experts in dialect, such as Shroppiemon (see Acknowledgements) and also the Shropshire Word Book by Georgina Frederica Jackson, published 1879.

All round the Wrekin: taking too long to get to the point
Anna: haven't
Babby: baby
Bait: food, a meal
Big-sorted: proud, stuck-up
Blethering: talking too much
Canna: can't
Chappers: lads
Chillun: children
Chunnering: chatting
Clemmed: hungry, famished
Darksome: gloomy, melancholy, sad
Darter: daughter
Didna: did not
Drodsome: dreadful, alarming
Dunna: don't
Earywig: earwig
Fadder: father
Frit: frightened

MEMORY LANE

From off: from outside the local area
Gunna: going to
Hadna: had not
Hobbety-hoy: a youth or adolescent
Inna: isn't
Lungeous: spiteful
Mon: man, often used as a term of address to males
Mun: must
Ow bist?: How are you?
Ow bist thee faring?: How are you doing? How are you managing?
Proper jam: lovely; really good.
Shoosby: Shrewsbury
Shoulda: should have
Shouldna: should not/should not have
Summat: something
Trow: a cargo boat used to transport goods
Wanna: want to
Wench: used for a young woman in a similar way to 'lass' and is in no way derogatory to females. See the *Shropshire Word Book* definition: 'a young girl, or young woman, of peasant rank, to whom it is applied in no unworthy sense – the good old word maintaining its respectability.'
Wonna: won't
Wouldna: would not have

MEMORY LANE

Rachel Woodvine's Fidget Pie

This recipe makes a traditional Shropshire fidget pie, just like Rachel Woodvine makes for her husband John and her daughter Anny to take to work for their lunch. A slice of a fidget pie is delicious and filling.

You will need

For the pastry:
500g plain flour
1tbsp salt
140g lard, diced
200ml water
2 tbsp butter, for greasing
1 egg, beaten

For the filling:
300g ham or gammon, diced
2 onions, peeled and diced
3 large apples, peeled and diced
3 large potatoes, peeled and diced
100ml cider
50ml milk
2 tbsp plain flour
2–3 tbsp soft brown sugar
1 tsp black pepper
1 tsp dried sage
1 tsp salt

Method:

1. Pre-heat the oven to 200°C/180°C fan/gas mark 6.
2. Mix together the flour and salt in a large bowl.
3. Heat the lard and water in a saucepan, until the water is simmering and the lard melted. Pour the hot liquid into the bowl with the flour.
4. Stir with a wooden spoon, then turn out onto a floured surface and knead to form a soft dough. Cover and set aside.
5. In a separate bowl, mix the ham, onions, apples and potatoes together. Add the cider, milk and flour, then the salt, pepper, sugar and sage. Mix together well.
6. Grease a cake tin (approximately 22cm) with butter.
7. Roll out two thirds of the pastry dough made earlier onto a floured surface, in a large circle. Line the cake tin with the pastry, letting it overlap the rim a little.
8. Roll out the remaining third of the pastry to make a lid large enough to cover the pie. Set this to one side.
9. Put the filling into the pie case, packing it tightly down.
10. Brush the pastry's edges with beaten egg, then cover with the lid. Crimp the edges together, then brush the whole lid with beaten egg.
11. Bake in the oven for an hour, then turn off the heat and leave in the oven for another half hour before removing.
12. Enjoy!

MEMORY LANE

An extract from Mollie Walton's next book, *The Secrets of Ironbridge*

Prologue

Queenie wondered where she was buried. A pauper's grave, no doubt. But which sorrowful patch of ground? Queenie pictured her now, a pitiful pile of bones in a crowded pit. She imagined the girl's spirit rising from its haphazard burial place, delighted to be free of its chaotic tumble of earth and human remains. Where would it go? Perhaps it would revisit the scenes and sights of its childhood: some sort of poor man's hovel where it was born, maybe a patch of ground where it used to play with other urchins. But once it was done with those, inevitably, it would come to the King house, to Southover. After all, the spirit was only a young girl when she had come there as a maid-of-all-work. And what if the spirit of this servant – this Betsy Blaize – were to come to Queenie's house now? What would she see? Even as she wondered this Queenie questioned why she had conjured the memory of Blaize's spirit after all these years of thinking of it rarely. Out of sight, out of mind. It must be because the house was draped in worry, waiting as it was for the death of her son.

She shivered and glanced at the closed curtains in her bedroom. In her mind's eye, she saw the spirit rise from its scrappy piece of earth across the river, floating up, up into the night sky. Over the tops of trees and industry it would go, seeing the fires of the furnaces emblazon the darkness with their hellish colours. It would skim fleetly over factories and forges, lime kilns and waggonways, pumping engines and brickworks. It might circle the pit-heads and the men labouring below them in the bowels of the earth. They would never see the spirit that passed over them, buried as they were like her body, or what was left of it. Onwards, to the river itself, the mighty Severn that scoured out the Gorge and rushed through it, relentless and temperamental. The spirit would travel its length to reach the iron bridge – it would have to visit the site of its creation, after all, the place where Betsy Blaize the girl had carried her newborn child, handed it to a passing Quaker and died. Across the iron bridge it would fly, up over the houses and shops and streets, all good folk sleeping peacefully in their beds, their mattresses soft or hard depending on their gentility. Up the hill to the great house that stood above the town, frowning down upon it. Southover, the house of the hated Kings.

Queenie envisaged the spirit approaching the house from the gravel drive, making no sound as it skimmed the stones, lifting up to the window of Mr Ralph King Junior, Queenie's son, master of the house and figurehead of the King businesses, struck down in his early sixties by sickness. If it glanced through the crack in the curtains, it would see the deathly pale face of Ralph sleeping fitfully in his bed, groaning in pain all the night through. But of course Ralph wouldn't be her final destination. It wasn't him who had wronged her. The spirit would float on, coming around the eastern corner of the house, slowing now, closer and closer, to arrive at its destination: Queenie's own window.

Queenie felt a chill down her spine again and the lamp on her desk guttered like a spent candle. She adjusted her favourite cashmere shawl closer about her shoulders. She had lost some weight in recent years and felt the cold more keenly. Her devoted lady's maid, Jenkins, kept trying to feed her up, complaining that Queenie would soon look like a skeleton if she didn't fatten up a bit. She stood up and walked to the window, then hesitated. A sudden, sharp fear came of what might appear behind it. She scolded herself for her silliness and yanked the curtain open. She saw only the night look back at her, blank and black. The vague shapes of trees moved mysteriously at the edge of the lawns. She did not look at the family graveyard, instead turning briskly and returning to her desk. Today, the doctor had advised Queenie to 'gather your family around you'. The others were here – her grandson Cyril and Ralph's wife Benjamina – neither caring much whether Ralph made it through the night or not. Indeed, Queenie suspected they positively hoped he wouldn't, so they could move on to the next stages of their lives. But there was family not present that ought to be.

Thus, she had sat down to pen this letter to the one person who was absent, who was over the sea, in a foreign city for nigh on twenty years now, her granddaughter Margaret. She pictured her now, her youth having left her, approaching middle age. Had the years been kind to her, Queenie wondered, or would she have aged badly? Margaret's relative poverty, as a teacher of English and pianoforte, would not afford her the King lifestyle, that was certain. Perhaps it would be a blessing to her to return home again, at last, after all these years. Perhaps she would welcome it, after all she had struggled through, as a widow and a lone mother to a daughter. Or perhaps she still considered her loss of riches a small price to pay to be free of the King family. Then, Queenie's thoughts coalesced around another, the girl, her great-granddaughter, Beatrice. Queenie had never met her. Would the girl favour her pale, yellow-haired mother or her dark, gypsy-eyed father? Queenie would soon find out if the answer to this letter were in the affirmative. She set to finish it, dipping her pen in the black ink and looping it out across the page in her neat hand.

As she wrote the words 'your father is close to death', she felt that chill again and hurriedly glanced back at the strip of window open to the dark night. There was a flicker of something there. Or was there? Just a spatter of rain. She stood once more and marched to the window, jerking the curtain over to shut out the night. But as she did it, she knew that it was never that simple to shut out memories – or guilt.

Queenie imagined the spirit she had conjured gliding down from her window and taking its customary place beside Queenie's long-dead husband's grave, standing beside it, looking up at the house. Watching and waiting in the coal-dark night, scored by the rain that fell across the King lawns and into the wild woodland beyond.

·MEMORY LANE·

Chapter 1

The coach trundled on, the horses struggling up a steep incline, their hooves slipping. Beatrice grasped her mother's hand again and squeezed. Her mother was still snoozing and stirred at her touch, then fell back into her stupor. *Maman always looks tired these days*, thought Beatrice. It was good that they were returning to her mother's family, after all these years. Good that her mother would get some rest, be waited on in the big house and pampered a little. If they were welcomed, that was.

Beatrice glanced at the other passengers opposite them in the coach, two women and a man, all in various states of restless slumber, jogged by the coach's swaying rhythm. But she could not sleep. She had never travelled far from home in Montmartre and never met her English family, so this journey was filled with excitement and tinged with fear. The coach to the port, the ship across the Channel. The sea voyage made her so sick, she told her mother she was dying. But they got through it and then came the long ride north-west. Nights were spent in coaching inns, fending off the lascivious looks and comments of Englishmen. She was eighteen years of age and she was lovely to look upon, or so Maman told her daily.

'We shall need to buy you a whole new wardrobe, Bea,' Maman said, awake now. 'Shropshire society won't be able to cope with your Paris fashion.'

'But how will we afford that?' she asked.

All her life, lack of money had been their constant, tedious companion. She knew how little they had left. The journey had cost them a pretty penny. To hear her mother talk of splashing out on new clothes was shocking.

'All will be different,' her mother replied. 'You do not know your great-grandmother yet, but she'd never stand for a King to be presented in society as anything but the height of sophistication.'

The coach was on the flat now, the horses fleeter. Beatrice leant forward and looked out of the window. The dark, tree-rooved roads they'd come through for miles were thinning out into more open country. She saw the Shropshire countryside broaden into beauty: rolling hills, deeply wooded areas, patches of water, cottages and a church nestled in a valley. Having lived all her life in the dense, populated world of a city, the landscape here was intoxicating to her. She loved her life in Montmartre and its busy, noisy character. She had imagined the town of Ironbridge to be simply a smaller version of what she was used to. But nothing had prepared for the splendour of the landscape here. The coachman called something to the horses and they slowed, then turned onto another road, the sign she'd spied at the junction: Broseley and Ironbridge. Not far now, she hoped.

They gathered pace along the Broseley road. Before long, the greenery faded into brown and a new sight took her interest, the signs of industry. There were brick buildings and a tall chimney, and behind it she could make out great mounds of grey earth. To one side was some kind of structure with a wheel and ropes, and to the other a stretch of grey ground, an open working of some sort, peopled by a blur of many workers and horses going to and fro. Some words painted in broad white lettering on the side of a building caught her eye: KING BRICK AND TILE WORKS. King was her mother's name – her maiden name, that was.

Beatrice grasped the window ledge and leant out further, so she could see the people, the first large group of locals she'd seen for miles. The coach was slowing down, as one of the female passengers, now awake and readying herself, was to alight here. Beatrice watched as the woman clambered out of the other door and was handed her bag from the roof. Beatrice looked through the window at the workers. She could see them clearly. They were digging great lumps of material from the open ground, placing it on handcarts or carrying it by hand. She saw now that some of the workers were children bowed down by the weight of their load. Some of them were so small, her heart went out to them. Surely they were too young for such backbreaking work? Everyone was covered in grey dust, making them seem as if they were people of the clay, arisen from the ground. Beatrice stared at them, until one came from an open-sided building, turned and looked in her direction. She could see his eyes fix upon her. She stared back for a moment, then looked away, abashed. She felt ashamed, to be gawking at this young man working so hard, while she lounged in a coach. She withdrew her head and sat back down beside her mother.

'We are on the road to Broseley and Ironbridge,' Beatrice told her.

'Ah, then we are almost home,' said Maman.

'Look at this place,' she told her mother who leant forward and peered out of the window. 'It has your name on it.'

'It does indeed belong to the Kings. Queenie told me in a letter that the Kings now own this site, as well as having interests in iron and mining.'

MEMORY LANE

Beatrice looked outside again to see the workers labour on, the smoke rising from the chimney, the young man who had looked upon her lost now in the dust and the muck. She struggled to imagine her family owning so much.

Her mother began talking to her of her family, reminding her of each member, telling her of the town of Ironbridge they were now approaching. France, Paris, Montmartre, their little terraced house on the corner opposite the *boulangerie*, the smell of fresh baking accompanying their every waking morning – all seemed very far away.

As the coach drew closer to their destination, Beatrice called up the sights and sounds of her home: the comings and goings of Maman's pupils; the tinkling sounds of piano pieces and the drumming monotony of scales practice; the halting tones of children learning English, while Beatrice assisted her mother with preparing learning materials, marking work and domestic duties. Sometimes, Beatrice would give lessons to the younger ones herself. She spoke English with her mother at home and spoke French outside of home. She had been raised perfectly bilingual, her English spoken without a French accent, so her mother said, yet with a tinge of French phrasing from time to time. Her fellow Parisians would say she spoke French similarly, with a perfect accent, yet a hint of Englishness in her turn of phrase. Her mother told her every day how proud she was of her, what a good girl she was, how clever and kind. Eighteen years they had been together, every day Beatrice had spent on this earth; they were the best of friends, the greatest team Beatrice could imagine. Their world had been that little house, the streets nearby, the stray yet sociable cats she fed on their front porch, the musical and artistic friends that would bring food and laughter and gossip of an evening. They had a life confined by poverty yet expanded by ideas, conversation and reading; a shabby-genteel existence. A happy one.

But then there came news that Ralph King was ill. It was her grandfather, her mother's father, a man Beatrice had never met. Her mother did not speak of her past often, but as Beatrice had grown older she had asked more and more. She knew that she had been born out of love, a great romance with her father, the artist Jake Ashford. That her parents had run away together from Ironbridge to Paris. Tragically her father had died of a fever before she was even born, leaving her mother a young widow, struggling to bring Beatrice up alone.

She'd never met anyone in her family. The word 'family' only meant Mother, or as she called her, in the French way, Maman. Her whole family was Maman. But now they were going to the house where Maman had grown up, where her grandfather Ralph lived with her step-grandmother Benjamina and her Uncle Cyril, and where her great-grandmother, who they all called Queenie, ruled the roost.

The day was waning and Beatrice suddenly felt very weary, worn out by her worry of what this mysterious family would make of her and Maman. The coach was tipping forwards as they descended another hill and again she grasped her mother's hand.

'Look!' said Maman, and Beatrice saw through the window a broad, roiling mass of water surging forwards and beyond it, spanning the River Severn grandly from bank to bank, the great iron bridge, its backbone covered in jostling traffic and people.

'Ironbridge,' said Beatrice.

'Home,' said Maman.

MEMORY LANE

Curious how small it looked to Margaret, her family home, Southover. As a child it had seemed like a mansion of endless rooms, with the tallest ceilings and longest corridors. But now, having alighted from the coach and standing before it, it was still impressive – far grander than their little house in Montmartre – but somewhat smaller than she remembered. *Strange how memories play tricks on the mind*, she thought. She realised that the house loomed large in her thoughts mostly because of its power over her childhood. It was still much larger than the majority of houses around these parts, and to Beatrice, she thought, as she glanced at her beautiful daughter gazing up at it, it must seem like the Palace of Versailles compared to the simple narrow house she'd grown up in. She felt a pang of guilt that her daughter had never had the finery she'd had growing up, then recalled that finery was no use if you were imprisoned in it. And that is how she saw her childhood, one long stretch of incarceration before she opened the cage door and she flew. And now she was back, nearly twenty years older, wiser and yet exhausted. Despite missing her beloved Paris, the thought of good food, hot water and servants to tend one's every need seemed like heaven to her now. Strangely, she was glad to be here, though a little nervous of their reception. She had left under a storm cloud all those years ago, after all.

Margaret watched as the butler and other staff came out to greet the coach and handle the luggage. Brunt, her family butler of many years' standing, was gone, replaced by a younger man only a few years older than herself by the looks of it. But that was all she had time to notice before she saw that they all wore black armbands and then she felt a shiver up her spine as she realised her father, Ralph King, must already be dead.

MEMORY LANE

Her grandmother had written to her weeks before, to inform her that her father was dying. Margaret had read the letter and sat staring at the walls of her little house for a long time, mulling over the news. To see her father and the rest of her family again, after all these years of self-imposed exile. To bring Beatrice and introduce her to the family Margaret had so longed to escape. It was fraught with worrying possibilities. She had never liked her father. He was a selfish, pompous man, who spent her childhood years dishing up disapproval and disappointment to his only daughter. She knew it was because her mother had died giving birth to her. The thought of seeing him again and having to submit to his rules in any way brought back the old fears of her youth. But she was no longer the young woman who'd run from the King house all those years ago. Though she'd hated her family – their coldness, their cruelty – they were still her family. To ignore a deathbed request . . .

And then there was Bea, who had never known any other family. Margaret was thirty-five years old now. Her health had declined in these recent years, with mysterious pains here and there, as well as piercing headaches and dizzy spells from time to time. Independence was fine when she was well, terrifying when she was not. Her ill health had lost her some pupils and it was increasingly hard to make ends meet. What would happen to Bea if something truly horrible were to befall her? What was more, Beatrice was coming of age and Margaret feared for her daughter's future. In the world of the Kings, a girl of Bea's age would be launched upon the social scene, ready to find a suitable husband. With their meagre lifestyle in Montmartre, such a thing was impossible. It had seemed romantic and worthy once, to live this life of fierce self-reliance, and Margaret was still proud of what she had achieved alone. But she was tired, and she wanted so much more for Beatrice. Maybe her family had changed. So they had come, but it seemed they were too late.

There she was, her grandmother Queenie, standing in the doorway, dressed head to toe in black.

'Margaret, my dear,' she said, in a strong voice. Her hair was pure white now, different from the bright stripes through deep brown and gunmetal grey she'd had when Margaret last saw her. She walked in a confident, upright stride towards them across the driveway, yet smiled wanly.

'Are we too late, Grandmother? Is Father . . . gone?'

Queenie arrived in front of her and took her hands, her grandmother's skin dry and papery yet her hands warm and firm.

'I am sorry to say you are too late. He passed away two days hence, but there was no way to alert you.'

It struck Margaret that she felt absolutely nothing at all. It was akin to being told the *boulangerie* opposite their house had run out of bread, annoying that she'd missed her chance, yet hardly more than an inconvenience. *Am I really so cold?* she thought.

'I'm grieved to hear it and so sorry for our family's loss,' she heard herself saying to Queenie, who cocked her head and smiled a strange little smile.

'Really, my dear? I didn't think you cared for your father one jot! But, of course, you are saying the right things and acting with perfect decorum.'

Queenie hadn't changed, then. She'd always said what she thought. Then, Queenie's face altered suddenly as her gaze shifted aside and fell upon Margaret's daughter, waiting patiently beside her.

'And this is Beatrice,' said Queenie with a kind of breathy wonder. Queenie's eyes were wide open and she swiftly removed her hands from Margaret's. It had been good to feel her grandmother's touch again, the only King who ever really cared about her. Indeed, her brother Cyril and stepmother Benjamina had not even come out to greet their arrival. Typical and, truth be told, something of a relief.

'Why, my dear, you are a stunning creature!' said Queenie and took the girl's hands. Beatrice glanced nervously sideways at her mother who nodded. 'You are the very picture of your father, with those dark eyes. I do not recall much about the artist Ashford, but one could not forget those eyes. And I see you have your mother's fine features. You will do very nicely, my dear. Will you not greet me as your great-grandmother, child? You speak English, I assume?'

'Indeed, I do, Great-grandmother,' Beatrice said, smiling. Yet another glance at her mother showed how nervous and eager to do the right thing she was. 'I would like to offer my condolences on your loss. I am so very sorry I did not meet my grandfather.'

Margaret watched her grandmother place her palms on her daughter's cheeks, who stood rigidly, trying to appear natural. 'You are kind to say so, but you may be the better for it. He was my son, but he wasn't the man I wished him to be. No doubt that appears wickedly unkind to you, but you will learn that your great-grandmother is honest as the day is long and will not brook any flim-flam. Come now, you must be fatigued from your travels. Come inside.'

Queenie led the way. Beatrice took her mother's hand and squeezed it, her face a sweet picture of concern, her eyes seeming to ask if her mother was well, after the bad news.

'I am fine,' Margaret said quietly to her as she squeezed Beatrice's hand back and they walked together into the was three, she started teaching her to play. Pupils came daily and their living improved, with enough money to buy some pretty things for her daughter and some decent wine for herself. They had friends, they had freedom, they had each other. There had been suitors from time to time – Margaret had always been a pretty woman – and though she enjoyed flirting with them, she never succumbed. She wanted no more husbands. Her whole life until that little house had been lived in thrall to others, particularly men, directing her destiny and limiting her choices. She'd vowed she would never do that again.

Margaret followed Queenie into the drawing room and she immediately noticed that the picture in her mind's eye was different from the room she now stood in. It had been fully redecorated since she left, with bright flock wallpaper in red and pale pink, quite gaudy, she thought. Benjamina's influence, no doubt. She looked about the room for her fashionable stepmother, wondering how the years would have treated her, so obsessed with her appearance she'd always been. She was only a few years older than Margaret herself – the 'child bride', as she'd always thought of her secretly. But Benjamina was not here and neither was Margaret's brother, Cyril. A wave of relief swept over her. He was the one she dreaded seeing most of all. And suddenly she felt icy cold and a phrase leapt to her mind: *We should never have come.*

MEMORY LANE

Introducing the place for story lovers – a welcoming home for all readers who love heartwarming tales of wartime, family and romance. Join us to discuss your favourite stories with other readers, plus get book recommendations, book giveaways and behind-the-scenes writing moments from your favourite authors.

www.MemoryLane.Club

/MemoryLaneClub

Praise for

The Ironbridge Saga

'A journey. Compelling. Addictive'

VAL WOOD

'The attention to period detail and beautiful writing drew me right in'

LYNNE FRANCIS

'An addictive, heartwarming book, with an unputdownable plot. I didn't want it to end'

DINAH JEFFERIES

'*The Daughters of Ironbridge* has that compulsive page-turning quality, irresistible characters the reader gets hugely invested in, and Walton has created a brilliantly alive, vivid and breathing world'

LOUISA TREGER

'Feisty female characters, an atmospheric setting and a spell-binding storyline make this a phenomenal read'

CATHY BRAMLEY

'Evocative, dramatic and hugely compelling . . . has all the hallmarks of a classic saga. I loved it'

MIRANDA DICKINSON

‘Beautiful and poignant’

TANIA CROSSE

‘Such great characters who will stay with me for a long time’

BETH MILLER

‘A powerful sense of place and period, compelling characters and a pacey plot had me racing to the end’

GILL PAUL

‘A story that is vivid, twisting and pacey, with characters that absolutely leap off the page’

IONA GREY

‘Hard-hitting storyline, clever blend of real history and fiction, and an atmospheric evocation’

LANCASTER GUARDIAN

The Orphan of Ironbridge

Mollie Walton has always been fascinated by history and on a trip to Shropshire, while gazing down from the iron bridge, found the inspiration for her debut saga novel, *The Daughters of Ironbridge.*

Also by Mollie Walton:
The Daughters of Ironbridge
The Secrets of Ironbridge

The Orphan of Ironbridge

MOLLIE WALTON

ZAFFRE

First published in the UK in 2021 by
ZAFFRE
An imprint of Bonnier Books UK
4th Floor, Victoria House,
Bloomsbury Square,
London WC1B 4DA
Owned by Bonnier Books
Sveavägen 56, Stockholm, Sweden

A CIP catalogue record for this book is available from the British Library.

ISBN: 978-1-83877-314-4

Also available as an ebook

3 5 7 9 10 8 6 4 2

Typeset by IDSUK (Data Connection) Ltd
Printed and bound in Great Britain by Clays Ltd, Elcograf S.p.A.

MIX
Paper from responsible sources
FSC® C018072

Zaffre is an imprint of Bonnier Books UK
www.bonnierbooks.co.uk

This novel is dedicated to the memory of Jude Corfield, who listened to her daughter Lu brilliantly narrating an Ironbridge *book and 'heard home'.*

Prologue

August 1861

The child sat down on the bed, shuffling herself back until her little legs stuck out over the edge. Her feet were bare and grubby from dusty adventures outside. She was holding a doll made from scraps of material, a floppy ragged thing that she loved to distraction.

Anny watched her draw the doll to her lips and kiss it tenderly. Beside her, stretched out under the sheets, pale and limp, the child's mother rested her trembling hand on the child's arm.

'Hettie,' said Anny, and the girl looked up sharply. 'Your mama wants to talk to you. Lean down close to her now, for her voice is small.'

Hettie nodded. She looked round at her mother, unsure, then clasped the doll to her breast and haltingly leant towards her mother's face. She glanced round at Anny for reassurance, and Anny nodded encouragement. *Poor child*, thought Anny, *and poor mother*. Martha had been unwell for so long that she had grown strange to Hettie and the child was a little afraid of her. It must break Martha's heart.

Anny sat down on the wooden chair near the door and took up some sewing. She wanted this to be a private moment for the two of them, but she was too worried about Martha to leave her.

'Sweet Hettie,' said Martha and smiled. She lifted her hand and touched the child's face, who watched her mother's gaze with wide eyes. 'I've things to tell you, child. As you are only three years of age, these are things you wonna be understanding now or maybe for a long time, but I mun tell them nonetheless.'

Her body is weak, thought Anny. But her voice was firm, though quiet. Anny guessed she must be using her last ounce of strength to talk to her daughter. It was perhaps her last chance to do so.

'Tell Lizzie,' said Hettie, and carefully placed her doll on her mother's shoulder, resting it against her hair.

Martha smiled. 'I'll tell you both. You were born in this house, Hettie. Born from love and into love. I was born in different circumstances. I never knew my mother or where she came from. All I know is that she died on the iron bridge, handing me over to a kind man who took me in. I dunna even know where they laid her to rest.'

Martha paused to draw a deep breath. *So*, Anny thought, *it was really true; Martha was the baby on the bridge*. She'd heard rumours of this from her mother, but never had it told from the horse's mouth before.

'This man was a good man, a Quaker. He took me in. He and his wife raised me as their own. I couldna been luckier, to land with such a family. I wish you coulda met them, as they were loving folk and they'd've loved you so. But they both were owd folk when they got me and they died afore you were born. They brought me up a good person and that's what your father, Adam, saw in me and he loved me for it. He is a good man too. But he inna here, as you know. And you havna met him yet. But one day, I hope and I pray, he will be returned from that faraway land they sent him to on the convict ship, and he will come to find you. Now listen, Hettie. Listen carefully.'

Anny watched Martha's face, her large green eyes intense. Hettie took fright. She snatched her doll back and clutched it.

'Lizzie scared,' she said.

Anny watched as Martha's intensity faded, replaced by a saddened smile, her eyes glistening in the dim light of the sickroom.

'Dunna fret, my angel,' said Martha, stroking Hettie's arm. 'I didna mean to frit'ee. But you mun mind me, when I tell you this. One day, if your father ever returns, you mun love him with all of your heart. And look after him, as I would, if I were here. He was the happiest man alive the day you were born, and it were never his fault that he were taken from us. He was innocent, Hettie. He did no wrong in this world, only good. You came from good, you came from love, my sweet lass. Never forget that.'

Martha stopped then and closed her eyes, coughing weakly. Anny put down her sewing and came to her. She touched her forehead, which was cold and clammy.

'Rest now, Martha, hmm?' Anny said.

Martha opened her eyes, her gaze hazy for a moment, until she seemed to remember where she lay and what her purpose was.

'No,' she murmured. Then, 'I mun speak. Hettie, my little duckie egg.'

Anny feared the child could take no more of this. She was too unsettled by her poor mother's illness.

'Just hear your mother one more time, Hettie. Then you may go play with Evan.'

Hettie's eyes lit up, then she glanced back at her mother. Anny's eyes pricked with tears as she watched Martha struggle to keep the little girl's attention. *She must be close now*, Anny thought. If only the child were older. If only she understood how significant this moment was. Anny vowed to memorise what Martha Jones said that day so that she could relate it to Hettie when she was older and had need of it.

Martha said, 'I mun tell you, my chick, for it may be my last chance. This life is not about where you came from, but where you are going. Always be good, be kind and treat others as you would wish yourself to be treated. Some are eaten up by hate or revenge. Some rail against the life they have, against the wrongs that have been done. Others meet hate with love and do all they can to build bridges. You must be the last sort, the good sort. Like your Quaker grandparents. Like I have tried to be. Like Anny and Peter and Evan Malone who will look after you when I am gone. Do good in this world. Once all is said and done, what folk need most is kindness. Be good, be happy, my child, my lovely lass, light of my heart.'

Anny sniffed and wiped the tears from her eyes as Hettie, sensing a break in the stream of words, hopped off the bed and ran across the room. Her swift steps showed how glad she was to escape.

'Hush now, Martha,' said Anny, stroking her dear friend's face. Martha closed her eyes, a faint smile about her lips. She had said her piece. She was happy now.

Anny looked up to see that Hettie had not left the house, but was loitering near the door to the sickroom. She moved towards her.

'Give Lizzie to Mama,' said Hettie, and thrust the doll at Anny.

'You are a kind, good girl,' she said and put her hand on the girl's little head, golden brown from the sun. 'Run along to Evan now. He's picking beans with his father, I warrant. Can you pick faster than him?'

'I can, I can!' Hettie yelled. She turned, skipping across the front room and through the open doorway to the dusty ground beyond.

Anny turned back to Martha. As she reached down to place the doll beside her face, she stopped. She drew back and held the doll close. Martha's eyes were half-open, her lips parted and her face as still as a mask.

'Oh, Martha,' whispered Anny. She sobbed as she held the doll to her mouth, tears for her dead friend rolling down her cheeks into the doll's woollen hair.

Chapter 1

January 1875

The sound of their clogs could be heard a mile away or more. It began before dawn, in the milky darkness of a foggy winter's morn. A rumble from afar, that grew in strength and breadth until it took on a more chaotic form. Each wooden clog that made its mark on the ground had nails driven into the sole; they struck a note with every step. The noise grew louder still, as the men and women of the pits appeared from front doors and back doors, from side roads and alleyways, joining the throng on its way to work. If any lucky person were still abed, they would be rudely awoken by the growing clatter of the clogs on the cobbles, ringing and bouncing off walls and windows of every street. Along with this came the chatter of the men and oftentimes the singing of the women. The pit bank lasses would rouse them all into sound, even at this early hour. No wonder they called it the clog chorus.

Hettie Jones could hear the singing from across the way as she pulled on her bonnet and grasped her basket. It was as if they sang only to her, calling for her to join them – and so she did, six days a week. So she had done for the past five years, since she left school aged eleven. For Hettie was a pit bank wench and proud of it.

'Make haste, Evan!' she called, as she went to the door. 'They're a-coming down the bank, singing all the way.'

'I am coming,' he answered grumpily. Evan Malone never did like the early mornings.

'Dunna forget your bait,' said his father, Peter. He passed one packet to Hettie, who put it in her basket, and one to Evan, who shoved it in the pocket of his greatcoat. Peter did the same with his own lunch.

'Ta-ta, Anny,' said Hettie and kissed her cheek.

Anny smiled at her. 'Careful on that pit bank. You know girls can fall down shafts if they're careless with their footing. Mind that's not you.'

'I always do,' said Hettie.

Out she went, Peter close behind and Evan following last, out into the bitter air of a January morning. The path was glittering with ice crystals.

'Jack Frost has been,' said Peter and shuddered.

Hettie drew her shawl closer around her and hurried ahead of Peter and Evan, keen to catch the other women as they came down the hill and onto the path that led by the Malones' house. Today they were singing one of her favourite folk songs. As she passed beside the river, swift and black in its winter dress, she could hear their voices rise above the ramshackle rooves of the houses.

Hettie joined in before she could see them, singing out and trotting forward, her clogs tapping in time to the beat of the song. She glanced back at Evan and saw him watching her. He lifted a hand and gave her a crooked smile. She smiled back and turned the corner to see the women marching forward, their voices raised as one. They all wore the same kind of clothes, an unofficial uniform: warm flannel dresses covered waist-down with a home-made apron, petticoats and thick leggings beneath. Some had greatcoats like the men and others had woollen shawls. Many sported patterned neckerchiefs, and all wore print bonnets and clogs. Their wooden shoes were made locally, cool in summer and warm in winter, and raised their feet up out of the mud.

'Morning, Hettie!' said Ada, her closest friend at the pit bank, falling into step beside her. 'Where's Evan today?'

'Back there.' Hettie gestured, then continued singing along.

'Such a nice face. And tall!' said Ada, looking back over her shoulder as they walked. 'You're so lucky to have such a handsome sweetheart.'

'He inna my sweetheart!' said Hettie. 'We grew up together is all. We're more like best friends than anything.'

‘Well, I wish he were my best friend,’ said Ada, grinning mischievously. ‘I’d like to wake every morning to that face, I can tell thee.’

‘Ah, stop your nonsense,’ said Hettie and broke into song again.

She did not like to talk about Evan with the girls. They all fancied him and it made her feel tetchy. Growing up together had brought them closer than most. And these days everybody seemed to think that they might one day be wed. The idea hung in the air like a question waiting to be answered. But was it the right thing to do? Would their precious friendship be spoilt if it changed? Hettie did not know. Nobody spoke of it directly. It was just there, as a constant presence. She sang extra loud to stop herself thinking about it.

But somehow she couldn’t stop thinking about it. She and Evan had been thick as thieves since before she could remember. They played together the whole of their childhood. Even when Evan’s siblings were born, Hettie and Evan didn’t play with the others much, instead rushing off to the woods or the river to be alone. Only school and chores took them away from each other. They had their own language that no one but them understood, which infuriated Anny and Peter. They would have crawled into each other’s beds each night and slept together if the Malones had let them, but Anny made sure they had separate rooms, which were soon occupied with other babies and toddlers as Anny's new children grew. They were all Evan's siblings, and Hettie was the odd one out.

She was a Jones, not a Malone, her mother dead, her father transported. Hettie had never met her father, Adam Jones. He'd been in Australia for sixteen years now, nine beyond his sentence. Everyone thought he was probably dead. In dark moments, Hettie thought of herself as an orphan. It was such a forlorn-sounding word when she whispered it aloud to herself: *orphan*. But the Malones had never made her feel left out and had treated her as one of the family. And Anny always told Hettie stories about her lost mother and father, so that Hettie could keep their memories alive, even if they were second-hand ones. Once school was done and she joined the ranks of the pit bank wenches, they felt like family, too. And now Hettie was never alone. She loved that; she loved gossip and good company.

They all marched together now, about thirty or so females, mostly young women from fourteen or so up to their early twenties, with a couple of middle-aged women and one older still. The walk was another two miles to the pit and they sang all the way, some breaking off to talk or laugh at a private joke. The roads were glassy with ice and some lost their footing as they went, tipping into those beside them. But there was always a pair of hands to catch and right them. They moved as one, the pit bank wenches.

As the pit workings appeared ahead, the crowd of walkers split, the women all heading right, towards the weathering heaps, and the men heading left, towards the shafts. Dawn was breaking now, as dreary daylight crept over the brow of the mound. The great grey heaps of clay studded with nodules of ironstone loomed above them. This was their place of work, their territory. They filtered in and out of the cabin, leaving their baskets and stopping to warm their hands by the fire. Someone would soon light the brazier that sat atop the bank, so that the pickers up there could have a bit of a warm while they were at their work.

And so it began, the Saturday shift.

The pit bank was a huge pile of weathered clay around thirty feet high. Teams of women and girls would go along it, picking out the lumps of ironstone. Hettie began collecting, still humming the song. She deposited each piece in an iron basket. Once it was full, she pulled out a rag from her pocket – an old cloth of Anny's – then folded it and placed it atop her head. She called Ada, who helped her lift the iron basket and settle it on her head, the folded cloth protecting her scalp and helping the heavy basket to balance. The first day she'd started work, aged eleven, Hettie had come home that night crying at her stiff neck. She hadn't thought she could go back and do it all again the next day. But she did and her neck got used to it. Now she could carry a basket with no hands, in perfect balance.

She walked over to the heaps of ironstone that everyone called 'ranks' and deposited her load. Then, back to the bank and the whole process was repeated.

Yes, it was repetitive, but there was a comfort in that. There were few horrible surprises in her workday, unless a girl fell down a mineshaft, as Anny had warned, or there was an accident down the pit. It did happen from time to time and was usually bad news, the worst. Other than that, it was the kind of job that meant you were free from a bossy overseer or the meddling of other workers. Everyone just got on with it, working mostly in good humour, enjoying the freedom to be in the open air. Many other girls her age were in service, and though she liked the idea of that on rainy days, Hettie enjoyed being outside. She loved the camaraderie and the confidence it gave them all. These were girls who had not been bowed by confinement, and it showed: each had a face in ruddy health, strong arms and thighs. And when Hettie took the corner of her neckerchief to wipe the dust from her face, anyone could see she had clear, peachy skin, bright green eyes like her mother and, beneath her bonnet, shining hazelnut hair. Every girl moved assuredly along the bank. It was honest, simple work and Hettie liked it.

The pit was in full swing now and the bursts of chatter from the girls were accompanied by the sounds from the pit mouth, chains clanking through the pulleys, waggons clattering over rollers. The women periodically stopped to stamp their frozen feet on the solid ground and rub their hands together. Hettie and Ada clambered up to the brazier, now burning brightly atop the bank, and held their hands to the heat, fingers reaching towards the flames as close as they dared. Hettie looked up above the mine, beyond the woods nearby and into the sky. It was glowing with a strange yellow-white hue.

'Looks like snow a-coming,' said Hettie.

'I canna wait till summer,' said Ada. 'Oh, Hettie – you are coming to London with us this year? Have you asked your . . . Anny?'

Hettie thought, *Ada was going to say your parents, your mother or father*. But Hettie had no parents to ask anything of. She tried to push the thought away.

'Not yet. I'm a-thinking on it.'

Ada replied, 'Oh, you mun come! Whatever might be stopping you? I wanted you to come last year, but you wouldna. But you shall love it, you'll see. We shall all take the train to London together. The gardens will be in full fruit and we shall spend our days picking strawberries and the like, packing them in baskets and carrying them on our heads to the markets and carrying our empties back. Then when the fruit is done, we go on to vegetables. Singing all the way. And lots of coin to be earned. And then you shall spend it – or some of it, leastways – on the prettiest dress that the fair ever saw. And in September, at Oakengates fair, we shall be the finest wenches in

Shropshire. You didna go to the fair last year for you didna have a fine enough dress. So you mun go this time, Hettie. You surely mun go!'

'I know all of that,' said Hettie. She turned, pretending she'd spotted some lumps of ironstone a few steps away.

The truth was that she did not know whether to go or not. She loved the sound of it, the annual migration of the pit bank girls to the fruit and vegetable fields west of London, where their skill for picking and carrying heavy loads was put to an alternative summer use. But she was nervous of leaving home alone, without Anny or Peter to look out for her. And without Evan – that was the truth of it. To go a whole summer without her Evan, without seeing his face every morn and night, without his words and whisperings when they walked together, without his shoulder to lean on when they sat in a cwtch, with the other children on the settle, before the fire. Without all of this, she did not know if she had the confidence to leave her home for three months, only in the company of the other pit bank wenches. But she did not want to admit it to Ada, or to anyone. It made her feel silly, to dote upon Evan so, but he was her sun and her moon, and that was that.

Yet the strawberry fields were tempting. She could only imagine how sweet the scent of the air must be in a field of fruit. And the thought of seeing new people and places, of the hustle and bustle of the

London markets, the fruit sellers and the other market folk shouting and cursing, as Ada had told her stories of. It would be thrilling! Hettie had been too afraid last year, but perhaps it was time. She was sixteen, after all, and most of her friends had done it now. And she would have some rum stories to tell Evan when she came back.

'All right,' she called over to Ada, who needed help with her iron basket. Hettie came towards her, slipping a little on an icy patch, her clog skidding down the bank a couple of inches, her breath catching in her throat. But she stayed balanced and went back to Ada, helping her up with her load. 'I'll do it. I'll come strawberry picking.'

'You wonna regret it, Hettie!' cried Ada. 'And what larks we shall have!'

There was a new boy today. Ten years old, trying to look taller than he was. Evan watched him clamber into the chain seat that would take them down the pit shaft. He climbed on beside him, followed by two other men. Evan could feel the new boy's shoulder juddering against his own, shaking and shivering. It wasn't just the cold that gripped the boy – they'd all taken their coats off and left them in the cabin – but it was fear, too. Each one of them was handed a lit candle, stuck fast into a lump of marl. Evan's eyes were drawn to the captivating flames, the only bright thing in this scene of greys and blacks.

The contraption that carried the men down the shaft was called the doubles by the miners. The banksman stood beside it to ensure a decent connection between the hook above them and the chain that carried them down. The bellman gave a quick ring of his bell to signal all was safe and ready for the men to go. All done, the slow descent began. The four candles threw swift, flickering shadows onto the brick-lined walls all around them.

There were four of them riding the doubles today. Evan's father was working above ground, supervising the loading of the coal into the waggons and fixing some of the equipment. Along with Evan and the boy were two of the oldest, most seasoned and sarcastic colliers that ever drew breath.

Boxer, the eldest, a man built like a brick privy, cleared his throat to speak, then coughed and coughed again. All colliers past a certain age had that cough. And one day the cough would carry them off. Everyone knew that.

'I think it be twelve month today since rope last broke,' said Boxer.

Evan rolled his eyes at the tasteless joke, but the new boy began to whimper.

'I believe this understrapper be afeard,' said Socksy, their other companion, a wiry little man with a thin neck but thick arms like two hams.

The boy said nothing.

'He hasna a scrap on him,' said Boxer. 'He'll be dead of hard work afore it's time for bait.'

'Leave him be,' said Evan, gruffly. He had no time for bullies.

'But mon,' Socksy carried on, 'this little nipper needs some advising, dunna he, Scrapper?'

All the colliers had nicknames and this was Evan's, in honour of his habit of falling into scraps with other boys from an early age. And pretty handy with his fists was Evan, too.

'Arr, he do,' added Boxer. 'Listen up, Daff.'

So, the new boy had his nickname already. Daff meant someone shy and a bit wet behind the ears. He'd never outlive that name. The die was cast.

'Now then, lad,' began Socksy, leaning over and speaking in the boy's ear, close enough that the boy must have been able to feel the tickle of Socksy's prodigious moustache hairs. 'There be only one thing that can kill you down there and that's all of it.'

This was followed by a guffaw of laughter that made the boy flinch into Evan's arm.

'Damp'll kill you,' added Boxer. 'And I'm not talking moist. I'm talking gas. Damps, we call 'em. Stinkdamp smells like rotten eggs and'll make you sick as a dog. Firedamp'll catch from your candle and blow you to bits. But worst of all is blackdamp – it lingers above you, no odour. Just one breath and you're dead.'

Evan decided to tell the boy later about the canaries in cages they used to test for blackdamp. But everyone knew that it came so fast sometimes that the men were dead in their tracks before they'd had a moment to even notice the canary's demise, leastways alert anyone. He wouldn't tell the boy that, though. No sense in scaring him even more.

Boxer and Socksy fell silent now, leaving the boy to his morbid thoughts. Evan closed his eyes. The winder was so steady that it almost felt as if they were not moving. But when he opened his eyes, he saw that most of the brick-lined shaft was above them and they were about to reach the bottom. He felt the speed slacken as the ground came up to them, and then it was time to extricate his legs from the chains and stand firmly on the floor. They were around eight hundred feet down beneath the surface, in a place no human should ever be.

'Off you pile!' cried Boxer.

Evan watched the new boy climb clumsily out of the chains. He tripped, dropping his candle. It hit the floor and promptly went out. Evan took it up, relit it from his own and handed it to the boy, who nodded in gratitude. His face was as white as a sheet as he gazed around at his new surroundings.

The first thing the boy would see was the stables: cut out from the rock was a recess in which a few ponies were kept all year round. Some of them had not seen sunlight for seven years or more. Evan knew that if you touched them their skins were smooth like velvet, because they'd been cocooned down here so long. Evan pitied them, of course he did. Though he sometimes had a short fuse, Evan hated cruelty in all its forms.

He pitied the boy Daff too, who was now gaping about himself and wiping his brow with his cloth cap. The heat was already building up here at the foot of the shaft. It would only get hotter as they went deeper into the earth. The others were taking off their shirts and hanging them up on nails driven into the rock. Evan followed suit and gestured that Daff should do the same. Everyone worked half-naked down here.

Evan had to get off to the coalface and the boy would be taken to his place somewhere else, perhaps to man the doors that kept the airflow controlled, or to pull a waggon of coal in some confined space. Before he went, Evan took Daff aside beneath the timber supports that arched over their heads at the commencement of the tunnels.

'Where's your bait?'

Daff still did not speak, but took a pitifully small package from his trouser pocket, wrapped in newspaper, as Evan's was.

'When you get where you're going, if you can, string it up with a bit of explosive wire, so it hangs above the ground. Either that, or eat it straight away. Otherwise it'll get pinched.'

'They'll take my food? But it's all I got,' said the boy, welling up.

'Not the blokes,' said Evan. 'The mice. And the rats. Watch out for them.'

He left the boy then, not wanting to waste any more time. He had to move along to the coalface and get started. Boxer and Socksy were already heading that way. Colliers were paid by weight, not time, so every minute counted. Evan left Daff clutching his lunch, still pale-faced and terrified. The boy would have to get used to it, that was all. Nobody could do it for him.

As Evan walked away from the boy and down the tunnel they called a 'road', he finally had time to think. His candle threw strange shadows about him, twisting, fleeting things that dipped and swooped like dark ghosts. It was common to think on such things down here, though why a spirit with free rein of the outside would ever bother to haunt a mine was beyond him.

He thought he'd seen one once, flitting between the gravestones at dusk, when he and Hettie used to frequent the ruins of Southover. They did it all the time when they were nippers. It was quiet up there, away from the other village kids. They liked nothing better than to play alone. When the other kids were about, there was always some trouble brewing. The children from different villages, especially those from different sides of the river, were perpetually at war, with lengthy, staged battles taking place all over. Evan was always commandeered for his skill at fighting, though if the truth be known, he'd much rather hang about with Hettie than anyone else.

Most folk avoided the ruins of Southover, saying that it was indeed haunted. But Evan couldn't stay away; it fascinated him. He knew it was the place where his brother Owen had died when Evan was still in his mother's belly, the brother Evan had never known. His parents never spoke of it, but Evan had heard the gossip, the story that Owen had loved a girl from the King family and it had been the death of him. He'd died saving her from the burning building.

Though he never knew Owen, this fact alone raised him to the status of hero in Evan's eyes. He often wanted to ask his parents more about his elder brother, but every time his name was mentioned, his mother's eyes would fill and his father's would cloud and Evan could not bear to see the pain in their faces, still fresh after all these years. So he was drawn to the ruins. But since he and Hettie had both started working, they had far less time to spend together. Though they were employed by the same pit, they worked in different worlds, Hettie above ground and Evan below, scouring away at the earth's riches, buried jealously away from man's endeavours.

Evan finally reached the coalface. First, he fetched his tools that he left in a recess in the rock each day, as all the men did. His pick was his own and no man must touch it. All the colliers felt the same about their tools. They were sacrosanct. Each had the owner's initials carved in the handle. Beside Evan's pick was his ringer, a crowbar with a spike at one end and a lever at the other, to break up the coal. He knelt down and shoved them along the ground, holding the candle in his other hand, crawling along to reach his place at the coalface.

It was about three feet high there. He set down his candle and sat on his knees, his clogs beneath him, each arse cheek resting on a clog. It saved his feet from aching too much. But everything else ached, his neck from bending, his back from crouching, his knees from kneeling. Now and again he'd stretch out on the floor and roll around to free his muscles up a bit, then back to it. In five hours he'd stop and eat his bait, there at the coalface. Then another five hours and it'd be time to go and see Hettie.

'Hettie,' he said her name aloud, then checked himself. But nobody was listening. The nearest collier was six yards away, already striking the coalface with his ringer and ignoring all other presence than his own two arms and the coal that spilled forth from his labour. Nobody chatted down here at the face. Nobody had the time or the strength. It was graft, pure graft. And Evan must start his for the day.

He took up his pick and with his sizeable arms, muscles straining, he heaved it at the coalface and struck it soundly. Only thousands more strikes to do and then his day would be done. Out of this godforsaken place and up, up into the waning day and his first glimpse of Hettie since dawn.

Hettie loved her job, but she always welcomed the end of the shift and the walk home with Peter and Evan. All the way back, her mind was filled with her decision to go to London, though she did not speak of it. She was not ready to tell Evan about it yet. Something told her he wouldn't approve. No, it was more than that; he wouldn't want her to go, for he would miss her company terribly. Perhaps even more so, he would fear that she would change, that she wouldn't be his Hettie anymore once her head had been turned by London ways. But that was precisely the reason Hettie wanted to go. She *wanted* to change and grow, to see a patch of the world beyond her own. And she found a kernel of resentment in herself that Evan and the rest of the Malone family might want to deny her that chance.

As they tramped home in the cold, for the first time she found herself thinking, *Nothing ever happens around here. Every day is the same.*

Once home, they were welcomed by Anny with a hot supper and they all shared the gossip of the day. Once the meal was done and they were clearing the table, Hettie took her chance.

She announced to anyone who would listen, 'I want to go to London to pick strawberries this year.'

Everyone stopped and stared at her. From their surprised expressions, Hettie could see that Peter and Evan were against it, but Anny was smiling and nodding, showing she was for it. Flora, aged ten, with a thatch of thick red hair, glanced earnestly at both sides. She most likely wanted to go to London herself one day, and would be picking up tips of how to achieve that when the time came. The younger ones, the twins with their blond curls – christened William and Lilian, but known to all as Billy and Lily – were ignoring the debate. They were aged only six and were far more concerned with Billy's set of jacks. They'd lost the ball and were traipsing around the cottage looking for it, whining from time to time and being roundly ignored by all.

'It inna fitting for a girl to go to London on her own,' said Evan, standing with his arms folded, glaring at Hettie.

'There'll be twenty other women with me!' said Hettie.

'A gaggle of wenches dunna mean you'll be safe,' said Peter, puffing on his pipe.

'Is anyone going to help me with these blessed dishes?' asked Anny impatiently, wiping her hands on her apron while the others stood about and bickered.

'But what do you think, Anny?' said her husband. 'This is important. We mun make a decision.'

'Listen to me,' said Anny, and everyone did – even Billy and Lily ceased their search for a moment. Anny was the matriarch of the family and what she said was followed to the letter. 'Hettie is sixteen and shall turn seventeen in July. She is a young woman. She can make her own mind up about these things. What do you want to do, Hettie?'

All eyes turned to Hettie. She raised her chin and spoke clearly. 'I want to go.'

'That's that, then,' said Anny, and went to the sink to pour in water.

'But there are dangers in London,' said Peter. 'You know what they say about girls who go there, unaccompanied as they are.'

'I will be accompanied! I've told you!' cried Hettie, exasperated now.

'But there'll be no man to keep you in line, lass.'

Anny turned swiftly round from the sink and gave her husband such a glare that he coughed a little on his pipe smoke.

'No man keeps me in line, Peter Malone,' she said in a low voice, laced with threat.

Peter shook his head and coughed a little more. 'Oh, I wasna thinking of such as you, my sweet.'

'But Father is right,' said Evan, hunched in a chair by the fire. 'You know what they say about the girls who go to London.'

'What do they say?' piped up Flora, even more interested now.

'Nothing,' said Anny. 'Just idle gossip.'

'Well, that Morrison girl wasna gossip, was she? She came back with . . .'

'With what?' said Flora, eyes wide as saucers.

Peter puffed again, then said quietly, as if that meant Flora couldn't hear, 'In the *family way*.'

'She was always like that, Olive Morrison,' said Hettie. 'Always after the boys. But I inna like that!'

'We know that, love,' said Anny. 'And anyway, Olive's young man came from London and took her there and they married and 'twas all respectable in the end.'

'But we dunna want our Hettie marrying some London feller!' cried Evan.

Anny gave him a sharp, curious look. Evan turned away. Hettie watched all this with interest.

'As I say,' Anny went on, 'Hettie is a young woman now and the decision is entirely hers to make.'

'But Mother,' began Evan, standing up from his chair.

He was interrupted by Billy and Lily, who had had enough of this tedious discussion and wanted to assert their own rights to attention now. Billy piped up, 'We've looked high and low!'

'High and low!' repeated Lily.

'And no ball!' cried Billy, which Lily again echoed. 'The only place we havna looked is the ceiling.'

'What ball?' said Anny, lifting a bowl from the sink and setting it down to drip-dry on the draining board.

A faint knock came on the front door. Only Flora noticed. 'Was that a knock?' she said, and everyone stopped to listen.

After a moment's silence, it came again. Definitely a knock, then another and another. Three knocks, louder this time, more insistent.

Peter said, 'Answer it then, Flossie.'

Flora skipped over to the door, lifted the latch and pulled it open. Everyone heard Flora gasp and they turned to see as a blast of winter air filled the room.

Hettie was behind the door when she saw Flora's face turn, with a touch of apprehension, to her mother. 'It's a mon,' said Flora in a small voice and stepped back from the door. She was usually chatty with strangers, and it was unlike her to be afraid.

'My God,' said Peter, his pipe held motionless, smoke spiralling from it in the cold air.

'Who is that mon with the long beard?' asked Billy, and Lily added, 'Proper long beard.'

Hettie stepped round to look at the man at the door. He did indeed have a very long beard, dark and bushy and threaded with grey. He wore a thin coat unsuited to the January cold. His trousers were muddy at the knees and ragged at the ankles, atop filthy boots. He wore a grey waistcoat and a chequered shirt, a grimy neckerchief knotted about his neck. On his head was a battered brown hat pulled down low over his ears, hiding his eyes in shadow.

'Come in, mon. Come in,' said Peter, who was now striding over to the door and reaching out to place his hand on the man's shoulder. He obviously knew him.

But, Hettie thought, *who is he?*

She turned towards Anny, to see if she knew the man. Anny looked white as a sheet. Then she glanced hurriedly at Hettie. The look was piercing, as if she had seen something in Hettie's soul. Hettie felt a sudden surge of confusion and alarm. What was happening?

As the man stepped into the room, nodding at all of its occupants, Anny moved towards him. When he looked at Hettie, he stopped and stared at her. He removed his hat and now Hettie could see his eyes. Black eyes, so dark and intense they gave her a shock.

The man looked at Anny, gestured to Hettie and said, 'Is this my girl?'

My girl? she thought. Then the knowledge came to her like a slap. This man was her father. This dishevelled, roughshod man was her own father, returned from certain death in Australia.

'That it be,' said Anny, placing her hands on his shoulders and guiding him over to the table. He sat down, never taking his eyes from Hettie. She stared back at him, unable to speak or move. He went to place his hat carefully before him on the table, but hesitated and put it on his lap instead. Perhaps he thought it too filthy to sully the Malones' table.

He turned his face up to Anny and asked, 'Where is my Martha?'

The younger children stood around like wax dummies, watching the man's every move.

Hettie saw Anny's eyes fill with tears.

'She's gone,' said Peter, and patted the man on the shoulder. 'Thirteen year ago now. She didna suffer. A short illness. We've kept Hettie ever since. She's been well looked after.'

The man turned and looked at Hettie again, pain in his eyes. Then he looked away and his head fell. He buried his face in his hands.

'Everyone,' said Anny, 'this man is an old friend of ours. His name is Adam Jones. He's Hettie's father.'

Chapter 2

Queenie looked out of her bedroom window at the swaying trees beyond. The temperature had not risen above freezing that day, and the branches were still draped in white. Queenie was swathed in blankets and shawls, with slippers made from fox fur. Sitting around was what she mostly did these days, and Jenkins kept the fire stoked up, but Queenie always felt cold, the kind of cold that went down to her bones.

She shivered and shifted in her seat. Just the same old trees to look at, nothing more. She had been in this house, the old brickmaster's place as many still called it, for sixteen years now. She had grown accustomed to it since the loss of Southover in the fire, torched by those errant brickmakers who had defied the Kings and destroyed the seat of their power. *But, as ever, the Kings were not to be beaten*, thought Queenie proudly.

She had led this family back to success – for three years after the fire, at least. Then her health had taken a turn for the worse, and against all of her better judgement, she had had to hand over the running of the business to her daughter-in-law, Benjamina. For thirteen years the woman had been in charge, and Queenie had to admit that she had done well. Very well, if truth be known. But Queenie would never let on that this was the case. She had always disliked Benjamina, and she knew the feeling was mutual. Now that Queenie was a very elderly woman herself, she knew that her daughter-in-law's deepest desire was for her to die. She should have died years ago, she knew that; ninety-six was a ridiculous age to attain. But here she still was, a needle in Benjamina's side. That fact at least pleased Queenie.

'Meeting soon,' came a voice, and Queenie turned to see Jenkins shuffle in. 'It's your meeting with Benjamina soon, and after that it'll be time for dinner, so you'd best look lively. Did you hear what I said, woman?'

'I heard you quite clearly,' replied Queenie in a haughty tone, 'but seeing as it is a weekly occurrence and I have not yet lost my mind completely, I was well aware of the fact already.'

The two women glared at each other, then their eyes softened. They had played this game of back and forth for so long that it was in their very blood. Behind the bickering was true closeness. Rose Jenkins, her beloved lady's maid, who had been with her for decades, had always stood by her, through thick and thin; she was Queenie's only friend in the world. Queenie was always aware that it was a business arrangement, that Jenkins was paid to be there. But in her softer moments, she liked to think that Jenkins had at least a portion of the regard – and dare she say, even love? – that Queenie had for her, after all these years. Queenie watched her approach with real fondness. Jenkins stopped and coughed, then coughed again. It took her several moments to recover herself, moments that Queenie spent encased in a creeping fear.

'Jenkins, that is the third time this week I have seen you overcome in this way.'

'Overcome? It is but a winter cough. I'm fine. Don't fuss me.'

'I don't know how many times I've told you – I've lost count – but you are too old for this job. You must retire and let me pay your pension. It will be generous, you know that.'

'I don't want to retire,' said Jenkins and huffed. She came to Queenie's chair and rearranged the blanket over her knees, tucking it in to ensure Queenie's legs were fully covered. 'And what would I do with a pension? I have no children to leave it to. And who would I talk to, down in Worthing or Weston-super-Mare or wherever it is old spinsters go to stay in cold boarding houses before their imminent death?'

'My dear, you are seventy-five years of age. You are often breathless. I worry for your heart.'

'Oh, there's nothing wrong with my heart. You know I have old Dr Fitzgerald check it every so often, as you pay him handsomely for it. And besides, I have Clayton to help me now.'

'Yes, you do. But you must allow her to do more.'

'How can she do more? I know she's young, all of twenty-five. And of course, being my cousin's child, she comes from good stock and would never be one to shirk work. But she's Benjamina's lady's maid, not yours. She has enough to do. I let her do the heavy work – not that there is much. I manage the rest. I am quite capable of working for a good few years yet, Miss Alice, you mark my words.'

'But you should not be working any longer. You should be resting,' said Queenie, gently placing her hand on Jenkins's own.

Jenkins gave Queenie's hand a quick squeeze, then went to her hair and fiddled with it, though Queenie knew it needed nothing. Jenkins's reluctance to retire and leave her bathed Queenie in warmth. Perhaps Jenkins needed Queenie as much as Queenie needed her, after all.

'I don't want to rest, Miss Alice. I'd be horribly bored. Now, I'll go and tell the girl to bring your tea.'

While she awaited her tea tray, Queenie made the decision to give Jenkins a week off all duties and insist that Clayton tend to her needs, whenever Benjamina could possibly spare her. Even though she could afford to hire as many new maids as she liked, utilising Benjamina's maid would madden her so very much, and this fact brought Queenie great pleasure. She was still grinning about it when Jenkins came back.

In fact, just to annoy Benjamina further, she told Jenkins to stay and have a cup of tea with her and not fetch the younger Mrs King just yet. That jumped-up shop girl could wait.

Presently, Jenkins got up and said, 'I'm off to get the dog botherer.'

Queenie smirked at Jenkins's nickname for Benjamina. How they both despised her! They always had done, since she was brought to the house by her unwise son to be his wife when she was aged just seventeen. She had only her beauty to recommend her, with no sense and no class. Benjamina had been a shop girl that Ralph had found in Shrewsbury, for heaven's sake. Hardly a suitable match for the King heir. But his first wife had died giving birth to their second child, and he had been heartbroken by it. He wanted this new wife to cheer him, and Queenie had not been able to find reason enough to prevent it. He had insisted and Queenie had let him win.

From that day forward she had begrudgingly put up with the child – for that is what Benjamina had been, more or less, when Ralph brought her home. She had been only a few years older than Ralph's own children, Margaret and Cyril. They were only twelve and fourteen then; now, both of them were dead and gone, just like her son.

Her memories were interrupted by the entrance of Benjamina, followed by Jenkins. Benjamina wore a midnight-blue silk dress with a bodice far too tight for her age, with a sizeable bustle at the back. She was carrying a sheaf of papers to make her look important. Queenie noted with satisfaction that her hands looked far older than her face, belying the age she took such pains to hide. But Queenie had to admit that Benjamina was an extremely handsome woman. Few would guess she was in her late fifties.

She took a seat opposite Queenie, perched on the edge due to her bustle, which made Queenie smirk. It was definitely one of the more ridiculous current fashions.

'Firstly, the weekly figures,' announced Benjamina imperiously. There was never any small talk between them. Queenie listened carefully to Benjamina's summary, although she'd already seen the figures herself; she had these sent to her regularly, as she liked to be prepared. Benjamina was wittering on now about how well everything was doing, as if it were all down to her and her alone, as if there were no workers labouring from dawn till dusk to bring this success about.

'I am sure you'll agree, Queenie, that the running of the companies has improved vastly since my late husband's day. His inept handling could have landed us in the workhouse!'

At this mention of her son, Queenie sighed. So many of her family were gone now. Her son Ralph had died of illness brought on by lazy living. Though she had had little feeling for him during his lifetime, she did regret his early death. Her grandchildren also both died young, Margaret lost in the fire and Cyril killed in a railway accident fifteen years ago, over in America. He had gone there after the fire, eager to escape the aftermath, and had been accompanied by Queenie's beloved great-granddaughter Beatrice.

Beatrice was Queenie's great love, but her mother's death in the fire broke her for a time and she would not stay in a place that plagued her with memories. She had told Queenie that there was a boy she loved, one of that Woodvine family, the Malones by marriage. He'd saved her life the night of the fire, but died himself in the burning house.

Queenie's eyes filled with tears, not for Owen Malone, though she was grateful to his memory for saving her darling Beatrice, but for Beatrice's absence. She had been resident in America for sixteen years now without a single visit home, and nothing Queenie wrote to her could ever persuade her to come back. Beatrice wrote letters to Queenie every three months to the day. She was a loyal child that way. But she would not come back. She'd once written to Queenie that she felt haunted by Ironbridge and all that had happened there, but somehow the ship to America had left those spectres lingering at the port, unable to cross the ocean.

'Queenie?' said Benjamina.

Queenie looked up to find the woman staring at her. 'Yes, yes, I am listening,' she said.

Benjamina raised her eyebrows to no one but herself, which annoyed Queenie intensely. Benjamina went on, 'I must now move on to another matter . . . one I know you dislike to discuss, but it must be said.'

Queenie knew what was coming; they had the same argument roughly once a month or so.

'Go on,' Queenie simply said. She liked to watch Benjamina work herself up into a lather.

'I do believe that the letters you receive from your great-granddaughter are a bad influence upon your decision-making.'

'Ah,' said Queenie and smiled. 'It has been a little while since you attacked Beatrice. Please do elaborate.'

Benjamina shifted in her seat. 'Attack is entirely the wrong word. Rather, I advise. Beatrice is a kind soul but she has been in America too long. Her brain has been addled by the talk of freedom they adore over there. Things work differently here in the old country. I know how fond you are of her, but her ideas are not suited to our way of life. She has encouraged you to change the business and include a philanthropic wing to our work – which is admirable, certainly, but it makes no sense in business terms. It is costing us dearly, and I fear it will place our business in a dangerous position if we continue in this same vein.'

'You cannot scare me into changing my mind,' said Queenie. 'You've never succeeded in scaring me, Benjamina, and you never will.'

Benjamina shifted forward in her seat. Was that meant to assert dominance? Queenie wondered. It just made her look even more precarious, as if the bustle would shove her off the chair imminently. 'I strongly advise you to disregard Beatrice's advice. You won't like me saying it, but it has to be said. You must cease this sentimental clinging to the ghosts of the past.'

At the mention of ghosts, Queenie glanced around. No ghosts here – not for years. She had not had a sniff of the spirit of her old maidservant, Betsy Blaize, since a few months after Beatrice had left.

Many years ago, Blaize had been raped and impregnated by Ralph senior, Queenie's husband, and Queenie had stood by and let it happen. Since Blaize's death when she was just sixteen years old, her ghost had visited Queenie continually, cursing her and the Kings for their actions and berating her for not protecting her daughter, the baby on the bridge. But then, sixteen years ago, Queenie herself had saved the husband of Blaize's daughter from certain death: her intervention in the trial of Adam Jones had led to him being sentenced only to transportation, not death, for organising the arson upon Southover. And she had done more than that for her fellow man, much more: once Queenie had heard from Beatrice that she was never coming back to take over the King business as Queenie had desired, she had decided to run her business in a new way, dealing with their workers in a more humanitarian fashion and devoting any surplus profits to charitable works. Since that decision, the ghost had stopped its visits.

Three years after the fire, Queenie heard from Jenkins that Blaize's daughter Martha had died, and that her child Hettie continued to live with Peter and Anny Malone. Queenie had arranged for Jenkins to take money to the Malones several times, to help with Hettie's upbringing, but it was always refused and returned. On each occasion, Queenie expected the vengeful ghost of Blaize to appear and berate her, but it never did. Either the spirit was satisfied or Queenie's former madness had passed. She was never quite sure where the truth lay, in supernatural causes or the vagaries of her own mind. But the ghost was gone, for good it seemed, and that was a comfort to Queenie.

She had become a better person in the last sixteen years, not only at the ghost's behest but also at the urgings of her darling Beatrice, who had told her again and again that things must change. Queenie had ensured that Benjamina continued her charitable business practices when she took over, and it was something they argued about incessantly. Benjamina did not have Queenie's reasons to be soft in business, and fought against Queenie's directions. But Queenie believed with all of her heart that if the Kings ever returned to the cruelty of their past, then the ghost would surely appear again, lighting up Queenie's room at night with its unearthly glow and bringing disaster to the King household once more.

'Queenie! Please concentrate!'

Queenie recalled where she was and who she was talking to. She might have been nearly a hundred years of age, but she still had a voice, and a strident one at that. And she still had her wits about her. 'If you wish me to remain present, then you must stop repeating your empty phrases like a trained mynah bird. The charitable contributions will remain as long as I am alive. And it would serve you well in the eternal hereafter, Benjamina, if you thought of others more than yourself. You never know who is watching.'

Benjamina looked queerly at Queenie. *She thinks I am mad*, thought Queenie. *Let her. I know I'm right about this one.*

'Is that all, Benjamina? I do believe it is time to prepare for dinner. You may go now.'

Benjamina got up in a huff, Queenie smiling serenely until she'd left the room. Once the door closed, she felt spent. It was a tiring business, thwarting Benjamina. But Queenie was determined she would continue these weekly meetings – to the very day she died, if she could.

It gave her great pleasure to aggravate the woman at every possible opportunity.

Hettie stared at the man. Flora, Billy and Lily all turned and gaped at her. She felt their astonished scrutiny and glanced at Evan. He was watching her, too, but with pity in his eyes. She hated it, this sharp attention on her. She wanted to run away and hide. Could this mess of a man really be her long-awaited father? He looked about a hundred years old and he smelt terrible. Now the door was closed and the icy air had gone, the unwashed stink of him wafted about the room and sickened Hettie.

Still, she knew that something was expected of her, so she stepped forward. The man lifted his eyes and fixed her with his dark gaze.

'Pleasure to meet you, sir,' said Hettie, her voice croaking a little in the middle, her mouth suddenly dry.

'I have dreamt of this moment for many a year,' said the man. She could not bear to think of him yet as her father or even as the fabled Adam Jones she had dreamt of when she was a young child. She was ashamed of him, she realised, and ashamed of herself for being so.

'Let us feed you and water you and get you to rest,' said Anny. 'We can talk more in the morning. Children, this man has travelled thousands and thousands of miles to be with us this night, and he must be sorely tired. You must all be quiet and get an early bedtime and leave him be.'

'But I wanna talk to the mon!' cried Billy.

'And ask about his beard,' added Lily. 'Are there sparrows living in it?'

Billy whispered loudly to Lily, 'I think I saw a spider in it. Also, he smells like pig dung.'

'Off with you now,' said Anny, and shooed the little ones away to their room. She tasked Flora with sorting them out, then came back to the main room, giving a concerned glance to Hettie.

Hettie was rooted to the spot, unable to move or speak. Her father was sitting with his eyes drawn to the fire that danced in the fireplace. He looked half-delirious. Hettie guessed he must be exhausted.

But then, abruptly, he sat upright, turned to her and spoke.

'I know my arrival will be a dreadful shock to you, Hettie. My appearance is not what I'd have hoped for my first meeting with my daughter since her infancy. But I want you to know that underneath this filth, these soiled garments and this crow's nest of a beard, is a father. A father who once loved you more than life itself, though you wouldna recall it, being just a babby when I saw you last. I have been through the circles of hell since then, and I have much to tell you, if you wish to hear it. But for now, I would like to eat and drink. I am exceeding weary from my journey.'

‘Yes,’ said Hettie, nodding. She was taken aback by this eloquent speech, which she had not expected from such a rough exterior. ‘You must eat and drink.’

She still could not move, but she saw Anny was fetching bread and meat from the shelves in the larder and bringing it to the table. She thought a drink of milk would be good sustenance for the man – her father, as she must now think of him – and she managed to move her rooted feet to fetch him one. She walked to the jug and exchanged glances with Evan, who came to stand beside her.

‘Are you well, Hettie?’ he said, kindly. His eyes searched her face. Evan always understood her. He would know how shocking this moment was for her and how important.

‘Quite well, thank’ee,’ she said quietly and poured out the milk into a mug.

She took it to her father and placed it beside him on the table. He looked up at her and somewhere in the midst of that bushy beard, there came a smile. His eyes softened as he gazed upon her and she could not help but smile back.

‘Thank’ee.’ He nodded at her, taking up the mug and downing it almost in one gulp.

‘You’re more than welcome,’ she said, taking up a seat on the other side of the fire, not far from Evan. She could still feel him watching her.

Peter and Anny went about their chores as her father solemnly ate his food. Bits of bread stuck in his beard, which he brushed off from time to time. Hettie knew he must want to eat in peace, but so many questions were racing about her head, and she felt she would burst waiting to ask them. So the three of them sat in an awkward silence, Evan, Hettie and her father, watching him eat, or staring into the fire, or glancing at each other.

When all three of the younger children were in bed, Anny invited Adam to sit by the fire in Peter's chair, the most comfortable one of all. Anny continued bustling about with jobs, while Peter found a spare pipe for Adam and together they lit up and puffed. Evan and Hettie watched all this with interest.

Then, Adam spoke again. 'Daughter, I suppose you would like to hear the story of what has happened to me these past years.'

'Yes!' said Hettie, then checked herself. She hadn't meant it to come out so eagerly.

'Good,' said Adam. 'For there is much to tell.'

'Are you not too tired, Adam?' said Anny, bringing him a steaming mug of tea to enjoy with his pipe.

'I find myself revived,' he said, a twinkle appearing in his eye, which made him look ten years younger. Hettie realised with a jolt that this man was probably the same age as Peter, or thereabouts. He must be in his early fifties, though he had looked ten years older than that when he first appeared at their door.

Anny settled in a chair with her knitting. Evan stood by the fire, leaning against the mantelpiece, watching Hettie watch her father as he began his story.

'I was transported on the *Palmerston* in November – the eighth of November, 1860. I'll never forget the date. There were just over three hundred souls on board. Most were sentenced to life imprisonment, some to seven years, like me, others to twelve or more. We left from Portland. There were some passengers on board, too, pensioner guards, wives and children, as well as soldiers and us convicts. I treated every man on that ship as an enemy until I had hard proof they were not. Eventually, I became friends with one man, Henry Adkins. He'd also been sent down for arson – he'd been convicted of firing a haystack, which he said he hadna done, just as I didna commit my crime. His sentence was ten and mine was seven, so I counted myself lucky.'

He paused for a moment, clearing his throat and breathing heavily. Hettie wanted him to rest and was about to say he should, when he started up again. She supposed it was more important to him to get his story out.

'We arrived in February in Western Australia at the Swan River colony. It was a rural place, small, like a village. The houses were little, made of brick or stone, some laid out with gardens and allotments for growing food. Some of the main thoroughfares had proper roads, but most of the place was paved in loose sand. It blinded you in the bright summer light and turned to mud in the infrequent rain.

'Convicts were stationed at a low, long, white building called the 'Establishment', where all the chain gangs were housed. We worked on road building at first. Later on construction of buildings, docks and bridges. Sometimes one of the other men tried to escape. Sometimes they were caught and received the lash, but most of the time the punishment was the land itself. There was no sustenance or comfort in the bush, and all escapees starved out there, or else returned to the chains to accept their punishment and survive. My friend Henry Adkins tried to persuade me to escape with him, but I saw it was senseless. They brought his body back some weeks later, a bag of bones, starved to death. They laid it out as a warning for all to see. That near broke my spirit, I tell you, but I persevered. Writing home was all that kept me going at first. I wrote to Martha again and again, but I never received any reply. Perhaps they never arrived. I don't know. I always tried to hope so. The thought that Martha had disowned me was too much to bear.'

'We never received a thing,' said Peter, in astonishment.

Anny's eyes were shining with emotion. 'How terrible,' she muttered.

'Well, I'm happy to know I wasna ignored and 'twas but a quirk of fate my letters were never answered.' Adam sighed. 'After four years, I was eligible for a pardon and was allowed to work as a wage earner for free settlers for the next three years of my sentence. I was given my ticket-of-leave. But the money I'd earnt was nowhere near enough to secure passage back to England. I worked for sheep farmers around and about for another four years before I was finally able to apply for my Certificate of Freedom. As soon as I had it, I saved up some money to board a ship to eastern Australia.

'It was difficult to find much work there. The people were prejudiced against convicts. I struggled for a while in Sydney before I returned to Western Australia, seeking the old masters I used to work for. I lived as simply as I could and I saved as much of my wage as I could manage without starving. I saved up for the passage home for the next five years.'

'It can't have been easy,' said Anny.

Adam shook his head. 'It weren't. I had to master my loneliness and desperation, remembering always that my goal was to return to my Martha and my child. My money was stolen twice, and I had to start saving again from scratch. But eventually I got there and bought my passage. It took four months for the ship to arrive. I came straight to Shropshire from the coast, walking mostly or hitching a ride on a waggon here and there.' He glanced at Peter and Anny. 'I've no money left, I'm sorry to say, so I canna offer you payment for your kindness to my girl.'

'No payment necessary, mon,' said Peter.

Hettie had listened to the whole narrative in awe. To think that this man, her father, had been alive all this time, when she thought he must have died; had been thinking of her all this time, when she thought he cared not; had been plotting his return to her and her mother all these years, when she thought she was an orphan and would never see a parent again in this lifetime. And here he was, alive, well-spoken and intelligent, sitting before her, large as life.

She stood then. She moved towards him and leant down, placing her hands on his shoulders. He gazed up at her with a kind of reverence, as if she were an angel descended from heaven to greet him. She leant down, trying to ignore the stench of his trials that lingered about him, found a bare patch of his skin on his weather-beaten cheek and kissed him there.

'Welcome home, Father.'

Chapter 3

Queenie awoke with a jolt. Before she opened her eyes, she knew. She had felt precisely this way before. It was many years ago now, but the mind never forgot such an experience. Her eyes were still closed, as she was too afraid to open them. It couldn't be *her*, could it? Surely not, after all these years?

Queenie willed herself to open her eyes to a slit, just wide enough to see if that same spectral blue-white light came through the crack in the curtains. It did not, but it did emanate from somewhere else in the room. She snapped her eyes shut again and screwed them up. Why now? What had changed?

There was nothing else for it but to look at her intruder.

There she was, standing by the wall, gazing straight at Queenie. She looked just the same. Queenie knew from before that this spirit never changed, never aged. The beautiful pale face of the spirit of Betsy Blaize stood before her, regarding her with ice-blue eyes. Queenie stared, getting used to the sight of her again. There was a time, just after the fire, when the ghost had been with her so much of the time that she became a silent companion. In a curious way, it was good to see the spirit again, like meeting an old friend. But her presence was always tinged with malice, and Queenie began to feel queasy. She knew that her appearance in the past had foretold dreadful events.

'Hello, old friend,' she said wearily to the ghost.

The spirit nodded slowly, never taking her eyes from Queenie's.

In the absence of an utterance, Queenie spoke again: 'I know not where you go when you are not with me. But wherever you have been, you may or may not have been watching my actions these last years. I wish you to know that I have been the very model of charity. I have directed my businesses to give some of our profits to those in need. I have also acted far more kindly to our workers. I had assumed you knew this and approved, and that this is the reason I have not seen you again.'

The ghost was not one for conversation. She continued to stare at Queenie, her eyes unreadable. Queenie felt a twisting inside her and wondered if the ghost was causing it. She knew there was more she wanted to hear.

'As for your child, the woman died young, I'm afraid. Perhaps you have met her again in your realm – who knows. I suspect you will not tell me. You only seem to speak in riddles. Or curses.'

Queenie involuntarily shuddered at this last word and pulled the covers closer to her chin. The ghost's presence and the cold room made her shiver. She was tiring of this interruption to her sleep.

'Since then, I have sent money to the Malones on a regular basis, as they kept your grandchild and have raised her. But that Anny Woodvine hates us Kings and will not take a penny from us. There is nothing I can do about that. The woman is as stubborn as a mule. Perhaps you should visit her instead, spirit.'

Queenie was warming to her theme now and felt a certain smug superiority over this silent ghost. But at that moment, the ghost moved swiftly to the bedside, making Queenie gasp with her sudden approach.

'*The child will cross the bridge. The child will make one house from two. The child is the answer*.' The spirit was close to Queenie now, her flowing white hair subtly shifting in the spectral air, her eyes piercingly blue.

'You said those words to me before, many years ago. But you were wrong. This did not come to pass. The child Beatrice went to America and never came home. And she most likely never will. So perhaps you are not such a powerful seer as you think, Blaize.'

'*Fool!*' cried the ghost, in such a screeching yet hollow wail that Queenie felt as if a poker had been thrust in her ear. Surely the house would wake at this unearthly sound. But nothing stirred. *I must be finally losing my mind*, Queenie thought.

'I am ninety-six years of age,' she said quietly. 'Please do not berate me, spirit.'

Queenie felt a waft of warm air on her cheek. When she turned, the ghost was inches from her face.

'*The wrong child*,' she said and pulled away, standing up, seemingly taller than ever, glaring down at Queenie.

'But . . . which child is it, then?' Queenie muttered.

'*Child of my child*.'

With that, the ghost fixed Queenie with a last stare, then faded from view, its eyes the last to go, leaving a bluish tinge to the air. Then it was gone.

Queenie stared at the space where the ghost had stood. Then, everything went black.

When she awoke the next morning, she realised she must have fallen asleep within seconds of the ghost's departure. She went through the motions with Jenkins all morning and was quite relieved when Jenkins went for a walk into town and left her to rest. Finally, she had a moment's peace to think.

Child of my child, the ghost had said. That must mean Martha's child. Hettie, her name was. Well, the child was well looked after. One couldn't ask for more devoted adoptive parents than the Malones. They were good people, Queenie knew that. And the child had lived a good life with them. She was now a pit bank girl, Queenie had heard. How would this child cross the bridge and make one house from two? What did that mean anyway? And why was the child the answer? What was the question, indeed?

When Jenkins returned in the afternoon, she looked more sprightly than usual. Queenie was happy to see that the week of rest had done her old friend no end of good and she looked more hale and hearty than ever.

'I bring news from town,' said Jenkins. 'Some interesting gossip concerning the Malones.' She settled down with a shawl of Queenie's that required a hole sewing up. Her fingers were still nimble, and her needle moved more swiftly through the fabric than her age would suggest.

Queenie turned to her, seated in her chair by the window as usual. News of the Malones after last night's visitation made her skin prickle. 'Spit it out, then,' she replied.

'They say that Adam Jones has returned from Australia.'

Queenie stared. 'After all these years? How many is it?'

'Seventeen years this summer since the fire. Everyone thought Jones must've died out there, so long past his sentence he was gone. But he's back, large as life.'

'Hettie's father . . .' Queenie muttered, her thoughts elsewhere, with the spirit's words.

'He is staying with the Malones for the time being. He came back a week ago. But they say he looked like nothing on earth when he appeared at their door. Anny

Malone has cleaned him up since, shaved his beard and so forth, but he came back stinking of drink and has been seen drinking the afternoon away at various inns hereabouts all week, setting up unpaid accounts all over town. The Malones have had to fetch him and half carry him home.'

This does not bode well, thought Queenie. The ghost's sudden reappearance must have something to do with it. The father come back, drinking himself silly. What must the child be going through? Yes, this was why the ghost had come back. Something must be done.

'Send money to him,' said Queenie.

'What?' said Jenkins, looking up from her sewing, her needle held mid-stitch.

'You heard me, woman. Send a goodly sum to him.'

'But he will drink himself to death with it!' cried Jenkins.

'Send it,' Queenie said. 'Then tell Benjamina to come to me. I have something to discuss with her.'

Jenkins put down her sewing and muttered her way out of the room.

As Queenie waited for her daughter-in-law to deign to come to her, Queenie made a decision. It was something she'd been toying with for a while. Now she knew it was the right time. The ghost's appearance and Jones's return told her that. She had a plan to put in motion and she would need Benjamina's assistance.

There was a brief rat-a-tat-tat on the door, quickly followed by the woman herself. She never waited after her knock and only did that from time to time, after Queenie had complained that she mustn't barge in.

'What is it?' asked Benjamina with impatience. 'I was about to set off for an afternoon tea.'

Queenie was not fazed by her bullying tone. 'Organise an architect to come and see me. The finest in the county.'

'Whatever for?' scoffed Benjamina.

'We are going to rebuild Southover.'

Benjamina spent her entire time at the afternoon tea in a fit of grumpiness after hearing Queenie's latest hare-brained scheme. The woman was getting far too old to be permitted to make decisions about the family finances. Rebuilding their old family home was pointless when they had plenty of room in the old brickmaster's house where they now lived. Here was yet another example of why Queenie should have taken retirement years ago and left everything to Benjamina.

Wasteful old fool, thought Benjamina as she mounted the stairs to her room to take a short nap before dinner. Entering her room, she expected her little dog Drina to welcome her, but discovered that the maid had not yet brought the dog back from her afternoon walk. If it wasn't troublesome old women, it was troublesome maids that plagued Benjamina's life. She could hear one of the stupid girls outside calling Drina's name.

Finally, there was a knock on the door and in came the scurrying sound of Drina's feet on the carpet, music to Benjamina's ears.

'Where have you been, you naughty little thing?' said Benjamina, scooping up the dog and fondling her velvety ears. Then she peered at the servant over Drina's bobbing head, as the dog panted in her arms. 'Why did it take so long? Where have you been?' This was one of the tweeny maids and not her own lady's maid, Clayton, who had been requisitioned to help Queenie while Jenkins was resting. Another ridiculous decision that made Benjamina hopping mad, and meant that other things in the house went awry.

'Begging your pardon, ma'am,' said the maid. 'When you let the little dog run about the grounds on its own, it does run off into the forest and chase squirrels and suchlike. It inna easy to get it back in. It dunna wanna come back.'

'Don't be an idiot,' snapped Benjamina. 'Of course she wants to come back. This is her home and I am her mistress. Next time, keep an eye out for her and don't let her go into the forest. She could be taken by a fox or heaven knows what. Just after my husband's death, one of my dogs was strangled by a worker that came out of those woods. Do your job with the same care you would take with an infant. She is that precious, do you hear me?'

'Yes, ma'am,' the maid replied, her eyes frightened at Benjamina's harsh tone. Benjamina could not even remember this one's name. Servants seemed to come and go far too quickly these days, getting themselves pregnant or uppity and finding other jobs. It was almost impossible to find a decent maid. And this one was a bit too bold for Benjamina's liking.

'Get away with you. Get out.'

Benjamina shoved the door shut with her shoulder, right in the girl's face. She knew it was a common gesture, but the girl had angered her. And she had her hands full. She buried her face in Drina's soft coat and kissed, kissed, kissed her dear one.

'You are my baby, my perfect little baby,' she said. 'Yes, you are. Yes, you are.'

Drina whined then barked. This was Benjamina's fifth King Charles spaniel, after Chloe and then Phoebe both died in quick succession when young; then the unfortunate Louise, murdered by one of those cruel strikers from the brickyard. Then there was Nancy, who caught distemper from a fox. And now there was Drina, the dear thing. Drina was the liveliest of the lot, and barked too much for everyone's liking. But Benjamina took pleasure in their annoyance. She adored Drina and disliked everyone else in her house. Drina was the only one that loved her and was loyal to her. Drina was her only friend in this cluttered prison of a home.

She kissed Drina again on the top of her soft head and whispered, 'I love you, little one. More than anything.'

The dog heard a sound outside and wriggled free of her mistress's grasp and ran to the bedroom window, staring pointedly upwards. She hopped up on a chair, then the dressing table, knocking over two items of Benjamina's toilette. She sat at the edge, where she had a perfect view out of the window, and whined and yelped at something down there, something of great import in a dog's world. But Benjamina felt too indolent to move. She lay back on her bed, full of her tea, feeling despondent at her dog's rejection.

She knew she was utterly alone in the world, a widow for seventeen years now. For all his faults, at least her husband Ralph had been hers. When she was given to him at sixteen, she had lost her freedom but gained money, lost her mother but gained a husband. Benjamina had come from nothing. Or rather, her father had left them nothing after he drank himself to death.

He had been of the middling sort, with ambitious merchant parents who educated him and spoilt him. He was set up with a hat shop, mostly catering to men. It was a tidy little shop in a good street in Shrewsbury and it did very well at first. But her father had a taste for gin, and it ruined him. It was a common occurrence in her childhood to be awoken from her bed in the middle of the night and dragged downstairs by her mother's hot, sweaty hand, then shoved under the stairs in a tight cwtch. Together they would hide in the cupboard there, to avoid her father's violent rants. He would find them and pull out her mother, beating her about the head until he collapsed in a drunken stupor.

He left when she was fifteen years old, thank God, and they heard some months later that he had died in the street. *Good riddance.*

It was a great relief to be free of the man. Benjamina and her mother lived in glorious liberty for a while. But they were saddled with debt that grew like mould. Her mother ran the shop adequately, but custom was down and getting less and less by the month. Fashions were changing, as Benjamina noted; she had a keen eye for the latest style. Waists were pinched in and hats were tall, but her mother continued to stock old-fashioned hats and recommend styles that were sometimes of the last century, let alone fit for the new decade of the 1830s. The younger male customers fell away and only older men appeared in the shop. Some days it seemed they only came to flirt with the proprietor's delicious daughter.

There was something about being a shop girl that seemed to invite all manner of indecent proposals. Benjamina laughed them away in her girlish manner, but soon realised it was the only power she had. She would woo clients and flatter them, trying to inveigle them into buying the more expensive items. It sometimes worked – but at other times, she only received a groping for her troubles. And all the while, the shop's profits were dwindling and the debt was rising, and the shadows under her mother's eyes darkened daily.

One day, a middle-aged gentleman with a pot belly came in and seemed struck by lightning when he saw her. His goggle-eyed fascination was disarming, if not rather alarming. Through conversation with her mother, the man revealed that he was widowed with two children not much younger than Benjamina. He fawned over her mother, who giggled like a schoolgirl, then kept glancing at Benjamina in a meaningful way. Benjamina did not like the look of those glances, not one bit. She disappeared into the back room, and was called upon to return. The gentleman introduced himself as Ralph King, an ironmaster from Ironbridge. The workings of iron and all such industry revolted her; she imagined it to be tainted by hard, manual work and the stink of chimneys. But her mother seemed delighted with this pompous fool, who returned the very next day and flattered them both by buying far too many handkerchiefs and two new hats. She did not want this man as her new father and was amazed her mother seemed to consider sacrificing her own freedom for this fat idiot.

But after a couple of visits, it became clear that another plan was afoot. And her mother would not be the one who made the sacrifice.

'Princess,' her mother had said to her, the name her mother always used with her when she wanted her to do something. 'My beautiful princess. You shall save us. You will marry this King and become his queen.'

'No, Mother! I hate the man!' Benjamina had cried, tears streaming down her face.

But her mother flourished the mounting bills at her and said, 'Do you want to see me in the workhouse before the week's end? That is what'll happen if you don't grab this gift from providence. It is up to you, princess.'

Benjamina married Ralph King when she had just turned seventeen. He promised to pay a lump sum to her mother to save the shop and off Benjamina went to Ironbridge with her husband, who was older than her own father had been when he died. They went to a large house on a hill surrounded below by the muck of industry. There lived two children who she knew immediately hated her. News came after a few months that her mother had died of a weak heart. She went to the funeral with her husband, who closed down the shop and sold the assets, pocketing the profits. Back they went to the big house in Ironbridge.

She was seventeen, owned by a man she disliked, forced to live with two unpleasant children who looked at her reproachfully whenever she spoke. And there she was, the lady of the house. Except that there were two others who ruled that house, and they did so with an iron fist. Her father-in-law, Ralph senior, who ran the business and assaulted the household maids whenever he got the chance. And his wife, her mother-in-law, Queenie. She could see that Queenie despised her from the first moment they met, even more than silent, boring Margaret and petulant, sulky Cyril. She had no words of comfort or advice from a soul in that house from the moment she arrived. She had never felt so alone, even as a child hiding in the cupboard under the stairs, her hands over her ears, cowering in terror that one night her father would murder her mother and then start on her. This loneliness was worse, a slow, creeping malaise that weighed her down, like the heavy burden of her husband's body on top of her each night.

Thus she decided there was nothing to do but embrace this new life, as desolate as it might be. At least she could enjoy the comforts of wealth. She used all her fashion acumen to purchase a new selection of the latest clothes, an ever-evolving wardrobe of which she was very proud, knowing how fine she looked in her exquisite gowns. She purchased a King Charles spaniel which she named Chloe – the name of the heroine in the first play her new husband had taken her to. She had never owned a dog before and this animal adored her, whatever she did or said. She had never known such fierce loyalty from any living thing and she could not have enough of it. Her spaniel became her only love and she petted and spoilt it from dawn till dusk, her only friend in that friendless house. Her husband she satisfied each night as he wanted and simply closed her eyes while it was happening, thinking about the shop or her dog or fine silks and ribbons or whatever else she could fill her mind with to escape the dreadful pounding of his flesh into hers. Worse even than this nightly misery was the thought of bearing a child. She had not one maternal bone in her body and she dreaded the time when a baby would come. But each night, she douched herself as her mother had once taught her, and it must have worked, or else there was something broken inside of her, as a pregnancy never appeared, much to her relief. After a while, she began to feign illness to avoid the nightly chore and he deferred to her at first, whining from time to time. Then she made it very clear she did not want him to come to her in that way at any time, day or night. At first he railed against her, shouting and stomping his feet, at which his jowls would wobble and his cheeks would go purple with rage. But eventually he gave up. He did not have it in him to attack her. He was not a violent man like her father. She was grateful for this at least.

And so decades passed, a life of indolence, fine things to eat and lovely things to wear and the love of small dogs who devoted their lives to her. From time to time there was a dalliance with a passing gentleman, the most notable of which was the artist Jake Ashford, who bedded her on the chaise longue on several passionate occasions when he was supposed to be completing her portrait. He never finished the painting, or even really started, as to everyone's amazement he chose the tedious little Margaret and ran off with her to Paris. Benjamina had had no particular designs on Jake herself, but she hated Margaret for taking him from her. She enjoyed their sexual encounters and the danger of fornicating in the drawing room, where a servant could walk in at any time. All her misplaced passion from the lonely years came rushing out into her lust for Jake Ashford. And then he was gone, off to a new life in France with that little harlot, her stepdaughter. The only satisfaction was that, according to the house gossip, Margaret left him with the daughter still in her belly and he died a while later.

She had once been envious of Margaret, for those brief months of happiness they must have had after the elopement. At least Margaret had tasted love for a while. Benjamina had never loved anybody, apart from her mother, and she was long gone. Now she had only a selfish, spoilt dog for company.

How pathetic! She scolded herself inwardly and stood up. She knew what the answer to loneliness was. It was power. It burned inside her like a perpetual furnace, this desire for power. It was the only desire she had left. Sex was dull, her beauty had faded, children or true friends she had neither (only acquaintances for whom she cared little), and her family was a joke to her. Hated and hating, she had whittled herself down to this one purpose: to be the ruler of the King business and household. For the past thirteen years, she had run the businesses and done an excellent job. The King fortune was stronger than ever. She had found her calling at last, after years of pointless existence. At the age of fifty-nine, she was an icon in Shropshire, an independent woman operating in a man's world, fully capable of anything a businessman could do.

But it was still not enough. Queenie held Benjamina's future in her hands. When Queenie's husband, Ralph senior, died, he left everything to Queenie in his will, not trusting his son to manage anything properly. And this meant that when Ralph junior died, Benjamina inherited nothing from her husband. It all still remained in Queenie's ownership.

Since Benjamina had taken over the business, Queenie had agreed to pay her a salary for her work. Benjamina had been careful with this money and stowed it away in the bank and in safe investments, so she certainly had a good stock of cash when she needed it. But Benjamina wanted her rights. She deserved it. She was owed it. She had married that oaf and put up with him for all that time. And, since all of Queenie's children and grandchildren were either dead or, as in Beatrice's case, refused to be a beneficiary, Benjamina had now been named as the sole heir of the King fortune in Queenie's will. But the old woman had lived till ninety-six! And still she seemed to show no signs of going anywhere. She had usurped Queenie and ruled in her stead; all of the other Kings were either dead or gone. There was nobody left to inherit but herself. She would have it all.

'Come, Drina,' she called and the dog looked alert, leapt down and followed her. Benjamina walked across the landing and knocked on her mother-in-law's door. Before she took her nap, Benjamina intended to argue with Queenie about this ridiculous decision to rebuild the old house. She knew she would not win the argument and that Queenie would go ahead with it anyway. But she loved to antagonise her, and she knew that by causing a row about it, and having her yappy little dog in the room, she'd successfully ruin Queenie's evening. Queenie did not like dogs, so Benjamina often brought Drina along to Queenie's room, just to watch her distress as the dog gambolled about, disturbing the peace.

How she loved to lord it over Queenie. And how she hated the old harridan and could not wait for her to die.

Chapter 4

Sitting by the fire with Hettie, watching the flames flicker, chatting about the latest gossip from the pit, Evan knew this was the best moment of his week. It was unusually quiet in the Malone household, as his parents were out with friends celebrating a new birth, wetting the baby's head, as they said. The younger children were asleep in bed. Hettie was darning some of Flora's socks and Evan was stretched out in his father's chair, the soles of his feet turned towards the heat, his eyes watching the flames and the lamplight play across Hettie's face and hair as she laughed at his jokes and bent her head to see her stitches.

Adam Jones was out too, thankfully. What a relief it was when he left their home. He had gone out every day since he'd received the King money a week ago. And though Evan was relieved to see the man leave, his return was always fraught; he had come back every evening drunk as a lord, much to Hettie's shame. After her father turned up that night a fortnight ago, he had been quiet for the first few days, sleeping a lot and talking little. But soon, he started going out drinking at the local taverns every single day. Each time he came home was worse than the day before. Hettie took charge of him, marshalling the drunken fool to his bed in the boys' room. Evan now had to squeeze into a narrow bunk with Billy, and more often than not, he'd lie awake and listen to Adam snoring, stinking of beer, dreaming of God knows what and calling out in his sleep, interrupting the rest that Evan so desperately needed to get through another day at the coalface. To his credit, Adam had given a portion of the King money to Evan's mother for housekeeping, but the rest he was drinking away and it made everyone uneasy. Hettie seemed to accept it. She clearly didn't want to discuss it, but Evan could hold it in no longer.

'It's nice, this,' said Evan.

'Yes, it surely is,' said Hettie, smiling.

'We dunna get much time to just be, me and you.'

'No, we dunna these days.'

'Indeed. These days . . .' Evan hesitated. He knew what he wanted to say, about Adam Jones, about how he was spoiling things. He didn't want to ruin this peace they had tonight with talk of that man, but it was so hard to get Hettie alone these days, he felt he couldn't miss this chance. 'Since your father came back . . .'

He saw Hettie's mouth purse, as if she were steeling herself for what was to come next. How could he say it so that it didn't sound like a criticism?

'It's a kind of miracle, really,' he said, hoping that's what she'd want to hear.

'Thank the Lord,' said Hettie, not lifting her eyes from her sewing.

'A marvellous thing,' Evan went on, pretending to sound as if he was merely musing, not planning. 'And I am proper pleased for you, to have your father back. I am, truly.'

'I know it,' said Hettie, still not looking up.

'But I mun confess . . . I do miss our old times. You know, the times we'd spend like this or out on our walks. But since your father's return . . . and dunna get me wrong, I know how important it is for you two to get to know one another. And like I said, it's a marvellous thing.'

Hettie said nothing in reply and Evan avoided looking at her. If he did, he might lose his nerve to continue.

'But the truth is, you've changed, Hettie. You used to want to spend all your time with me, but now you're always with him.'

It came out wrongly. He didn't mean it that way. He sounded like a jealous child.

'I think I might turn in,' said Hettie, stabbing her needle into a sock and putting the sewing aside.

Evan sat up, pulling his legs in, resting his elbows on his knees. 'Dunna go, Hettie. I'm sorry if . . .'

'I'm tired, is all.' She glanced at him, her eyes shining.

'Please, Hettie, dunna go. These times with you alone . . . well, they are precious to me.'

'And to me,' she said and looked at him again. He was sure she had tears glistening in her eyes and it shamed him. 'It's a pity you spoilt it.' She stood up then and turned as if to go.

Evan stood too and reached out to her, touching her arm. 'Dunna go, Hettie, please! I am sorry. I just wanted to . . .'

She turned abruptly back to him and now he could see anger in her eyes. 'You were right about one thing. It is marvellous to me to have a father return as if from the dead. And I'll do everything in my power to look after him and make up for the years we lost. I'd hope you'd understand that. And what that means for me.'

'Course I do! But he's . . .'

'He's what? A broken man? Wouldna you be, after what he's suffered? Wouldna anyone?'

'Yes, course, but it's the way it pains you I canna bear. The drinking . . .'

A sound came from behind them and stopped their argument. It was Flora, appearing at the door, rubbing her sleepy eyes.

'I woke up,' she muttered. 'Bad dreams.'

'Come on, Floss,' said Evan and went to her. Flora often suffered from vivid dreams. She was a clever girl with an active imagination which spilled over into her sleeping life and often caused nightmares. Evan was used to it and always knew how to solve it. 'Let's get you a sip of milk.'

He put his arm about his sister's narrow shoulders, and she rested her head on him as he led her over to the kitchen table. He was aware that Hettie had sat down beside the fire again and taken up her sewing. That was good. Perhaps once he'd got his sister back to bed, he could make amends and regain the lovely atmosphere of earlier, before he'd ruined it. He sat Flora down at the kitchen table and fetched her a splash of milk in a mug. Somehow, tasting some goodness like that always chased her dreams away. He'd done it for her since she was a little nipper and she always came to him when she was upset at night. She was a sweet child and loved him simply, as he loved her. They had a knowledge of shared ancestry that made their love pure and effortless. Certainly, they annoyed each other from time to time, as all siblings do. But their love was quiet and ever-present, never questioned and never a trial.

As he watched Flora sip her milk, he glanced back at Hettie. She was his first love, his first companion, thrown together as infants and as thick as thieves ever since. There was nothing simple about the way he loved Hettie. Everything about their friendship, their relationship was intense and urgent. It pained him and delighted him equally. And it confused him terribly.

He had always known that the love he bore Hettie was not like the love he bore the rest of his family, but it was only these last few years he had truly understood that he loved her not only as a friend but as a girl, as a young woman, as a companion – and one day, he hoped as a lover and wife. The thought of marrying her had filled his mind for months, if not years. He was sixteen now and he could ask her. It was constantly in his mind.

It wasn't simple, though. Where would they live? If they stayed at home, no doubt they'd be given the boys' room and Billy would have to go in with Flora and Lily. It could work, for a while, but they'd have no privacy and it would start married life off badly. He kept meaning to sit down and work out how much money they both earnt at the pit and see if they could have afforded their own place. But something stopped him from doing so.

As he watched her now, sewing by the fire, he realised that what stopped him was fear. He was terrified that if he had everything in place, he would have to ask her to marry him and there was the alarming prospect that she would say no. If that happened, how could he continue to live with her, knowing she had rejected him? How could they possibly remain the friends and companions they had always been? It would be intolerable. Every couple of weeks or so, he'd look at her and think, *do it. Ask her.* And then he would turn away, afraid of what her answer would bring.

Flora finished her milk and looked up sleepily at her brother, a white rim along her top lip.

'Come on, Floss,' said Evan and led her back to bed. He saw his littlest sister Lily asleep on her front, knees tucked under, bottom in the air. Her quirkiness made him smile. He looked in on Billy to find him in the exact same position as his twin.

He knew that he took his love for his siblings for granted. They were part of him and would always be there. But his love for Hettie ran faster in his veins. There was little peace in it. It was flighty, unobtainable as a butterfly; if you caught it, you'd crush it. He'd always been afraid he'd lose her one day. And now, her father had returned like a ghost from the past, raking up old feelings and opening old wounds. His presence was splitting the family and separating him from Hettie.

Somehow, he needed to show Hettie that he understood how important Adam's return was to her, but also that she needed to realise he was not her responsibility. Adam was his own man and he would have to learn how to stand on his own two feet; she did not need to be at his beck and call. Surely if he explained this to her calmly, she would understand.

He went back into the front room. There was Hettie, still seated by the fire, and Evan was about to make his reasonable speech, when the front door was flung open and in stumbled Adam Jones.

Immediately Hettie was up and by his side. The man was incoherent, muttering something about bones and blood. Everything the man said, did and was felt hateful to Evan. He knew he ought to help Hettie, as Adam slumped against her and she fought to assist him. But he was too resentful and self-righteous, slumping instead into his father's chair by the fire and staring into the flames. He ignored the two shuffling figures beside him as they headed for the boys' room. He heard Hettie shushing Adam, getting him into bed as quietly as she could so that he didn't disturb Billy and the others. *If he wakes the little'uns, I'll tear a strip off him*, thought Evan.

Presently, Hettie came back in. She fetched a glass of water and took it back through to her father. Then she appeared again and said, 'I'm off to bed.'

'Please dunna go yet, Hettie.'

'I am tired. I must sleep,' she said and drew a trembling hand across her eyes.

Evan went to her. He wanted to reach out and take her in his arms, but he didn't. He couldn't. He was too afraid she'd push him away.

'*He* is making you tired, Hettie. It's not right, what he's doing. He's wrecking you. He shouldna be spending King money on drink like this. He should be using it to set himself up in a new place, a new life. Instead of drinking it all away. It inna fair on you!'

Hettie looked up at him, her eyes fiery. 'Show some charity, Evan Malone! He's been through hell. He relives it every waking moment and every night in his dreams. He's just found his family again and it tortures him daily, what he lost. He's finding his feet now. He'll stop drinking once he's settled, you'll see. Show him some kindness, for my sake if nothing else.'

It was an eloquent speech. Hettie had always had that gift.

'I'll do it for you,' said Evan, trying to say the right thing. Yet he couldn't help adding, 'But not for him.'

She shook her head at him and left the room. Evan knew he could've made himself more agreeable to her. But he was headstrong. And he was convinced he was right about this. He did not believe that Hettie's predictions of her father's recovery would ever come to pass. Adam Jones was broken beyond repair and he would bring Hettie down with him.

Well, Evan thought, *I won't stand by to see that happen. Not ever.*

A week later, Anny was hurrying along High Street with her three smallest children, eager to get home and out of the cold after a long day's work.

'Come on now, no dawdling,' said Anny, turning round to see Flora daydreaming with her head in the clouds, as usual, while Billy and Lily were conspiring over something in Lily's hand. A swift look confirmed it was a woodlouse, which Anny batted away onto the road.

'Mother!' cried Billy.

'Mother!' echoed Lily.

'I said, no dawdling! We need to get home so I can get on with chores. Now, everybody stop at the roadside and wait for this carriage to go by. Then hold hands . . . and go.'

The four of them hurried across the street, filled with late-afternoon shoppers and strollers, farmers driving animals, workers walking home weary and children picking pockets, given half a chance. They approached the iron bridge and Anny put down her basket, empty of the pies she'd just sold and delivered, to look for the toll in her own pocket.

At that moment, she heard a commotion nearby. She looked over to see a couple of burly men manhandling a fellow out of the Tontine Hotel bar. Immediately she realised it was Adam Jones. They pushed him forward and he lost his footing, landing on his outstretched palms and losing his hat in the process.

'Blast that man,' Anny muttered. She turned to Flora. 'Here, watch the twins and my basket. Do not move, you hear me?'

'Yes, Mother,' said Flora, her eyes wide as she watched the forsaken figure of Adam Jones grovel in the dust.

He managed to right himself before Anny reached him. He lent down to retrieve his battered hat, but Anny got there before him and swiped it up, thrusting it at him. He looked at her blearily. He used to be such a handsome man, thought Anny. Dark, good looks. Now what she saw was the alcohol he consumed every day swimming in his red eyes. His skin was patchy and aged, no doubt from years of Australian sun. There was pity in her heart for him – of course there was – but it was fast running dry.

'Come on.' She tried to keep her voice kind, but it wasn't easy.

'Dear Anny,' he muttered and let himself be led by her, acquiescent as a sleepy toddler.

Anny linked arms with him and marshalled him to the bridge. Flora's eyes were wider than ever, the twins watching warily, holding tightly onto each other's hands. Flora picked up Anny's basket and followed, chiding the twins if they lagged behind.

She's a good girl, thought Anny; she could usually rely on Flora to do the right thing. How utterly thrilled she'd been when she had her, late in life, her first girl. She'd been immediately besotted with her, tiny little thing she was, with a shock of red hair. Evan and Hettie paired off and disappeared much of the time, leaving Anny to adore her first daughter in peace. Then the twins came four years later and were such a joy to her. Her brood, just as she'd wanted, as her mother had once wanted and never achieved; Anny had been an only child. Until recently, everything felt like it was coming together nicely. Her little'uns were growing fast and true, and Evan and Hettie were near coming of age, ready to start their own lives soon, maybe even their own family together. Anny and Peter had always felt they seemed made for each other.

But then this happened: this man she now struggled to keep upright as they crossed the bridge, receiving disgruntled or disapproving looks from passers-by as they did so. This ghost from their past who'd returned. A cuckoo in their happy home.

As they struggled on down the roads towards home, Anny inwardly scolded herself for thinking of him that way. After all, Adam Jones was family, in a way. His first wife, Juliet, had been Peter's cousin, and even after her death and Adam's remarriage to Martha, Peter and Adam had remained close. And since he had been away, he had been through so much suffering, it was almost unimaginable. Anny herself had had her own stint in prison and knew the horrors of it. It had never left her, despite it being decades ago now. She dreamt of it some nights and woke in a panic. And if she felt this, after just months in prison, how must Adam feel after all those years? She knew he had nightmares, too; they all knew, as he had woken up shouting, waking the whole household. Hettie would get up and go to him, infinitely patient with her new-found father, stroking his brow and soothing him back to sleep. The poor girl was half asleep on the way to work these days, with her careworn evenings and sleepless nights worrying about this man. Hettie was always a kind girl, a thoughtful one, who wore her heart on her sleeve and cared for all living things. Now she had a new parent to care for, she seemed to pour all her love into the man, despite his absence most of the time at the local taverns. He was still a good man underneath, Anny was sure, but a broken one. She could see it was exhausting for Hettie, and she knew that Evan did not like it. He was restless and grumpy much of the time these days; he seemed jealous of Hettie's attentions to her father, though Evan must know it was wrong to feel that way. Anny knew her son better than anyone else did and she could see the envy seething in him. Peter was struggling with his presence, too, though he felt obliged to keep him there for the sake of their family ties. And the little ones were scared of Adam Jones.

In their small house there were three bedrooms for seven occupants, and now an eighth who slept in with the boys. It was overcrowded, to say the least. But it wasn't just that. There was a change in the atmosphere of the home, which before had been good-natured and busy. It was as if a cloud had arrived over their house, a dark cloud that cast shade across their daily existence. This man and his drinking had brought it. For her own part, as sorry for Adam as she'd always been, for his wrongful conviction and the terrible years he had to spend away from home, there was still a stone of resentment buried inside Anny. It was lodged down deep, but she could still feel it there: Adam had been with her son Owen the night the burning King house fell upon and killed him. Adam had led him there and Adam had been out cold on the ground when Owen went into that burning house. She knew it was wrong to blame him, but in Anny's mind Adam Jones had let her son die. She could never forgive him for that, whatever the rights and wrongs of it were. It was a primal, unreasoned hatred that she had buried when he had been away, had disappeared and was assumed to have died across the oceans. But now he had come back, as if from the land of the dead. An uncharitable thought came into Anny's head; she tried to brush it away, but its stain remained: Adam Jones should never have come back from Australia. It would've been better for everyone if he had died out there.

Arriving home, she ushered Adam into Peter's chair by the fire and stoked it up, adding precious coal to heat the room. The twins fell to playing and Flora helped her mother set the table and prepare the dinner: slabs of fidget pie for all with stewed apples from a jar for afters. Anny boiled up turnips to go with the pie and soon the house was filled with the scents of good food. Adam dozed in the chair – Peter's chair, Anny thought sourly.

Then the clog chorus signalled that the missing members of the household were about to appear, and soon enough, there they were, red-cheeked from their cold walk home and eager for food. Peter, Evan and Hettie came in as one, laughing and joking, but the moment they were inside, Hettie immediately went to her father dozing in his chair by the fire, and all amusement ceased. Peter and Evan removed their coats and scarves in silence and Anny felt irritated, yet again, that this man threw a shroud over their lives by his very presence.

She served up dinner and everyone took their places at the table. Hettie woke Adam, who came meekly and sat beside her, waiting quietly and bleary-eyed for his food. Unlike usual family dinners in the days before, this one was subdued; even the twins did not complain or bicker much as they used to. Everyone stared at their food and passed the odd pleasantry. But the stink of alcohol emanating from Adam was enough to put anyone off their dinner. Anny had had enough of it.

'This has to stop, Adam Jones.'

Everybody halted, mid-chew. Adam looked up vaguely.

'I said, this has to stop. D'you hear me?'

'Now then, Anny,' began Peter, but Anny shot him such a glare. It stopped his mouth and instead he shovelled another forkful of pie into his face, blackened with coal dust.

'Now then, nothing. Are you listening to me, Adam?'

Adam looked up from his dinner and managed to fix Anny with a stare. The deadness in the eyes arrested her for a moment and she regretted her tone. But she had something to say and she knew it needed saying.

'We all know you've been to hell and come back. I cannot imagine the trials you have suffered to bring you to this table this night. But we have all been through trials. We have all suffered losses, some too painful to mention.'

There was dead silence around the table now. Even the twins were transfixed.

'But life goes on. It must. And we have moved on. We have forged new lives and not mistreated others or ourselves while we have done so. But you, Adam Jones, are making our lives a misery.'

'No, Anny,' began Hettie, her eyes shining with tears, her voice cracking with emotion. How hard it must be for her, caught between the family who raised her and this new addition, her blood father, a wreck of a man who brought her nothing but trouble. But she must hear this, decided Anny.

'Yes, Hettie, it needs to be said. Your father must change his ways. No more drinking. No more. He's been drinking daily for weeks now and it's going to ruin him. If he stops now, he has a chance of recovering his strength, of being able to work some day and be useful. Only if he gives up the drink will he have a chance of regaining his life.'

Adam spoke then. His voice was low and gravelly, cracked with despair. 'Regain my life? My life, you say? I had my life wrenched from me. My freedom, my youth, my wife. Everything was stolen from me. And I was hurled across the world and left to rot there for a decade and a half, beaten and abused, tortured in the unbearable heat and forced to wear the chains all day and all night, until they chafed me to the bone. It was no life, it was a living death. I had a life once, here. But everything was taken from me.'

It was a stirring speech which affected everyone. A stifled sob came from Flora, tears rolling down her cheeks. Hettie looked as if she were holding back tears, trying to be strong, in that stubborn way she had. But Anny was undeterred, though her voice was softer now.

'Not everything was taken from you, Adam,' she said. 'You have Hettie. And she is worth more than gold.'

'Truth,' said Evan and the twins nodded their joint agreement. Hettie's eyes were filled with tears now too, and she could not look up at those around the table, so her tears fell straight into her lap, splashing onto the backs of her hands.

Anny went on, 'And you owe this girl a father. She is the best of people and she deserves the best father you can be. So far, since your return, you have failed her. Now is the time to step up and change that. No more drinking, get yourself well, get yourself working and earning, find yourself a place and make a home. Because you will not be staying here forever, and that is a fact.'

It rang harshly, but Anny knew it was right.

'I have found a place,' said Adam, his chin raised in defiance, his eyes coming to life now. 'If you had but asked, you'd've discovered it.'

'What place?' asked Peter, his voice uncertain yet tinged with hope.

‘A place down yonder, along the river. An old butty has offered it to me. I just need to find the first month’s rent and I’ll be gone there, dunna you fret. It has two rooms, one for me and one for Hettie.’

Anny hadn’t expected that. It was out of the question, of course. Adam should go – he could go to hell for all Anny cared right now – but he would not be taking Hettie with him.

‘A room for me?’ said Hettie, her eyes shining.

‘Oh no, that will not be happening,’ said Anny. ‘Hettie lives here. Her home is here.’

Adam fixed Anny with a hard stare. ‘She is my daughter and she will come with me.’

‘It inna right,’ said Evan, his voice higher-pitched than usual. The twins followed the argument agog, turning their heads in perfect synchronicity to each speaker in the argument. ‘Hettie mun stay here, with us.’

‘Nobody should speak for me, but me,’ said Hettie. All eyes turned to her. Anny knew she was headstrong, but hoped against hope that the girl would see sense. Living in some hovel with a drunken father was not the place for her. Anny wouldn’t allow it.

‘Hettie, dear,’ Anny began.

‘No, please, Anny,’ Hettie went on. ‘Please let me speak. I made a promise many years ago, that if my father returned, I would look after him. You were there, Anny, when my mother asked that of me. You told me about it, in great detail, after the event, as I was just a little'un then. And I made my promise. I feared it would never matter, that I made that promise, as I was sure my father was dead and gone, never to return. But by some miracle, he has survived and he has come back to me. I must honour my mother's wishes and go with him.'

The tears were rolling down her cheeks now, her chin quivering as she raised it, in just the same gesture as her father's. Anny's heart broke to see this brave girl squander her affection in such an undeserving place. She glanced at Evan and saw in his face that his heart was breaking too, at the thought of losing his soulmate, his Hettie. His anger a moment before seemed all turned to pain. Love like that was the mighty river behind the dam and any crack would send it charging through.

Anny said gently, 'Your mother would not have wanted this for you, Hettie.'

'My Martha?' cried Adam. 'How dare you speak for her! She was my wife.'

Anny stood up from the table. She was not having this. 'How dare I? *How dare I*? Only that I nursed Hettie into the world and nursed Martha out of it. Only that I tended to her all the days she had left, after you'd gone and she came to live with us, when she fell onto hard times. Only that she was the best friend I ever had and I was hers. Only that I raised her daughter as my own. Only *that*, Adam Jones. I think I have earned my say in this matter.'

Hettie stood up then. She was about to speak when a knock came at the door.

'Who the devil will't be this time, Mother?' piped up Billy, and Lily added, 'Who the devil?'

'Hush, you two,' said Flora. Peter stood and went to the door.

Anny saw it was the errand boy from the King house. What was he doing here again?

'For Mr Adam Jones,' said the lad, and handed over a package of brown paper. 'From old Mrs King, over at the old brickmaster's house. With 'er compliments.'

And with that, the lad was gone.

Peter shut the door and stood holding the packet for a moment. Anny could see it had a crimson wax seal on it. She knew those packets, for they had come before. The ones for her she had always turned away, every single one. But when one came two weeks back for Adam, he had taken it greedily and kept it without comment. She knew that quite a bit of it had gone on drink, as well as some to her. She hadn't wanted to take it, but she had no choice; Adam's bed and board needed funding somehow.

Now Adam stood up and took this new packet quickly, tearing it open. Inside was a suede purse filled with coins. It looked double the amount he had previously received.

He snapped the purse shut and pushed it into his pocket. Then, he looked up defiantly at Anny, his eyes clear and black now. 'Now you shall see how I will make good for Hettie. All of you. I will take her to this place and we shall make a life. I thank you, Anny, and you, Peter, for your hospitality these past weeks. But now it is time for me to go.'

'Tonight, Father?' said Hettie, wiping the tears from her face with her neckerchief.

'Yes, child. I shall go tonight and see this mon I know and take possession of our place, my dear. Tomorrow you shall bring your things and live with me there. How does that suit you, eh? You have a father of means now, with this.' He patted the purse in his pocket, and it chinked with coin.

Anny had no argument left. Adam had his money and his daughter's devotion. What could she say to that?

'He will go out this night and drink all that money away,' said Anny, folding her arms firmly.

'I will not.' Adam spoke loudly and deeply, his voice shocking the little ones, who cuddled up together in fright.

'We've heard that before,' said Anny, knowing she had lost the argument now, but too stubborn to give up, for she knew she was right.

Then Hettie spoke. 'I will only come with you tomorrow, Father, if you promise me that you will not drink again. Will you promise me that, as I once promised my mother I would take care of you, if you ever returned?'

Adam took a step towards Hettie and placed his hands on her shoulders. Whatever argument Anny had faded as quickly as it had erupted, as Hettie looked into her father's face, awaiting his response.

'On my life, I promise you, my darling daughter, that I will never take a drink again.'

'Then I shall go with you, Father, and we shall make a home together. And it shall be neat and clean and proper and good.'

The children were overcome at this vision of contentment, and Flora broke out into a little peal of applause, while the twins cheered. It created a festive atmosphere as Hettie and Adam hugged and she kissed him on the cheek. Peter looked approving too, though there was a wary look in his eye.

Evan and Anny did not join in the celebration. As they glanced at each other, his eyes were willing her to do something. He shook his head faintly at her and Anny knew he could not bear to see Hettie go with this man. But what could they do? The decision was made.

Chapter 5

'We are only down the road,' said Hettie, pulling out a hankie to wipe Flora's tears. 'Only a short, brisk walk. You can visit whenever you wish.'

But everyone knew that Hettie's new home, the place her father had found for them, was a tiny hovel and there would be no room for visitors there.

'Or I will visit you, often,' said Hettie, and tried to beam a smile at the Malones, gathered as they were in the front room. Billy and Lily were crying too, clinging onto their mother's skirts. Peter was trying to look supportive and Anny was fussing over the little'uns, unable to meet Hettie's eye. Evan was standing at the kitchen window, his back to her, refusing to be a part of this.

Anny ushered the fretting twins towards her husband, then came towards Hettie. The look they gave each other was fraught with meaning. Anny folded Hettie into her arms and Hettie thought she might sob. She had to fight to stop herself from breaking down. She wanted to be with her father. Of course she did. She wanted to look after him and tend to him, to make that plan of his recovery, of which she'd spoken to Evan, come true. But the stark fact of leaving her home and her family was upon her now and she could hardly bear it. To leave her loved ones and live elsewhere, with a man she barely knew, was a hard, cold choice, but one which she felt was impossible to refuse.

After a tight hug from Anny that Hettie never wanted to end, Anny withdrew and held Hettie at arm's length, her hands firmly about her shoulders.

'You are a brave girl,' she said, nodding resolutely at her. 'A good and kind girl. You have made your choice and I admire you for it. But Hettie, know that you are part of this family and you will always have a home with us here, whenever you need it. Know this in your heart.'

'I do know it, I do,' said Hettie and felt her eyes fill. She had to look away then, or she knew she would bawl like a baby. It was daft, really, all this emotion. She was only moving to the other side of town. She would still see Evan and Peter at work. But it was more than that. It was leaving home, giving up comfort and security for the unknown. Partly the idea excited her, but it also terrified her.

A new life beckoned, and she did not know if she was up to the challenge.

The truth was, Hettie's new home was a dump. It did have two bedrooms as promised, thankfully, but the main room consisted of a dirt floor and an inefficient range that was choked with soot to begin with. It took Hettie a whole day to clean it out and get it to burn without billowing smoke. The house itself had been thrown up by some canny developers looking to make some quick cash, and was built with walls as thin as paper. One night Adam put his foot through a wall when he came back drunk and angry, bitter at the world and all its miseries. Peter came to fix it for them, shaking his head at Adam, who scowled at him and then tried to pay him for his trouble, which Peter refused. Adam always seemed to have a coin about him, which then disappeared before the end of the day, spent on everybody-knew-what.

Money kept arriving from Mrs King, and Adam gave some to Hettie and kept the rest for 'sundries', as he called it. He was drinking still, of course. He had broken his promise. But he told her that he was in constant pain from his old injuries, aching all over every day due to the physical hardships he had suffered. A little drink took the pain away, he explained, and he was too ill to work. Hettie's wages and the regular packets from Mrs King kept them just about afloat.

Hettie soon gave up hope of him seeking out productive work that would keep him from the taverns or drinking great pitchers of beer at home. He didn't get as drunk as he used to, but it was more that he was slightly inebriated all of the time, rather than sober in the mornings then roaring drunk in the afternoon. After a few weeks of this, Hettie could hardly imagine him sober.

She cooked for him every night after returning from work. He did the washing well enough on Mondays and the ironing on Tuesdays; he had a real talent for that. He told Hettie that for a time in Australia his legs had been injured and, unable to do the construction work at the colony, he had been put on laundry duties for a few weeks, cleaning all the clothes of the prisoners and their masters at the Establishment, the building in which they were housed at the Swan River colony. He had tried his very best at it, to provide the cleanest, smartest laundry he could under the circumstances, so that they'd keep him there and not make him go out in the chain gangs on the roads again. But it had not turned out that way, and he was sent back out as soon as his legs recovered. Other than that peculiar skill at laundry, he was not much good at anything else around the home. He swept up a bit, but the rest of the cleaning and house care was done by Hettie on Sundays.

Anny had told Hettie she could come home any time she wanted to, that she didn't have to live like this. Oh, how tempting it was: Anny's motherly care and her excellent cooking; the children's laughter; Flora's sweet companionship; and last but not least, Evan. The first few weeks she missed Evan's presence like a hunger. She still saw him part of the way to and from work, but it wasn't the same as cwtching with him before the fire of an evening. She missed her family desperately. Evan came to see her on Sunday afternoons, but she was often too busy with housework to go for a walk with him. She could see the resentment, too, in his eyes when she talked of her father or when Evan saw or spoke to him. His disapproval of Adam became too difficult to bear and at last she asked Evan not to come anymore if he couldn't be civil and find a place in his heart for her father. He hadn't been back after that, too proud to agree to her demands. But Hettie could not abandon her father. He had nobody else. And she had promised her dead mother.

Getting used to the idea of having a father at all had been difficult, but it had had its little joys. The Malones only saw the broken drunk her father presented to the world, but over the months they lived together Hettie began to see a different side to him. In the evenings, after they had eaten and tidied away, they sat before the fire, Hettie mending, patching and knitting, Adam puffing on a pipe and telling Hettie stories about the time before he was sent away. He told her all about her mother Martha, how they met, what a good wife she was, how beautiful she was and how Hettie had inherited her bright green eyes. He spent a whole evening telling her the tale of how Hettie was born, how Miss Beatrice came from the big house with the lady's maid Jenkins, who fetched the doctor and saved not only her mother's life but Hettie's own. Hettie liked the sound of Miss Beatrice and was curious about the suggestion that she and Evan's dead brother, Owen, had had a forbidden romance. Adam related to her all the events of the brickmakers' strike, the way the Kings behaved so shabbily, his friendship with Owen and the bitter sadness of Owen's death and Adam's subsequent arrest and conviction.

Hettie had heard snippets of these stories from the Malones, but it was an eye-opener to hear someone else's version of events. Certainly, Adam came out of it as the hero of the day, in Hettie's eyes, at least. This was despite the fact that Adam tried to blame himself for the failure of the strike and also for Owen's death. Hettie chided him for this; as far as she could see, her father had done his very best and bad luck had caused the results, not bad judgement or bad acts on his part.

He also told her about his time in Australia. He spared her the most grisly details, and instead told her of the beauty of the strange land in which he found himself for all those years. He described to her the spectacular red sunsets that glowed across the wilderness that surrounded them. He told her about the strange creatures of the place that sounded like something from a storybook – an animal which kept its babies in a pouch on its tummy; a bird that laughed and laughed; a little bear with fringed ears that lived in gumtrees. The stories filled Hettie with wonder and a desire to travel. She knew she would most likely never sail the seas and visit anywhere as exotic, but she knew she wanted to see something beyond Ironbridge one day.

The first step towards this was her trip to London to pick fruit and vegetables from late May to August. Her father was against it. This was the only thing that Adam and Evan agreed upon. But Hettie was adamant; she'd told her father again and again that the money she earned would be considerable and would help improve their home. Secretly, she intended to keep a chunk of it to buy herself a pretty dress, as Ada had suggested back in January. All the unmarried girls who came back from London did this, spending their hard-earned wages on the best dress they could afford to wear to the Oakengates fair in September. She couldn't wait for that.

But her mind was conflicted about the trip: the truth was, she was afraid to leave her father. He drank steadily these days, but was still able to perform some domestic duties and remain civil. She hoped this was because of her calming influence. But with her gone for three whole months, would he have the self-discipline to maintain the house, keep cooking and cleaning for himself, and not drink himself to death? She worried about that most of all.

Before she went, she had a quiet word with Peter and asked him to keep an eye on her father, and Peter agreed. She knew she couldn't ask this of Anny or Evan, because they would have refused. She just hoped her father could keep himself from misadventure for those twelve or so weeks.

The night before she was to leave for London with the other pit bank girls, Hettie could not sleep. The thought of leaving her home without Anny or Peter for the very first time and travelling by rail to London to live there for three months, was too thrilling to induce rest. She lay awake in her bed, listening to her father snoring behind the thin wall that separated their rooms.

The next morning she was up with the lark and kissing her father goodbye while he was still sleepy. He roused himself as he saw her pick up her carpet bag and head to the door.

'Hettie, wait!' he said groggily and hauled himself up and out of bed, standing unsteadily.

'Father, I mun go. The girls will be waiting for me.'

'Will you write to me, child?'

'Only if you will write back in return, Father.' She hoped that the incentive to write letters might keep him on the straight and narrow a little.

'I surely will. You have brought me back to life, my love.'

'Nonsense,' she said and took his hand. 'You are doing that all by yourself. Promise me you . . . will . . . take care of yourself?'

She wanted to tell him not to drink too much, but he hated it when she mentioned drink, as if it were a figment of her imagination. He had a large capacity for self-deceit.

'Course I will. You too. And dunna get yer head turned by any of these London folk. They be no better than you or I, with their fancy ways. Do your work, earn your wage, mind your business and come home to me as soon as you can.'

'I will, Father. Dunna fret.'

She kissed him again and he threw his arms around her, squeezing her tight, nearly knocking off her bonnet.

She withdrew and left him standing there in his nightshirt. She gave him a smile and a nod, before taking her luggage and leaving, closing the door gently behind her so as not to vex him. His head was always fragile in the mornings. The moment she stepped into the street, she realised how much she had been looking forward to escaping that little house – and her father – and this wracked her with guilt as she walked along the way to meet the others upriver. But there was no reason to feel guilty, she knew that; she was going to work, not for a holiday. It would be hard work, no doubt, so she had nothing to feel bad about. But she fairly skipped along as she approached the meeting place on the corner not far from her old home, where Ada and the other pit bank girls were waiting for her.

Chapter 6

'Come on, slow coach!' cried Ada as she saw her friend approach. They all had a bag each and were wearing warm travelling clothes. It was early, and despite being the end of May, there was a bit of a nip in the air. She fell in with Ada and they walked together, gossiping about this and that. Before long, they reached the railway station at Coalbrookdale. They queued up at the ticket office window in a gaggle, all talking at once and fishing in their bags for the money to pay for their tickets.

From here, they were to take the train to Wellington, change there and get the train to London. Both the train to Wellington and the next to London were not too busy and they all found a seat with ease. The open sides of the second-class carriage gave a marvellous view of the countryside and villages they went past, which fascinated Hettie. She'd never been far beyond Ironbridge in her life. But the lack of windows also made this morning journey distinctly chilly, and Hettie drew her shawl around her and cuddled up to Ada to keep warm. She was thankful it wasn't raining that day.

There was an atmosphere of excitement and anticipation amongst all the women. There were about twenty of them, many around Hettie and Ada's age of sixteen or so, with a couple of older women who had done the trip many times and knew the route inside out. The eldest and the one thus seemingly in charge was Nora, a woman in her early forties who had a sharp tongue and kept the women in line as they changed trains at Wellington. As their train swayed around a long curve and began its approach to Paddington, Nora called to the girls to pay attention.

'Now listen, wenches. When we get to Paddington station, it'll be sniving with folk bustling about hither and thither. We mun stick together. Find yourself a butty to keep an eye on you or a couple of butties. We need to cross the station and find a train on the GWR line that stops at Hayes and Harlington. You hear me? Hayes and Harlington. That be the one we need. So, choose yer butties now to keep an eye on and we'll soon be off.'

Hettie and Ada immediately linked arms and nodded. As the train pulled into the vast station, Hettie's eyes filled with wonder. She looked up at the massive arched structure built with iron girders that might have been cast at Coalbrookdale – who knew? It was the largest building she had ever seen in her life, let alone entered. It gave her a thrill to move along under its lofty curved ceiling and see the pigeons flap about up there.

As the train slowed to a halt, the next wonder was the people. There was a veritable army of people outside, filling the platform. There were many minutes of pushing and shoving to alight from the train, while others tried to fill it at the same time. Hettie grasped Ada's hand so hard she feared she might break her bones, but she was terrified of losing her grip and not being able to find her way back to the other women.

As they made their way along the platform, Hettie gazed up at the signs hanging above them signalling all manner of rooms beyond: cloakroom, general offices, gentleman's lavatory, telegraph office, and so on. Paddington felt like a village in itself, complete with inhabitants and shops and businesses all its own. The crowds of passengers moving hurriedly to and fro along the platform were joined by dozens of railway workmen and men in uniform, who she saw were porters being paid a penny here and there to carry bags. The turmoil of noise and movement assaulted her ears and confused her eyes, as bells rang out left and right and the sound of hundreds of folk talking and shouting and laughing filled the steamy, acrid air. She still held tight onto Ada's hand and made sure she kept her eye on the bobbing feather in Nora's hat that moved a few feet before them, weaving its way through the crowds to the ticket office for them to queue up yet again to purchase the ticket for their next train.

That achieved, they headed back into the melee and finally reached the correct platform, expertly sourced by

Nora. The train to Hayes and Harlington was waiting for them there. Again, hordes of people filled the platform. Everyone wanted to get into the carriages furthest back from the engine, pooling there at the near end of the platform. The train stood empty and Hettie soon realised everyone was waiting for some signal to climb aboard, fidgeting and jostling to get the best position to do so.

Suddenly a loud bell rang out and everybody moved. There was a great push towards the nearest carriages. Hettie saw Nora's feather bobbing away along the platform and she followed it, Ada grasping her hand as tightly as ever. All the carriages they passed were soon filled, so the women continued their way forward and most of them ended up in the very first carriage at the other end of the platform, right next to the engine itself, about which lolled the driver and his men, smoking cigarettes and winking at the females. The rest of the women climbed into the next carriage along.

Once in, they managed to sit on the wooden seats more or less together, with the odd seat taken up by another passenger, all of whom looked disapprovingly at the gaggle of wenches with the funny Shropshire voices filling up the seats around them. Nora popped out onto the platform and into the next carriage, then returned, carrying out a total headcount to make sure they were all there, then sat down herself. Hettie was relieved they had all got through the station in one piece and that nobody was lost along the way.

It was not long until the train set off and Hettie soon realised why nobody wanted to sit near the engine. The carriage filled with smoke, which billowed in and out of the open sides. Ashes floated on the air and landed on their clothes, some still hot, which left black burn marks on the skirts and cloaks of some. As the train picked up speed, the smoke and ash were not as bad, but still rolled in from time to time and made them all cough and brush themselves down. Her excitement at the newness of taking the train soon changed to annoyance that the conveyance was such a mucky, tiresome way to get about, so unlike walking or hitching a ride on the back of a waggon, as she sometimes did at home. Horses left their dung in the road and always smelt ripe and earthy, but at least they didn't throw burning coals at you. What was more, the train bounced around and jerked the passengers to and fro quite violently at times. At one point, one of their girls fell forward into the lap of a woman opposite, who cursed her clumsiness, at which the girls all laughed. It wasn't their fault after all, just the rough riding of the train.

After what seemed an age, and was in fact most of a day's dirty, crowded, exhausting travel, the train pulled in to Hayes and Harlington station, and Nora shepherded all the girls towards the doors. Coming out onto the platform was quite a relief. The day was waning but still warm in the late-May sunshine.

The women all gathered and Nora led the way again, walking out of the station and onto a long straight road lined with houses, along which the women began to walk in pairs or threes. The sun beat down upon them and Hettie removed her cloak and threw it over her arm. The sun on their faces felt good, and she was so relieved to be out of the train and away from the madness of the railway stations. She imagined what it must be like for folk who worked every day in London, who had to navigate their way through that chaotic bustle every morning and every evening, just to get to and from work. She had never been so grateful for her walk to the pit. Even on the coldest, rainiest mornings, she would rather do that than ride in those infernal trains every day.

The houses soon thinned out to be replaced by fields and farms. They walked for about an hour or so, taking glugs of water from bottles they'd brought with them, as well as bites of food. Hettie had eaten all of her bait on the train journeys, and she was so weary and hungry now that she wished she'd kept something for later. Ada kindly gave her an apple to eat, which tasted so sweet after the trials of the day.

At long last, Nora turned back and said, 'This be the place!' They turned off the main road, walking up a dusty path bounded on one side by a long row of apple trees, and thence through a gate to a collection of several wooden huts that stood empty with their doors wide open.

'Home sweet home!' said Nora, and went straight into the first hut. Hettie followed her, along with Ada behind and a friend of Nora's called Edna. There was straw on the floor and that was all, with enough space for four to sleep. Hettie had been told to bring a blanket and something to rest her head on. She'd found a small flattish cushion at Anny's that would fit in her bag. The girls deposited their bags, took off their hats and cloaks and went back outside.

So, this motley collection of huts was to be their home for the next three months. It was basic in the extreme, but Hettie found herself grinning from ear to ear. What an adventure! Nora and another woman had fetched some pots to cook in. All the women pooled the food they had brought with them to find a goodly collection of potatoes, onions and leeks, as well as a bit of bacon and some apples. There were two trivets in one of the huts which they brought out, collecting sticks to make fires underneath. Nora had the matches and set up the campfires, while others helped peel and chop the vegetables. They used a standpipe nearby for the water. They soon had a hearty stew of vegetables and bacon bubbling away. Some of the women had little leather bottles from which they swigged and passed round from time to time. Hettie recognised the smell of alcohol all too well, so declined when it came her way. Her father's predilection for the stuff had turned her off for life. Instead, she went to her hut and collected the bowls and spoons she and Ada had brought with them and took them back to the others. The stew was ladled out and they sat quietly and ate it quickly in great mouthfuls; they were all so hungry. Hettie was shattered, filthy from the journey, footsore and achy – yet sitting there cross-legged on the dusty ground with those twenty or so women shovelling stew into their mouths that May evening, she felt she had not been so happy in years.

In the morning, Nora was outside the huts at first light, calling everybody to wake up. Hettie had worried that sleeping on the hay would be so uncomfortable that she would toss and turn all night, but she had been so shattered from the day's exertions that she did not even remember falling asleep. The women prepared themselves with a quick wash from the standpipe and pulled on their dresses and aprons brought from home. Some had been made from flour bags, and the manufacturer's name could be seen emblazoned across it: SAMPSON FLOUR. They all wore bonnets and neckerchiefs to protect their heads and necks from the afternoon sun.

Once up and ready, they travelled out to the strawberry fields in horse-drawn carts. There was much good-natured chatting between Nora and some of the other old hands and the men who drove the carts. Hettie realised that they were probably old friends; Nora had been coming here annually for years. It also dawned on her that she had agreed to this job without asking one question about what the work was actually like. She suddenly felt a little nervous about it.

'Ada,' she said as they trundled along a dusty road, bordered by hedges beyond which lay orchards and fields on both sides. 'What do we actually do all day? What will our duties be?'

'We'll be picking the strawberries and packing 'em into pottles first.'

'What's a pottle?'

'It's a little basket, shaped like a dunce's cap. We put all the fruit in there, then pack those into round baskets. We'll be hoeing the fields, too, scuffling for weeds. Some of us will be sent to carry the big baskets on our heads to market on some days. We sell the pottles there then bring the baskets and money back to the masters here. They pay our wages at the end of the week. Later in the season, we'll be picking other fruits and hoeing the vegetable fields as well.'

'How far is the walk to the London market?'

'Oh, a good ten mile. Takes about three hours or so.'

'Danker me!' cried Hettie. 'I had no clue it was such a trek.'

'Ah, well, 'tis easier than the picking, which fairly breaks your back after a few hours. I always like to go to the market, and you must too, Hettie, for it is rare fun.'

'Fun? Walking for miles and miles there and back?'

'But just you wait till you see the market. Full of interesting folk and some nice-looking lads, too! Even more handsome than your Evan. You'll see . . .'

Ada winked at Hettie, who sat quietly for a moment. She was so busy thinking about the London markets that she barely registered what Ada had said about Evan. It would be good to see the world, and she was used to walking to and from the pit every day, though it was not half as long a walk as this. Either way, she'd had her curiosity piqued by Ada's account, and wanted to go into London very much.

Once they'd arrived, the women got down from the cart and went through a gate into the strawberry field. It stretched out before them, the brown earth dotted with what seemed like thousands of bright red spots, fringed by green leaves rustling in the breeze, seeming to crawl across the land in low mounds. To the right was a rough structure, a three-sided shed, where could be seen the large round baskets and conical vessels Ada had described for packing the strawberries into for market. Also piled up were smaller baskets that Hettie guessed were for carrying with them in the fields to pack the picked fruit into before it was transferred.

Hettie followed the others as they went to the shed and collected their baskets, then fanned out into the fields and began to bend over to pick the strawberries. She was sorely tempted to snack on them, but had been told she must not taste even one, so of course she did not. But how she longed to feel the sweet taste of a strawberry on her tongue! The sun was soon up and it was warm, threatening to be a proper hot day. Now and again, a worker would traipse back to the hut and take a drink from a standpipe there and rub some cold water across her face and neck. Hettie followed suit. Soon, her basket was full and so was Ada's. Hettie watched as Ada took the fruit carefully from her basket and packed it into the pottles, then into the big baskets.

'You mun keep the very best strawberries at the top,' said Ada. 'These are called the toppers, because that's where we put 'em. It makes the whole pottle look fairer to the customer. The little squished ones we put at the bottom, which wonna be seen before the pottle is bought.'

'Clever,' said Hettie and followed suit, picking out the best strawberries from her basket last in the process.

The first morning was long and increasingly hot. Ada had been right about the picking; after a few hours, Hettie's neck, shoulders and back were aching. She watched a selection of women go off before lunchtime to the markets and envied them their escape, though carrying the heavy baskets full of laden pottles on their heads for ten miles would certainly not be easy. But she knew she wanted to be chosen one of these days. She'd carried iron baskets of ironstone on her head for years – not for ten miles, admittedly, but she hoped that strawberries and wicker baskets would be lighter, at least.

At lunchtime, a man from the farm came on a cart and brought baskets with cheese and bread in and beer to drink. Hettie found she was ravenous and ate quickly.

After lunch, she went back to the field and carried on, her body protesting against the constant bending and righting, up and down. There had been conversation and a bit of jollity in the morning, but now, in the heat of the afternoon, with everyone growing weary, all the women picked silently. The sounds were not of chatter but of their labour, accompanied by the soft sigh of the wind through the orchard trees beyond the hedge.

Then, into this came a new sound: a melody. Someone was whistling a tune. Hettie looked up to see which woman was so cheerful, but it was none of them. She looked in the direction of the music and saw a hat, bobbing along atop the hedge that bordered the field. Then, a man appeared. He stopped, not pushing through into the field, instead leaning on the gate. He was a gentleman, anyone could see that, with his morning coat, ascot tie, smart trousers, waistcoat, pocket watch on a chain, and felt hat with a band – every inch the city gent. So what on earth was he doing here near Isleworth, leaning over a gate into a strawberry field?

Hettie looked away, aware she was staring. But she soon glanced back and saw that he was watching them all of them, the women picking the strawberries. Then he looked directly at her and she swiftly looked away. He had dark eyes which had a way of picking you out and pinning you to the spot. She looked back again and he smiled at her, then reached down and fiddled with the latch on the gate. He was coming into the field! Perhaps he was an overseer, maybe the landowner.

Hettie fell to working even harder, in case he should come and scold her for not picking his strawberries quickly enough. He stepped into the field, closed the gate in a leisurely fashion and strolled along the edge of the field to the packing shed. He nodded to the workers there, who nodded back. Then, Hettie heard the women around her start to mutter and giggle. They too were aware of the gentleman and some were making comments about him.

Her hut mate Edna called out, 'Tell us the time then, Master!'

Hettie envied her the nerve to shout at a gent like that. Hettie would never have dared. The man smirked at her and began to approach. As he came closer, Hettie could see those dark eyes again. They turned with interest from girl to girl in the field, nodding and smiling.

'Good afternoon, ladies,' he said, stopping at the edge of the field and removing his hat in a salutatory gesture.

'Ooh, ladies!' said Nora, and laughed sarcastically.

'I can see by your dress that you are from Staffordshire or Shropshire, perchance?'

'Yes, Shropshire,' said Nora, sounding a little wary of him now. 'What be your business here?'

'I happen to study the lives of working women all over our great country. I'm particularly interested in seasonal labourers such as yourself, who spend part of the year here and the rest elsewhere.'

'What is there to study about us?' Nora replied, bending down to pick more fruit and toss it into her basket. 'We bend down, like so. We bend up, like so.'

Hettie was awed by Nora's fearlessness. She was always mouthy at the pit with the lads, but this was a gentleman and a London one at that. Yet it seemed to have no effect upon her. Hettie resolved to be more like Nora, if she ever had occasion to.

'There is much to study, my dear,' he went on, unfazed. 'I'm fascinated by all aspects of your lives. From the details of your labour, the skills you demonstrate, the manner of your dress, your travel habits, et cetera, et cetera.'

The girls had stopped their work now and stared at the man, one and all. One or two had giggled at first, but now all smirking had passed and their faces were quite serious.

The gentleman spoke again: 'Are there any pit-wenches amongst you?'

'Aye!' cried Edna.

There was a general nodding and mutterings of, 'That be true'.

Nora added, 'We all be. Every one of us. Most of us have worked on the pit bank most of our days.'

'And you travel here in the summer months, when pit work is slack, is that right?'

Everyone nodded and agreed.

'And what do you do with the money you earn here?' he went on. Then turning to Edna, he said, 'Do you use it for a dowry for your sweetheart?'

Edna giggled and it was infectious. Lots of the girls tittered then and some covered their mouths in embarrassment. Nora was not smiling, but Hettie could not help it. The gentleman had a wicked little grin on his face and it had set them all off.

'No, sir,' managed Edna between snorts of laughter. 'Leastways, not yet.'

'And you?' said the gentleman and turned his eyes directly on Hettie. She felt rooted to the spot. Was he really talking to her?

'Me, sir?' she said quietly.

'Yes, my dear. What will you spend your money on?'

'I shall give it to my father,' Hettie said, straightening up. It was the truth and it pained her, but she wanted to give an honest answer. She knew no other way in life but to speak the truth.

'And buy a pretty dress for the fair,' said Ada, a saucy look on her face.

The gentleman said, 'Ah now, that is far more interesting. You wish to impress the young men at the fair, my dear?' he said to Hettie, looking at her directly again. She could see now that he was quite young, perhaps only in his twenties. She had to look away from those eyes. There was something dangerous about them.

'I might buy a dress,' she said quietly. 'But if I do, it shall be for myself. It inna to impress boys.'

She surprised herself by speaking back to the man, but he seemed impressed with her response. He stepped closer to her, wending his way into the field itself to stand before her.

'Quite right,' he said and smiled. 'You are young. Have you come here before?'

'My first year,' she said. 'And this be my first day in the field.' The other girls were muttering now and falling back to their work, glancing at Hettie and the man as they continued to talk.

'Even though you've just arrived, I suppose you must be heartily sick of strawberries after eating them all day, my dear.'

'Oh no, sir. We inna allowed to eat the fruit.'

'You've been picking strawberries and haven't tasted one? Not one?'

'No, sir.'

'Well, then, we must see what we can do about that.'

He looked about him, then turned from Hettie and walked over to the packing shed and had a quick word with one of the women there. He passed her some coins and she gave him a pottle. He brought it back. Hettie watched him approach her and glanced at Ada, who had a sly smile on her face.

Ada whispered behind her hand, 'He be sweet on you, Hettie. Sweets for his sweet!'

'Hush your noise, Ada!' said Hettie, then turned to see him holding out the pottle to her.

'For you, my dear. A whole punnet for you to eat yourself.'

'I canna take a gift from a stranger,' said Hettie, shaking her head. 'Thank'ee all the same.'

'Thank'ee, thank'ee! What a charming phrase! Oh, but you must, my dear. And I am no stranger now, for we have been talking. Please, do take it and share with your friend, if you like. I can see she wants some.'

He smiled at Ada, who was agog at the idea, eyeing the large, juicy toppers. So, Hettie took the pottle and nodded a thank you to the man. She passed some to Ada, who grabbed a couple and immediately started munching away. Hettie offered one to the gentleman, who shook his head and said, 'No, not for me. All for you, my dear. It is a crime that you should have to pick these beautiful, ripe fruits all day and not have the pleasure of partaking in them. Please, go ahead.'

Hettie felt embarrassed now, eating in front of this gentleman, and wished she could save them for later. But he was waiting for her, and it seemed rude to disappoint him. So, she took a strawberry and raised it to her mouth, blushing all the while, then took a bite. The soft sweetness exploded in her mouth and filled it with pleasure. A little juice escaped and she had to wipe her lips with the back of her hand. The gentleman looked on appreciatively.

'Does it taste good?' he said.

Hettie's mouth was filled with strawberry, so she merely nodded.

'I'm so glad. You girls work so hard, you deserve a treat.'

Hettie swallowed down the fruit and said, 'Thank'ee again for your kindness, sir.'

'The pleasure was all mine,' he said, smiling. Then he fished about in his inside pocket and brought out a little silver case, which sprang open as he touched a clasp. Inside was a pile of tiny pieces of card. He took one out, put away the case and handed the card to her.

'Can you read?' he said, with no hint of embarrassment about asking such a personal question.

'I can indeed, sir,' Hettie answered, with some pride.

'Good. Then you'll see my name and address on there. If you ever come in to central London, or if you ever find yourself in any kind of need of assistance, I hope you will consider me an old friend and seek me out.'

Hettie thought it unlikely that this might ever come to pass, but she merely nodded and held the card awkwardly before her in one stiff hand, the pottle of strawberries in the other. Above the man's address in London, the card was headed with three words in flowing, elaborate script: *Laurence Maxwell Ripley*.

'Good day, Miss . . . to whom do I have the pleasure of speaking?'

At first she wasn't sure what he meant, then worked out he must be asking for her name.

'Hettie Jones,' she said.

'Well, then, Miss Hettie Jones, I bid you and all you ladies farewell, until next time,' he said, removed his hat with a flourish and gave a little bow.

Hettie watched him walk away, then heard Ada snort with laughter the second he had gone through the gate and disappeared behind the hedge, the only sign of him being his hat bobbing along the path away from them.

'Ooh, he was all over you, Hettie!'

'What rot!' said Hettie.

'A gentleman admirer! I never did!'

'Oh, do stop your noise!'

Ada took another couple of fruits from Hettie and laughed again, staring at her now.

'You like him! I can tell! You be all crowsty about it. A sure sign!'

But their argument was abruptly ended by Nora calling out across the field for them to get on with their work. She approached and added rather spitefully, 'Now the King of England's gone, you might have time to pick some fruit, eh?'

Hettie put down her own fruit to save them for later. She took another look at the gentleman's card, then placed it carefully into her pocket, hoping it wouldn't be too damaged by the time she had the chance to look at it again that evening. For she knew she would be looking at it again, and again.

She went back to picking, trying to fall into a rhythm of it in order to take her mind off the extraordinary meeting she'd just had. But she couldn't stop thinking about it, about the sweet, luscious taste of the strawberries, the pure white, clean and unblemished card, and about the gentleman with those eyes, Mr Laurence Maxwell Ripley.

Chapter 7

The days and nights went on just as the first one, long hours in the field, short hours in the evening, then sleeping the sleep of the dead at night. Hettie bonded with the others in her sleeping hut and they told each other long stories of the boys they loved and hated. Hettie did not once speak of Evan. It seemed wrong. Ada mentioned him from time to time, with a twinkle in her eye, but Hettie did not react. Evan was private to her, nobody's business but her own.

After a month in the fields, Hettie was chosen to take the fruit to market. Much to her annoyance, she was not permitted to go with Ada, who had been chosen to go another day. Nora was there, and two other girls who Hettie did not get on with so well. She felt out of sorts about the whole thing and was not looking forward to it.

Mid-morning came and she was called to the hut to load up. The large baskets were filled with pottles and she put a folded cloth on her head – the same kind she always used for carrying the ironstone, but this one was new and clean, brought from home. The basket was weighty but no more so than the ironstone. It fitted quite comfortably on her head and off they went, Nora in front with the other girls, Hettie behind, alone.

The day was warm but not sweltering. Even so, it was a hard trek from the market gardens near Isleworth to the busy streets of central London and their destination, Covent Garden. They walked down long lanes flanked by fields, that soon gave way to more and more housing, more and more people, as the way grew wearier and hotter. Hettie's neck began aching about halfway and got worse and worse by the time they walked through the busier streets of the city. But the sights she saw fascinated her, and took her mind off the pain.

Ironbridge and the surrounding towns were busy, especially on market days, but London was something else. The people flowed through it like a river, a mucky, jumbled river full of flotsam and jetsam. Hettie wondered who they all were, where they were all going, what they were all thinking. There were hawkers and pedlars and costermongers everywhere, who Hettie and the others had to manoeuvre their way around, stepping into the gutter at times in order to avoid them. Hettie's biggest fear was that she would lose her balance and the basket would topple, so she steadied it with her hands from time to time, whenever she had to avoid people barging past.

The street sellers were fascinating though, selling all manner of goods: cough lozenges, dolls, buns, pipe tobacco, combs, ornaments, flowers, books, chirping birds in cages, healing ointment and harmonicas. There were street musicians on every corner, playing everything from accordions to penny whistles, and there was one boy in a cap too large for his head strumming quite tunefully on a full-size harp.

Also evident on the streets was the appalling poverty of the metropolis. There were people grovelling on the ground for scraps outside eateries and being kicked or stepped on by passers-by. Hettie saw a mother with twin babies sitting almost comatose on some steps, the babies crying weakly and the mother as thin as a sapling. Hettie felt sickened by it and looked away. She felt very fortunate that she had her family and her friends to support her, and that she lived in a small town where people looked out for each other, not in a sprawling, uncaring city like London, as thrilling as it was to walk through its streets.

At last, after over three hours of walking, Nora announced that they would soon be approaching Covent Garden market and that they should, as ever, remain together at all times. Horses clip-clopped by, jingling their harnesses, pulling a bewildering variety of vehicles behind them in the streets. As they passed by, they threw up great clouds of dust that lingered in the warm air and settled on Hettie's clothes and face and irritated her eyes. As the market drew nearer, the roads tapered and thus grew busier and more chaotic. The passages leading to the main square of the market were very narrow indeed, causing vendors to jostle and argue with each other over space. Hettie held onto her basket in alarm, lest all should be lost. Yet, eventually, they were allowed to pass through and into the market proper.

It stretched out across the piazza and was a sight to behold. Every manner of fruit and vegetable could be seen, ranged on stalls peopled by noisy sellers. The air was filled with the thrum of humanity, pierced by the calls and songs of the vendors shouting out their wares and their bargain prices. Two girls laden with flowers in baskets strolled past her, one singing out 'Two bundles a penny, primroses!' while the other called, 'Sweet violets, penny a bunch!' The scent of the flowers, as well as that of a thousand foodstuffs, mingled with the sharp notes of soot, smoke and the stench of animal dung and foul mess in the street gutters all about. Hettie felt her eyes widen like saucers as she struggled to take in the rambling madness of it all, as well as keep her wits about her and follow Nora and the others to their spot.

It turned out their masters had a stall at the western edge of the piazza, so they negotiated their way through the thronging crowds in that direction to find a sleepy and wrinkled old woman selling the few pieces of fruit she had left, and who was very pleased to see them. At last, they could remove the baskets from their heads and place them down onto the stall. The little old lady had looked half-dead when they arrived, but she soon perked up. As she reorganised the stall, she lifted her chin and began to sing out, 'Ripe strawberries! A groat a pottle, today. Only a groat a pottle, is what I say!' The voice that issued from the old woman was high, sweet and clear as a bell, and Hettie was surprised at the pure, angelic sound issuing from such a wizened vessel.

Nora told the others to wait there while she bought them something to eat. Hettie passed the time by watching the buyers of London flock past to haggle with the sellers, easing her neck ache by rubbing it with her sweaty hand. Covent Garden was quite the spectacle, and she was glad she'd seen it.

Ada had told her about the young men hereabouts, and Hettie looked out for them. Opposite was a collection of flower stalls and a group of men busied themselves in hats and caps, brown jackets or waistcoats and shirtsleeves, picking up blooms and placing them in baskets to take to other stalls or deliver to girls who carried them about, singing. Their faces were weathered and bronzed by the outdoors, unlike Evan and the other miners who were pale from working underground. They looked healthier for it, just as Hettie and her fellow pit-wenches and strawberry pickers did – working outside gave you that healthful glow. Ever since Evan had started working down the mine, Hettie had had a dreadful fear of the underworld, as she called it, when they talked of conditions underground. 'How goes the underworld?' she'd say to him, when they were walking home of an evening. 'Deathly and dull,' Evan would reply.

Evan . . . the thought of him gave her an ache in her belly, made worse by her hunger. Where was Nora with their food? She watched the flower boys move with ease and confidence, one catching her eye and winking at her. She turned quickly away. He was a good-looking lad; they all were. But they could not hold a candle to her Evan. Or indeed to Mr Laurence Maxwell Ripley.

Nora returned with slices of pie filled with some indeterminate pale meat, probably some sort of offal. They were tasty and hugely welcome. She also got them beer to drink and apples to put in their pockets for later.

That done, it was time to start the walk home. At least their baskets were lighter now, empty save for yesterday's pottles which they stacked up inside. The walk back was easier, of course, with less weight, but Hettie's feet were wearier. She thought about her bed on the straw most of the way out of the city and into the suburbs, looking forward to the moment when she could acquaint herself with sleep again. There was some idle chatter with the others, but the three of them knew each other better than they knew her and she felt too tired to make the effort with conversation and yet also disappointed that none of them tried to engage with her. But mostly, she was too drained to think. She plodded on, following Nora's striding gait, as ever.

They were about two miles or so from Isleworth when she heard her name spoken aloud, her full name, preceded by the word 'Miss'. It was so odd to hear that she thought she must have imagined it and almost dismissed it, until there it came again.

'Miss Hettie Jones?'

She turned around and saw that the gentleman, Mr Laurence Maxwell Ripley, had appeared behind them and was striding up to her. She knew she ought to be polite and say how do you do, or some such thing, but she was so astonished to see him again that she merely stared at him.

He stopped before her and gave her a quizzical smile. 'I am addressing Miss Hettie Jones, am I not?'

'Why, yes,' she managed, her voice dry from not talking or drinking since London. She cleared her throat.

'I knew it was. I never forget a face, certainly not one as memorable as yours. It's Mr Ripley, from some weeks ago. I visited your field and gave you my card?'

Hettie stared at him. Then she realised that Nora and the others had not seen her stop; they were far ahead of her on the road towards the fields.

'I mun . . . I mun go,' she said, and turned to trot off in their direction, feeling a fool for such a graceless exit – but in truth she had not concentrated on the walk to London and so was afraid she would lose her way back.

But Mr Ripley soon caught up with her. 'I assume you are returning to the fields from London?'

'Yes, sir,' she said, peeking at him, then immediately looking away. Those eyes. He was not a tall man; in fact, he was exactly the same size as her, slight of figure, with black hair that emerged from his hat in dark sideburns and a few locks that escaped across his forehead from under the brim.

'Please, call me Max. It is not my given name, but a corruption of my middle name. Everybody calls me Max.'

Hettie said, 'I canna call you that!' His boldness with her had given her an ounce of courage to answer him back. What was he thinking, accosting her in the street and asking her to call him by a nickname? She was glad she wasn't in Ironbridge. Imagine the gossip!

'Of course, of course. My mistake. Mr Ripley, then? That is proper, surely.'

'If you say so,' she said, hurrying to catch up with Nora and the others.

'Miss Jones, I was wondering if I could talk to you as we walk. I was actually on my way to visit your field to discuss something with you ladies when I saw you. A happy accident.'

'Discuss what?' she said.

'I believe I mentioned to you something of my work.'

'I didna think gentlemen did any work,' she said and smiled at her own cheek. She was warming to this now, talking to a gentleman and giving him a bit of trouble about it.

He chuckled. 'Well, yes, you are quite right. It certainly is not work in the sense of what you achieve each and every week of the year, Miss Jones. Indeed not. But I do my best to make myself useful in the world. As I mentioned, I am studying the working women of England. Their work, their habits, their dress, and so forth. I am interviewing as many as I can and making sketches of them, as well as taking notes on everything I can find out. I was wondering if you would allow me to ask you about your work as you walk back to the fields.'

'If you're strolling the same way,' said Hettie, 'I canna stop you.'

She glanced at him and they shared a smile.

'Splendid!' he said.

The last few streets of the village near the farmland thinned out and soon they were on the long, dusty path back. As they walked, Mr Ripley asked Hettie a series of questions about her work at the pit, the hours, the conditions, and so on, as well as detailed queries about how they travelled to Isleworth, their working times and what they did in the evenings. She liked the timbre of his voice; it was quite low and mellow and it took her mind off her aching feet. He seemed genuinely fascinated by her kind and yet was not overly enthusiastic, remaining a little reserved, which made her want to please him more, to bring forth his praise. From time to time he said extraordinary things, calling the pit-wenches 'courageous women' and describing the walk they did to Covent Garden market with the baskets full of strawberries on their heads as 'the stuff of heroes'.

After a while he returned to the subject of her work on the pit bank.

'And how do you find it, Miss Jones? Is it not a hardship to be outside all through the winter?'

'I like it fine,' she said. 'It is healthful, being outside. And we wrap up proper warm when we need to.'

'Did you know that a few years ago there actually took place a government enquiry into the degradation of women working on the pit bank?'

'The *what* of women?' Hettie had had some schooling and thought herself quite bright, but she had never heard that word before or anything like it.

'Ah, forgive me. The report complained that the women should not be working on the pit bank, as it was shameful. In some parts of the country women wear trousers to do this work, and it was felt by some to be immoral. They feared the women mixing with the male miners could become indecent.'

'I dunna understand all of what you said, but I think it a good job for a woman. I canna fathom why some people hundreds of miles from us want to stop it.'

'There was a concern that women working outside in such jobs would become too independent and unfeminine.'

'And what is wrong with being independent? A woman at home has to work every day of her life without a helping hand, and yet at work she is expected not to be able to look after herself? Sounds like rot to me. But will they win? What shall we do without our jobs if they do?'

'No, indeed. The enquiry found in favour of allowing women to continue. The report showed no evidence that women working on the pit bank were . . . how to say it . . . lacking in morals or decency.'

'How could they think it? All us pit bank women are decent and upstanding! And if we didna work there, we might end up in the workhouse, or worse. Many of our number are the children of miners and some are widows of miners, who wouldna be able to keep their own children if they didna do this work.'

'I agree with you. It was a badly conceived enquiry. We can only be grateful that common sense prevailed. After all, why should any woman be prevented from earning an honest wage? I for one am delighted to see women working outdoors. It's healthy work, better than being cooped up inside. I do believe women should indeed have been banned from working underground in the mines: it is indecent to be in mixed company down there with so much . . . well, to be frank, so much nudity.'

Hettie felt her cheeks colour. Everybody knew that miners stripped off to work in the terrible heat down there, but it was too much to hear the word 'nudity' from this gentleman in general conversation. He seemed to sense her embarrassment, as he glanced at her and coughed nervously.

'My opinion is that pit bank wenches such as yourself have a perfectly respectable profession. It is a joy to see you all so hale and hearty and full of confidence and independence.'

'I agree,' said Hettie. 'And I'm proper glad those fools who tried to stop it were beaten!'

'Me too, Miss Jones. Me too.'

They were now nearing the farm gates that led to the strawberry fields. Hettie would have to finish her shift there before she could rest. She felt exhausted all of a sudden, and realised that the entire time she had been talking to the gent, she had not noticed her sore feet or her weariness. She had been transported to a different world for a short time in her monotonous working day.

'I mun go now, sir,' she said, noticing that Nora and the others were eyeing her coldly. It seemed they did not approve of her conversing with such a man. *Most likely just green with envy*, thought Hettie.

'Miss Jones, I want to thank you for your kindness in talking with me today. Your answers have provided an excellent level of detail for my studies. I am so very grateful.'

'You're welcome,' said Hettie quietly, allowing herself now to look him square in the face. She wanted to look at those eyes for a long time.

'You have my card. Remember what I said. If you ever are in need of assistance, please do not hesitate to get in touch. It would be my pleasure to see you again.'

'Thank'ee,' she said, and bobbed a curtsey.

'Oh, Miss Jones, please. There is no need to do that. We are equals, you and I. In fact, I would propose that you are my superior; I play at working, and yet you are the true worker. You labour to bring us not only the iron from the earth but also the fruit of the land. I have great admiration for the working women of this country and that is why I study them. Thank you again.'

'Hettie!' cried Nora. Her face looked like thunder. 'Hurry up, child.'

'Coming,' called Hettie. She did not wish to displease Nora and the others, but oh, how little did she want to go back to the field and end this conversation. 'Goodbye then, Mr Ripley.'

'Farewell, Miss Jones. Until another time, I hope.'

He smiled at her and she smiled back. Then he turned away and walked back the way they'd come.

Hettie rushed onwards to join up with Nora, who gave her a sharp look and said, 'Evan Malone wouldna like the sight of that, you all familiar with a gent.'

Hettie's cheeks burned as she walked on. She wanted to argue with Nora, but she knew that Nora was their self-appointed leader as well as her hut mate, and she didn't want to get on her wrong side. The truth was that nothing was set in stone with Evan, was it? People just assumed it. And anyway, the gentleman had a professional interest in Hettie – that was all. And now it was done and she would never see him again.

As they reached the gate to the field, she turned to look at him once more. She saw him, Mr Lawrence Maxwell Ripley, strolling away down that dusty road, banked by fields of strawberries on one side and orchards of apple trees and gooseberry bushes on the other. The late-afternoon sun ahead of him hit the trees and made them glow, his shadow lengthening behind him.

All this was burned into her memory like a painting – a moving one, filled with life and longing.

Chapter 8

September 1875

It was the first week of September and the sun was rising over a still, clear day that promised much. Hettie was up before the sun that day; she had her chores to do before she could thoroughly wash all the dust and grime from herself in good time for leaving for the fair. She made her father a breakfast of eggs and yesterday's bread and roused him from his sleep. She encouraged him to breakfast well, as he often did not eat again until the evening. He had grown worse while she'd been away in London, and had been resentful and needy at first when she returned. But she'd now been back a full week, and he was growing kinder to her and was drinking less. She was pleased to see his progress.

'Come on then, Father,' she encouraged him, brushing off the suit she'd bought him especially for the fair. Her own new dress hung in her bedroom, pristine, ready to make its debut out in the world.

Once he was ready, she said, 'You scrub up well!' and her father grinned.

'Go get yourself ready then, wench,' he said. 'I canna wait to see you in your new frock. You'll be the belle of the ball.'

She smiled and went into her room. There it was, her London dress, as she thought of it. The money from all her summer work had paid for a few things around the house, as well as her father's suit and this dress. It was worth the months of labour to see him handsome and smiling. It was also worth it for the experience of being away from home and seeing the world through new eyes. She was now someone who had left their town and journeyed to bigger, brighter things, and coming back to Ironbridge somehow made everything at home look small. Hettie didn't think this in a critical way, but suddenly the parameters of her experience had widened and she felt her life as it had been was narrowed.

And the summer of work had also brought something else: Mr Laurence Maxwell Ripley. She could not stop thinking of him, although she knew it was pointless. She only met him twice, and it was months ago now. But she had never met such a person and she knew he had turned her head.

She had not been to see Evan and the rest of the Malones since her return. Indeed, she had not seen them now in person for several months. She had moved on from them and their sphere of influence so much since she'd left for London and she felt like a different person, a new creature, emerged from the cocoon of her Malone years. She was blossoming into a fresh incarnation.

Now, Hettie stood in her bedroom, gazing at her new dress. It was made of panels of dusky pink and pale green, with neat little pink roses on green backing here and there. The bodice hugged her frame snugly, with an open neck suited to the warm weather, fringed with green ruffles. The skirt was formed of layers of material, alternating pink and green, with an underskirt striped in both colours, a slice of which could be peeked at the front. There were two large green bows, one at the lower back and another beneath the bust. The sleeves were three-quarter length and close-fitting. The whole dress was fashioned from a fine cotton, which made it light and easy to wear in the summer heat. She could not afford new shoes to wear with it, and the walk to the railway station and from there around the fair would make them impractical anyhow. So, Hettie had polished up her best boots to a shine instead.

She dressed her hair simply, held up at the sides and front with pins, while the rest tumbled down her back. She was proud of her light brown hair and her green eyes and wanted to show them off today. The colour of her dress enhanced them. She took it down from the hanger and laid it out on the bed. It was the most precious thing she had ever owned. And she was thrilled she had bought it with her own money, earned by her own hands. She stepped into the skirt and buttoned it at the waist, followed by the bodice, which she fastened all down the front, loving the feel of the tiny buttons slipping through the holes, each one decorated with a single pink rose bloom. They were the most beautiful buttons she had ever seen, let alone worn.

She had no full-length mirror to view herself, so she took a hand mirror to hold at various angles to see the shapes her figure made against the drab background of her room. What she saw thrilled her; she was indeed a new person in this stunning dress. She felt a stab of nerves at the thought of being seen in public in such fashion and how it would surely bring the gaze of others, something she'd never craved before. She hated to be the centre of attention in anything, but she was proud, too, that she would be a beauty at the fair, and who knew what that beauty would bring her?

But there was a kernel of disappointment that Mr Laurence Maxwell Ripley would never see her in this dress. He'd only seen her in her dowdy work clothes with the home-made apron and her hair in a mess from her labour. But she must put thoughts of him from her mind today and focus instead on enjoying the thrills of the fair.

She left her room and went to find her father, whose face looked pained.

'The image of your mother,' he said with a choked sob. 'The very image!'

'I am so happy to hear that,' she said, and gave him a kiss on the cheek.

'She would be so proud.' He dried his eyes, smiling broadly now as he looked her over again. 'And so am I. My beautiful girl.'

She linked arms with him. 'Come, let us go out and make merry.'

They took the train to the fair. It was worth the small expense, as she did not wish to muddy her dress on the long walk. They strolled arm in arm to Madeley Market station, where they caught the train that went through Stirchley and Mallinslee before arriving at Oakengates Market Street station. The carriages were stuffed with fairgoers, the men in their Sunday best and the ladies in their new dresses. Hettie found many a face turned towards her, the women in approbation or envy, the men with something else in their eyes. Her dress was demure, but it hugged her figure perfectly, and she felt their eyes trace her curves. Her father spoke to some of the other men on the train, while she looked out of the window, keeping her thoughts to herself. She had not seen Evan for months, and wondered what he'd make of her. The thought troubled and excited her in equal measure. For all that the London gentleman had turned her head, another part of her still wanted Evan to think she looked nice.

From the station, it was a short walk to the fairground. All paths were thronged with fairgoers and a noisy hubbub of excited gossip. The Oakengates fair was held at the same time as the Wakes, a series of entertainments that took place over several days in September. The fair was the highlight for most people, a feast of superior food and drink, attended by every family, every lad and lass, every labourer and maid alike, folk coming in from all over the county. Some workers were given the full day off work for the fair, and those who were not would rise early, so that before dawn on the day of the fair a passing field mouse would be surprised to see ploughmen out on the fields completing their work, so that they could finish early and attend the fair.

All along the main street, Hettie walked arm in arm with her father, who was beaming his pride at every passer-by. They saw stalls set up with every sort of good thing to eat for sale. There were little cakes, oranges, hot sausages and buns, with many a stall selling different varieties of ale and sweet drinks such as ginger beer and lemonade. They stopped and bought some gingerbread to munch on, one of their favourites.

The throng thickened as they approached the entrance to the fair itself. The air was filled with the sounds of celebration: music emanating in waves across the ever-warming late-summer air, mixing and jangling with the shouts of sellers and the air of hilarity from the revellers. Hettie scanned the crowd for the Malones. She'd received a message through a mutual friend that they would all meet at the coconut gallery at some point during the morning, and Hettie was eager to see them, if a little anxious, too. She had missed them all over the summer, and she wanted them to see her new dress.

But before they found the shy, her father spent a few pennies taking her on a roundabout, which whipped them round at quite a rate and made Hettie cry out in delight, her father laughing heartily. How good it was to see him laugh! She caught a glimpse of the whole man he must once have been, before life took him up so roughly and broke him.

From the raised height of the roundabout, Hettie spotted the coconut shy, and after they'd finished their ride she led her father in that direction. The Malones were not there yet, so Hettie bought her and her father a strawberry ice in a glass cup each, which they licked out until not a vestige remained, handing the cups back to the stall when they were done.

'Hettie!' called a deep voice, and she turned to see a tall young man walking towards her.

She was astonished to realise it was Evan. He had had a phenomenal growth spurt over the summer, and now his sixteen years – soon to be seventeen in October – looked more like twenty. He had turned into a man in her absence. He looked inches taller, his voice had lowered considerably and he had the hint of a pale beard about his jaw. His blond hair was thicker and darker, his neck bulged with a prominent Adam's apple that she had never noticed and his legs looked longer and broader. As he strode towards her, she could not take her eyes from him. He too was gazing at her with intention and fascination. He looked her all over, his eyes bluer than ever in the sunshine. She was so thrilled to see him she could not stop herself, and threw her arms about him. He laughed and hugged her back, hard and urgent. She stepped back, alarmed at her rash behaviour, unbecoming to her smart dress. But nobody around them seemed to care; everyone was too busy with their own merrymaking.

'Hettie, my dear!' came Anny's voice, and soon the whole Malone tribe were upon them, the twins hugging her waist, Flora touching her hair and the tiny roses on her dress with a grin. Anny and Peter gave her warm hugs and kisses, and many a pat on the shoulder was given to Adam, who Hettie was proud to see stood beaming and chatting good-naturedly with Peter. *Perhaps this will be the turning point*, thought Hettie, *the moment where Father sees the error of his ways and stops drinking forever*. Perhaps they would look back on the day of the Oakengates fair as the time when everything changed for the better.

'Come with me,' said Evan, taking her hand. Hettie nodded eagerly, and a quick glance at her father in the company of the Malones reassured her that he would be in good hands. She could go and have some of her own fun. Evan pulled her onwards, into the heaving crowds, his large, manly hand clasping her own, warm and sticky in the rising heat.

'Where are we going?' she said, and Evan replied, 'You'll see.'

Then there they were at the swing-boats, which rocked back and forth at an alarming height and pace.

'Is it safe?' she asked Evan.

'Course,' he said and squeezed her arm.

While they waited for the current ride to finish, they suddenly became aware of each other and Hettie stepped away from him slightly. There was an awkwardness between them, different from the distance they'd had since she left, the opposite of their childhood closeness. There was something in the air that vibrated with meaning. It was attraction. Hettie looked up at him, now so much taller than her. He was no longer just her Evan – he was a young man and he was staring at her. When their eyes met, a message flashed between them, so exquisitely painful she had to look away.

'Your dress . . .' Evan began. He was never very good with words, and she waited patiently for him to form them. 'Your dress is the prettiest thing I ever saw.'

'Thank you,' she said and did a little curtsey, which made them both laugh and broke the spell a little.

Then, the swing-boat man called for new customers as the ride came to an end and its occupants dismounted. Evan took Hettie's hand to climb in. She did not need it, being a pit bank girl who clambered on steep slopes in all weathers, but it was nice to feel his hand again. They snuggled up on the slatted wooden seat and were joined by another pair opposite, a young courting couple. Before the boats began to swing, the young man opposite had his arm around his girl and was whispering things in her ear that made her giggle. Hettie glanced at Evan and they both burst out laughing. They were embarrassed and amused, but there was also a hint of envy as they glanced back at the couple, just before the boat began to move.

As it rose higher and its angle grew steeper, Hettie found herself reaching up to grasp Evan's arm. He swiftly drew it out and around her, pulling her in close so her head was beneath his shoulder and the whole length of her frame pressed into his side. The thrill of the ride mingled with the thrill of their closeness. How much Evan had changed was foremost in her mind. She had gone to London and left him a boy. She had returned to a man. The boats went higher still and she felt his arm clutching her closer. The females in the boats were squealing, the men laughing or cheering. The air rushed past Hettie's face, taking her breath away, while the feel of Evan holding her made her feel safe. She did not turn her face to look at him, as the ride made all small movements impossible, but she felt his presence course through her as the boats reached their top height and speed. She held onto him tightly and though the ride made her feel giddy, she wished it would never stop and she could stay in his arms with a good excuse for doing so.

After the rush of the swing-boats, her head felt light when she stepped out onto solid ground again. Evan smiled at her and she found herself laughing; she felt as if she had been drinking ale. Evan laughed too and took her hand again, leading her off into the crowd.

They stopped at a stall selling sausages and bought some with onions and bread, a delicious, hot, spicy treat. They ate noisily, talking about the local gossip, Evan giving her some choice facts about lads and lasses he saw passing by, telling her what she'd missed while she'd been in London. Their awkwardness was waning now, replaced by the ease they once had, but peppered with their physical awareness of each other. How good it was to be with him in this easy way again.

'So, how was strawberry picking then?' he asked, polishing off the last of his food and wiping the crumbs from his mouth.

'It was proper hard work. Nearly broke my back, all that bending and carrying. And walking ten miles or so to the market with the basket on your head. And standing in the hot sun in the fields all day. The huts we slept in were proper simple, just straw on the floor.'

'Sounds like hell,' said Evan.

'Not really. It was hard. But it was fun, too, messing about with the other wenches after dark. And going into London was proper jam!'

Evan made a face and said, 'I always thought London sounded like a drodsome place. Just the word sounds horrible.'

'Oh, it had its bad points, surely. There were some poor souls in the streets that looked like ghosts, so thin they were, with eyes that looked black and wide, like holes in their faces. Fair broke my heart. You dunna see that round here in the same way, except at the workhouse perchance. There's a fair amount of those around. But the market was full of life and the living. All sorts of colour and noise and smells, and people from all over. It was something to see, it truly was.'

'Sounds better here,' was all Evan wished to say on that matter.

Hettie felt disappointed with his response. She wanted to impress him and delight him with all the details. But he was not interested. Or perhaps it was something else.

Then he said, 'You meet anyone there? Anyone turn your head, eh?'

Hettie knew he was just teasing her, but an image of Laurence Maxwell Ripley leapt to her mind and she felt her cheeks go hot.

'You did!' he said, looking more closely.

'I didna!' she cried, and turned away. 'Who would I meet working in the fields all day? Dunna be daft.'

'You were blushing.' He stepped round her, so that she had to face him. 'Did you meet someone?'

'I've given my answer. Now stop badgering me, Evan Malone! Let's see more of the fair.'

She grasped his hand and led the way this time, straight to the shooting gallery. It would be good if Evan could impress her with his aim. It might take his mind off what had just happened. But Hettie could not stop thinking of it, of Mr Ripley and of Evan. She had built the gentleman into an object of perfection in her mind, but Evan was Evan, and she knew that what she felt for him ran deep. Watching him raise the weapon and expertly hit the target, winning her a posy of artificial flowers, Hettie felt a thrill. Mr Ripley had those dark eyes, but Evan had this body, a body that worked hard and showed it in its curves and dips. Looking at his strong arms made her feel a little faint, and she had to look away.

They strolled on as the sun rose higher in the sky, passing by clowns, an Aunt Sally and a test-your-strength machine; men boxing and women dancing; boys assaulting people with water pistols and screaming with laughter at their antics. For a while they watched a man walking on a high wire with a net beneath him, which was thrilling and bizarre. Hettie could not believe her eyes; it seemed impossible that a person could walk on something so narrow. She laughed with Evan and they held hands and talked. All in all, a perfect day.

They were strolling back towards the coconut shy to see if the other Malones and her father were there when a commotion broke out nearby and a man fell to the ground before them.

'Ignore it,' said Evan, manoeuvring her gently out of the way as the man scrambled on the floor. 'Just some drunken fools.'

But someone was shouting at the man, who was standing up now, brushing himself off and shouting back. Hettie looked up to see where the noise was coming from. There, beside a beer stall, upon which was a nine-gallon cask of beer and a mess of dirty mugs, was her father.

He was pointing at the man on the ground and cursing him in the most filthy language, worse than any miner on a bad day. His face was distorted with anger and beer, his cheeks a deep red, his eyes swimming, his movements erratic. The horror of seeing her father that way in front of everyone at the fair rooted her to the spot. She knew she should go to him, but she dreaded having to admit to all around them that he was related to her. The day had been wonderful, her dress was beautiful and Evan was everything. And now, here was her only kin making a spectacle and ruining everything. A drunken fool, as Evan had said, before they realised her own father was involved.

Evan seemed to read her mind, as he always had. 'I'll deal with him. You go.'

'No,' she said. 'No.'

She couldn't desert him. She'd promised her mother. She went to him, Evan behind her saying, 'Hettie,

Hettie.' But she went on, pushing her way through a gaggle of other drunks holding mugs of beer, which slopped this way and that. One man tripped sideways as she came through and raised his voice at her, lurching towards her, his beer sloshing up in a great splash which landed right on Hettie's front, soaking her green bow and staining her bodice a dirty brown. She stopped and looked down at her dress in horror. Her beautiful dress – ruined!

Things moved very quickly then. The man was in Evan's grip within a moment and she looked up to see Evan land a fist on his cheek. He was floored in an instant. She saw her father's face, confused and alarmed, raising his mug and shouting about how it was just a bit of fun. She grasped his mug and threw it to the ground, then took his arm and manhandled him out of there, ducking the men, who were now in a chaotic fist fight. Evan was in the centre, taking no prisoners, punching out every man that came near him.

'Evan!' she cried, trying to hold her father up. He now looked like he was going to collapse. He lurched forward, nearly toppling her, then fell onto all fours and vomited copiously onto the ground. People walking by gave him a wide berth, laughing, shaking their heads, gasping and complaining. Hettie felt as if she would die of humiliation.

She looked round to see Evan step away from three men groaning on the ground, wiping his hands on his waistcoat. He always had been handy with his fists. Now he was tall and strapping, he had finished them off with no trouble.

Hettie stood, her dress stinking of beer, her father still coughing up half-digested beer which ran in rivulets through the dusty ground, his new suit wrecked as he grovelled there.

Evan took her arm and said, 'Go find Mother. I'll deal with him. And after this, you mun leave this fool forever and come home to us. You've done your best by him. But home is where you belong, with us. With me, Hettie.'

Chapter 9

The trees lining the road up to the Southover plot were dressed in rich autumn colours. Copper-coloured leaves drifted down as the carriage climbed the hill. Queenie regarded the outside world largely with mistrust these days, yet she was surprised to find that she'd enjoyed the feel of this short journey, from her present home to her real one – for that was the way she thought of Southover: her proper home. It had belonged to her long-dead husband's family, but she had made his family, his name and his legacy all her own, and so she had made Southover her own. The loss of it in the fire went deeper than anyone else knew, and the wound still smarted.

And so, for reasons known only to herself, she had made the decision in January to have Southover rebuilt, and now was the time to inspect its advancement. The carriage's progress up the gravel drive and onto the sweeping frontage of the house was like something from an old dream. How many times she had once done this, and how much she had missed it when it was gone years ago! Jenkins climbed out of the carriage first and came round to open the door for Queenie.

'Do you want to stay in the carriage?' said Jenkins. 'You can see things from there. No need to fuss yourself.'

'No,' said Queenie, firmly. 'I wish to see my house with my feet on the ground.'

Jenkins made a face, which could have been annoyance but which looked a little like pain. Queenie knew Jenkins thought this trip was a bad idea; the weather was unseasonably cold for October, and she had told Queenie to wait until the house was fully finished in the spring. But too much of Queenie's life was left to others to manage and she wanted to do this for herself, to see the progress of her house with her own eyes. She had been looking forward to it for a long time.

Jenkins put out her hand and helped Queenie down the steps onto the gravel. The ruins were long gone and in their place were new foundations, with new walls rising brick by brick. Local bricks, from the King brickyard, of course. Some of the fancier bricks and tiles for patterning around the doors and windows were purchased from her old associates, the Elkins, at their yard that specialised in such designs. The layout of the new house would mirror that of the old one. The architect had tried to convince Queenie to go with a more modern design, but she would not be turned. She wanted the same house, an exact copy, as if the old one had never burned down.

Walking slowly towards it, leaning on Jenkins's arm, she found herself smiling as the shape of her beloved home was forming before her. The builders and other workers had stopped their work and lined up on the gravel with their hats and caps in hand to receive her. She waved them away and said, 'Continue with your work.' They did so, looking relieved that none of them were required to speak to her.

She watched their progress with interest for a while, Jenkins beside her, adjusting Queenie's shawl to keep her warm. The bricklayers fascinated her. She watched them scoop up the mortar and slap it down, placing the bricks so carefully, so perfectly. There was such skill in building a house, yet these poor fellows would never be rich from their skills, as impressive as they were. Queenie made a mental note to instruct the site manager to raise their wages for this job, the surplus of which she would cover. *Always appeasing the ghost of Blaize*, she thought. Or was it that she had truly changed and become a better person? Either way, she was proud these skilful men were making her home, and she wanted them to be rewarded justly for their sacred task.

She moved on and performed a tour of the whole house, walking around it twice to get a feel for how far the building work had come. It would surely be ready for them to move into in the spring. Ah, to see the clouds of white blossom on the hawthorn trees from her bedroom window again – that would be quite something. She pictured it all as she ambled around her own grounds. The garden was overgrown and needed some brutal care. She would engage gardeners soon, to clear the growth of weeds and begin again. Regrowth, renewal and new life all felt like gifts at this late stage of her life. The thought of it made her smile again as she rounded the eastern corner to arrive upon the gravel drive once more, Jenkins beside her for support.

After a while, Queenie's legs began to tire. She was delighted with the progress of the building, and had seen enough. She turned to Jenkins to instruct her to take her back to the coach.

But Jenkins did not seem to hear Queenie's command. She had let go of her mistress's arm and was standing oddly bent over, staring at the ground.

'What is it?' asked Queenie, with alarm.

Jenkins's hands came up suddenly and clutched at her chest. Her face crumpled into an expression that fluctuated between fear and extreme pain.

'Help!' cried Queenie. 'Help us!'

The coachman came running, as did two of the builders. But they were too late to catch Jenkins, whose knees buckled beneath her as she fell forward onto the gravel. Queenie cried out and felt a rush of faintness come over her. She could not kneel down beside her friend to help her. All she could do was cry out, 'Help her! Help her!'

One of the builders was talking to Jenkins, asking her what was wrong, but Jenkins was still clutching at her chest, grimacing, and could not speak.

The coachman stepped over to Queenie and said, 'Come with me, Mrs King. Let's get you safely back in the carriage, eh?'

'But Jenkins!' Queenie cried.

'I can help her better if I know you're safe and sound, ma'am. May I escort you to the carriage? And then we can fetch help and get you home at the same time.'

Queenie was too upset to reply. She allowed herself to be taken by the arm over to the carriage and helped onto the step. Before she got inside, she turned back for another look at Jenkins. Two builders were leaning over her as she lay helplessly on the ground.

'Go straight to the doctor's house,' she told the coachman. 'Do not take me home first.'

'But ma'am . . .' he replied.

'Do as I say!' she said, as loudly as she could manage. She felt feeble and breathless, as if she might pass out at any moment. He helped her onto the seat and closed the door.

Soon they were off, and as the coach rattled across the gravel, Queenie sobbed at the thought of Jenkins left there with only strangers for company, in her hour of direst need. She closed her eyes and slumped against the side of the carriage. She was so upset that she could not bear to look outside.

When the carriage came to a halt, she prepared herself to face the doctor, but saw instead that they were at home. She heard the coachman calling into the house for help. Her anger boiled up that he had dismissed her orders and taken her home instead of helping Jenkins first. She was fully prepared to raise her voice at him or even raise her fists.

But the next thing she knew, she was in someone's arms. She was being carried. A man was carrying her. It was the most extraordinary sensation, of being weightless and helpless, like a child carried by a parent. What on earth was happening?

Then, there was nothing for a time. The next moment of consciousness was waking at night. She called out for Jenkins, wondering if she were still doubled over on the ground at the building site, nobody to help her as the builders would have gone home for their suppers and sleep. But a voice came, and hands. It was not Jenkins. It was Benjamina's maid Clayton, who was talking soothingly, stroking Queenie's forehead. So she closed her eyes and slept again.

The morning came greyly, a thin strip of light through the curtains that someone had not closed properly. Everything was wrong. Nothing was right without Jenkins here. And where was Jenkins? That fool of a coachman had better have got the doctor to her without delay. Jenkins would be recovering there, perhaps, or here, at home. For it was Jenkins's home as sure as it was her own. The woman had devoted her life to this family, to Queenie. Surely Benjamina would have dealt with it all fairly, ensuring the most senior maid in the household was taken care of appropriately.

'Clayton,' said Queenie, her voice dry and almost silent. She cleared her throat and tried again.

The door opened and in came the young woman. She had a nice face. But it was not the right face. She went to the curtains and opened them a few inches to let in more light.

'Now then, ma'am,' she said softly. She came to Queenie, helping her to sit up slightly against her pillows. She held a glass of water to Queenie's lips without even being asked. She seemed to divine that she would be thirsty. Queenie sipped the water gratefully.

'Where is Jenkins?'

'Oh, ma'am,' said Clayton, and her face fell. 'I am ever so sorry, ma'am.'

'No,' said Queenie. 'No!'

'Please stay calm, Mrs King. You need to rest.'

'Where is she? Where is Jenkins?'

'She's with the undertaker, ma'am. The funeral is tomorrow. You've been asleep on and off for two days yourself. I am so very sorry, ma'am. They said it was her heart gave out.'

'Rose,' whispered Queenie.

'She's at peace now, ma'am,' said Clayton. 'Take comfort in that.'

'Rose Jenkins. My oldest friend.'

'Let me fetch your breakfast, ma'am. You'll feel so much better once you've had a bite to eat.'

Queenie turned away from Clayton's young, pitying face and stared at the gap in the curtains. Through it she could see that fog had engulfed the house, as if they were at sea. Her head felt light and airy, as if the fog had wended its way inside her mind as well. She felt utterly lost.

Queenie was incapacitated for over a week, her strength seemingly lost with Jenkins. She slept for the first day, then spent the next one half awake, half asleep. That evening, she was possessed with a sudden fear and called for Benjamina, only to tell her as clearly as she could in her weak voice one thing: that Jenkins must be buried in the King family plot. She said it three times to Benjamina, to ensure the woman listened properly. After this, she told Clayton that she did not wish to see Benjamina again until further notice.

Queenie was not well enough to attend the funeral. The knowledge that she could not say farewell to her friend brought a mild relapse. She would speak to nobody but Clayton. She turned her face often into her pillow and wept. Nothing consoled her. She simply wanted to die. There did not seem any point in continuing with this pointless, overlong life if Jenkins was not there to share it.

And the cruelty of not being able to help her in her final moments or even say goodbye to her at the church was too much for her. She was glad at least that she had ensured Jenkins would be buried in the family plot, which was still situated in the grounds of Southover, tended carefully by a servant from the house. Thus when she recovered she would at least have the meagre comfort of being able to visit her friend's grave whenever she wanted in her own private grounds. Soon, Southover would be her home again and she would be close to Jenkins forever. She would insist that she was buried next to her when her own time came. Queenie thought of the ghost's curses, how frightened she had been of them, how worried she had been for the risk to her life at moments, over the years. Now, she felt that her long survival, living to nearly one hundred, was the curse. Lying there in her bed, too weak to move for much of the day, she wished now that she had been killed in the fire with Margaret. What good had come from her life since then? Nothing good. Beatrice and Cyril had left, never to return; Benjamina had taken over the business; and Jenkins was dead and gone.

All she had now was Clayton. Benjamina's lady's maid had worked for the family for just over a year. She was in her late twenties and had come with impeccable references from another good house in Wrockwardine. She was a relation of Jenkins, her cousin's child, and that was a comfort to Queenie. Clayton was not pretty, but rather handsome. Tall, a squarish face, mousy hair in a neat bun, small brown eyes that seemed to comprehend meanings swiftly and strong hands that were quick and capable. When Jenkins had needed rest, Queenie found that Clayton had filled in admirably. She possessed all the cleaning, mending and styling skills a lady's maid required and, best of all, she was sympathetic. Heaven knows how she found working for Benjamina, who was petulant and demanding. In the terrible days after the loss of Jenkins, Queenie turned to Clayton and put her life utterly in her hands. And the young maid took great care of Queenie and helped ease the passage into her new life without her rock. Queenie was grateful beyond words.

Yet, as Queenie's health and strength recovered, a plan began to form in her mind that would hopefully mean she would not have Clayton by her side for much longer. It would be a wrench, but Queenie knew it was what she needed to do. Someone demanded it. Or rather, something demanded it.

So, two weeks after Jenkins's death, on a chilly Saturday in November, Queenie wrote a letter, sitting up in bed, and had it sent. Then she told Clayton to prepare her favourite green day dress and matching shawl, for she was to receive a visitor on the morrow, first thing in the morning.

'Yes, ma'am,' said Clayton.

'And prepare my beige dress for this afternoon, as I do believe I am strong enough to venture for a walk to the graveyard today.'

'But ma'am, it is bitter cold out, and you have only walked about this room these past days. You've not even been down the stairs yet. I think you best stay in bed a while longer.'

'No,' said Queenie. 'I need to visit my dear friend. It has been two weeks since her passing and I have not visited her grave yet. I imagine the stone has not been put in place as yet, but I would like to see her resting place at Southover. Tell the men to get the carriage ready for after luncheon.'

'Southover, ma'am?' Clayton said, doubtfully.

'Yes, Southover, of course,' replied Queenie, a little tetchily.

'The grave of Rose Jenkins is not at Southover, ma'am.'

Queenie stared at her. 'Of course it is. I insisted upon it to Benjamina.'

'I am sorry, ma'am, but Jenkins was laid to rest in the town. Many old friends from Ironbridge turned out for her. It was a fine service. I omitted mention of it, ma'am, as I wanted to avoid upsetting you.'

'What? What? But she should be on King ground! This is terrible!'

'Please, you'll make yourself ill, ma'am!' said Clayton, stepping towards Queenie, her hand outstretched to placate her.

But Queenie would not be calmed. This was the worst injury Benjamina had inflicted upon her yet. How cruel could a person be? How *dare* she!

'Send Mrs King to me immediately,' said Queenie with more strength and resolve than she'd had in weeks.

Clayton nodded and left the room, while Queenie sat bolt upright in bed, seething. Her anger gave her strength, but woven through her anger was also a burgeoning sorrow, that her bosom friend was in a town plot with all those strangers, abandoned by the Kings at her last hour. It was almost too much to bear.

The door opened and she steeled herself for the showdown with Benjamina. But it was only Clayton.

'Mrs King wishes me to inform you that she believes you are yet too weak to receive visitors, and will delay her visit until such time as you are fully recovered. She said she wished to have no part in delaying your recovery.'

Clayton said all this with a blank look on her face. Queenie could not yet read her with accuracy, but she was certain she detected a note of judgement in Clayton's voice.

'So, she hides from me,' muttered Queenie. 'Well, she will rue it. She will rue all of it. Mark my words.'

Chapter 10

Hettie received the letter from old Mrs King on Saturday evening, on her return from work. Her father had already broken the wax seal and opened it, which she scolded him for.

'It was a letter, is all. I didna know it was for you, until I saw Dear Miss Jones at the top. I didna read the rest. I have some honour, you know.'

'I know, Father,' she said.

Hettie took the letter and read it quickly. It summoned her to a meeting with Mrs King at the old brickmaster's house the following morning at eight. She was curious, of course, but regretted that she would lose the luxury of her Sunday-morning late sleep.

'What is it, then?'

'Old Mrs King wants me to come to a meeting with her tomorrow morning.'

'Whatever for?' Her father's voice was low and his face was fixed in a scowl.

'It doesna say.'

‘That woman,’ said her father, taking a deep puff on his pipe, leaning against the mantelpiece as if for support. ‘She was the death and the life of me. Her family took my freedom away, but she begged for clemency for me and saved me from the noose. I hate her and I am indebted to her in the very same breath.’

‘I know, Father. Dunna fret. Maybe it is regarding this money she’s been sending. Perhaps she is to stop it and she’d rather inform me than have to deal with you directly, who knows? It is most likely for the best, if so. I do believe it may be time for you to look for work.’

It was something she’d wanted to raise with her father for a while now, and she was glad to have this letter as an excuse to bring it up again.

Her father sighed, staring into the fireplace. ‘You know my nerves are not up to working, my dear.’

Hettie came to him and put a hand on his shoulder. ‘I believe that your nerves would do better out of this house and out of the taverns and in the fresh air.’

‘And what sort of job would anyone give me, an old convict?’ he replied, bitterly.

‘I dunna have an answer to that, Father. But you wonna know until you look.’

He grumbled some unintelligible response to this, and she chose not to ask him what. She had just finished a long shift on the pit bank and she was tired. This week had exhausted her. She’d had another argument with Evan last Sunday and it had been hanging over her for days. He had told her again that she ought to leave her father once and for all and come home.

Evan meant well, she knew that, and it was hard to keep disappointing him. But she could not seem to make him understand that she would never abandon her father. It wasn't only the promise to her mother that stopped her, but the fact that this man, however trammelled by circumstance he may be, was her only kin on this earth. After her mother's untimely death, she had grown for the past thirteen years without a member of her true family about her. She had nobody she could look at and say, *this is where I come from, this is who I am*. The Malones had given her the best childhood an orphan could desire, filled with love and acceptance. But this man, this broken man, was part of her, and she was part of him. She'd rather die than leave him.

The next morning, she was up and about long before her father, dressing in her Sunday best for this unexpected meeting with Mrs King. She carried out her early chores and put out a breakfast of boiled eggs and a little bit of ham for her father, before leaving the house quietly.

She was out in plenty of time and did not need to hurry, so walked in a leisurely way along the river, over the iron bridge and through Benthalledge Wood towards the old brickmaster's house, the King residence. Walking along the woodland path, deserted on this Sunday morning, she felt at peace amidst the sound of birdsong and the river burbling away beyond the trees. It was quite a while since she had been alone, and an age since she had walked through a wood and had the time to listen to the sounds of nature. Her life always belonged to other people and other things – her work, her father, her responsibilities. She had little or no control over anything she did. Walking in this quiet place, hearing the birds singing and seeing them flit from branch to branch, she felt some envy for their freedom. They were masters of their own fate, and best of all, they could fly away from everything whenever they wanted.

With this thought in her mind, she saw the King house edge into view. She swallowed nervously as she rounded the house and went to the servants' entrance at the back; she knew full well it was the appropriate door for someone of her low status. As she recalled her reason for this peaceful walk, her stomach lurched with nerves. What could old Mrs King want with her? Surely it would only be about the money. Hettie murmured a little prayer, hoping that it was not bad news. She was too tired to face any more drama in her life.

But something told her that any dealings between the Joneses, the Malones and the Kings never ended well.

Inside, the house was grand but not overly so. She liked the jolly look of the chequerboard tiles in the hallway. She followed a maid up the stairs, but did not know the girl, who was a few years older than her. The maid had given her a swift look of dissatisfaction when she had presented herself. At the top of the stairs, the maid went down a corridor, then knocked lightly on a door at the end of the landing.

'Enter,' a voice said.

The maid went in and Hettie followed. It was a large, bright bedchamber, sparsely furnished. In an armchair by the window sat a very old woman, her face deeply lined and wrinkled, her ice-white hair swept away from her face in a chignon, her shoulders slightly humped and her body wrapped in a shawl and blanket. But her eyes were bright and piercing, staring now at Hettie. She had never seen Mrs King, because the old woman hardly ever ventured out these days, but Hettie presumed this must be her. Her penetrating gaze was disconcerting, but Hettie tried her best to face up to this strange meeting and stepped forward when the maid introduced her as Miss Jones.

Another woman came in at that moment, a more senior maid. She gave Hettie a quick up and down glance, then gestured that she should sit in a chair that had been placed opposite Mrs King. Hettie did so, and the two maids left the room.

Hettie finally raised her eyes to look again at Mrs King, who it seemed had not taken her eyes from Hettie.

'Miss Jones,' said Mrs King. Despite her advanced age, her voice was as clear and strong as her gaze. 'You have your mother's green eyes.'

This was a shock, to hear her long-lost mother spoken of by a stranger. Was she allowed to speak? She imagined so, since she had been summoned by name for an audience. 'Thank you, ma'am,' she began meekly, then took courage and continued, 'Did you know my mother, ma'am?'

'I met her once,' said Mrs King. 'She was heavy with child – with you. She had the most extraordinary green eyes, and you have inherited them. In fact, you are the spitting image of her. It is quite disconcerting.' She paused. 'I suppose you have little memory of her.'

Talking to this local dignitary was peculiar enough, but speaking of something so personal was even more so. But it was welcome to Hettie, somehow, as she had always had a hunger to talk of her mother – and here was another person, outside of the Malones and her father, who had known her first-hand. 'I have some pictures in my head, ma'am. Little things. Passing things.'

'I suppose that such early memories must be mingled with dreams and wishful thinking, so that the thoughts one possesses could be seen as unreliable. You may have a recollection of your mother that has been placed in your mind by what others have told you, or even what you wanted her to be.'

It was a complex utterance, but Hettie believed she had the gist of it. 'I think that is true, ma'am. I think dreams can feel real. So it inna always easy to tell 'em apart from the waking world.'

Mrs King smiled and nodded her head approvingly. 'Good. Good. You are a clever child. I was hoping you would be. Your father was always a very intelligent man, so it seems you have inherited his brain, as well as your mother's looks.'

Again, Hettie did not know quite how to respond. 'Thank you,' she said, as she perceived it was a compliment, though Mrs King's voice had a slightly disparaging tone to it when she mentioned Hettie's father.

'Now then, I have some business to discuss with you. My lady's maid, Rose Jenkins, died recently. She was my maid for decades and her loss is keenly felt.'

Mrs King stopped and looked down at her hands. Hettie felt the old woman was overcome with emotion, which seemed peculiar for a lady to have when talking of a mere servant. As the silence continued, Hettie felt compelled to speak. 'Sorry to hear it, ma'am.'

Mrs King recovered herself and looked up again at Hettie. 'That is the reason I have summoned you here today. I wish to offer you the role of my new lady's maid.'

Hettie stared at the old woman, so shocked she could not speak. Her, Hettie Jones – pit bank girl and strawberry picker – a lady's maid, one of the most senior female servants in the house, second only to the housekeeper? Hettie had no idea how to respond.

'I understand this will come as something of a surprise to you, to say the least. You have had no experience in service. I understand that. But I will ensure that you will receive training, not only from my current maid Clayton, but from the entire staff and also from myself. I will ensure that you are paid well. I would estimate it will be almost twice the wage you currently receive as a picker at the mine. And of course, the conditions will be vastly superior, working indoors with me as opposed to out of doors, facing the elements day in and day out.'

This was not the time to protest how much Hettie enjoyed working outside, how much she liked the freedom of it. And how she had always dreaded the fate of service, cooped up in a house with masters and mistresses bossing you about all the livelong day, with the starchy smart uniforms and the bowing and scraping. She'd never seen service as something to aspire to and had always been glad of her job.

But now, this extraordinary offer was being placed before her. And more than anything, her first thought was spoken as a question, a loud, piercing question that needed to be answered before she could even entertain the proposal that was being put before her.

'Why me?' she said suddenly. It almost shocked her that it came out aloud, rather than in her head. She wished she could take it back, as it was the height of rudeness. But it was out there now, and so be it.

Mrs King smiled. 'That is the pertinent question, and you have hit upon it instantly. A clever girl, as I said. So, why you, Miss Jones? The answer is a complex one and you will understand it more as time goes on. I promise you that in the end all will become clear. But for now, what you need to know is that I require a lady's maid and I have a notion to train one up. And since your family has links to mine, from regrettable events in the past, I feel that offering you the position will serve to mend those rifts, or at least attempt to. I would urge you to consider my offer carefully. It will change your prospects in life immeasurably. It will provide security for your future. And, though this will make no difference to you presently, I am sure, it will make a very old woman very happy indeed.'

Hettie did not know how to respond. All of the information had landed in her lap with a thump, and she felt pinioned to the chair by it. Mrs King seemed to perceive this, as she continued to speak.

'It will not be an easy decision. There is much for you to consider. Go back to your nearest and dearest and discuss it with them. I will offer one warning to you, though. There will be factions about you that will try to talk you out of accepting this position. I won't mention names, but I think you know how certain families around here feel about the Kings. I would counsel you to listen to all arguments, but remember, make your own decision based on your own needs, desires and aspirations for your future. All of us only possess one gift, and that is life. It is your choice what to do with your life. Please have that in the forefront of your mind when you make your decision. And it is your decision, Hettie Jones. It is your life.'

Hettie knew Mrs King must be referring to Anny and the Malones. Who else could it be? She knew Anny would hate the idea, and so would Evan. Her father might, too, although the position it gave her and the money it brought might tempt him – and he quite liked to be on opposing sides to Anny over any issue, merely out of resentment. Hettie knew there would be arguments ahead.

But Mrs King was right: this was her decision, her life.

'Thank you, ma'am,' she said, as Mrs King watched her closely, a slight smile about her wizened lips. 'It is a very kind offer. I will think about it, proper careful.'

'That is all I can ask. Consider it well. Will you come to see me again next Sunday at the same hour, to give me your answer?'

'I will, ma'am. And thank you. Again, I say thank you. I never had such a meeting in my life. And such . . . consideration. I hope . . . I inna being rude or . . . unladylike in my manners. I am in a bit of a shock, that's all.'

Mrs King smiled more broadly now. She seemed genuinely pleased with Hettie, though Hettie herself had no idea why. 'You have behaved perfectly, my dear. Now off you go and have a good think about it. Let the decision be yours and yours alone.'

Hettie thought of her determination to go strawberry picking and how it had been opposed by Evan and Peter. It was Anny who had counselled her then, who had told her she was a young woman now and that the decision was her own.

'It is my decision, ma'am,' she said with some pride. 'And I shall make it myself.'

'Good girl,' said Mrs King. Her eyes were twinkling now as she smiled at Hettie. And Hettie couldn't help but smile back at her.

As long as Hettie could remember, this old woman had been an object of awe and contempt, known as the 'owd witch' or even the 'owd bitch', and other awful insults that the townsfolk and in particular the Malones had often been heard to throw at her from afar. And now she, Hettie Jones, was sitting quite cosily with this local legend, sharing a smile. Hettie found herself basking in the wonder of it. As each day came, you never knew what might happen by the end of it. And this day, this meeting, and this offer might well change Hettie's life forever.

Chapter 11

After the meeting with Mrs King, Hettie went straight home and told her father. His eyes lit up, especially when she told him her wage would be double that at the pit. It seemed like a dream come true, except for the fact that it was an offer from the Kings. That name had resounded in the house like a curse throughout her life. She knew she would have to discuss it with the Malones and get their views on it. They knew far more than her about the Kings, and she needed to hear both sides.

'My advice is dunna go and talk to 'em about it,' her father said. 'This is a once in a lifetime chance, wench. Gifts like this dunna come along twice. It'll be the making of you. This is your way out of labour and poverty. You wonna be young forever, and the pit bank and the fruit picking is a younger wench's way of earning a crust. This lady's maid post will be easier on your bones and your back. But mark me, the Malones will try to talk you out of it because Anny Malone hates the Kings. By God, I hate them too, but old Mrs King did save my life, and I owe her that. Besides, if she feels enough guilt about us and what happened to give you this job, then I say we grasp the opportunity with both hands.'

Hettie agreed, but she still wanted to hear the Malones' views. She walked over there that very afternoon, apprehensive of how her news would be taken. She was greeted with good cheer, as she had not seen them all for a while. Evan in particular was delighted, and greeted her in a somewhat awkward fashion, yet his eyes were sparkling at the sight of her.

But as soon as she revealed her news, the mood dropped with a thud. Anny's face was like thunder. Peter shifted uncomfortably. The children watched with wonder as to what would happen next. Evan shook his head in disbelief.

Anny said, 'None of us will ever work for the Kings again. We made this choice years ago.'

Hettie wanted to say, *But I'm not one of you.* She didn't really mean it, not in a cruel way. These people had been all the family she'd had or needed from her earliest memories. But this feud with the Kings was not her battle to fight.

'It's a good chance for me,' Hettie said.

'You canna do it,' said Evan, folding his arms.

Hettie had never followed Evan's advice, and she wasn't going to start now. 'That will be my choice,' she said firmly.

Anny came to her across the room and took her hand, looking into her eyes feverishly. 'Listen, lass. I know that us telling you not to will make you wish it more so.'

Hettie shifted uneasily. Anny knew her so well. Of course she did. She was her second mother. Hettie hated to disappoint her. She could feel tears pricking in her eyes.

'But that's no reason to do it,' Anny went on. 'The Kings are poison. I know that's not what you want to hear. I know you think a great opportunity has come to you and you'd be a fool not to take it. But those Kings . . .'

Anny's eyes glistened with tears. She dropped Hettie's hand and turned away to Peter, who came to her and took her in his arms. Anny was the towering strength of the family, and to see her like this upset Hettie more than anything.

'Anny, please,' she said.

Peter held his wife and said to Hettie, 'The Kings' money is blood money.'

Hettie knew the stories, of Anny's imprisonment after a false accusation of theft from Cyril King, who had wanted to bed her and wed her but instead took out his revenge on her; of Owen, Evan's older brother, who was worshipped as a saint by the Malones, how he'd died when the King house crashed down on him as he saved a King girl from the fire at Southover. It was a bitter legacy indeed.

'I know there is hatred for the Kings. I know terrible things have happened. But good has come from them too. The Kings' money paid for the doctor who saved my mother when I was born, which saved me too. And Mrs King saved my father's life.'

'And look what he's done with it!' said Evan. 'Drunk it down the drain!'

'Dunna speak ill of him!' cried Hettie, shocking all those in the room. Even the children stopped fidgeting. 'I am sick and tired of having to explain my father to all of you. He is what he is. But most of all, he is my father. He is my kin. I never had kin in my life, not in the life I remember, leastways. You all have each other. You always have. The Malones are like . . . are like a kind of castle. You have the walls to keep others out and keep you safe inside. And I am grateful you kept me safe within these walls for all those years. I know you raised me as your own and loved me as your own. I will always be grateful for that, believe me, to my dying day. But my father is my kin and I will never desert him.'

Anny had recovered enough to leave her husband's arms and turn to Hettie. 'Nobody is asking you to, love.'

'Evan is!' said Hettie, pointing at him.

'And so I am!' he said. 'You shoulda left him at the fair and never looked back. I told you that then, but you never listen.'

'Because he is my blood! Because I come from his blood! Blood makes all the difference. Blood is everything!'

She didn't mean it to hurt, but she could see it did. The Malones seemed to shrink from her then. It felt like the final step away from them, on a journey she had begun the moment her father turned up on their doorstep all those months before. She regretted it, but there was a part of her that desired it, too. She felt she was finally moving towards something of her own, after years of being the cuckoo, though she was never, ever made to feel that by them. It was something she had put upon herself, and now she felt ready to fledge and fly.

'I am so sorry to bring any of you heartache,' she said, holding back the tears that would surely come. 'First by leaving you to go and look after my father. And now this post I've been offered. But you mun see that I have a life before me and I mun make of it what I will. I love you all. I hope you know that. But I mun go now and forge my own path.'

She turned to go to the door, but Evan caught her arm as she passed. His eyes were wide, imploring. 'Dunna go, Hettie.'

'Try not to hate me,' she said, and stared at his hand until he removed it from her.

'Hettie, that will never be,' said Evan, and the emotion in his voice nearly broke her will.

She looked back as she opened the door. The children were shifting about uncomfortably, and Anny and Peter would not look at her. She could not look at Evan again.

She left and closed the door gently behind her.

Hettie gave notice straight away and had to work one more week before she was permitted to leave. The pit bank girls greeted her news with equal amounts of incredulity and resentment. She knew then that they would never again be her friends. Her closest pit bank companion Ada seemed the most resentful of all, immediately transferring her affection to another girl on the bank, leaving Hettie to see out her week's notice largely alone. There was no celebration, no grand goodbye. At the end of her final shift, she slunk off home. That Sunday, Hettie arrived at the King house just before lunchtime. She was shown to her room by a sullen tweeny maid who had no interest in speaking to her, let alone making her feel in any way welcome. All the maid said when they reached the room, which was next to Mrs King's bedchamber, was, 'Jenkins's room.'

Hettie knew that Jenkins had been Mrs King's old lady's maid, and she felt she was trespassing.

Unpacking her carpet bag in this room was a strange sensation. She had few things to unpack: two day dresses for Sundays, underclothes, two hats and shawls, a spare pair of boots, some items of toilette and a book of poetry for children that Anny had given her on her tenth birthday. It was a precious item; she liked to read the poems when alone and be taken back to the days of childhood, before the pit bank, when she still went to school and played with Evan in the ruins of the old King house. And now she was working in the old brickmaster's house for Mrs King. Could she have predicted such a turn of events? Never, not in a thousand years.

Once she'd unpacked, she wasn't sure what to do next. She had been given no instructions. She put her ear to the door that separated her room from old Mrs King's, to see if she could hear if the lady was in there. She did not have the nerve to knock on the door and enter as yet. She sat on her bed for a while and waited, growing increasingly nervous. Should she go and ask someone what to do? Would that be a black mark against her?

Then, the door opened.

'Jones, is it?'

It was Mrs King the younger. Hettie knew her by sight. She was a beautiful woman, old – not half as old as old Mrs King, but still old to Hettie – yet she was still a fine woman.

'Yes, ma'am,' said Hettie, standing up abruptly and giving a quick dip of a curtsey.

'I am Mrs King. I am in charge of all the servants.'

'Yes ma'am.'

Mrs King looked at Hettie's feet, then slowly worked her way up to Hettie's face. 'So, this is the new lady's maid.'

Hettie didn't know what to say to that.

'Come with me.'

'Yes, ma'am. Thank you, ma'am.'

Hettie was trying to be as polite as she could, but she felt something was off about this Mrs King. She seemed to sneer at Hettie and make her feel small.

She took Hettie to meet the other servants in the kitchen. Everyone stared at her. Nobody smiled. Young Mrs King told Hettie everybody's names, but in her nerves she couldn't take in a single one. Hettie was told to sit near the top of the table, next to the butler, who grimaced at her. Surely there was some mistake and she should be further down. But Mrs King made it clear that the lady's maid must sit near the head, as she carried that privilege due to her high status in the servants' hall. A titter went around the servants. Mrs King smirked too, then left, sweeping her skirts out of the room.

Hettie sat down to a lunch of mutton stew, with tapioca for pudding, and nobody spoke to her. When Hettie stood up to help clear the table, a young maid with black hair grabbed Hettie's arm and said, 'Excuse me, *miss*,' then kicked her sharply in the calf, throwing her arm down and leaving the room afterwards.

It all happened so quickly that Hettie just stood in shock, unable to respond. Nobody seemed to notice or, if they did, they didn't say a word.

As Hettie left to mount the stairs to her room, she saw the girl again, who gave her a vicious smile and spat out the words, 'Pit-wench', as if it were poison on her tongue.

Hettie hurriedly fled up the servants' staircase to her room – or rather, to Jenkins's room. She sat on her bed and felt the tears pricking in her eyes.

'Dunna cry!' she scolded herself in a harsh whisper. She was determined to be strong. But as she waited in her room, again unsure what she was supposed to do next, she felt the tears begin to roll down her face. She brushed them away smartly and told herself to get on with it. She stood up straight and marched across the room to the door and, after a brief, trembling hesitation, she knocked firmly on the door.

After a moment, she heard a voice say, 'Come in, Jones.'

Hettie opened the door to see Mrs King sitting up in bed, smiling.

'Come closer, Jones.'

Hettie walked over towards the bed and stopped at a distance she felt was respectful.

'I am glad you've arrived. Have you had luncheon?'

'I have, thank you, ma'am,' said Hettie and curtseyed.

'No need for any of that nonsense. You never need curtsey to me again, do you understand?'

'Yes, ma'am.'

'Now then, I don't suppose Mrs King the younger has told you a thing about your duties. She does not approve of you, as I'd imagine you've guessed. But never mind that. She is of no consequence. You are here at my behest and you answer to me. Understood?'

'Yes, ma'am.'

'Now then, this afternoon you are free to make yourself comfortable in your room and not to worry about any duties for today. Your training will begin on the morrow. Later you will be visited by a seamstress to measure you for your uniform. Attend dinner after that downstairs, and in the morning Clayton will wake you and talk you through your duties. Any questions?'

'No, ma'am. Thank you, ma'am.'

'Good, good. Leave me now. Clayton will tend to me today. Tomorrow is the beginning of everything.'

'Yes, ma'am,' said Hettie and curtseyed again, then stopped halfway and said, 'Sorry, ma'am.'

'Off you go, Jones,' said Mrs King.

Hettie left and went back to her room. She sat again on her bed, puzzling over the conversation. Had she done well? Mrs King seemed to have something of a twinkle in her eye after she did that ridiculous half-curtsey. She seemed to be tolerant of Hettie's inexperience, far more so than anyone else in the house. Hettie wondered what this Clayton would be like, and tried to remember if her name had been amongst those in the servants' hall.

When the seamstress arrived, she was brisk and businesslike, with no time for conversation. Hettie stood stiffly as the woman measured her all over. That was the only person she saw for the rest of the day, sitting in her room, staring out of the window or flicking through her poetry book. A young maid fetched her for dinner without a word. Again, nobody spoke to her at dinner and she was too nervous to attempt a conversation. She went upstairs in silence and retired to her room for the night. At least nobody had kicked her this time.

Lying awake in bed, Hettie suddenly felt very alone. She knew nobody here, she had not been met with kindness, and she had no idea what she was supposed to be doing. She felt as if Ironbridge were a hundred miles away. She wondered if she'd made a terrible mistake. But she told herself that change was always hard, and change was also good. She'd get used to it. She'd do her best.

The next morning, she woke up very early. She was wide awake in the darkness. She had had a dream about Mr Laurence Maxwell Ripley. It had been a kissing dream and Hettie had awoken sharply, wishing for that moment between sleeping and waking so that she could drift down into it again. But she knew it was over and she was here, in the King household.

She tried to hold onto the image of Mr Ripley from the dream. She wondered what he would think of her new post, if he'd find her half as interesting now she was a servant, as he seemed to be much more fascinated with the rougher trades. She felt proud that she had attained such a position, but she was confused, too; there was a part of her that knew she had not been given it through merit, but instead some old debt, wrapped up in her father and mother and the Malones and all the secrets of the past. Despite her rise in fortunes, she had begun to think that her destiny was more than ever not her own. Here she was, sleeping in the next room to old Mrs King; soon she'd be tending to her every need. But she took comfort in the fact that her doubled wage would secure her future and her father's retirement in comfort. She just hoped he would be able to keep off the drink in the meantime. She missed her pit bank friends and Evan and the Malones, and she hated the fact that they disapproved of her working here. But she also felt excited that her life had changed so very much. It just showed that you never could tell what was waiting for you, just around the corner.

Then, she heard footsteps outside her door and a light knock.

'Yes?'

The door opened and in came a young woman, a few years older than Hettie. She recognised her from dinner last night, but they had not spoken, though the woman had looked at her curiously a few times.

'I'm Clayton, Mrs King the younger's lady's maid. I'm here to talk you through your duties. I'll give you a few minutes to get yourself dressed and then I'll be back.'

'All right,' said Hettie, then paused, as she did not know whether to call another senior servant ma'am or by her surname, or what. But Clayton didn't wait to correct her and shut the door swiftly.

Hettie scrambled up and got herself dressed as quickly as she could. She had brought her Sunday best winter dress to wear in her first few days, before a uniform could be organised. She brushed her hair and washed her face and made herself presentable.

Then Clayton came back and Hettie's instruction began.

'They tell me you have never worked in service, so I shall go over everything in detail with you and assume you know very little. Does that sound fair?'

'Very fair,' said Hettie, and smiled.

Clayton did not smile back. She went on, 'Firstly, you must rise just before your mistress and carry out your own toilette first. I will knock on your door each morning to wake you. Your first task will then be to look over your mistress's clothes that have been worn the day before, check for any stains or mending needs and put them away or aside for later work. If your mistress has been out, it may be necessary to remove mud from hems or boots, but since Mrs King rarely goes out, you will usually be spared this task. But all shoes need a regular clean, despite lack of use. Kid leather boots need a polish with a sponge dipped in milk to keep their shine.'

Clayton paused and looked at Hettie.

'Thank you,' said Hettie, unsure of what was required.

'Do you have any questions so far?' said Clayton, looking peevish.

'No, not really. You make it all very clear. Thank you for that.'

Clayton said, 'You're very welcome,' and there was a hint of a smile. But as soon as she'd said this, she seemed to regret it and she set her mouth firmly in a straight line again. It was peculiar. It felt almost as though she'd been told to be horrid to Hettie, but couldn't go through with it all the way.

Then it occurred to Hettie that perhaps this was exactly what had happened. Old Mrs King had said the younger Mrs King didn't approve of her. Perhaps that was why all the servants were mean to her; perhaps they had been ordered to be so.

Hettie listened carefully as Clayton went on with her instructions. There was so much to learn and remember, Hettie felt her head begin to swim with the enormity of it all. Once her mistress was awake, she must bring her the breakfast tray and either draw her bath, if required, or prepare her jug and basin for washing.

Then came assisting Mrs King in dressing and styling her hair, which was past shoulder length. Since Hettie had always had long hair, she had some experience of putting it up into attractive styles, as she often did on Sundays. But she had no idea of the fashions for ladies of advanced age, other than what she'd seen Mrs King sport so far. Hettie would need to learn what products her mistress required on her hair and how to keep it looking shiny and bright white. It must be washed with a mixture of rosemary water and borax, then, once the hair had been thoroughly dried, an amount of pomade must be applied. Clayton said Mrs King also liked to use a variety of creams and other potions on her face and body and Hettie needed to learn which was which, as well as order the ingredients for most of these and concoct them herself. Hettie must also ensure the reordering of such essentials at regular intervals.

Once Mrs King was washed and dressed, Hettie must then tidy the room. Clayton explained that this would normally take place after the mistress had left the room for the day, but that Mrs King liked to sit in her armchair and look out at the woodland and was quite happy for her maid to clear up about her and chat. The dressing table, toilette table and linen would need attention. Combs would need to be cleaned but not with water, as this would damage the teeth and make the tortoiseshell rough; they required the use of a comb brush, a small object made specially for the purpose and kept with the range of other brushes Hettie would need. Her mistress's hairbrushes must be cleaned carefully, in water that had a little soda dissolved in it, the bristles cleaned thoroughly but not left for too long in the liquid in case they turned soft. When it came to her mistress's clothes, Hettie must learn the particular care for materials such as tweed and silk. Some would need laying out on a table and brushing, others a light beating with a handkerchief to remove dust.

Though the laundry was done elsewhere (by people like Anny), Hettie would need to sort the clothes to be sent out and reorganise those that had been sent back. She was also expected to keep a written inventory of all items that left the room and a record of costs of laundering those items, so that the household was never cheated on its bills. The same went for the costs of cosmetics. Hettie was given an accounts book for this. She was glad Anny had ensured she'd been educated, or this part of the job would be far beyond her. Clayton told her that Mrs King often dropped food down the front of her garments and that these stains needed careful attention by the maid immediately and were not to be left for the washerwoman to deal with. The room would need airing once a day as well, especially after the mistress had used the commode, the clearing away of which was also Hettie's duty.

All items used must be cleaned, the wash basins rinsed of soap scum, fresh water and clean towels replenished. Though Hettie was not responsible for dusting every tiny object, as another maid would do this, she had to ensure the room was spick and span at all times, with not one spare thread or hair to be seen on the carpets or furnishings. It was also necessary to keep a strict inventory of every object in the mistress's rooms, to keep an eye on any thieving servant who might remove small objects of value thinking their absence would not be noted.

Once the room was inspected and tidy, the mending work began: darning stockings and other jobs for the needle and thread. Clayton said that most lady's maids had to be tolerable seamstresses and milliners, able to even make outfits from scratch if necessary. This alarmed Hettie, who had never made a whole outfit, though she had mended her own and her father's often enough. But luckily, as Mrs King rarely left the house and never attended events these days, new outfits were rare.

In a way, old Mrs King was the dream mistress for a lady's maid. She afforded so little wear and tear on any of her items. If she did leave the house, her bonnet or hat must be either brushed or dusted with a feather plume before putting away. Any clothing items that had feathers or flowers would need adjusting; perhaps the feather might need recurling with a warmed knife or any crushed artificial flowers would need amending with a pair of flower pliers. Again, these were to be found in Jenkins's armoury, left behind in her room to be passed on to the next lady's maid.

Once all of these tasks had been carried out – or even while doing them, since Mrs King rarely left her rooms – Hettie's other main duty was to provide companionship for Mrs King. Her life was to be wedded to that of her mistress; she was to be on hand at any moment of the day or night. A younger mistress would be out of the house for periods of time, but not Mrs King.

Clayton also explained that Mrs King was still mourning the death of her previous maid, Jenkins, to whom she had been very close.

Clayton added, 'You will never replace Jenkins. She was here for decades and many said they were more like sisters than mistress and maid. But you can do your best to be civil and solicitous at all times, listening to Mrs King's complaints or stories and nodding or providing comment if asked.'

Hettie said, 'I've heard of Jenkins.'

'She is well known,' said Clayton. Then, after a moment's hesitation, 'She was my mother's cousin.'

Hettie nodded. 'She was there when I was born.'

Clayton gave her an inquisitive look and asked, 'How did that come about?'

'It was in the strike days. Anny Malone –who raised me after my mother died – she told me that Jenkins came with the young lady of the house when my mother was in labour. Things had gone bad and they didna think she'd live, nor me. So they fetched a doctor and the Kings paid for it. I was born and my mother didna die and nor did I.'

Clayton frowned. 'But why would Mrs King pay for a physician for the likes of you? No offence.'

Hettie thought about it. 'I anna got a clue,' she said and smiled. 'It is a story from before my memory and I've often thought of it, how the Kings helped me.'

The Kings had also done far worse to those she loved, but she wasn't going to mention that to Clayton.

Clayton eyed her curiously. She hesitated, then said, 'Anyway, I cannot stand around here talking to you all day.'

'I'm Hettie, by the way. What's your first name?'

Clayton drew herself up and said haughtily, 'First names are not required for lady's maids. The under-servants should call you miss, and your mistress and I will call you Jones.'

'I know that,' said Hettie, smiling. 'But I'd be grateful to know it anyway.'

Clayton shook her head to dismiss such silliness and walked to the door. But she stopped, turned and said quietly to Hettie, 'It's Kezia. Kezia Clayton.' Then she left.

Kezia's instructions had taken up much of the morning. Luncheon was quiet and miserable; Hettie was universally ignored. In the afternoon, she sat with Mrs King, who asked her to read to her from an old novel from the last century. Hettie was a good reader, but she struggled with some of the words. Mrs King didn't seem to mind, and was soon napping in her chair anyway.

Hettie took the opportunity to acquaint herself with the tools of her job, all tidily packed away by Kezia in Jenkins's room. She made a mental note of each brush and what it was for, reminding herself to ask Kezia of the ones she'd forgotten.

Mrs King slept a lot that day. Hettie watched as Kezia helped her mistress get ready for dinner. Hettie saw how gentle Kezia was with Mrs King and was touched. Kezia had a tenderness about her that was lovely to watch.

Lying in bed that second night, wide awake with fretting when she should've been sleeping, Hettie decided she would make a friend of Kezia Clayton if she could. For whatever reason, the other servants all seemed to hate her, and the one who'd kicked her had chosen Hettie as her mortal enemy. Nobody spoke to her at mealtimes and she was universally shunned. Kezia Clayton was the only person other than Mrs King who had shown her a moment's kindness.

The varied and innumerable tasks of a lady's maid, and everything she must learn, were daunting, but more worrying still was the feeling that she had come to a house that wanted her out of it. She had no idea why. She'd never felt this way before. All her life she had been surrounded by love and affection: at the Malones' house; at school, where she always had plenty of friends; at work, where the camaraderie of the pit bank girls was rough but constant; even with her difficult father, who despite his problems loved her truly. Her childhood feeling of being a cuckoo at the Malones' house was magnified a hundredfold in the King household. She missed them all and pined for a kind word, a gentle look, someone who was glad to see her.

'Jenkins!' came a call from the next room. 'Jenkins!'

Her mistress was calling. She threw off her bedcovers and shrank from the winter chill as she padded across the floor to the connecting door between their rooms.

Hettie went to her and asked, 'Can I help you, ma'am?'

Mrs King, eyes screwed shut, held out her hand. Hettie didn't know what to do with it at first. A maid or a pit-wench didn't go round touching the hands of dignitaries like Mrs King. But as well as being an upper-class lady, Mrs King was just a person, an old woman who needed someone's help.

So Hettie took her mistress's hand and felt it relax in her grasp. Mrs King sighed contentedly. Hettie stroked the old lady's hand, papery and cool to the touch. She waited there, quietly, until Mrs King fell peacefully back to sleep.

Whatever fears and sorrows Hettie had, one thing was clear: old Mrs King needed her and wanted her. And she would do her best to serve the lady well, whatever the rest of the household did to thwart her.

Chapter 12

Evan Malone did not like change. He knew this about himself. He never was any good at it. He liked routine. He found it comforting. He liked the fact that he was always woken at the same time each morning by his mother; that he always took the same bait to work; that his work rarely varied from day to day; that the walk home was with the same people as yesterday, down the same streets and past the same houses; that his Sundays were always spent the same way, playing a bit of chess with his mother, helping his father in the vegetable plot behind the house, playing hide-and-seek or pirate ships with the little'uns; going for a walk with Hettie. He liked his routine.

But these days, that last joy was often denied him. Hettie was now working at the King house, looking after the old woman. Evan had not seen her at all in the month since she'd started there. He'd sent a note to her at the King house four times. Three were answered with a reply in the negative, something along the lines of *Not this Sunday. Too tired. See you presently. H.*

But this Sunday, at last, Hettie had agreed. Well, she had her caveats, but in theory, she'd be there: *Meet you at Southover midday. Only if the weather be fine. Otherwise not. H.*

Evan hoped the weather would hold. It was a foggy winter morning on the way there, but as he arrived, at least a half hour early in his enthusiasm, the fog began to lift and a weak late-November sun threw a yellowish light over the Southover building plot. The place was empty of workers, being Sunday, and so they would have privacy.

Evan wondered if Hettie was avoiding him or if she really was simply too tired. The agony of not knowing gnawed at him. They had fallen out over her father, and now this. He felt as if unseen forces were moving against him when it came to Hettie. Once her father appeared from nowhere, the special place Evan had held in her affections was supplanted by this ghost of a man. Nothing Evan could say or do would shift her from him. It seemed that Adam Jones could have set fire to their house with Hettie in it and she'd still forgive him and take him back. Evan knew it was madness to compete with a girl over her father – but he could not help himself. Adam Jones was bad news, the worst kind. A good man gone bad, no good now to himself or others, especially Hettie. Evan tried to understand, tried to support her in her decisions, but he missed her too much. He wanted her back in the safe embrace of the Malone family; he wanted her home. He wanted *her*.

And now this, the job with the Kings, was fate moving against him again. His mother had said as much, many times over the years, bemoaning the curious fact that the Malones and the Kings seemed destined to be tangled up like wool forever, however much they wrangled with the knots. Evan knew he could not contend with that; he couldn't fight decades of feuding between these two families. And now Hettie had happily stepped into that muddle and embraced it, working not only for the Kings, but with the head of the whole nasty heap of them, Mrs King herself! What was she thinking?

He had to pull her out of it, somehow. He had to make her see that her fate was doomed if she stayed beholden to those forsaken bastards, as his mother often called them, out of the earshot of the little ones. But he'd have to be clever about it; if he told her outright what to do, she'd never listen. Hettie Jones never did take orders from Evan Malone; never had, never would.

These were the scrambled thoughts that plagued his mind as he sat on a stone bench, covered by years of creeping moss, in the grounds of Southover, awaiting his love. For she was his love, Hettie Jones, and now they were both seventeen years of age, he felt ready to declare it to her.

And here she was, crunching up the gravel drive towards him. She was dressed well. Her wages must be good, or else the Kings had given her new things. She wore a dark maroon dress striped with grey. Around her shoulders was a thick shawl the colour of red bricks. She wore gloves. She'd never had such smart walking clothes, and it made him swiftly glance down at his own Sunday best and find it wanting. His suit was handed down from his long-lost brother Owen and had been mended many a time by his mother, the patches showing clearly if you looked close enough in a good light.

I inna good enough for her now, he thought, hopelessly. But at that moment, she raised her eyes and saw him, giving him such a beaming smile that he forgot his previous doubts. He took off his hat and rose up to meet her, grinning all the way.

'Well, inna you a picture!' he said as he walked briskly towards her.

'And you, Evan.'

'Oh, I dunna think so. You've seen this old suit a hundred times.'

'But you look well in it,' she said, still smiling.

'Shall we take a stroll about the grounds?' he asked. He was suddenly nervous. He knew what he wanted to ask her, what this meeting was for, but he knew he'd have to work up to it gradually and he needed some mileage to get there.

'I am tired,' she said, and sighed. 'Do you mind if we sit here a bit instead? I need the rest.'

'Yes, surely,' he said, minding his language, trying to echo her new voice, tinged with a new properness about it that she'd never had in her pit days. She must be learning by listening to the Kings. Another sign she was slipping away from him.

They sat beside each other, a good twelve inches between them, so unlike their younger days when they'd sit in a cwtch beside the fire at home.

'Tell me about your new post, then,' he said, turning slightly so that he could see her face. He felt suddenly all fingers and thumbs and did not know where to put his hat. In the end, he placed it on the ground beside the bench. He needed his hands free for later, he hoped.

'It is good,' she said and nodded. 'It is a lot of work. I am up with the mistress and tend to her needs all day. And she dunna sleep well at night. I'm often in and out, as she calls for help. She can sleep in if she wishes, but I mun get up at the usual hour and carry out my duties. But I mun say it is easier than the pit bank and the strawberry fields, by far. Much, much easier.'

'I warrant it is,' said Evan, watching her face. Her eyes were greener than ever, her lips plumper and rosier. She did have shadows beneath those pretty eyes, but she looked even more beautiful now than she did in his imagination. Her light brown hair was down, over her shoulders, silky and thick. She must have washed it that morning. How he longed to touch it.

'And you? How is your work? I think of the pit and my days there. As hard as the work was, I miss it. I miss it something terrible.'

'Do you? How can that be? It sounds like a proper lollocking job you got there.'

'Oh, it inna idle or easy, by no means. But not back-breaking. No, it's other things I miss.'

Hettie looked away, towards the half-built structure of the new Southover. He couldn't see her face but knew her of old, knew every nuance of her moods and reactions. He knew she was upset. He reached over slowly and touched her arm gently.

'What is it, Hettie? Tell me.'

She turned back and he was right. Her eyes had filled, and one fat tear rolled down her cheek and dropped onto her shawl.

'I inna wanted there.'

'But why? Mrs King asked for you herself!'

'Mrs King likes me. She is kind to me. Very kind. But the others. Everyone. They all hate me. I dunna know why.'

'Oh Hettie, how could anyone hate you? I canna fathom it!' How he longed to wipe her tears away. And then kiss her better. When they were little, they had kissed on the lips all of the time. They had cuddled and held hands. But when they reached a certain age, it stopped and they grew wary of each other. How unfair it seemed that now he wanted to kiss those lips so very much, there seemed a barrier between them thicker than a castle wall.

'They have taken against me. All the other servants. Except one – Kezia Clayton, her name is. She is Mrs King the younger's maid. She is that kind to me, it gives me some small comfort. But she's shy about it, as if she's been told not to be nice to me.'

'Who woulda told her that? And why?'

'I dunna know. I think maybe Mrs King the younger. She looks at me as if I were a crawling thing beneath her dainty feet. I know there's no love lost between the two of 'em, the elder and the younger Mrs Kings. Maybe that's the reason. But the worst is one of the younger maids. She is proper vicious with me. How I do hate her so!'

Hettie's tears were drying up now she was warming to her subject. It was good to see her old feistiness return.

Evan asked, 'How so? What does the wench do?'

'She pinches me and kicks me, pulls at my cap or my hair. She spreads lies about me amongst the other servants, saying dreadful things about me . . . saying . . . I am easy and lie with the messenger boy or whoever I fancy.'

Evan felt the rage boil up in him. He wanted to kill this maid. How dare she hurt his girl! And to say such things about Hettie! She was pure as spring water and no mistake. 'I shall murder her,' he said in a low voice.

Hettie reached and took his hand. It was a thrill to feel her touch. 'Dunna say such things, Evan. I tell you this because I have nobody to talk to. I need you to listen and do nothing. I must fight my own battles. And I will win them, one day. I am kind to everyone in the house, sweet and gentle with them all. I will win them round, you'll see.'

'But it makes me proper furious, Hettie, to hear of you being hurt. All it would take is to see if this girl had a brother . . . I could sort him and sort her too with one strike.'

'You'll do no such thing, Evan Malone!' Hettie's voice was raised. She let go of his hand and he regretted his outburst.

'I just want everything in your life to be good,' he said, taking her hand again.

She squeezed it and replied, 'I know, I know. But what I need is for you to listen to me when I need it. And to be my friend.'

She was looking right at him now, right into his eyes. All it would take was one swift movement and his lips would be on hers. But he faltered. She had said 'friend'. That was not what he wanted. He struggled over how to reply, but he was not quick enough. She was speaking again.

'And my father is suffering from my absence.'

Oh, not her damned father again! he thought. But Evan had to look sympathetic or she would shun him. And besides, he knew all about it. Everyone did. Adam Jones had been seen to frequent the inns hereabouts again in the past month, something he'd all but given up under Hettie's care, preferring to drink at home instead – still enough ale to make him merry but not like he'd put away when he was at a tavern.

'I know it,' said Evan. It was all he could muster.

'I was wondering . . . if you could look in on him from time to time.'

'You ask much of me with that, Hettie,' he said. He forgot for a moment that he'd intended to be everything she needed, so that he could ask her to be everything he wanted. 'I mean, I will if that is what you ask of me.'

She looked at him a little quizzically and replied, 'Of course that is what I ask of you – I have just this minute asked it! You are in a queer mood, Evan. What is the matter?'

Was now the time? Her hand was still in his. He squeezed it again, for courage, and she squeezed back.

'I have a question for you, Hettie.'

'And what is it?'

Did she really have no clue? He looked searchingly into her eyes. And there was a flutter there and she looked away. He could not read her so well these days. He did not know what it meant. But now was the time. He might not get another chance for a long while.

'Hettie, I wish to see you more.'

'I am so busy, Evan. And so tired.'

'Not like that. I wish to . . . well . . .' He faltered. Could he come out and simply say it? 'I wish . . . I wish you and

I were children again and could play in the ruins here as we used to.'

Hettie turned from him and took her hand away. She smiled at the memory. He had lost his nerve and the moment had passed.

'Happy times,' she said, still smiling. Her eyes scanned the new building work, perhaps recalling their childhood antics as she looked.

'They were the very best,' he went on. 'Just me and thee, galloping around like ponies. Free as birds. Careless as the wind.'

'Oh yes, Evan. That we were.'

'And could be again . . .' he tried. She turned to him, that same little arch of her eyebrows showing her curiosity. 'If . . . you were not so far above me now, Miss Hettie Jones, lady's maid. If that were not who you are now, one day we coulda been married. And be together always, with a brood of little'uns to bring us joy.'

Ah, how clever he had been! Surely she would turn it round now and make it right.

'Yes . . .' was all she said, and she looked away again. That wasn't supposed to happen. Then she added, 'It's a lovely idea . . . but . . .'

But? She trailed off and left him desperate. 'I dunna like the sound of that *but*.'

'We're a bit young to be talking of such things, I reckon.'

‘Too young? Many folk around these parts are married off by now.’

‘And my post . . . I’d have to give it up. And I only just started it. And learning the ways of it. And it is a great chance for me, Evan.’

‘So . . . so you’d rather work for that forsaken family than . . .’

‘Than what?’

‘Than marry me!’ he blurted out, infuriated now.

She looked round at him. ‘Evan, you haven’t asked me to marry you.’

‘Well . . . I . . . not in so many words, lass, but . . .’

‘You see, you inna ready for it neither. Even if it seems a lovely idea.’

‘You have changed,’ he said, annoyed at himself now, more than her. She was right. He should’ve prepared it properly, with a speech all ready for her. She deserved that and so much more. He was a fool to think a shabby suit was enough for Hettie Jones. ‘You woulda never said *lovely* in former times. You woulda said *proper jam*.’

‘You’re right. I have changed. I inna the girl I once was. I’ve new responsibilities now. To my father. And to Mrs King.’

To hear the name King in the midst of his marriage proposal was more than his short temper could bear.

‘Over me? And us, all of us?’

Hettie sighed and shook her head. ‘Dunna start a row now, Evan. I dunna wanna fight with you.’

'It's just . . . we all feel . . . me and Mother and Father . . . we all think you need to show . . . more . . . be more . . .' What was he even saying? He needed to stop this and get back to the matter in hand, to marriage, to his love for her. But she had angered him and now his mouth was running and he couldn't pull back.

'Grateful?' she asked, and her eyes turned cold on him. 'You want me to be more *grateful* to you all?'

'No,' he said, exasperated. 'But, well, yes! You've gone and left us and . . . you dunna seem to . . . wanna know us no more.'

'I'm here now, aren't I? And anyway, how do you want me to show how grateful I am? Shall I get myself on bended knee? Whip myself with a cat o' nine tails, such as my father had on his back in the colonies?'

'Agh, wench, you are so vexing!' That was that. He had lost his temper now and she had caused it. Impossible girl!

'Since I dunna agree with every little thing you say, Evan Malone, then I am vexing.'

'You surely are! I came here today to . . .' Her face softened now. But he could not finish his sentence. He could not take more rejection. 'Never mind.'

'You came here today to be my friend. So, please honour that. Do not box my ears. I have no one to talk to down there. I must listen and follow orders. I have not one friend in my new world, not a true friend. Not like you. Will you be my friend, Evan?'

So, now it was her asking the question, and it was not the one he wanted to hear. But how could he refuse her simple, plaintive request?

'Course. Course I will. Always. You know that, Hettie.'

'And I thank God for it. For you. Thank'ee for listening. And for coming. I mun go now. I need my rest before tonight and another round of fitful sleep.'

She stood up, and he knew it was done. His chance was gone.

They walked down the hill together in silence. She seemed lost in a dream, staring ahead as he glanced at her. At their parting of ways, they said farewell, without a hug, without the kiss he had been dreaming of for weeks. All that was gone. He had come to Southover to make her his bride, and he left there with nothing.

Except her friendship. He did at least still have that. And it was a prize he valued more than any treasure.

Chapter 13

Christmas came and went and the dark days of January followed. Much of this Hettie spent with her mistress in her room, reading to her or listening to her stories. Over these past months, old Mrs King had transformed in Hettie's eyes, from the old witch some people in the village felt she was, to a warm, clever and witty person for whom Hettie genuinely cared. She was constantly amazed at how sharp her mistress was; she was ninety-seven years of age and frail of body, but her mind was all there. She did get a little tearful at times, especially when she reminisced about the past, as she had done more and more in recent weeks. She told Hettie stories about her son Ralph, her grandson Cyril, her granddaughter Margaret and her great-granddaughter Beatrice. One afternoon, she shared stories of her childhood with Hettie. She had been a child in the later decades of the eighteenth century, a time that seemed impossible to Hettie to have lived through, it was all so long ago.

'Something you might not know about me is my real name. Do you know it, Jones?'

'No, ma'am. I only know you as Mrs King.'

'Once I married I became known as Queenie, because I ruled this place and this family like a regent. But before that, I was Alice Hinton. That was my true name. I had a sister, Selina. She was beautiful and kind. And told wonderful stories. I loved her very much. But . . . well . . . she died.' Her voice trailed off and her eyes clouded.

Hettie said, 'I am sorry to hear that, ma'am.'

Mrs King shook her head and forced a smile. 'Oh, it was ever so many years ago now. Well, let me tell you something. When we were children, Selina and I had a piano teacher come to the house called Miss Simkiss. She was an elderly lady, but very sharp and a talented pianist. She was kind to us, though she could be a bit of a taskmaster. One day, Selina and I were permitted to visit Miss Simkiss at her home. It was a terraced house by the river towards Buildwas, painted white with a magnificent wisteria that climbed gloriously across the façade. The house was neat and tidy and comfortable. Two cats lived there – now what were their names? Ah yes, Pusskins and Smudge! Extraordinary how I can remember such useless information from eight or nine decades ago. Another woman lived there, too, another Miss Simkiss. We were introduced and the lady bid us good afternoon.

'As our teacher poured us glasses of cordial in the small, homely kitchen, I remember thinking how much I pitied Miss Simkiss, that she was an old spinster, that she had never found a husband and had to live with her sister, poor old thing. We went back out into the pretty garden and I sat quietly with Selina and the Misses Simkiss. We listened to the birds chirping and the river flowing and the breeze ruffling the uppermost branches of the trees. The two old women were at peace and completely at ease with each other and their surroundings. I found myself yearning for such peace, though I did not understand why. It was as if a knot in my stomach had unravelled itself, and the relief was immense.

'I was too young then to understand it, but years later I have looked back on those ladies, after they were long dead, and realised that I had envied them. They had mastered the art of living. To have stayed with my dear sister Selina forever, in a tidy little house, with pea plants and wisteria, with two indolent cats and that perfection of peace – no husbands, no fathers, no children, no grandchildren to spoil it – that would have been the best life I could imagine. How happy we would have been! Selina and I, alone in perfect companionship. If only my life had been that way.'

Hettie listened with fascination. Throughout these conversations about her mistress's past, Hettie would listen or ask polite questions as Mrs King spoke. She often talked fondly of the past, but sometimes spoke with true vitriol when she described her husband, son or grandson. For the female members of the family, she had nothing but praise, and sometimes she would weep a little, for the death of Margaret and for Beatrice's absence. Hettie realised that, whatever terrible things the Malones and Anny's family, the Woodvines, had been through due to the Kings, Mrs King had suffered too.

Mrs King turned to look at Hettie. Her eyes were shining with tears, an apologetic smile on her face. Hettie knew that if she said a kind thing now, Mrs King would weep. But perhaps that was not what she needed, to be exhausted by tears and regret when she had so little energy already. So Hettie only said, 'Keep your chin up, ma'am.'

Mrs King shrugged her shoulders and smiled wider, then jutted her chin out and said, 'Is that better?'

'Much better, ma'am.'

They sat in companionable silence after that. Hettie knew she would never replace Jenkins. But she was proud that she seemed to bring some scrap of comfort to this extraordinary lady in the winter days of her life.

It was the most curious feeling. When Queenie awoke that February night, she was aware of the cold first. It always crept into her bones in the middle of the night, no matter how many blankets Jones gave her. Sometimes she felt weighted down by bedding, as if she could not move, but still the cold would come for her. But this morning, something else had crept into her body, something new and foreign.

She opened her eyes and found there was a fogginess there. It must just be sleep in her eyes, she guessed. Lying on her right side, she went to raise her left hand to wipe it out and found that her left arm was immobile. Again, just sleepiness, she thought. She tried again. But her left arm would not move, nor her left leg. She opened her mouth to speak and said, 'Beatrice.' She hadn't meant to say that name. She'd wanted to say Jenkins, even though she knew it was Jones she wanted, her dear Jones, her Hettie. How fond she'd grown of the girl since she'd started there a few months before.

'Jenkins,' she said. 'Cyril,' she said next, now alarmed. Why on earth would she be calling for him, her grandson who had passed away? And besides, she was only whispering. If all these people she'd called had been standing at the other side of the room, they would not have heard her.

'Blaize,' she said next and then felt truly frightened. She would never willingly summon the ghost of the long-dead servant. Oh, if only Jones could hear her!

She tried again to move her left side, and nothing happened. She lay there for some time in a state of terror. She stared across the room at the doorway to Jones's room, as if glaring long enough would wake the girl. But her eyes were still foggy and the doorway shimmered, the door jamb beginning to waver and undulate like a snake. She closed her eyes and felt a sudden rush of dizziness, so disconcerting that she opened them again.

She decided to stare at the pillow, as its comforting whiteness blanked out everything else.

She must have slept eventually, for when she came to daybreak had lightened the curtains.

'Jones,' she said, relieved to hear the name she intended to say and also that her voice was stronger. 'Jones!' she called again and this time she heard, at last, movement from the next room.

In came Hettie, her light brown hair in a long plait over her shoulder, her green eyes shining in the early-morning light. For a moment, Queenie thought she was Martha Jones, come back to haunt her. It seemed her room was filling with ghosts.

'Morning, ma'am,' said Hettie, going to the window to draw open the curtains. 'We have both slept in a little today. I am so sorry. I should've been up by now. Please forgive me.'

'Jones, I am ill,' said Queenie.

Hettie turned to her and came closer. 'In what manner, ma'am?'

'I cannot move anything down my left side. Help me to sit up. I have been trapped like this for hours.'

Hettie rushed to her then and put the back of her hand against her forehead. She then grasped Queenie's shoulder and turned her body to lie on her back. What a relief it was to be off her side. Her right arm felt numb from being underneath her so long, but feeling was coming back to it. Her left side, however, was still useless.

When Hettie looked down and saw Queenie's face, she gasped.

'Help me sit up,' said Queenie, and now that her face was freed from lying on her side, she realised that the left side of her mouth was not moving. Only the right side was forming the words. Hettie tried to pull her up, reaching to drag an extra pillow behind her head. She was propped up now at least – not fully, but enough to feel a touch more dignified.

'I shall send for the doctor immediately,' said Hettie.

'What is wrong with my face?' said Queenie.

'The left side . . . has dropped, ma'am. I shall fetch the doctor, do not fret.'

Even in the shock of the moment, of confirming her fear that something was very wrong with her, she was pleased to hear that Hettie was learning to speak more correctly, losing the *dunna* of her previous self and using the standard form of *do not*. Queenie had been training her well these past months, not only in the duties of a lady's maid, but also in the correct etiquette for ladies themselves. Only Queenie knew why she had begun this process of transforming Hettie. And now Queenie had woken up incapacitated and – who knew? – perhaps that much closer to death, she was content that her work on Hettie was well under way. She might not have much time left to complete her plan.

The doctor had been sent for and Queenie rested her eyes while she waited. The dizziness had gone, at least.

Hettie, now dressed in her smart maid's uniform, fed Queenie her breakfast of porridge with honey. Queenie could have used her right hand, but had little vitality to move and was glad of Hettie's help. The girl was kind-hearted and never spoke too much. She had adjusted to this new post and her new life with decorum, fortitude and a willingness to learn. Her manner was gentle but never cloying. As she thought on Hettie's good qualities, Queenie realised that tears were streaming down her face.

Hettie took a handkerchief from her sleeve and dabbed at Queenie's face. She looked into Hettie's green eyes, smiling with compassion, and said, 'Thank you.'

Hettie merely nodded, but a moment passed between them, a knowledge that the maid was more than a maid and the mistress was more than a mistress. It made Queenie's heart sing, even in the midst of her distress.

A knock on the door announced the arrival of Dr Fitzgerald, physician to the King family. He was looking old these days. Indeed, he was around the same age as Jenkins had been and probably should have retired by now. But Queenie trusted nobody else with her health. In he came, placing his hat on a side table as he crossed the room to her bed. One look at her face and he nodded. Hettie took away the mostly finished bowl of porridge and stood at the end of the bed, awaiting instructions.

'Mrs King,' said Fitzgerald softly, offering her a pitying smile. 'What an odd state we find ourselves in this morning, hmm?'

'None of that,' said Queenie. 'Tell me my prognosis.'

'I'm glad to hear your speech is normal. As acerbic as ever.'

He carried out an examination of her body, looking into her eyes and taking her pulse, then asking her to move certain things she couldn't move on her left side, but could on her right.

'All done, dear lady,' he said at last, and stood up. 'I shall have a word with your daughter-in-law and give her instructions. You must rest now for many days, until you feel better.'

'First you shall tell me the prognosis, as I have asked.' The paralysis of half of her face made talking awkward, but her voice was as clear as it could be. She did not wish that Benjamina should have any say in what happened to her. She wanted the truth, so that she could plan accordingly.

Dr Fitzgerald sighed, then sat down on the bed and crossed his legs and his arms. He then looked Queenie right in the eye and said, 'The prognosis is not good. You have suffered from a bout of apoplexy. There are some invasive procedures I might try with a younger patient, such as bloodletting, but to my mind, considering your great age, the kindest approach would be to leave you be. It is highly likely that you will have another bout within weeks, days or even hours, and that the next one will be fatal. So I believe the best course of action is to make you as comfortable as possible and ensure you have your affairs in order.'

Queenie had feared this, but it was almost a relief to hear it, to know the facts. She hated being in ignorance more than almost anything. Now she knew exactly what she must do.

'Thank you, Fitzgerald,' she said and gave what must have been a lopsided smile.

The doctor smiled back at her. 'You've lived a long and fruitful life, Mrs King,' he said. 'And it has been my honour to serve you through these many years.'

'I will join Jenkins soon, and Selina and my babies,' she said and again those tears began to stream down her face without warning. Hettie came over and dabbed at her cheeks.

Fitzgerald had his own moment of emotion, for Queenie knew he had always been sweet on Rose Jenkins and that she had spurned him in favour of her post as lady's maid. Her death must have moved him tremendously.

'Leave me now,' Queenie said. 'Give instructions to Jones here, not the other Mrs King. Jones may be young, but she is more than capable.'

Fitzgerald nodded and took his leave. Queenie saw him talking in hushed tones as Hettie went with him to the door. She lay alone for a moment, as Hettie saw him out. Thoughts rushed in. So, she was to die soon.

To die. To leave this place, to go . . . where? To another place? Or to oblivion? She had never had much faith, though she went through the motions of churchgoing.

Other thoughts crowded in, of those 'affairs' the doctor had mentioned. She must instruct Hettie the moment she came back into the room. Hettie must write immediately to Beatrice, demanding that she come home from America to see Queenie before she went. It was probably a hopeless request, as according to the doctor's prognosis, Queenie might not last the day. But he had mentioned weeks. Weeks could be months – who knew? Queenie had defied all odds living to nearly a hundred as it was. Well, Beatrice must be summoned.

Even more pressing was her need to see her solicitor. She was stupid to have left this so long. She needed to see him immediately, today. When Hettie returned from speaking with the doctor, Queenie would order it. She only hoped that he would arrive before the apoplexy returned and finished her off. She decided that if she began to feel seriously unwell again when she was waiting, then she would have Hettie bring her paper and a pen and she would sign it herself, asking Hettie to write down the necessaries. Would it be legal? It would have to do. She could only hope she would not die before her solicitor came and she could ensure that Benjamina did not thwart this closing act of hers. Then all would be well, the future secured for those who awaited her final deed.

So, the letter to Beatrice and the solicitor's visit first. Then, she must speak with Hettie, for she had something to tell the girl, something only Queenie knew – something that would change Hettie's life forever.

Chapter 14

As the doctor was leaving, he stopped Hettie on the landing and said, 'I was present at your birth, young lady.'

Hettie was taken aback by this. She knew the story, of course, but she did not know it was this doctor who had been summoned by Rose Jenkins to save her life and that of her mother. Her family never had enough money to see him, relying instead on various potions Anny made or bought. She was moved to meet this doctor at last, the man who had ensured that her passage into this world was a safe one.

'Thank you!' she said. 'Thank you so much!'

He waved away her gratitude and bustled off down the stairs saying, 'My pleasure, Miss Jones. I'll see myself out.'

Hettie stood for a moment, thinking how things would have been so different if the Kings had not sent for him that day. She might not have been standing here now. Then she recalled herself and went back to her mistress, the same woman who had paid for that doctor to save her life. How curious and strange life was, its web of connections mysterious.

She found Mrs King quite agitated. First, she insisted that Hettie send a note to the family solicitor, demanding his presence immediately, which Hettie arranged straight away. Next, she feverishly dictated a letter to Miss Beatrice Ashford, her great-granddaughter, requesting her to return home from America as soon as possible, due to her dangerously ill health. Then, she made Hettie sit on the edge of the bed, and said she had something to tell her.

Hettie was wondering what it could be when Clayton popped her head around the door to say that the solicitor had arrived, and Mrs King said that she would speak to Hettie afterwards.

The solicitor, Mr Steadman, was shown in, and Hettie was told to leave and sit in her room to await instructions. She waited there, preoccupied. She could hear the voices of Mrs King and the solicitor murmuring in the next room, but could not make out any of the words. She shouldn't, of course, because it was private business. But she did wonder what it was that Mrs King felt she needed so urgently to tell her. Now she had the time to sit and think about things – unexpected in the daily routine of a lady's maid – her wonderings crowded in. What would happen now? If her mistress died soon, as it seemed she would, what would Hettie do next? Could she go back to her pit life, or would she take her experience gained and go on in service? If her mistress wrote her a reference, she surely could. But she would have to ask her, as she was certain that young Mrs King would not bother or would write her a terrible one; she seemed to hate Hettie so, though Hettie still had no idea why.

For some reason, Mr Lawrence Maxwell Ripley came into her mind, the vision of his handsome face as large as life before her. She had thought of him often since beginning her work here at the King household months before. It was something about being in a well-to-do environment that prompted it. She would enact grand fantasies in her mind, of going to London with Mrs King as her maid and accidentally bumping into Mr Ripley in a restaurant or hotel foyer. He would seek her out again and declare his love, defy society's expectations and ask her to marry him.

It was all folly; she knew that. But it kept her warm on cold nights. At other times, she thought of Evan, his strong arms, the beautifully thick blond hair that she would love to run her fingers through. It hadn't been easy turning him down when they met that day at Southover. She knew he was in love with her. And she loved him – of course she did. But she could not get Mr Ripley out of her mind, and marriage to Evan would mean giving up her post; she could not bear that, not when she had only just started it and her future was shining more brightly.

Since then, Evan had not brought it up again, and she half wondered if he had changed his mind about her.

They certainly were drifting apart. Her new post altered not only her appearance in her finer clothes, but her voice too, as she took on Mrs King's daily advice about her language and deportment. If she married Evan, a life in the pit beckoned – her old life, back again. Sometimes she missed it, but other times she thanked her lucky stars that Mrs King had given her this opportunity and laid her future open to so many new possibilities. Now it seemed it would be coming to an end, and she feared what might happen next.

'Jones!'

Mrs King was calling her from the next room. She went through to find the solicitor packing away some papers and writing materials into his bag. She went to open the door for him, looking briefly at Mrs King to see she was propped up comfortably. She looked better than she had all day. Her face was still odd to look upon, with its slanting left side, all the features drooping. But she had a smile playing about her lips, and looked truly content.

'Show out Mr Steadman and then come straight back to me, Jones.'

Her voice sounded stronger, too. That was good. The solicitor was ready now and followed her out onto the landing.

Once Hettie had shut the door behind her, Mr Steadman turned to her and smiled. He was a short, sturdy man with little remaining hair and spider veins on his cheeks.

'You serve your mistress well, Miss Jones,' he said, a definite twinkle in his eye.

'Yes, sir,' she said, unsure how to proceed. 'I do my very best.'

'Evidently,' he said, with a smile. 'But listen, my dear.' He moved his bald head closer to her, took a quick glance about him and lowered his voice. 'Keep your wits about you. Look out for yourself. And don't let anyone tell you what to do. Strange times lie ahead, and you'll need all of your guile to get through them. Something tells me you'll be fine.'

What in God's name was the man talking about? Hettie just stared at him, knowing she should respond but entirely lost for words. He tapped his nose and winked at her. She had not been winked at by a man since she'd worked at the pit.

'Sir, I . . .'

'All will become clear,' he said and his face changed, from one of amusement to that of utter seriousness. 'I will see you again soon – before too long, I expect. And if you ever need help, you know where to find me. I'll be happy to assist you, at any time. Remember that.'

He did not allow her to reply to this odd statement, and instead turned and trotted down the stairs, leaving her on the landing, agog.

A few moments later she heard Mr Steadman talking to someone in the hallway. She went to the bannister and peered over. It was Mrs King the younger, returned from a ride she had taken out early that morning with a gentleman friend. She did not even know about the elder Mrs King's condition. Hettie hoped Clayton would inform her, so that she did not have to speak to her. Meanwhile, she saw that Mr Steadman was talking to her in low tones, perhaps giving her the news himself. But at that moment, Mrs King looked up sharply and saw Hettie. She said good afternoon to Mr Steadman and came quickly up the stairs.

Hettie turned away to go back to her mistress, but the younger Mrs King called out to her, 'You. You there.'

She never called her Jones, only *you* or sometimes even just *maid*. Hettie wished she had not been so nosy; she could've been safely back in her mistress's room if she'd not been so stupid as to have eavesdropped on them.

'Yes, ma'am?' she said and turned to Mrs King, who was now at the top of the stairs and making towards her.

'What was he here for?' she snapped at Hettie.

'Mr Steadman, ma'am?'

'Yes, Mr Steadman. Who do you think I mean?'

'I'm sure I do not know, ma'am. He came to speak with Mrs King the elder and then he left.'

'You were not in the room?'

'I was not, ma'am.'

'Are you lying? You're lying, aren't you, you little schemer. You were there or you listened in. I would wager ten guineas you know exactly what was discussed in that room.'

Mrs King's face was now only inches away from her own. Hettie had always thought of Mrs King the younger as a handsome woman, but now her viciousness showed in her twisted expression and Hettie wanted to get as far away from it as possible. But she stood her ground and did not flinch. Something told her that battle lines were being drawn. She did not know how or what would become of this, but she sensed that her mistress needed protection from this woman.

'Indeed not, ma'am. I was in the next room and heard not a word.'

Mrs King gave a dry bark of a laugh, with not one ounce of humour in it, only mockery. Then she turned and marched downstairs, her fine riding clothes rustling expensively as she went.

Hettie gathered herself and went back in to her mistress. Mrs King the elder was clearly waiting for her, as she reached out with her right hand and patted the bedspread.

'Come sit with me. I must speak with you now.'

The child sat on the bed beside her. Queenie still thought of her as the child, for Hettie was so young. Eighteen in July. Not so young, perhaps. But at ninety-seven, everyone seemed like babies to Queenie, even the doctor and the solicitor. Besides, Hettie was the child of the baby on the bridge, the child of Blaize's prophecy, the child who would bridge the divide. Queenie felt as if the past seven decades of her life had somehow been leading to this moment, ever since she had watched her long-dead husband rape the poor maid Blaize, and Queenie had stood by and done nothing. Now, finally, she was able to make amends. Now, perhaps, the ghost of Blaize would approve and leave her in everlasting peace.

'My dear,' Queenie began, suddenly feeling very weary. She wished to sleep, after a busy day of visitors and the settling of affairs. But she had no idea how much time she had left and this last duty must be done. 'I have something to tell you. When you hear it, it will change you. But I hope it will do so for the better. Your life now will alter immeasurably, as will your future. You must listen carefully and not interrupt. Do you understand?'

Hettie's green eyes were narrowed with curiosity, her brow furrowed. She nodded.

'Many years ago, when I was a new young wife, my husband used to assault the servants that worked in our house. One day, I found him forcing himself on a young maid called Betsy Blaize. Later, that maid left our employ. No, I must be truthful. I dismissed her. I regret this deeply. But there it is. Betsy Blaize had a child, the bastard child of my husband, Ralph King senior. She carried it across the iron bridge and gave it to a passing Quaker man, and then she died. The Quaker was called

Beddoes and he brought up the baby on the bridge with his wife, as their own. This baby was Martha, your mother.

'So you see, my dear, your grandfather was Ralph King senior. You are related to the Kings. You are a King, more so than myself or my daughter-in-law Benjamina, for we are Kings only by marriage, not by blood. My granddaughter, Margaret, was your cousin, and her daughter Beatrice is your first cousin, once removed.

'When Beatrice comes here from America, you will be reunited as the family you are. She was present at your birth and she cared deeply for you, your mother and father, as well as the Malones, whose son Owen she was in love with before he died. So, you see, the Kings, the Malones and the Joneses are all intimately connected, though it has brought us nothing but trouble. The feud has raged on these sixty years or so, but now you are the one to bridge that divide and bring harmony to these families. You are the one true connection between us all. *The child will cross the bridge. The child will make one house from two. The child is the answer.* That is you, my dear Hettie. *You* are the answer.'

The relief of having said it all in one speech was immense, but so was the effort expended. Queenie closed her eyes, inhaled deeply and breathed out slowly, her breath slightly ragged. She had watched Hettie's eyes grow wider and wider as she listened. Now

Queenie had said her piece, she felt so exhausted, she decided not to open her eyes again. She had no energy left to answer the child's inevitable questions. She heard Hettie's breathing, but she kept her eyes closed.

A peace had come upon her the likes of which she had not experienced for a lifetime; the last time she felt like this was in her youth, with her sister. But Selina had gone strange, been put away in an asylum and killed herself. And Alice had married Ralph King, a cold, cruel rapist of young women. She had sacrificed any peace she might have had for a marriage to a monster. He made her pregnant and she lost twin girls to tuberculosis before they were six months old. Eventually, she produced her son Ralph junior and from then on, she devoted her life to this family, to making it the greatest in the county and beyond.

But oh, what terrible losses they had suffered along the way. Now, in her final days, she could see at last that everything was coming to fruition. The King fortune was considerable, but almost all of its descendants were dead or had abandoned the family. Yet this child, this baby of the baby on the bridge, this Hettie Jones, would be Queenie's final act. Queenie smiled inwardly and felt a great wave of peace wash over her, as if she lay at the bottom of the River Severn, the water flowing over her lazily, as her mind drifted away from consciousness and she slept.

Time passed. It might have been hours or days or even weeks, Queenie had no idea. She was just so tired, so very, very tired. Sleep felt like a comfortable bath, continuously topped up with more deliciously warm water. She had no inclination to leave it and step out into the cold glare of waking life.

Her dreams were muddled and shifting, scenes from her long life filing past her like a motley parade. She was aware of Hettie at times, Benjamina and Clayton at others. She believed the doctor was there at points, but couldn't swear on it. He might have been another dream.

But then, one night, she opened her eyes and the room was bathed in a bluish-white light. She knew that light. It was the spectral garb of her old companion, the ghost of Betsy Blaize.

She's come for me, thought Queenie.

She forced herself to focus and moved her eyes lazily across the room, seeking the source of the light. And there she was, the spirit, clothed in a brilliant white gown, her hair flowing in a gentle zephyr, her blue eyes shining out and gazing upon Queenie with infinite pity and love.

'*It is time*,' a voice spoke in Queenie's mind, the voice of the spirit.

'*I am ready*,' answered Queenie, without moving her lips.

'*Look*,' said the spirit and raised her hand, gesturing towards the bed where Queenie lay.

Queenie saw the forms of others materialising, coming into being as if a fog was lifting. First was Jenkins, her beloved Rose, her smile knowing, mischievous and yet kind, just as she often looked on her mistress in life. Beside her were the beautiful blonde locks and large blue eyes of her granddaughter Margaret, who clasped her hands before her and nodded at her grandmother, smiling. Beside her stood two identical little girls, ribbons in their hair, both broadly grinning, their teeth a brilliant white – Queenie's daughters, lost as babies, grown into the girls they would have been. Queenie's heart overflowed with joy.

Then, last, came the one she lost the longest ago, a slim, willowy figure with the same large blue eyes her great-niece had inherited; it was Queenie's dear sister Selina. In life, those eyes had been clouded with trouble, but now, in death, they shone clearly and brightly.

Selina held out her hand to Queenie.

Chapter 15

The morning was an extremely cold one. Hettie shivered as she went to her mistress's fireplace to remake the fire. She cleaned out the ashes and lit a new one, all the while expecting her mistress to wake at any moment to complain that Hettie was making too much noise.

But Mrs King did not wake up and berate her as she usually did, and once finished with the fire, Hettie approached the bed slowly. As she drew back the bed curtains, a chill ran down her spine, which at first she thought must just be the cold. But something stopped her, and as she looked up at Mrs King's face, she saw that her eyes were open, staring to the side of the bed. Her arm was outstretched, her palm open. There was that chill again and as Hettie bent over Mrs King, she knew immediately that she was gone. The dead look in the eyes was beyond that she'd seen when her mistress had been very ill. This was death and it was unmistakable.

Hettie stood still and looked down upon her mistress. She had never seen a dead person before. She didn't know if this was the correct thing to do, but she felt very strongly that she should close her mistress's eyes. She gently did so. Then she placed her arm beside her body, so that it was not outstretched. The skin was ice-cold.

Hettie knew that Mrs King the younger must be told, and that the woman would be delighted; everyone in the house knew that she wanted her mother-in-law dead. As Hettie stood next to her mistress's small, slight figure, dwarfed by blankets, and looked down at her still, pale face, she felt a wave of sadness overcome her and her own eyes welled up. She would miss her mistress very much. She would miss her company, her stories and the twinkle in her eye when she smiled at Hettie. And though she knew it was selfish to do so, she also worried for her own future. With old Mrs King gone, Hettie knew that her work here was done. She would have to move on and find another position. She had not even had the heart to ask her mistress to write a reference for her before she passed away. Now she would be stuck with no reference, or a very poor one from the younger Mrs King.

Hettie thought about the pit bank and returning to work there. It felt like another country now. She could move back in with her father and resume her job – but how would the others be with her? She had barely seen Ada and the others since she left. She had been in service, working at the big house, as a lady's maid, no less. She knew she could be a pit girl again – that girl had never left her – but she also knew that she had moved on from their world and would not easily be accepted back, perhaps ever. She was caught in between two worlds, with nowhere to go except the uncertain future.

With a heavy heart, she went back to her room, dressed herself quickly and walked through to find Kezia to tell her the news, so that Mrs King the younger could be informed. She stood by her mistress's bed and waited until the doctor came to pronounce her formally gone. Hearing his words brought the truth of her loss closer. Somehow it wasn't real until Dr Fitzgerald said it. He shed a tear too.

Once he was gone, the reality of Hettie's situation sank in and she expected at any moment to be dismissed from the premises. But before the undertaker arrived to take Mrs King away, a note from the solicitor came, informing them of a two o'clock meeting, which he summoned Mrs King the younger and Miss Hettie Jones, lady's maid, to attend, in order to discuss an urgent matter relating to the death of Mrs King the elder.

At two o'clock, Hettie found herself sitting in the most uncomfortable of silences in Mrs King's study, awaiting the solicitor's arrival. She sat bolt upright in the chair she'd been given. The atmosphere in the room was so thick with menace, Hettie was sure she could have cut it with a cheese knife. Benjamina King could not keep still. She kept shuffling in her study chair, the rustle of her silk gown slicing through the air. She was pretending to look at papers on her desk, but Hettie, even without looking directly at her, could tell it was all for show. Hettie stared straight ahead at the wall, desperate not to catch Mrs King's eye.

Hettie's mind would not keep still. It was filled with the events of the last few days – old Mrs King's revelation, old Mrs King's death. Her mistress was dead, and Hettie was a King. She was the daughter of a woman whose mother had been raped by Ralph King senior. Just being the product of such violence was disturbing enough, but to discover that she was related to the hated Kings was another matter entirely. The new knowledge of her origins burned a hole in the fabric of her mind. Her overwhelming feeling was of shame. Utter shame. She felt embarrassed and appalled that her mother was not only a bastard in the eyes of the law, but also a product of rape. It seemed that this despicable fact somehow followed her through the generations and infected her, too. She felt disgusted to be related to a man who could do such a thing to an innocent young girl. She wondered if she would ever tell anyone: her father? Anny? Evan? She could not imagine framing the words. She did not want them to look at her differently, or to look at her mother differently. No, she would keep it to herself always. Nobody should ever know. It was her shame and she would carry it for the rest of her life. The only people who knew the truth were now dead.

Hettie looked up at the sound of footsteps, and the butler Busby finally showed Mr Steadman in. They had been waiting for him for only five minutes or so, but it felt like an age.

Pleasantries were exchanged between Mrs King and Mr Steadman, who took a seat next to Hettie.

'I must say,' began Mrs King, splendid and regal behind her enormous desk, 'that the haste in which you have demanded to be seen is very unusual, Mr Steadman. It is only a few hours since we found that my dear mother-in-law had passed away during the night, and yet here you are.'

'I understand your concern, madam. But I must tell you that the elder Mrs King's instructions were absolutely clear,' said Steadman, confidently.

Hettie had no idea why she'd been summoned to this meeting, but she was glad that Steadman wasn't afraid of Mrs King like everyone else was.

'She clearly stipulated that I must attend as soon as possible after her death, in order to give you and Miss Jones fair warning.'

Mrs King shot a glance at Hettie, who unfortunately caught her eye, then looked away swiftly. What was happening here?

'Warning?' said Mrs King, in a low, almost threatening voice. 'Of what?'

'The reading of wills is always a delicate matter. Under normal circumstances we would schedule this meeting in a few days in order to let . . . the dust settle, if that is not an unfortunate metaphor to use . . . but Mrs King made it clear that she wanted the contents of her will to be revealed within a day of her death to the two parties hereby present, so that one of the parties did not unwittingly throw the other party out of the house at the first opportunity.'

Now the atmosphere was thicker than ever. Hettie could feel the anger and confusion emanating from Mrs King in waves. Her own mind was racing. Why on earth was she in this room with these people? She should have been packing her bags to leave by now.

'What the devil are you talking about, man?' Mrs King's mask of respectability was slipping.

'I must inform you both that Mrs King the elder was the sole owner of the King fortune, stock, businesses and houses. Therefore, upon her death, it was her duty to dispose of these riches as she saw fit. She had a will drawn up some years ago that left all of this to you, Mrs King, on the proviso that if her great-granddaughter Beatrice ever returned from America to seek her fortune again, the whole must be given up to her. However, Mrs King the elder called upon me very recently and drew up a new will. This is the document I have here today and will make known to you presently.'

'If my mother-in-law has in her final days made this . . . maid . . . a beneficiary of some trifle in her possession, surely this could have waited? I am a very busy woman, Mr Steadman.'

'I will read you the main points first,' said Steadman, ignoring Mrs King and looking straight at Hettie, who met his gaze. He gave her the briefest of smiles, which only confused her further. Then he took out a document and held it up to read from it. 'This being the last will and testament of Alice Mary King, née Hinton, on this day, et cetera, et cetera . . . Ah, here we are. That the entire King fortune owned solely by the aforementioned Alice King is hereby bequeathed upon her death, in whole, to Miss Hettie Jones.'

There was a low guttural noise from across the desk. Hettie realised it was Mrs King saying, 'What?' For herself, Hettie did not believe the words she was hearing. None of it made sense. It created a kind of schism in her brain; on one side was common sense, telling her that what was happening was real. On the other was the certainty that this was a daydream and she would come to her senses at any moment.

Steadman went on. 'Thereby Miss Hettie Jones is the sole heir of all monies, businesses, stocks, houses, other goods and chattels, et cetera, et cetera. Nothing will go to Mrs Benjamina King, apart from the clothes, jewellery and other trinkets she already owns. The will stipulates that Miss Jones is now the sole manager of the King businesses, that she can employ Mrs King to run said businesses if she wishes, but is under no obligation to do so and can choose to turn Mrs King out of the house immediately if she wishes to. However, on the occasion that Miss Jones refuses the inheritance or passes away without issue, rather than the inheritance going to Mr Adam Jones or to the crown, the sole heir will be Mrs Benjamina King, being the last living survivor with that name.'

Hettie sat stock still and so did Mrs King.

'I refute this madness,' said Mrs King, slowly and carefully.

'You may do as you wish, but the meaning of the will is transparent and was drawn up by myself very recently. Your maid Kezia Clayton was called in to witness the signatures and therefore the will is valid and legal. You may contest all you like, but you will not change one word of the meaning of this last will and testament. Mrs King the elder knew her own mind . . .'

'That is where you are wrong, Steadman,' spat Mrs King. 'The old woman's mind was failing her, for months, if not years, before her death. The servants heard her talking to someone when in her room alone. She then hired a pit girl as a lady's maid, further evidence of her addled mind. So if you think I'm going to sit back and allow this travesty to . . .'

'And now,' said Steadman loudly, cutting off Mrs King, which left her agog, 'we come to the reasoning behind Mrs King's decision. Miss Jones is aware of this information already. But it is time to reveal the reason why Miss Jones is named as sole heir.'

Hettie felt as if all the blood drained from her head and pooled in her feet. Surely Mr Steadman didn't know . . . surely?

'Sir . . .' she began. But Steadman was already speaking.

'The fact is that Miss Jones is . . .'

'No!' cried Hettie.

Mrs King glared at her, then her expression changed to a kind of evil fascination. 'Do go on,' she said, smiling disgracefully.

'Miss Jones is in fact a King heir,' said Mr Steadman. 'She is related in blood to Mr Ralph King senior. He had relations of a forcible kind with a maid, Miss Betsy Blaize, which produced a child, Martha, who married Mr Adam Jones, and thus Miss Hettie Jones was born. Therefore, she is a King by blood and due her inheritance, gifted by Mrs King senior.'

Hettie wanted the ground to open up and swallow her. The shame dripped from her like sweat. To have known this fact was bad enough, but to have it paraded so gaily before an enemy was too much to bear.

'Well, well, well,' said Mrs King and stood up from her desk. 'We have a bastard in our midst.'

Mr Steadman stood up too. 'Now then, that's enough, Mrs King. And inaccurate. Miss Jones's mother may have been born out of wedlock – through no fault of her own, I may add – but Miss Jones was born firmly within wedlock. I am sure that if any one of us were to look back into our own ancestry they'd find a bastard or two along the way. Even amongst royalty, as history clearly shows!'

'But she had no claim,' said Mrs King. 'There is no proof!'

'I have Mrs King the elder's word and that is enough for me. In any case, it is of no consequence, as Mrs King could choose to leave her fortune to whomsoever she desired. She could leave it to your little dog if she wished. But she did not. She left it in whole to this young woman, whose kindness she hugely appreciated these past months. And that is something that could never be said of you, Mrs King!'

'How dare you!' she cried.

Hettie felt as if her head would split open if she had to hear any more of this. She felt so hot in this room – the atmosphere was so close. She wanted to run.

Steadman was putting his papers back into his briefcase. 'I must confer with my client now. Miss Jones, will you take a turn around the garden with me? We can talk there.'

Hettie glanced at Mrs King, whose cheeks had two round red spots of rage blooming upon them. Her eyes were like ice. Hettie wanted nothing more than to get out of that room, so she nodded meekly and stood up. She had no idea what to say, so she said nothing.

'This is not over,' said Benjamina, staring down at the desk now.

'That is your opinion, but not a legal fact. I will provide more details in the coming weeks of the extent of the King fortune, of course. But for now, Mrs King the elder made it very clear that I must give the two of you this news within a day of her death, so that you,

Mrs King, did not force you, Miss Jones, to leave the house in the mistaken knowledge that you were now in charge. It is you, Miss Jones, who are in charge now. Come, let us walk and I will explain things further to you. I take my leave of you, Mrs King.'

With that, Steadman went straight to the door and held it open, nodding at Hettie. She did not look round at Mrs King, but could feel the hatred flowing from her, as real as a roaring fire. She left the room and then Mr Steadman walked before her silently, leading her across the hallway and through a side door, out into the grounds. As she followed him, her mind was screaming. Mrs King had left her entire fortune . . . to her. To Hettie Jones, pit girl, strawberry picker, maid. Everything: the houses, the businesses, the money. To her. It was daft. It was impossible.

Once outside, Mr Steadman turned to Hettie and smiled.

'Good to get out of there, hm?' he said, and gave a sly look towards the house.

'Mr Steadman, please,' said Hettie, her voice shaking.

His expression changed and he reached out and patted her on the shoulder. 'It's a shock for you, I know. But you must bear up under it. Your life has changed in a moment. Do you feel faint, Miss Jones?'

Did she? Perhaps she did. Her head was swimming. But he was right, it was good to get out of the house.

‘Could we walk a bit?’ she said and stepped onto the path away from the house that led into the woodland. She needed time to think, to breathe.

‘Of course, my dear. We shall walk and talk a little.’

Steadman explained to her what would happen next. He would arrange for her to sign some papers at his office. He said something about ‘probate’, but she didn’t know what that was, so she just nodded. He explained some details about the businesses and who ran each one and what Mrs King wanted, but he lost her after the first few seconds and she just let his voice flow over her and she walked slowly onwards, the birds chirping around them in the trees, oblivious.

‘Excuse me, sir,’ she said, interrupting. ‘Surely it’s a mistake.’

‘In what sense?’ he said.

‘All of it. Mrs King must have been losing her mind to do this.’

‘Not at all, my dear. She was absolutely lucid. She knew exactly what she wanted to do and why. She explained it all to me. And do not fear: Mrs King junior’s bark is far worse than her bite. She can do nothing to refute this. The will stands. You inherit, and Mrs King does not.’

‘You said something about “issue”. If I “pass without issue”. What does that mean?’

‘If you die before having a child, the heir will be Mrs King junior.’

‘I see.’

'Yes, Mrs King senior added this stipulation to the will for a particular reason. You see, she originally wanted Miss Beatrice Ashford to be the sole heir, but Miss Ashford refused it, and she wondered if you might do the same. Also, she feared that if you passed away before your time and had not yet married and had children, that the estate would go to your father – with which outcome I'm afraid she was not happy – or to the crown. She could not bear that idea. She wanted the King name and houses and businesses to live on in perpetuity. Is there any risk that you will do that, Miss Jones?'

'Die without children?' she said, shocked at such a question.

'Ah no, my dear. I meant, that you might refuse the inheritance.'

Hettie had not considered it. The Malones would, she was sure of that. And Beatrice had, for all the right reasons. Should she herself refuse it too?

'Can I use the inheritance in any way? In whatever way I see fit?'

'You can do whatever you wish, with the businesses, with the money, with Southover when it is completed and with the old brickmaster's house here, as we still call it. You are in control of the entire estate, and may use it or dispose of it as you will.'

Hettie stopped walking and turned back towards the old brickmaster's house, her home for the past five months. She stared at it, outlining with her eyes the windows, doors and bricks that built it.

'Are you feeling ill, Miss Jones? Can I assist you?'

'No, thank you. I am well. But I have a question. I have plenty of questions. But one in particular is gnawing away at me.'

'Never fear. In a day or so, you can come to my office and we'll go through it all together. I will see you through this strange time. But what is your question?'

'When can I move my father into this house?'

Chapter 16

Benjamina still sat at her desk, rigid with shock. She could hear her dog Drina barking intermittently upstairs. It was time for her walk, after which Benjamina would normally take her afternoon nap. That was the unchanging pattern of her life for the past few years: up early, business in the morning, luncheon, dog walk, nap, dinner, entertainment, bed. She had taken the monotony for granted. She had sometimes complained of it, to her dog, to her acquaintances, to her lovers – how hard she worked every day to manage the businesses, how little time she had for shopping, or socialising, or dancing. But she'd been happy with it, too – delighted, in fact. After all these years of being an ornament, she had finally had a use. And it all had a higher purpose: it led towards the conclusion of the inheritance. One day when the old bitch had died, Benjamina would own everything: from the mines to the forges and the brickyards, every wine glass in the cupboard and tulip bulb in the garden. It would all be hers. She had no child to leave it to, but she didn't care. She had no interest in what happened to the King name after her death. It could go to the dogs for all she cared. But she had waited for this all of her adult life.

And now it was gone, in a moment. To this slip of a girl, this pit-wench, this *maid*.

Her thoughts fell heavily on Hettie Jones, the object now of all her hatred. Hettie was the same age now as Benjamina herself had been when she was given to Ralph King. Given, like a gift, like a possession, like a transaction. She'd never had her own life until now. And this child had strolled in from the pit bank and taken it from her. One girl was sold to a man and the other girl was given a fortune. The comparison gave her physical pain, a gnawing in her gut that had just begun. The injustice of it! Benjamina could well imagine the pleasure Queenie must have felt as she added that stipulation to the will, that if Hettie refused or passed without a child, the next heir would be herself. So close and yet so far. The old witch must have delighted in knowing how much that would torture her. Benjamina clenched her fists and looked down at them, her perfectly manicured nails digging into her palms. She felt positively murderous.

She heard someone enter the house from the garden door and assumed it must be the girl, back from her walk. Benjamina had to face up to her situation. She would contest this will – of course she would. But in the meantime, she had to deal with the girl. Shouting and screaming would get her nowhere. And the horrible truth was, the girl could have her thrown out. That very day, thrown out of her home, the house she had renovated in every detail, down to the spoons and the vases and the other thousand tiny details of a home. Benjamina wasn't going to lose all that because of anger or pride. She would have to be clever now.

She left her study and went into the living room, where there was a door out to the garden. There she found Hettie, standing by the window, looking out at the woodland beyond. The girl turned swiftly upon her entering the room. Her face looked shocked and pale. Her eyes darted about the room, before looking back at her.

Benjamina guessed the girl must feel awkward and even a touch guilty about standing in a room that had so recently been the leisure room of her employers. She wondered if the girl would dare even touch a chair, let alone sit in one, leaning her head back on an antimacassar. Benjamina realised she could take advantage of the girl's astonishment at her new situation. She was a babe in the wood. Benjamina still had the power here.

'Miss Jones,' she said and forced herself to smile.

The girl looked at her blankly, then tried to smile as well.

'Mrs King, can I speak a bit with you?'

Ah, so the girl had more nerve than she'd given her credit for.

'Of course, my dear. Won't you sit down?'

'Oh no, I couldna do that.'

Benjamina noted that, in her nerves, the local dialect was coming back, after weeks of Queenie schooling her against it. Well, the girl was rich now. Benjamina supposed she could talk however she pleased.

'But you must,' said Benjamina, forcing another smile. 'This is all yours now. You must make yourself comfortable.'

But the girl was not comfortable – far from it, standing stiffly by the window, her eyes still wide with the surprise of it all. She reluctantly came forward and chose a chair to the side that was not generally used by either Queenie or Benjamina and sat awkwardly on the edge of it.

'Thank'ee, ma'am,' said Hettie.

Benjamina's mind was feverish with plotting. How should she handle this girl? She could steamroller her into agreeing with her terms, which would be quite easy, she felt, as the girl was so confused she would probably defer to her on anything at this moment. But Benjamina needed to know her intentions, so it might be best to play the subtler game and let the girl talk a while, to see where her thinking lay.

'No need to thank me. Now, you wish to speak with me. I think that is a capital idea. We have much to discuss and organise. So, please, do begin.'

The girl sat bolt upright, as if a broomstick were strapped to her back.

'I want to say plenty of things, ma'am. It's hard to know where I should start. But the very first thing to tell you is that I had no clue that anything like this could ever happen to a girl like me. I didna know a thing about my mistress's plans. I promise you that. But I mun confess I did know about my origins. Mrs King told me about it the day before she passed. I couldna ask no questions, as she slipped into sleep just after and never awoke. So I'm as perplexed by it as the next person.'

She still had those frightened rabbit eyes, but once she started talking, her demeanour changed and she seemed to grow in confidence. Benjamina needed to assert some control over this now, as the girl was dangerously close to being assured, and Benjamina couldn't have that.

'My dear, it must have been a terrible shock to you, to understand that you came from . . . well, such inauspicious circumstances.'

The girl looked blankly at her. Benjamina knew how to use words as weapons.

'I inna sure I know what that means. But yes, it was a dreadful shock. And I want to say summat else. The idea that I own this house and everything in it and all the businesses and all that – it boggles my mind, it does. And I know that you, ma'am, have been in charge of all this for many a year, and that is your world, not mine. There was summat Mr Steadman read out, summat about you running the businesses or being thrown out onto the streets.'

The girl stopped talking. Benjamina felt the blood rush to her cheeks. Was she trying to humiliate her? Was she playing with her? She had to remember that not everybody thought as she did, in a scheming manner. She must control her own anger and resist striking this girl down with it. She had to be cautious and courteous.

'Yes, Miss Jones. I recall it very well.'

'Well, ma'am, I want you to know that this idea of you, the mistress of this house and family, being thrown out onto the streets is a heartless thing. Of course that mun never happen. Everyone in the county knows you and admires you for being so clever at your business. And you mun carry it on and be paid a fair wage for it. No question of that, ma'am. The thought that you, at this time of your life, would lose your home and all you are used to, in an instant, and because of me – well, it inna right. And though I was proper fond of my mistress, I believe this a cruel thought and one I want no part in.'

For once in her life, Benjamina didn't know what to say. The girl had disarmed her. She'd only known of this extraordinary change in her circumstances for such a brief time and already she had come to terms with it and was beginning to make decisions about how to proceed. This was not what Benjamina expected and it unsettled her greatly. Perhaps this girl would not be as easy to mould as she had thought. But she was not giving up as yet.

'Miss Jones, I can see that my dear, departed mother-in-law made a wise choice when she gave you the role of lady's maid. You have a natural refinement that belies your origins. I thank you for your kind remarks regarding my . . . new situation. And of course, I would be delighted to remain here, in my family home, as I believe is right and proper. I have designed and refurbished every inch of the interior of this house. It is my home. Southover is being rebuilt presently, as you know. You may find that residence more to your liking, perhaps, when it is ready. But until then, I can see from your courteous demeanour that you and I will get on famously.' She paused. 'But there is something else I feel I must put to you. Something about your family.'

'My family? I have little. Only my father. I'll be moving him in here tomorrow.'

What was this? The girl had already planned this out? Benjamina knew about Adam Jones, the man who had been transported for burning down Southover, whatever he claimed about his innocence. Benjamina always quizzed the servants for their gossip, as knowledge was power, so she knew the rumours about Hettie's father being a hopeless all-day drinker. It reminded Benjamina of her own father's violent drunken bouts. It brought an old fear back to her, clutching at her heart, of hiding under the stairs with her mother, awaiting his terrible fists. She felt a tightness in her chest at the mere thought of a drunk living in her beautiful house, let alone one who had committed arson against her family. But she must remain in control.

'That is one idea and a good one. I'm sure it will be a great relief to you to provide a stable environment for your father. But . . . a thought occurs to me. This will be a great change in your life, and in his life. As you say, I will be running the businesses and carrying on my life as before in many respects. For you and your father, this will be an enormous challenge, a metamorphosis in comparison to the way you've previously lived. So, let me make a suggestion. The money that is coming to you from the will . . . I am sure that Mr Steadman could forward you an advance, which would allow you and your father to seek alternative accommodation, perhaps a nice, cosy house in Ironbridge. Something that would suit you both well. I would continue to reside here, in my home and to continue my work to keep the King name and businesses thriving. You could live at your leisure, in town, amongst . . . your people. Indeed, you may find that the idea of accepting this will and becoming the sole heir is not to your liking, that it will remove you from the bosom of your family and, as I say, your people. Miss Ashford made a similar choice, when she emigrated to America and started a new life.

She knew where she wanted to belong and it was not here, in this house. And I know you admire Miss Ashford hugely and one must admit, she certainly seems to have thrived after such a wise decision. Mrs King senior was well aware of this fact, mentioning in the will that you might follow suit. And . . . if you were . . . to *refuse the inheritance*, you would not be going against Mrs King's wishes, as she predicted in her will that you might indeed do so. I wonder if you understand how much your life will change – being the sole heir – and whether you are ready for that change? Might it not be better for you, for your father, for your adoptive family and your friends, if you refused this inheritance and instead I make a generous donation to you for your services here? It would be more than generous, enough for you to live comfortably for the rest of your lives with . . . your people.'

Benjamina was unsure if she had pushed things too far. But the thought of this wench and her drunken father living here, under the same roof as a King, was utterly ridiculous. And more importantly, perhaps she could turn the girl away from the inheritance altogether, upon which happy day she herself would become the heir and all would be as it should be again. Surely, the girl had to see that. Hettie had looked down at her hands, clasped in her lap. Now she looked up and met Benjamina's eye.

'There is a part of me that is a King. I know that now. I was born a Jones. Then I grew up as a Malone, but apart from them, not being of their blood. Now, for the first time, my mistress has given me a chance to make myself anew, to become the person maybe I was always meant to be. And I mean to grasp it with both hands, Mrs King. I will not be refusing the inheritance. And I will be staying here. And my father will live here with me. And we will all have to do our best to get along.'

Damn this child!

Benjamina managed a simpering smile. But this was not over. Not by many a mile.

'Of course, my dear. Whatever you wish.'

'But I would ask one thing of you – that you dunna tell a soul about my . . . about how I came about, how I'm related to the King family. It inna a fact I wish to be gossiped about by all and sundry. It is my business, and my business alone.'

Oh, the little, trusting fool. Now she had shown a weakness. Still, it would not strengthen Benjamina's own case for it to be common knowledge that the girl was related to the Kings. She had already decided that tomorrow she would travel to Shrewsbury and see her own solicitor, and ask him to bring a suit against Hettie Jones, claiming that Hettie bewitched Queenie and preyed upon a weak old woman, that the will was changed through coercion upon a very elderly lady who was not of sound mind. If Hettie was keen to keep her relation to the Kings quiet, that would only serve Benjamina the better.

Still, it was good to know that the girl was ashamed of it. Benjamina might be able to use that against her one day. For now, she slipped it into a mental pocket for another time.

'Why, of course, my dear. It would never cross my mind to speak of it. It would be better all round if enquiring minds who wish to know why this extraordinary event has come about be instead directed towards the idea that the late Mrs King was aged, infirm and confused in her last days. That would explain everything to our satisfaction, don't you agree?'

Hettie shook her head. 'No, it wouldna, ma'am. I spent every moment I could with my mistress and I am sure this was her choice and one she made with a clear head. Mr Steadman says the same and he has the law on his side.'

It was time to end this meeting. Benjamina was tired and running out of parries for this surprisingly feisty pit bank wench. She knew now what she was up against. This was no village idiot. The girl had a brain and she had spirit. A troublesome combination, but not a match for Benjamina King. The girl might have been thinking she had won this battle. But this was a war.

So Benjamina smiled at the girl and took her leave, claiming a need to get back to business as it wouldn't run itself. She left the room determined to go to any lengths to beat this upstart and to win this war, by any means fair or foul.

Chapter 17

As much as Anny loved raising all of her children (and Hettie – she always considered Hettie one of her own), she was delighted when they began to develop more independence. It made her life easier but also gave her a mother's satisfaction of knowing she had nearly achieved her goal of getting them through childhood and into early adulthood without disaster befalling them. Or death. After Owen had *left them* (to that day, she could use few other words for it, as it still hurt so much), she had such a fear of losing her children. As each completed the next stage of development, it was as if a checklist was ticked off in her mind on the journey towards adulthood. Each goal reached settled her fears somewhat. Once they were grown and gone, she would still worry for them, but her charge of keeping them alive would not feel as urgent.

So when Hettie had talked about going to London and Anny could see her spreading her wings, she had been all for it. It would be marvellous for her independence. But then Adam Jones came into her life. And then the job from Mrs King. These unexpected twists of fortune had forced Hettie suddenly to complete her final stage of growing up. Hettie not only moved out of the house, but out of the family too, somehow. Living with the Kings was the final insult.

Now that old Mrs King had died, Anny wondered what would happen to Hettie. She would be out of a job, surely. Anny didn't think the younger Mrs King would want to keep Hettie on, after the gossip she'd heard about how mean she was to Hettie. Anny dearly hoped that Hettie would be back to work in the pit and all would be as it was. Perhaps she'd even come home, tired of her father.

One chilly Sunday, Hettie turned up with Adam unannounced at the Malones' door. It was wonderful to see her. She had filled out a bit, her cheeks fuller and her hips dipped in a greater curve. She looked like a woman now, confident and well dressed in her Sunday outfit. Anny saw that Evan found it difficult to keep his eyes from her, but also that he was awkward in her presence. Anny's heart went out to her son. She knew this separation had been hardest on him.

She looked back at Hettie, who was staring at her. There was something wrong. Anny knew it from Hettie's eyes the moment she looked at her. Hettie had news to tell them, and it looked like the telling of it would be uncomfortable. Was she moving away? Please let it not be that. Anny had always feared that

Adam would find slotting back into his old existence in Ironbridge impossible, that he might use the King money to move on elsewhere and start his life anew. Anny wished he would – but not with Hettie in tow. Now Hettie had had a taste of the service life, maybe she would go with him, looking for another post as a servant elsewhere.

No, it looked worse than that. Adam had gone to stand by the fireplace, looking smug. Oh Lord, what was it? Anny caught Hettie's eye and saw her hesitate.

'I have news, for all of you,' said Hettie.

Anny glanced at Evan, whose eyes were round and worried. Peter looked over at her too, and fielded the twins to sit down on the hearth rug to keep them still, while Flora perched on a chair, excited to hear the latest turn in the fortunes of Hettie Jones.

'Go ahead then, lass,' said Anny. She could not sit down herself; she was too agitated to move.

'Summat has happened, summat unexpected and . . . well, strange.'

'Spit it out then,' said Evan gruffly.

Adam was still preening at the fireplace.

'I'm sure you've all heard about Mrs King's death. As it turns out . . .'

Hettie paused and her cheeks flushed. She faltered. Nobody spoke. It was as if everyone held their breath.

'Well, I'm her only beneficiary. She left it all to me. All of it. The house, the businesses, the money. All of it.'

There was a moment's stunned silence.

'What's a ben-fish?' asked Lily, unusually speaking before her brother.

'Oh, everyone knows that,' scoffed Billy, but he looked uncertain.

Anny stared. Was she hearing right? Could it possibly be true?

'Are you sure, lass?' said Peter, standing up now, his eyebrows furrowed in confusion. 'It inna some mistake?'

'It be true, all true,' said Adam. Anny could hardly bear to look at him, now she knew the reason for his complacency.

'It is all confirmed by the solicitor, Mr Steadman,' Hettie explained. 'He helped Mrs King draw up the new will near the end.'

She looked intensely uncomfortable. She did not look like a young woman who was in receipt of astounding good fortune.

The room was utterly silent. Anny glanced at Evan, whose face was a picture of confusion. He was in shock and could not hide it.

'Congratulations, Hettie,' said Anny. Somebody had to speak.

'Is Hettie rich now?' asked Flora, the gravity of Hettie's announcement finally beginning to weigh.

'Rich?' said Billy.

'Rich?' said Lily. 'What's that got to do with fish?'

'Yes,' said Adam.

Anny refused to look at him; she knew that his face would be trained upon her, lording it over her. 'It is astonishing news, Hettie. Truly astonishing. And I'm happy for you, love. Truly happy. Congratulations.'

'Yes indeed,' said Peter, and went over to Hettie and hugged her. 'Congratulations, lass!'

The children were still unsure as to what was happening, but they were happy to join in with the general air of good news and they hugged Hettie too, said, 'Well done,' and did a few little jumps afterwards.

Hettie looked painfully at Anny and gave her a lopsided smile. Anny came and put her arms around Hettie, though she felt stiff as she did it and knew that she was withholding herself from fully embracing her dear girl. The truth was, this latest news was more than a wedge between them. Her previous post of the King servant had been bad enough, but now there yawned a chasm. It was Evan she worried for most. He looked as if he had been punched in the stomach.

Hettie explained to everyone about what had happened in the days leading up to Mrs King's death, about the will and Mr Steadman the solicitor, about the younger Mrs King being disinherited (*which will cause no end of trouble*, thought Anny warily).

'Hettie, I know you are the best kind of person and it is no surprise that others think the same,' said Anny. 'But did you have any inkling that Mrs King was going to do such a thing? Did she give you any warning of her intentions?'

'Not at all. We had grown closer in recent weeks, that was all. She relied on me a lot. I was . . . fond of her, I was. And I believe she was fond of me. But no, I had no idea.'

'What will Mrs King the younger do about all this?' said Peter, echoing Anny's thoughts.

'It is said she wonna let it lie. So we shall see,' replied Hettie.

'Watch out for that one,' said Anny. 'She could cause you grief and no mistake.'

Hettie said, 'I have Mr Steadman in my corner. I believe he will see me right. And that's something else I wanted to say. I want to see you all right. All taken care of.'

Another silence fell then. Peter glanced at Anny.

'We have no need of anything,' said Anny, aware her voice sounded cold.

'I know that, but I will have surplus and I want to use it wisely. I want to help. I want to change your lives, if you will let me.'

Peter was watching his wife closely and Anny looked away. She knew they would be discussing this later, perhaps even arguing about it. But she was resolute. She had guessed, moments after Hettie revealed her news, that this would be coming.

'Hettie, you know I'd accept any gift from you but this. We will never accept King money. It is blood money. We've said this before and so I say it again.'

Hettie looked physically pained by Anny's words. 'But it is not King money anymore. It is mine. And I want to repay the love and kindness you have shown me all my life.'

'You think we want your money for that?' said Evan, speaking up at last. 'You think we want paying for loving you?'

'No! Course not!' Hettie's tone was exasperated.

'Let them refuse it,' said Adam, still leaning infuriatingly on the mantelpiece. 'Bloody fools.'

'Now then,' said Peter. 'No need for that.'

'Father, please,' said Hettie. She looked back at Anny. 'It would grieve me sorely if you did not take what I am offering you. Money is not evil in itself. Only what is done with it can be called a good or evil thing. And this would be a good thing.'

'We dunna want it,' said Evan, folding his arms. 'Any of it.'

'That's right,' said Anny. 'Thank you for thinking kindly of us. But we respectfully decline.'

Now the atmosphere had moved beyond strained to soured. Hettie looked at Evan, then at Anny, then at her father. Her face remained confused, her hands twisting her gloves round and round. Anny just wanted to hug her, to tell her not to fret, that she was still their dear girl. She took a step towards her and put her hand on Hettie's arm.

'We are happy for you, love. It is marvellous news. And a testament to the good work you have done for that lady, no doubt about that. Your kindness and companionship have been rewarded. It is wonderful. Be happy and enjoy it. We will always be here, if you need us. But we are not part of your world now, nor shall we ever be. Go freely into it and never fret for us. We are doing well and we shall prevail, without help from any quarter. You can rest assured of that.'

Hettie still looked pained but she gave a weary nod. 'It is as I suspected. And I respect you for it. But let me assure you that none of this turnabout in my fortunes will affect the love and regard I have for you all. I wish us to be easy with each other, as we always have been. I intend to remain unchanged by it and to be true to myself always.'

'Good girl,' said Anny. She reached out and hugged Hettie again, this time full of proper feeling, and it was returned heartily.

But over Hettie's shoulder, Anny glanced at Evan and saw in his face that his dreams had been crumpled up like autumn leaves held in the hand, crushed to smithereens.

Chapter 18

April 1876

Stockings, knickerbockers and a chemise came first. Hettie asked Kezia to help her with the stockings as Hettie's hands were still rough from her working days and snagged on the fine material. Kezia tied up her corset next, pulling the laces quite tight and crossing them at the back, then bringing them round to tie them in front.

Next, Kezia helped her lift the crinolette over her head, a caged and fabric construction that had a bustle on the back. Hettie buttoned it at the waist. Kezia threw over a white petticoat with lace at the hem, which Hettie pulled down and arranged neatly over the crinolette. Then came the camisole, a sleeveless cotton top, buttoned at the front, which hid the corset ridges. The skirt, made of green silk with maroon piping, was pulled over her head and put in place, buttoned at the back by Kezia. At its base was an extra row of detachable ruffles designed to protect the skirt from the dusty, dirty ground; she'd need this later, as she intended to go for a walk that afternoon.

On top of this came the overskirt, in maroon silk with yellow bows, cut away at the front to reveal the green skirt beneath. Then Kezia helped her on with the bodice, a waist-length silk jacket, with frilly cuffs and fitted style, in matching maroon and green. First a waist stay was fastened to keep it in place, then Kezia started buttoning at the bottom and Hettie at the top, meeting in the middle. Each tiny button had a perfect five-pointed star embroidered upon it. Hettie pinned on an extra yellow bow at the waist to complete the outfit.

It was a pleasure to put on colourful clothes again. The household had been in mourning clothes for a month until the end of March, but now it had been decided that it was seemly to wear the full wardrobe again, since no one in the house had been a blood relation of Mrs King. If she were going out immediately, she would have added a hat, her little boater with yellow ribbons perhaps – but the meeting she was going to attend was here at home, so she did not need to leave the house as yet. Kezia had pinned up her hair at the sides, which fell down at the back in a waterfall of ringlets.

Throughout this long procedure of dressing, Hettie and Kezia, her newly appointed lady's maid, gossiped and laughed and chatted the time away. Hettie knew that custom dictated she should call her maid by her surname, but Hettie refused to call her Clayton. She considered Kezia a friend, not a servant. How grateful she was to have Kezia here with her, helping her learn the ways of this new world, not in order to be a maid to another, as in her previous life, but in order to be the lady herself. For that was what Hettie had to be now. A lady.

And a businesswoman, or at least, the owner of the businesses. Benjamina, as Hettie now called her, was still in charge of running the businesses, but Steadman had insisted that Hettie attend a monthly meeting with Benjamina and the managers of the three industries – iron, coal and brick – in order to keep her hand in and hold Benjamina to account. Steadman attended too and gave Hettie a debrief after each one. Hettie dreaded them. She had been to one in March and she was about to attend her second. She had sat through the first in utter confusion, listening to the numbers being thrown around that meant nothing to her. She'd tried to keep up and nod politely from time to time, always hotly aware of Benjamina's smug face watching her. The woman knew that Hettie had no idea what they were talking about.

Their relationship was strained further by the fact that Benjamina was suing to have the will overturned. Steadman had told Hettie that nothing would come of it, that she would never prove that Mrs King was not of sound mind. But it was a constant worry, of course. Hettie's relationship with Benjamina was a seething mass of resentments topped with a thin veneer of courtesy.

At least Steadman was there for Hettie. He was her one friend in this echelon of society. Hettie smiled at the thought. Friends came from unexpected places when you most needed them. When she had been a new maid, it was Kezia. Now she was a new lady, it was Steadman. Her only friends in her new life.

She thought of her old friends, Ada and everyone else at the pit bank, Evan and the rest of the Malones. She thought of that awful day in late February when she had walked to their house from her father's, after giving him the news about the inheritance. He was full of it, crowing and whooping about their good fortune. He had warned her not to see them, as they would disapprove and put a dampener on it all. He'd said she should write to them instead, but Hettie knew she couldn't just write. She had to tell them in person, because they were family. Two months had passed since she'd told them, and she had not seen them once. It was as much her fault as theirs, perhaps hers more so. She had not sought them out and it was hardly likely that any of the Malones would troop up uninvited to the old brickmaster's house for afternoon tea. She decided she must rectify this soon, but truly, she did not know how. It was easier to put it off and think about something else, like this fearsome meeting she was about to attend. Or like her father.

She had moved him in within days of the announcement. He had turned up sheepishly at first, but once installed in his rooms, with his own valet, he soon acclimatised himself to his new position and began enjoying himself immensely. The truth was that he was enjoying himself far too much, with the brandy and whisky kept at home, and in the taverns he still frequented, now dressed up in his new gentlemanly finery, from which his valet had a damnable job of removing stains after his nightly excursions into town. With more or less unlimited funds, he had run up huge bills at various establishments and would not stop doing so, despite Hettie asking him to steady himself.

She had discussed it with Steadman, who came up with a plan. He had her father come to his office in town and informed him that he would be giving him a weekly allowance, to be collected by him from the office every Monday morning at 9 a.m. sharp. If he did not arrive, he would not receive it, and he was told that all of the shops and public houses in town had been informed not to give anything on account to him. Her father was livid and shouted the house down when he heard this plan. He called it a humiliation, said he was being treated like a child. And what was the point of all this money if he could not spend it how he wished? He had been through hell, he told Hettie, and now his reward should be to do whatever he liked.

But Steadman stuck to his guns and so did Hettie. Adam lived on his weekly allowance and it meant he could not perhaps get as drunk as previously, not if he wanted to drink every day anyway. Hettie felt that at least he had some portion of control exerted over the worst of his nature, which gave her some relief. It was not enough, of course, and she still feared for him, but it was the best she could do for now.

In the last few weeks, Hettie had spent her time learning more and more about the etiquette of ladies from Kezia and about the businesses from Steadman. She had also tried to learn how to control her father, though she felt she was failing at this. He was as drunk as ever, but at least there were days when he ran out of money and could not go out to disgrace himself. Then he'd take a decanter upstairs to his room instead.

Benjamina ate all her meals in her room, so often Hettie ate alone, her father out or ensconced in his quarters. Of course, Kezia could not come to eat with her, though Hettie wished she could. She had never felt more lonely in her life.

Now she picked up her fan from her dressing table; although it was only April, the sun was warm that day and she knew she would feel it, especially in the dreaded meeting that was to come, with all those people she did not understand packed into Benjamina's study.

Just as she was about to leave the room and face the music, she heard the sound of carriage wheels approaching the old brickmaster's house. Hettie went to her bedroom window and saw an unfamiliar coach arrive and pull up to a halt, the horses stamping and shaking their heads. She presumed it was one of the business managers, perhaps come in a new coach as his was being repaired. But out came a woman in her thirties or thereabouts, with a shapely form and a beautiful face. She stepped down from the carriage and stood very still, staring up at the house, wide-eyed and pale, as if she were looking at a ghost.

Intrigued, Hettie left the room and headed downstairs. As she reached the front entrance hall, Benjamina's office door opened and her disagreeable face appeared.

'Didn't you say you wrote to Beatrice Ashford about Queenie's death?' said Benjamina to Hettie, walking towards the sitting room, scowling.

Hettie replied, 'I did. Two days after Mrs King's passing.'

'Well, it clearly didn't get there on time. Or else the girl was determined to come anyway. Blast it. I could do without entertaining her for God knows how long. We never liked each other.'

'That lady outside is Beatrice Ashford?' asked Hettie.

'Yes, of course it is. Come, we shall await her.'

Hettie had heard much of Miss Ashford from her mistress – and she had held a fascination for her long before, since Beatrice had been present at Hettie's birth and had had a love affair with Evan's older brother, Owen. As she had assured Benjamina, Hettie had written to Miss Ashford informing her of Mrs King's death, and Mr Steadman too had written, explaining about the change to Mrs King's will. But now Hettie was secretly pleased that it seemed both letters had not arrived in time, as Beatrice cut a romantic figure and she was eager to meet her.

Normally, visitors would be greeted by the butler and brought into the sitting room, but Hettie was not as interested in custom at that moment as in meeting Miss Beatrice Ashford. She went straight out of the front door herself, to find Busby greeting Miss Ashford. Busby turned in surprise to see the lady of the house approaching them across the driveway, but when Hettie told him she would take care of it, he took his leave.

Miss Ashford look tired and yet so handsome, her brown eyes and brown hair shining in the April sun. She looked curiously at Hettie and raised her eyebrows.

'Miss Ashford?' said Hettie. She did not know whether to hold out her hand or curtsey, but she had heard so much about Beatrice from her mistress that she felt like they were old friends already.

'Yes,' she replied, hesitantly, her face tired and slightly confused. 'And you are?'

'I'm Hettie Jones.'

Now Miss Ashford looked positively shocked. 'Are you really? Little Hettie Jones? Why, you're all grown up!'

She had a tinge of a foreign accent about her voice. It might be the American influence, but she'd also been told Beatrice had been raised in France, so maybe it was a mixture of both.

Hettie replied, 'Well, yes, I reckon I am! I'll be eighteen in a couple of months.'

'My great-grandmother told me in her letter that you were now her maid, which astonished and delighted me. I am also most eager to see her. How is she?'

'Miss Ashford, I am so sorry to be giving you bad news, but Mrs King passed away back in February.'

Beatrice's eyes dimmed and she nodded her head. 'I suspected as much. I came as soon as I could, but I was not sure if I would make it in time.'

'I wrote to tell you, and so did the family solicitor, Mr Steadman, but I think the letters must've arrived after you left. I am truly sorry you've been put to all this bother of coming, only to find . . . Well, I am sorry.'

'Please, do not apologise. It is not of your doing.'

'You'll stay with us a while, though, Miss Ashford? Come in, please.'

Beatrice did look weary and nodded firmly. 'I would love to stay. And to get to know you, Hettie.'

They crossed the driveway, and Beatrice stopped just before the front door. 'I suppose Benjamina is still in residence.' This was said with a slight grimace, which gave Hettie a thrill. It seemed she might just have a supporter in her ongoing war against Benjamina.

'Yes, she is. She now runs all of the King businesses.'

'Indeed,' said Beatrice thoughtfully. 'Hettie, I hope you don't mind me asking, but I cannot help but notice you are not dressed in a maid's uniform. Can you explain to me what has changed in your situation?'

Hettie felt a slight dig of shame. Perhaps she was still an interloper, dressed as a rich lady but still a poor girl inside. But she knew that Miss Ashford approved of such things as poor folk bettering themselves; her mistress had told her all about Beatrice's kind ways.

'That's what the solicitor wrote to you about. Mrs King left her fortune to me. I know it must be a proper shock. Nobody expected it. But it is legal, I assure you. Mr Steadman the solicitor will be here soon, as we have a business meeting planned for today. I'm sure you could ask him any questions you want and have it all explained.'

Beatrice stared at her in amazement, the O of her mouth expanding into a delighted smile. 'Why, my dear! This is most welcome news! Good old Queenie! What a marvellous final gesture!'

To hear Beatrice's approval was much more than Hettie could have hoped for. She had worried that Beatrice might argue with it, as the old will had mentioned that if she changed her mind about renouncing the King fortune, she could inherit everything. But she seemed to have no interest in that whatsoever.

'Really? You dunna mind? I mean to say, you do not mind, miss?'

Beatrice took Hettie's hand and held it between her own. 'Firstly, never apologise for speaking in the way you were raised. To hear the Shropshire dialect again after all these years gladdens my heart.' At this, her eyes filled and she glanced round at the house. 'And secondly, many years ago, when I first left Ironbridge, I wrote to my great-grandmother and asked her to look out for you and others like you. I'm thrilled to hear that she took my advice to heart. To think, little Hettie Jones is the sole heir of the King fortune. It's a stroke of genius. Well done, Queenie!'

Beatrice laughed, yet the tears were falling down her cheeks now.

'Oh, Miss Ashford, I dunna know what to say. You are as kind and beautiful as my mistress said you were, even more so. I know we dunna know each other, but I am proper glad you're here. It's . . . been hard, miss. So hard these past weeks.'

Beatrice retrieved a handkerchief from her pocket and dabbed her eyes. 'I imagine that Benjamina has been appalled to be disinherited. I am sure she has not made things easy for you. But I am here now. And we will talk of many things. And you will stop with this "Miss Ashford" and so forth. You shall call me Beatrice.'

'All right, I will!' said Hettie. 'Now, you mun be tired and needing of rest. Come in, do.'

Hettie watched as Beatrice and Benjamina met again for the first time in years and saw there was no love lost between them. They were stiff and formal with each other and both looked as if they could not wait to escape the room.

Hettie was glad her father had gone out early and had not yet returned, yet she dreaded him coming back. She was aware that Beatrice and her father had known each other back in the old days, and didn't know what kind of reception he would give her. Those stories were all wrapped up with pain and resentment, with her father's false conviction, with Owen Malone's death. It was a heavy burden for any new friendship to bear. But Hettie felt freer of it than most, only being a baby when it had happened. She took to Beatrice immediately and was overjoyed to have her here, a reminder of her mistress and an ally against Benjamina.

Soon, the carriages began to arrive for the monthly business meeting, and Beatrice went up to her room to rest. She said she was too weary to meet anyone unknown to her, but asked Hettie to pass her regards on to Mr Steadman and thank him for writing. She would visit him in due course during her stay. She told Hettie she would stay around a week or ten days, after which she would be going on to Paris to visit old family friends. Hettie wished that Beatrice could stay forever, but was at least glad it would be a week or so.

The meeting went well, particularly as Beatrice's arrival had given Hettie such a boost that she felt more confident in this meeting and actually spoke twice, giving her approval to certain items. She could see this was infuriating to Benjamina, whose response to Beatrice's arrival was clearly severe displeasure.

Afterwards, Steadman congratulated Hettie on her success at the meeting. Beatrice slept in her room all afternoon, then came down for some afternoon tea. Benjamina took it in her rooms as usual, leaving Beatrice and Hettie alone together.

What a delight it was to have a female companion to talk to, other than her dear Kezia. Beatrice told her stories of America, of her work there as a journalist, of the fact she had decided not to marry thus far and instead still lived with her friend Dinah, an artist, who had once been her maid. This fact fascinated Hettie. Dinah had graduated from maid to lady's companion, to now having a career in her own right, and it made Hettie feel as if she were not such a freak of nature after all. It taught her that the strict lines of separation between the classes were not as set in stone as others would have her believe. It was freeing to think on it. In fact, everything about talking to Beatrice was freeing. Hettie felt her mind being opened wide, as if she could step out of it into a new world.

After eating substantially at afternoon tea, Hettie and Beatrice had decided to forego dinner. Hettie told the cook to only provide meals for Benjamina and her father that night, in their rooms, and she and Beatrice remained in the sitting room, where they talked into the early evening. The topic of conversation eventually turned to Hettie's father.

'He lives here with me,' she told Beatrice. 'But he's out just now.'

'Ah, Adam Jones.' Beatrice nodded thoughtfully.

Hettie wondered whether to keep his drinking quiet for the moment, but she was worried how Beatrice would react if he came home appallingly drunk, as he sometimes did. He wouldn't know they had a visitor, of course, so would not think to curb his behaviour.

'I mun tell you that he is not the man you once knew. The years havna been kind to him. The time in Australia broke his body and nearly his spirit. And then, once he came home, the demon drink has taken him and he canna escape its clutches. I do what I can to discourage but I am afraid to say he is a heavy drinker, and it pains me every day.'

'I am sorry to hear it, though considering his experiences, I suppose one could say it is understandable, though selfish. He should be supporting you, Hettie, not causing you more problems. I must be honest and say that I have complicated feelings towards your father. I do believe he was innocent of the charge of arson made against him. Queenie at least did what she could to lessen his punishment, and indeed saved his life – but he was there that night when . . . the fire happened. And some say he should not have been and that he should have protected Owen Malone . . . who died, as well as my mother, of course.'

'It must've been awful,' said Hettie quietly. All of these events took place so long ago, before her memory began, but she saw how such happenings scored their place deeply into family history and remained a scar upon the memories of others. 'Do you mind me asking, what was Owen like? I grew up with his family after my mother died, but Owen was gone when I were a babby. They never talk about him. I think it's because it's too painful for them. I've seen Anny's eyes fill up just at the mention of his name.'

Then Hettie was surprised to see that Beatrice's eyes were full of tears, too.

'Oh, I'm so sorry! I've caused you great upset. I'm a fool.'

'Oh, no, not at all. It is nearly twenty years ago, give or take a year or two. I really should be able to think of him now without blubbing. But it is being here with you, in this place. The memories are crowding in. I do feel somewhat overcome by them at times. But I am fine, I assure you.'

'Let's speak about summat else then,' said Hettie.

'No, no. It's good to air these things. And you must be very curious about these events. They happened when you were an infant but they still play out now in your adult life.' Beatrice smiled. 'Owen Malone was a good person, the best person I ever knew, I think. And so handsome. My, he was a fine-looking man. And I loved him. I loved him very much. I wanted to build a life with him. You know yourself the barriers that are in place even today for those from different classes. In fact, you are living it yourself, at this moment! So, you will know that the odds were utterly against us. But love knows no barriers and will range freely, where it will. I lost him and I lost my mother in that fire. It created a deep hollow in me that took years to fill, with work, with friendship and with a new life. Oh, it is strange to be back here, haunted as it is by the past. I am glad to see it again. It seems smaller, somehow than it has been in my memory. I'll visit the graves tomorrow. And I'm so glad to have met you, Hettie. Perhaps knowing you and being back here will help to exorcise those ghosts a little, who knows.'

'We both lost our mothers, then,' said Hettie. It had slipped out without her meaning it to. It was a thought that became words. She looked swiftly up at Beatrice to make sure she hadn't been too forward to say it.

'Yes, so I heard from Queenie. I am sorry to hear about your mother. I met her twice and she was a good, strong, fearless woman. And you have certainly inherited her beauty, especially those magnetic green eyes of yours, Hettie. I'm sure you're the belle of Ironbridge now and the young men will be swarming round soon.'

'I mun say, I canna think what it must be like to lose the man you love. I'm proper sorry it happened to you.'

'Is there not a special young man in your life, Hettie?' said Beatrice, smiling.

Hettie thought of Evan and Laurence Maxwell Ripley in the same moment. She had sometimes thought recently that now she was a lady, she should write to Mr Ripley and inform him. But every time she thought of doing so, she was crippled by embarrassment. How would he view her now? With fascination as an object of study, or as an eligible young woman? Was it even proper to write to him? The rules of propriety confused her. She kept putting it off, aware too that she felt guilty for even considering another man when she thought of Evan. She knew some part of her loved him, but it was now more complicated than ever considering her new position in society. Hearing Beatrice talk of her love for Evan's brother brought her own feelings for Evan to the surface and she missed him with a twinge in her heart, like a deep hunger. But would he want to see her now? Would he judge her harshly in her finery? She looked down at the yellow bow on her bodice and wondered if he'd hate it and say it was foolish, or think her prettier than ever.

She did not know Beatrice well enough yet to explain any of this, so she simply replied, 'No, not yet.'

At that moment, Hettie heard her father arrive home. Her throat felt tight as he began arguing with Busby in the hall. When he'd first moved in, he'd made a big show of treating the servants as equals, but this soon dissolved into them becoming scapegoats for his changing moods. And it sounded as if his mood tonight was a bad one.

'That'll be my father. I'll just go and see what is vexing him. I'm sure it's nothing.'

Beatrice smiled at her, but her eyebrows showed she was perturbed by the noise.

Hettie rushed out into the hall to find her father remonstrating with Busby about his hat. Apparently the butler had taken it roughly from him.

'Father,' said Hettie and put her hand on his arm, trying to keep her voice sweet. 'We've a visitor. Please, calm yourself.'

'What visitor?' he said. He was not as drunk as he could be. He was able to stand up straight, talk coherently and walk. But he was in a foul mood.

'Beatrice Ashford, come all the way from America. She's a lovely person, Father.'

'Beatrice . . . what, the King girl?'

'Mrs King's great-granddaughter. Maybe you're tired and you'd like to meet her tomorrow. Maybe you'd like to take your dinner in your room. We inna having ours now, you see, as we had a big tea earlier. So, would you like to go upstairs now, Father?'

'No, I would not. I would like to see this King girl. What's she doing back here after all these years?'

'I told you that before. Mrs King wrote to her before she went, urging Miss Ashford to visit before she died.

But she's got here too late, of course. Father, surely you'd rather . . .'

But her father was striding forward to the sitting room and it was too late to try and stop him now.

'Miss Ashford,' Hettie heard him say, as she came in behind him to watch things unfurl.

'Mr Jones,' she said and stood, offering her hand for him to shake in manly fashion. He looked awkwardly at it for a moment, then decided to shake it. His face showed his begrudging respect for such a move.

He flicked his coat-tails back and sat down heavily on the settee opposite Beatrice.

'It's been nearly twenty year,' he said.

'It has,' said Beatrice.

'And you look so much the same as the last time I saw you. It puts me to shame!'

'You are too kind,' said Beatrice, smiling gently. 'I have aged and yet I would recognise you anywhere, Mr Jones.'

'You are the one being kind now. I am a wreck of a man and I know it. I weathered those years on a chain gang in Australia. And since, I have been ravaged by drink – by my own hand, I'll not deny. I know I am not what I was.'

Hettie had sat down, her bustle dictating she must perch on the edge of an armchair. But she felt as if she would faint with embarrassment if her father carried on roughly like this. She wished he would vanish in a puff of smoke.

'You have suffered much,' said Beatrice. 'And I am sorry for it. But you are right that some of your suffering has been of your own making.'

'And what do you mean by that exactly?'

Hettie swallowed hard. Things were heating up between them already and she felt powerless to stop it.

'I believe that a man who has been given a second chance in life should not abuse it by drinking it into oblivion. You have a duty to your daughter to be a good father to her and help her, not drink yourself to kingdom come.'

'Well, well, if it isn't Miss High and Mighty come all the way from America to teach us foolish country folk how to live.'

'Father, please,' said Hettie, reaching out her hand towards him.

'Father, please, what?' he cried, his face reddening. 'She's insulted me and I'm meant to stand for that?'

'I speak the truth and that is all,' said Beatrice.

'Well, missy, try this truth on for size. I suppose being back here has brought back memories for you. I suppose you've been thinking on Owen Malone and your great love affair. There's summat you dunna know about all that and it's this. Owen was only ever with you for me. He worked for me, as a spy for the strikers. I told him to befriend you and win you over to our cause. He used you to get information. That's all.'

Hettie watched Beatrice's face fall. She looked down at her hands, then back up at him.

'That may be how it started. And I see now how you used his good nature to suit your own purposes. But it was not how it ended. Owen and I loved each other, that I know. You were not there in our secret meetings, you did not understand the workings of his heart. I did. And I know he loved me.'

'He was playing at it! He got carried away, is all. Dunna flatter yourself.'

'But he saved her life!' cried Hettie. 'He ran into a burning building for her!'

Her father looked shocked to hear her jump in to defend others. 'That's because he were a good lad, that's all. He'd'a done that for anyone.'

'But he did it for me!' cried Beatrice, her eyes shining with emotion. She fought to control herself, but her breathing was heavy. 'I live with his sacrifice every day of my life. Since then, I have striven to make my life worthwhile, so that his death was not meaningless. Through my writing, I work hard to bring ideas of democracy to the public, to argue for equal rights for all. But none of this will ever assuage the guilt I carry with me every day that Owen Malone gave his life so that I could live. The only thing that helps in some small part is the knowledge that he acted out of love. And nothing you say, in your petty, mean need for absolution, will ever take that away from me.'

Hettie saw her father shake his head, but he seemed a little chastised by her words. 'Well, that's not how it began, even if it ended differently. The fact remains if he hadn't gone in after you, he'd'a been here today, a fine grown man.'

Beatrice countered with, 'And there were those who say that you should never have allowed him to come that night to Southover, that you were his father's cousin by marriage and should have known better than to put him in harm's way, an innocent young man as he was. So perhaps there is blame on both sides, Mr Jones.'

Hettie felt pity for everyone involved, for the suffering of the families and the two people in this room. What a mess this feud was between the two families! How much misery it had triggered and was still causing.

In the silence that fell between them, Hettie spoke quietly but firmly. 'There are losses on both sides. I've seen it from the Malones, from my father, then from Mrs King and now from Miss Ashford. Everyone has suffered through these terrible things that have come to pass between these families: the Kings, the Woodvines, the Malones and the Joneses. But here we are, sitting together in a King house that I now own. And whatever power I have due to my inheritance, I want to end this feud and go forward into a brighter future, where old miseries are laid to rest, where new friendships are made and old ones are made like new again.'

Beatrice nodded at her and smiled. Her father sighed and looked up at her.

'You've become a poet,' he said. 'A good one. And a wise one.'

'I dunna think so, Father,' she said gently.

He clapped his hands on his knees and stood up. 'I find that I've outstayed my welcome, as usual. So I shall off to bed and sleep off this rotten mood of mine. Miss Ashford, Hettie, I take your leave. Dunna stand up. Not for me.'

And with that, he left the room and closed the door behind him.

'Beatrice, I'm so . . .' began Hettie, her voice apologetic.

'He is a good man, deep down. And he loves you more than anything in the world, Hettie. Despite his problems, he is still your father. I never knew my father, and since my mother's death, I am of course an orphan. You at least have him and he has you. Never forget that.'

Beatrice took her leave of Hettie, claiming tiredness from her journey. Hettie sat alone, cursing her bustle for making her seat so uncomfortable. She missed her old clothes. She missed Anny and Peter and the little ones. She missed Evan.

She was feeling sorry for herself and found tears building in her eyes when the door opened and Beatrice was back.

'Do you need summat?' said Hettie, standing up and walking to meet her at the door.

'No, my dear. I am fine. I just wanted to say something else to you. I am so very glad that Queenie made this decision and named you as her sole beneficiary. I think it is an act of genius.'

'Oh, that means a lot, coming from you. I wondered if you might feel . . . cheated. It should be you in Mrs King's will. Not me. I'm nobody.'

'No, my dear. I made it very clear to Queenie years ago that I wanted no part of the King fortune. It was poisoned for me by the terrible losses I suffered. And I was determined to make my own life, and I have certainly done that. So yes, it is right and proper that it should go to someone deserving. If anyone can bring these families together and help atone for the past, it is you. You're a good, kind soul, but you're also clever and determined, in a quiet, calm way, which is necessary. I was always a hothead, and that has gotten me into no end of trouble. But it won't be easy for you. You're living between two worlds now, that of the rich and that of the poor. It won't be easy. Neither side will accept you easily. But I believe you'll find your way. You will make a success of this inheritance, I am sure of it.'

'Thank you,' said Hettie. 'Your words are kind and mean so much. But it may not be mine for much longer. I havna had a chance to tell you yet, but there may be trouble ahead. Benjamina is suing to change the will, saying I made Mrs King do it and she had a weak mind.'

‘Sounds ridiculous,’ said Beatrice. ‘It will be thrown out, I’m sure.’

‘Well, it’s made me wonder whether I should leave this place and set up elsewhere. It was Benjamina’s house for years. Maybe a house in town. Maybe Southover, when it’s rebuilt.’

‘They’re rebuilding Southover?’ said Beatrice, shocked.

‘Oh yes, I’m sorry. You didna know. Mrs King ordered it last year.’

‘Such a strange idea. I think it would have been better left a ruin.’

‘We played in it as little’uns,’ said Hettie. ‘Me and Evan. That’s Owen’s brother.’

‘Did you?’

‘Sorry,’ said Hettie, suddenly realising how heartless that must sound to Beatrice, who had lost both her mother and her lover there. ‘That was a stupid thing to say.’

‘Not at all. I’m glad to think of you playing there, shooing away the old ghosts. Perhaps that’s what Queenie had in mind. Perhaps Southover is the place for you, Hettie. Once you’ve decided what you’re going to do with the rest of your life. What will that be, I wonder?’

‘Oh, Miss Beatrice, I am running to keep up with my present life, let alone make plans for the future.’

‘But one day you will. And I predict you will do something extraordinary, Hettie Jones.’

Beatrice smiled warmly at her.

Hettie hesitated. Now would be the perfect time for her to tell Beatrice the whole story: not only were they connected by their past and by Queenie's regard for them both, but they were also linked by blood: Hettie had worked it out in her head while they were talking. She was Beatrice's mother's cousin. But the thought of the good news of that connection strengthening their bond was scarred by the fact of how it happened: a product of rape. Hettie opened her mouth to say it, but faltered and stopped.

'Are you quite well, my dear?' said Beatrice.

'Oh, yes. Proper jam,' said Hettie and smiled.

'Good. Now, Hettie, I was there at your birth and believe me, heaven and earth were moved to bring you into this world. You've earnt your place in it. Now I have no doubt you will do something wonderful with your life.'

Beatrice then bade her good evening, turned and crossed the chequerboard hallway. She stopped for a moment and Hettie watched as she looked about her at the floor, reliving something perhaps. Then she shook her head and wearily mounted the stairs.

Hettie was left with a mind riddled with thorny thoughts, and yet glimmering behind these was something new and warm and comforting. Instead of seeing her origins and the inheritance as an unending series of problems, Hettie saw that her life really was open-ended now. With this money, she could do anything, for good or ill. She had the freedom of the woodland birds she'd seen fly away as she walked by. And it was Beatrice who had shown her this. She saw now that Beatrice had given her two marvellous gifts: hope and wonder.

Chapter 19

Beatrice stayed eleven days, and she and Hettie became fast friends. Beatrice showed her such kindness it gladdened her heart and gave her courage to go on. Even Hettie's father seemed to come round to her a little. He sometimes stayed at home and had dinner with them, which was a nice change. He was begrudgingly polite to Beatrice at first, then seemed to warm as the days went on.

But the day she left, he fell into a black mood once more. Hettie tried to talk with him about it, but he refused. All he would say was that her coming 'stirred up bad old memories.' Hettie had been hoping that this would help her father to heal, but it seemed to have the opposite effect. When Beatrice left, it was a terrible wrench for Hettie and she too felt saddened and downhearted. She did not want to go on alone with this strange new life.

Soon after, Hettie was on her own in the sitting room one day, reading a book of poetry she used to read to Mrs King, strange little poems by John Donne, that made her mind wander along unusual paths. She was thinking about this and feeling a little sad, when her father came in, dressed smartly and newly shaven by his valet. She hadn't seen him look so well in ages.

'Hettie, can I speak with you a little?'

'Course, Father. What is it? You look as if you've an appointment somewhere.'

'I inna going anywhere, but I wanted to look the part. For this very morning, I have made a decision and I wanted to share it with you. Seeing the Ashford girl had a bad effect on me for a while, as you know. And I am sorry for it, for my black moods. But this morning I awoke with a clear head and I had cause to think on my turnabout in fortunes and everything it meant. And I decided to turn over a new leaf. I have been self-indulgent and weak.'

'No, Father,' said Hettie, reaching out to him.

'No, no, dunna interrupt, child. It is the truth. I have been weak. And Evan Malone was right that I have been a burden to you. No, let me finish. That all ends now. I am going to embrace my good fortune – not the money, but finding you again. You're worth more to me than any heap of gold. I will give up the drink and find a useful occupation to fill my days. I dunna know what it shall be yet, but I shall use my clear head to think on it. And you will be proud of me, Hettie. That is my dearest wish.'

'Oh, Father!' she cried and threw her arms about him. How often she had wanted to hear such words from him. How many times she had rehearsed such a speech in her head, imagining that the day would come when she would hear him come into his own and change himself for the better.

In the days following, he was true to his word. He stopped drinking and got up each morning. He went for long walks and came back weary yet with a look of satisfaction on his face. The walking was good for him, anyone could see that. It was such a relief to watch her father leave the house without the fear that he would return in a terrible state. The weather matched her mood and all through April the sun shone down on the spring flowers. Everyone said how strange it was that it was the warmest they could remember for many a year.

But then, at the beginning of May, heavy rain came. It came down hard and it did not leave. It poured down solidly for days on end. At first, it was somewhat of a relief to see it, as Hettie always loved the sound of the rain and had missed it. But this rain seemed unnaturally prolonged, making the paths and roads churn with mud and become almost impassable. Her father's mood was affected by it too. Trapped in the house, he began to look depressed again. More worrying still, the river was rising and there was fear in town of flooding.

One night, the wind got up and buffeted the house. Hettie lay in bed listening to it whistling through the eaves and making the walls creak and groan. Then came a new noise, one of commotion downstairs. She got out of bed and went to her door, met there by Kezia who had awoken too. Hettie said she'd deal with it and told Kezia to go back to bed and get some sleep.

With a sinking heart, Hettie headed downstairs. She knew it must be her father. She had heard him come in like that so many nights in the past. Though Kezia was kind and never judged him, Hettie was still embarrassed by him and wished to deal with him herself. She could hear him shouting now and hurried her step down the staircase and towards the kitchen, from where the noise emanated. Her heart felt heavy in her chest, crushed by disappointment. All his fine words and long walks and lighter moods had come to nothing. He was a drunk again, and perhaps he always would be.

Then she was shocked to hear him call out a name, a name that was very dear to her.

'Evan!' he cried. 'Leave me be!'

Hettie rushed into the kitchen and found them there, Evan holding her father up, as he pushed him away, a rash of vomit down his front, remnants of it clinging to his mouth. A look passed between Hettie and Evan, a complicated look mingling shame, frustration and acceptance. Hettie took up a kitchen cloth and came to her father, wiping his mouth and trying to clean down his front. Evan took one arm and she the other. The butler Busby and her father's valet, Towers, appeared on the stairs and Hettie shook her head at the butler to tell him that he was not needed. He retired, while the valet and Evan helped her father mount the stairs and stumble towards his room. He was singing an old Shropshire folksong now. Once they'd got him into his room, he seemed to come to himself and realise what was going on. As they tried to manoeuvre him onto the bed, he pushed them both away, complaining bitterly.

'I dunna need your assistance. I dunna need any of you. I survived by my wits alone in the Swan River Colony, all those years living hand to mouth in the damned desert with chains about me. And you think I need you now? A slip of a girl and a stupid servant and a village idiot?'

'Father!' cried Hettie. 'Behave yourself, I beg you. I am so sorry, Evan.'

'Dunna be sorry about him, the stupid old drunk,' said Evan, crossing his arms and shaking his head.

Towers, a tall, long-faced, sombre young man, said, 'If I may, ma'am, I shall prepare sir for his bed, shall I?'

'Get out!' yelled her father at Towers. 'I dunna require anything from the likes of you.'

Hettie was exasperated. She feared her father might strike Towers, so she whispered to him to go back to his room and said she would call him to clear up the clothes and the rest of the mess later. He left unwillingly, and Hettie turned to see her father leaning forward with his head in his hands, starting to weep. She went to him and placed her hand gently on his shoulder.

'No pity for me, my dear,' he said morosely. 'No pity for the convict. I let that boy die.'

'What boy?' she said gently, thinking of some lad in the colonies perhaps, another cryptic reference to his convict days he sometimes threw out but never explained.

'My brother,' said Evan, still standing with his arms folded. 'Is that who you're going on about, Jones, eh? My brother Owen?'

'It was all my fault,' sobbed Adam. 'I was the man. He was only a boy.'

'It was all an age ago,' said Hettie, trying to curb this conversation before it got out of hand.

'Not to my parents,' said Evan. 'It lives in them to this day, every day.'

Hettie said, 'Oh, please, now is not the time, Evan!' She tried to cajole her father into removing his waistcoat so that she could give it to Towers to clean. All his clothes were wet and muddy from the rain and his trip to the gutter, and they were soiling the bedsheets. But she'd have to deal with that tomorrow – or rather, his poor valet would. Hettie wondered if Towers would stay much longer; her father was such a handful to manage. His face was in his hands now and she couldn't wrest them free to remove his clothes. Instead, she sat down next to him and put her arm about his shoulders, as she had done many a time. It always seemed to calm him, but tonight it had the opposite effect.

'No, my dear!' he cried and flinched from her. 'No sympathy for me. I mishandled everything. The strike, the ones who starved. All my fault. Then Owen, who should never have been there, in that danger with those ruffians determined to cause trouble. Again, down to me. My own conviction was not of my doing, but it was my punishment for Owen's death. I see that now.'

'No, Father, you are too hard on yourself. We all make mistakes.'

'Him more than most,' muttered Evan.

Hettie shot him a look, which he took and looked down sheepishly.

'But, you see, my own life was ruined when Owen died. If he had lived, he would've testified for me, that I wasna part of the plot to burn the house down. He was my only salvation. I would've gone free. I would've come home. Martha may still be alive, who knows? I was out cold, on the ground. I wasna strong enough to wake up and stop him going in that house. It's all down to me. I ruined my own life.'

'Enough of this now, Father,' Hettie said and put both arms about him. 'Nothing is solved by harping on in the small hours this way, and certainly not when you are that far gone. You wonna recall a word of this in the morning. Let us get you to sleep and we shall talk it all out tomorrow.'

'I dunna wish to sleep – or rather, I wish to sleep and never wake up. I dunna wanna live further, child. I dunna wanna exist on this earth. My life is forfeit. What is the point in my living further? Even this new life, this fortune, has made no difference to me. I detest myself in my very bones. I promised you I would give up the drink. I have promised it so many times, I have forgotten how many. I am a liar and a fraud. I had purpose once. I had a cause and a wife and a child. I had a life. Now I have no life worth living. I canna mix with my old kind in town, and I wonna mix with the new kind. If I went to fine establishments, I would be laughed at and banished. I am at home nowhere. I am a nowhere sort of a person, a nothing.'

'And yet you have this gold!' cried Evan. Hettie looked up at him, shocked to hear such emotion in his voice. 'You have a daughter, mon. She loves you far more than you'll ever deserve. She is here beside you at this minute. The finest wench in all of Shropshire, in all of England. You have more money than you could ever use. And you're pissing it all away! The things I'd do with your fortune. Why, the very first thing I'd do . . . I'd . . .'

Evan looked directly at Hettie, a yearning look in his eye. But he could not finish his sentence, and instead made a noise of frustration and ran his hands roughly through his hair, leaving it sticking up on end. He turned away and rubbed his eyes.

Then Adam groaned and slumped forward. He seemed to lose consciousness for a moment. Then he came to and looked around, confused.

Hettie took the opportunity to persuade him to lie down. He did so, led like a sickly child into lying on his side. Hettie removed his muddy shoes and placed them on the floor beside the bed. He was sleeping soundly now, snoring noisily.

Then she glanced at Evan and beckoned for him to follow her in leaving the room.

She closed the door behind them and turned to Evan. 'Come to the kitchen. You're drenched. I'll warm some milk up.'

'I wonna say no to that,' he said.

Downstairs, Evan seated himself at the large oak table in the centre of the room. Hettie was suddenly aware that she was dressed only in her nightgown. She knew Evan had seen her many a time in her nightclothes, but somehow it felt quite different now. She felt him watching her as she stoked up the range and put a pan of milk on to warm slowly. She sat down at the table as they waited.

'Thank you for bringing him home,' she said.

'I was out with some lads. I found him in the street. I couldna leave him there. Much as he deserved to be left in the gutter.'

'Let's not fight about that,' she said and sighed, suddenly very tired. 'Let me just say thank you and be done with it.'

Evan was leaning his chin on his fists, watching her closely. 'You've changed,' he said.

'Course I have. My life has changed.'

'In the old days, you woulda said thank'ee. But you talk different now.'

'In some ways. I felt I had to change myself to fit in. But I might'a changed my mind on that a bit.'

'How so?'

'Miss Ashford came to stay. You know who she is.'

'Arr, she inna a person the Malones like to speak of, as you well know.'

'Well, you oughta change your opinion on that, since you never met her. I spent days with her, and she is the best kind of person you could ever hope to meet. And she loved your brother with all her heart.'

Evan gave a mocking laugh.

This infuriated Hettie. It was just like him, like he had always been when they were children. Always knowing best, despite being ignorant of many of the things he professed to dismiss. 'There you are again, making fun of something you know nothing about!'

'I know all I need to know. My brother's life was taken by that woman.'

'He gave it willingly because he loved her. And she has lived ever since trying to make up for that. She is a good person and she does good things in the world. She tries to make it a better place. You shoulda seen the emotion in her, being back here, the place where she lost both of them, her mother and the man she loved. It was still raw in her, Evan. It would break your heart to see. She's never married, you know. She truly did love your brother and still does.'

Evan looked at her directly and then looked down. She knew of old this was his way of admitting she was right without actually saying it.

Then he looked up again and spoke. 'So, how did she change you then? You said you changed your mind about things when she came.'

'She said she loved to hear the Shropshire way of talking in me. Old Mrs King tried to school me out of it. My maid Kezia Clayton has taught me, too, how to smooth out the rough ways of local talk. But Beatrice loves it. She says it's our character and our soul, buried there in those local words and ways of saying things. She says never to feel forced to change myself to suit others, that they should be more accepting and choose to change their opinions on such things, more than I should change my nature.'

'Fancy talk,' said Evan and sniffed.

'Oh, you drive me to distraction,' she said and got up to check the milk. She poured it out into two mugs and sat back down, pushing his towards him roughly, so the milk slopped over the side a little.

'What are you angry at me for? A minute ago I was the hero of the hour, saving your father from certain death in the streets of Ironbridge.'

'Because you always dismiss things you dunna understand.'

'Your dear father might call me the village idiot, but you know I inna so stupid.'

'I didna call you stupid! I'd never think that of you!'

'And give me some credit, wench. I understand you perfectly about this Miss Ashford. And I'm sure she is honest and believes what she tells you. But the truth is it is easy to have such lofty principles and try to change the world when you are rich. Folk with money can afford opinions. Those without canna and never will.'

Hettie sighed and took a gulp of the warm milk. She knew he was partly right, but she was as stubborn as he was and never enjoyed admitting she might be wrong to Evan Malone. The wind was getting up, rattling the shutters and whistling down the kitchen chimney. A spattering of heavy rain lashed the window and the sound of a downpour filled the room with a smothering, rushing noise that made them sit very quietly and listen.

'Sounds like a storm,' he said. 'I'd best be off.'

'No, Evan, you mun stay. I'll show you to a room and borrow some nightclothes from Towers.'

'No thank'ee. I wonna be doing that,' he said and swigged down the last of his milk, before standing up.

'Dunna be soft-headed. It's blowing a gale out there.'

'I wonna be staying in the house of a young lady. It inna . . . seemly.'

'And when have you ever cared about what is *seemly*, Evan Malone? I know I dunna care. And you and I, we are old friends. And that is enough reason for me to offer you a bed for the night in my house when there is a storm a-raging outside.'

'Friends? Is that all I am to you?' he said, glaring down at her.

'*All*?' Hettie stood up too now. She wouldn't have him leaning over her like that. 'Is that *all* you are? A friend is worth more than gold. A friend is what I need. I had no idea how precious a friend was until I had none.'

'But Hettie,' he said, his face changing now, his eyes burning, 'I want to be so much more than that. Surely you know . . . my regard for you . . . Hettie, you offer me a bed in your house . . . when there is only one bed I wish to have with you.'

At that moment, something crashed upstairs. Then a bang. A sound like the front door opening and being blown back on its hinges. Hettie moved first and Evan followed her. Up the stairs to the hallway they went and found the side table that held the plate for visitors' cards overturned, the plate smashed. And her father's coat was discarded on the doorstep, one arm turned inside out, as if he'd struggled to put it on and abandoned it.

'I'll look outside. You check he's not upstairs,' said Evan. He stepped over the coat quickly and went out into the rain.

Hettie took the stairs two at a time and burst into his room. Her father was gone, his shoes still beside the bed. He'd gone out into the storm without shoes or coat. She went to wake up Towers to ask for his help, explaining that his master was gone. He said he'd get dressed and join her directly. Next Hettie went to her room, pulled on some warm bloomers, stockings and boots. Kezia came and gave her a woollen dress of her own to keep warm, which she threw on over her nightdress. Then she rushed downstairs and retrieved her cloak and bonnet from the cloakroom, tying the bonnet tight onto her head to save it blowing away in the gale. Busby was up and asking how he could assist her. When she told him what had happened, he went to get dressed too.

She ran outside and called, 'Father! Father!' but her voice was lost in the wind. Then she called for Evan, but there was no sign of him either.

Soon, Busby and Towers joined her. They agreed to split and go in three separate directions, though the two men both said she shouldn't be out and they would take care of it. She wouldn't have that, and instead went off in the direction of the woodland path towards town. Evan appeared along it and ran to her.

'Any sign?' she shouted in the wind.

'No, he's proper vanished. Get yourself home.'

She shook her head violently and went forward. He grabbed her arm and shouted, 'Go home, wench!'

But she wasn't having any of that and wrested her arm free, running forward on the path, calling, 'Father! Father!' as she went.

Evan came up behind her and joined the call. Wind-battered trees waved violently in the gale. Just ahead, a branch was torn from its tree and crashed across the path. Evan stopped her again and held her arms fast so she could not proceed.

'It's not safe!' he yelled. 'I'm taking you home.'

Hettie saw the branch whipped up by the wind and smash into another tree. He was right. It certainly was not safe on this path. She nodded and back they went towards the house. All around them, the trees whipped back and forth as if possessed by demons and the wind howled through them. The rain lashed into their faces, almost blinding them by the time they reached the front door.

Inside they went and Hettie rubbed her face with her cloak so she could see. She turned to tell Evan they should call back Busby and Towers, as it wasn't safe for them either – but Evan had already gone back out into the storm.

She could not stop him now. She went to the kitchen to find the cook and kitchen maid up with the house-keeper, preparing a hot breakfast for the men when they returned. Hettie stayed with them. They told her to go, that all was in hand, but she could not bear to. Kezia came and stayed too, all of them bustling around the table as Hettie and Kezia sat and she told her what had happened with her father.

Since Hettie had become mistress, relations with the servants, though cold at first, had eased. She had proved to be a kind and thoughtful mistress, and everyone had warmed to her – except Brooks, the young dark-haired maid who had bullied her at first, and who was now Benjamina's lady's maid. Sitting at the kitchen table, listening to the gossip of the servants and drinking hot, sweet tea prepared by the cook, Hettie felt she would rather be with these fine folk than anybody else while she waited and worried herself sick about her father.

'I fear he will try to harm himself,' she said to Kezia in a low voice.

'He is most likely asleep under a bush and will come to by morning,' said Kezia, but her voice didn't sound convinced and Hettie found little comfort in it.

After an hour or so, they heard the servants' door open in the hallway along from the kitchen and Hettie rushed out to see Busby, Towers and Evan appear. Behind them came no one. Her father was not there.

'I brought these fellows home,' said Evan. 'It's too dangerous out there.'

Hettie agreed and knew it was unfair to ask any of these men to risk their lives further for her father.

'Then I mun go,' she said and stood up.

There was a universal cry of 'No!' Busby told her that she should absolutely not, that her father would find a place to rest and come home in the morning, and the housekeeper and the others agreed. Nobody could convince her this was the case, but she soon found that none of these good people would let her go alone, and she didn't want them in danger either.

Evan accepted the offer of a bed for the night, but not in the guest room. He agreed to sleep on Towers's floor and that was that. Towers arranged fresh clothes for him. The men ate the breakfast of bacon and eggs the cook had prepared first, then everyone trooped up to bed. Hettie bid all good night and went to her room in weary anxiety.

Kezia wanted to fuss over her and sort her damp clothes, but Hettie sent her to bed too. She could sort herself this one time. She became her own lady's maid, removing her clothes and towelling herself down, retrieving a fresh nightdress and wrapping herself in a shawl, as she felt shivery. She opened the curtains to watch the storm and climbed into bed. The sky was lightening, but there were no birds brave enough to sing the dawn in. Hettie leant back on the pillows but did not close her eyes. She would not sleep until her father returned, she thought. And as soon as the sky was light enough, she would get dressed and go out to continue the search.

But her body had other ideas and before she realised it she was fast asleep.

When she awoke, the sky outside was grey, the rain had stopped and the wind had died down. She leapt out of bed and went straight to her father's room. His bed was empty, the room unchanged since she had last seen him there. She knocked on Towers's door and waited. No answer. When she looked in, she saw that both Towers and Evan were gone. They must be out continuing the search.

She went to find Busby and discovered he was gone too. She was descending the stairs to the chequerboard hallway to ask the housekeeper if she had seen the men go, when she heard the front door handle squeak. She turned to see Evan on the doorstep, his cap in his hand, waiting to come in. She knew he wouldn't normally give a damn about ceremony and would walk straight over any rich man's threshold, just to make a point. And especially hers. But he just stood there, his eyes wide and his face white.

'What is it?' she asked as she approached him. 'Evan?'

But all he could do was shake his head. His eyes were filled with pity.

'Tell me.' Her whole body turned cold as ice. She felt as if she were made of glass. One shove and she would fall over and smash into a thousand pieces.

'We found him,' he said. 'Too late.'

'What? Too late for what?'

She could hear the words coming from her mouth, but she had no control over them. She knew how pointless they were.

'The river flooded,' said Evan. 'Half the town's been out escaping from their houses. Roads are impassable. Strewn tree limbs are all around, and other wreckage. It is a fearsome mess. Three people drowned in the flood last night. Hettie . . .'

'Was my father one of them?' she said.

But even as she said it, she knew the answer.

Chapter 20

Evan wore his best suit to the funeral. He had scrubbed and scrubbed at his face and hands to remove the coal dust. He wanted to be clean and smart for church and to show Hettie he'd made an effort, for her father, for her. A funeral service was always hard at the best of times, but to see Hettie there, her eyes red from weeping, and to know that he could not cross the church and put his arms around her . . . it was torture. But Hettie was a lady now, and thus sat alone at the front. The Malones came and took their places on the other side, where the general ordinary folk sat. Hettie had greeted everyone at the door, barely able to speak and trying to force a small smile at each person. But it was all very formal, of course. There was no room for comfort or hugs.

As he listened to the few words that were said about Adam Jones, Evan experienced a stab of guilt for the relief he felt that the man was dead. On that terrible night, he had wanted to be the one to find Adam, to deliver him safely back to Hettie. But he still felt infuriated with the man for causing Hettie all that trouble.

Once he had known Adam was dead, he had dreaded delivering the news to Hettie. She wept and wept afterwards and blamed herself. It was torment to watch her suffer like that, and Evan wished he could take that pain from her. To see her now so composed at the church, so stoic and strong, had a tremendous effect on him. He admired her more than ever and it ate away at him.

That afternoon, after the funeral, he moped about at home, stewing in his sorrows. Then, in the evening, he suddenly got up and left the house, saying he was going out to meet friends. But he took the woodland path instead without thinking about how wise the decision was, and somehow found himself at the door to the old brickmaster's house.

It was after nine o'clock on a Sunday. Would they let him see her or send him away? Evan knocked on the servants' door, hoping Busby wouldn't be the one to answer. He wasn't sure the man would let him in, even though they had bonded on the night of the storm. The man would be a stickler for the rules, he was sure, and say it was impossible for the lady of the house to be disturbed. But if a maid answered, perhaps Evan could charm her into letting him in . . .

The door opened. It was a maid. He didn't know her name but she was scowling.

'What the devil do you want this time of night?' she said.

'Urgent news for Miss Jones.'

'Give it to me, then,' said the maid, now looking self-important. 'I'm Mrs King's lady's maid and I dunna have time to be wasting on townsfolk.'

'I was told I mun deliver it in person to Miss Jones herself and Miss Jones only.'

'Concerning what?' she said, and narrowed her eyes at him.

He wanted to say *concerning none of your damned business, wench*. But charm always worked better than anger, in his limited experience.

'Concerning Miss Jones and not for you, I am sorry to say, miss.'

She squinted at him, and he smiled at her. It was not easy to find a female who didn't respond to a smile from Evan Malone. But it never did him much good. He knew the effect he had on girls, but all he did was compare each one to Hettie and find them wanting.

The maid smiled back and dropped her eyes. 'Well then, come in, if you mun. Sit at the kitchen table and I'll deliver news of your arrival to Miss Jones. But I canna think she'll see the likes of you. Even with your Sunday best on, you still reek of the pit.'

Evan had to force himself to keep the smile on his face, when all he wanted to do was slap her. He had done his very best with his suit for today's funeral, and he'd kept it on for this visit, hoping it would show him in a good light to Hettie. He wanted to remind her that he was not always caked in coal dust and could scrub up well when the occasion demanded.

He followed the maid to the kitchen, where the cook was finishing up for the night and nodded at him when he came in. They had an acquaintance now since the terrible night of Adam Jones's disappearance, and though the maid had been a pain, the rest of the house were generally quite warm towards Evan. The maid left and the cook made him a cup of tea and asked, 'What're you doing here then?'

'Message for Miss Jones,' he said.

The cook, Mrs Guest – a short, stocky, middle-aged woman with enormous forearms – winked at him. 'You're sweet on 'er,' she said and crossed her forearms over her bosom, presenting quite the formidable stance.

'Dunna be daft,' he said and took a sip of the welcome tea. 'She's like family. And anyway, she's a lady now.'

'You're still sweet on 'er. I inna blind. And Hettie Jones is good and kind, despite her new airs and graces. Any man would fall for that beauty. But you've no chance, lad. A gentleman will turn up afore long and snap her up.' Then she looked up, raised her eyebrows alarmingly and said, 'Can we help you, ma'am?'

Evan swivelled round and saw Hettie standing in the kitchen doorway. She still wore her black funeral dress from today and despite its sombre tones and her pale face, she managed to shine from it, her green eyes dulled but still wonderful. Evan stood up.

‘Evan. Are you well? Everyone at home well?’

It gladdened his heart to hear her call it home, but he knew it was not her home any longer and had not been for a long time.

‘Yes, all is well. I came . . . with a message for you.’ He glanced at Mrs Guest, who was busying herself putting away the tea things.

‘Will you come up to the sitting room?’

Mrs Guest said, ‘I’m all done for the evening, ma’am, if you wish to talk here.’ She nodded politely at Hettie and left the room.

‘The cook dunna approve of me, I wager,’ said Evan and grinned at Hettie. He was trying to make her smile, but he realised it was a stupid thing to do on this day and he cursed himself for being so crass.

She took a seat opposite and sighed heavily. ‘Thank’ee for coming today,’ she said and managed a small smile back. Perhaps it was not such a bad idea to smile at her. He guessed she needed a smile these days.

‘Course I came. It must’ve been . . . a difficult day for you.’

She nodded and drew a hand over her eyes, dropping her head wearily. ‘What was the message?’

‘No message. I just wanted to see you.’

‘Thought so,’ she said and smiled wanly. She looked shattered.

‘It’s late. I shouldna come,’ he said. ‘What was I thinking? I’ll be going.’

'No,' she said urgently and looked up at him. 'I dunna wanna be . . . on my own here.'

'You're surrounded by folk,' he said and smiled at her again, trying to win one back from her. 'At your beck and call day and night.'

'It inna the same. They're paid to be here. They're good people, I know that. But they're not friends. Or family.'

At the word family, her voice cracked a little and she looked down again. Her eyes were brimming, but she raised her head and sniffed, using her hands to dispel the tears that threatened to spill onto her cheeks.

Evan said gently, 'You can weep if you wish.'

'If I start, I fear I shall never stop.'

How he wanted to take her and kiss those tears away. But on the night of her father's funeral? It wasn't . . . seemly. That was the only word he could find in his mind for it. He'd have to be more careful than that, if he was to win her.

'I am here,' he said, simply.

'I know. I'm so glad of it. To see a friendly face.'

Every mention she made of the word friend annoyed him. He did not want to be only her friend. But he understood now that it meant more than anything to her. It was, in its way, a high compliment.

'We will always be friends to each other, Hettie.'

She looked up at him. 'I am an orphan now. I had not thought of it until this very evening. I used to think on it much as a child, when I thought my father was dead and gone, like my mother. I hated the word orphan. It sounded so forlorn. But now I have known my father and lost him, the loss is worse somehow. I wonder sometimes if it'd been better I never knew him. And then I scold myself for my selfishness, for it meant the world to him that he found me again. That is why . . . I dunna understand . . . why . . . oh, Evan . . .'

She could not hold back the tide now. He could not hold himself back either. As she sobbed into her hands, he pushed back his chair and was round the table in a second. He crouched down and put his arms about her. She turned and sobbed into his chest, and he felt her tears on his skin, warm and sacred.

Then, she suddenly sat up and said, 'Do you think he meant to drown himself? It haunts me all day and night. I will never know if it were an accident or if he wanted to die. He said he did, that night, remember? But why, when he . . . why would he throw away his life when he had me?'

Evan wanted to take away her pain with some magic spell. It was too much. Every thought he had about Adam Jones was bad and she wouldn't want to hear that. 'Some people were not meant to live long,' was all he could think of to say at first. 'But there were two others drowned that night. It's just as likely your father was the same as them. An accident. Just an accident.'

Now that she was sitting up, he felt foolish crouching beside her. He stood up and took his seat opposite her again.

'You're right,' she said, looking for a handkerchief in her sleeve and dabbing her eyes. 'I'm sorry about all the upset. I just feel . . . so alone. So very alone.'

'Dunna be daft. You're allowed upset on this day of all days. And you inna alone. You have me and the family with you forever. We all love you and would do anything for you – you know that. We are family. We are bound together by our past, if not our blood. You know, Hettie, blood inna everything. Blood doesna matter as much as you think.'

He watched as her face changed. There came the most extraordinary expression in her eyes, something akin to fear. And shame. She looked away.

'What is it, Hettie?' He knew her so well that every glance was easy to read.

'I canna say,' she said, so quietly he could barely hear her.

'Yes, you can. And you mun say it. Summat awful has come over you. What is it?'

'It's summat I carry with me. Summat I wish I never knew. But it's such a burden. I havna told a soul. Not even my father. Or Miss Ashford.'

'But . . . why would you tell Miss Ashford?' His mind boggled. 'Whatever burden you carry, share the load with me, Hettie. I will not tell a soul either. You know that.'

She looked up and fixed him with her eyes. Those eyes that he adored, shining green, now worried him. There was true fear there.

'If I tell you, you mun promise me that you will never think on me differently. That I will always be your Hettie.'

To hear her call herself this gave him such joy that all thoughts of fear were banished for a moment. 'Course you will. You'll always be my girl!'

'I am a King.'

He frowned at her. 'Not truly. Inheriting their riches doesna make you one of 'em.'

'No, there is more. Mrs King told me afore she died. My mother was a bastard, born of rape. By Mrs King's husband, old Ralph King. He took a maid, Betsy Blaize, and put a child in her by force. That child was my mother, Martha. So, you see, I am joined by blood to the Kings. I am a King.'

As he stared into her fearful eyes, Evan felt as if the room about them tipped to one side. All his life, the name King had been impressed upon him as a wicked word, a terrible thing of monstrous proportions. He had grown up knowing that the Kings had imprisoned his mother and killed his brother.

And now, his best girl, his true love, his Hettie. She was a King? It was unthinkable. He wouldn't have it.

'It could be a lie,' he said slowly.

'Why would Mrs King have lied? What good would it do?'

'Maybe the old bitch was mad. Maybe she made it up like a story in her head.'

'She wasna mad. And she wasna a bitch. Dunna ever call her that.'

'Oh, you would defend her, being a King.'

He had not meant to say it, but Hettie always riled him. He couldn't bear it when she told him off. He always answered hotly. But it was an awful thing to say. He had spat the word *King* from his mouth as if it were bitterness on his tongue.

Hettie stood up abruptly. 'I think you better go now,' she said. She clasped her hands before her, her chin jutting out proudly.

'No, Hettie, please. I'm sorry. I didna mean to say it. I didna . . .'

'Please go,' she said. Her eyes were pleading, yet as she looked away, there was that shame again. She was ashamed of who she was and he had made it worse by insulting her. He could punch himself.

'I will, Hettie. But I mun say . . .'

'No,' she said, firmly and loudly, so much so that it shocked him. 'No more tonight. Thank'ee for coming.'

With that, she left the room, her black gown swishing along the kitchen floor as she went. No goodbye, no kind word. He had hurt her badly and he was a bloody fool.

There was nothing for it but to skulk off out of the house and walk the dark path home. But as he neared town, he couldn't face going to his house. He didn't want to be where his family was, didn't want to have to face his mother. She had an uncanny ability to read his thoughts in his face. She would know something was very wrong from just one glance at him. And he would not be able to hide it.

No, he needed something to distract him before he had to see her. He turned towards town instead and headed for his favourite tavern. He would partake of the local ale, and only then would he be ready to go home and face his mother, so drunk, he hoped, that she would not bother to question him about anything.

As he walked through Ironbridge, Evan thought for the first time in his life that his love for Hettie had changed, not by anything he or she had said or done, but by invisible forces beyond their control. Could he love a King? Should he tell his mother the truth about Hettie? Did he now look at Hettie differently, knowing her mother was a King bastard? He didn't want to think any of these things, but he couldn't help it. Blood had changed everything.

Chapter 21

'You want to get out, don't you?' said Benjamina. 'Not yet, not yet, little one.'

Benjamina fondled Drina's ears. The little dog loved a carriage ride. She would sit on Benjamina's lap and stare out of the window, tongue hanging out, absorbing the atmosphere and intense excitement of the outside world. Now the carriage had come to a halt, Drina's tail was wagging so hard her whole body was lurching from side to side. Benjamina had instructed her driver to pull in to a clearing at the edge of the woodland on a road above Ironbridge. They were parked opposite the Holy Trinity church at Coalbrookdale, the iron railings framing its long, slim grounds, beyond it the thick woodland stretching for miles, punctuated by the steaming trails of chimney smoke and other signs of industry. It was a quiet spot at this time, so early in the morning. It was thankfully cool, as the July weather that week had been particularly hot and uncomfortable. Benjamina had chosen this time of day for its coolness, but mostly to avoid people as much as possible. She did not want any passers-by to witness the meeting she was about to have.

It was not something she would ever have planned, but it had become essential. It was a necessity due to the cruel actions of others. The final straw had been the meeting with her solicitor last week. He had told her that her lawsuit ought to be dropped, that it would come to nothing, that there was no evidence and no witnesses to support her claim that Queenie was losing her mind or that Hettie Jones had inveigled her way into the old woman's affections and subsequently her will. Benjamina had argued with him for some time, but she had not persuaded him. He did not want any more part in it. She could have engaged another legal man, but she trusted his judgement and knew that if he said it was pointless, it must truly be so.

She was bitterly disappointed. And she was furious. She had come home that day determined to scream at the Jones girl, to strike her in the face, even. She did not, of course, but she pictured doing so often as they spoke to each other across the sitting room or wherever it was in the house – Jones's house now, not her own. Benjamina felt that she was no better than a lodger in her own home.

A couple of days after her meeting, the Jones girl came to her directly and said she had been speaking to her own solicitor, too, that he had given her the news that Benjamina was to cease pursuing her claim. Jones had simpered and said how glad she was, that they could move forward and put it behind them. Benjamina had smiled and nodded and agreed with the little fool. But inside, she was wracked with rage. She had gone back to her study and picked up a fountain pen, wanting to stab herself in the hand with it. It was the only thing she could think of to calm her fury, to focus on physical pain rather than her internal storm. But she did not. She had more control of herself than that. Instead, she sat at her desk for hours that day, mulling it over. If legal means would not bring her what she deserved, then she would have to circumvent the law and take matters into her own hands.

She had formulated a plan that grew into a brief note, a letter sent to this man to meet her here.

He was late and Benjamina scolded him into Drina's ear, telling her all about the silly man who kept them waiting. Finally, she heard her driver speak to someone and the carriage door opened. There he was, looking much worse than the last time she had seen him, years before. Drina barked madly at him and he looked alarmed. Benjamina calmed her down and called her driver to take Drina for a walk, so that they could talk in peace.

'Mr Troon,' she said. 'Please.' She gestured to the seat opposite her. He climbed in somewhat clumsily, for he was a man unaccustomed to riding in carriages. He had been fine-looking once, many years ago. But time and circumstance had not treated him kindly and he looked haggard now.

'Mrs King,' he said and nodded. He took off his cap and held it awkwardly in his hands. He was looking at her now, at all of her, a hungry survey of her figure. An image from nearly twenty years ago popped into her mind, of a time he had kissed her neck when they stood in the shadows behind Southover. It disgusted her now, this thought. But that had been in the times when he was the foreman at the King brickworks, often coming for meetings with Queenie and loitering about afterwards to liaise with Benjamina when she allowed it, when he was a younger man, virile and darkly handsome. Now, the thought of this ghost of a man coming anywhere near her made her feel queasy.

'Thank you for coming to meet me. I have a business opportunity for you. Would that be of interest to you?'

'It would, ma'am, yes. I've fallen on hard times since last we . . . knew each other.'

'I can see that,' she said, with some distaste.

'I wasna always this . . . shabby a man. I'm hoping you recall . . . how I used to be.'

'I do, Troon. And I can see that you are in need of a new prospect.'

'I am, Mrs King. All that business at the brickyard broke me. After the strike and that poor lad Brain. After he died, it was never the same. Then Mrs King let me go. I dunna wanna speak ill of the dead, but that wasna fair. I'd worked myself to death in that job, and she just dismissed me. Since Mrs King let me go from the brickyard all those years ago, my life has taken a terrible turn. My wife left me with our children and I've spent a spell in the workhouse. I barely saw my little'uns growing up and now they are grown they will not even speak to me in the street. My life has been cursed, ma'am. Truly cursed.'

'Well, then. Stop your complaints about the past and listen. I do have a job for you. And you're the man for it. The pay will be significant. But you may find it distasteful. It is beyond the law, you see. It is very much against the law. And afterwards, you must leave the area and never come back. But I will give you a year's wages that you would've once earnt at the brickyard. Will that be enough to persuade you?'

Troon leant forward, his eyes like saucers. 'A year's wages? A whole year, in one go?'

'Yes. That is what I said. Are you interested?'

Troon blinked. 'And it is against the law of the land?'

'It most certainly is. But if you are not capable of taking such a risk, then I shall find another who has more about him and . . .'

'No, I am your man for this, Mrs King. I am your man. Dunna deny me. For a year's wages, I'd raise a pistol at the Queen, may God forgive me for saying so, ma'am.'

Benjamina smiled and leant forward, placing her hand carefully on Troon's thigh. 'Good, Troon,' she said, in a treacly voice. 'Good man.'

He was desperate for the money and desperate for her. Yes, he would do nicely.

Chapter 22

July 1876

First class was rather different from second or third. Hettie recalled her strawberry picking railway journey with clarity: the buffeting breeze, the sooty steam and the hard seats. This time, her trip to London was characterised by comfort. Hettie's tickets, as well as those of Kezia and Mrs Elkin were all numbered and reserved, so there was no pushing and shoving to find a seat. The seats themselves were far more comfortable and the compartment had glass windows. For the first part of the trip, a gentleman lit up a cigar, which filled the small space with choking tobacco smoke, especially unbearable in the warm July weather. Mrs Elkin pointedly yet politely informed the gentleman that smoking of any sort was prohibited on the railways, but the man simply flicked his newspaper on his lap and ignored her. Kezia opened the window and everyone was glad when the man alighted at the next stop. Hettie wondered if her clothes might stink of cigars forever.

Mrs Elkin kept up a steady stream of conversation for most of the first half of the journey. For a trip of any length, an unmarried young woman such as Hettie required a chaperone, and Mrs Elkin was an old business acquaintance of Mrs King the elder. She had also once met Beatrice Ashford and extolled her virtues at length to Hettie, which Hettie was able to join in with, and they had a very pleasant conversation as they recalled Beatrice in all her ways. Mrs Elkin was a widow, her husband Edwin – a local tile manufacturer – having died ten years before. Hettie thought Mrs Elkin seemed cheery yet lonely, and she had been eager to join them for the trip, to escape her business affairs and home and get away to London for a few days.

Hettie too was eager to escape. That was the purpose of her trip, though the reason she had given to others such as Mrs Elkin was that it was a treat to celebrate her eighteenth birthday, which had recently passed uneventfully. The truth was that since the news that Benjamina's suit was unsuccessful, the atmosphere at home had been intolerable. It did not help Hettie's spirits that since telling Evan her secret about her origins, he had not visited once. She wondered if he had told anyone: his mother and father, perhaps? What would Anny make of it? Would she detest Hettie now? There had been no news from them, so Hettie did not want to visit and find out. She could not have borne seeing a look of disgust in Anny's eyes. It was bad enough when she was working for the Kings. Now she was one of them, would Anny and Peter ever accept her as the child they'd once raised?

Too many questions plagued her. Instead of facing them, Hettie simply wanted to vanish. She was miserable, stuck at home with a woman who hated her and separated by circumstance from the one person who could ever lighten her mood and truly understand her: Evan Malone. She missed him so, more than she ever had before. She could only hope that his distaste for her secret would have compelled him to keep his mouth shut and not tell a soul. Hettie certainly intended never to tell another living person.

In the second half of the journey, Mrs Elkin's late middle age caught up with her and she fell into a slumber to which the rhythm of the train played useful accompaniment, keeping her snoozing most of the rest of the way. When Hettie heard a snort of a snore from her, she glanced at Kezia and they smirked at each other, then had to cover their mouths to stop themselves giggling, lest they wake up the talkative Mrs Elkin. It was a relief to have some peace. Nobody else in the carriage wanted to converse, thank heavens, so Hettie was able to relax and look out of the window, watching the countryside roll past them.

It wasn't only Benjamina's fury and Evan's absence that she wanted to escape. It had only been two months since her father's death. The night of the storm and its aftermath was like something out of a nightmare to her now, from which she felt she had never awoken. Her father had been a worry from the moment he arrived back in her life, but he had been *her* trouble, and all that he was belonged to *her*. He was her only kin.

She was an orphan now. How she hated that word. It felt so final. She had not seen her father's body; Evan told her not to and she had acquiesced. She wanted to remember him in his best times: sitting by the fire, puffing on a pipe and telling her stories about her mother, the brickyard, her baby days, the old times . . . The years and his woes seemed to drop from him then. She saw him as he could have been, the father he once promised to be, before fate took him and ravaged him, turned him into the half-man he became.

Through it all, despite the evidence before her eyes and the faithless stance of the Malones, she had still believed that one day he would turn a corner and give up the drink for good, settle into a quiet life and become the father she'd always wanted. Instead, he was taken from her too soon and she was tortured by the feeling that if only she had sat with him that night, she could have stopped him leaving, seen him through his dark night of the soul and kept him safe. Perhaps after that, he might have improved. Perhaps she could've taken him away on a trip somewhere – a European tour perhaps, where he would not have the time or opportunity to drink so much, where he could have his eyes opened, his horizons broadened, where he could have realised there was more to the texture of the earth than the landscape of his failures. Perhaps, if only . . . these were the words that haunted her.

Thus, she had hastily planned a trip to London, to escape the house and its memories. She had no particular plan, other than to stay in a hotel recommended by Mrs Elkin and to frequent some of the smart London shops and enjoy some entertainments.

But Hettie was lying to herself. She knew that there was one particular reason she wanted to visit London and it had nothing to do with shopping or museums or parks or theatres. It was Mr Laurence Maxwell Ripley.

On arrival at the railway station, the porters swarmed around them, and they chose one to carry their luggage. Mrs Elkin was in charge of tips, and paid them generously, as the porter was civil and most helpful. He informed them that their residence while in London, The Great Western Royal Hotel, was immediately adjacent to the station, and thus they could walk. He pointed it out and allowed them to walk ahead, to spare them the embarrassment of having to walk with him.

As Hettie approached with Kezia and Mrs Elkin, she looked up in awe at the building. The hotel was a magnificent many-windowed structure, made from a caramel-coloured stone. It was admittedly stained with the sooty deposits of London, but still looked beautiful. Carriages, porters, guests and staff came and went from its doors like busy bees at a hive.

Mrs Elkin dealt with the bookings and before long, they were being shown around by another porter, this one dressed extremely smartly in the crimson and grey hotel uniform. He showed them briefly to the general coffee room on the ground floor, a long room sweeping the whole length of the building, peppered with people enjoying their drinks and snacks. On the first floor, they were shown a reading room, its walls lined with books and its table strewn with newspapers. Next was a music room furnished with a highly polished grand piano, and then they were shown a private coffee room. They were asked to follow the porter to their room along the deep-piled carpets which rendered all footsteps soundless.

Their suite was a series of rooms, one for each of the three women, with a dressing room besides, all spacious with tall ceilings and elaborate stucco work. Heavy silk curtains hung at the windows, and the main one opened on to a balcony. Outside, the view of the street gave Hettie the impression of a postcard depicting a typical London scene, with carriages and horses and omnibuses and hard-working folk going to and fro about their business. Inside the apartment, the furniture was fine and served their every need. There was a writing table, and even a sofa and armchairs for the ladies to use when they wished to escape the hubbub of London life outside. Mrs Elkin, to whom Hettie had given a substantial sum of money at the beginning of their trip in order to take care of tipping and other small bills, gave the porter a prodigious amount; she clearly felt delighted to be able to splash other people's money around.

Over the next few hours, Mrs Elkin rested in her room, while Kezia unpacked the two ladies' belongings. Hettie wanted to help but Kezia refused, as usual, so Hettie went to the writing table and took up pen and ink. Before beginning, she thought for a while about how she should frame this letter to Mr Laurence Maxwell Ripley.

Dear Sir, she began. Was that too formal? They had spoken on two occasions, and she was now a lady, after all. She put that piece of paper aside, cursing herself for the wastage, though she knew it didn't matter. *Dear Mr Ripley*, she wrote. Yes, that would do. She knew his name, after all. Why not use it?

> *You will not remember me, I'm sure. We met at the strawberry field and you gave me your card. Since then, I have had a very surprising turnabout in my fortunes. I am now an . . .*

She had no idea how to spell *heiress*. After all, it was not a word she ever thought she would need when she was learning to read and write. She thought it might start with an *a*, but after that she was lost. And she didn't want to seem like a dunce to Mr Ripley, though she felt like one.

She asked Kezia, who wasn't convinced by the *a* but couldn't think what else it would be, so Hettie went through to find Mrs Elkin supine on her bed, reading a novel. Mrs Elkin told her the correct spelling, which seemed so outlandish that Hettie doubted she could possibly know what she was talking about. But with no other authority to ask, she would have to trust her.

> *. . . I am now an heiress. I was left houses and businesses and money by my employer, Mrs King, on her death. She was very kind and wanted to see me right. As we have met before and also as I suppose I am now a lady, I wondered if we might meet for a stroll and a talk, if you think such a meeting would be seemly. I can tell you many more things about Shropshire ways for your research and so it might be a useful meeting to you, who can tell? I will be with my friend Mrs Elkin so it will be seemly. If this is not something that you wish to find time to do or if it is not in good taste or seemly or not something you desire to do for any reason, and other things I know not a lot about then . . .*

She ran out of steam and read over the last sentence, wondering where on earth she'd been going with it. She'd used *seemly* three times. But it was a good word, and so it should be used as much as possible, she thought. It summed up everything she felt she didn't know about being a lady. But how to finish this stupidly long sentence? The point was, she wanted him to be able to safely say no without fear of offending her. After all, she knew it was probably a ridiculous thing to be contacting him in the first place. It was highly likely he would have no memory of her whatsoever. He was luminously memorable to her, of course, as meeting him was a highly unusual occurrence in her life, but with his work researching women of the working classes, he must come across wenches like her daily – or like the wench she had once been, at any rate. So she wanted to ensure there was ample room for him to decline and not seem ungentlemanly. She decided to abandon that sentence and put a full stop at the end of it, as surely it was long enough now. She then added:

> *This is all very well understood and not to be questioned by myself or anyone.*

Yes, she liked that sentence. Now, it was time to finish this thing off. How to end a letter was a mystery to her, lost in the schooldays that had passed so many years before. She could hear Mrs Elkin snoring again now in the next room, so did not wish to wake her to ask. At last she decided on something which sounded appropriate without being too familiar.

Regarding,
Miss Hettie Jones
The Great Western Royal Hotel
Paddington
London.

Kezia arranged for it to be sent to the address on his card, which Hettie had always kept safe and sound and had brought with her to London. When the letter had gone, she held the card in her hand and looked upon it again. It was creased and worn, now having been handled by her on many occasions since it was first proffered to her by its owner. The thought, however unlikely, of seeing him again perhaps today or tomorrow or the day after that brought a warmth to her cheeks and made her smile.

And it had been quite a while since a thought of anything had made Hettie smile.

The following morning was to be spent in the pursuit of shopping. This was something that Hettie had never done for pleasure, only necessity. At first, she had to be persuaded by Mrs Elkin that it was worth doing at all; shopping had always been a chore to her, not something to be pursued for entertainment. Her chaperone said it would be a marvellous experience for her, as she could spend all she liked. Kezia accompanied them too, at Hettie's request, though Mrs Elkin did not see the need to bring a maid. But Hettie secretly wanted Kezia to enjoy her stay in London, too, for Kezia was much more a friend than a servant, though Hettie could not or would not explain this to the likes of Mrs Elkin. She had been well off all her life and was not a creature of two worlds, like Hettie. She would not understand.

They travelled in the carriage to Regent Street, where some of the best shops were, according to Mrs Elkin. The experience of seeing London from a carriage was vastly different from that of traversing it on foot with a basket of strawberries perched on your head. Walking through the streets made Hettie feel a part of it, but the view from the carriage removed her from the action and made it seem like a puppet show, where the passers-by were there only to furnish the scene with spectacle. Hettie tried to dispel that strange, isolated feeling of distance from these ordinary people by picking one at a time and trying to imagine where they'd been and where they were going. It made her feel more of a connection to them, something she'd felt sadly lacking since she'd become an heiress. At times she felt locked up in a castle; her situation was so removed from that of her previous life and acquaintances. She hoped that London would make her feel part of the world again, but here, in the coach she felt more removed than ever.

Hettie's favourite shop was Liberty. It was like a treasure chest full of pretty things, the likes of which she'd never seen before. Mrs Elkin told her that much of it came from far away, from the East, exotic places like Japan, of which Hettie had so little knowledge she could not even begin to imagine what life was like in such a country. Mrs Elkin, who seemed to enjoy shopping for Hettie more than Hettie did herself, encouraged her to buy some ornaments for the house, but Hettie had no idea what to choose, as everything looked so exquisite. When Mrs Elkin was engaged talking to a lady at the perfume counter, Hettie said to Kezia, 'I want to buy gifts for the Malones, for all of them. But I dunna know what to buy. What would they like from here?'

Kezia thought a moment. 'It's hard to say. Maybe some nice fabric for Anny, tobacco for Peter. Toys for the children, of course.'

'Yes, yes! You're so clever to think of it all, Kezia. But what for Evan?'

They both pondered and decided to find the other items first, while still considering Evan Malone. Hettie wanted to buy him something he would like, that would bring some pleasure to his everyday life, that he wouldn't judge her for or turn his nose up at. She couldn't think of a single thing. A hat or gloves or other item of clothing from Liberty wouldn't fit into his world and would be left on the hook or in a drawer. He didn't smoke much, unlike his father, so tobacco would not suit. It seemed impossible to buy the man a gift! She tried to think through his day at the pit and his time at home. What did he need?

'I've got it!' she told Kezia, and led her back to a part of the shop where they sold tin boxes decorated with attractive scenes. 'He can put his bait in it to keep it safe from the rats.'

'Capital idea!' said Kezia. They looked through the piles of tin boxes, discarding anything with flowers or small animals on. Everything was too feminine. But Hettie found one with a woodland scene painted on it, tall trees and a blue sky behind with cottonwool clouds. It reminded her of their walks in the woods up to Southover when they were children. There was even a hint of a river in the picture, a splash of blue twinkling in the sunshine through the trees. Yes, this was perfect. Big enough to hold his lunch yet small enough to put in his greatcoat pocket.

Hettie was thrilled with all of the gifts she'd selected for the Malones, and once she'd purchased them she turned to Kezia and said, 'Now, what would you like?'

But Kezia firmly shook her head. It was not the done thing. Hettie didn't care and insisted, and in the end, Kezia accepted a writing set with pretty paper and envelopes, to write to her mother in Staffordshire, which she did every week. Hettie was glad to think that Kezia would have a nice thing that she could use, something that would bring her a little joy every time she used it.

Money was a necessity, Hettie realised, but when you had a surfeit, it could bring little joys like these and make life easier and more pleasant. She still worried that the Malones would find her gifts extravagant and ridiculous, and she so wanted to please them. Another unpleasant thought crept into her mind, that they might think she was trying to buy their favour, especially if they now knew from Evan that she was a King. She dismissed the idea, as the gifts were purchased now. And after all, whatever they knew or thought about her, she loved them and wanted to treat them.

When they arrived back in their suite, after shopping and luncheon, Kezia came to Hettie with a letter received that morning at the hotel while they were out. She did not recognise the hand, so turned it over to see the sender had written his full name on the back. In that moment she ripped open the letter with her fingers, not waiting to use the paper knife on the writing desk that ladies were supposed to use.

Dear Miss Jones,

Why, of course I remember you. I recall our meeting and conversations with perfect clarity. To hear from you is nothing short of a miracle. I never imagined I would but I gave you my card in the small hope that one day our paths might cross again. To hear of your change in fortunes is like something from a romantic novel! I am delighted to learn of it. Nobody could deserve such luck more than you, Miss Jones. I could tell from our meetings that you are a good, hard-working person.

I would be delighted to meet with you. May I suggest the Royal Aquarium, which has only recently opened to the public? We could meet there and have a stroll around the exhibits and talk as we do so. I think this would be supremely 'seemly', a word of which you seem excessively fond! I am free tomorrow afternoon, if that suits. I look forward to seeing you again, Miss Jones, very much indeed.

Yours sincerely,
Laurence Maxwell Ripley

Further arrangements were made by letter and a plan to meet was decided upon, at the hour of three the following day. Hettie and Kezia chose her smartest mourning frock. Something about the blackness of the dress made her eyes shine more greenly than ever, Kezia said, which Hettie was pleased about, as her competition was the dark, dangerous eyes of Mr Ripley. She wanted to dazzle him as much as she knew he would dazzle her, whatever he was wearing.

Mrs Elkin was all a-flutter at the idea of meeting a gentleman, and Hettie hoped she would not take over the entire conversation with him. After some whispering with Kezia, they secretly planned that Kezia would fall behind with Mrs Elkin, pointing out things of interest and thus allowing Hettie and Mr Ripley to converse with each other with a modicum of privacy.

Arriving at the aquarium, Hettie was again astounded by the size of the buildings in London. As with the hotel, it was one of the biggest buildings she'd ever seen, though this was even more spectacular. The main hall was covered by a curved roof of glass and iron. The room was huge and long, filled with tall, exotic plants and sculptures, amongst the many water-filled glass tanks. Overwhelmed as she was by the spectacle, Hettie's eyes flicked from person to person, looking for the one person she wanted to see more than any other at this moment in time. It was the dark eyes she searched for, those eyes she had pictured so many times in her mind. She looked hurriedly about for them, amongst the many hats and bonnets that bobbed along, stopping and starting, admiring the exhibits. They had agreed to meet by the largest tank, so Hettie headed that way, passing by several smaller tanks filled with fish darting to and fro, pointed at by onlookers. Amidst the hubbub of chatter, the sound of a musical instrument sliced through, followed by others tuning their instruments, ready for a performance. She looked over and saw the musicians seated, chatting amongst themselves and playing snatches of tunes. If she had come here without the plan to meet Mr Ripley, she would have been completely taken up with the spectacle of what surrounded her. But she was intent on only one thing.

And there he was, standing in a leisurely fashion, his back to the main tank, staring at her with a gentle smile on his face. He had seen her first and waited for her to approach, watching her all the way. She had to look away. Seeing those black eyes again did something to her she couldn't explain. He took off his hat as she neared him and she saw that his hair was longer than the last time she'd seen him, curling at the sides about his ears and halfway down his neck, jet black and perfectly outlined against the water in the tank behind him. His smile grew wider and she saw his neat white teeth. He was beautiful; there was no other word for it. He was even more handsome than she recalled, and that was truly saying something.

He stepped towards her, shaking his head, smiling all the while.

'Why, Miss Jones, you are transformed.'

She didn't understand his meaning for a moment, but as he glanced over her figure, she felt a thrill akin to nothing she had felt before. Then she realised what he meant.

'Smarter than last you saw me,' she said and found she was grinning at him. Things felt so easy between them, as if they had spoken only that morning.

He leant in and said more quietly, 'To me, your fruit-picking garb was just as charming. Yet that is not what a young lady wants to hear, of course. Your dress becomes you. I am sorry to see that you are in mourning.'

'My father.'

'Ah, Miss Jones. Please accept my heartfelt condolences.'

'Thank you,' she said quietly, unable to look up at him as she said it. Those eyes made her feel like she couldn't concentrate.

'May I ask, was it a long illness?'

Hettie was about to explain about her father when Mrs Elkin came suddenly was upon them and introductions had to be made. Mr Ripley was so kind and solicitous to Mrs Elkin that she was utterly charmed.

They strolled in a three, Kezia behind, as Mr Ripley pointed out the names of some of the sculptures and the fish in some of the tanks, explaining that the larger tanks were empty as the aquarium had only been open for a few months. He teased Mrs Elkin by telling her they would be housing whales, which she believed for a moment, then collapsed into giggles when she realised what a foolish idea that was. Hettie enjoyed the chance to watch him talk and move, but she was beginning to get frustrated with her chaperone's presence. Then Mr Ripley seemed to read her mind, for he told Mrs Elkin that she looked weary and suggested she might like to be seated a while and listen to the orchestra, which was about to play. Mrs Elkin readily agreed, never refusing a chance to sit down. She agreed that Mr Ripley could show Hettie the other amusements while she was sitting down, as long as she could see them at all times.

They readily agreed, and Kezia winked at Hettie as she took a seat beside Mrs Elkin.

At last, they were alone. They were surrounded by hundreds of people, but to Hettie they all fell away, leaving only herself and this man, his hair and his eyes. They strolled slowly, not wishing to complete their circumference of the hall too quickly, for then their time alone would come to an end.

'Now we can speak of our true minds and dispense with small talk,' he said with a twinkle in his eye.

'Dunna be cheeky,' she said, and enjoyed his smile at her Shropshire way of talking.

'Oh, I can be far cheekier than that,' he said, his voice low and delicious. 'But Miss Jones, what I would like to tell you is how much more fascinating you are to me now than before. Not because you are now a lady. No, that is not it, even if that's what you were thinking. It is the process of that transformation that interests me. I see your life as that of two phases: your working phase and your leisure phase. I would love to study the differences between the two, how your daily life has altered, your physical state, even how your thoughts and feelings have changed, if you would be willing to explain such things to me.'

She loved having his full attention, but as they passed by the tanks filled with tiny marine lives, she felt a little like a lobster or limpet or some such specimen, only interesting to him as an object of study, to examine and file away. She wondered if he genuinely liked her as a person, or only as an object of curiosity. She could have given him a long speech about how much her life had changed, but instead she decided to be brutally honest.

'I am more lonely and miserable now than I've ever been in my life.'

He stopped walking. She turned and faced him, wishing she had not said it. She had meant to appear gay and joyful to him, for she assumed that was what a man like him would find attractive in a lady.

'I can see it is true, Miss Jones. There is an intense sadness about your magnificent green eyes. I am much aggrieved to hear it. Please be assured you can speak to me about your father's passing, if it would assist you.'

She looked away and continued to stroll forward and he fell into step beside her. 'My father drowned in a storm two months back.'

'Oh, I am so sorry. How terrible for you. This is awful, Miss Jones.'

'Yes, it was. He was a troubled man but he was my only family. I am alone now.'

'You are an orphan?'

'Yes.' How she hated the word.

'I am an orphan too.'

'You are?' She never imagined rich people as orphans. It often happened to poor folk. but she never imagined it with the wealthy. She supposed she had always thought of them as living charmed lives, though she knew from her own experience how wrong she'd been about that.

'Yes. My mother died when I was a small boy and I was sent away to live with an aunt. I saw little of my father, and then he died abroad the year I turned twenty. So I have been an orphan these seven years. It is a curious feeling, is it not? Like a boat without an anchor.'

'Yes, it's exactly that way. I grew up feeling like that, as my mother died when I was a little'un and then my father only came back . . .' She hesitated. She certainly did not wish to tell him that her father had returned from Australia as a former convict. '. . . from being away, and we spent a year and a half together. But then . . . I lost him.' That was how she still felt about it. *She* had lost *him*, for if she had only stayed with him that night, she would have kept him.

'I know how hard that must have been for you. I am sorely sorry to hear it. At least you have your friends to sustain you at this difficult time. I know I have relied on my own friends far too much these past years. But they don't seem to mind. They indulge me.'

'I never see my old friends now. We canna be easy with each other, like we would in the old days. And I canna make new friends, for folk look at me as an odd thing, without a place. I feel as if I live between two worlds and I canna be in either without wanting the other.'

'I see. I am ashamed of myself, Miss Jones.'

'What for?'

'When I asked you to tell about your experiences, I imagined you regaling me with amusing anecdotes about how strange it has been to discard your old ways and adopt new ones, how using the right spoon at the dinner table or negotiating the vagaries of a lady's dressing routine had flummoxed you. And that we would chortle about such things, and I would see delight in your eyes at your new situation and enjoy it with you. Now I see I was a blind fool. Of course the truth is that such a drastic change in anyone's life brings with it trauma. And my heart aches for you, Miss Jones, for the loss of your father, for the estrangement from your friends and everything sorrowful that has befallen you since we last met. Please accept my apology.'

'No need to say sorry,' she said quietly. His words had moved her very much, though she had not understood every one. But she knew he was humbled by her suffering and that was enough. 'It inna your fault, Mr Ripley.'

'Please, won't you call me Max now, as I asked you to all that time ago? If we are to be friends – it is what my friends call me.'

'I'll call you Max if you'll call me Hettie.'

'Agreed,' he said and beamed a smile, which she shyly returned. 'It is good to see you smile. I am hoping that the very least I can do is offer my friendship. If, as you say, your old friends have abandoned you . . .'

‘Oh no, not abandoned. It’s not like that.’ She thought of the Malones and particularly Evan, and wondered if perhaps it *was* like that. Had Evan abandoned her? Could he still love her now he knew who she was? Maybe he had abandoned her. Maybe it was true.

‘Of course not, I did not mean to judge harshly. Let me rephrase. If you feel that relations with your old friends are troubled and you have not yet found new friends, then let me be your new friend. In fact, I am your old new friend, as we met over a year ago, did we not? I hope you will always look upon me that way, as your new old friend or your old new friend, it matters not. The key word is friend.’

‘Yes, I need a friend more than anything in the world,’ she said and looked round at him. He was staring at her so intently that she held her breath.

‘None of my friends have your honesty, Hettie. Not only in your directness and your words. It shines from your eyes somehow. They are so clear. So beautiful. So purely and perfectly . . . green.’

By now, their circle around the hall was complete and the orchestra had just finished their last piece, the audience before them erupting into applause. Hettie had not heard a note of it, had not taken in a single thing in the aquarium. All that she saw and heard was Laurence Maxwell Ripley.

Mrs Elkin was up now and coming at them with overtures of rapture about the music and how she hoped they had enjoyed their stroll, and saying that there was now a performance of bell ringers which was not her favoured instrument, it always sounding a bit tinny to her ears, and perhaps they would be better taking a look at the aquarium's gallery room, which housed some fine art, apparently . . . and so she rattled on, while Hettie glanced up from time to time at Mr Ripley, who was not listening to a word Mrs Elkin said and instead was gazing at Hettie. She drank it in, that look, those eyes. She wanted the world to freeze in time – like the merry-go-round at Oakengates came to a halt and the passengers clambered off the galloping horses, so she wished London would stop, so she could step off with Max, take his hand and vanish into a world of their own making.

Chapter 23

August 1876

It was warm already, even at dawn. The night had been hot and sticky. Evan hadn't slept much. On the walk to work, he clutched his new bait tin in his hand. As it was August, he wasn't wearing his greatcoat to work so had to carry the tin, which invited merciless teasing from his fellow miners. Some of the others had tins, but nothing so fancy, with trees painted on it and from Liberty of London. He knew he'd be ribbed for it, but he didn't care. He wanted it with him all day in that dark place. It gave him a taste of the outdoors, of nature and of Hettie.

He still carried a torch for her, of course he did. It didn't matter that she was out of reach now. He couldn't help the way he felt; he had felt it since before he could remember. She had always been with him, in his heart. The bait tin was physical proof of it and he kept it close to him at all times underground.

When the gifts had arrived – delivered anonymously, though they all guessed they were from Hettie – there was general delight from the kids and his parents were also touched. Billy and Lily were overjoyed with their wooden train set, and Flora adored her fan decorated with pictures from somewhere far away and strange. She treasured it and kept it very safe, barely using it lest it break, instead opening it out carefully to gaze at it every day.

But they were all disappointed that Hettie hadn't visited with the gifts in person, and everyone felt her absence even more. It was nice to know she was thinking of them. But, Evan felt, why couldn't she come herself? Did she believe she was too good for them now? No, he couldn't believe that of her. She'd never be that way. Maybe she was embarrassed, about what she'd told him . . . well, he didn't want to think about that right now. Just the thought of it flushed his cheeks as he strode along the road to work, his father chatting with Socksy and Boxer behind him. He'd done something that night after he'd left her, something he wasn't proud of. But hopefully it would blow over. He brushed it aside in his mind, just as he arrived at the pit and Socksy clapped him on the back with one of his huge hands.

'That tin be proper jam! Wheresoever did you get a winsome tin like that, Scrapper?'

'Jealousy. That be your problem, Socksy. For the rats will carry your bait off, while mine'll be safe.'

He shoved it inside his shirt and wondered if he should keep using it. Did it make him look foolish? Was he indeed a fool, to still hang on thoughts of her, when she could not even bring herself to visit the family?

Maybe he should give up on her, see other girls. There were plenty around, plenty who wanted a taste of Evan Malone, he knew that. He saw it in their eyes when he caught them looking. He could have his pick. He ought to, really. But his heart wasn't in it.

He took a look over at the pit girls gathering for work. There was the odd pretty one, but none of them could hold a candle to Hettie, so what was the point? He had to snap out of it, that was for sure. Or his life would pass him by.

Then, to his surprise, his mother appeared, walking around the girls and coming towards him, looking straight at him.

'Evan!' she called him. His father turned. She was carrying a load of other people's dirty laundry to take home and she looked vexed. Angry, if truth be told. The other miners glanced around.

He walked up to his mother and his father came, too. Evan said, 'We were just about to go down. What's the fuss about?'

'I wanna word with you, Evan Malone.'

Dear Hettie,

I hope my latest letter finds you well and hearty. I have highly enjoyed our correspondence these past weeks. I hope you realise by now that I am eager to see you again. I wish to inform you that on Tuesday next I will visit Shropshire to meet with you. I will send a note upon my arrival to see if you are free to receive me at your home. If not, I will wait at my lodging until that happy moment when you send for me.

Yours in great anticipation,
Laurence Maxwell Ripley (also known as, your Max)

The day had arrived. Hettie read over the letter again, for perhaps the twentieth time since she'd received it a week before. A note had that morning come to announce that Max was staying at an Ironbridge inn. She had replied that the time was perfect, and now awaited his arrival. He had come all the way to Shropshire to see her.

Since she'd seen him in London, she had thought of little else. They had indeed been writing long letters to each other for a month and every time one arrived, she felt a thrill of excitement. But there was something there, something that clouded these happy blue skies a little: a niggling doubt. His letters were charming, interesting, full of his thoughts and ideas. But there was nothing about his feelings for her in them, only about his work and how much she could help him with it. She wondered if he was shy about sharing his feelings . . . yes, perhaps that was it. So, to hear that he was coming all this way to speak with her made her heart soar. Would he now pour his heart out to her? Would he tell her how beautiful she was, how her eyes or her hair or her figure made his heart sing? She knew it was vain to think such things, but she also knew that she wanted to hear those compliments more than anything. She knew she was interesting to him related to his work, but she wanted more, much more. She wanted to be his great love. And she was not convinced yet that she held this place in his affections, or anything like it. That he was travelling all the way from London to see her promised much excitement. Kezia had helped her pick out the perfect dress with just the right amount of bare skin about the neckline, but not too much as to be obvious.

The sound of a carriage pulling into the drive alerted her. He was here. It was time. How would her life change within the next hour or so? She felt light-headed with excitement and sick to her stomach with nerves.

'What is it, love?' said Peter to his wife.

'Evan, you have some explaining to do,' said Anny. 'One of my laundry clients just told me that the night of Adam's funeral, when you got roaring drunk, you blurted out in the tavern to all and sundry and anyone that would listen that Hettie was a King bastard. Everyone is gossiping about it, apparently. Is it true? What does it mean? What do you know? And why haven't you told us about it?'

'What's this?' said Peter. 'What does that mean – a King bastard?'

Evan felt his face burn hot as he recalled his behaviour that night. He sometimes blacked out when he got properly inebriated, but he remembered every little thing he did and said that night, as the shame ran deep. Yes, he'd been mouthing off about Hettie. He'd started on Adam, saying he didn't wish to speak ill of the dead, but it was good riddance to that waste of Shroppie air. Then he'd started on Hettie, that she was all hoity-toity now she was rich. But she had no reason to have airs, for she was a King bastard, after all. Folk had started to ask him questions about it: what did he mean? Whose bastard was Hettie Jones? He'd brushed them off and stood up to tell them all to get lost, when he tripped over and didn't remember much after that, except arriving home at some point and sleeping it off.

''Tis true. Hettie told me, the night of the funeral. Her mother Martha was born of old Ralph King, who took a maid against her will.'

'And why am I only hearing of this now, and from townsfolk, for heaven's sake? Why am I the last to know?'

'I dunna believe it,' said Peter, shocked.

'It makes sense,' said Anny. 'Explains why old Mrs King left everything to Hettie. She was her kin, or at least, kin of the Kings. But why keep it from us, lad?'

Evan heard behind him the bellman ring the bell for the miners to descend the shaft. He looked away from his mother's accusing eyes. 'I didna know how to tell you. It was shameful.'

'How is it shameful?' said Anny. 'How is it Hettie's shame what her grandparents got up to?'

Evan did not know what to say. Whatever the truth was about Hettie's origins, he knew that the shame was with him, for rejecting her for it, for blurting it out to a bunch of gossipy townsfolk and for not having the nerve to tell his parents. Anny pinpointed him with her fierce gaze and added, 'I never raised you to be judgemental, Evan.'

Then Evan heard a whistle from across the way and turned to see Boxer gesturing to him and his father.

'Come on then, lads,' shouted Boxer. 'We're the first lot down today. Look lively.'

Boxer and Socksy climbed onto the doubles to ride down to the coalface.

Peter turned and called out, 'We'll go on the next one. Set Daff and the new boys on. See you down there.'

Evan glanced back and saw Daff, now an old hand and no longer afraid as he had been last year. He helped on three new boys, so there were six riding the doubles. It was too many folk on there, really, but the boys were only small and light, so he supposed it would be all right with one more.

'Coming!' said Evan, glad of the escape. Then to his mother, who he tried never to disrespect, despite her testing him at times like these, he said, 'We'll talk about this later.'

'You stay right here, Evan,' said Anny, still fuming.

Socksy called to Evan, 'You coming or what, Scrapper?'

Kezia had brought tea, cake and sandwiches. Max sat opposite her, talking away about his work and ignoring the food. Hettie sipped at her tea, marvelling in his presence. His letters had been thrilling enough, but to see him again was almost unbearable. His eyes flashed as he described to her the chapters he was writing on the various pit women of the Black Country, Yorkshire and Lancashire, how their clothes and accents differed. It was interesting, of course, but she was eager for the conversation to turn towards her, or his feelings, or their future. Perhaps he was nervous and that made him talk so much on other subjects. Whatever it was, she was tiring of it and decided to take matters into her own hands. After all, even when she was a strawberry picker, she had been quite forward with him. Why stop now that they were equal?

'It's a proper long way from London to Ironbridge,' she said, 'so I'm wondering what's brought you all this way.'

He smiled and his eyes locked with hers. It was so very hard to look into those eyes and not want to drown in them. Now was the critical moment. What would he say next?

The banksman at the pit was a widower. His wife had died in her sleep a few months back. They had been childless and now he lived alone. When he stood at the pit head and did his work, he often thought of the happy times they'd had together, once upon a time. Nobody knew why she'd died in her sleep. It was just God's way. Even the doctor couldn't explain it, muttering something about a weak heart. He was thinking about his wife that morning when he heard Anny Malone calling to her son and husband. She was a fine-looking woman, with that red hair. But even she wasn't a patch on his Sarah.

The men were coming over, climbing onto the doubles. He needed to focus now, so he banished thoughts of his beloved from his mind and concentrated on his work. The hook and chain on the doubles had to be checked, to ensure they were secure. The chain had a ring at its end that connected to the hook. That was the crucial part of his job. He checked it and checked it again, to make certain. Yes, all was good. The doubles began to descend. He glanced back to see if that Anny Malone was still around, as he liked her red hair and it did him good to see it.

That was when it happened.

The engine man, whose job it was to lower and raise the chain, shouted out, 'Gone slack!'

Those two words were filled with horror for every man at the pit head. Something was wrong, very wrong. Everyone around rushed over and looked keenly down the shaft.

'Wind it up!' called the banksman.

'The doubles fell,' said another miner, as the chain was being wound up.

The banksman and others were shouting down the shaft, asking if anyone could hear them, if anyone was there, if they were hurt, if they were in pain. But there was no reply, only the blackness of the shaft looking back at them.

Up came the chain, with the horrifying absence of the doubles. All that appeared from the shaft was the chain and hook, with a short section of chain below it, snapped off. The doubles – and all the men it carried – were gone. The banksman, whose heart had been in his mouth until the chain was brought up, nearly fainted with relief that it had not been his fault. The hook and ring were still intact. It was the chain below this that had snapped. He'd complained to his boss only last week that it needed replacing. A new chain had been purchased but not fitted yet. Whose fault was it, then? The banksman did not have time to think about that. All he knew was that it wasn't his.

And that the men down there must be dead.

They had fallen from such a great height, taller than a clock tower.

Things moved very quickly then. An alternative doubles was brought and four miners volunteered to go down and look. As the men and boys on the broken chain had been the first on their shift, there would be nobody already down there to help them.

A miner said, 'Sure these men are safe to go down? Is the chain weak? Will it hold? There could be four more men dead.'

But the banksman and others said the upper chain was good. It was the chain connected to the doubles that had snapped. Four men climbed aboard the doubles. They were given candles and sent down the shaft. All at the pit head were grim with grief. The banksman was too, but it was tinged with guilt that he had been thinking mostly of his own actions not being the cause of the tragedy. How he wished his Sarah was still with him, so that he could go home and hold her, put his head in her lap as he used to and tell it all to her. And she would stroke his hair and listen and understand him.

'As ever, you are straight to the point with me, and so I shall come to the point with you.'

Max put down the cup of cold tea he had been holding onto for some time. Hettie steeled herself for this moment. She found herself sitting up straighter and her eyes widened, as if to drink in every last drop of his next utterance.

'Hettie, my dear, dear girl, I am in love with you. Yes, it is true. I have thought of nothing else but you since I saw you that day in London. The truth is also that I thought of you for months after I first met you in that field. The memory of you only faded slightly at that time, since I had little if not no hope whatsoever of laying eyes on you again. So to receive your note asking to meet me in London – and the news of your extraordinary change in fortunes – was an absolute delight and, dare I say it, has changed my life. Not only does it promise of joys to come, in the nature of love and marriage and family and so forth, but also in terms of my work. If you agree to be my wife, I foresee a delightful collaboration between us that would enrich my work and make it even more enlightening for the general reader, as well as profitable.'

He stopped then, picked up his cup again, took a sip of its cold contents and grimaced.

Was that it? Was that a marriage proposal? He did mention the word 'wife' in there somewhere, but had he actually asked her to marry him? It did not feel as if he had. Hettie felt deflated. She tried to formulate what she would say next, but it seemed he wasn't finished.

'What I have in mind is this: we could do a series of illustrations – or perhaps even photographs – of you in the different working woman's clothes you used to wear, that of the pit-wench and the fruit picker. We could then compare and contrast these with images of you in your finery as you are today. It would be fascinating for the general public to read your story and see your transformation. I know that this is more than merely a story. It is, of course, your life. And I know it has not been easy for you, and indeed you have suffered great loss and heartache because of it. I hope that marriage would ensure that you need never suffer again for a moment in your life. I would take care of you for the rest of your life. You need never again worry about your Shropshire businesses, as I would ensure that these are well taken care of, too. Instead, you would lead a life of leisure in London with me, with travels to Europe from time to time, dinner parties and balls and exhibitions and oh, so many things to fill your time in our great capital! There would be fun and friends galore for you in London, my darling. So yes, that is what I am offering you if you were to become my wife.'

Instead of the overwhelming excitement she should have felt at hearing a marriage proposal from Laurence Maxwell Ripley, she felt nervous, tinged with disappointment. She had thought of him often these past weeks, of course she had. She had brooded upon his dark eyes many times a day, had imagined his lips kissing hers, his arms touching her back as he embraced her. She had delighted at his letters, full of anecdote and charm. But now, this. She had wondered about his feelings for her, wondered if he saw her only as a friend, or even a curiosity, perhaps part of his work, her story being that much more interesting now it was a rags-to-riches tale. She had hoped that he felt the same desire for her as she felt for him, hoped that the looks he gave her in London that day were reciprocal and long-lasting, evidence of his regard for her and not merely a passing fancy or moment of lust.

Now she had absolute proof of it, an answer to all the questions her heart had been asking for weeks. But what was this? No joy, no excitement. She had built up so many expectations of a proposal from a man she desired that the moment itself was probably bound to fall a little short. But it was much more than that. There was something of the business arrangement about the proposal, as well as a hint of the scientist in there, too. If she married him, would he expect to share her fortune? Might he want to use it for his own work? From her conversations with Beatrice, Hettie had already been toying with the idea that she should do something more useful with the gift of wealth she had been bequeathed, and she did not know what Max would make of that. She had continued the regular donations to charity that Mrs King had begun, but she also had an inkling of what more she could do with it. Perhaps something more useful than mere money . . . some sort of organisation that would truly help people less fortunate in practical, everyday ways that were much needed. All of this was just beginning to coalesce in her mind and was far from certain. But it was something she was considering. If she married, that would not be her choice alone.

In scientific terms, his words also disturbed her. From all of her interactions with Max, she knew he was obsessed with his work. It was his one true love. Nothing was as interesting to him as his book, as yet unfinished after years of his studies. She was reminded of the animals in the aquarium, trapped and stared at, taken out of their natural environment and imprisoned for the entertainment of others.

The proposal felt as if it were not a declaration of love; instead he was laying out the terms under which she would spend the rest of her days. She would be given comfort (which she already had, being an heiress) in exchange for her worth as a subject of study. Yes, he was offering far more than that – and the potential pleasures of their companionship were attractive indeed – but there was this niggling feeling that, once she had escaped the misery of being holed up with Benjamina in this comfortable Shropshire prison of hers, she would swap it instead for a London version, complete with a charming, striking husband and all the trappings that would furnish, yet still a prison in its way. He was a handsome man, that was certain and she felt a twinge in her belly when she looked at him. He was beautiful on the outside and he seemed to admire her, but was he beautiful on the inside, too? Of this, she was less than certain.

Suddenly, she felt very hot on this sweltering August day. How much easier it was to cope with the heat in her old poor Hettie clothes, than her new rich Hettie frocks with layers of undergarments!

Hettie tried to focus. What on earth should she say to him, looking keenly at her, waiting for her response?

Then, thankfully, a knock came at the door. In walked Kezia, who Hettie was so pleased to see, saving her from having to answer Max directly. But Kezia's face showed alarm.

'What is it?' said Hettie.

'An accident at the mine. Where the Malones work.'

'Is it them? Is it Evan? Or Peter?'

'No names yet.'

Hettie started up. 'I'm going down there.'

Kezia nodded and said, 'I'll go and make arrangements for the carriage now.'

'You are leaving?' asked Max. In that moment, Hettie realised she had entirely forgotten about his presence.

'I must go, I do apologise.'

'Do you own that mine?'

'No, but I used to work there. These are my friends.'

'Then I shall come with you.'

'No!' she said sharply, then wondered why she had. 'I am sorry for that. I didna mean to snap.'

'Well, you must go. Don't worry about me. Just go and do what you need to do.' His voice was reasonable and solicitous, and she felt momentarily guilty about her own sharpness with him.

'Thank you. I will return presently.'

Hettie got up and went to fetch her hat and purse. The carriage was ready outside. She walked away from Max and did not have a single thought in her head but the lives of Evan and Peter, and the horror that they might have ended while she took tea with a London gent.

Chapter 24

Once out in the carriage, Hettie's imagination took full flight. She could picture the dead bodies of her loved ones stretched out at the pit head, all the miners and pit bank wenches standing about, heads down with sorrow.

She told herself that there were many men who worked at that mine. It could easily be someone else. She did not wish death on any of them, but she prayed in her carriage, so hard she screwed her eyes shut and clasped her lace-gloved hands tightly together, that the deaths were not Evan or Peter Malone. *Anyone but them*, she thought, *and may the Lord forgive me for that.*

She arrived at the mine and swiftly descended onto the dusty ground. There were many people milling around. The pit-wenches and the miners who would normally be hard at work on their shift were standing about in groups, talking in low tones. It seemed all work had halted for the day. This was not a King-owned mine, so Hettie had no influence here, but she noticed as she walked forward that many eyes were on her. People parted like a wave as she walked towards the pit head, where she could see the owners standing, marked out by their suits rather than working clothes. Her eyes were scanning the folk for the faces of her beloved ones, but she could not see them. As she walked closer she feared she would faint if the answer to her question involved their names.

Her old foreman spotted her and stepped in front of her, stopping her progress towards the mine owners.

'You're not needed here,' he said roughly.

She had never liked him much when he was her boss, but now she didn't work there anymore, he seemed to hate her.

'I heard some have died,' she said.

He nodded.

'Evan and Peter Malone. Were they . . . ?' She could not finish her utterance.

'Hettie,' came a voice behind her and she turned to see Anny. Hettie stared at her face, so beautiful in its familiarity. She ran towards her. Each step seemed to take an age.

The men on the doubles watched the flickering candle-light as they went down. They all guessed this would most likely be a retrieval situation, not a rescue. But you never knew for sure. It all depended how far the men fell. Perhaps they had broken limbs and had been in too much pain to call out. Maybe they had been knocked out by the fall and could not reply to the shouts above. All four men on the doubles stared down into the gloom to try and catch a glimpse of what they were facing. None of the men spoke.

As they neared the bottom of the shaft, they lifted their candles to throw light at the base. The first thing they could make out was splinters. The oak planks that lined the base of the shaft had been smashed. The remains of the doubles were half in and half out of the hole, and wrapped inside them was a pair of legs, the torso that belonged to it buried beneath the smashed planks. Everyone knew that beneath the floor of the shaft was a sump, where many feet of water accumulated. They could see now that all of the men had smashed through the planks and must now be underwater. Only one was halfway out, but his head must be submerged. The moment they were close enough, all four men wriggled out of the doubles and leapt to the site of the accident.

Peter and Evan got there first and glanced at each other. Without saying a word, both knew the meaning of that look. They knew that if Peter had not stopped Evan from going down on the first descent, along with Socksy, Boxer, Daff and the others, it would be him in that sump, broken and drowned. It was only Peter's insistence that Evan respect his mother and finish their talk that had saved Evan from this fate. But there was no time to think on that. Who knew if one or more of the men could still be breathing?

They quickly began the grim task of lifting up the fractured planks to get to the bodies. They pulled out the doubles, and tangled with them were the top man's legs. Evan hoped against hope that once freed, perhaps the man might breathe again. It was Socksy, those huge arms trailing out of the water last as they dragged him onto the shaft floor, his face deathly pale and his hair dripping with filthy sump water.

'Put him on his front,' said Peter, who knelt down and started to push against his back rhythmically.

Evan knelt down. 'Socksy? Socksy, mon? Wake up. Wake up, mon.'

The other two were looking down into the hole between the broken floor and the sump. There was no sign of any of the other men. They must have sunk into the sump and were completely submerged. There was no question that all would be drowned, if the fall hadn't killed them first. Socksy, Boxer, Daff and three brand-new boys, their first day down the mine. All dead, in an instant.

Men above were shouting down the shaft for news.

Evan called up, 'All dead. Six dead.'

There was only silence from above.

'We'll need ropes,' said Peter, who had given up on trying to pump the water out of Socksy. 'Ropes and hooks to drag 'em all out of the sump. We'll have to go back up. We'll take Socksy.'

One of the other men stayed below, in order to be the hooker-on, in charge of supervising the connection of the hook and chain for the doubles to ride back up the shaft. Evan and the other man helped Peter take Socksy over his shoulder as he sat on the doubles, then he climbed aboard and helped his father keep Socksy's body balanced. They rose up the shaft, Socksy's drenched body dripping down into the darkness, Evan's hand aching from holding him steady on Peter's shoulder.

As they ascended, Evan felt a wave of nausea wash over him. He swallowed and screwed his eyes shut to stop himself from vomiting. He thought of his mother, whose face always calmed him down in moments of panic and realised with a shock that not only had his father unknowingly saved his life by making him stay, but his mother had too, by coming to talk to him at all. If she hadn't come to ask so urgently about Hettie, he would be dead in that sump right now. And so would his father.

He felt a cold chill on his neck so clearly, so tangibly that he turned his head to see if some spirit with icy breath was floating behind him in the gloomy shaft. He used his upper arm to wipe away from his eyes the damp hair that was plastered to his forehead. He thought, *It's as if Hettie's secret saved our lives.*

Hettie held onto Anny, not wanting to let go. Anny's embrace held years of comfort in it. Hettie was determined not to cry with relief at the news that Evan and

Peter were alive. All around her were the friends, colleagues and family of the six who had died, and her tears of relief would not go down well. As she pulled away from Anny, a look passed between them that expressed all of this and more. Being here, amongst her people, was overwhelming. She hadn't realised until this moment just how much she had missed them all.

They turned to watch the grim spectacle of the first body retrieved from the mine being brought up. Hettie saw Evan and Peter carrying the body, which was taken by other miners at the pit head and placed on the ground with infinite care. The foreman tenderly draped a jacket over the dead man's face. Hettie watched Evan and Peter climb out of the doubles and stand beside the body, shaking their heads. After that, they went down again and brought up more bodies. Hettie waited with Anny, arms linked, quiet and watchful as the grim recovery operation unfolded. Six bodies were brought up, three of them small. When the mothers and fathers of the boys arrived, their grief was dreadful, the sound of their sobbing piercing the thick summer air.

There was nothing more for Evan and Peter to do to help. Hettie watched as they looked about for Anny and then spotted Hettie beside her. Evan came first, striding towards them, Peter following wearily behind.

Evan came close to Hettie and said, 'So glad you're here.'

'I had to come,' she said. 'I had to know. I'm so happy it inna . . . I mean, I'm so sorry . . .'

She felt the tears of relief build again in her eyes and lifted her gloved hand to wipe them away. Evan's face showed signs of exhaustion and struggle, dark patches under his eyes, his hair plastered to his head, as if he'd been dunked in a dirty pond. But his eyes showed pity for her and concern for her feelings, which made her want to let those tears fall even more. As she smiled at him, Anny and Peter came closer.

'Hettie, it's good of you to come,' said Peter, smiling. Now his kindness would set her off again, but she knew she mustn't cry in front of these brave people. This was their struggle, not hers.

'I was so worried,' she said, and tried to smile back at them.

'Dunna fret,' said Peter. 'Evan is all in one piece.'

Hettie smiled at Peter, Anny and Evan in turn. She wanted to throw her arms around them all and sob with relief. But then she heard her name.

'Miss Hettie Jones. Miss Hoity-Toity.'

It was a woman's voice. She looked to see that it was Nora, her leader on the strawberry trip, standing nearby, next to Hettie's other hut mate, Edna.

'Miss King, more like,' said Edna.

'Yeah, the King *bastard*,' said Nora, spitting the words as if they tasted bad.

Hettie shot a look at Evan, who shook his head hurriedly, his pale cheeks blooming red.

'You're not wanted here, bastard,' continued Nora. 'You always thought you were better'n us. Well, now we all know. You're nothing but a bastard. A King bastard at that. Why dunna you run off back to yer mansion and leave us poor folk be?'

Hettie wanted to run. How could this be? How could Nora and Edna possibly know her secret?

'Hettie, I didna mean to,' said Evan, and she looked at him, horrified. 'I were drunk and I blurted it out at the tavern. I didna mean to. Please, Hettie.'

'Bastard!' said Nora again.

'That's quite enough of that rubbish,' said Anny, striding towards Nora with her hands on her hips. 'This is not the time and the place for any of this. And what's more, that girl is a good girl. I know because I raised her myself. It matters not where she came from, only how she acts in her time. And she is a good, kind person, as you all know. She came down here today out of concern for her loved ones, as anyone with a heart would. And you judge her. For what? For what her grandparents did scores of years ago?' Anny raised her voice and turned to address all the onlookers. 'And anyone who has a problem with Hettie Jones has a problem with me. So, anyone else like to open their stupid damned mouths to me, eh? Anyone?'

The huddles of people shifted uncomfortably. Nora turned away and marched off in the direction of the pit bank, Edna following her dutifully.

'Thank you, Anny,' said Hettie quietly.

'Come on home with us, love,' said Anny. 'Come and have a drink and a pie with us, like old times, eh?'

'Yes, I'd love that,' she said.

'Hettie, I'm so sorry,' Evan said. 'Can yer forgive me, Hettie?'

She looked up into his face, wracked by fear and worry, already exhausted by the events of the day.

'There is nothing to forgive,' she said quietly. 'What happens here is important. This is life and death. Who knows or doesna know who my grandfather is . . . well, what does it matter? I'm glad it's out now. I dunna have to worry about it no more.'

Evan and Peter had to stay at the mine, so she bid them farewell, so glad to see Evan's face smiling at her through the grime and tiredness. She told the coachman to go home, that she would send for him later. The walk back to the Malone place with Anny was wonderful, just like old times. They linked arms and Anny told her all the gossip about Flora, Billy and Lily and the scrapes they'd got into, while Hettie told her the particulars of her life, about Beatrice's visit back in May, about Benjamina's failed suit and Hettie's trip to London. But she stopped short of telling Anny about Max. She knew that Anny knew how much Evan loved her. And she loved him back, more than she loved her own self. Her crushing fear at the possibility of his death had taught her that, if nothing else.

Once back at the Malone house, the children greeted her with the most effusive hugs and whoops and cheers. How good it was to play with the feisty twins and chat with Flora about her hopes and dreams! Hettie helped Anny bake a batch of pies for the miners and then all of them went back to the mine, the twins tagging along behind, finding items of interest on the ground as they went, bringing each little thing to Hettie as a gift.

The pies were handed out and, though she received a couple of sidelong glances, Hettie was more or less ignored, as she had hoped to be. The Malones all walked home together, along with Hettie. She found herself feeling more at peace than she had in weeks, if not months, despite the horrors of the day. In fact, seeing the dead brought up from under the ground had made her feel keenly grateful for her own life and those of the ones she loved, her dear Malones.

Back at their home, they invited her to stay the night, but everyone knew it was not 'seemly', and instead Evan offered to walk her home, which she accepted gladly.

On their walk, she asked him to tell her about the accident, if he wished to do so. He said it would help him, if she didn't mind, and he told her the whole story, how they'd used hooks and ropes to secure the bodies from the sump and drag them up. She learnt the names of the men and boys who'd died. She shed a tear for them all. And as usual, Evan wanted only to comfort her.

When they arrived at the old brickmaster's house, she turned to Evan and touched his face. He stood stock still and let her do it.

'You are the best of men,' she said.

He shook his head violently. 'No, I inna. I let you down, Hettie. Badly.'

'No, you didna. I told you, I'm glad the truth is out. It were a terrible burden to carry alone. Now everyone knows, it canna hurt me no more. That's a good thing. You did me a favour, Evan, in a way.'

'I'm proper glad you feel that way. But I still know it were wrong. Thank you for being such a forgiving person. I dunna deserve it.'

'Will you come in and sit with me a while, Evan?'

He looked up at the house and down at her. 'No, I dunna think so. This be your world, Hettie. I oughta go back to mine.'

'Are you sure?' She wanted to keep looking into his blue eyes; she was beyond happy to see they still looked upon the world and were not glassy in the sump at the bottom of the mine.

'Yes. I am glad you came. To the mine. And home. We've waited for that.'

'I'm glad too. And Evan, about the mine – I want to do summat.'

'What?'

‘I want to give some money to the families of those that were lost. A gift, not charity. To see them right. And I want to pay for a memorial stone to be placed in the graveyard where they are to be laid to rest. The town should remember them and what they gave up for the mine.’

‘That is proper jam, Hettie Jones. Proper jam.’

With that, he gave her a little bow, then turned and walked away. She watched him go, the evening sun throwing shadows of the shifting trees onto the ground behind him as he disappeared along the woodland path. Then she went into the house and stood in the hallway for a moment, looking down at the black and white chequered floor.

She knew now that she would never fit into either world, the rich or the poor. They were as opposite as the black and white squares beneath her feet. She inhabited the grey area in between. It seemed an impossible place to survive, but she knew at that moment that it gave her distinct advantages, too. She could use her knowledge of the working folk and her resources of the wealthy to effect real change. She could do this small thing for the families of the miners who were lost. But she could do more, much more than that. She could use her money to do real good in the world. If she married Max, surely her future would look very different. She would be a married woman, with responsibilities to her husband. For all his interest in working women, she had no idea if Max would approve of her schemes. But if she stayed a spinster, she would always have full control over her life – and her money and the good it could do.

She looked up around her at the old brickmaster's house – Benjamina's house, as she still thought of it. It would never feel like home, and she did not want to stay in it any longer than she had to. It was time to make a decision. She had been informed recently that the building of Southover was now finished and ready to sell or occupy, whichever she preferred. Now she knew what she wanted to do. She was going to move out of this place and into Southover. It would become her home. She would arrange a meeting with Steadman and think about some organised way she could do the good in the world that she wanted to achieve. Southover would be her base, and she would use it to create something that would change the lives of needy people in the local area and, who knew, perhaps even further afield. She didn't know what yet, or how it would be shaped, but the idea was blooming in her mind. So she was the pit bank wench, the strawberry picker, the rags-to-riches girl, the daughter of Adam and Martha Jones, the King bastard. She was all these things and more, much more. She was Miss Hettie Jones, and she was going to stay that way. And now, she had a plan for her future.

Busby appeared, full of concern for his mistress and clearly eager for news from the mine. Hettie told him everything she knew and they spoke in hushed tones about those who were lost. Again Hettie felt more at home with the servants than the new class she was supposed to now be a part of.

Max! Thinking of his proposal, she suddenly remembered that she had left him to go to the mine.

'Is Mr Ripley still here?'

'No, ma'am. He left just after you did. Let me fetch the note he sent for you.'

Busby went over to the hall table and handed her the note, then gave a small bow and left. Hettie opened up the note.

My dear Hettie.

I waited for a time at the inn, but then felt it would be best to take the evening coach back to London. I am about to board it now. I will await news of your response to my proposal there. It was unfortunate that we were interrupted by such tragedy, but I am glad I managed to say what I needed to. I do hope you look upon my offer favourably. As I hope I conveyed to you, I do think we would make a marvellous team.

Yours in anticipation,
Max

She thought back to the moment he had said he'd come with her to the mine and she'd snapped at him. She hadn't had time to understand it then, but she did now.

Firstly, the pit was not his place, it was hers. Or at least, it used to be hers. Secondly, she feared he would be seen as some sort of ghoulish tourist, turning up to witness the tragedy of others. And she didn't want to be associated in any way with that. Lastly, and most importantly to Hettie, she did not want the Malones – and especially Evan – to know about Max, to even be aware of his existence. The thought of Evan and Max coming face to face was unbearable.

As she pictured this fictitious meeting, she compared the two men in her mind. Evan, tall, blond, muscular, a proud working man; Max, the small, slight, dark-eyed gent from the big city. Thinking of him again gave her that familiar lurch in her stomach. She still had a pang for him – of course she did. Could she really turn down a proposal from him, after wanting him for so long, since that day in the strawberry field? Could they be a team, as he suggested, and really make it work? But what about Evan? Wouldn't they make a better team? Could Evan accept her now she was a King, after everything he'd said?

So many questions, and no answers. Only the wash of relief that her loved ones were safe and she was thankfully alone with her thoughts once more. She ascended the stairs and fell on her bed.

Soon, she slept. It had been an exhausting day.

Chapter 25

It was a sultry September morning, the air heavy, the atmosphere stifling. A sticky, uncomfortable day. Benjamina stood at her bedroom window, waiting for the carriage to leave with Hettie inside it. There was a haze of sweat on her forehead. She was so hot, she wished she could tear all her layers of clothes off and plunge into the River Severn. But a lady would never do such a thing. And anyway, she had work to do. Today had come at last. It was the day when her plans would come to fruition.

Finally, Troon had agreed to her plan. Once he'd heard the precise nature of it, she had to raise the payment to two years' salary for him to acquiesce. No matter. Once the plan had been executed successfully, she would be independently rich. And Troon would earn his money, of that there was no doubt. He'd need a decent amount to hide afterwards, somewhere very far away. Benjamina didn't want Troon hanging around like an idiot waiting to be caught and confessing all. The fee would be worth it, in the end.

Benjamina heard footsteps outside her room. She had listened to Hettie and Clayton packing all week, ready for the move to Southover. She was delighted when Hettie had told her the plan a month back, just after that pit incident. Whatever happened, Benjamina would have her house back and the little interloper would be gone.

That morning at breakfast, Hettie had informed her that she was going over to Southover that afternoon to supervise the arrival of furniture and where it was to be placed in the house. As usual, Hettie Jones had mistaken her role and taken on activities that only a maid or servant should be doing. But the stupid young woman could not leave her lower-class origins behind. This was another reason why the girl should never have become an heiress. Benjamina remembered her own transformation from shop girl to lady of the manor. She had had to learn fast and adopt the airs and graces of a lady quickly, in order not to embarrass her new husband, Ralph King junior. She had been desperately lonely, without a soul to advise or comfort her. And she had managed it magnificently.

This one, this Jones girl, had moped about the house for months and made a mess of everything, including the death of her wastrel father. Now at least she had made a good decision: to move out. But, Benjamina reminded herself, none of that would matter after tonight. She looked down at the driveway before the house and watched the landau carriage leave, Hettie inside. Now, it was time to act.

Benjamina left her room and went to find Clayton, who she discovered in Hettie's room, cleaning one of Hettie's hats. Hettie had such crass taste in millinery that it would be an embarrassment to be seen with her, if Benjamina ever bothered to accompany her anywhere. Benjamina smirked as she thought of it. At least as a shop girl she had known about fashion and used this to her advantage when she became a rich wife. Hettie always looked like a jumped-up poor child mimicking wealth.

Clayton looked up as Benjamina entered the room without knocking. She put down the hat and brush, then stood up immediately. 'Ma'am?'

'My dear,' said Benjamina, using a term of endearment she would never normally adopt with an inferior, 'I bring news of your mother.'

Clayton looked confused. 'My mother?'

'Yes. I was outside taking the air and a boy approached the house, saying he brought news of Kezia Clayton's mother. He said that she is gravely ill in Staffordshire and that she has requested your presence as soon as possible.'

'Oh, my word! Thank you, ma'am. May I have your permission . . . ?'

'Of course, Clayton. I will arrange for transport for you to the coaching stop just outside town. I understand there is a weekly service to Staffordshire that leaves later this afternoon.'

'That is so kind of you, ma'am, but I couldn't accept . . .'

'Oh, but you can and you will, Clayton. We always look after our own in the King household. And you have been with us some years now and have always proven yourself to offer good service. Now, do go and pack a bag and I will organise your transport.'

'Thank you so very much, ma'am. May I ask, did the boy say who he was? Is he still here? I would like to reward him if I can for his kindness in bringing such a message. I can't imagine who he was or where he came from, Staffordshire being such a trip. '

'Ah no, I gave him a coin and sent him on his way.'

Benjamina knew that when Kezia arrived at her mother's house and found her hale and hearty, the falsehood would be revealed. But she relied on her position in society to be assured that nobody would believe a servant's doubts over her word, and that she could easily claim there had been a misunderstanding or even a prank of some sort and blame the phantom boy. After all, nobody could prove he did not exist.

'Thank you for that kindness, ma'am. I'll pack directly. Please, you do not need to concern yourself any further with this family matter of mine. I am so grateful for the solicitude you have already shown.'

'But I would be remiss if I did not assist any person under such circumstances. I will tell Busby to prepare the cabriolet to take you to the coaching stop. You pack your things now. No need to find me to say goodbye, my dear. I will inform Miss Jones of your departure.'

Then Benjamina gave Clayton her best approximation of a sympathetic smile and left the room.

Good, she thought. *That's the first obstacle out of the way.*

Benjamina went back to her room and rang the bell for Busby, who arrived within less than a minute. She informed him that she had decided to visit friends in Shrewsbury. She would take the barouche and would be gone for two days, taking her maid Brooks with her. She informed him also of Clayton's imminent departure and that Miss Jones would be without a maid.

'However,' she explained to Busby, 'Miss Jones has often said to me in the past that she is in no need of a lady's maid, being aware of all the accoutrements a lady requires, having once been a maid herself. I am sure she can manage without one for a day or two. May I suggest that Towers, our former valet and now footman, be assigned to be on hand to assist Miss Jones if she needs any particular jobs doing – other than dressing, of course?'

'Yes, ma'am,' said Busby, although he did look alarmed at the thought of Towers serving as lady's maid in any capacity, however temporarily. 'I will instruct

Towers accordingly. I will prepare the barouche for your departure.'

'I will be taking Drina with me, so make sure there is a blanket for her on the seat. And send Brooks to me. We need to pack for Shrewsbury.'

Her maid came, and was all a-flutter at the thought of a couple of days in the county town, away from the boredom of her usual routine. Benjamina feigned tiredness and let her fuss on, lying down and watching her plan unfold. Soon, Clayton would be gone to Staffordshire, and she would be gone to Shrewsbury. When Hettie came back from Southover later, nobody would be present in the room next to hers for the whole day and night to come. This was what Benjamina needed and it was all nicely coming to pass. This night was what all these years of struggle had been leading to, and Benjamina was delighted to be on the cusp of success at last. Tomorrow would be delicious. The first day of the rest of her life.

Drina ran in from wherever she'd been creating havoc and leapt on Benjamina's bed. The dog had cottony fluff all around her chops, suggesting she'd been destroying some item of furniture or clothing somewhere in the house.

'Good girl,' said Benjamina, and gave her a kiss on her wet nose.

In the early evening, Hettie stepped down from the carriage and thanked the coachman. She looked up at the sky, where dark grey clouds were gathering in the distance. There had been some rumbles of thunder far away as she'd been coming home, and now it looked as if the storm was heading her direction. She welcomed it in one way, as rain would hopefully dispel the humid heat that had felt stifling for days. But storms brought sadness with them, reminding her of the night of her father's passing. She associated them with melancholy.

She tried to put this from her mind as she walked towards the front door of her old house, and instead filled her head with visions of her new one. Seeing the writing desk and bookshelves being delivered, and supervising their placement in her new study was an absolute delight. This study – which she learnt had once been the site of Mrs King's office when she lived at Southover – would be Hettie's base of operations for her new endeavours. She had had meetings with Steadman these past weeks, firstly outlining her vague plans to him and then discussing possibilities for how best she could bring them about.

They had come up with the idea of a foundation, an organisation she would run from Southover that would require funding not only from her own fortune but from a wide range of donors. Steadman was delighted to be involved and gave her many ideas about how the foundation could be managed and become successful. They discussed at length which kind of recipients would be most in need. Hettie was adamant that charity must begin at home, and that the first groups of people to be helped should be Ironbridge folk and those of the locality that found themselves out of work or otherwise incapacitated, who would otherwise be forced to starve or end up in the dreaded workhouse. Money could be used to set up a hostel of some sort, or two, one for women (and their children, if they had any) and one for men. Her other concern was that of men or women who had had their lives blighted by alcoholic abuse. She wanted a safe place where people could go to save themselves from the ravages of drink, stop their drinking and recover. This could be situated in Ironbridge or another town nearby. These were her first two plans. Steadman said that was quite enough and would be very expensive as it was. Hettie had so many ideas in her head of how she could help people further, but Steadman was right. The King fortune was finite and needed to be treated carefully in order for it to be managed well and for the charitable endeavours to become successful.

For the first time since the arrival of her father in January of the year before, Hettie felt that she had some modicum of control over her life. At last, she had a purpose in this world. It felt wonderful.

Hettie was met by Busby as she came into the house. He informed her of a number of unusual events that had occurred in her absence. Firstly, Benjamina had gone to Shrewsbury, taking her maid Brooks with her. Secondly, Kezia had received a message stating that her mother was gravely ill and thus had left on the afternoon coach for Staffordshire. Apparently, Benjamina had suggested that Towers wait on Hettie in Kezia's absence. Hettie could see how worried Busby was about this last case in particular.

'Please dunna fret,' she said to Busby. 'I'll be fine without a maid for a day or so. Tell Towers I'll call on him for anything I might need, but other than that, I'll make do.'

'Yes, ma'am. Please be assured that under my watch, this household will always exceed any idea of "making do". We will always do our utmost to serve you, ma'am.'

'Oh, I know that, Busby. And I thank'ee for it. But I will be fine.'

Hettie went to her room, full of concern for her friend Kezia. When she arrived at her writing desk, she saw a note in Kezia's hand and also a letter from Max. She took up Kezia's first and read of the same particulars Busby had already told her. She decided that in the morning she would arrange for flowers and wholesome fruit to be sent to Kezia's mother's house, as well as some extra money for Kezia in case she had medical expenses.

Then she turned to Max's letter. She almost wanted to leave it unopened, for she was unsure how to face whatever it contained. She had not replied to his suggestion of marriage and had further left a subsequent letter from him unanswered. More rumbles of thunder came and she looked up at the sky, those storm clouds now closer than before. A knock came at her door and Towers appeared, looking ill at ease in his new role of lady's maid. Hettie assured him that she would most likely be in no need of him tonight, except to bring her dinner in her rooms. She didn't want to dine formally tonight downstairs, as the house would be mostly empty except for herself and the servants.

'I think it'd be a nice idea for some of the servants to have the night off. What do you think, Towers?'

'If that is what you require, ma'am?'

'Yes, it'd be good for them. I'll just need you and Busby and the cook here. Everyone else can go out or visit friends or family if they want to. I'll give you a night off another time instead, Towers.'

'Thank you, ma'am!' he said, very pleased, and she sent him off to deliver the news.

So, it would be a quiet house tonight. That suited Hettie. She had so much on her mind that she liked the idea of a mostly empty house to think in. Now it was time to open Max's letter.

My dear Hettie,

Firstly, I am concerned that a previous letter I wrote to you has perhaps not arrived, as you have not replied to it, and I am certain you would have if it had arrived. Therefore I can only assume it was lost in the post. It has been a month since my proposal and though of course it is the woman's prerogative to keep a man waiting, I must say I grow anxious at the lack of news from you. Indeed, I would say that keeping a man waiting this long is decidedly 'unseemly' – to venture a play on one of your favourite words, I seem to remember! What a funny little thing you were in that first letter you wrote to me, the new heiress. How far you have come, my dear! So, please put a gentleman out of his misery and tell me you will marry me, darling. If I hear nothing more in response to this letter, I will hereafter complain most vociferously to the postal service, which has caused me such distress. And then I will forthwith take another coach to Shropshire and press my suit in person again, hopefully not interrupted by local matters once more!

Yours in rather desperate anticipation,
Max

Hettie didn't know if he was trying to be clever, or stupid, or what he was being. The letter felt crass and unfeeling, even selfish in the extreme. Perhaps it was arrogance; a gentleman like Max had probably never had to wait for anything in his life. And a man as handsome as him had never had to wait for an answer from a woman. All she knew was that, despite his beauty, she did not possess the feeling for him she once had. On first meeting, their situations had been so different that she was in awe of him. Once she had become an heiress, their levels were more equal in society, and she had been blinded by his eyes and his hair and his skin and his frame and everything that made him irresistible.

But now, the truth of what their marriage would be – and all she would stand to lose if she went through with it – suddenly lost him his sheen. She began to see him in a new light, that of a gentleman who lived a life of leisure, whose good fortunes had always fallen into his hands. He was not a bad person. He wanted to study working women and thereby enlighten the world of the good they were doing by their hard work. But she felt she would always be an object of curiosity to him, rather than a wife. And the final nail in the coffin was that in this letter he had again teased her about her use of the word 'seemly'.

'Enough of this,' she said aloud. She did not want to be married to a man who constantly sought to remind her of her little flaws, however amusing they might be. And he could not truly understand her if he thought that mocking her speech might endear him to her. She hated the way he teased her about the word *seemly*. This annoyed her more than anything, as small and insignificant as it was. For it was Evan's word, and she felt that not only was she herself being ridiculed, but her dear Evan too. And she would not stand for that. One joke was more than enough, but to continue the joke on and on went beyond funny to something akin to scorn. All of these things could have been borne, she realised, if she really loved Max.

As the first spots of welcome rain spattered against her window pane, she took up her pen and ink to write him a letter thanking him for his kind proposal but turning it down, as she wished to remain a spinster.

But the truth was that she did not love Laurence Maxwell Ripley. She loved Evan Malone. She always had and always would. Marriage between them was impossible – she knew that – so she would remain a spinster and dedicate her life to deserving the good fortune that had been given to her.

Troon had been told to wait until the cover of darkness to approach the old brickmaster's house. As it was August, this meant waiting until eleven or twelve at night. He was already feeling sleepy at nine. He had been drinking too much those past few days, using the money Mrs King had given him as an advance. But tonight was the night she'd said and he must do the deed.

When the rain started at seven or so, it soon became heavy and the skies darkened so much that night came early. Troon left the one room he lived in and trudged through the rain to the woodland path to the old brick-master's house. He thought of his children, now living in Wales with his wife, who had left him all those years ago. Mrs King had told him he must meet her in Shrewsbury on the morrow to collect the rest of his fee and thereafter flee the country and never come back. Well, he could go to Wales first, couldn't he? How would anyone know to look for him, anyway? He could go to Wales, spend some money on his wife and children, see if his new-found wealth might encourage them to accept him again as father and husband. His children were now grown, but everyone needed money. Yes, that's what he'd do. Mrs King did not need to know.

This thought bolstered him as he slogged on through the woods, every inch of him drenched, looking up from time to time to see the lightning flash and hear the thunder rumbling about him. To be out on such a godforsaken night was foolishness, but he had a job to do and after all, the storm gave him the perfect cover. As he saw the house looming ahead in the darkness, he went into the trees to get a better look. He didn't want to be seen by someone watching the storm from a window.

Once he'd decided that nobody was present, he skirted the house at a distance and saw the back door for which he'd been given a key. He crossed over, slotted the key in the door and turned it. He opened it slowly and quietly. Thunder crashed behind him and made him flinch. As another boom came, he quickly shut the door, using the sound to mask its closing. The storm was serving him well.

He was inside the house now, and nobody would have heard a thing.

Chapter 26

Evan sat in the chair by the fireplace. The little ones were in bed, but nobody was asleep, as the storm kept them all jittery and nervous. His mother and father were at the table, sorting through a series of bills and organising their accounts for the next month. He knew he should be helping them, but his mind was filled with other things – namely Hettie, as usual.

Seeing her again recently had been an absolute tonic, especially watching her here in his home, playing with the children and helping Anny with the pies, just like old times. The only thing that had been out of place was her fancy frock. Other than that, she slotted right back into her old ways and he hadn't seen her smile and laugh so much in a long time. Walking her home, he had felt their old closeness was there again. When she'd invited him to come into her house, of course he'd been desperate to agree – but every time he was there, he felt like the hired help. It did not suit him for her to see him there, in his poor excuse for clothes. And he figured it would do her good to have him say no to her for once, so that she would think of him in his absence and perhaps call on him again.

She hadn't called on him again, though. His plan had not worked. Ever since, he had been ruminating on how to solve this conundrum. He loved Hettie, he always had. And she loved him, in her way, he was sure of that. But they lived now in two separate worlds. How could he bridge that divide, in a way that would make both of them happy?

Another crash of thunder made the children call out from their beds, so he got up and went through to comfort them. Once they were settled, he went to the kitchen window and watched the storm for a while. White sheets of lightning lit up the ground outside, rendering it bright as daylight for a split second. Evan realised its significance with a pang. The storm would remind Hettie of Adam and the night of his drowning. She'd be sitting there right now, in her house, thinking of that night, sad and utterly alone. Evan's heart ached to be with her, to comfort her. But what could he do for her, truly? He couldn't bring her father back. He could not offer her a thing. She had everything she needed, didn't she? She was an heiress, after all.

But he remembered something she once said to him, that a friend was worth more than gold, more than anything. After a lifetime of friendship, obstacles had piled up between them in this past year or so. She was a King, he was a Malone. She was rich, he was poor. But really, what did any of that matter? The one thing they had in common was their feelings for each other. And surely that was enough to declare his love for her, to marry her. He didn't want any other girl, ever. He only wanted Hettie Jones. He was sure now that she loved him back, he was sure she would be sad this night and he was sure it was the right time to go out and find her. He was going to Hettie's house and he was going to ask her to marry him.

At that moment, as the storm raged around his house, he decided that he couldn't live without her and he needed her to know it. He wanted to tell her that her relation to the Kings meant nothing for him, that he would always love her, and that they should marry and damn what people think, and damn the money! He had to be with her, on whatever terms.

'Off out,' he said, grabbing his coat and cap.

'On a night like this?' his mother cried. 'No, you're stopping in, lad.'

'I wonna be long,' he lied and opened the front door.

'Dunna be daft,' said his father. 'It's treacherous out there!'

But he was already out, slamming the door behind him. He did not want to hear their reasons why it was ridiculous. He ran away down the path before either could come after him. He glimpsed the front door open as he turned the corner onto the next path and away down into town. Now sopping wet, he went across the bridge and into the woods, on his way to the old brickmaster's house, to Hettie. His ambition to marry her kept him warm and dry in his heart. And somehow he welcomed the rain, as it seemed to wash away all his old pride and leave him fresh and clean of excuses, ready to make her his wife.

Hettie was at her writing desk, the curtain open to see the storm. When something frightened her, she'd rather see it than hide from it. She liked to have the lightning about her, as somehow it was more disturbing to hear the thunder without it. The room itself was dim, as she had only a small lamp on her desk, and without Kezia here to light the other lamps around the room, she had not bothered. She sat in a small pool of lamplight, the rest of the room shrouded in darkness.

She was trying to decide how to sign off her letter to Max. She knew now that 'Regarding' was wrong. He'd told her that in another letter. *Always correcting me*, she thought. He was probably trying to help her, by telling her what she was getting wrong. But it was another indication to her that she was making the right decision in turning him down. She didn't want a teacher for a husband. She wanted an equal, someone she felt comfortable with and could share her failures and successes with, as well as his own. She decided to sign off with *Yours sincerely*, as she knew now that it was correct when you were acquainted with someone. They were more than acquainted, of course, but she felt it was right to begin to distance herself from him. After all, she never intended to see Mr Laurence Maxwell Ripley again after this letter was sent. She would never see those dark eyes again. *Good*, she decided. They were far too dangerous.

She was folding the letter when she heard the creak of footfall behind her. She turned round swiftly to see a pair of dark eyes coming at her through the dim room. For a crazed moment, she thought it was Max, come to propose. But it was not Max. It was a man she'd never seen before and he was lunging towards her.

She went to stand up but he was upon her before she stood fully, his full weight forcing her back onto the desk. His body was sodden and she felt splashes of water land on her skin as he grappled with her. His hands were about her throat and as she twisted away from him, the single lamp was pushed to the floor and extinguished, the room thrown into utter darkness. Her hands grasped at her throat as the man's closed about them. The strength in his fingers was intense and she could feel the air being squeezed out of her.

But she was a pit girl and a strawberry picker and she'd always had the upper body strength that had kept her going through the long days of work. She called on it now and grabbed at his arms, twisting her body violently to the side, which dragged him across her as they slipped from the desk and collapsed onto the carpet.

In the moment of confusion, she tried to cry out for help, but one of his hands was on her neck again, the other hand forcing its way into her mouth, the taste and texture of his three thick fingers on her tongue gagging her with disgust and terror. He pushed himself onto her and she bit down hard on his fingers. He cried out and she yelled, 'Help me!' But the storm was raging and her voice was lost in the thunder that crashed about them. He grabbed her head with both hands, one now bleeding from her almighty bite and smashed it backwards. She felt it crunch into the lamp behind her head and a searing pain took over her consciousness.

She heard him whimper and say, 'My hand!' in a pathetic voice, but her own pain was too much and she blacked out for a moment. But her body felt him reach for her again and reacted, kicking away at him through her skirts, causing him to cry out again. It gave her enough time to scramble up, but he was coming up with her, and now he had her against the window. She was flailing her arms at him. The pain in her head and the darkness of the room rendered everything like a dream, and as in dreams, she found she could not speak or cry out.

Instead, time slowed to a crawl, as she saw a flash of lightning create his outline for a moment, his black eyes like pools of ink on his face as he threw himself towards her again, his arms outstretched. And a thought came to her that this was the last thing she would see. She would die here, now, on a stormy night, just as her father had.

There was only one light in a window of the front façade of the old brickmaster's house. Evan knew it was Hettie's room, on the right-hand side of the house, as she'd told him about it before. He smiled at the sight. It felt as if she had left a light burning for him alone. All the other rooms on this side of the house were in darkness. He guessed the kitchen would be lit at the back of the house and perhaps some of the servants' rooms, but from here it looked as though Hettie was upstairs and everyone else was out or asleep.

Then, suddenly, the light disappeared. Had she blown it out? He hadn't seen her at the window before, but now there was someone there. Not someone – two people. There were two people struggling in the window. Then he saw that it was Hettie, her head being pushed back against the glass.

Evan broke into a frantic run, the likes of which he'd never felt. His legs seemed as if they were flying off in all directions and he nearly fell flat on his face as he hurtled across the frontage to the kitchen door at the back. He threw himself at the door, not waiting to see if it was locked or to bother knocking. Someone was attacking Hettie, and no other thought was in his mind but to stop it.

He turned the handle and it opened. He nearly fell again getting across the step, so violent was his forward momentum. His legs pushed him onwards as he ran into the front hall, one dim lamp in the hallway lighting his approach as he hurtled up the stairs, taking them two at a time, and then he was on the landing and heading for Hettie's room.

He threw open the door and there they were, a hunched, dark form by the window, the man's hands around Hettie's neck as her arms slapped wildly at him. In two strides Evan was there. His fist landed heavily on the man's lower back, making him loosen his grip and reach for the site of his pain. In that moment, Hettie dropped down, and Evan landed another punch on the man's side, winding him until Evan could grab him and drag him away from Hettie, whose hands were now around her throat as she coughed and gasped. Even when he hacked the coalface with his pick, Evan had never felt such strength as now when he grabbed this man, surely as tall and broad as himself, and dragged him away from his beloved.

The man stumbled and Evan laid another punch in his gut. He fell backwards as Evan rammed into him, punching for all he was worth. He pummelled the man's stomach, making him stagger backwards towards the far wall. Evan rushed forward with him, landing punches wherever he could. But the man had broad arms and still some strength, for he landed a punch on Evan's jaw which rattled him for a moment. Then the man stood upright and Evan saw he was even taller than himself. He threw another punch, catching Evan on the ear and making him see stars. Then came another punch on the side of his head and he felt his body bend at the waist like a hinge. He must stand upright, he must! He had to finish this bastard.

As Evan opened his eyes to throw another punch, a flash of lightning lit up the room, and he saw Hettie with a smashed lamp in her hands, the glass jagged in the white light. She raised it above her head and brought it down with brutal speed onto the man's ear and down he went like a skittle. Evan stepped forward and brought his boot down hard on the man's genitals, causing him to double over and curl up, whimpering and blubbering like an infant.

The man was no threat for the moment and so Evan turned to Hettie. She stood beside him, breathing heavily, her hair wild, her dress ripped. Another bolt of lightning lit her up like a picture and he saw a trickle of blood running down her neck into her bodice.

Evan said, 'You're hurt.'

The man groaned and tried to move, but Evan lifted his boot and kicked him back down at the chest. He didn't move then.

'I'll survive,' Hettie said, her voice croaky.

A thin moaning now came from the man. He was still alive, but incapacitated now. Lightning came and in the same moment thunder crashed again and the very house seemed to shake. The storm was immediately above them now.

As they stood there, gasping to get their breath back, Evan and Hettie glanced outside at the raging storm and saw a perfect zigzag of forked lightning rent the sky, a strange pinkish tinge to it. And as the thunder shook the house again, their eyes met in the dim moonlight and they laughed with the madness of it all. They actually laughed.

Chapter 27

A light threw two shadows on the wall at her door and Hettie started. Would it be friend or foe? Nothing would surprise her tonight.

'Ma'am, sir!' came a voice. It was Busby, with Towers close behind. They came through the open door, both carrying lamps. 'Are you well? Oh, my word! I did not hear this. An intruder! Towers, go fetch the constable and the doctor, for heaven's sake – hurry, man!'

Hettie's throat ached horribly. Her love was standing before her also the worse for wear, and at their feet was the man with the black eyes who had tried to kill her, still breathing, but otherwise motionless. And all she wanted to do was reassure Busby. She tried to speak out but it hurt, so she motioned for Busby to come closer.

'The man came in the storm,' she croaked. 'Evan helped me.'

'I must offer my most humble apologies, ma'am. I am the keeper of safety in this house and I have let you down most heinously. I will tender my resignation on the morrow.'

'No, you wonna be doing that,' she said hoarsely. 'You didna do a thing wrong. The storm drowned everything out. I need you, Busby. Dunna desert me now.'

Busby's face was a mixture of pride and mortification. 'Of course, ma'am. I see you have been injured. Please sit down or lie on the bed until the doctor arrives. You must rest, ma'am. Please.'

'He's right. Come on,' said Evan.

'I'll sit here. Something tells me if I lie down, I might not want to wake up.'

Evan righted her chair that had been pushed over in the fight. As she sat down, she saw Busby peering closely at the intruder.

'Well, I never. It's Troon. He was the foreman at the King brickworks years ago. Mrs King senior dismissed him and he went to the dogs, so they say. What on earth was he doing here?'

'Trying to kill me,' said Hettie.

Evan said, 'Most likely robbing the house. Maybe he had a grudge against the Kings.'

'No,' said Hettie firmly, her throat twinging with pain in response. 'He was trying to kill me. He had no other intent. He could've robbed the house easily under cover of the storm, but instead he came to me and went straight for my neck. He wanted to murder me. There inna a doubt about it.'

Mrs Guest, the cook, was up and about now. Hettie was brought warm milk with honey and a little rum in it and Evan was given a glass of whisky, which he seemed to particularly savour. Mrs Guest brought warm water and washed the blood from Hettie's neck and inspected her head. There was a wound there but it was mercifully small and she would leave the doctor to dress it, as he would know the right way. She also had some cream in a small jar she said was arnica for bruises, which she dabbed on Hettie's neck. She offered some to Evan, which he refused. Busby did not want to leave the room while Troon was still there, and nobody wanted to move him lest he should wake. He stood guard by Troon's sleeping form, as Evan sat in an armchair and Hettie drank her milk slowly, each swallow an effort. The storm was moving away and she watched the rain subside, as the rumbles of thunder grew quieter.

The constable arrived first. Hettie told him the bare facts, to which Evan added his part in it. When Troon was lifted up by Busby and Towers, he began to grumble and moan. Hettie flinched at the sound of him, terrified he should wake up, despite the room being filled with people to protect her. She knew she'd never forget the sight of those black eyes coming at her.

Evan was suddenly there, crouched beside her chair, his hand on her arm, looking up at her with concern.

'He'll never get to you. He'll never get anywhere near you again. I'll make sure of that.'

Everyone had left the room now and they were alone. Hettie looked down into Evan's blue eyes and was overcome. Her own eyes filled with tears.

'My darling girl,' said Evan and put his hand on her cheek.

'Dunna ever leave me again,' she said.

'Never. You know it. You've always known it.'

'Stay with me, Evan. Stay forever. For the rest of our lives.'

'I will. Oh, my love.'

He leant in and kissed her tenderly. How she had imagined this moment over and over; her first kiss. She had imagined it chaste or filled with passion, but never had she pictured that it would be so tender and full of love that it would make her weep with emotion.

The tears were flooding now as Evan put his arms about her awkwardly, still crouched on the floor at her side. She held onto him and sobbed. The feel of his cheek against hers, the strength of his arms around her, the smell of his damp hair, mingled with blood and whisky and honey. She would never forget this moment.

As her sobbing subsided, he pulled back to wipe the tears from her face and he smiled at her. Evan was often scowling at things, often dissatisfied or annoyed. It was a long time since she'd seen his face at peace like this. It reminded her of the look he had as a child, at the end of a carefree summer's day, when they were exhausted from playing out but utterly happy. She went to stand up and he said she mustn't, but there were some things that needed to be said standing up and this was one of them.

Hettie stood before him, his hand reaching tentatively for her to catch her should she fall. But she felt stronger than ever, for love was coursing through her.

'Evan Malone, will you be my husband?'

He looked shocked. Then he grinned. 'Course I will. It's what I came here this night to ask you.' He grasped her two hands. 'And as usual, you've shown me up. I was gonna ask you first.'

'Ask me then,' she said.

'Hettie Jones, will you be my wife?'

'Yes, I will. We be quite the team, eh?'

'Yes, we be that all right. We can beat anything, face anything, take on anything. As long as you're in my arms, Hettie.'

'Take me in your arms then, Evan.'

And he did. Their next kiss was long, slow, deep and glorious.

Epilogue

October 1876

Anny Malone was tidying her desk. Every item on it delighted her. She counted back the years, to the last time she had sat at a writing desk in an office. It was back in 1839, thirty-seven years ago. Back then, she had worked in the Kings' estate office and had her whole life ahead of her. She'd had visions of promotion to a legal clerk or something of the sort in Shrewsbury. But then the curse of the Kings came upon her and her life was blighted. Now, here she was, back on King property – but inside Southover this time, rather than banished to an estate office – back at a desk, ready to start her new job as clerk of the Hettie Malone Foundation. At the age of fifty-three, she had finally achieved her dream of an office job.

She thought about the events of the past months, how much had changed, the shocking events of that night on which she feared her second son might be lost to the storm. She had spent that night wracked with fear at Evan's absence, remembering the death of her firstborn, Owen, all those years before. Peter had gone out to the taverns to look for Evan, but he was nowhere to be found. After the storm had subsided, still no sleep came for her. She had worried herself sick for hours, until she heard the sound of carriage wheels and a horse, and went outside, thinking it would be some official telling her that her son was dead. She was stone-cold sure of it. But out of the carriage stepped Evan, looking like nothing on earth. Bruised and beaten, hair sticking up in a thousand directions. He had been brought home in Hettie's carriage. Anny's mind had filled with questions, but her body was weak with relief. She took him inside and cleaned him up, listening to the extraordinary events of that night.

As the days followed, more revelations came thick and fast. Troon had recovered and told the whole story to the police, who arrested Benjamina King in Shrewsbury. She had hired Troon to murder Hettie so she could inherit the King fortune. She had sent away Kezia Clayton on a false errand, telling her that her mother was ill in order to get her out of the house, so Hettie would be unguarded. The malice of it was wicked. Anny had never liked Benjamina King, but to hear of this cruel plan was shocking in the extreme. Troon was charged with attempted murder and Mrs King with conspiracy to commit murder. Both were in prison, awaiting trial.

It was the scandal of the decade. All tongues were wagging about it for weeks – until the wedding of Hettie Jones and Evan Malone, that was. Then they had something else to gossip about.

The wedding was a beautiful yet simple affair, as they both wanted. It took place in the local church, attended by family, friends and assorted pit workers. Hettie looked a picture in her dress, her green eyes shining with love for Evan, who had never looked more handsome. Anny's heart had nearly burst with pride and joy that day.

Now, Evan and Hettie were living at Southover. On their wedding day, instead of being the ones to receive gifts from her, they told Anny that they wanted to give her a gift instead: the old brickmaster's house now belonged to her and Peter. They were to go and live there with Flora, Billy and Lily. They could retire from their long years of work and live in peace.

Peter adored his new life of leisure, spending his time developing a new vegetable and fruit garden in the grounds of his new home. But Anny at first missed having a purpose in life and needed industry to make her feel necessary. Then, she and Hettie came up with the plan for Anny to help her with the running of the foundation.

And here she was, at her desk, beginning her first day of clerical work in decades.

Anny thought back to the time she sat with Martha Jones, Evan and Hettie at their feet. Martha had said they were proper sweethearts already and that maybe they would marry one day. Poor dead Martha's prophecy had come to pass. For Anny back then, Owen's death was still raw in her mind. And she had said to herself that this would not come to pass, that she would raise Evan to want more from life than she had had. She promised herself then that she would raise him to leave this place forever and forge a new life away from the daily grind, away from servitude to rich masters, away from the Kings and away from the secrets and lies of Ironbridge.

But, as more children came into her life and they settled into a routine of contentment, her feelings had subsided, though she often wished her son had a better life than toiling underground all the livelong day. And when Hettie had become entangled with the Kings again, Anny had felt the old shadow looming over her, this fear she'd carried for years that the Kings and her family would never escape each other, and that one day it would bring her death, or worse than that, the mortal hurt of those she loved.

But it had not come to pass. Anny realised now that Ironbridge and even the Kings were never the problem, that it was some curse that hung over them all that now seemed to have lifted.

Anny had no time for ideas of the invisible world, but she did feel as if other forces had been at work, and that somehow now they had moved on. She felt lighter than she ever had; all those years carrying a worrisome burden since Cyril's attack, the loss of her father, through her imprisonment, Margaret's disappearance and taking her sweetheart Jake away from her, her mother's passing and Owen's death. All of these felt like a heavy sack, heavier than any load of laundry or trayful of pies, that she carried with her always, that she had dragged behind her for years. Yet now, it was as if the load had dispersed like soap bubbles on the wind and Anny was free to go on her way, lightened and at liberty.

Without fear, Anny was content and had achieved her goals at last. She had work that finally utilised her intellect. Her family were safe and provided for forever. Her husband would never have to work down the mine again and could tend the garden at the old brickmaster's house for the rest of his days. Her son was happily married to the girl he loved. Anny could finally contribute towards helping others poorer than herself. And lastly, the feud between the Kings and her family had been vanquished forever, not only by Benjamina's incarceration, but also by Hettie joining the two houses together.

Anny took up a pen, dipped it in the green ink she had ordered to keep a record of accounts and began to write. She could not be happier.

October 1877

Hettie put her baby girl in the pram. Though Kezia fussed her and wished to help, Hettie told her friend that she was quite all right and so was baby Martha.

She was well-named, for she had her grandmother's green eyes, just the same as her mother's.

Kezia helped Hettie down the steps with the pram and Hettie set off across the grounds. It was a misty autumn morning, wisps of fog still lingering in the trees around Southover, and she wanted to take Martha to meet someone. She pushed the pram across the bumpy, grassy ground and rounded the house, heading for the graveyard. Last week, she took baby Martha to visit her mother and father's graves in the local churchyard and now she wanted to do the same here. She came to Queenie King's grave and stopped. She looked down and saw that Martha was already asleep.

'Well, you'll have to listen in your dreams then, little'un. For as Anny always told me, never wake a sleeping baby.'

Hettie put a hand into the pram and tucked the blanket more closely around her beautiful child. She caught her breath in a little gasp at how overwhelming her love was for this tiny person.

Then, she turned to the grave and she spoke to it.

'Now then, Queenie. I think we know each other well enough for me to call you by your nickname. And you certainly earnt that name, didna you? You ruled the Kings like a Queen and you were never beaten, not even by Benjamina, who now rots in gaol, you'll be glad to hear. Well, Queenie, this is my daughter, Martha. I married my love, Evan, and here is our child.

'I want you to know that we are all well, that my family prosper and that we have put your fortune to good use, just as your great-granddaughter wanted. Beatrice is coming to see us in the spring, in fact, to meet Martha and to write about our foundation. We are helping many people hereabouts and further afield. We are living good lives and strive to be good folk in our hearts. I hope you'd be proud of us, Queenie. I think you would. For we're happy, and everything is proper jam.'

Hettie found there was a tear in her eye. She missed old Mrs King. As she stood by her grave, listening to the sound of the autumn wind lifting the tree boughs in the woods beyond, and hearing her sleeping daughter snuffle, Hettie thought she heard a whisper of an answer in her ear. She looked about her, but dismissed it as a natural thing, leaves falling from the trees perhaps and rustling on the woodland floor. She nodded at the grave of Alice King and turned the pram around and pushed it back to the house.

The front door opened before she got there and out stepped Evan, his blond hair thick and brushed back, his blue eyes shining at her. He was dressed in a simple yet smart pair of brown trousers and a cream shirt, tucked in to reveal his fine chest and strong, flat stomach, his sleeves rolled up to show his broad, muscled arms. Ah, he was a fine figure of a man was Evan Malone. And he was all hers.

He smiled at her and took the pram with infinite care to carry it up the steps, placing it carefully down inside. Then he leant over and kissed her tenderly.

Hettie smiled and closed the door, safely inside Southover, away from the autumn chill.

And if the good ghosts of Southover could see Hettie go inside her house that day, what would they think of how things had come to pass? Perhaps they would gather about the graveyard – Betsy Blaize, John Woodvine, Queenie King and her twin daughters, Margaret Ashford, Owen Malone, Martha and Adam Jones, and even Rose Jenkins might be there, shining in a blue-white spectral light. They would see this happiest of couples and their new child inhabit this once fire-ravaged house, now built anew, order restored from chaos. The feud was no more, the divide had been bridged. And perhaps the spirits would smile on this, and at last leave this place, vanishing into the mist, finally at rest.

Acknowledgements

Shroppiemon, for continuing dialect and historical help, for again reading the early draft quickly, as well as moral support when I really needed it.

Katie Lumsden and Claire Johnson-Creek at Bonnier Books UK, for providing such expert edits and support, as well as Tara Loder for commissioning the trilogy and believing in it all the way. Brilliant, insightful editors are a gift to any writer and I have been blessed in this regard with Bonnier! Particular thanks also to the wonderful design team for producing such gorgeous covers.

Lu Corfield, for doing a perfectly beautiful job of narrating the previous *Ironbridge* books and bringing the characters to glorious life.

My excellent agent Laura Macdougall and also Olivia Davies at United Agents for their constant support and vigilance.

Memories of Shropshire Facebook group, for helping with my post about coal mining places to visit in the area: in particular, comments from Colin Armfield, Kate Cadman, Geoff Fletcher, Margaret Sheridan,

Rosemary Perry, Graham Hickman, Gareth Maverick, Nicola Edwards and Louise Bremner. Also, Juanita Gennard from the group for sharing the story about her father as a child listening to the clogs of miners walking past his window. Also, thanks to Alison Utting from the same group for telling me about the term 'clog chorus'.

Oakengates History group on Facebook: Gwyn Thunderwing Hartley, for help on pit girls' dress as well as on the Oakengates Wake; Dave Baker for excellent, detailed help on the railways, particularly the route from Ironbridge to Oakengates and the trip to London.

All the members and administrators of the various other Shropshire Facebook groups who have continued to give great advice on the subject as well as support the *Ironbridge* saga:

- Shropshire Tales, History and Memories
- Telford Memories
- Ironbridge and Coalbrookdale pictures
- Ironbridge through the Dales

Bill Scriven, ex-miner and font of knowledge about mining, with whom I had a fantastic phone conversation listening to his memories of working down the pit.

Joanne Smith and Sarah Roberts at the Ironbridge Gorge Museums Trust library and archives. Joanne, for finding materials on coal mining that were waiting for me when I arrived, and Sarah, for looking after me when I was there and showing me where all the coal mining materials were.

The Friends of Ironbridge Gorge Museum Trust, for inviting me to do a talk in November 2019 on the research for the *Ironbridge* saga. The audience's enthusiasm and help with coal mining research was awesome.

Ray Farlow, who I met at the IGMT talk, for sending me news articles from 1870s newspapers.

Steve Dewhirst of Broseley Local History Society, for articles about local fairs.

Andy Rose of Madeley Town Council, for resources on the pit girls and pit conditions.

Martine Bailey, for direction to useful resources on transportation to Australia.

Jé Maverick, for info and ideas on convicts.

Essie Fox, for information on the London Aquarium.

Early readers – my darling friends Lynn Downing, Pauline Lancaster and Lucy Adams, for reading so quickly and enthusiastically, as ever.

Melissa Bailey, Lynn Downing, Kerry Drewery, Kerry Hadley, Kathy Kendall, Bee Lewis, Fiona McKinnell, Beth Miller, Jamie Pearce, Louisa Treger and Sue White, for always indulging this chatterbox and drama queen.

Sumaira Wilson of SpellBound Books, for the best memes and moral support when any normal human would be focusing on their own battles. An absolute queen of a woman, publisher and friend.

My dear Facebook friends, for seeing me through difficult days and always making me laugh, for messaging me to check how I'm doing, as well as shamelessly encouraging me to post ever more highly inappropriate memes.

Readers, reviewers, book bloggers and booksellers for reading, selling and sharing your thoughts on the *Ironbridge* saga. A particular thanks to every single reader who has contacted me via social media to tell me how much they've enjoyed the books. Your messages and comments mean the world to this author.

Bev Johnson, for keeping me healthy.

Clément Barbin, for bringing me the sweetest of treats.

Fiona Cooke – you know why, babe. Suffice to say, the greatest and truest love story of lockdown. Grateful forever for your friendship.

This book was written and edited throughout the Covid pandemic, from first lockdown to third. I'd like to take this opportunity to thank my daughter, Poppy, and our family, as well as all our lovely friends, who helped me get through this period with camaraderie, humour and patience. Let's hope that by the time this book goes out into the world, there is hope on the horizon of a return to some semblance of normality. Love and gratitude to all of you.

MEMORY LANE

Welcome to the world of Mollie Walton!

Keep reading for more from Mollie Walton, to discover a recipe that features in this novel and to find out more about Mollie Walton's inspiration for the book . . .

We'd also like to welcome you to Memory Lane, a place to discuss the very best saga stories from authors you know and love with other readers, plus get recommendations for new books we think you'll enjoy. Read on and join our club!

MEMORY LANE

www.MemoryLane.Club

/MemoryLaneClub

MEMORY LANE

Dear Reader,

Thank you for reading the third instalment of the *Ironbridge* trilogy. If you're new to the *Ironbridge* saga, then welcome. And if you've followed all three books, then I hope you've enjoyed them all. I must say I've loved writing them.

For this book, some aspects of the research could not be as hands-on as usual, as it was mostly written during the Covid pandemic. However, luckily, before the first lockdown, I was able to visit Ironbridge and nearby Coalbrookdale and spend some time in the Ironbridge Gorge Museums Trust archives, to learn about mining in the nineteenth century. Through a Shropshire Facebook group (one of my most treasured resources) I was put in touch with Bill Scriven, an ex-coal miner from the area. We had a phone call that lasted hours, where I mercilessly quizzed him about his career. Luckily, he didn't seem to mind! His reminiscences were marvellous and gave me a fascinating, luminous image of these brave men and the work they did underground.

I've found that throughout the writing of this trilogy, my research into the lives of working people – such as ironworkers, brickmakers and colliers – have transformed my understanding of the industrial revolution and earned my eternal respect. It's one thing to be aware of their hard work and sacrifices; it's another to try and put yourself in their shoes. Not only did they suffer, but they also lived with camaraderie and community spirit which can sometimes feel lacking in this day and age. I will always feel grateful to them and in awe of the difficult lives they led.

So, it's with a heavy heart that I say farewell to the *Ironbridge* saga with this third and final book in the trilogy. I first had the idea for this story five years ago, when standing on the iron bridge itself. To see that story come to fruition is a very emotional moment for any writer. I must confess I did have a little cry when I finished this book. I've lived with these characters in my head for all those years, following their fortunes and – let's face it – putting them through hell! To say goodbye to them and see them go off into the world without me is a very peculiar feeling – part relief, part sadness. I've grown excessively fond of them all. I like to think of them living their lives into the rest of the nineteenth century and beyond. Maybe, we'll revisit them one day, who knows . . .

Looking back over the last five years of writing about these characters, one thing above all else stays with me and that is the delight of discovering

MEMORY LANE

Shropshire and its people. I'd like to sign off with a thank'ee to all the folk of this beautiful county that I've connected with, and I hope to visit you soon, when lockdown lifts. I miss my Ironbridge friends and I will be back. You're all proper jam.

Best wishes,
Mollie

Glossary of Shropshire Dialect Terms

Arr: yes
Babby: baby
Bait: packed lunch
Butty: mate, friend
Coulda: could have
Couldna: couldn't have
Crowsty: bad-tempered
Cwtch: a cuddle or sitting up close to someone
Daff: someone who is shy, silly or inexperienced
Didna: didn't
Doesna: doesn't
Drodsome: dreadful, alarming
Dunna: don't
Frit'ee: frighten you
Hadna: hadn't
Hasna: hasn't
Havna: haven't
Inna: isn't or am not
Little'uns: babies or children

Lollocking: easy, idle
Mon: man, a term of address for males
Mun: must
Owd: old
Proper jam: lovely, really good
Scuffling: weeding with a hoe
Shoulda: should have
Sniving: overrun with
Summat: something
Understrapper: boy
Wasna: wasn't
Wench: used for a young woman in a similar way to 'lass', in no way derogatory to females
Wonna: won't
Woulda: would have
Wouldna: wouldn't

MEMORY LANE

Strawberry Ice

At the Oakengates fair in Chapter 8, Hettie and her father, Adam, eat a strawberry ice each from a glass cup. An 'ice' was a Victorian precursor to ice cream, and would have been made with fresh strawberries such as the ones Hettie herself picks in the earlier chapters of the book.

You will need:

2 lb fresh strawberries
¾ pt cream
3 oz caster sugar

Method:

1. Cut the stems off the strawberries, slice them into small chunks, then either mash or blitz in a blender.
2. Push the mashed fresh strawberries through a sieve, getting out as much juice as you can.
3. Pour the sugar into the strawberry juice and stir until the sugar dissolves.
4. Whip the cream in a separate bowl until it forms stiff peaks, then slowly stir in the strawberry juice.
5. Spoon the mixture into individual glasses.
6. Freeze these overnight, then eat with a spoon.
7. Enjoy!

Praise for

The Daughters of Ironbridge

'A Journey. Compelling. Addictive'

VAL WOOD

'The attention to period detail and beautiful writing drew me right in'

LYNNE FRANCIS

'*The Daughters of Ironbridge* has that compulsive page-turning quality, irresistible characters the reader gets hugely invested in, and Walton has created a brilliantly alive, vivid and breathing world'

LOUISA TREGER

'Feisty female characters, an atmospheric setting and a spell-binding storyline make this a phenomenal read'

CATHY BRAMLEY

'Evocative, dramatic and hugely compelling . . . *The Daughters of Ironbridge* has all the hallmarks of a classic saga. I loved it'

MIRANDA DICKINSON

'Such great characters who will stay with me for a long time'

BETH MILLER

'A powerful sense of place and period, compelling characters and a pacey plot had me racing to the end'

GILL PAUL

'A story that is vivid, twisting and pacey, with characters that absolutely leap off the page'

IONA GREY

'Hard-hitting storyline, clever blend of real history and fiction, and an atmospheric evocation'

LANCASTER GUARDIAN

The Secrets of Ironbridge

MOLLIE WALTON

ZAFFRE

First published in Great Britain in 2020 by
ZAFFRE
An imprint of Bonnier Books UK
4th Floor, Victoria House,
Bloomsbury Square,
London WC1B 4DA
Owned by Bonnier Books
Sveavägen 56, Stockholm, Sweden

A CIP catalogue record for this book is
available from the British Library.

ISBN: 978-1-83877-068-6

Also available as an ebook

5 7 9 10 8 6 4

Typeset by IDSUK (Data Connection) Ltd
Printed and bound in Great Britain by Clays Ltd, Elcograf S.p.A.

MIX
Paper from
responsible sources
FSC® C018072

Zaffre is an imprint of Bonnier Books UK
www.bonnierbooks.co.uk

To my dear friend Lynn Downing, who always listens and is in all ways lovely.

Prologue

Queenie wondered where she was buried. A pauper's grave, no doubt. But which sorrowful patch of ground? Queenie pictured her now, a pitiful pile of bones in a crowded pit. She imagined the girl's spirit rising from its haphazard burial place, delighted to be free of its chaotic tumble of earth and human remains. Where would it go? Perhaps it would revisit the scenes and sights of its childhood: some sort of poor man's hovel where it was born, maybe a patch of ground where it used to play with other urchins. But once it was done with those, inevitably, it would come to the King house, to Southover. After all, the spirit was only a young girl when she had come there as a maid-of-all-work. And what if the spirit of this servant – this Betsy Blaize – were to come to Queenie's house now? What would she see? Even as she wondered this Queenie questioned why she had conjured the memory of Blaize's spirit after all these years of thinking of it rarely. Out of sight, out of mind. It must be because the house was draped in worry, waiting as it was for the death of her son.

She shivered and glanced at the closed curtains in her bedroom. In her mind's eye, she saw the spirit rise from its scrappy piece of earth across the river, floating up, up into the night sky. Over the tops of trees and industry it would go, seeing the fires of the furnaces emblazon the darkness with their hellish colours. It would skim fleetly over factories and forges, lime kilns and waggonways, pumping engines and brickworks. It might circle the pitheads and the men labouring below them in the bowels of the earth. They would never see the spirit that passed over them, buried as they were like her body, or what was left of it. Onwards, to the river itself, the mighty Severn that scoured out the Gorge and rushed through it, relentless and temperamental. The spirit would travel its length to reach the iron bridge – it would have to visit the site of its creation, after all, the place where Betsy Blaize the girl had carried her newborn child, handed it to a passing Quaker and died. Across the iron bridge it would fly, up over the houses and shops and streets, all good folk sleeping peacefully in their beds, their mattresses soft or hard depending on their gentility. Up the hill to the great house that stood above the town, frowning down upon it. Southover, the house of the hated Kings.

Queenie envisaged the spirit approaching the house from the gravel drive, making no sound as it skimmed the stones, lifting up to the window of Mr Ralph King Junior, Queenie's son, master of the house and figurehead of the King businesses, struck down in his early sixties by sickness. If it glanced through the crack in the curtains, it would see the deathly pale face of Ralph sleeping fitfully in his bed, groaning in pain all the night through. But of course Ralph wouldn't be her final destination. It wasn't him who had wronged her. The spirit would float on, coming around the eastern corner of the house, slowing now, closer and closer, to arrive at its destination: Queenie's own window.

Queenie felt a chill down her spine again and the lamp on her desk guttered like a spent candle. She adjusted her favourite cashmere shawl closer about her shoulders. She had lost some weight in recent years and felt the cold more keenly. Her devoted lady's maid, Jenkins, kept trying to feed her up, complaining that Queenie would soon look like a skeleton if she didn't fatten up a bit. She stood up and walked to the window, then hesitated. A sudden, sharp fear came of what might appear behind it. She scolded herself for her silliness and yanked the curtain open. She saw only the night look back at her, blank and black. The vague shapes of trees moved mysteriously at the edge of the lawns. She did not look at the family graveyard, instead turning briskly and returning to her desk. Today, the doctor had advised Queenie to 'gather your family around you'. The others were here – her grandson Cyril and Ralph's wife Benjamina – neither caring much whether Ralph made it through the night or not. Indeed, Queenie suspected they positively hoped he wouldn't, so they could move on to the next stages of their lives. But there was family not present that ought to be.

Thus, she had sat down to pen this letter to the one person who was absent, who was over the sea, in a foreign city for nigh on twenty years now, her granddaughter Margaret. She pictured her now, her youth having left her, approaching middle age. Had the years been kind to her, Queenie wondered, or would she have aged badly? Margaret's relative poverty, as a teacher of English and pianoforte, would not afford her the King lifestyle, that was certain. Perhaps it would be a blessing to her to return home again, at last, after all these years. Perhaps she would welcome it, after all she had struggled through, as a widow and a lone mother to a daughter. Or perhaps she still considered her loss of riches a small price to pay to be free of the King family. Then, Queenie's thoughts coalesced around another, the girl, her great-granddaughter, Beatrice. Queenie had never met her. Would the girl favour her pale, yellow-haired mother or her dark, gypsy-eyed father? Queenie would soon find out if the answer to this letter were in the affirmative. She set to finish it, dipping her pen in the black ink and looping it out across the page in her neat hand.

As she wrote the words 'your father is close to death', she felt that chill again and hurriedly glanced back at the strip of window open to the dark night. There was a flicker of something there. Or was there? Just a spatter of rain. She stood once more and marched to the window, jerking the curtain over to shut out the night. But as she did it, she knew that it was never that simple to shut out memories – or guilt.

Queenie imagined the spirit she had conjured gliding down from her window and taking its customary place beside Queenie's long-dead husband's grave, standing beside it, looking up at the house. Watching and waiting in the coal-dark night, scored by the rain that fell across the King lawns and into the wild woodland beyond.

Chapter 1

The coach trundled on, the horses struggling up a steep incline, their hooves slipping. Beatrice grasped her mother's hand again and squeezed. Her mother was still snoozing and stirred at her touch, then fell back into her stupor. *Maman always looks tired these days*, thought Beatrice. It was good that they were returning to her mother's family, after all these years. Good that her mother would get some rest, be waited on in the big house and pampered a little. If they were welcomed, that was.

Beatrice glanced at the other passengers opposite them in the coach, two women and a man, all in various states of restless slumber, jogged by the coach's swaying rhythm. But she could not sleep. She had never travelled far from home in Montmartre and never met her English family, so this journey was filled with excitement and tinged with fear. The coach to the port, the ship across the Channel. The sea voyage made her so sick, she told her mother she was dying. But they got through it and then came the long ride north-west. Nights were spent in coaching inns, fending off the lascivious looks and comments of Englishmen. She was eighteen years of age and she was lovely to look upon, or so Maman told her daily.

'We shall need to buy you a whole new wardrobe, Bea,' Maman said, awake now. 'Shropshire society won't be able to cope with your Paris fashion.'

'But how will we afford that?' she asked.

All her life, lack of money had been their constant, tedious companion. She knew how little they had left. The journey had cost them a pretty penny. To hear her mother talk of splashing out on new clothes was shocking.

'All will be different,' her mother replied. 'You do not know your great-grandmother yet, but she'd never stand for a King to be presented in society as anything but the height of sophistication.'

The coach was on the flat now, the horses fleeter. Beatrice leant forward and looked out of the window. The dark, tree-rooved roads they'd come through for miles were thinning out into more open country. She saw the Shropshire countryside broaden into beauty: rolling hills, deeply wooded areas, patches of water, cottages and a church nestled in a valley. Having lived all her life in the dense, populated world of a city, the landscape here was intoxicating to her. She loved her life in Montmartre and its busy, noisy character. She had imagined the town of Ironbridge to be simply a smaller version of what she was used to. But nothing had prepared for the splendour of the landscape here. The coachman called something to the horses and they slowed, then turned onto another road, the sign she'd spied at the junction: Broseley and Ironbridge. Not far now, she hoped.

They gathered pace along the Broseley road. Before long, the greenery faded into brown and a new sight took her interest, the signs of industry. There were brick buildings and a tall chimney, and behind it she could make out great mounds of grey earth. To one side was some kind of structure with a wheel and ropes, and to the other a stretch of grey ground, an open working of some sort, peopled by a blur of many workers and horses going to and fro. Some words painted in broad white lettering on the side of a building caught her eye: KING BRICK AND TILE WORKS. King was her mother's name – her maiden name, that was.

Beatrice grasped the window ledge and leant out further, so she could see the people, the first large group of locals she'd seen for miles. The coach was slowing down, as one of the female passengers, now awake and readying herself, was to alight here. Beatrice watched as the woman clambered out of the other door and was handed her bag from the roof. Beatrice looked through the window at the workers. She could see them clearly. They were digging great lumps of material from the open ground, placing it on handcarts or carrying it by hand. She saw now that some of the workers were children bowed down by the weight of their load. Some of them were so small, her heart went out to them. Surely they were too young for such backbreaking work? Everyone was covered in grey dust, making them seem as if they were people of the clay, arisen from the ground. Beatrice stared at them, until one came from an open-sided building, turned and looked in her direction. She could see his eyes fix upon her. She stared back for a moment, then looked away, abashed. She felt ashamed, to be gawking at this young man working so hard, while she lounged in a coach. She withdrew her head and sat back down beside her mother.

'We are on the road to Broseley and Ironbridge,' Beatrice told her.

'Ah, then we are almost home,' said Maman.

'Look at this place,' she told her mother who leant forward and peered out of the window. 'It has your name on it.'

'It does indeed belong to the Kings. Queenie told me in a letter that the Kings now own this site, as well as having interests in iron and mining.'

Beatrice looked outside again to see the workers labour on, the smoke rising from the chimney, the young man who had looked upon her lost now in the dust and the muck. She struggled to imagine her family owning so much.

Her mother began talking to her of her family, reminding her of each member, telling her of the town of Ironbridge they were now approaching. France, Paris,

Montmartre, their little terraced house on the corner opposite the *boulangerie*, the smell of fresh baking accompanying their every waking morning – all seemed very far away.

As the coach drew closer to their destination, Beatrice called up the sights and sounds of her home: the comings and goings of Maman's pupils; the tinkling sounds of piano pieces and the drumming monotony of scales practice; the halting tones of children learning English, while Beatrice assisted her mother with preparing learning materials, marking work and domestic duties. Sometimes, Beatrice would give lessons to the younger ones herself. She spoke English with her mother at home and spoke French outside of home. She had been raised perfectly bilingual, her English spoken without a French accent, so her mother said, yet with a tinge of French phrasing from time to time. Her fellow Parisians would say she spoke French similarly, with a perfect accent, yet a hint of Englishness in her turn of phrase. Her mother told her every day how proud she was of her, what a good girl she was, how clever and kind. Eighteen years they had been together, every day Beatrice had spent on this earth; they were the best of friends, the greatest team Beatrice could imagine. Their world had been that little house, the streets nearby, the stray yet sociable cats she fed on their front porch, the musical and artistic friends that would bring food and laughter and gossip of an evening. They had a life confined by poverty yet expanded by ideas, conversation and reading; a shabby-genteel existence. A happy one.

But then there came news that Ralph King was ill. It was her grandfather, her mother's father, a man Beatrice had never met. Her mother did not speak of her past often, but as Beatrice had grown older she had asked more and more. She knew that she had been born out of love, a great romance with her father, the artist Jake Ashford. That her parents had run away together from Ironbridge to Paris. Tragically her father had died of a fever before she was even born, leaving her mother a young widow, struggling to bring Beatrice up alone.

She'd never met anyone in her family. The word 'family' only meant Mother, or as she called her, in the French way, Maman. Her whole family was Maman. But now they were going to the house where Maman had grown up, where her grandfather Ralph lived with her step-grandmother Benjamina and her Uncle Cyril, and where her great-grandmother, who they all called Queenie, ruled the roost.

The day was waning and Beatrice suddenly felt very weary, worn out by her worry of what this mysterious family would make of her and Maman. The coach was tipping forwards as they descended another hill and again she grasped her mother's hand.

'Look!' said Maman, and Beatrice saw through the window a broad, roiling mass of water surging forwards and beyond it, spanning the River Severn grandly from bank to bank, the great iron bridge, its backbone covered in jostling traffic and people.

'Ironbridge,' said Beatrice.

'Home,' said Maman.

Curious how small it looked to Margaret, her family home, Southover. As a child it had seemed like a mansion of endless rooms, with the tallest ceilings and longest corridors. But now, having alighted from the coach and standing before it, it was still impressive – far grander than their little house in Montmartre – but somewhat smaller than she remembered. *Strange how memories play tricks on the mind*, she thought. She realised that the house loomed large in her thoughts mostly because of its power over her childhood. It was still much larger than the majority of houses around these parts, and to Beatrice, she thought, as she glanced at her beautiful daughter gazing up at it, it must seem like the Palace of Versailles compared to the simple narrow house she'd grown up in. She felt a pang of guilt that her daughter had never had the finery she'd had growing up, then recalled that finery was no use if you were imprisoned in it. And that is how she saw her childhood, one long stretch of incarceration before she opened the cage door and she flew. And now she was back, nearly twenty years older, wiser and yet exhausted. Despite missing her beloved Paris, the thought of good food, hot water and servants to tend one's every need seemed like heaven to her now. Strangely, she was glad to be here, though a little nervous of their reception. She had left under a storm cloud all those years ago, after all.

Margaret watched as the butler and other staff came out to greet the coach and handle the luggage. Brunt, her family butler of many years' standing, was gone, replaced by a younger man only a few years older than herself by the looks of it. But that was all she had time to notice before she saw that they all wore black armbands and then she felt a shiver up her spine as she realised her father, Ralph King, must already be dead.

Her grandmother had written to her weeks before, to inform her that her father was dying. Margaret had read the letter and sat staring at the walls of her little house for a long time, mulling over the news. To see her father and the rest of her family again, after all these years of self-imposed exile. To bring Beatrice and introduce her to the family Margaret had so longed to escape. It was fraught with worrying possibilities. She had never liked her father. He was a selfish, pompous man, who spent her childhood years dishing up disapproval and disappointment to his only daughter. She knew it was because her mother had died giving birth to her. The thought of seeing him again and having to submit to his rules in any way brought back the old fears of her youth. But she was no longer the young woman who'd run from the King house all those years ago. Though she'd hated her family – their coldness, their cruelty – they were still her family. To ignore a deathbed request . . .

And then there was Bea, who had never known any other family. Margaret was thirty-five years old now. Her health had declined in these recent years, with mysterious pains here and there, as well as piercing headaches and dizzy spells from time to time. Independence was fine when she was well, terrifying when she was not. Her ill health had lost her some pupils and it was increasingly hard to make ends meet. What would happen to Bea if something truly horrible were to befall her? What was more, Beatrice was coming of age and Margaret feared for her daughter's future. In the world of the Kings, a girl of Bea's age would be launched upon the social scene, ready to find a suitable husband. With their meagre lifestyle in Montmartre, such a thing was impossible. It had seemed romantic and worthy once, to live this life of fierce self-reliance, and Margaret was still proud of what she had achieved alone. But she was tired, and she wanted so much more for Beatrice. Maybe her family had changed. So they had come, but it seemed they were too late.

There she was, her grandmother Queenie, standing in the doorway, dressed head to toe in black.

'Margaret, my dear,' she said, in a strong voice. Her hair was pure white now, different from the bright stripes through deep brown and gunmetal grey she'd had when Margaret last saw her. She walked in a confident, upright stride towards them across the driveway, yet smiled wanly.

'Are we too late, Grandmother? Is Father . . . gone?'

Queenie arrived in front of her and took her hands, her grandmother's skin dry and papery yet her hands warm and firm.

'I am sorry to say you are too late. He passed away two days hence, but there was no way to alert you.'

It struck Margaret that she felt absolutely nothing at all. It was akin to being told the *boulangerie* opposite their house had run out of bread, annoying that she'd missed her chance, yet hardly more than an inconvenience. *Am I really so cold?* she thought.

'I'm grieved to hear it and so sorry for our family's loss,' she heard herself saying to Queenie, who cocked her head and smiled a strange little smile.

'Really, my dear? I didn't think you cared for your father one jot! But, of course, you are saying the right things and acting with perfect decorum.'

Queenie hadn't changed, then. She'd always said what she thought. Then, Queenie's face altered suddenly as her gaze shifted aside and fell upon Margaret's daughter, waiting patiently beside her.

'And this is Beatrice,' said Queenie with a kind of breathy wonder. Queenie's eyes were wide open and she swiftly removed her hands from Margaret's. It had been good to feel her grandmother's touch again, the only King who ever really cared about her. Indeed, her brother Cyril and stepmother Benjamina had not even come out to greet their arrival. Typical and, truth be told, something of a relief.

'Why, my dear, you are a stunning creature!' said Queenie and took the girl's hands. Beatrice glanced nervously sideways at her mother who nodded. 'You are the very picture of your father, with those dark eyes. I do not recall much about the artist Ashford, but one could not forget those eyes. And I see you have your mother's fine features. You will do very nicely, my dear. Will you not greet me as your great-grandmother, child? You speak English, I assume?'

'Indeed, I do, Great-grandmother,' Beatrice said, smiling. Yet another glance at her mother showed how nervous and eager to do the right thing she was. 'I would like to offer my condolences on your loss. I am so very sorry I did not meet my grandfather.'

Margaret watched her grandmother place her palms on her daughter's cheeks, who stood rigidly, trying to appear natural. 'You are kind to say so, but you may be the better for it. He was my son, but he wasn't the man I wished him to be. No doubt that appears wickedly unkind to you, but you will learn that your great-grandmother is honest as the day is long and will not brook any flim-flam. Come now, you must be fatigued from your travels. Come inside.'

Queenie led the way. Beatrice took her mother's hand and squeezed it, her face a sweet picture of concern, her eyes seeming to ask if her mother was well, after the bad news.

'I am fine,' Margaret said quietly to her as she squeezed Beatrice's hand back and they walked together into the hallway of Southover, tiled in colourful, geometric patterns, shiny and hard beneath their feet. A new floor in the hall then, using the local tiles, no doubt. Margaret began to feel a little shaken that so much had changed. She felt as if she were in a dream, where a place was familiar yet foreign. The new butler and maids took their cloaks and bonnets as Queenie looked on, never once taking her eyes off Beatrice, whose every nuance seemed to delight her. Margaret was proud of her daughter's beauty, sweet temperament and strength of character, yet there was something in the pit of her belly that made her feel uncomfortable at her grandmother's attentions.

'I believe that Cyril and Benjamina are in the drawing room,' said Queenie, adding, 'And Beatrice, I'm glad to hear that you speak our native tongue beautifully with no trace of an accent! A French accent around these parts would not go down very well. Many of us are old enough to recall the wars with France and we do not forgive easily.'

The butler opened the drawing room door for Queenie, who had waited imperiously for him to do so as if she could not do it herself, which of course she could. Margaret noticed all of these little touches. After nearly two decades away from such a life, it would take her a while to settle back into it. How strange it was to act as if one had lost the use of one's hands to simply open a door. But she decided at that moment that she would not let the maids dress her or wash her or anything like it. She had forged her own dignity in Paris at great cost, an independence hard fought for and won.

The story she had told Beatrice about her father was a lie. Beatrice's father was dead, that was true. But it did not happen when Margaret carried her child, but five years later. And it was not from a tragic fever, but something far more distasteful. Margaret had told her daughter these untruths to protect her from the squalid reality.

After a foolish affair and a runaway marriage, she had left her husband in the early months of pregnancy and walked off into the streets of Paris alone. In the weeks before she'd left, she would lie on the hard cot in the tiny apartment with one window she shared with Jake and daydream about a place she could escape to, a place to call her own, away from his drinking, his womanising, his blaming her for all of his failings.

Their great romance had soured the moment Jake realised she wouldn't beg her family for money. She could hardly believe it when she first took possession of her little house, months later, the birth not long away. It was in a street full of shops and businesses. It had before then been a seamstress's home and she would find scraps of material or the odd pin from time to time. It was basic but it was clean. And it took the last of the family money she'd taken the night she left Ironbridge. The main room had four windows and let in plenty of light. She put an advertisement in the front window for English lessons and soon had her first pupils. She wore the black clothes of a widow, although it would be some years before that became a fact. When the baby came, a neighbourly midwife helped her and the birth went smoothly.

Once she was up and about and the baby sleeping better, she began advertising as a piano teacher and left Beatrice with a friend who was a clockmaker's wife, who was childless and adored babies. Every day, she bought a small bouquet of flowers and placed them in the window. In time, she was able to purchase her own pianoforte, her friends helping her manoeuvre it into the house. She learnt how to tune and maintain it herself. When Beatrice was three, she started teaching her to play. Pupils came daily and their living improved, with enough money to buy some pretty things for her daughter and some decent wine for herself. They had friends, they had freedom, they had each other. There had been suitors from time to time – Margaret had always been a pretty woman – and though she enjoyed flirting with them, she never succumbed. She wanted no more husbands. Her whole life until that little house had been lived in thrall to others, particularly men, directing her destiny and limiting her choices. She'd vowed she would never do that again.

Margaret followed Queenie into the drawing room and she immediately noticed that the picture in her mind's eye was different from the room she now stood in. It had been fully redecorated since she left, with bright flock wallpaper in red and pale pink, quite gaudy, she thought. Benjamina's influence, no doubt. She looked about the room for her fashionable stepmother, wondering how the years would have treated her, so obsessed with her appearance she'd always been. She was only a few years older than Margaret herself – the 'child bride', as she'd always thought of her secretly. But Benjamina was not here and neither was Margaret's brother, Cyril. A wave of relief swept over her. He was the one she dreaded seeing most of all. And suddenly she felt icy cold and a phrase leapt to her mind: *We should never have come.*

Chapter 2

Owen Malone stretched his arms out, hearing his bones crack. His back ached. He shook his head to wake himself up. Since he'd seen the girl in the coach he had been in a daydream and had found it difficult to concentrate on this last hour of his working day. He yawned noisily, prompting his father to glance at him and say, 'Nearly time to go.'

'I'm not done with you yet,' snapped another voice. It was his father's cousin, Adam. They were arguing again.

His father looked more exhausted than anything when he replied, 'We shall go all round the houses and nowt will be settled, mon. We must agree to disagree. Come, Owen. Your mother will be setting the table.'

But Adam stepped forward and grasped his cousin's arm. 'We must be united or we shall fail. Is that what you want, Peter?' Owen did not like the look of this. He admired Adam, always had. He idolised him, if truth be told – his passion for what was right and wrong, for how the working man and woman must be treated. Owen's father knew right from wrong: there was no better man alive. Yet he did not have Adam's fire for change and this disappointed Owen at times.

Peter Malone slowly looked upon his cousin's grasp around his arm and then he smiled. 'After thirteen hours in this place, all what I want is my supper. And I shall have it, cousin. If you dunna mind.'

Adam released his grip, grumbling to himself as he returned to his moulding table. A boy staggered up to the bench and unloaded onto Adam's table a lump of clay from his head that must have been nearly forty pounds in weight. The boy turned wearily to trek back the thirty yards or so to the clay heaps to collect the next lump. He could not have been more than eight years of age, but his face appeared grey and lined, weathered and ancient. Owen grimaced at the sight, grateful that at seventeen years old, he was now an experienced brick-burner trained by his father, working alongside him in the kilns and not a child bearing the clay any longer.

The other workers were arriving to take over from them, as Owen and his father finished their shift. The two of them walked across the brickyard, nodding at their colleagues as they passed them, too tired to talk to anyone, focused only on putting one foot afore the other to make the journey home to their little house, to food and comfort. They left by the main gate, past the stacks of bricks and tiles in symmetrical piles, the finished wares displayed for customers to see from the road. They walked along it in easy companionship, passing by the woods on one side, the river on the other, the marks of industry everywhere about them. Here was a smithy, there the lime kilns, and further along a corn-mill and another brickworks. Men and women were returning home, falling into step behind or before them, coloured by the dust and muck of their trade, whether grey, reddish-brown or black, all dressed in grime-stiffened clothes, heads down, pushing their legs forward.

'Father,' Owen said.

'Arr?'

'If a master were to look upon us, all of us, us working men, trudging home as we are. What do you think he'd see?'

Peter strode forward, quiet, considering.

'He'd see money.'

'Yes, but what would they think of us?'

'I doubt they think on us at all. But if they do, they would see only money, as I say. Their means to make money. That's our role to play on this earth. The working man.'

'You're right,' said Owen, warming to his theme. 'He'd see only a working man, walking along. He'd see only our clothes and our dirty appearance and he'd likely think to himself, what empty-headed clots they be. But every man a-walking along here has thoughts, of plans he makes and ideas for things. He might be thinking on regrets or memories of loved ones. Or he might be dreaming up inventions that could change the world. But a rich man – or woman, for that matter – looking upon us from great heights, from the King house on the hill or . . . from the comfort of a coach, maybe. They would see only our shapes and our filth and if they thought on us at all, they would think we only be like creatures. Or machines, even. With nothing inside but blood and bones, or even that brick-dust filled our heads.'

'Arr, that be true,' said his father. ''Twas always thus and always thus shall be.'

Owen wanted to ask his father another thing, but he kept it to himself. He wasn't ready to share this with anyone yet. The moment he'd come out from the drying shed and spotted that coach pulled over by the brickyard entrance, he'd seen her eyes. The girl in the coach with the bonnet and the hair – what colour was it? It was a shining kind of brown, like a new conker hazed with dew. He was pleased with that description in his mind's eye. His mother always said his father was a poet and that Owen had inherited it, had inherited her cleverness too and her deep thoughts. But he had no deep thoughts about the girl he'd seen staring at him from the coach, only feelings. A spark of something that coursed through him the moment their eyes latched on. What was she looking at, he wondered? What would she think of him? He'd always been proud of his work at the brickyard, toiling alongside his family gang of cousins and uncles and aunts, learning his way up the trade to be a skilled brickburner like his father. But now he'd felt a pinch of shame when that girl looked upon him from the coach, the gloves she wore, that beauty, those eyes . . .

'Son,' his father said, startling him from his reverie.

'Arr?'

'Dunna be giving your mother werrit about all that talk at the yard, all the chunnering about brickmakers' unions and strikes and so forth. You know she'll only fuss.'

'And you know full well she'll be firing questions at us about that very subject.'

His father breathed out heavily. 'I do. But there be no need to encourage her.'

Owen thought for a few steps, as to his next words, which he chose carefully. 'I do think as she thinks though, on this subject, leastways. And I am a man now, entitled to my own views on matters of work and pay and suchlike.'

Another father might have laughed at that, scorned him, his boy. But not Peter Malone.

'I know it. And I am proud of you. You are everything a father could want in a son: upright, hard-working, good-hearted. And you know I worship your mother and she always was a person far cleverer than me. She was going places, Anny Woodvine. Until the sad times overcame her family. She was never the same after that. And I was lucky to have her even glance at me, let alone take me for a husband. But cleverness and anger can be a bitter brew. Think on it. That is all I ask.'

They walked on, Peter frowning, Owen thoughtful. They were passing down the steps beside the bridge now, along the riverside to the cluster of cottages where his home was, where his mother and father had grown up together as neighbours, where he himself was born. His grandparents had passed on some time ago, but before that they'd lived their whole lives here. The door stood open to the springtime evening, the smells of supper wafting over them as they stepped inside, the heat from the hearth filling the small space. And there was his mother, bent over the pot in which she boiled a sheep's head for their supper, her cheeks flushed from the steam. She raised her head and saw them, her dear face weary and careworn as ever, but at the sight of her beloveds, a smile lit up her face and turned it ten years younger.

After supper, Anny Malone liked to sit by the range and knit or sew, chatting with her husband Peter as he puffed on his clay pipe. She kissed him goodbye each morning and kissed him welcome home every evening. After eighteen years of marriage, she marvelled at how little they argued, how fond they still were, while all around them they heard couples rowing day in, day out, threatening all sorts of dreadful outcomes if she didna shut her trap or he didna move his backside, and so forth. But Anny and Peter had always been easy together. Of course, they had disagreements when the squalls of life knocked them about. Everyone did that. But there was a deep and abiding sense of calm between them, bonded by physical closeness. They had always hugged a lot and kissed a lot and embarrassed their only son with it in his younger years, who would cry, 'Leave off, you two!'

Anny smiled upon Owen now, watching him sitting beside them, carving chess figures from bits of wood he found lying about by the river. They already had one chess set that they used on winter evenings and now he was carving another. He'd always been good with his hands, Owen. A good mind too, sometimes beating her at chess, but not often. He'd learnt it a few years back from the master at school and borrowed a set from him to bring home. She'd kept her son in school as long as she possibly could, but he was needed at the brickyard in the warm months and once he'd had that taste of work, he grew tired of the schoolroom. She wouldn't allow their son to be a clay carrier for long. She'd seen the damage it had done to other children, their backs bent, their legs swollen. She did not want him to work at the brickyard at all, truth be known. But he wanted to be with his father. He adored him, followed him everywhere, every chance he got. So she agreed to it, as long as he still went to school in the winter till he was twelve and he learnt to read and write properly and to do his numbers. She'd revelled in watching him learn and worked at the table with him each evening when he was younger. She had even learnt chess from him and took to it quickly, a reminder that her brain had once been used for a higher purpose than the washing and sewing she took in at home. She had also started up a small business of making fidget pies, from her mother's time-worn recipe, in small individual portions that she sold to laundry customers for a good amount and to friends and neighbours cheap. It made a good few pennies and it comforted her, as it was her departed father's favourite and she thought on him every time she shaped the pastry. In summer, she made Mucky Mouth Pies from wimberries too, when the delicious blue fruits were ready to pick from the wild or buy from the market. Those were Owen's favourite, ever since he was little.

Dragging herself from her musings she turned to Peter and Owen and asked the question she knew they'd both been waiting for her to ask.

'What's the talk at work, then?'

Peter took a long draw on his pipe. She could see Owen wanted to answer, but deferred to his father.

'More nonsense from Adam.'

'They argued all day, on and off,' added Owen.

'Ruined my day,' muttered Peter.

'I don't know why you let him get to you,' said Anny. 'He's not even your blood. He was your cousin's husband and she died, poor soul. And now he's married again, within a few months.' Anny thought about Adam's new wife, Martha. People did marry after they'd been widowed – of course they did. But when Peter's lovely cousin, Judith, died young, nobody had predicted that her widower would marry again so soon. And Anny's mother had told her a rumour once, that Martha was found by her Quaker parents as a baby left on the iron bridge, but it had remained a rumour and never been proven. She seemed a nice woman, Martha, but Peter's family weren't too happy with Adam's choice and the speed of it. It left a bad taste in the mouth. 'You don't owe him anything. Why let him talk rubbish at you and get under your skin?'

'We are family,' said Peter. 'Cousins by marriage are still cousins. Just because we bicker dunna mean we inna family.'

Anny smiled to herself. Her ploy had worked. She winked at Owen who winked back. Both of them were trying to get Peter to come round to Adam's point of view. Anny knew well that if she criticised Peter's family, he would defend them. He always did.

'So, it wasn't all nonsense, what Adam had to say?'

Peter fell silent again, taking another thoughtful puff. Her son answered this time.

'Adam is talking of a strike!' said Owen, a kind of whispered awe in his voice betraying his excitement at the thought.

The word 'strike' fell into the room with a thud. Anny knew that it appealed to the young and impressionable ones, like her son. But to the old hands, the prospect of a strike was a huge worry. No pay for days, weeks, months even? It could mean the workhouse for some, even starvation for others if it went on too long. But if it worked? If they could twist the Kings into changing their unfair practices quickly, surely it would be worth the risk.

'Conditions of work at the brickyard have been awful for many a year,' said Anny. 'The long hours, the accidents. But what's starting this talk of a strike now? What's changed?'

Now Peter spoke. 'There is a rumour that the Kings are going to drop the pay per thousand bricks by thruppence. That's the talk hereabouts.'

The anger bloomed now in Anny. Her hatred of the King family of nearly two decades rose like bile in her throat and she was in no mood to swallow it. 'They seek to reduce pay when the price of everything else is shooting up?'

'Yes!' cried Owen. She could see he was glad she had spoken. He wanted to voice his opinions, despite his father's ominous silence. 'And I'd wager the selling price of their wares will stay the same, or even rise.'

'Well said, son,' replied Anny. 'And all the while you work longer hours than ever and risk more injury through exhaustion. Will those Kings never stop? I said this would happen when they took over the brickyard. I said you should leave and take up work elsewhere. Those Kings will never change. They let my poor father die, drove my mother to illness and ruin, and put me in prison for naught. How can you go on working for them?'

A pause followed while wife and son both looked at Peter, awaiting his response. But he said nothing, still puffing thoughtfully away. This was the only thing on which Anny could never agree with her husband: the King family. Then, Peter looked at her, his eyes serious and his mouth set in an annoyed grimace.

'I've told you a hundred times, woman, that nothing would change if I moved. All the brickmasters have made an agreement. They fix the prices and blacklist troublemakers. If we moved yards, we'd have yet further to walk to and from work each day. We'd be newer and lower in the pecking order. Any trouble and it'd be last in, first out. We'd have to put up with those outsiders who come from off, who've taken over the local brickyards hereabouts and set up their communes on the riverside, drinking and womanising till all hours. You know all this! At least at our yard there are decent, local families working there and have done for generations. So what if the Kings own it now? Our last master got himself bankrupt and nearly shut the whole yard down. Would you rather poverty and the workhouse, than us work for Kings?'

'Yes!' spat Anny. 'I would rather die than work for them myself.' And with that, she threw down her knitting and stomped outside.

She regretted raising her voice to her husband, she always did. Though since it was so rare, it felt like a small crime to lose her temper with him. But she was proud and did not want to go back in and apologise, not yet at any rate. And besides, she did not regret her words or their sentiment, as she felt it keenly.

It was a warm March evening, still light and busy around the houses, with neighbours feeding their animals and chatting. The smell of boiling sheep's head drifted on the air, as a few of them had bought it this week, a rare deal going cheap. Most of the men she saw wore the same caps as her husband and puffed on the same kind of pipes, made up the river from the local clay. The same pipes, the same clothes, the same food. The same lives. She had wanted more once. She had worked in the King office as a clerical assistant and had been tipped for greater things, maybe even an office worker in Shrewsbury one day. But the Kings had ruined it – the cruel and lecherous young son of the house had tried to woo her, had been rejected by her and had framed her for theft. She could not even bear to think of his name, let alone say it aloud, but yes, Cyril King had sent her to prison with his treacherous lies. It was disproven eventually, but while she was gone, her father had died at the King furnace explosion, an accident that was no accident, that could have been avoided if Ralph King had spent more money on taking care of his ironworks. Her mother never fully recovered and died a few years on.

And what of Anny Woodvine, as she was then, she thought? Had she ever fully recovered? She fell in love with her husband Peter, when he and his mother nursed her back to health after her desperate prison days. She still missed Peter's mother.

She had her beloved and only child, Owen. She'd learnt to put aside the ambition of her youth and see the value in a simple life. The only vestige of the Anny she used to be was that she'd taught herself back then to speak without the rhythms of the local dialect, forcing her speech to echo that of her masters. She still had that touch of the other girl about her, but that was all. That other Anny was gone, long ago. She was proud of their home, which she kept spick and span, just as her mother had taught her. Anny was proud of the work she did and the customers who valued her neat and tidy laundry and mending, always perfectly done, perfectly folded and doing so well she now was able to hire local girls and boys to help with deliveries. She was proud too of the delicious pies she made and the money they brought in. Her father – God rest his soul, taken from this earth too soon – would have been proud to see her do so well and have married such a good man. They loved each other. They had secure jobs. They had a beautiful boy, growing into a fine young man. They were complete. They were happy. But the poison of the Kings and what they had done to her family still crept in her veins. There was no escape from it. She would hate them with all of her heart until her dying day, beyond if truth be known. *When I die*, she thought, *I shall come back and haunt them, the forsaken bastards.*

Chapter 3

Queenie watched the procession of mourners follow the hearse up the road towards the church on the hill. It was a paltry gathering. Cyril had insisted that all the King workers be forced to attend, but Queenie had refused to allow this. First of all, they would lose a day's work and earnings if all their workers were off. Secondly, she knew none of them cared for Ralph King and it would be a spectacle of falsehood. And she couldn't abide false things, lies and mendacity of any sort. Her son was disliked and that was the truth. Nobody would weep for him or even honour him.

She'd loved her son once, but even she had trouble mourning the man he'd become. By the time her husband had passed on more than two decades before, she had grown completely cold towards him. And now for her son, she felt the same. Sadly, Ralph King Junior was a small-minded, self-centred and cruel man, with little natural intelligence. Left to him the King fortunes and name would dwindle to nothing. The best thing that could be said about him was that he lacked the appetites of the flesh that his father had been so prone to. He made a hash of everything he involved himself in, even this, his death, dying before her. The doctor had said it wasn't the gout that killed him as such, but that his overindulgence in food and wine had put such pressure on his liver and other organs, that the unwholesome mixture had poisoned his blood and caused his body to give up the ghost.

Yet there was a small part of her buried deep that had looked upon her dying son in his sickbed and had mourned the baby she had once doted upon. He was a fat, jolly infant and she had adored him so, especially after losing her twin baby daughters to consumption before him.

She was glad he had died before Margaret and Beatrice arrived. Queenie would not want them to have to see him as he was in his last days. That was no way for a man to be remembered. Especially for Beatrice. *Ah, Beatrice!* she thought, and sighed contentedly as the procession reached the churchyard. The pall-bearers, including Cyril, were gathering to carry the coffin inside. But Queenie's eyes were seeking out her great-granddaughter and there she was, standing demurely beside her mother, watching the proceedings with interest. *I wonder what she makes of us?* thought Queenie. As the thought entered her mind, she was surprised at it. She never gave a damn what anybody thought of her personally. It was the King reputation that was crucial and must be protected at all costs. But suddenly, at this late point in her life, this pretty little half-French thing had entered stage left and Queenie could think of little else. Beatrice was in her house and in her life now and Queenie could not be more delighted with her. She watched her now and tried to get the measure of her.

Beatrice was standing with her mother near to the church door. Her hands were demurely folded before her. Her eyes glanced down from time to time, showing she was a little reserved, and she also looked to her mother for reassurance often. But she was nothing like Margaret had been as a young person, desperately shy to the point of infuriating Queenie. With Beatrice it seemed more a kind of watchfulness, taking it all in and working on it in her mind. There was something very intelligent in the girl's eyes.

Now the girl was looking at Benjamina, her step-grandmother. Beatrice had a weakness for fashion, that was clear. Her outfits were a little fussy and flouncy for local tastes; it must be the French influence. Beatrice seemed to be looking at Benjamina's vulgar black creation today with interest. She wore a frilly black bonnet with a veil, a lacy mantle and embroidered gloves. *The grieving widow*, thought Queenie wryly, inspecting Benjamina. *Ha!*

She remembered her own relief when her cruel husband had passed. But this one was still young – by Queenie's standards anyway. Benjamina had been seventeen when Ralph had married her and now she was free and rich at only forty-two, with no children to encumber her. Queenie wondered what she would get up to next. *Let us hope she finds another wealthy fool and leaves us alone*, thought Queenie. She had noticed in the past few days that Beatrice, despite liking Benjamina's clothes, soon ran out of conversation with her. Benjamina was tedious and had little to discuss other than fashion and dogs.

Queenie looked away from her in disgust and focused back on Beatrice. Something else had caught the girl's attention now; Cyril was taking the coffin on to his shoulders, but was saying something, loudly.

'Watch out, there!' he cried, in his petulant voice. The King family butler, Busby, shouldered the opposite corner to Cyril. The coffin swayed dangerously and tipped, but was soon righted by the butler who kept his decorum at all times, unlike the idiot Cyril, who huffed and puffed and shot evil glances around, blaming everyone but himself, as usual. Queenie looked back at Beatrice, who actually grimaced and looked away. Queenie could see from the first day that Beatrice was repelled by Cyril. What an excellent judge of character the girl must be. Each passing day, Queenie grew more and more fascinated by her.

There was a tap on her arm and Queenie's reverie was interrupted. It was her faithful lady's maid, Jenkins, who nodded her head towards the church.

Queenie acquiesced. Jenkins could always be relied upon to keep her eyes and ears open. She entered the church, Jenkins leading her to her place of honour in the front row. Queenie watched as the coffin bearing her son's corpse was lifted into place before the meagre congregation. *I wonder if he'll haunt me, like the other?* she thought.

Later, at the wake at Southover, Queenie's feet were beginning to ache after all this standing about.

'We sincerely commiserate with you for your great loss at this difficult time.'

I wonder if they know how much I disliked my own son, thought Queenie, but said aloud instead, 'Thank you most kindly.'

Her son's wake was nearly over, thank heavens, but there was still a good deal of tasty food remaining, so some of the greedier guests continued to gobble it down. Queenie nodded politely as the wife of a local tile manufacturer wittered on about the cost of black silk these days. These types of people were the only reliable ones they could find to attend Ralph King's funeral, business associates of his – mostly of Queenie's to be frank as Ralph was never any good at running the business. He was the male figurehead of the King fortune, but everyone knew that it was herself who ran it all and had done for twenty-odd years. Her grandson Cyril had done his bit, visiting the works from time to time and chivvying on the foreman and suchlike. He wined and dined the other brickmasters and made connections in the counties beyond with other industrialists. But he had no true business acumen. It was Queenie alone who ruled the King businesses and she did so with an iron fist.

The wife was still talking to her and Queenie was nodding sympathetically and hoping she wouldn't be required to respond to any particulars, as she hadn't heard a word of it. She was watching Beatrice again, who was now standing near to the window and gazing out of it, with rather a lost expression. The poor girl must be bored to tears and feeling very alone at this gathering of strangers, all from England, from Shropshire, speaking of things Beatrice knew nothing about, and gathered for a man Beatrice had never known.

'Mrs Elkin,' Queenie interrupted the wife who stopped abruptly, mid-flow. 'Have you met my great-granddaughter, Beatrice?'

'I have not had the pleasure,' simpered the Elkin woman, while Queenie swept past her, gesturing her to follow. She advanced towards Beatrice by the window, who turned to notice her approach. Queenie was greeted by a dazzling smile, which delighted her.

'Beatrice, this is Mrs Elkin.'

'Delighted, I'm sure,' said the woman.

'And I too am delighted to make your acquaintance,' said Beatrice.

The girl speaks well, thought Queenie. *More than well. Her English is excellent.*

'May I offer my condolences for the passing of your . . . grandfather?'

'Yes, my grandfather. Thank you. I never had the fortune to meet him, but I understand he was a great man.'

Queenie raised her eyebrows a touch. She was impressed by Beatrice's diplomacy. How many girls her age would be arch enough to play that game so well? But Queenie was eager to steer clear of discussing her son.

'Beatrice, I should explain that Mrs Elkin's husband manages a decorative tileworks along the river.'

'Decorative tiles?' said Beatrice to the wife. 'Are they very pretty?'

'Oh, yes! Very pretty they are. I cannot pretend to understand the business itself, but I know a pretty thing when I see it. These decorated tiles are the latest thing. We have them all over the front of our house. It is like a show house, you see, to show off our wares. You must come to see us one day for afternoon tea, Miss Beatrice.'

'I would love that,' said Beatrice. Queenie's pleasure at the girl's social skills grew with every word. She could not be more different from her mother at that age, who had always cowered and hidden from every social opportunity.

'Oh and this is my husband now,' said Mrs Elkin, gesturing to a short man of broad girth who had manoeuvred past a range of snacking guests to appear at his wife's side.

Introductions were made and Queenie continued to watch as Beatrice responded to this dull couple so deftly.

Beatrice said, 'I understand you make beautiful tiles, Mr Elkin.'

Husband and wife smiled at each other and Mr Elkin attempted to laugh it off, but was clearly charmed.

'Well, I say, I find them so, as does my wife. Just recently, my tileworks has specialised in producing a range of encaustic tiles, with elaborate designs. Quite lovely. Exquisite, some might say.'

'And where do you sell such lovely things?' said Beatrice. 'We all know the world needs bricks, but where do you find your customers for such fancy work?'

'Why, all over the country, Miss Beatrice. All over the world, if I have my way! We do such fine work, it is a joy to behold. Very attractive. The ladies love it. You must come and see our house.'

'I said the very same thing, Edwin,' added Mrs Elkin. 'We'd be delighted to have you, my dear.'

Queenie watched Beatrice as she went on with the conversation, talking with these two stuffed shirts as if she'd known them for years. The girl had managed to flatter them, appear interested and even knowledgeable about a business she surely knew nothing about and had garnered an invitation to tea from both husband and wife in just a few utterances. Queenie was delighted her first impressions of the girl had been correct, that she was not shy but instead watchful with a busy mind. Her company was as lovely as her appearance, an excellent coupling in society. But she was no mere society belle, practised in the art of small talk. She showed real interest in Elkin's business. They were talking of which clays they used in its manufacture now. Queenie stared at Beatrice as she negotiated each turn of the conversation with ease, and at that moment, Queenie made a decision. She vowed that she would take the girl under her wing, introduce her successfully into society and teach her about the business. Her son Ralph and grandson Cyril had been such disappointments when it came to running the King businesses, whilst her one hope, Margaret, had run off with an artist and forfeited her place. Now here was a bright young woman who possessed a true spark of life. This girl would be her protégé and Queenie couldn't wait to get started on her. With the right influence Beatrice might even one day lead the King family.

Chapter 4

Beatrice was taught the waltz first. Madame said that the galop and polka would come next, with the mazurka last, as it was the most tricky.

'You are coming of age at the most thrilling moment in the history of dance!' exclaimed Madame at the end of her first dance lesson. 'Dancing closely with a man is now the fashion. Lucky you, Beatrice! Ah, to be young in 1858.'

Beatrice smiled uncertainly as Madame fanned herself in dramatic fashion with one hand, while touching her forehead with the back of the other. Maman had told her that Madame was actually called Mrs Prescott and was Shropshire born and bred, yet had taken the name Madame and a fake French accent to attract more pupils. When introduced to Madame, Beatrice had begun speaking in French, glad to speak it again after a couple of weeks of only English. But Madame had looked at her somewhat aghast and Beatrice realised that her dance teacher did not speak a word of French.

'Are you not excited by the thought, my dear?' said Madame.

'The idea of dancing with a young man?' said Beatrice.

'Why, yes!'

'Well, I can't see that the huge crinoline under my skirt would allow me to get closer to a man than an arm's length, or even further!' laughed Beatrice.

But Madame did not appreciate this and pursed her lips with disapproval. For a fake Frenchwoman, she certainly seemed to disapprove of any nod to Beatrice's slightly risqué sense of humour. She ignored the comment and went on, 'Are there are any young men you have had the pleasure of meeting here in Ironbridge?'

'I am newly arrived and have not yet had the pleasure.'

'Well, there is not much choice hereabouts. Shrewsbury would suit you much better. Some lovely young men there. But around these parts, you'd better seek out the masters' sons. Ironmasters, brickmasters, coalmasters. They are all educating their sons these days and I teach them all to dance. The gentry on the country estates have their own dance teachers, of course. But for the rich in town, like your family, then I am the one they come to. You are lucky I managed to fit you in, my dear. I am so busy. So very much in demand!'

And so Madame went on, rattling through stories of her first dances back in the day, which boys made eyes at her and how many hearts she broke and so forth. Beatrice listened with a polite, fixed smile but inside her stomach was groaning and all she could think of was finishing this dance lesson and meeting Maman. She would ask if they could visit a tea shop and have cake.

English cake was her new obsession, especially the sponge sandwich with jam and cream. She had not eaten since luncheon and it was now late afternoon and she felt ravenous. Beatrice's attention began to wander. She did not find dancing particularly interesting.

And it was not only dancing that bored her; the whole idea of being a debutante, of 'coming out' – something her grandmother and now her mother seemed obsessed with – it all seemed rather silly to Beatrice. In Paris she walked to the local shops alone, she met friends in the street and chatted, she ate snacks when she felt like it.

On arriving at the Kings' beautiful house, she was bowled over by the furnishings, the clothes, the servants. This last confused her the most. She had been expressly told by her great-grandmother that the servants were there to serve, no more and not to be friendly with them in any way. But Beatrice was used to talking to everyone, to anyone. There was a girl, her own maid, called Dinah. She had round pink cheeks and a shy smile, a nice soft voice with that local lilt of the Shropshire accent that Beatrice found so lovely, like music. When Dinah came to Beatrice to help with her clothes or hair, or to clean her room, or make up her fire, Beatrice would ignore the rules and try to engage Dinah in conversation. But it hadn't worked yet. Dinah was not only shy but she adhered to the house rules admirably – or disappointingly, for Beatrice. She was not used to this, this lack of conversation, this stiffness. It was the thing she disliked most about England.

But her favourite thing about England so far was her great-grandmother. She could see that some might find her a difficult woman, but with Beatrice Queenie would sit for hours telling her stories of the family – of Margaret as a shy girl and Cyril as a naughty boy and of her own sister Selina who sadly died young. She told her about the Kings, their history and their place in society. Queenie's eyes sparkled when she told these stories and Beatrice was pleased to hear them, her hitherto shadowy understanding of her background coming into the light and seen in sharp focus, a whole world of family she'd known little about until now.

Her other favourite thing about England were mealtimes. Such hearty meals, of several courses, cooked for you and brought to you at the table. But she had to wait so long for each mealtime and there was no opportunity to wander into the pantry and grab an apple or pop opposite to the *boulangerie* and have a croissant, as at home. Here everything was orchestrated at set times, with no exceptions. The formality of it all was beginning to grate. She had so much more freedom in Paris and virtually none here. She would have to be met by her mother after this class to be escorted home, even though it was only a short walk up to the house from town. She had admired Benjamina's clothes immensely but now her mother was at the dressmaker ordering some outfits for both of them and she wondered how restrictive the English styles would be; Benjamina never looked relaxed or comfortable, but perhaps that was her way, rather than her corset.

If Beatrice were honest with herself, she was confused by her new life here. She loved being spoiled, being waited upon, the richness of clothes and bedding, the bath by the fire filled for her by a maid. She loved the way her great-grandmother sought her out every day and talked to her. She was happy too to see her mother rest for once, at last, after years of work and struggle. It was a joy to see her being indulged, taking an afternoon nap, with no pupils to bother her, no bills to pay, but Beatrice missed home, its freedoms and their friends. She did not want to tell her mother that, as she seemed so happy here. Despite her new privileges, Beatrice secretly preferred her old life.

The window in the dancing room was ajar and through it came the savoury scent of freshly baked goods, which made her insides twist for food even more. She followed her nose and glanced past Madame's shoulder, through the window to the back yard outside. There, she saw a young man had come to the back door, carrying a basket covered with a cloth. He was tall and had yellow hair. The thin April sunshine caught it in that light and made it shine golden. A servant came out and questioned the young man. He lifted the cloth and showed her his wares, a batch of pies. Beatrice's stomach groaned in return. The servant was shaking her head at the young man and having words with him. Beatrice could hear the shrill tone of the servant and it caught Madame's ear too, who simply spoke more loudly, droning on now about the correct use of fans.

At last, Beatrice said, 'I think it is time, Madame. I must go and meet my mother now.'

'Ah indeed, our time is up. See you tomorrow for your next lesson. Send the next one in, will you? If she is there, that is. That girl is always tardy.'

Beatrice gathered her bonnet, shawl and purse and headed out into the corridor. Instead of going right to the front door, she took a glance behind her, then went left instead, towards the back of the house. She found a door to the outside and opened it. There was the young man and his pies and the servant still arguing with him.

'I ordered only four pies, Owen Malone. I dunna care what yer mother says.'

'But she has made five and she expects the money for five,' said the young man.

Beatrice spied the pies again, each one identical and beautifully turned, each one small and individual, perfect for one person to hold in their hands.

'I shall buy it from you,' said Beatrice.

Both faces turned to her in shock, the servant crossing her arms, the young man staring.

‘How much for the pie?’ she asked, reaching into her purse.

‘There y’are,’ said the serving woman, taking the four pies and piling them two by two on her arm and disappearing behind the door, which she kicked shut.

The young man did not speak, simply stared at Beatrice as if she had landed that very moment from the sky.

‘Please, I really am ever so hungry and those pies look very good,’ she said.

‘Then you must have it, miss,’ he said and held out the basket towards her.

‘How much?’ she said.

‘Try it first,’ he said, the corner of his mouth turning up. He was nervous but he was finding his way now. ‘Then you may judge how much it be worth.’

Beatrice smiled and took the pie. In Paris, they often ate street food. But here in Ironbridge, the Kings only ate at the table with a full set of cutlery dazzling in its complexity, one of the many new things Beatrice was having to learn. It was good to take food sealed in its own container and simply bite into it, no napkin, no knife and fork, no decorum to speak of. She took a big bite, at which sight the young man’s eyes grew even wider. As Beatrice chewed, the tastes of pork, onion and a hint of sweetness enveloped her taste buds. It was still slightly warm, so must have been freshly baked that afternoon.

'Hmmm,' she said as she polished off her mouthful. 'It is magnificent! Pork and apple, is it? What a lovely combination.'

'It is a fidget pie.'

'Fidget pie? What a curious and charming name! What can it mean?'

'Some say it is from the shape, being somewhat five-sided. Fidget can mean five round here.'

'How delightful! And your mother bakes these fidget pies?'

'Yes and makes a pretty penny selling them.'

'Please tell her from me that it is the best food I've eaten in England yet.'

'In the whole of England?' he scoffed.

'Well,' she said, desperate to take another bite but enjoying the conversation too much, 'I have only seen Ironbridge so far and some places en route from the port. But this is by far the best, in that limited experience.'

'You are from off then, miss?'

'From where?'

'Not from round here. An incomer, as they say? You dunna sound local. And you dunna look like an Ironbridge lass, if you dunna mind me saying.'

Beatrice laughed and said, 'Indeed no. I am "from off", as you say. I come from France.'

His eyes were wide again. Beatrice took another bite and savoured the delicious taste. He watched her with amusement as she wiped the crumbs from her mouth. She wondered what he thought of her.

'You sound English though, miss.'

'I learnt both languages growing up in Paris, as my mother is English. Oh! My mother! I forgot all about her!'

She glanced around and saw a wooden gate that she guessed led out into the street.

'Where is your mother?'

'She's coming to meet me out at the front of the house.'

'Here, miss. I'll show you. It's just through there.'

'Thank you so much,' she said and took another bite. He opened the gate for her and they both stepped into the street. The young man looked both ways, then something caught his eye down the road. Two men were walking their way and the young man must have known them, as they nodded to each other as they passed, staring at her and glancing back at him, their heads falling close.

'I'll show you to the main street, then be on my way, miss,' he said.

'Your name is Owen, is that right?' said Beatrice.

'It is,' said Owen and looked curiously at her. 'But how . . .?'

'I heard the maid at the house call you that.'

'You have sharp ears, miss,' he said and smiled.

'My name is Bea.'

'Bea? Like the buzzing kind? Or like the letter?'

'Just Bea. With an A.'

He touched his forehead and nodded with a simple gallantry. 'Charmed, Miss Bea with an A.'

She took another bite of the pie as they walked up to the main road. There was no sign of her mother yet, so she walked up to the steps of Madame's house and turned to see Owen turn the other way.

'But are you not going to say farewell?'

Owen looked about him and replied in a low voice, 'I dunna think you want to be seen talking with the likes of me on the main street.'

'I happen to like talking to the likes of whomever I please, wherever I please,' she said and smiled.

It must have been infectious, as Owen smiled back. 'That the French way, is it, miss?'

'Perhaps. Or maybe it is just my way, just Bea's way.'

'I inna sure that Ironbridge is ready for Bea's way quite yet,' he said and she smiled. He was teasing her.

She laughed and said, without thinking, without pausing, 'I don't think I really fit in here. I don't have any friends here yet. I feel rather lonely.'

Owen's face was hard to read. She immediately regretted her honesty, as it seemed to have embarrassed him, this lad, this pie-seller. But he was kind to her and had such a friendly manner. And such a nice face.

'It must be very hard,' he said quietly. 'Leaving your home behind. And everything you know.'

'It is!' she said. 'Nobody understands that. Until you.'

There was a moment where they looked at each other and she felt her cheeks warming. She looked away, taking one last mouthful of the pie to cover her embarrassment, not wanting to look at him, though she wanted to very much at the same time.

'Farewell then, Miss Bea,' she heard him say.

'But the pie,' she cried as he turned away. 'How much for the pie?'

Owen glanced back and said, 'The pie is my treat. Take it as a welcome to Ironbridge.' And with that, he turned and strode off down the street, his basket knocking against his hip as he went.

'Beatrice!'

And there was Maman.

'I'm so sorry, *chérie*. The dressmaker took so long finding the silk we wanted for . . . But what is that around your mouth?'

'Tidget pie,' she said dreamily, as she wiped her mouth and stared down the road, her eyes searching. But there was no sign of Owen Malone. He had been swallowed up by the crowds of folk going to and fro about their business.

The girl from the coach. It was surely the girl from the coach. Those same dark eyes, that same chestnut hair, even more shiny close up. Newly arrived in town. Her clothes, so curious, so different from the local girls. And she loved fidget pie. She loved his mother's fidget pie and ate it in the street, the crumbs dropping all over her shoes. Pink shoes.

'Malone, mon! Watch yerself!'

'He's in a dream. He's dreaming of the King girl!'

He turned in shock to see the two mates from the brickyard he'd spotted in the street earlier. It was Royce and Brain, two lads from the brickworks. Royce was around the same age as him and mostly worked as a labourer who dug out the clay. Brain was Royce's cousin or second cousin or something, and was as tall as Owen, though only being twelve years of age. Brain did a variety of jobs around the works, whatever he was bidden to do. They were all right lads, not too bright. Brain was thick-headed, which caused great hilarity due to his name. Royce was cleverer but not as genial as his cousin, more dour and even a touch bitter was Royce. But both were generally good to work with. And loyal, to the workers and to the yard, particularly to cousin Adam. They did anything Adam said and listened rapt when he spouted forth about workers' conditions. But what was it Royce just said?

'The what girl?' said Owen, stepping out of the flow of people on the pavement.

'Who you were chunnering with. That's the new King girl,' said Royce.

'She's a King?'

'You didna know? It's the talk of the town. The King daughter came back from France, after running off there with 'er fancy man all those years back. She brought her own darter back with 'er.'

'That's her? She's a King?'

'What did she want with the likes of you?' said Brain.

Owen stared off up the street, as if the girl from the coach might appear like magic before him. Bea, she said her name was. Bea. So, she was the Beatrice he'd heard tell of, the King. He'd heard the gossip, paid little attention to it. He wished he'd listened more now. She was . . . something he couldn't put into words, clear thoughts eluding him. She was so many things, so new and astonishing, it confounded his mind. But there was only one thing that sounded clearly in his head like a knell, she was a King.

'What did she want, mon?' insisted Royce. Owen looked back at them. He felt momentarily embarrassed by his distraction. They were smirking at him.

'She bought a pie,' he replied and knew that it was a lie, but a small lie. What did it matter, if she bought a pie or he gave her one for free? That was his business. But he suddenly realised with a jolt that he'd have to account for the lost coin to his mother and what would he say? *I'll tell her I ate it*, he thought.

'What would your cousin Adam say to see you talking with the enemy, eh?' said Royce.

Owen focused back quickly. 'I just sold her a pie, that's all. Making money inna a crime now, is it?'

'Depends whose money it is,' said Royce, an allegation hanging in the air. 'Listen, we're going to a meeting at the tavern now, with Adam and the others. Come with us. We'll be talking of the strike.'

'Arr, come with us, mon,' said Brain cheerfully, as if it were an invite to a picnic. 'It's at The Swan. The one on The Wharfage, not Lincoln Hill.'

Royce added, 'Adam'll want you there. It's a Sunday, you've got nothing else to do. You're needed there.'

'Not today, lads. Father is expecting me with this money. He has to pay a neighbour back who he borrowed from.' Another lie. Normally, he'd be excited at the prospect of a workers' meeting. But his parents had been rowing about it all more and more lately. And their arguments confused and upset him. He was not sure these days what he thought about the situation at work. He agreed with his mother's arguments that the masters were exploiting them, making coin while they went without and their children were forced into back-breaking labour just so their families could put food on the table. Something must be done, yet he understood his father's concerns too. The masters were in cahoots and had them tied up proper, with their price fixing and their stiff contracts. His father was worried about what would happen to local families if a strike came to pass; with no money coming in, essentials would soon be unaffordable. And strikes so often meant violence, as they'd heard of riots and trouble with the law in other parts of the country during strikes. So, his father maintained that nothing good would come of action. Owen agreed with parts of both, though his parents could not see an inch of common ground. He felt as if his home was battling itself, as well as his own mind.

'Another time, then,' said Royce and looked meaningfully at Owen. 'It would be good to see you more useful with all this. You believe in the cause, dunna you?'

'Course I do.'

Royce squinted at him. 'Your cousin leads us and I hear your mother is keen on action. But your father lets the side down.'

Owen bristled at this, though he knew it were true. 'Every man is entitled to his own opinion and must listen to his own conscience.'

'Arr, that be true,' said Brain, nodding. But Royce was not so congenial.

'Not when it comes to war. And that is what we are engaged in, mon. Make no mistake. We are skirmishing at present with the masters. But it wonna be long before it's war.'

'You'd be good on the stage, Royce,' said Owen. 'Natural flair for drama. Or a politician. You'd have to be good at lying though.' He had always liked Brain. But he had never been sure of Royce.

Royce narrowed his eyes at Owen and leant forward. 'Oh, I will lie and cheat and play dirty if needs be, when it serves our cause. And so will you, Malone. This meeting you had with that'un today could prove useful. I'll be telling your cousin that you've been seen talking with the King girl and ooh, how she did smile upon you and simper and blush like a sweet apple in your very presence! Most useful, that could be. We'll see what plans your cousin might have for you with that choice piece of news.'

'Tell him what you like,' said Owen and stepped aside from Royce's attention, too close for comfort. 'Brain,' he said pleasantly, nodding at him. The implications of Royce's words were beyond the likes of Brain. He just wanted to be involved, like a loyal dog.

Owen began to whistle a merry tune as he walked away from them and headed for home. But he knew it was fakery. Inside, his mind was churning like the river in a winter storm.

Chapter 5

'Wake up. Wake up, Miss Alice.'

Queenie fought the hands that held her shoulders, urging her to wake. Even half asleep, she knew it was Jenkins, her lady's maid, who was trying to wake her. Only Jenkins called her by her real name, Alice.

'What is it, for heaven's sake? Is the very house on fire?'

'No, the brickyard is.'

Queenie's eyes snapped open. Jenkins had lit a lamp and Queenie could see Jenkins's alarmed face, looking old, deep shadows beneath the eyes. 'What's this?'

'The foreman is here. Shall I send Cyril?'

Queenie's brain was still in a bit of a fog. But she knew what she thought of that. 'Lord, no. Don't send that idiot. Here, fetch my robe.'

'The foreman can't see you in this state, you silly old thing! What will he think?'

'I do not care!' insisted Queenie. 'Hurry or I shall face him in my nightdress.'

Queenie pulled herself out of bed while Jenkins did her best to make her presentable, helping her on with her robe and fixing her hair with a couple of pins. *Fire at the brickworks? Why was the foreman here instead of there, dealing with it?* Jenkins held Queenie's arm to walk her to the door, but she did not require it. She felt perfectly strong now.

'Enough, Jenkins. I shall proceed alone.'

She walked out onto the landing, to see the butler waiting for her, stiff as a rod.

'What is occurring then, Busby?'

'Mr Troon awaits you in the hall, ma'am. Shall I send him to your study?'

'No, the hallway will do fine,' said Queenie.

Then, a door off the landing opened and Benjamina appeared, a picture of languorous beauty in her dishevelled night attire.

'There is nothing to concern you here,' snapped Queenie. 'Go back to bed.'

'Is there trouble at the house?' she said in a fragile voice, a mock-feminine voice if you asked Queenie. 'Busby?'

Queenie hated the way Benjamina turned to the servants for answers when she herself refused. It only embarrassed them.

'This is business,' she said, and then to Busby, 'Lead on.'

'Yes, ma'am,' said Busby and swiftly turned to go below and tell the man to wait. He motioned with one quick sharp hand movement to a footman, who swiftly held up a lamp to guide Queenie down the stairs.

'Thank you, Grainger,' she said and followed him. She took pride in knowing the name of every member of staff, however humble. When she had acquired the brickworks a year ago, she had done the same thing with the list of workers' names. She insisted that the foreman, Troon, sent her updates regularly on who was hired and fired, so that she could keep a track of the families that worked there, where they lived, which family members they hired themselves and who came from outside the area. She had asserted that they try to keep to locals only. Those outsiders who came down from Lord knows where looking for brickmaking work were her last choice for workers. She wanted the tried and tested local folk the most. They were bad enough with their grumblings, but the ones who came down from elsewhere, they were the troublemakers, the drinkers and the talkers of uprisings and charters. Local people just wanted to make a living and that suited her fine. But there were not always enough of the locals to fill the skilled work, like the brickmoulders or the brickburners. There was one from Liverpool, another from Manchester. She had told Troon to keep an eye on them. She didn't know if he did or not. She didn't know if she could trust Troon yet.

Troon was standing in the middle of the hallway, cap in hand, watching her come down the stairs as if he'd seen a ghost. Busby stood to the side, near the doorway to the drawing room, his hands folded before him, his eyes lowered, awaiting instructions. Queenie decided to keep him there. His stalwart service was comforting to her, especially at times of vexation, like this might prove to be.

'Troon, there is trouble at the brickworks, I hear,' she said to the foreman as she approached.

'I didna mean to wake you, ma'am. I thought it might be Mr King a-coming.'

'No, I am your superior here, Troon. Now, what is this business that requires waking me past ten at night?'

'There was a fire at the brickworks. But it's out now. Someone came in and set fire to one of the sheds. The kiln men were around and they saw two fellows running away into the woods, so they chased them but they eluded them, ma'am.' He was pleased with the word 'eluded', Queenie could tell. 'Then the kiln men put the fire out. All is well now and the damage inna too bad.'

'Was anyone hurt?'

'No, ma'am. Just some damage. No injuries.'

Queenie chose her next words with care. 'Is it possible, do you think, that it might have been one of the kiln men that started the fire? Perhaps it was . . . an accident.'

Troon looked affronted. 'That would never be, ma'am. They are good men, through and through.

Worked at the yard nigh on ten year. Trust 'em with my life, I would. All good men, at the King brickworks. All good men.'

'Then, who set this fire? And for what purpose?'

'That I canna say.' Troon's face was blank.

'You "canna" say? Or you "wonna" say?' Queenie narrowed her eyes at the man. He was a good foreman in his way, excellent with facts and figures, liked by the workers and always on time with their meetings. He knew the business inside out, had worked in it since he was a boy, carrying clay to his father's table. He was a tall, broad man in his thirties, family worked with him at the yard, quite handsome with a bit of a twinkle in his eye. But his face at times was so difficult to read and she had not found the trick of it yet.

'If I knew, I would surely tell you, ma'am. We dunna want trouble at the works. Why would we set fire to our own livelihood?'

'To make a point,' said Queenie, raising her bony finger and pointing it directly at him. 'I've heard tell of meetings in town, Troon. Seditious talk.'

'Workers grumble and talk, that is true. Always have. There is nothing in it.'

Queenie looked at him but again, the face gave nothing away.

'Thank you for coming to give me notice of this occurrence, Troon. It was good of you. I am most grateful to know that no one was hurt.'

'Ma'am.'

'Tomorrow, you should surmise the cost of the repairs and supervise the rebuilding of the shed. And I want you to look into this occurrence further. Talk to the workers and find out if anyone knows anything. Report back to me by evening.'

'Yes, ma'am.'

'I do not like this turn of events, Troon. I do not like it at all. And it is your job to keep order in that yard. Make sure you do so. I shall see you tomorrow. Get home to your wife and children now.'

'Ma'am,' he said again and turned to leave.

'Mr Troon,' said a voice behind her. Coming down the stairs, fully clothed and hair loose about her shoulders, was Benjamina. Queenie felt herself colour with rage. What on earth did she want, dolled up like that?

'Yes Ma'am?' said Troon, his eyes agog.

'What do you want here?' said Queenie, turning at the foot of the stairs to stand directly in between Benjamina and Troon. What on earth was she up to, interrupting them?

'I think the man deserves some refreshment, don't you?' said Benjamina, looking past Queenie and offering a dazzling smile to Troon.

'This is business and does not concern you,' snapped Queenie. Benjamina had never had as much as a sniff of business matters before now. Why was she involving herself?

'But I understand Mr Troon has had a terrible night of it,' replied Benjamina and stepped past Queenie, swiftly positioning herself beside him.

'As I said . . .' began Queenie, dismayed that the woman was interfering with her meeting. But Benjamina interrupted her and continued to speak to Troon directly.

'Please accept our hospitality in return for your good service in coming all this way from the yard to tell us of the trouble. You must feel free to come to me with anything. With my dear husband gone, I know he would want me to step in, to ensure that the brickworkers are well taken care of. Busby, will you take Troon to the kitchen and furnish him with food and perhaps some ale?'

'Thank'ee most kindly, ma'am!' crowed Troon, who caught Queenie's eye then looked suitably chastised. Queenie saw too that Busby was appalled by the suggestion, yet had to follow the mistress's orders. He said gruffly to Troon, 'This way', and led him off.

Benjamina stood smiling sweetly at Queenie, who really wanted to slap the strumpet in the face. What was she thinking, interfering like that? Ingratiating herself with one such as Troon? Anyone watching might have felt that Benjamina was being kind. But Queenie knew better. That woman gave not one jot of care for those below her. Before Queenie could summon up the energy to give her a tongue-lashing, Benjamina turned and ascended the stairs languidly.

‘I don’t know what you think you’re up to!’ cried Queenie after her.

Benjamina turned and looked down upon her. ‘Carrot and stick, mother-in-law,’ she said enigmatically, then went back upstairs, too quickly now for Queenie to continue the conversation. Whatever did she mean? Oh, the damned woman. If she’d shown even a spark of interest in the business before, Queenie might have welcomed the help. But she’d known Benjamina for years, and while she was certainly clever enough, she was a schemer who was only out for herself. She’d squeeze every penny of profit out of the works to buy pretty dresses and fabulous jewels, but her inability to think outside her own interests would soon see the business fail. If she thought she was going to used Ralph’s death to gain a place in the business she had another thing coming. The sooner she was gone, off with a new husband, the better. Queenie would have to seek one out and marry her off.

But something told her that would be a much harder task than it sounded, with this vixen to deal with. Queenie and Benjamina had never liked each other, but she had been easy to deal with when Ralph was alive. She’d never had any interest in anything beyond herself. This new development of Benjamina interfering with the business was a new addition to Queenie’s daily stresses that she did not need.

The whole experience had greatly fatigued Queenie and she hauled herself up the stairs to find Jenkins waiting for her on the landing. Her maid put her to bed and though she lay awake for a minute or so wondering about this mysterious fire, she was soon fast asleep again.

It was the witching hour. Queenie awoke with a start. It took her some moments to become aware that she was not in the dream, a dream of being lost in a crowded marketplace, jostled by people all around her, pushing and shoving. But she had pushed on, as she was frantic in the dream, looking for her lost child. A horrible dream, losing your child like that. It wasn't Ralph she'd been searching for in the dream; it had been her daughters. She dreamt of them often, yet always as little girls not as the babies that were gone. She thought, *If my girls had survived, all this would be different. They'd have been strong characters, like me. Not like the King men. All of them are weak fools.*

She felt a tear escape her eye and settle on her cheek. She wiped it away and suddenly felt forlorn, overcome with grief and worry. All her children were dead, and though she hadn't been fond of Ralph, he'd been her son.

'Jenkins,' she muttered. But her lady's maid in the next room would never hear that, even as devoted as she was. 'Jenkins!' she called and soon heard movement and the door opening.

'What now?' said Jenkins, looking a bit of a fright with her grey hair in a plait over her shoulder, the fringe sticking up at all angles, lit up like a spirit from the lamp she held up.

'Jenkins, you're getting old,' said Queenie.

'You woke me up at this hour, to tell me that? You stupid goose.'

'No, no. I had a dream. An awful dream of common people, all around me, manhandling me. It was atrocious!'

Jenkins came over and helped Queenie sit up by rearranging her pillows. She did look aged and tired. Jenkins had been in her employ for fifty years, coming to this house as a kitchen maid aged only nine. She was the person that Queenie relied upon for everything. Jenkins sat down on the bed and sighed, pushing her messy hair back from her face.

'You had that dream because of the trouble at the brickyard tonight. It's all about that, dealing with those scurrilous people. If we can call them people. Setting fire to things now, are they? Animals. No, that's too good for 'em. Monsters, they are.'

Queenie nodded and wiped her eyes again. 'I do not understand these people. We give them paid work, freedom to hire their own families if they wish. And still they treat us like the very devil.'

'Ungrateful, they are,' said Jenkins. 'And they will never learn. Now, enough unbroken sleep tonight. Get some rest. All this kerfuffle is aging me terribly. I cannot be doing with it at my advanced years. I need my sleep, woman!'

'I am sorry, Jenkins. Please forgive me,' she said, her voice catching in a little sob.

'Now, now. Don't upset yourself. Just sleep now. Nothing for you to worry your head about at this hour. We shall talk it all through in the light of day. I'm going back to my bed. Good night, Miss Alice.'

'Good night, Jenkins.'

Jenkins shuffled out of the room, taking the lamp with her. The room fell into inky darkness again. Queenie had never liked the dark. As a child, she and her sister had shared a room all of their childhood and most nights shared a bed. They had cuddled up together, sleeping like spoons, she stroking Selina's hair or Selina stroking hers, whispering secrets and stories to each other until sleep took them.

But their parents split the two of them up when Selina began acting strangely in her later teens. And then, Queenie was married off to Ralph King Senior and they took Selina away and put her in that asylum. That made it sound like a place of rest, a kind of hospital, but it wasn't. It was a prison for mad people. Queenie's new husband forbade her from seeing her sister in that place. She was found hanging there. Selina. Beautiful, clever and kind Selina had killed herself. It had broken Queenie's heart.

Since then, the only person she had given her heart to was Jenkins, but always in the back of her mind was the hard fact that it was a business arrangement, of course. She paid Jenkins to be with her. Yes, Jenkins was fond of her, she was sure of that. And Jenkins knew no other life or family, had left her own at such a tender age and lived here with Queenie ever since. But still, it was not true family, not true love, unsullied by money or duty. The last time she had fallen for anyone had been those few months before marriage, a kind of madness she thought of it now. Once married, she discovered the cold truth about her husband: that he had no capacity for love and that he wanted to bed virgin maids, not her. And so he did, regularly. Sometimes with tragic consequences.

She lay in her bed, determined to sleep, but the light was bothering her eyes. What light? She screwed her eyes tight shut, but still she could somehow feel it playing across her eyelids. She opened up one eye speculatively, determined not to be roused from her warm, cosy position. And there it was, a strip of light coming through the gap in the curtains. Surely she had not slept the night through and the dawn had come. She opened both eyes and stared at the light. It was not daylight. It had a silvery quality to it. And then, with a sinking feeling of nausea, she knew where she had seen that light before.

She stared at it, watching that same shifting shimmer she had seen all those years before, coming through her curtains, just the same as when the ghost had visited her after her husband's death. She had seen it again at the grave of her husband. It had spoken to her, cursed the family, the house, their future. She had believed it then. But since, she had come to think that it was just her nerves that caused that false vision, just a belated reaction to her husband's death. An imaginary thing concocted in her addled mind, twisted by grief. Though she had hated her husband, grief was an odd fish. Nobody knew how it could affect you. Seeing things could happen to anyone placed under great strain. And after all, none of the ghost's wild curses had come to pass. It was all nonsense. She had come to know this. She had convinced herself. She wasn't like Selina . . .

It was the ghost of Betsy Blaize who had visited her, beneath her window and beside the grave. Twenty-four years ago Blaize had died penniless on the iron bridge, her newborn child in her arms, taken in by someone. The baby on the bridge, they called it. The bastard child of Queenie's husband, conceived by violent rape upon that poor servant girl in their employ, young Betsy Blaize. She had visited Queenie in this ghostly guise those two times, foretelling disaster for the King family, '*This house will fall . . . Dark times are ahead . . .*'

Yet despite her fear then, nothing had happened to Queenie or any of the family to confirm this horrible fate. Yes, Margaret had eloped soon after, which threatened scandal on the family, but people soon forgot and moved on. The daughter of the house had at least married the artist, which Queenie ensured was reported in the local newspaper. Since those days, the King fortune had gone from strength to strength, acquiring land and businesses galore. They were now richer than ever. So, the flame of her fear had guttered and gone out over the years, replaced by disbelief that it had ever happened at all.

But now, eighteen years since she saw it last, that same flickering light was here again. But perhaps it was not a ghost. It could be moonlight. She shut her eyes with the thought and willed herself to sleep. But it seemed to burn brighter through her closed eyelids and she could not bear to keep them shut. It was brighter, almost white in its intensity now. She felt drawn to it, the mystery of it. But also, a dread in the pit of her stomach. She felt her body move almost without her will. She pushed back the covers and stood up from her bed. She walked over to the window and paused at the gap in the curtains. She felt as if the spirit were moving her, not herself. She pulled back one of the curtains and looked down, into the light.

Blaize stood there, in the family graveyard that Queenie could see from her bedroom window. The same bright white hair and skin, the same spectral blue eyes. She had dreamt of this vision many times since, but never seen it again with her waking eyes. And despite her determination over the years to disbelieve it, she could not deny its terrible presence there beneath her.

Just as before, its words came to her in her mind, without its lips moving.

'Have you forgotten?' said Blaize. 'Have you forgotten my words?'

Queenie thought, *You said the house would fall. But it has not.* Then Queenie grasped the handle to the window and opened it to the night air. She spoke aloud, 'I am not afraid of you now!' She had tried to be brave but her voice came out as a squeak.

'You *have* forgotten. I told you once, the crucible will purify. After the fire, I will come again. A baby will bridge the divide.'

Queenie had forgotten those last words. They were said to her by the grave in the second visitation. Somehow, over the years, she had blanked them out. Not understanding them at the time, she had simply forgotten them. But now, tonight, after Troon's visit and news from the brickworks, she felt a prickle of recognition. The fire. *After the fire, I will come again.*

'So, here you are again, after the fire.' Queenie spoke more steadily now. She felt stronger, more able to reason with this creature. 'What do you want this time?'

The spirit's eyes burned bluer than ever. They seemed to bore a hole in Queenie's gaze, so bright she wanted to look away, but could not.

'Justice.'

Justice? Queenie thought. *I have been a good woman. I have managed my family and my businesses well. My workers are paid fairly. What else can I do? Give all our riches to the poor? Ridiculous!*

The spirit answered, 'You lie to yourself.'

Queenie felt intensely uncomfortable. Blaize could read her mind, it seemed.

Suddenly, the ghost raised its arms and cried out, 'My baby! Where is my baby?'

The face of Blaize was horrifying, twisted in its misery and glowing whiter than snow beneath the sun. Its eyes seemed to expand, its black mouth too, gaping open. Queenie had to steel herself against this horror and keep her wits about her.

'I do not know,' said Queenie firmly, though it were not strictly true. She had heard rumours, from Margaret first back then, and more recently from Jenkins, that the babe was taken in by a local family back in '34. She knew no more than that. If it had lived, it would be a young person now with children of its own, perhaps. If it had lived. And she had decided long ago, that although the child were a King, a bastard child of the head of the King family, it had no place here at Southover. It had done well to escape the poisonous men of the King family. She was happy for it, just as she had been happy for Margaret when she escaped. She had seen that a wrong had been done to this girl, to Betsy Blaize the maid, raped from the age of twelve, pregnant at fifteen, dead at sixteen. It was a terrible wrong, but what could Queenie do for her now? It was all a long time ago and the child was lucky. It had escaped not only the Kings but a life with an outcast for a mother, an unmarried mother. It should count itself lucky. 'What do you want from me?' Queenie asked.

'Find my child. Improve her lot in life.'

So, it was a girl then, the baby on the bridge. A girl that had been taken in and looked after by a local family. Queenie remembered what she'd said to Margaret, all those years ago, *It's a fortunate child that escapes the King family*. 'And what if she doesn't want to be found? What if she's happy as she is?'

The ghost said nothing. It had no answer to that. Queenie was emboldened by this and went on, 'And what can you, a mere spirit, do to me if I do not follow your instructions?'

Blaize's arms fell, her mouth closed. It stared at Queenie for what seemed like an age. Then it spoke again, quietly, almost a whisper, though Queenie could hear it as if the ghost were speaking into her ear, 'The fire will wash you clean. *All of you*.'

Chapter 6

'Brothers and sisters of the brickyard, I bid thee welcome. Our spare time when we are not slaving at work is precious and so I doubly thank'ee for meeting here today. Let us not waste this time with pleasantries. We must state our aims and draw our plans together.'

Owen glanced around the room at the men, women, children, infants and babes gathered there in the arched brick cellar of The Swan Inn. There had been smaller meetings in past weeks, but this was the largest yet by far. The majority of their number were women, as female workers made up the bulk of the brickmaking force. Most brickmoulders were women, though some men had made it their skilled trade as well. Men did the heavy digging and brickburning, and operated the machinery. Child brickworkers were numerous too, with boys and girls hired equally as clay carriers and to do other odd jobs around the site. Thus, the whole family could be employed as brickies. As Owen surveyed them all, it felt to him as if all human life was present, all the poor folk of human life at any rate. The men puffed on their pipes, the women held their babies or knitted. Always knitting to do and never a moment wasted, those women. Some men drank their time away in taverns but Owen never saw a woman in his community waste her time, though he knew some of the outsiders that camped along the river had just as many drunken women as their men. Not in his area though, where he lived. The women were the salt of the earth. Many here were nodding at Adam Jones's words. Some squinted at him, their faces betraying that they were unsure about him or perhaps they just required spectacles they could never afford. Everyone here was listening intently and the sheer number of people squashed into the meeting room in the tavern basement was enough to show the strength of feeling.

Adam went on, 'Afore the King family bought our brickyard a year hence, most of you will remember our old boss, Mr Cotterhill. Yes, he was a bit of a fool with business and yes, he sadly went bankrupt. Nobody can deny that. But hc was a good mon and a good manager of people. He was fair and he was just. He could see the skill in what we do. He and his good lady wife celebrated champion brickmakers, rewarding those moulders who worked not only the quickest but with the highest quality, and even the child who lugged the clay on his head wasna below Cotterhill's attentions. He gave bonuses on a weekly rotation, so that every good worker received his or her due. He had plans to train his workforce to produce more fancy wares, decorative tiles and so forth.

He built houses for us and charged low rents. He organised a meal every Easter Sunday for the whole workforce at his own expense. And our children were hired by Mr Cotterhill himself. He paid 'em fairly and charged his overseers to look out for their safety. He was a good mon, a fair mon, a just mon.'

Owen saw the nodding heads increase and grunts of approval all round.

'But now we have the Kings. They believe we have no skill whatsoever. They believe we are the lowest sort of folk. Some of us have overheard Cyril King say as much in his rare visits to the yard. They have put up our rents, left our houses to fall into rack and ruin with no repairs, no maintenance. There is an end to the annual meal and to the bonuses the hardest workers enjoyed. There has been a simplification of our wares, so that all plans for expanding the works and the benefits of new training have gone. Our hours are longer than ever. They have introduced the unfair "back pence" system, whereby they withhold part of our wages until the end of the season, which is only paid if there have been no unforeseen incidents that year to reduce their profits. The Kings have also callously changed our contracts in another way, so that now the children are hired by the moulder him or herself, so that no legal responsibility resides with the Kings in respect of any child on the site. If a child is injured or overworked or hurt in any way, the moulder must answer for it. And this, when brick moulders are already engaged in producing a thousand bricks a day at a minimum, they are being asked to look out at the same time for the welfare of the dozens of children that work all over the site? This was once the responsibility of the owner and his foreman. But now each moulder must become an overseer with none of the pay to go with it. It is a nonsense.'

Each of these points was greeted with a disgruntled cheer, a cheerless cheer of angry agreement.

'And now, brothers and sisters, the latest degradation. There is talk of reducing our wages.'

Some men stood up at this point and yelled out a hearty 'boo', shaking their fists and cursing. Women were shaking their heads and patting their babies' bottoms furiously.

'I am sure you will agree that this is the final straw that will break our backs.'

Adam's head fell and he shook it slowly, then wiped a shaking hand across his eyes. Women frowned in sympathy, men puffed thoughtfully on their pipes and grimaced in solidarity. Owen recalled his dad telling him Adam should've been an actor, with all his theatrics. Owen had to agree. But at least Adam was putting it to good use, not using his dramatic skills to charm women or cheat working folk as a confidence trickster; he was using his charisma to help his fellow brickworkers. And Owen loved him for that. Worshipped him, if truth be known.

Adam looked up and scanned the crowd, his gaze seeming to fall on each face in turn. His next words were spoken so low, the crowd seemed to edge forward as one to hear them. 'But are we to be broken so easily?'

There was general muttering.

'Are we, my friends?' Adam said, louder.

There were a few cries of 'No!' and someone called out, 'We inna, by God!'

'Then it is time for us to join together. Just as the brickmasters are joined, so should we be. They conspire to lower wages. So we should combine to stand against them. All gathered here today and those not here due to other commitments must join together as one. We must form a union of brickworkers, with the same aims and objectives. Strength in numbers, brothers and sisters!'

This was met with a hearty cheer by many voices. A baby started to cry.

'No to lower wages! No to longer hours! No to poorer contracts!'

Each was cheered on by the whole assembly now and many were up on their feet, including Owen.

'Yes to respect!'

A great cheer.

'Yes to a fair wage for a fair day's work!'

An even greater cheer.

'Yes to the United Operative Brickmakers' Benevolent and Protective Society of Ironbridge, Broseley and Vicinity!'

A yet greater cheer, showing a hearty approval of the idea of a union of brickworkers, yet some confused muttering as to what a mouthful it was.

The meeting had been a wonderful success. A table had been set up near the door, manned by Owen, Royce and Brain, writing down names in a ledger and taking the dues of tuppence to join the society. Meanwhile, Adam stood beside them fielding queries and slapping men on their backs and leaning in to women with a smile and ruffling the hair on the heads of children. Almost every person in the room joined up and the air was filled with plans of when the next meeting would be, what would be discussed and what action might be agreed upon to be taken against the Kings. And the name of the Kings rang around the room like a curse to Owen's ears.

There was a light pat on Owen's shoulder and he looked up to see Adam looking down seriously at him.

'A word, cousin?'

Adam moved over to a darkened corner and Owen followed him.

'Owen, lad. Well, I suppose I shouldna call you lad any more, now that you are grown. It should be mon!'

'Yes mon!' laughed Owen.

'Now, to business.' The smiles were over and Adam was frowning down at him. 'I hear the King girl is sweet on you.'

'Oh well, I wouldna go that far or anything like it. I met her in the street and sold her a pie, is all.'

'I hear different. I hear she couldna take her eyes off you. All blushes and how-do-you-do.'

'That be from Royce and Brain, would it? I wouldna trust either of them to report a rainstorm even when they're drenched in it.'

'I see,' mused Adam. 'Did she seem well disposed towards you? Could you approach her again without a fuss, d'yer think?'

Owen felt his own cheeks start to flush at the thought of Beatrice and cursed himself for it. Adam didn't miss a thing and added, 'I see she's had quite the effect on you.'

'She is a pretty thing, there's no denying.'

'Well, dunna be fooled. All those Kings are poison. Your mother knows that more'n any. But we need someone inside there. We're trying to get to some of the staff working in the house, but it's proving tricky. If you could ingratiate yourself with Miss Beatrice, now . . . that would be summat. Get to know her a bit, get her on side a bit. Find out what the Kings are planning. There's talk, but then there's knowing. Ask a few questions, find out a bit of this and that. She'd be interested to talk with you again, you reckon?'

Owen's thoughts were racing ahead. He had thought of little else but Beatrice since their meeting a few days ago. Of course, he hadn't told a soul. He had tried to find a reason to justify speaking to her again and had come up with nothing. And now a reason to talk to her was being handed to him on a plate, encouraged and required, even. He had licence now to pursue this girl, this marvellous girl. But it left a taste behind it, something slightly bitter. To see the girl and talk to her, to help the cause by doing so, yet at the same time lying to her by doing so. She was a King though, he must remember that.

'I do reckon I could do that. I am certain I could.'

'Good mon,' said Adam and put a rough arm around him, grinning and winking. 'I knew I could rely on family. And a good-looking lad like you'll have her eating out of your hand in no time. Report back to me once a week, whenever you can get away from your father. I think it best to keep your parents out of this, dunna you? Just between ourselves, like. Dunna want to upset them, eh?'

'Arr, wouldna wanna do that,' said Owen and nodded.

Secrets and lies. This is how they begin, thought Owen.

Beatrice looked through the window again. Still no sign. Madame was droning on about the etiquette of the ballroom and how one should comport oneself in regards to the filling in of the dance card, but Beatrice wasn't really listening. She was waiting to see if Owen the pieman was going to turn up again. But the lesson was almost over and he wasn't there. Her disappointment was acute and surprised her. She had thought about the lad a few times in the past few days, but had put such thoughts out of her head. What was the point? He was not the sort of person anyone in her family would encourage her to make an acquaintance of, a door-to-door pie salesman. She had noticed that his nails had been grimy with grey dust and wondered how much of that muck went into the pies, but perhaps none, as the pie certainly tasted good. She ran her tongue over her lips and could almost taste it there, the savoury pork, the sweet apple. Delicious.

Madame was coming to an end and ushering Beatrice to the door. She was a little ashamed that she had listened to so little of what had been taught her and knew she would regret it once her first ball came along and she had no idea what to do. But she cared so little about such things, despite her mother's insistence that she must learn the correct protocol for 'coming out' – such a strange expression. Coming out of what? Into what? Childhood to marriage, she supposed. She did not feel ready to be married.

She left her dancing teacher's house by the front door this time, shut it behind her and descended the steps, glancing up and down the street for her mother. Late again. Her mother was the worst timekeeper. She sighed and considered going back inside, but she couldn't be bothered. Then she saw a figure walking towards her and smiling right at her. It was him. It was the pie boy.

'Miss,' he said and touched his cap respectfully.

'Owen!' she cried. 'I wondered if I would see you today, at the back door. But you did not arrive.'

She knew she was gushing, but she didn't care.

Owen had stopped before her, still with a smile on his face. Such a nice face.

'I inna selling pies today, miss. Day off.'

'Do you sell pies all over town, then? All over Shropshire, I wonder? They are such good pies, I'm sure they're in great demand.'

'Did you think I was a pie-seller? That it was my trade?'

He was still smiling, with an amused look in his eye that he knew something she didn't. 'Well, I thought . . .'

'Ah, well, you know what thought did.'

'What did thought do?'

'Followed a dust cart and thought it were a wedding.'

Beatrice stared at him, puzzled at this nonsense. But his smile got to her and she grinned broadly, then laughed aloud and so did he. 'I have no idea what you are talking about!'

'Neither do I, much of the time, miss. May I walk you to your destination?'

'Ah, I am waiting upon my mother again and do not know when she will arrive. She is always delayed by something. But we can talk here on the steps a while. And you must tell me, what is your trade, if it is not selling pies?'

'I just sell pies on a Sunday sometimes, to help out my mother. But it inna my trade. I'm a brickburner, just like my father.'

Beatrice looked more closely at him. 'You work at a brickyard?'

'I do.'

Was his the face she saw from the coach that day? It couldn't be. Could it? What were the chances?

'Not the King brickworks?'

'The very same. Your family are my bosses, so it probably inna the done thing to be talking to you like this in the street.'

She ignored that last comment – the done thing never really interested her – and put her hand to her mouth. 'But this is extraordinary. I saw you, I'm sure I did. The very first day I arrived in Shropshire. Our coach stopped beside the brickworks and Maman – that's what I call my mother – Maman told me that it belonged to the Kings. And I saw a young man and we looked at each other. Could it be you? Tell me it was you. How marvellous that would be!'

Owen's smile had gone and his cheeks were reddening. He looked away from her and muttered, 'I dunna think so, miss. I dunna make a habit of staring at young ladies.'

'Well, perhaps you could not see me clearly from where you were, but I saw you, I'm sure I did! How wonderful! And now we are met again, by chance. How strange the world is!'

He looked back at her now, not smiling, cheeks still flushed, his eyes meaningful. ''Tis a strange thing indeed.'

'Certainly. So tell me about life as a – what did you say you did? A brick something?'

'Brickburner, miss.'

'What does that involve?'

'I bake bricks.'

'Tell me more. I want to know. What is your average day like?'

'It will be tedious for a young lady like yourself, surely.'

'How can you say a young lady like *yourself* when you don't even know me? Once you do know me, you will find that I want to know everything. I am hungry to speak to every person who ever lived, if needs be, to discover the truth about the world and all that is in it. So, please, if you will tell me what the life of a brickburner is about.'

He looked taken aback by this little pronouncement – people often did, not expecting a girl to be interested in anything other than dances and little dogs – but he soon recovered himself and went on.

'I work in the kilns with my father. We are responsible for the baking of the bricks until they are ready. We have a great responsibility, as if we mess up our job then the bricks will be ruined. They have to be stacked just so, and the fires must be maintained just so. It is a job of some serious responsibility.'

'I can imagine,' she said, though she could not. And, as usual, her mouth ran faster than her thoughts. 'Actually, I cannot. I must admit I have never once in my life thought about the making of a brick. I have seen thousands of them, tens of thousands most likely. And never once have I considered where they all come from.'

'Like most people,' said Owen. 'When people look at a house, most don't even notice the bricks. But there's blood in those bricks.'

'Whatever do you mean?'

'Blood and sweat and misery. Long, hard shifts of boys, girls, men and women. Digging the clay from the ground, weathering it in great heaps for months, carrying it on their heads or in heavy, unwieldy handcarts, feeding it into the mills, to cut it and wet it and flatten it and make it easier to work with. Then moulding it into bricks on tables, a thousand a day. Then carried to the kilns and stacked and arranged just so and baked, the fires burning and watched like hawks do, for days and nights on end. Then carried and stacked again, transported by horse and cart and barge all over the county, the country even. Nobody thinks of all that, when they pass by a house, a row of houses, a whole street of 'em. The time it took to make each brick, the effort and the backbreaking hours and the accidents at the brickyard that took young lives. Like I said, there is blood in those bricks, every brick.'

Beatrice gazed at Owen. The whole time he had been making this extraordinary speech, his eyes had been on hers and she had felt paralysed by them, their blue intensity. 'You are truly an astonishing person, Owen.'

Now she had embarrassed him. He looked askance, nervous and out of sorts, but she did not regret what she had said. She meant it. Her great-grandmother, uncle and step-grandmother – her new family would probably have thought it akin to a crime to be standing here, talking to a brickworker. They saw their workers as objects, she knew that from the way they spoke of them, moving them about here and there like so many chess pieces. But this young man was no object. His mind was alive. It flowed out through his words and through his eyes.

'I ought to go, miss,' he mumbled. 'I've said too much.'

'No, I fear you have not said enough. I wish to know more, about my family's brickworks and what life is like for you there. Can we meet again, here next week? I will tell my mother I need a chaperone no longer and will walk home alone. I'm sure I can convince her. Then perhaps we can talk a while, on the way. What do you say, Owen?'

'I say yes to that, miss.'

'Won't you call me Bea?'

'Maybe next time, miss,' he said, and with that he smiled again at her, touched his cap and turned away. She watched him walk down the street but then he stopped. He turned back and looked at her. His smile was gone and he stared at her intently, a worried look upon his face. She raised her hand a little to gesture farewell, but he turned quickly back and hurried away. His face was like the weather here in Shropshire, constantly on the move and as predictable as a moth. She was sure he felt deeply about things, sure he thought deeply about things too. But how did Owen feel about her? That was the question left burning in her mind, as she saw Maman hurrying up the street to meet her, thankfully and gloriously late as ever.

On their walk home, she said to her mother, 'When you were a little girl, who were your friends here in Ironbridge?'

'I didn't have many,' said Maman, with a bit of a sigh. 'I was a loner and loved to read and play on my piano. I was schooled at home, as you know, so I did not have much of an opportunity to meet friends.'

'You did not have any friends, not one?' gasped Beatrice. 'Nobody like my Juliette or Ana?' Beatrice thought with a pang of her friends from home and reminded herself she must write to them. How she missed her dear friends and their laughter, their secrets and giggles. She wondered when she would see them again, when they would end this extended visit to England. Were they to stay for a month, a year? Forever? Each time she asked her mother, she had no answer but 'a while, Bea'. For the time being Maman seemed to be in no hurry to leave this place she called home.

'I did have one friend, yes. A dear friend. But . . . we fell out, sadly.'

'Why did you fall out?'

'It's a long story.'

'What was she called?'

'Her name was Anny,' said Maman in a small voice. Beatrice stole a glance at her to see that she was frowning. 'But that is enough about that,' she added, peevishly.

Beatrice knew that tone well. Maman did not want to speak about it any further. They walked on, along the street that led from the town square towards the hill that took them up to Southover. She watched the folk walk past, some well dressed, some poorly dressed, all consumed with their own thoughts and business and lives. It often hit her with a little shock how placid a person might look on the outside, yet inside their heads was a whirlwind of thoughts and memories, feelings and passions. Though she walked silently beside her mother, her own mind was consumed with curiosity into this friend of her mother's, Anny, about whom she had never heard a word mentioned. She kept trying to phrase and rephrase her next question about this Anny in her mind, to make it sound by the by, of passing interest, as if she didn't really care. But her mother spoke first.

'I'm sorry I snapped, *chérie*. It's being here, back at home. Makes me think of the past and I become maudlin. And I mustn't. It is all water under the iron bridge, long ago and long gone. Now, the future, that is something I'd much rather talk about. Tell me about your dancing.'

Chapter 7

'You've seen her then?'

Owen met up with Adam in the basement of The Swan. Adam bought him a pint of beer and the taste of it was good and earthy. He smacked his lips and answered, 'I have.'

'What is she like?'

'She is a talkative girl and not stupid – clever, in fact. And open to talking to anyone, it seems, myself included.'

Adam was pleased. 'She'll be easy to handle, if she's friendly and trusting.'

'She is that,' said Owen and in saying it, felt the truth of it and the distaste of how easy it would be to fool her.

'But how did it go, talking with her? Did you make any headway?' said Adam with impatience.

'It went well.' Owen sensed he needed to impress him further, adding, 'It went better than I could've planned.'

'How so?'

'She asked me – *she* asked *me*, mind – if I wanted to walk her home from her dance lesson next week and talk further.'

'That be sebunctious news, mon! I knew you'd manage it. Now, we need to know more about their plans. Do you think she'll talk about her family a bit? Or too loyal?'

'That I dunna know, as yet. I shall figure it out the next time. I aim to tread carefully.'

'Arr, tread lightly, agreed. But we have little time. The Kings will make their move soon, as they'll have had wind of our meetings and will want to curb it. The fire at the sheds will have unnerved them. Try to find out all you can but dunna look like you're trying to find out anything.'

'Yes, mon. Understood.'

'Now then, enough of that. Do you have your eye on any local girl?'

Owen was taken aback. His father's cousin had never shown an interest in him to this extent. He'd always been roughly affectionate with him, since he was a little boy lugging the clay to Adam's table. But he'd not sat with him and talked like this.

'None in particular,' said Owen, thinking of Beatrice. Yet another lie, then.

'Find yerself one, mon. Handsome type like you needs a girl. Take his mind off things. Seek some pleasure in this weary road to death we call life.'

'I suppose.'

'No suppose about it. And make sure she's the right sort. A girl like you, from around where you live. She'll understand you, listen to you. Her parents and your parents will know each other and get on. These things matter, lad. They matter.'

Owen realised that Adam was not so subtly warning him off any thoughts of Beatrice.

'After I lost my Judith, I thought I'd never want another. But when I met my Martha, I knew she was the right one. And her Quaker parents were good, kind folk and they approved the match. And now she is with child, I couldna be happier. It is a wonderful thing, to know you'll be a father. A settling thing. Secures a man's place in the world, to start a family.'

'Arr, you're right, of course. I shall keep my eyes peeled,' said Owen, to placate him. But the only girl who really seemed to understand him was Beatrice. The real him, the poet in him, same as his father, who'd been lucky and found a local girl who understood this about him. His mother would often speak of how thoughtful and interesting his father was. Beatrice had seen it, too, she had called Owen 'an astonishing person'. What local girl would ever say something like that? He was smitten; he knew he was.

A week later, Owen was waiting for Beatrice when she came out of her dance teacher's house and stood on the step. He saw from her searching eyes that she was waiting for him, too.

'Owen! I am so glad to see you. I was so hoping you'd come, but didn't know if you would.'

She was an open book about her feelings and thoughts. She didn't seem to care who knew it. *No fear in her*, he thought. *Not a bit of it.*

'Miss. Shall we walk?'

'Yes, let's. My mother agreed to no chaperone, as I know my way about the town now. Let us walk along the riverside and then I can take the woodland path home, up to Southover. I have explored the woods a bit too and find I adore them. I was brought up in the city of Paris, as you know, so woodland and countryside are all new to me.'

She did rattle on. But he loved to listen to it. Her accent was English through and through but there was a touch of the foreigner about it, something you couldn't quite put your finger on. She was from off, as they said around here, and however good her accent was, the foreign nature of her way of speaking and her dress, even the way she held her head to one side or flourished her hands while talking, all spoke of something exotic.

'What is Paris like?'

'It is a huge, smelly city. But it is my home and I love it. There are street vendors calling and singing their wares. There are boatmen on the River Seine, crowded and shouting, not unlike here with your River Severn. There was music everywhere, in our home, a singer with an accordion on the streets or a violinist two doors down. Artists painting, bakers selling sweet pastries. The best wine in the world. Yes, I have tasted a little,' and she smiled coquettishly at this.

They had crossed the road and gone down the steps below the iron bridge to the river path. This sunny May Sunday was the perfect day, apple and pear blossom snowing in wafts from the trees that lined the river, drifting into the water, muddied and lost there. Every word she said was like a sip of wine to him, delicious, bittersweet and intoxicating. But he must keep his wits about him.

'It all sounds a bit too good to be true.'

'Oh, I have only said the good things, for the most part. There is poverty, terrible poverty. Beggars on the streets, worse than here. People starving to death. I've seen corpses in the gutter with my own eyes.'

'People starve here too.'

'They do?'

'In the winter, a lot of the brickworkers are laid off, as there is not so much work to be done. They look for other jobs, the men in the iron trade, the women whatever they can find. But some find their way to the dreaded workhouse. And some never find work and they starve.'

Beatrice gasped. 'Is there nobody to help them, in this small, welcoming town? I thought it would only be the big cities of the world that cared little enough of their thousands of poor to let them starve. I assumed here would be different. Everyone seems so caring and friendly here.'

'Family help, friends help, where they can. But when you have precious little for your own, it is hard to share it with others. We do what we can. But we must live. We earn so little for our labours. It inna possible to spare even a penny some days.'

They walked on, Beatrice quiet. He glanced at her, the pretty profile in repose, biting her lip. He had to walk slightly behind her, her skirts too wide for the riverside path. It gave him the perfect opportunity to study that profile, the curve of her neck and the way her dark hair was swept up at its nape. One strand was loose and he could not take his eyes away from it.

'Owen, may I ask you something?'

'You can ask. No harm in asking.'

'Do my family treat you well? At the brickworks, I mean. Are the Kings good bosses?'

The girl was making it too easy for him! He was glad, knowing how pleased Adam would be at his progress. Then he swallowed down a lump in his throat and coughed. Pride and shame, in the very same moment. Never in his life had he felt so muddled.

'Do you want to hear the polite answer? Or the truth, miss?'

'Why, the truth, without a doubt.'

She had stopped on the path and stared at him, awaiting his answer.

'You might hear some things that inna to your liking.'

'Before you go on, please understand something about me. I was brought up with Maman and Maman alone. You have probably heard from gossip that my mother had run away from her family because they did not approve of her match. It was a great, romantic gesture. But what you may not know is that my father tragically died when she was with child. So, I grew up with a widow for a mother, who made her way in the world alone. We never had pomp and finery when I was a child. My mother taught pupils at our small home, which never brought in riches. I was not raised a King. And I had no concept of family, other than my mother. So I am not a King and do not wish to be. I am Beatrice Ashford. I am myself and always will be. Anything you say to me about the Kings, I will listen to without prejudice. I merely want the truth, from my friends, my family, from the world. I want to *know*. So, if you please, go straight ahead.'

He had watched her mouth and eyes as she spoke. He wanted to take her by the shoulders and kiss that mouth. What was he doing? What was happening to him? He wanted to say so much. He wanted to tell her the truth, about Adam, about his role as a spy. He almost said it. Who could resist such a pure, simple appeal to truth? But unlike her, he did not stand alone. He had loyalties, deep ones, rooted three hundred feet down in the Shropshire earth, down in the layers of Ironbridge clay.

‘The Kings dunna treat their workers well.’

‘But how? What do they do?’ She stared at him, her eyes welling with tears. She could be so moved, by only this? He could not look her in the eye any longer. Her straightforward honesty shamed him.

‘Let us walk on, miss. I’ll tell you how.’

They fell back into walking, but slowly now, his words slowing to match their pace, thoughtfully chosen, carefully.

‘We had an old master before the Kings, who treated us well. Fair contracts, good hours, useful training to better ourselves and solid housing, well maintained. Now we have lost all of those.’

‘Who is responsible? My uncle? My great-grandmother?’

‘Both, I believe. We do not see the elder Mrs King, but Mr Cyril King appears down the works from time to time. And it is never a good day when he comes around.’

‘I am sorry to say that I concur with that,’ she said, her voice small. Perhaps she had a little loyalty to her family after all, but could not help but speak the truth. ‘I do not like him.’

‘Few do, miss. You inna alone in that.’

‘I have not fallen foul of him myself, but there is something in my belly that tells me he is a cruel man.’

‘That he be, miss. That he be.’ He thought on his feet and felt it might be the right time to push a little further.

'Does he speak of us? Do they discuss such things as us poor folk at home?'

'Oh yes, well, from time to time. I have overheard things. And I am not pleased by what I hear. Uncle speaks of workers as "things".'

'Things?'

'Yes, objects. Things. I heard Cyril say once, "A worker is a damnable thing."'

'*Things*,' he repeated. 'I am not a thing. My father is not a thing.' He thought of his conversation with his father, that the masters saw only money when they looked at them. He assumed it were true. Now he heard it from the horse's mouth. They sickened him, the Kings.

'Oh, indeed not! I know that. You believe me, don't you?'

This girl though, she was not one of them. And yet she was part of them, the youngest of them and with the pig Cyril having had no children, she was the heir. The heir to the King fortune. And she was walking beside him – Owen Malone, brickburner – sharing confidences with him. A stroke of luck for the brickworkers' union, a blessing and a curse for him. He was torn between kissing her and betraying all of her confidences.

'I do believe you,' he said, then added with a small smile, 'I think.'

'Oh, please believe me. Maybe I could even help.'

There she went again, laying his path so conveniently for him. She was too kind, too rash. Too lovely.

'Do they talk of the brickyard?' he said. 'Of their plans?'

'What kind of plans?'

Had he pushed it too far? Perhaps he should have saved this for another conversation. He did not want to spook her, as a young horse must be coaxed into having a man on its back and only in its own time.

'Oh, nothing particular. We worry, that's all. About the future.'

'The future of the brickworks?'

'No, not as such. Bricks are needed everywhere. People need houses. We line shafts and tunnels in the mines with bricks these days, over timber. On farms, barns are being built in brick, as well as stables and other outhouses. We need bricks. We need clay too. Think of all of the stuff men dig up from the ground. Which would be the most precious to mankind, do you think? Gold? Or clay?'

He glanced at her to see her face had changed from cloudy to sunshine.

'Now you've explained it so well, my answer must be clay. But until then, I would have said gold, I think.'

'Why gold?'

'Well, now that I think of it, there is no worth in gold. It is not ideal for making anything but something pretty and decorative. It is swapped as a thing of value, but is not particularly useful in itself.'

'So which is more precious? Gold? Or clay?'

'I would say you have proved your point admirably. It is clay, of course!'

'I would say so, miss.'

'The more one thinks of it, the more things one finds that are made of clay. Why, clay has contributed more to our comfort and well-being than gold ever did, or perhaps any other substance, save coal.'

'You are quite right. Coal, clay and iron. We dig all three from the ground round here and all three power the world.'

'What you do is mightily important, Owen. I hope you are proud of that.'

'I would be more so, if our wages were higher.'

There came the clouds across that pretty, pale face again. Had he done it again, ruined the moment, startled the filly?

'I heard them talk of wages the other day. They say . . . I heard them say . . . the wages of the brickworkers were to be lowered. I heard my great-grandmother talk of it, and Cyril and Benjamina. They were arguing but it was decided in the end.'

And there he had it. What he wanted. Exactly what he wanted. Adam would be pleased as punch with him, for wheedling that information out of the girl. But all he felt was sick, sick with the knowledge that their pay was soon to drop and how hard that would make his life, his mother and father's lives, all of their lives, sick with betraying this girl who told confidences so easily.

Now they had reached the woodland path. There was a moment of complicit understanding that he would not proceed further with her than the river. This path was open and peopled by passers-by. But the woods were hidden and shadowy. A respectable girl would not be seen alone with a young man there.

'You are silent, Owen. What say you to this news? Have I helped you by telling you this? I do hope so.'

What could he say to this? The girl was too good, too nice. Was there ever such a girl, so honest and true? And could such a girl really be a King?

'We suspected it,' he muttered, intending to say no more, to play it down and leave her now, not wanting to pry more from her, to leave her be. But he couldn't help himself. 'I have never . . . I have never met such a person as you, miss. Most of the rich care nothing for us. What makes you interested in us? In the brick-works? In clay and the people who work it? Why do you care?'

Beatrice cocked her head and gazed into middle distance. How lovely she was when she was considering, the deep brown eyes darkening with thought. 'I suppose it is because I was not raised in wealth. I am new to it. It is as foreign to me as your Shropshire words, your dunna and inna and so on.'

She laughed, a clear, sweet laugh like water tumbling over smooth pebbles. But her face clouded again and she looked closely at him.

'But also, Owen, I do care. I am part of the King family now and I do not wish it to be part of something cruel. There's good in my family . . . I want to visit the brickworks and see more. I want to speak to the other workers and hear their views.'

Owen couldn't have that. He was supposed to be gaining information. If she demanded her family take her to the yard they would start asking awkward questions and Adam's plan would be over before it even began. 'It wouldna do any good, miss. If you came, it would be announced beforehand and everyone would clean themselves up and speak only good things to you. Troon the foreman would make sure of it. He is a lackey of the bosses.'

'Then, I shall come unannounced one day. You shall see.'

'I do hope not, miss. It is a filthy, smelly place. Much worse than your Paris, I'm sure.'

'We shall see,' she smiled that kittenish smile again, playful and inviting. 'I may surprise you.'

'You do surprise me, Miss Beatrice,' he said and they both laughed, good-naturedly. 'Well, you best get going or they'll be sending out a search party for you. Will you make it through the trees with that . . . that contraption on?'

Beatrice looked affronted but laughed at the same time, showing she took it in good humour.

‘I see you do not approve of the crinoline! Is it because we women are taking up more room in the world? We command more space in one of these and push the men to the side! Is that your objection?’

‘I just like to see a woman’s natural form, is all. There’s nothing finer.’

There was a moment of quiet between them.

‘Meet me next week, same time, same place?’ she said, as she turned to ascend the forest path to her home, the big house on the hill.

‘I wouldna miss it for the world,’ he said, taking off his cap with a flourish. He watched her figure move lightly through the trees, until all that was left of her was the tread of her footsteps through the bracken and the warning sounds of little birds that foolishly fled as she passed them by.

Chapter 8

Beatrice stood outside the kitchen door holding an empty pillowcase, listening intently. She was wearing her travelling dress, the simplest garment she now owned. She heard someone chopping and someone else gossiping about their neighbours. They seemed to be fully occupied. She glanced up the corridor, to ensure nobody was coming. As quietly as she could, she opened the cupboard door before her. Inside were stored piles of clothes. They belonged to the servants who did not live in with the Kings. They walked to the house in their own clothes, then changed into their smart service uniforms on arrival. Beatrice had spied them coming and going and discovered this place where they stored their home clothes. She recognised her own maid Dinah's chequered shawl and took the whole pile and stuffed it into the pillowcase. She looked down at the base of the cupboard and grabbed a pair of boots that looked about her size. She would only be gone an hour or two and she'd replace the clothes exactly as she found them. Nobody would need to know and no harm would be done.

Off she scampered, out of the back door without seeing anybody, thank heavens. She didn't want to have to explain the pillowcase she carried conspicuously. She felt like a thief in her own home and all of it was thrilling. She slipped unseen from the garden into the woods. Once the house was no longer visible, Beatrice found a likely tree and quickly undressed, laying her clothes out on the branch and pulling out Dinah's, a calico shirt with woollen skirt and shawl. Once redressed, she stuffed her own dress into the pillowcase and stowed it in the hollow of the tree, mightily pleased with herself for this cunning plan.

The walk through the woods was easy enough. Beatrice could remain unseen there until the short stretch of road she had to walk along, before turning once again into the cover of the trees behind the brickworks. On the way, she rubbed her hands in some dust and smeared it across her face, as well as running some dust through her hair, hoping to disguise herself further as a working person. She made sure that the grime was lodged beneath her fingernails too. She could not roughen up her hands to mimic years of manual labour, but she had done enough of their household washing in Paris to make her hands not as smooth as other debutantes her age. Though dusty, her hair still had the lustre of someone who had it washed often, but she had used Dinah's cotton mob cap to cover it, tying its frayed ribbons tightly beneath the chin to make sure the hair did not slip out and show. All the way, she kept looking down at her garments, unable to get used to their fascinating newness to her. She knew from seeing people of all classes in town that perhaps she was even too well dressed for a girl looking for brickwork, which is what she intended to be. Dinah's hobnail boots, which walked her between her home in Jackfield and the King house seven days a week through all weathers, were suitably worn and muddy. But Dinah's clothes, Beatrice noticed, had been carefully mended in several places. Dinah took pride in her appearance and, Beatrice realised, could not afford to buy new ones when her clothes ripped.

She came to the back of the brickworks through the trees, seeing the great shadow of the weathering heap loom up before her. There was no fence as such, just a shallow trench dug around the site to mark its boundary here. She clambered across it, thankful the ground was dry and crusty due to a recent lack of rain. She came up behind the huge heap of clay and edged around it to get a good look at the yard that spread forth beyond it. As she loitered, she saw the workers engaged in their various tasks, too wrapped up in their business to notice her. There were tall, broad men digging into the weathered clay heap, their spades portioning huge lumps which were dumped to one side. A series of children, boys and girls, of a range of ages from twelve or thirteen down to some very small ones. Could they be as young as five or six? Or maybe, Beatrice grimaced, they were so underfed as to be older yet with stunted growth. All of the children were grey with the clay that stuck to their bare arms and legs.

She could see that she was indeed dressed far better than the majority of these children, many of whom were half naked. On their heads, they all wore caps or scarves of some sort, upon which they balanced a lump of clay that looked far too large for those small heads to accommodate. They would squat down without bending their bodies and take another lump in their arms, the clay mass shoved up against their stomachs, and then they would stagger off. She watched one girl with thin bandy legs and a stumbling gait, walk with difficulty carrying her double load, down the incline of the yard, past a variety of buildings and workers coming to and fro, all the way to a three-sided shed, and disappear inside. Within moments, out she came again, free of her burden and trudged her way back up to the heap again, her head bowed and her shoulders sunken. The girl moved in a strange, unnerving way, an awkwardness in her step, as if her muscles and joints were not on speaking terms. Beatrice could only imagine that this was the result of years of the same debilitating work rendering her growing body malformed in some way. When the girl looked up at the heap of clay before her, her cheeks were pale and there was a deadness in the eyes that chilled Beatrice. The girl took up her double load again and off she went. Beatrice watched her make the same trip three times, before she guessed that this is what the girl must do all day, every day and by doing so must walk for miles and miles and carry tons and tons of clay on her head and in her arms every single shift.

The sight of these children made Beatrice's heart lurch. She had seen dire poverty on the streets of Montmartre, begging orphans in rags hanging around in miserable clumps. But there was something about these grey children slogging through life with no rest, no hope, that seized her sympathy and shook her to the core. And to know this was her family's business, it removed any distance that she might have kept between her and those Parisian children. She didn't have the means to help back then and now the fine meals she enjoyed were paid for by the work of these poor waifs.

She wanted to see more. She came forward and was spotted by a clay digger, who stared at her with amazement, as if she had stepped down from a cloud. Perhaps her disguise was not enough, perhaps they knew what the new King girl looked like. She sincerely hoped not. She gathered her courage and said boldly, 'Looking for work.'

'Down on yer luck? Got yerself in trouble?' said the digger, smirking, looking her up and down in the way only a man could.

'Who do I talk to?' she said.

He pointed downhill. Which building or structure that indicated, she could not tell, but she stepped forward as if she knew anyway and turned her head away from him. 'Miss Hoity-toity!' she heard him say and laugh at her. She carried on walking as if she knew exactly what she was doing, but with every step she felt less and less sure of her rash decision to come here. More than anything, she hoped she would not see Owen. The thought of it had excited her on her walk, but now she was here, she felt how ill-advised her plan had been, to spend a morning playing at brickmaking. Inwardly she cursed her folly and regretted it sorely. What had she been thinking? She decided to ask one of the brickmoulders briefly about work then turn and leave as soon as she was able.

While walking down to the shed where the brickmoulders stood, she saw yet more young children, taking the bricks from the benches and delivering them to another shed, where she guessed the bricks were dried out. Men came and went from the drying shed, one man was leading a horse down towards the gate, others carrying tools into a building where she could hear some sort of machine at work. Further along, she saw more children coming and going from another structure, a round building dotted with a range of entrances, out of which each child was carrying four or five finished bricks at a time in their arms, their neck muscles straining, whilst their bowed legs looked about to snap. She turned her attention back to the open-sided shed, where the brickmoulders stood in rows, each one standing before a bench.

There must have been around twenty or so. At first she thought she saw one or two women amongst their number. But then as she looked more closely she realised that most of them were women, made sexless by their uniform grey colour and turbaned heads. Beatrice caught a quick glance at the dexterity of one moulder, who dashed the clay into the mould, pummelled it with a stick, threw a piece of cloth onto it and beat it with a stubby bat, then smoothed it off with a sweeping motion, using a tool that seemed the union of a cheese wire and a bow. And there, the brick was done. She whacked the mould on the bench to release the brick, which was taken up by a waiting child and removed from the bench. And now the next lump of clay was deposited and the moulder did her magic again, so quick, so skilful.

Beatrice could see that the moulder job must have been sought after in the brickyard hierarchy, as though you'd be on your feet all day, at least you didn't have to carry the clay or bricks and did not move from your bench. It seemed to her that those least able to do the heavy work were forced into that very role, with hideous and tragic consequences. The children she saw there looked more like creatures of nightmare arisen from the mud, ghoulish and haunted. One such boy who was coming down to deposit his clay on a bench lagged behind the others and she watched as a woman stepped out and swiped at him with one huge flat hand the size of a paddle, hitting him so hard he fell flat on his back. Not a word was spoken, as the boy struggled to his feet and the moulder carried on her work.

'Leave him alone!' cried Beatrice, before she thought to stop herself. Almost as one, all heads turned in her direction. She saw the boy staring at her, his mouth open in amazement. 'Are you all right?' she asked him. He shot a glance at the woman who'd hit him.

'Friend of yours?' the woman said to the boy.

'No, Mother. Never seen her afore, I swear!' he cried, then hobbled off uphill as fast as his spindly legs would carry him.

'That is your *son*?' said Beatrice to the woman, aghast.

'Who's asking? The Queen of Ironbridge?'

That raised a laugh around the workers and attracted the attention of an overseer, who turned sharply and stormed over towards Beatrice. 'Get on with yer work!' he shouted at the others as he approached, then turning to Beatrice, he lurched towards her face and yelled, 'Stop loitering there!'

'I came to ask after some work,' she said and felt her face turn hot.

'What manner o'work?' said the man, squinting at her. 'You dunna look like you ever done a day's work in yer life.'

She did not know what jobs they did at such a yard and suddenly heard how different her voice was from all those around her, how unmarked by toil she must look. *What a fool I've been, coming here, trying to fit in,* she thought. But others were staring at her and she had to say something.

'I was a teacher once. Fallen on hard times.'

'Teacher?' scoffed the man. 'That inna work. What good would yer be round here? Get away.'

'All right,' she said and jutted out her chin, defiantly. 'I'm going. But you better mind that your workers treat those children better. Or I'll report you all. Just you see if I won't!'

And with that, she darted away from the man, whose eyes had grown wider with every word and she'd feared he might strike her at the end of her little speech. She half ran, half stumbled up the incline, past curious looks and sniggering laughs, back out into the woods again.

The walk home was long and tiresome and with each step she repeated the scene at the brickyard in her head. She'd been foolish to think she could pass as a brickworker, but still she was glad she had seen the state of the yard for herself. She went down to the riverside and managed to scoop up a bit of water to clean the worst of the mud from her face and hands. She found her clothes in the pillowcase and managed to get them back on, but her hair once the mob cap had been removed was a fright, she could feel it. If seen, she would have to face the music and make up a story. At the edge of the garden, she waited a while to see if anyone had appeared at a window to see her passage, but there was nobody there. She whisked across the garden and into a back door. Upon opening it, she found herself face to face with Jenkins, her great-grandmother's lady's maid. Jenkins stared at her, dumbfounded.

'I got lost in the woods and could not find my way home. I followed the river but the wrong way. Silly me! What a fool I am! I was caught by the vegetation and it messed up my hair a bit. But I am all right. Please do not concern yourself with it, or bother my mother or great-grandmother. I have learnt my lesson and will not go exploring any further.'

All of this was said in a tumble of words that Jenkins appeared to regard with smug amusement, also eyeing with interest the pillowcase Beatrice grasped in her hands. Beatrice did not wait for a reply and instead dashed up the servant staircase, remembering halfway up that Jenkins would wonder why on earth the daughter of the house was taking that lowly route. But it was too late to go back down now, so she ran up the last few steps and across to her room. Once inside, she rebraided her hair, then took out Dinah's clothes and folded them neatly. Later, she'd have to find a time to replace them in the cupboard, but for now, she was exhausted and could not face leaving her room and bumping into Jenkins again, or anyone else.

She sank down onto her bed. Again, visions of what she had experienced filled her exhausted mind, like scenes from a night terror. But despite the misery of it all, she told herself that something good had come of all this. She was appalled at what she had seen, what those brickworkers had to endure, day in, day out, just to earn enough to live. With every passing moment, her disgust at her family's complicity deepened and by the time she heard the gong sound below for luncheon, she was resolved. Something had to be done.

Chapter 9

Queenie had tried to put the vision of the ghost out of her mind for weeks now, but with little success. She had told no one about it, yet the morning after the visitation, fresh from the ghost's plea, she had asked Jenkins to find out what she could about the long forgotten baby on the bridge. Jenkins had not approved, but in the end had agreed.

That had been weeks ago and nothing had been said since. But now she was watching Jenkins pin her hair up and she pressed her on it. 'You have said nothing about the baby on the bridge. Have you forgotten?'

'I'm not losing my mind. I don't forget things. I was waiting until I had all the information.'

'So, you have some information then? Oh, do not be tiresome, Jenkins. Tell me what you have discovered thus far.' Queenie was eager to hear of it, but tried to cover this fact.

'I spoke to the old school mistress, Miss Millington, who hears most of the gossip because the children tell her things. She said the baby was taken in by a Quaker family, but she didn't know which one or if they still lived. She thought the midwife Mrs Lunt might know, but she's been away from town this month visiting family up north and has only just returned. I was planning to go into town this morning and ask her. Satisfied?'

Queenie nodded respectfully and said, 'Yes, thank you, Jenkins.'

'I still think raking over those ashes is a bad idea. Leave them dead and cold as they are.'

'I am aware of your opinion on the matter and do not wish to hear it again. Leave me now. I shall finish my own hair today.'

Once Jenkins had gone, she looked hopelessly at her pins on the dressing table and thrust one in somewhere at the back of her head to feel that she had done something. How helpless she would be without Jenkins. She was not capable of even managing the hair on her own head.

She was annoyed at Jenkins for withholding information that could have eased her mind these past weeks. She guessed that Jenkins had done that on purpose, because she didn't approve of Queenie's interest in the baby on the bridge. But she was not about to admit to Jenkins the truth behind why she was really asking about it, and worse still, what she had seen from her window. She was haunted not only by the spirit of Betsy Blaize but also the ghost of fear that clutched at her about her sister. She'd told Bea that Selina had died young, but not that she had spent her final years in an asylum. Queenie feared that Selina's fate of madness and suicide would afflict her too, that it ran in families and she was losing her mind, seeing ghouls like that. She would not admit that to anyone, even Jenkins. It was the thing that frightened her most and kept her awake at night, even without ghostly manifestations to disturb her sleep.

'Enough of this folly,' she told herself in the mirror. Patting her hair uselessly, she stood up and made her way downstairs to her study.

It was one of her favourite rooms in the house, the walls lined with French novels that Queenie had no intention of reading. But they had belonged to Margaret, who had pored over them as a child and left them all behind when she eloped to Paris. After Ralph's death, Queenie had taken over his study, changing the décor and some of the furniture to suit her own taste. She had had the books moved in there from the library and all of her son's tedious magazines and journals removed. Having Margaret's old novels all around her gave her comfort. She liked to be surrounded by the happier memories of Margaret as a child, when things were easier and she had company in the house, someone to play cards with, other than Jenkins. She had failed Margaret all those years ago, but she was home once more. Now she smiled to herself that she had Margaret back and now Beatrice, her joy. Such a sweet girl and such fun to talk to.

Queenie felt better already and went to her desk, scrupulously tidy with dustless inkstand and blotter before her, and she sat down. She glanced at the clock and saw it was ten minutes before the hour. She liked to take her seat and prepare herself mentally and physically before any planned event and always insisted that Jenkins checked her hair and tidied up any stray strands and made it perfect. She saw any hint of messiness in a woman's hair as a character flaw. There, she was ready now, waiting for Troon to arrive for a meeting about the brickyard.

Busby the butler was as fastidious as she was about timing and as the clock in her study chimed the hour of eleven, she heard footsteps approach her room. In he came and said, 'Mr Troon and a Mr Jones are here to see you, Ma'am.'

'A "Mr Jones"?' repeated Queenie with disdain. 'Whoever is that?'

'I believe he works at the brickyard with Mr Troon. He introduced himself to me as Mr Adam Jones, a brickmoulder. Shall I send him away?'

'No, no. Troon must have a reason to bring him, I surmise. Show them in, Busby.'

In came Troon, that handsome face marred by a poorly disguised sneer sneaking about his lips, Queenie felt. And behind him this Jones chap. He was stocky and ill-shaven. Black sideburns, black moustache, black eyes. He had made an effort to wash his arms and face, as well as wearing a clean jacket. But his boots were caked in clay and Queenie knew the maids would be cursing him for traipsing it through the house.

Queenie spoke first. 'I was expecting you, Mr Troon. But not this other . . . gentleman. Please indicate your reason for attending this meeting today, Mr Jones.'

Both men had taken off their caps. Troon fingered his cap but Jones stood stock still and looked directly at her.

'I am a brickmoulder at your yard, ma'am. I am also the General Secretary of our union.'

'Of your *what*?'

Before Jones had a chance to answer, a knock came at the door and then it immediately opened. Her grandson Cyril's red-cheeked face appeared. He strode across the room and stood beside Queenie's desk and turned to address one and all, as if he had been expected, as if he were wanted, which, Queenie thought, he decidedly was *not* on either count.

'I hear there are brickworkers in the house,' he said loudly. How Queenie hated his strident voice, pitched rather too high and with an edge of sarcasm about it, as if the world were a great joke to him. 'So I took it upon myself to invite myself to the proceedings.' He then flicked the tails of his brown frock coat and sat down upon a chair to the right of the desk, crossing his legs and folding his hands across his stomach, showing off his royal blue waistcoat and purple cravat, the height of informal morning wear.

Queenie was about to tell him to get out, when she stopped herself, aware that Troon and this Jones fellow would see it as a weakness that the family were quarrelling. So she swallowed her rage and addressed the two workers standing before her.

'Mr Jones,' she said imperiously. 'Your appearance here is unorthodox, without prior arrangement. However, I will hear your concerns.'

'I wish to inform you of our union of which I spoke earlier. Us brickworkers have formed a union. I have come today to advise you that we intend to negotiate with you on the rates of pay for all brickworkers under your employ.'

Queenie saw Cyril shift forwards in his seat and unfold his arms. She wished to keep this meeting brief and civil, yet if Cyril got involved with all his customary bluster, she feared things would take a darker turn. She was about to explain her position to Jones, but Cyril was younger and swifter and he got there first.

'Egads! The impertinence of the new breed of worker! This one has the look of a gypsy, don't you think, Queenie?'

Could the fool not be quiet for even a moment? He'd have this man up in arms before they even began talking. And to use her nickname in front of outsiders. But again, before she had a chance to reply, the Jones man was speaking yet again.

'Personal comments are unnecessary, Mr King. I come in the spirit of justice for all to inform you that we are united, that we speak with one voice. And we say to our masters, all we ask for is fair pay for a hard day's work.'

'Mr Jones,' Queenie began, raising her voice a notch to cut off a brash response from Cyril, who appeared to be winding himself up for one. 'We appreciate you coming here to inform us of your union and your concerns. Unfortunately we have a full meeting today. If you could speak to Mr Troon about your concerns in the first instance, that would perhaps be best.'

'And if I may ask, ma'am,' Jones said with a deferential nod of the head. The man was trying to show respect at least, thought Queenie. 'There is a rumour that a deal has been struck between all of the brickmasters, to lower our wages, and that this is to come into force imminently.'

Queenie was annoyed that Jones had heard of this. The brickmasters had agreed that the pay would go down at the beginning of the next month. *Nothing is secret in a small town like Ironbridge*, mused Queenie. But there was no way she would confirm it before talking to the other brickmasters. She began, 'This is not a matter . . .' but was shouted over by Cyril, who was now on his feet.

'You are absolutely correct in that and your new rate of pay per thousand bricks will be far more than you deserve. Of course we must lower pay, when you and your cronies work like lazy sluggards, always loafing off down the public houses. I hear you get tramps to man the kilns at night, so you can sneak off down to the inns and get drunk. Yes! I keep my ear to the ground too, you know.'

Cyril was utterly infuriating! Queenie glared at him. What was he thinking? All the other brickmasters would hear of it and think her a traitor for letting the news out before their set date. But she had to tread carefully; there was no way on earth she could let Jones and Troon know she thought her grandson was an idiot.

'Mr Jones,' she said in a conciliatory voice. 'Be aware that no final decisions have been made at this time, despite my grandson's . . . enthusiasm. We regularly look into the cost of wages and materials to ensure the profitability of our business. Brick prices rise and fall and we must move with the tides of change. Our main interest is to ensure that this brickyard remains open.'

'Yes, indeed!' cried Cyril. 'And let that be a warning to you, Jones or whatever you call yourself,' said Cyril, taking a threatening step forward, as if readying himself for a fist-fight. 'Any talk of strikes and such foolery will be met in severe terms. The harshest of terms, man. Do you hear me?'

Troon took a step forward too – at which Cyril took a stumbling step backwards – but Troon had his hands out, palms down. 'Nobody has spoken of strikes, Mr King, ma'am.'

'I'm no fool,' spat Cyril. 'I've heard whispers about town of secret meetings and plans to strike. Deny it, if you dare.'

'There is no secret about it,' said Jones, jutting out his chin. 'We make no secret of our union, hence my visit here this day. We have not mentioned strikes but be aware, that if pay is to be cut in any way for any workers, then we *will* strike and it'll be on your head, let me warn you.'

Cyril continued, 'And allow me to warn you, you . . . you ruffian! Remember that a great many of our workers live in housing provided by this family. If you whip them up into insurrection and call a strike, every one of them will be summarily evicted. And if you're one of them, be assured you will lose your home and it will be the workhouse for you and everyone you care about.'

Cyril had gone too far! Queenie felt quite ill at this turn of events. She wanted to retract what her grandson had said. Evictions was a trump card to be used much later on in the process, if necessary. To threaten it now was idiocy. But she could not show division in the family. It would be a sign of weakness. While she wrestled with what to say next, she looked at Jones. He stared directly at Cyril and showed no sign of wavering. He spoke again, just as plainly and coolly as before.

'I am one of your tenants, sir. My wife and I have lived there together these past two years.'

'Then you'd better watch yourself or you'll be out on the street!' said Cyril, his voice raised.

'With all due respect,' continued Jones, 'let me remind you that we have our union. We shall look after one another. We have no fear of a strike and no terror of the workhouse. But Mrs King, Mr King, I must say this meeting has not proceeded in the manner in which I had hoped.'

'Listen to the gentleman!' scoffed Cyril. 'Speaking like a Lord!'

Jones ignored this and continued, 'And my wish to negotiate seems to have fallen on deaf ears. Please let me finish by saying that I have worked hard for this brickyard for twenty years, that I am a highly skilled brickmoulder who contributes daily towards the success of the King brickyard. I value my work and my colleagues, and do not wish to cause trouble unnecessarily. I hope we can talk again in the future in a more productive manner. Thank you for your time. I will take my leave of you now.'

With that, he made a short bow, turned and left the room, closing the door gently behind him.

Troon looked shocked and Cyril laughed. Queenie was left infuriated by Cyril. She was also impressed by Jones. There was intelligence in him, to be sure, and he had spoken sense and attempted to be respectful towards the end. It was clear that, if Cyril's rumours were to be believed, Mr Jones had the ear of all the workers and he was charismatic enough to lead them all against the King family and never give in. She would have to be careful with this one. He would take cautious handling.

'I do apologise for any offence caused, ma'am,' said Troon, his voice polite yet oily. 'It was my understanding that Mr Jones was coming here today to introduce himself as the union leader. I didna sanction any talk of strikes, nor do I at the yard neither.'

'Understood, Troon,' said Queenie. 'You are not to blame. Thank you and please take your leave. I shall see you again tomorrow, when tempers are cooler.'

'Yes, ma'am, sir,' said Troon, bobbing his head twice, then leaving quietly.

'Well, well,' said Cyril in a tone that showed how mightily pleased with himself he was. 'I knew something was going on with those blackguards.'

Queenie turned a cold eye on her grandson, who looked at her, pleased with himself, until he saw her thunderous expression.

'How dare you inflame the situation so! What were you thinking? What possessed you to pepper your speech with such inflammatory terms as "strike" and "eviction"?'

'Well, I must say, I'm surprised at you. You've always been tough as old boots with these types. Are you going soft in your old age?'

Queenie sighed and put her hand to her head. It would be easy to dismiss him as a fool, but she felt she must attempt to explain it to him, to prevent another such embarrassment. Cyril was in his late thirties now and not a young man any more. Although he was usually napping or supping or otherwise engaged, he did show some interest in the business and could be useful to carry out site visits and suchlike. She had to try to make him understand, at least.

'It is not a case of weakness. Negotiation must be handled with great care. Think of it as a politician might, when a great battle looms on the horizon. Attempts must be made to avoid it before letting slip the dogs of war.'

'I don't see why. They are but a rabble of rag-tags, half drunk much of the time and plotting our demise the rest, so people say.'

'What people? And what talk have you heard of this around town, Cyril? And why have you not brought it to my attention before?'

'It was only rumblings. But they're saying that the brickworkers meet in the basement of inns hereabouts and talk of sedition. I had no proof, only some drunken gossiping.'

'I see,' said Queenie. 'But this does not forgive your rash behaviour here today. You must curb yourself in future. I shall pursue matters from here on. I shall think on it.'

'But there is no thinking to be done. We must stamp on them. We must dismiss that Jones, immediately.'

'It is not that simple,' snapped Queenie, suddenly very tired of him and the whole situation. 'These things are delicate and need to be handled cleverly.'

'Delicate? What rot! Dismiss the lot of them.'

'Just like that! And where do you presume we shall find a whole brickyard's worth of trained workers, at a moment's notice? It would cost us a fortune to halt production and find a whole new workforce. That would be the last resort, or at least a threat to hold over them later in the process. Can't you see, that we must play our cards cleverly?'

'Nothing clever required with that lot of scoundrels.'

'Oh, do shut up, Cyril!' she cried. 'You have no idea what you're talking about. You are no help at all, just like your useless father.'

She walked past him, noting the lack of response as she went through the door and into the passageway. A wave of exhaustion came over her, tinged with guilt. She shouldn't have said that to Cyril, but he made it so hard to respect him.

Once in her room, she closed the door behind her with relief. It would be lunchtime soon and she would need to face the family. She made the decision to have her lunch sent up to her. She was about to ring the bell to summon a servant to give her luncheon instructions, when a knock came at the door.

'Saving me the trouble,' she muttered to herself and called, 'Come in.'

But it was not a servant. It was Beatrice.

'My dear, you do look tired. And very serious. What can the matter be?'

'I've had a very trying morning,' she said.

'Come and sit with me on the bed,' said Queenie and patted the covers. Queenie pushed her pillows up so she could lean against them and make herself comfortable.

As shattered as she was and as much as she longed for rest, she could not resist Beatrice and wanted to hear every last detail of whatever it was that had happened. Beatrice sat down opposite her, at the end of the bed, her feet curled under her. 'Now, tell me everything.'

Beatrice looked down and sighed. 'I have a secret to tell you. But first I ask that you must not be angry with me.'

Queenie was immediately rapt, but could not imagine the child could do anything that would make her angry. So she replied, 'I will listen without prejudice.'

Beatrice bit her lip. 'I do hope so . . . I went to the brickworks this morning.'

This was the last thing Queenie expected to hear. 'And how did this come to pass? Who took you there?'

'Myself. I took myself there. Indeed, I took it upon myself to dress up in the clothes of a working woman and go to the brickyard to see it for myself.'

Queenie was on high alert now. 'Were you seen? Were you recognised?'

'I was seen and spoken to, but I believe that my disguise worked and I was not recognised.'

'You believe?' probed Queenie. The scandal, if it were discovered! How humiliating for a King to be found dressing up as a commoner and rattling around with Ironbridge working folk. This was the opposite of what was needed just before Beatrice was about to be launched in society. Queenie was trying to keep her temper. The child had surprised her. As before, with Margaret's elopement, she was half shocked and horrified, half secretly pleased that the girl was showing spirit. But this, this madness? What on earth could the girl have been thinking?

'You are not angry, Queenie?'

'Why did you go, my dear?'

'I wanted to see for myself. I had heard bad things about the yard. It is owned by my family. So I felt I ought to know the truth.'

Queenie bridled at this, but fought to remain calm. She would come back to the accusation of 'bad things' presently. 'But why not request a formal visit, with me or your uncle, or even your mother? Why this theatrical subterfuge? Why lie and dissemble?'

Beatrice sniffed and looked blankly at her. 'I knew that if I went openly, the truth would not be shown to me. Everyone would be on best behaviour.'

'I am impressed by your reasoning. Now, tell me everything that happened, from beginning to end.'

'I saw the children there, half clothed and exhausted, lugging lumps of clay about that look twice as heavy as they are themselves. Some were deformed, it seems by the backbreaking work they must do. A child was struck viciously.'

'Well, what you may not know is that most of those children are working for their own families.'

'Yes, it was the mother who hit her son.'

'There you are, then. The moulders are at liberty to hire their own kin and how they treat them really is their own business.'

'But the whole place is riven with misery and want. If they were not worked so hard, were not in such dreary circumstances and were not driven by desperation to stay in such a job, perhaps they would not act so. The children are so downtrodden and pathetic, they tear your heart in two! Their faces are like that of old men, placed on young, weak bodies. And some of them were no more than five or six years of age. What of their schooling? What of their minds? What possible parents can they grow up to be if this is their education? But none of them have such choices, if they are worked into the ground in such a place. If I hadn't gone there myself and seen it with my own eyes, I never would have believed it were possible, in this day and age, in England, in this fine county, in our family business! Queenie, I do believe—'

But Queenie had heard enough. It was time to rein this one in.

'My dear child, you are young and passionate, but in one trip to the brickyard you could never begin to understand what it means to run a business. I'm sure you think you saw something, but we have people in place to manage the brickworkers, people trained to run the business. Your decision to go incognito to a King-owned business was rash and foolhardy. If anybody there discovered that you were a King, we would be laughing stocks. Listen now. I am learning that you have a fine mind, that we can put to use in the business one day, I am sure of it. But you are still young and callow. What you did was rash and badly thought out. Luckily, it seems that you escaped without being recognised.'

'But, Queenie! Did you know these terrible things were occurring in your own brickyard? Did you?'

Queenie bristled at this. From anyone else, she would not have stood for such insolence. She could forgive Beatrice most things, but the girl was sailing close to the wind on this one. 'My business is to make a profit for our family and our shareholders. My foreman's business is to oversee my brickyard. Your business is to profit from all of this and to sleep in a warm bed, eat your fill at mealtimes and wear the prettiest dresses in Shropshire. Please do not tell me my business, child.'

Usually this kind of Queenie pronouncement formed the end of most discussions. But Beatrice was not to be stopped.

'But you are the owner. You should know what is going on with your own workers.'

'What they do is their business. I am no foreman and I hope you are not suggesting I drag my skirts through the brick dust in my silk shoes and shout at people.'

'No, of course not. But you are guilty by omission! You are culpably unaware of the goings-on in your own brickyard. The children are being worked to death. It is a place of neglect and misery and violence.'

'And that is because of the brickworker breed. Coming from France, you may not be aware of this. But if you read our newspapers and the thoughts of our foremost thinkers, you will find that the brickworker in particular is not well thought of in any vein of society, including their own. The brickworker is known universally as the lowest type, the lowest of the low,' pronounced Queenie, sure this point would end this insufferable argument.

'That is not true,' returned Beatrice, tenacious in her dispute. 'As with all people, there are good, bad and indifferent. I was brought up in a small, narrow house without refinement or privilege.'

'That is not the same thing at all. Your mother was educated and taught you well. And she had the best of breeding, coming from my line, and the King line. It was born in you to be refined.'

'But not all educated, privileged people are refined. Look at Uncle Cyril! And not all brickworkers are like the one I saw strike her child. Some are the most wonderful, intelligent, even poetic people.'

'What drivel! How could you possibly know that from looking at them?'

Beatrice looked askance. 'I know one, personally. He is a friend of mine.'

'He?' gasped Queenie. This was going from bad to worse! 'Who is this "he"?'

'I bought a pie from a young man of around my age. He turned out to be one of our brickmakers. We have become friends. He is everything I claim. He is good and kind and clever. He would never raise a hand to a child or a woman. He reads and is well-spoken. I am proud to call him my friend.'

Queenie's alarm bells were pealing at full volume. She steeled herself for the lecture that was to come. A young male brickworker that reads, friends with her Bea? Never! 'Now listen, my girl. Only trouble will come of that. Ask your mother. It was that business with Anny that caused all the trouble years ago.'

Beatrice's face lit up. 'Ah! Mother has mentioned Anny but won't tell me any more. What happened between them? Was Anny poor?'

'Ask her,' said Queenie, with venom. 'Ask your mother what befell that friendship and all who suffered because of it. All I shall say is that your mother knows full well that friendships between the classes never work and will end in disaster. Mark my words, girl!'

'But this is about more than him. It is about the whole brickyard and the fate of its workers. I have heard that plans are afoot to lower their wages. Just yesterday, I heard you say that the price of bricks is on the rise. Could we not afford to pay our workers a reasonable wage? Should our workers not share in our success?'

'That is not how business works, Beatrice. Brick prices rise and thus our profits rise. We then invest that money back into our businesses to grow them evermore. The brickworkers are used to their old brickmaster's ways and he was inefficient and became a bankrupt. We must tighten our belts when it comes to wages, or our profits will fall and eventually our business will fail. Then everyone will be out of work, including your friends the brickworkers and this fine house here and everyone in it.'

'I do not believe it is that simple. There must be a way to run a successful business and still take care of your workers. Great-grandmother, I beg you. Please do not lower their wages. Please, go down there and see them for yourself.'

'I will do no such thing, Beatrice!' Queenie was about to launch into a final sermon to end this madness, but the child had boundless energy for a fight and would not stop.

'But how can you stand by when those who rely on you suffer? You must do what you can. You must strive to improve things for them. It is your duty to improve their lot in life.'

A chill clutched at Queenie's throat.

'What did you say?' she murmured.

'I said you must improve their lot in life. Have I said the phrase wrongly? Maman says it, a good English phrase I think. Their lot in life.'

'Stop saying that!' cried Queenie and realised her hands were shaking.

'Queenie, what is it?' said Beatrice, visibly distressed. She moved towards her great-grandmother and took her hands in her own, massaging them gently.

Improve her lot in life, the ghost of Betsy Blaize had demanded for her child. Was the spirit working through her nearest and dearest now?

Queenie snatched her hands away. 'Leave me,' she said. 'You have upset me greatly.'

Beatrice looked guiltily away, stood up from the bed and walked slowly to the door. 'I am sorry for upsetting you. I am very sorry for that.'

Queenie was glad to hear it and waved her hand feebly to signal her acceptance of this. But the girl was not finished.

Before she left the room, Beatrice said quietly, 'But I am not sorry for what I said, as it is the truth. All of it.'

Beatrice went out and shut the door. For the first time in years, Queenie feared she might actually weep. The child had upset her so, with cruel accusations and worrying news. But the stress of hearing the spirit's words come from the mouth of her darling girl was too much.

'Jenkins,' Queenie said, knowing that her faithful servant was not there. 'Jenkins,' she said again, for comfort. But as if the call had summoned her existence, the door between their bedrooms opened and there she was, dressed up in her bonnet with the cloth flowers and her beige day dress, from her trip into town.

'You don't look right,' said Jenkins, coming over quickly to Queenie and taking her wrist, feeling for her pulse. Simply the touch of Jenkins's dry, firm hands was a relief.

'Must I be beset by troubles at this time of my life?' sighed Queenie. 'I ought to be seeing out my autumn years in peace and relaxation.'

'Winter years, more like,' said Jenkins, but then cocked her head and peered at her. 'But this is not like you. What's been going on?'

'Miss Beatrice has been playing merry hell with my nerves. I shall tell you all about it later. I want to stay up here for lunch. Tell them in a moment, will you? I've had the very devil of a morning. But first, Jenkins, news. News from you and then I must rest. What news from town?'

Jenkins undid the bow beneath her chin and removed her bonnet. She liked to delay her revelations, to draw out the drama. She did love a bit of gossip, did Jenkins.

'I have news. The Quaker midwife told me the baby was called Martha, brought up by the Beddoes family, good people. Both the Beddoes are dead now. This Martha – the baby on the bridge – she is now married to one of our very own brickmakers called Jones. They are with child, the midwife says, as she's visited them already.'

She knew that name. Oh no, could it be? The man who had stood in her study just that morning, the union leader, the cause of all her troubles at the brickworks? But it was a common name thereabouts, very common in Shropshire. There could be any number of Joneses.

'Did she say the man's Christian name, this Jones?'

'Now, let me see. Yes, she did. Adam. Adam and Martha Jones, she said. A brickmoulder at the King brickyard. Now then, you have your news. You know where the baby on the bridge is. Happily married and her own baby on the way. I'd say that's the matter closed, wouldn't you? Now, let me sort luncheon. Tongue sandwiches today, I think. You need a bit of meat in you. You look so pale.'

Queenie slept that afternoon, shattered after her day of strife. She was hungry and ready for something good and filling to eat as the dinner gong sounded its hollow ring downstairs. She left her room and saw Benjamina appear, dressed up in a blue silk gown with bell shaped sleeves trimmed with broderie anglaise. It was a fine ensemble, Queenie had to admit, but surely a tad overdressed for a simple family dinner. Benjamina was pulling the door to gently, shutting her dog Louise in.

'You are the sweetest thing,' said Benjamina to the dog, who was wriggling through the gap in the door, trying to come out and join her mistress for dinner. 'Yes, you are. Yes, you are. The most loveable, most pretty, most sweet, most wonderful little creature that ever did live! But you must stay here. Mama is going for dinner now. I shall see you in less than a shake of your dear little tail.'

Queenie rolled her eyes. Benjamina managed to shut the dog in and turned to her, nodding and simpering that fake smile of hers.

'Benjamina,' said Queenie and walked forwards, assuming the lead, of course.

'Are you well?' came Benjamina's voice behind her.

'Quite well, thank you.'

'You do look a little pale. I do wonder if you take on too much these days.'

Queenie stopped on the landing halfway down the stairs and turned to Benjamina, who was still smiling that smile, with an overly concerned look in her eye. Queenie had never got on well with her daughter-in-law, but recently, the woman seemed to be up to something. Whatever it was, Queenie was keen to ensure that Benjamina knew her place, which was well down the pecking order from herself.

'Not at all, my dear. I have never felt stronger in my life.'

'If you're sure, Queenie,' said Benjamina, touching the blue ribbons in her hair, as if to adjust them, although they were quite perfect just as they were. 'We wouldn't want you to suffer under too much stress and vexation. Not at *your* age.'

Queenie ignored the remark and descended the stairs with a quicker step than usual. She swept into the dining room at quite a pace. Seated at the dinner table, she listened with distaste while Benjamina uncharacteristically filled in time by making conversation with the others. She began with indulging Beatrice by asking about her Paris friends, flattering Margaret by asking her favourite pieces to play on the pianoforte and next she came up with a topic she seemed to know would annoy Queenie.

'The old brickmaster's house,' Benjamina said. 'It's still boarded up. Shouldn't we open it up and use it? It is such a lovely location in Benthall Edge Woods, just along from that pretty church. I would be delighted to take over its renovation. It'd be a marvellous project to get my teeth into. If we are honest with ourselves, one would say it is a finer house than this, being built much more recently. Cyril agrees with me, don't you?'

'It is a good, solid house,' he said, with his mouth full, not letting that stop him. 'But too secluded and far away from town for my liking. I prefer it here, up on top of the hill, looking down at everyone.'

'Which house is this?' asked Beatrice.

Margaret answered, 'The Kings took over the brickworks when the old brickmaster went bankrupt and the house came to us. Is that right, Grandmother?'

Queenie nodded, finishing her mouthful. She did not deign to look at Benjamina, who again was sticking her nose into things that had never been her business, trying to reorganise where they lived, for heaven's sake.

This woman was definitely up to something, jostling for position since the death of her husband. Well, Queenie was having none of that. She dabbed the corners of her lips before answering. 'There is no question it is a fine house. But if Benjamina thinks we can afford to run two large houses with a full staff in the same environs, she's lost her reason. We shall sell it at some point, I'd imagine. But I haven't decided its fate quite yet. When the time comes, as head of the house and the company, it will be my decision and nobody else's.'

That put an end to that. Queenie glanced round the table to see Margaret looking blank, Beatrice looking thoughtful, Benjamina smiling an infuriating little smirk, and Cyril looking bored. But he caught her eye and said, 'Ah Queenie.'

'What is it, Cyril?'

'I forgot to inform you this afternoon. You'll be proud of me, as I have finally taken some initiative in the family business and shown those ruffians who's the boss.'

'What have you done?' Queenie said in a low voice.

'I've had eviction notices served on all of the brickies who live in King housing. Imagine their surprise when they finish their shifts and discover they must vacate our properties by tomorrow evening. That should sort out the blackguards once and for all. Now they'll know who they're dealing with. It'll take the wind out of their sails.'

Queenie could not believe her ears. After everything she had tried to explain to this fool, he had done this?

She was about to rain fire and brimstone down upon him, when she was interrupted.

'How could you!' cried Beatrice.

'How could I? Quite easily, my dear. I marched down to Brotherton's office and gave the order.'

Queenie could hold back no longer and with a great voice that scratched her throat and seemed to make the very walls quiver, she shouted, 'You *imbecile*!'

But there was no time for reaction, as in came Busby and approached her. He whispered to her that Mr Troon was here to see her. The door was opened roughly and there was Troon. Busby looked round, horrified that an outsider had passed the threshold to the inner sanctum. Would Busby try to manhandle him? It was unthinkable, a kerfuffle in the King drawing room. And Queenie knew that Troon's arms as sturdy as a sailor's would make quick work of the wiry, middle-aged butler.

'News has reached us of the eviction of all brickworkers from King housing,' announced Troon, standing at the foot of the table with his arms crossed. 'So I have news for the King family. Every last worker at your brickyard has downed tools and we have put out the kiln fires. From tonight at seven of the clock, we are officially on strike.'

Chapter 10

Owen was waiting for her on Madame's steps the next morning, as usual. They looked at each other without smiling.

'I am glad you're here,' Beatrice said. 'I didn't think you'd come.'

'Course I did,' he said and tried to smile, but it didn't quite work and came out as a smirk, then a grimace.

'I thought they'd tell you not to see me anymore.'

'Who?'

'Mr Troon and the other brickworkers.'

'I follow my own path,' he replied and smiled properly this time.

'Last night, my great-grandmother told me I was not to speak to you again.'

'You'd told her about me, about . . . us? Our friendship?' He looked nervous.

'Only that I knew a brickworker as an acquaintance. After we received the news about the strike, she found me upstairs later in my room and said I was forbidden to "fraternise" with anyone from the brickworks.'

'I see,' he said and fiddled with his cap he held in his hands.

Beatrice glanced up and down the road, checking her mother or anyone else from the house wasn't about to spot them. She leant in and whispered, 'But I know a place we can meet later.'

Back at home, luncheon was a quiet affair, sitting only with her mother. Benjamina was indisposed in her room with her yappy little dog, Louise, while Queenie and Cyril were ensconced in the study all day having meetings with some of the staff. Four visitors arrived and were shown in to join the meetings, local brickmasters, apparently. Beatrice could hear raised voices coming from that room, when she loitered near it, but could not make out what they were saying. After lunch, Beatrice told her mother she was going for a walk along the riverside that afternoon with Madame. Her mother did not question her, as she seemed very pleased to see her daughter exercising. She did harp on so about Beatrice's waist these days, but never had in Paris. It made her feel quite low, this hint that she was plump and ought to do something about it. Maman had said, 'When you wear tight silk across your back, one can see a little roll of flesh bulging atop the line of the corset, which won't be seemly when you attend balls.' *Well,* thought Beatrice, *the flesh has got to go somewhere!* Also, it seemed more sensible to Beatrice to have the silk cut so that it wasn't so tight. Of course she was happy she had been given a whole new wardrobe, but she felt like she was wearing somebody else's clothes, outfits that never quite fit or sat right on her body. That morning, she had looked at a milkmaid in town carrying her wares on a yoke and thought how pretty she was, how pleasing her round cheeks were and her large bosom and hips that curved like hillsides. This obsession with the tiny waist was tiresome and silly. It seemed so unfair that women were not encouraged to look like women, but instead like a cool hourglass without feelings, breath, flesh or character.

Beatrice asked her maid the way to the old brickmaster's house and Dinah kindly drew her a little map to get there, which impressed Beatrice with its fine detail. She made sure she mentioned to her maid that it was beautifully done. Once out of the house and alone, Beatrice felt giddy as she hurried down the hill to town. Passing along the main street, she delighted in the sights and sounds of ordinary folk going about their business. There were sheep, cows and geese to be seen, chivvied along by their owners. Animal noises merged with the hubbub of chitchat and sellers calling out their wares. She smiled at everyone, receiving some pleasant looks in return, whilst others looked surprised to see a girl so nicely dressed walk among them, beaming at everybody. Some days here in England she felt so out of place, as lonely as a single boot on a roadside. But today she felt part of the world, a piece placed in the giant puzzle of humanity. Her friendship with Owen had somehow linked her with everyone in this town and at last she felt a connection with her mother's home.

Walking up from the bridge she passed the halfway point marked by a waterwheel. She heard it before she could see it, the sound of rushing water growing louder as she approached. She expected something the size of a carriage wheel, perhaps a little bigger, but rounding the path and beholding it for the first time, she gasped at its size. It towered above the brick house beside it and was turning at a great pace, the splish-splash of water spraying from its spokes as it went around, catching the sun in twinkling cascades. There were a couple of well-dressed visitors looking and pointing up at the wheel, nodding appreciatively. Beatrice wondered if they had come especially to see it, a wonder of the industry that made this place so remarkable.

She remembered her mother telling Beatrice that her father, Jake Ashford, had come to Ironbridge to paint the industries and that is how they had met. Her mother never liked to talk about him. Beatrice had accepted this, growing up. That was just the way things were. She wondered sometimes if it were her mother's grief that prevented her from discussing him. But being here, in the place where her father and mother had met, she began to yearn for more information. She wondered if her father had stood here, gazed up at the same waterwheel and sketched it, all those years ago, before she existed. She must ask her mother. She would like to see his drawings, if any survived. If she had her father's skill – which she had definitely not inherited, drawing stick figures or horses that looked like dogs – she would sketch this magnificent waterwheel.

The final part of her walk was undisturbed in that part of the woods, away from town and the sounds of industry. It was so quiet there, she saw a deer, standing alert in a narrow clearing, which leapt away from sight in the blink of an eye. This was an animal she'd never seen outside picture books and it thrilled her.

She reached a fork in the path and looked at the map. The right-handed way was the one to take and it took her closer to the river. Its constant murmur was comforting, punctuated by the odd splash of a fish leaping. At that moment, she realised that it would be very hard to leave this place and return to the city. Its beauty had crept into her heart, curled up there and made itself comfortable. As she walked on, she heard the river grow in sound, the water rushing over something, probably a small weir beyond the trees. The sound was joyful and crystal clear. She listened to it and loved it. She wondered if she had come into existence in Maman's belly before she had left Ironbridge, wondered if she had been surrounded by these woods or even heard a glimmer of the wandering river beyond her mother's frame and that's why it felt like home, despite the fact that Paris was where she had grown up. The woods, the river and the bridge over it had cast a spell over Beatrice. Ironbridge tugged at her heartstrings as if it had full claim to do so.

A house came into sight. It was not as large as Southover, but was more interesting to look at – Benjamina had been right about that. It had two tall brick chimneys, one on either end and many windows all along the two floors. There were rounded bays surrounded by wisteria that grew rather wildly and drooped over the windows, covering some of them completely. It needed taming. Beatrice approached a downstairs window and looked inside, to see a couple of items of furniture, swathed in white sheets. Other than that, the house seemed mostly empty of furnishings, all carpets, rugs and wall hangings having been removed. It had a sad air about it, as if the previous owners had left suddenly and the house longed for company. Beatrice wondered if there was a door that might be unlocked. Or at least might be easy to force open.

Then, footsteps on the path made her turn and stare, alert as she was to being alone. As she saw Owen walking towards her, framed by the swaying trees, she suddenly felt a strange certainty that she would never return to Paris. It frightened yet exhilarated her alike.

When he saw her, his face lit up. She was suddenly very aware of her solitude in that place, with this boy. She knew what they were doing was wrong. But she did not care to think about that.

'Afternoon miss,' he said and removed his cap with a flourish, at which they both laughed.

'Please, you must call me Bea. We are good friends now.'

'Bea,' he said simply.

She wished she could spend the whole day with him, but she wasn't sure how long she could stay away and this walk had taken far longer than she expected just to get there. 'So, the brickworkers are on strike.'

'Yes, we are.'

'Is that what you wanted?'

'It's more about need than want.'

His face was serious now and even more handsome that way. She felt a little unsteady – perhaps it was the long walk or simply the excitement of seeing him again – but she pushed on. She must tell him what she had planned to say.

'Owen, I have a confession to make. I have been to the brickworks but I came incognito.'

'In a what?' he frowned.

'No,' she smiled gently, 'I came in disguise. I borrowed my maid's clothes and came pretending to look for work. I did not want to be lied to or have the truth covered up, as it would have been had I come in my normal attire. I wanted to see the truth.'

'When was this? I never saw you there.'

'Yesterday. I did not see you either and I am pleased I didn't. It was terrible.'

'Terrible? How?'

'I saw a child struck viciously there and I defended that child to its mother and to a man who was some sort of overseer. They didn't seem to care.'

'Well, it's quite normal for folk to give a good clout. It happens all the time at the yard.'

'I can see it happens all the time. I saw it with my own eyes! How can you live like that?'

'Like what?' he said and narrowed his eyes at her.

'Amid such violence! How can you defend such actions? To strike a child so violently! It is criminal. And these are your colleagues. Explain yourself!'

'Explain *myself*?'

'Yes, you must give me an explanation. I am on your side. I have already spoken to my great-grandmother about improving things there. I have told her she must do something. But these are your people. What are *you* doing about it?'

'Me? It inna me doing the beatings!'

'But you've said it happens all the time, around you. Do you stand by and do nothing? What kind of people are they, that will beat a child, a child so malnourished and weak and beaten down by life already? It is monstrous!'

Her blood was up too now and she did feel faint. *This damned corset*, she thought. She glared at him, not afraid, not willing to back down, ever. These were his people behaving in this awful manner and she wanted him to explain it to her. She was already taking sides against Queenie and her own family. Now she needed some hope that it was the right thing to do.

'Listen here,' he said. 'You know nothing. You understand nothing. These people have been brought up in this life, the brickmakers' life. Most of 'em were born to it, carrying clay as soon as they were able, at five year, some of 'em. And most have never had a day of schooling. They're worked until they're ready to drop. But when they're done they dunna go home to some mansion and eat a three-course meal. No, they go home to a small house, where they sometimes sleep three to a bed, head to toe just to make room. And their supper? If they're lucky, they might get a good price on a sheep's head for a thin stew, so that tomorrow they can do it all again. Malnourished and weak, you say? You're right. And if the whole family dunna work fast enough then malnourishment slips over to starving. So they push their children to work harder. And your family has done all it can to make matters worse. Our cottages leak and mould grows up our walls, our wages drop and we have even less to eat. There inna time to think about what's right. My mother insisted I went to school every day for years, but we were the lucky ones. Most canna afford to have a child not working for any length of time. Education hasna played no part in their lives so they see no part of it in the lives of their young'uns. But I want change, I want reform. I want all children to go to school, of course I do, so that the little'uns are able leastways to read and write afore they are dragged into this way of life. But for that to happen, the brickmakers need higher pay and shorter hours, they need decent contracts and homes and conditions, so that they can send their child to school instead of being forced to hire them to make ends meet. It's the system that needs changing and then the people will change right enough with it. And *that* is in the hands of the brickmasters. They are the ones with the power to change for good. That is why we are on strike. Like I said, it's need, not want. What do you say to that, Miss King?'

She had watched his face twist into fury as he spat out the last two words.

'I am not a King. I am an Ashford.'

He was breathing heavily and glaring at her.

'If you're not one of them, then prove it.'

'How?'

'Help us.'

'I am trying to do just that. It's why I went to the brickyard.'

'You'd be more use to us at home than dressing up. Keep your eyes and ears open. Tell us what the brick-masters are planning. Speak up for us. Will you do that? Will you help us?'

She would be a spy – that's what he was asking. Could she do it? Did she want to?

'I want to help, of course I do. But I am no natural liar. I am not practised in the art of spying or dissembling.

But I will do what I feel is right. And you have right on your side. Yes, I will help you. Together, you and I could make a marvellous team!'

'I believe you're right about that,' he said and they smiled at each other. Then, their smiles faded as the intensity between them grew. His blue eyes became the centre of her vision. The world and all its troubles faded behind them. She reached out and grasped his hand.

The touch of her hand on his rooted them both to the spot. He looked down at their hands and stared at them, as if they belonged to somebody else. Then he moved his hand gently, letting his fingers slide between hers and lock the two of them together. He lifted her hand slowly to his lips and kissed it, his eyes closing.

She stepped towards him and then they kissed, mouth to mouth, her hands reaching up into his hair – how she had longed to touch it! So fair and now she knew, so soft. She felt his hands around her back. Her eyes were closed and the whole world had vanished into this one moment, this one kiss. She never wanted it to end.

But end it must, as they came up for air, gasping like dreamers rudely awakened. Owen was trembling, she saw, which astounded her. She had never imagined a man could be affected like that, especially by her. But she knew the strength of her feelings for him and hoped – no, she knew – that his were just as potent. He kissed her again.

When they stopped and came to, the life of the forest around them seemed to hold its breath, the whole world seemed to. They held hands and looked at each other. Their happiness was overflowing and they could not help but smile, then laugh. It spilled out of them like the bubbling water she could hear, frothing over the weir beyond. They looked into each other's eyes, searching for something there, some certainty perhaps, as she felt as if her legs were standing on a coracle in the river, whirling round and round. But now he frowned, he looked down and shook his head, still squeezing her hand tightly.

'Is this wrong?' he whispered. He kissed her hand tenderly and then kissed her mouth again and they held on desperately, as if they drowned in the air.

'It is not,' she said breathily, into his ear, then kissed his neck and heard him groan. 'It is right. I know it is right.'

He had to walk to the inn at Broseley, but he was walking on air and never wanted to arrive. He had seen her to the edge of the wood, making sure she went on to the main road safely. He wished he could have walked her home, like a local girl, seen her to her door, tipped his hat to her parents, noted their interest that a local boy had walked their daughter home, seen her blush as she crossed her threshold into her cottage. But this girl was not a local girl, the girl he loved. She was a stranger to Ironbridge and she did not smell of clay or iron but the scent of flowers and powder and money. He could not walk with her through town, hold her hand, kiss her on the cheek or take her to a dance. He could not bring her to his mother and father and watch them become acquainted with her ways, her frankness and curiosity, her kindness and her temper. He was a Malone and she was a King, whatever her father's name was. She was one of them and she was the enemy.

His lips felt bruised with desire, tingling and heavy as if stung. His insides churned and a heat emanated from deep within and flushed his entire body. He felt as if desire was written all over his skin that everyone could see it, it felt so alive to him. He had taken a liking to local girls before. But nothing like this, nothing like her. Beatrice. Bea.

He was coming up to the Jitties now, the rabbit warren of lanes and alleyways where poor folk lived in higgledy-piggledy squatter cottages, the names of each lane representing the names of families who'd lived there or old folklore. He walked along Spout Lane, past the pipe out of which poured spring water and by a woman carrying two buckets of water on a yoke back to her house. He went on down Quarry Road, left onto Carters Jitty, down Mission Jitty, along Simmonds Jitty, down Crews Park, then turned onto King Street, seeing the King's Head tavern before him. He stopped and almost turned back. He could not face what was to come, not right now. He wanted to run to Bea. Then, he cursed himself for his weakness. To lose your mind over a girl, and the enemy at that? But she had agreed to help him, to help them. Perhaps they were no longer enemies, perhaps they could even have a future. But he was still lying to her. How would she feel about him if she knew he'd courted her from the start for Adam's rebellion?

Head down, hands shoved in pockets, he stalked across the road and went into the tavern, seeking out the meeting room and hearing the hubbub of noise drift up the stairs as he descended. It was full of his fellow brickmakers and their children, talking excitedly, some angrily. A table was set up at which people queued to sign the open book. They were paying the subs that would help to see the worst affected families through the strike days ahead. Owen hoped that it would indeed only be days and no longer. He feared what would happen to those families that were poorest if the strike lasted longer than the weekend, let alone weeks on end. The pennies they collected in subs wouldn't last long if that were the case. Surrounded by his people, his desire dissolved like river mist in sunshine.

Adam saw him across the room and caught his eye, gesturing him to come over. As he made his way through the crowded room, Owen glanced about to see if his parents were there, but he couldn't see them. He knew his father was against the strike and wouldn't want to come, but he'd wondered if his mother might force him. Once she made her mind up, she was difficult to refuse.

'Owen,' said Adam and took a puff on his pipe. He looked grim and tired. Owen nodded at him. 'Have you been with her?'

'I have.'

'Any news? What did she tell you?'

Owen thought of her lips and swallowed hard, trying to erase the memory.

'She told me she came to the yard dressed up like a poor lass.'

Adam looked incredulous, then laughed. 'She didna! Did she?'

Owen took up his laugh, but it rang hollowly to his ears. 'Arr, she said she came to see what the brickworks was all about and she got the shock of her life.'

'Danker me! What possessed the wench? Why didna she come with her family?'

'She wanted to know what it was truly like. She was angered by it. She wants to make things better, I reckon. For us. For all the workers. She's already spoken out for us. Asking her family to improve conditions.'

Adam listened carefully and watched Owen as he spoke. Owen could feel his true feelings for her simmering over and believed Adam could see right through him.

'Is she sweet on yer, lad?'

Owen willed himself to be stony-faced. 'I reckon so.'

'And she wants to help us, you say?'

'Arr, I believe so. I know. She said as much. She said she'd help us in her own way.'

Owen waited while Adam puffed thoughtfully on his tobacco and blew out a stream of blue-grey smoke. Then, he grinned. 'You've done a fine job! The daughter of the house following you about like a puppy and all in a fluster as to how she can help the common folk. I couldna planned it better myself. Well done, lad!'

Owen felt a hearty clap on his back from Adam and he grinned back at him, but it was fakery and inside he felt sickened by it all.

'Thank'ee,' said Owen, having no other words, as he just wanted to get out of there and get away.

'Now then, the next time, see what you can wheedle out of her about the other brickmasters, what they're up to, what the Kings might be leaning towards. We need to know their intentions if we are to outrun them and win the day. See what you can find out, lad. But be careful, be wary. Dunna give away much about our side. When do you see her next?'

'We agreed to meet tomorrow afternoon. Now I'm not at work, there is more chance to see each other.'

'But where? You canna be seen with her.'

'Dunna werrit, we have a secret place.'

Adam raised his eyebrows in wolfish approval. 'Good lad. Good lad! Come see me after and report the latest.'

Owen walked home slowly. If his legs had been in charge, they would've run all the way to the old brickmaster's house and taken his girl in his arms again and kissed her. But she would be gone, back to the King house and he was due back at his own. The impossibility of what they were doing assaulted him – the stupidity of it! How could he have let himself be beguiled by a King? But in the same moment he condemned himself in one ear, a voice in his other told him she was a good person, a lovely girl, a beauty too and mad for him. But then the nausea came again as he remembered that he was a spy, that he had fooled her into trusting him and she had responded faithfully. But his feelings were true. He did not have to tell her the truth about the spying. He could keep that to himself until . . . forever. Why not? And then, in the future, when this was all over and they could . . . could what? It was exciting to meet in secret, to fool them all and steal kisses in the shelter of the forest. But what would come of it? Secrets never lasted long in Ironbridge. Everyone knew everything about everyone. And one day their secret would come out. What future was there for the brickmaster lass and the brickburner lad? But she could help them, help all of them. Maybe, just maybe, it would be the making of them. Secretly, he and Bea could hatch plans to bring the two sides together. She could persuade the Kings and he could persuade Adam and the rest. Could it work?

So consumed was his mind, he had barely noticed the journey his feet made to take him home. He was coming around the bend and up the incline to his house, when he saw his parents standing outside it, his mother in his father's arms, smiling at each other. It was strange to see them so happy, when all around was fret and worry. The strike was making everyone else grumpy and scowling. His father saw him first and his face broke into a great, big smile.

'Son! There is news!'

'What is it?' he said, breaking into a trot to reach them.

'I'll let your mother tell you. It's all her doing.'

'With a little help from you, Peter Malone,' she said and smiled at her husband. 'Owen, I am expecting.'

Owen almost said, Expecting what? But then the meaning of the words found him.

'You mean . . . ?'

'Yes, lad!' cried his father. 'Another little Malone is on the way. After all these years. Can you believe it!'

His mother laughed and came to Owen, taking his face in her hands and kissing him on the forehead. The touch of his mother's rough, dry hands was like balm, calming him and making him feel that all was right with the world.

'It is a marvel, is what it is!' he said and went to hug her, but held back, looking down at her belly. He saw that there was indeed a bump there and said, 'I must have been living in a daydream not to have noticed it before.'

'Maybe you thought I was just getting fat!' she said.

'You have been in a daydream these past weeks, son,' added his father in a solemn tone. 'Time to wake up. There's a babby on the way and all the extra work that will mean, for all of us. Hard times are ahead.'

'Oh, let's not think on that today. Only happy thoughts today!' said his mother. 'You know, Owen, I never thought I'd have another. I lost three babbies, after you. You never knew. My mother was the same. She had only me, then no more. I thought I'd be the same as her. But now, this one is clinging on and there have been no signs of trouble. He's a strong'un, that's for sure. I have high hopes for him.' Her face was full of faith and it squeezed his heart to look on it.

'Me too,' said Owen and kissed his mother's cheek. She beamed at him, her face filling with laughter lines, yet looking younger than ever. Expecting a nipper agreed with her. But Owen felt ten years older. Now, the strike took on a different colour, a threat to his family rather than a triumphant act. With a baby coming, they'd need their wages more than ever. His mother needed rest, not to work harder to compensate for their lack of pay. Now he must focus on her and not on anyone else, certainly not on the King girl. The old loyalties to hearth and home were pulling at him. He felt an awful tug inside him, as he looked at his dear mother and thought of all she had suffered.

Owen didn't know she had lost babies before, or that his grandmother had too. He had never thought about why he was an only child. As a boy, he had asked his parents over and over if he could have a brother, not a sister – he didn't want one of those, and they would just smile at him and change the subject. To think, his lovely mother had been suffering all that time, mourning the loss of the children that never were. But she never said a word, never betrayed her grief to him. He looked at her dear face and realised how little he knew of what went on behind it. He thought about how little folk really knew of each other, of the people they live with every day. They thought they knew them so well, because their faces, their hands, their movements and habits were so familiar. But the inside of someone else's head was as mysterious and unreachable as the moon. Only the moon knew its own secrets and the same went for the mind of every person living and every creature that crawled upon the earth, swam through the water and flew against the sky. The world was alive with secrets.

Chapter 11

Queenie lay in bed listening to the house creak on Monday morning. She had had Jenkins inform everyone she was to spend the morning in her room, alone, with no interruptions. Her fury of Saturday night had only abated after a drink of something strong and acrid, given to her by Jenkins, which helped her sleep. She had not asked what it contained. She had slept through the night, with no dreams she could recall and no visitations, thank heavens. She had awoken on Sunday in a bit of a fog but once she had eaten her porridge with honey and had drunk down a strong pot of tea with plenty of sugar, she felt human again. She had immediately sent word to the other brickmasters and they had come later that day. After a day of vexatious meetings, arguing amongst themselves as to the best course of action, she had gone to her bed late, exhausted. She had awoken with an idea at the back of her mind and wanted the morning to mull it over.

She dispatched Jenkins to take a message to Brotherton. He and his wife had worked for the family for nearly thirty years now and they were wholly loyal. In her note to Brotherton, she had asked for the address in Ironbridge of a particular brickworker and his wife.

When Jenkins returned with Brotherton's reply, Queenie sat up sharply and said, 'I will go out this afternoon.'

'Not one of your wisest ideas. You need rest, woman.'

Queenie smoothed the covers over her lap and sat up straighter. 'I feel quite well now and moreover, needs must. I will be visiting the home of Mr Adam Jones and I will need you to accompany me, of course.'

Jenkins shot her a glance. 'Jones? Not the union fellow, Jones?'

'Yes.'

'The baby on the bridge's husband? *That* Jones?'

'The very same,' pronounced Queenie, holding Jenkins's fierce gaze.

'What in all that is holy do you want to do that for? That is the worst idea I ever heard!'

'I have my reasons. And if I succeed, this strike will be over before it's properly begun. And what's more . . .' But Queenie faltered, aware she was about to mention the curse of Betsy Blaize. She had nearly let it slip to Jenkins – how clumsy! She had known Jenkins longer and in more depth than any other person living and she knew this woman's character was built on the rock of hard facts. If Queenie gave a hint of the supernatural or a curse or anything of the like, Jenkins would scold her and not hear another word of it. She must keep it her secret. Yet Queenie's fears over Blaize's curse had intensified since the weekend's events. The baby on the bridge was to be evicted, the wife of a union leader, an enemy of the King family. How could she improve her lot in life now?

'And what? What's more?' said Jenkins.

'Then, amends will be made. I will reverse Cyril's eviction order, save their home and Jones will be so grateful, he will capitulate and end the strike.'

'Just like that?' said Jenkins, folding her arms, her face smug with sarcasm.

'Yes, just like that. I can be very persuasive.'

Jenkins shook her head and came to sit on the bed. 'Miss Alice,' she said, knowing the power of Queenie's real name to tug at her heartstrings, 'I'm telling you, do not do this. Everything you've built over the decades, everything you've fought for . . . in all those years, you've never kowtowed to anyone, not once. If you see this Jones now, on his home ground, you will weaken your position so much, this strike will likely last for months.'

'But why will it do that? Why?' demanded Queenie. She could only see the positives in going to see Jones personally, a show of good faith.

'Because he'll see your weakness. He'll think he can hold out till you give in. But he doesn't know you like I do. He doesn't know yet that you'll never give in.

So you and he will dig your holes deeper and deeper until you are both buried. Families will starve, the brickyard will go under. Nobody will win. Everyone will suffer. And the King name will be damaged, probably beyond repair. Is that what you've struggled all these years for?'

Jenkins looked at her closely. But she did not press it further, raised her eyes to the heavens, then went out to fetch what was needed for Queenie to get ready.

Once she was prepared and her hair a picture of control, she asked that Jenkins summon Beatrice, who appeared looking radiant. A strange way to be when all around was trouble.

'You look well, child.'

'I am well, thank you,' said Beatrice and beamed at her.

'Come and talk with me, you on the stool and I shall sit here, in my favourite armchair.'

Beatrice came and took her seat.

'I was going to ask if you were upset about our disagreement the other day, but you seem to have got over it.'

Beatrice nodded and her radiance faded a little. 'Yes, of course, I have been worried. I hate the thought that we should ever fall out about anything.'

'Please do not concern yourself. We are family and we support each other, mm? I may disagree with your actions but I can see that your heart was in the right place. You are a good person, Bea. You are my dear girl and I love you very much.'

'And I love you, too and I always will,' she said and gave Queenie a sweet peck on the cheek.

'I am glad to hear it, child. Perhaps there is a way you could prove the truth of that. I need to ask you a favour and I very much hope you will accept it.'

'Of course I will!' she cried. 'Anything! Name it.'

'First, I must have your word that nothing of what we shall discuss will be repeated to another living soul.'

Beatrice looked intrigued and energised by the thought of such a secret. 'Of course!'

'Even your mother? You must not speak a word of it to her either. It must only be between the two of us. Will you agree?'

Beatrice frowned slightly, her hand tensed against Queenie's hands. But then she seemed to make some internal decision and said, 'Agreed. Just the two of us.'

'Good. Today I will make an unannounced visit to the leader of the strike, Adam Jones. I will attempt to talk him round by assuring him that the eviction notice was not of my doing and is to be immediately revoked. You will accompany me, Beatrice. Your presence will soften proceedings, from a confrontation between masters and workers to a more social call. And your friendship with the brickworker you mentioned and your sympathy with him will help us to provide a reasonable front to this man and show a more human side to our negotiations. I want you to know that I am no monster, Beatrice. I do what is right for our business to flourish, yet at the same time I do wish for my workers to be provided for appropriately. Agreed?'

Beatrice had listened to all of this with a growing smile. 'Oh yes, indeed. I would be thrilled to accompany you. I will do my best to help, but I will take my lead from you. Thank you for asking me! Thank you most of all for listening. And for trusting me.'

When Jenkins saw Queenie was to go out with Beatrice, she gave Queenie a queer look. It looked like a mixture of scorn and envy. Queenie ignored it and enjoyed the walk out with her great-granddaughter, climbing into the landau together and holding hands, cuddling up on the seat. Queenie had never met a young person so affectionate. It was utterly disarming. She had not told the child everything – how could she? Instead, she had given her an edited version of events. She had said that Adam Jones was the leader of the strike, a fact. That his wife Martha was found as a baby on the iron bridge, another fact, her mother dying the same night, also a fact. That her dead mother had once worked as a maid at the King house, true. That since Martha's mother had once been employed by the Kings and Martha had been through enough difficulties in life, the Kings should not be the cause of any further hardship, also true. Beatrice had agreed wholeheartedly with all of this and looked delighted that Queenie was proving how kind she could be, after their horrible argument. Beatrice did not seem to have it in her to look smug, but Queenie could see it gladdened her heart to be on this mission of mercy with her great-grandmother.

'It's all so colourful and romantic!' cried Beatrice after hearing these facts. 'A baby found on a bridge!'

Queenie smiled at her girlish notions of romance. However, as they trundled down the hill to the centre of Ironbridge and through its bumpy streets to the poorer part of town, the facts she had omitted whispered their secrets in her ear. That the dead mother had been raped by Bea's great-grandfather, when she was still a frightened, powerless child. That Queenie herself had dismissed the girl when she started to show and Queenie had done worse before that, much worse. She dismissed these distressing thoughts. *Rome was not built in a day*, she decided. This was a good start and it would have to do, for the moment.

The landau took them through the town and over the bridge to the street that the Kings owned, taken over when the previous brickmaster had gone bankrupt. These were the dwellings not far from the brickworks upon which Cyril had served eviction orders the night before. The ten houses were built from the local brick, a row that shared walls all the way along, so the whole street looked like one house with ten doors and twice as many windows. Queenie could see that several of the cottage doors were open, with people toing and froing, carrying all manner of domestic items out into the street and loading them onto handcarts. There were stools and settles and other bits of plain furniture piled up in the small square yards in front of each house. The residents had answered the eviction order already, wasting no time. Queenie had thought they might resist it. She felt a tightness in her chest at the role she was about to play, the bountiful owner come to reprieve the workers. As the carriage trundled slowly along the short street, she saw every one of those folk in the road turn and stop to look, unaccustomed to such a fine carriage appearing at their doorsteps. The landau pulled up outside the fourth cottage along, the Jones's house.

Queenie said, 'Out you get first, child. Then give me your hand and help me descend.'

Their coachman opened the door and Beatrice descended first, turning back to offer her hand to Queenie, who stepped gingerly into the muddy road. She looked up to see that several people in the road were still staring, now at her. On every face was a look of recognition. And hatred. Queenie linked arms with Beatrice, for comfort more than support, and lifted her chin, ready for anything. She considered making a speech to these people right then and there, telling them that the eviction order was quashed. But her innate dignity stopped her from making pronouncements in the mucky road and instead she turned towards the Jones's cottage. He could tell them all after she had spoken with him. That would be far more fitting.

As Queenie and Beatrice approached the door, it opened. Out came Jones, not seeing them at first, turning back briefly to say something to a figure behind him, presumably his wife. Then, he looked back and stopped. Queenie was a good reader of faces. His expression was that of triumph. Perhaps Jenkins had been right. Perhaps this was not a good idea.

'May I speak with you, Mr Jones? Inside?'

Jones nodded, said not a word and disappeared inside. Queenie looked at Beatrice, who swallowed nervously.

'Come, child,' said Queenie. They entered the dwelling. There was one room downstairs, L-shaped, with a pantry in the smaller part. The room was dominated by a range against the wall and in one corner was a steep narrow staircase going up to the room above. Standing before the stairs was a woman, her hands resting on her rounded belly, a few months pregnant with a little time to go. Her face was pale, her hair hidden beneath a greyish cap, but those large green eyes, staring in shock at her unexpected visitors, shone out in the gloomy room. Queenie was assaulted by the resemblance to her late husband and it made her feel faint. She glanced about the room, looking for a seat to sit on, but the room was empty, all the furniture gone. With nothing to obscure the walls, Queenie could see that mould blossomed blackly along each wall from the floor upwards. How she wanted to turn tail and flee, to sit down, to lean on her great-granddaughter's arm at least, or even merely pull out her handkerchief and hold it to her nose. But she did none of these things.

'Come to gloat?' said Jones.

All pretence at professionalism had left him, Queenie noted. *It is time to change this tune*, she thought.

'Not at all, Mr Jones. I have come to meet the family. Now then, Mrs Jones,' she said, looking directly at Martha, the sight of those green eyes still bothering Queenie, they were so like her husband's. She swallowed her discomfort and pushed onwards. 'We have not been acquainted before now. Allow me to introduce myself. I am Mrs King and this is my great-granddaughter Beatrice Ashford. Please forgive us descending upon you with no notice, but time is of the essence, I see.' She gestured vaguely behind her.

'Ma'am, miss,' said Martha and bobbed a slight curtsey, then glanced nervously at her husband.

'What do you want with us?' said Jones. 'We are leaving in a matter of minutes. You could've sent a lackey to see this. But I'm supposing you wanted to enjoy the sight of it yourself.'

Queenie heard the anger in his voice and saw defiance in his stance. 'You do me a disservice, Jones,' she said and smiled, which seemed to increase the fire in his eyes. 'I am here to overturn the eviction and inform you that you may stay. All of you. The whole street. The eviction order was not sanctioned by me. It has been a misunderstanding.'

She awaited the gratitude and the turnabout of their chilly reception. But the Joneses simply stood and stared at them. Martha glanced at Adam, but nobody said a word.

'I hope I have made myself clear,' tried Queenie. 'The eviction is overturned. You do not have to leave these dwellings, any of you.'

Jones said, 'That may be so. Tell the neighbours if you like. I shanna be living in a King house no longer.'

'Mr Jones,' Queenie began. 'It would be pure folly to . . .'

'Dunna try to persuade us. We have a place to go, Martha 'n' me. A place where we are welcome and wanted. Unlike here. And they'll be expecting us. So, if you dunna mind . . .'

Jones held out his hand, to show them the door. Queenie stuttered, 'But . . . but Mr Jones.' She glanced over at his wife, hoping to appeal to her reason instead. 'Surely, Mrs Jones, in your condition, you do not want to leave your home.'

But Martha was silent and tight-lipped.

'Please, may I say something?'

It was Beatrice. Well, if the girl could make them see sense, it might help.

'Of course, my dear,' said Queenie.

'Mr Jones, I am friendly with Owen Malone.'

Jones said nothing, but glanced downwards at the floor. *An odd reaction*, thought Queenie.

Beatrice continued, 'He had told me of the conditions at the brickyard.'

Oh no! thought Queenie. The girl was not going to admit she'd been there, was she?

'I was unhappy to hear that things were not good there. I spoke to my great-grandmother about it. And I know that my great-grandmother came here today to make things right. I am sure that we can all work together to end this dispute.'

At least the girl did not admit her humiliating incognito visit to the brickworks. But she was rushing too far forwards, with these ideas of conciliation. Queenie must interrupt her before she weakened their position. But Jones got there first.

'You're saying the Kings will meet our demands?'

'The eviction is the pressing matter,' said Queenie, attempting to delay answering that question or anything like it, until she had a more formal setting in which to discuss terms. 'Please be assured that you are welcome to stay in these houses. They are your homes, you and your neighbours.'

'Not much of one.'

It was Martha, speaking up for the first time. Queenie turned to look at her.

'Look at the walls,' she went on. 'The damp grows and grows and never stops, however much I scrub it. Like a black, creeping death. I dunna want my babby exposed to it. We tell your man about it every month, when he comes to fetch our rent. We tell him about the hole in the roof too, where we have to put pots and pans upstairs to catch the rain when it comes in. But he hasna done a thing about it. After two years of telling. Not a thing.'

Queenie glanced at the black mould creeping across the walls and felt a shudder of disgust, tinged with shame. 'I will admonish my man for not responding to your requests and not informing me of these necessary repairs. It will be addressed on the morrow and all necessary repairs paid for by my family. We will make this a home fit for your baby, never fear, Mrs Jones.'

'Too little, too late,' said Jones. 'We do not wish to discuss housing with you. We have made our plans and are now delayed in carrying them out. All I wish to know from you is the question I have already put to you. Will you meet our demands?'

The man was a dog with a bone. 'We are not going to discuss such things now, here,' said Queenie sharply.

'Then, our conversation is over.'

'Please, Mr Jones,' said Beatrice. 'I am sure we can come to some arrangement, Great-grandmother? Can we at least discuss pay?'

'Yes! Pay. Tell me the wage per thousand bricks will not go down.'

Queenie regretted bringing the child with her now.

'I can make no such promise. The brickworks must remain competitive. Do not forget, Mr Jones, that the previous owner went bankrupt and nearly caused the closing of the brickyard. The Kings saved the business and we must run it as we see fit, in order to make it a profitable enterprise. With our competitors lowering their costs, to remain competitive so must we.'

'But you have the power, the standing in this community,' said Jones. 'You could stand alone from them, if you saw fit. You're rich enough, by God.'

'And where will it all end?' cried Queenie, exasperated. 'A penny today, a guinea tomorrow!'

'And why not?' spat Jones. 'We work ourselves to an early grave for it. Why should we not be paid in gold for our sacrifice? Without workers this country would crumble and fall in a week. And where would you be then, without your servants and your brickies and all the poor folk who prop up your comforts?'

'These are the rumblings of sedition, Mr Jones. And I will not stay to hear them.'

Queenie turned and looked at the open door. Through it, she saw that all of the neighbours that had been filling their carts with their possessions were now gathered in a silent, grey crowd outside, listening to every word, blocking her exit. Panic rose in her throat and she feared she would faint.

'Beatrice,' she said, summoning her last ounce of dignity. 'Please lead the way to our carriage.'

She felt the girl's arm link with hers and a warm flow of vitality flooded back into her from her beloved

Beatrice's touch. She lifted her head and fixed her eyes at the cloudy sky above the heads of the little mob at the door, allowing Beatrice to make the excuses to part the throng and get her safely into the landau. She sat back onto the carriage seat and did not look up as they left. She and Beatrice did not speak as the carriage laboured up the hill, homewards. Queenie did not wish to explain herself and the girl seemed to be keeping quiet out of embarrassment. Queenie spent the whole journey staring at her own gloved hands. Only when they came up the gravel driveway to Southover did Queenie lean forward to see the welcome sight of her own beautiful house, thankful to be back, away from the world and all its filth. But she glimpsed the family graveyard and it chilled her for a moment, before she heard her inner voice answer the request of another employee of the King family, long ago dead and now haunting her with its demands.

I did my best, Queenie said in her thoughts, to the spirit of Betsy Blaize. *I went to them on their own home ground and said they could keep it, for heaven's sake. It is not my doing that they rejected sense. I did try.*

Not hard enough, came the ghostly reply.

Chapter 12

They came at night. Nobody knew about them until a tramp who used to mind the kilns was passing the brickyard, bemoaning the fact that the kilns were cold and gone were his nice warm nights. And he saw them filing through the front gate, dozens of them, walking up the incline to the huts where it looked like they might be sleeping for the night. He'd heard them talking. They spoke English but with a strange accent. Irish maybe? Scottish or somewhere north? He had never left Shropshire, so did not know the accents beyond its boundaries. He'd run back to Broseley and told a brickie friend of his and then word spread fast.

Word arrived at the Malone residence early the following morning. Owen was asleep in his new position on the floor by the fireplace. It'd been all change in their house to accommodate the new arrivals. Martha slept in with his mother, both pregnant women deserving and needing the best bed, of course. Adam and his father shared Owen's bed, top to toe. Sometimes one would tire of the other's snoring and settle on the floor instead. It wasn't ideal, but at least the men weren't working these days, so they did not desperately need every moment of sleep like they had before. Owen was closest to the front door when the knock came. He heard the others muttering as he leapt up and ran to it, so urgent the knocks became.

It was the boy Brain, eyes agog and breathing hard.

'What is it?' said Owen.

'The Kings got in scabs to break the strike!' cried Brain, overexcited.

'How do you know? Have you seen 'em?' said Owen, regarding much of what Brain said with scepticism.

'Not me but word come from old Furlong the roadster. He saw 'em going in. Speaking in a strange tongue. They come from off. Maybe Irish'uns.'

Owen's father and Adam were up now and approaching the door. Adam got there first and reached out, shaking Brain's hand, much to the latter's surprise.

'Good lad, Brain. Well done for coming with the news.'

'Thank'ee!' said Brain, delighted.

'Go find Marshfield, Lunt and Deeley. Tell 'em to call their teams to The Swan by lunchtime at the latest. We must hold a meeting this day.'

Owen noted his father hanging back, rubbing his eyes. Peter had followed the strike orders like all of his colleagues. He was no blackleg. But Owen could see that he did not like to get involved. His mother, Anny, on the other hand, was as militant as ever, appearing from her bed, wrapping a shawl about her and asking what was going on. Brain had gone by now and soon the family – with their new members – were seated around the table eating a breakfast of bread and dripping, with a few fried-up potato slices left over from dinner the night before.

'Only two weeks in and already they have shipped in scabs,' said Anny, shaking her head in disgust and serving up more potatoes onto a central serving plate from which everyone took their share.

'They have no shame,' added Martha, dunking some bread in her cup of tea.

'We all knew this would happen,' said Peter, quietly. There was no tone about his voice, no suggestion of 'I told you so'. He was simply stating a fact. But his words hung in the air, as the voice of fact against the voice of anger.

'Well, yes. It was expected,' said Adam. 'But not so soon, I must admit. I dunna think they're from across the sea. And I dunna think they're Irish. I've heard tell that Cyril King has connections in Liverpool. I reckon he got the scabs in from there.'

'What does it mean, though?' asked Owen. 'What happens now?'

He was looking at his father, out of deference, but it was Adam who answered. 'Now we stop the talks. Every meeting I've had with the Kings and the other brick-masters this past fortnight has got us nowhere. And now they have broken their word and got in workers. We will cancel our next talk with the Kings and instead we must proceed directly to the yard and start the next stage of our campaign.'

Owen saw his father grimace, then poke a finger in his mouth to pick his teeth. His sour face could have been at something lodged in there. Or it could have been distaste at what his cousin was saying.

'What will that be?' asked Owen.

'We must set about harassing these workers and seek to drive them away. We shall protest at the gates each day and night, all of the day and night. We shall take it in shifts. We shall never let up or give in.'

'Never!' cried his mother and Martha added, 'Nor ever!'

'Come, lad,' said Adam, pushing back his chair and standing up. 'We must get on to the tavern and be there to greet our fellow strikers before the meeting starts. You coming, Peter?'

Owen saw his father continue to pick his teeth, taking his time to answer, staring straight ahead and not at Adam or anybody. 'Not today,' he said. Owen caught a glimpse of his mother, her eyes falling, her mouth set in a hard line. 'Work to do round here. Ground won't weed itself. We'll need those vegetables to grow out there more than ever now.'

Adam said nothing and went to the door, pulled on his boots and grabbed his cap. Owen did the same and out they went. Part of him wished his father was coming too, as he felt embarrassed by his lack of commitment. But part of him was glad, as he had something to talk to Adam about, out of his father's earshot. The two of them set off at a good pace, eager to get to the tavern, see their comrades and make plans.

'I had a plan to see the girl today, in about an hour,' Owen told Adam.

'Good, good. Then you must go. Dunna fret about missing the meeting. You are doing our work yer own way. I'll make excuses if anyone asks and I wonna be saying you're doing housework neither.'

Owen sensed a dig at his father, but did not respond. 'I'll walk with you far as the bridge then turn off.'

'Not much chance to talk to you about her these days, being so much in yer parents' good company. Any progress?'

Owen thought of how to measure progress in his meetings with Bea over the last two weeks. He had moved from kissing to putting his hand in various places on her body where he had never before touched a girl. That was certainly progress in his book.

'Nothing about the scabs. She didna know about them. She'd've told me.'

'There be only so much use in the girl unless she can become a bit more of a spy. Can you ask her? She must loiter about more and listen in on things. Otherwise, we are wasting our prize asset. Surely, she is useful already, being in the house. But the stakes are higher than ever now and we must make more use of her.'

'I see that, but to be fair, she is arguing our side with her elders every chance she gets. As for more spying, I'll see what I can do.'

'And make sure . . . well, how can I put it? There must not be any . . . complications.'

Owen watched their boots stamp forward as they walked along the river path briskly onwards to the bridge. 'Not sure what you mean,' Owen said and glanced over at him.

Adam was not looking at him, instead staring straight ahead with his hands in his pockets. 'I suppose you've been cwtching and so forth. Kissing and such foolery.'

Owen said, 'Summat like that.' He did not want to talk about this with Adam. But also, he couldn't appear as if he did not want to talk about it. All along, he felt he had managed to keep up the façade of a lad toying with a girl's affections, not taking any of it to heart. Adam would not be happy with the truth, that his heart was gone, given fully to Bea Ashford.

'Well, make sure it goes no further'n that.'

'Course,' said Owen, but was not entirely sure what he was agreeing to.

His uncertainty must have come out in his voice, because Adam let out a harried sigh and said bluntly, 'Dunna get the girl in the family way.'

Owen gulped down a lump in his throat.

'Course,' he said again, in a small voice.

'All hell will break loose if you do.'

Neither spoke further. There was a grunt between them as they parted ways at the bridge. Owen went on alone, ducking into the woods to follow the path to the old brickmaster's house, where he was due to meet Bea in a short while. There was nothing he wanted more than to lie with her and be with her in that way, to be unclothed and alone, skin to skin. To see her in all her glory and to feel her as nobody else ever had, closer to her than any had ever been. He had thought of little else these past weeks. He dreamt of it by night and daydreamt of it the rest of the time, picturing the scene and haunting his own body with imagined feelings. He had never done that with a girl and so did not know what it might feel like. He could only think it must be like heaven. What a miracle it was, that amidst the drab routine of everyday life, there was this secret rapture at the heart of every home. The act of becoming one with another body was as forbidden as mortal sin and yet as common as muck. And he wanted it, not when he had a wife to make it lawful, but now, with this girl, with the King heiress. Her money, his poverty, her family and his – none of this mattered when two bodies met. He was her Owen and she was his Bea. That was all.

As he rounded the path and the house came into view, he knew it was all hopeless. Adam was right. There was no way he could bed the King girl. A child would be a disaster. And however much he would give his right arm to make such a girl his wife, he knew they could never marry. So it would never happen. He had to swallow these bitter facts.

But here she came, hurrying along the path after him, calling his name. And he feared that the iron will he needed to resist her would melt like molten metal the moment she touched him.

They did not speak at first, their greeting consumed with passionate kisses.

Bea pulled away, her face aglow and full of excitement.

'Here!' she cried. 'I have the keys to the house. I stole them from Great-grandmother's office!'

She flourished a set of keys from a pocket in her dress and jangled them.

'What house?' said Owen.

'This one, silly! The old brickmaster's house. We can go inside.'

'Should we?'

'Yes, why not?'

He looked at the building and raised his eyebrows. 'Folk say it is haunted.'

'Ooh, do they?' she gasped and turned to stare at the house, her hand on one cheek and eyes wide. 'Now we simply must go in!' She grasped his hand. He let himself be pulled towards the house, feigning reluctance. 'Come, come! Let us scare the spirits away.'

She reached a side door and tried a key, that didn't fit. She tried another and this one caught. She turned the key in the lock. The door was large and thick, made of carved, dark wood. Beatrice walked in breezily. Owen had never stepped across such a threshold. The smartest building he'd ever entered was the church. He stepped in guardedly and found himself in a dim passageway leading to a corner. Beatrice had already disappeared around it. He followed, listening to the click-clack of her shoes ahead of him on the stone floor. He came upon a large hallway to the main part of the house, an elaborate pattern of tilework on the floor, in shades of terracotta, white and black. The tiles looked old, like a ruined floor of an abbey. The decoration on each tile was simple, like a kind of flower, yet together the floor created a complex pattern of light and dark that confused the eye.

'It's pretty,' said Beatrice, quietly.

'It's owd, very owd,' said Owen, also in a quiet voice. There was something about the house that made him want to speak in hushed tones. Every door that faced onto the hall was closed, giving the space a muffled, dense atmosphere. Beatrice strode over to the nearest door and opened it confidently, letting in light that streamed across the floor in a sharp-angled shape.

They went inside to find it had once been a sitting room. Largely empty, there were some chairs near the window shrouded in white sheets. Dust motes floated in the light, disturbed by their entrance.

She turned to him and said, 'I thought it would be fun to come inside. But actually, it feels sad.'

'It is a sad place. And for good reason.'

'What happened to the brickmaster who used to live here?'

'You dunna wanna know that, wench,' said Owen, stepping towards her and drawing her near, leaning in to kiss her, so they didn't have to talk about it any further.

'I certainly do. Tell me!'

'It is a tragic tale.'

Her face fell. 'But now I must know. What happened to him?'

'When he lost his business and all his money, he drank himself stupid at a tavern. The men tried to take him home, but he would have none of it. He was found the following morning, on the mud by the coracle hut. Drowned.'

Beatrice shook her head. 'That is awful. I'm so sorry.'

'We were sorry too. Everyone was. He was a good man.'

She turned from him and folded her arms, thoughtful. 'Is there no end to my family's crimes?' she said in a low voice.

'The old brickmaster lost his business himself, nothing to do with the Kings. He never was good with money, so they said.'

She turned back to him, her eyes bright. 'But the Kings still profited nicely from his misfortune, did they not?'

'That they did.'

She looked at him searchingly. 'Do you blame me, for my family, making life so hard for you all?'

'Of course not. You've done nothing wrong.'

'I profit from them though,' she said, looking down at her dress. 'My things, my luxuries. Living there with them. Even taking the key to come into this house. Now I know what was lost here, I wish I'd never brought you inside.'

'Why did you bring me here, Bea?' he asked softly.

'I foolishly imagined it would be an adventure. But also . . . I thought . . . we might have some privacy. Was I wrong to do so?'

Her face was serious, her eyes searching his for an answer. He wondered if she had any idea what a man and a woman might do, when they are alone in a house.

'I canna stay here, Bea. I'm sorry.'

Her face fell. 'Why? Must you go?'

'No, I can spend a little time with you. But we shouldna be in here.'

'Is it because of him, the old man, and what happened?'

'No, it inna that. I shouldna be in this house with you, alone. It inna . . . right. Or safe.'

'But, whatever can you mean? What isn't safe? The house is perfectly well made. Benjamina was even talking about us moving in there.'

'No!' he raised his voice and it took her aback. 'I'm sorry, Bea. It inna that neither. Listen, if I stay in here with you, I fear what we will do. I fear what will happen between us. Dunna you?'

Bea glanced at her feet, then lifted those beautiful brown eyes up to him, twisting his insides like wringing a sodden cloth. 'I was hoping something might happen,' she said, quietly. 'Is that very wrong of me?'

'Yes,' he said, firmly. Then, at the sight of her forlorn face, added, 'I mean, no. It inna wrong. I mean, it is because we are not husband and wife. But I know I want to . . . lie with you. But we might get you . . . into trouble.'

'Nobody will find us here,' she said.

'No, Bea.' Was she really this innocent? 'You know what happens when a man and a woman lie together? A child might come of it. And we canna have a child.'

'Why not?'

He was perplexed now. Was it not innocence of the facts, then? Something else?

'Why not? Because we inna married.'

'Then let's get married!' she said and smiled. 'Let's run away together.'

'What?'

'My mother did it and started a new life in Paris. All right, it didn't end too well for her, but we would not be like that. We would make it work. We love each other so much, don't we? And that is all that you need in this world. Love.'

So, perhaps she wasn't so innocent about the sexual act. Instead, she was innocent about the world.

'There is more at stake than that.'

'Than love? Nothing is more important.'

'Bea, I canna run away with you. This inna no storybook. This is my life, my family, my friends. We are fighting here for our very lives.'

'I know that. I don't really mean it. I know we must stay and fight to make things better for you, for your family and for all the workers and children at the yard. But sometimes, I confess I feel selfish. My love for you makes me feel that way. There are times when I think of nothing else but you. Aren't you the same, sometimes?'

'Yes, but no. Thoughts of you fill my mind, it's true. But I do not have the same leisure to think as you. I must earn for my family and strive for them and for my people.'

'They are your people, yes. As thc King family are mine. But we are more than that, we are individuals in our own right. And you are my love. I love you and you love me. Love conquers all!'

How little she understood. It exasperated him, even as she stood there with her stunning dark eyes and pouting mouth, making him want to hurl aside this stupid argument and just kiss her again.

'It inna just my mother and father, though that is enough. I would do anything for them. They have been the best parents a lad can imagine. Dunna you feel like that?'

'About my mother, yes. She has been my heart and soul as long as I can remember. I would do anything for her. I would die for her.'

'Me too,' said Owen. 'But it's beyond only close family. You may not know this, but the strike leader and his wife are living with us now. The very centre of the strike is in our home.'

'Mr Adam Jones? And his wife Martha, the one who's expecting a baby? I have met them. Mr Jones has been to the house. But my great-grandmother and I visited them, at theirs after Uncle Cyril evicted the workers.'

'Yes, I heard about that.' He did not say more, as he had been told an account of the meeting by Adam and it was not flattering to either old Mrs King or to Bea. Adam had characterised them both as royalty forced to converse with the gutter. Owen had smarted at the description. He knew that underneath Bea wasn't like that, however she had come across to Adam Jones.

His feelings must have shown in his face, as she continued, 'It was a wise idea, I believe, to try to speak with him and his wife. We went to try to make them stay. But they would not.'

'No, they wouldna. For good reason.'

'But why are they with you, now? Of all people, why are they staying with you?'

'Adam is my father's cousin. Well, he inna his blood cousin. Adam was once married to my father's . . .' His words trailed off. He had fallen into the trap of sharing confidences with her, but suddenly recalled who he was talking to. The daughter of the enemy.

'To your father's cousin, was it?' asked Beatrice, guessing at the end of his sentence. Was she simply interested or digging for information? His own spying had made him paranoid. Surely Beatrice was not engaged in the same pursuit as him. Was she a spy for the Kings as well? Had he been duped, all along?

'What is it, Owen?' she said and reached out to touch his arm. He flinched at it and she withdrew, hurt flickering in her eyes. He steeled his heart against it and chose his next words carefully.

'Listen. You must listen. This strike is killing us. There are children of brickies hereabouts grown dangerously thin. They dunna have enough food to eat. We get money to them, whatever we can, but there are too many and not enough food for us all. We must fight to end the strike as soon as possible. But for that, I need you. Only you hold the key to solving this crisis. Can you help us further, Bea?'

'Anything! Ask me and I will do whatever I can, you know that.'

'Speak to your great-grandmother again. Ask her to get rid of the scabs and get us back to work on our usual pay. We can talk about other conditions, but we must go back on the old pay. Nothing else will do.'

Bea frowned but nodded. 'She is a tough old bird and that's for sure. She is hard to persuade of anything. But I shall see what I can do.'

'Good!' he said.

'If I manage it, to get the strike ended, is there a future for us?'

So, this was what was at stake. The community's future rested on the strike outcome, as well as his family's. But even closer, his own happiness with the love of his life. Could it work? His mind raced forward, madly imagining a possible future, where the strike was done, the workers were back at good rates of pay and everyone's lives were better. And beyond that, himself, standing beside this beautiful girl, in a white dress with blossoms in her hair. It was madness, surely. Or was it?

'I cannot promise that, though I wish it with all of my heart. All I know is, once the strike is over and we are back to work, and nobody is starving, then we can talk further and make plans.'

'I will do it!' she cried.

Her face lit up with hope. It was a delight to see and he kissed her joyfully. Then, they kissed more deeply and joy gave way to a melting bliss, that flowed through his body like warm honey. He pulled away and they gazed at each other. All happiness was subsumed in passion now, serious and utterly compelling.

'You see the effect you have on me, Bea?'

'I know,' she said and pulled in close, her head beside his, resting her cheek on his shoulder. 'Me too.'

'And that's why we must be careful.'

'Yes,' she said and stepped backwards. 'But now we have a plan. We have a future, Owen!'

She moved to the door and beckoned for him to follow. She ran across the hallway, the dust flying in swirls as she passed through it. He ran after her and they came out into the day.

She locked the door and gave him a peck on the cheek. 'I will make things better. I will make it work. You'll see!'

And with that, she blew him a kiss, turned and trotted off up the path, homeward.

I hope to God she's right, he thought.

Beatrice tried. She really did try. But Queenie was having none of it. Beatrice hardly saw her these days anyway, for she was either ensconced in her study with a variety of angry men coming and going or she was in her room, not to be interrupted, resting after the exertions of the day. The latest news was that two of the other brickyards had gone on strike too, and it seemed that some of the masters blamed the Kings for starting it. Beatrice could hear the arguments through the walls and floors of Southover, creating a constant air of disagreement in the house. The strike was not easy on anyone. What's more, the late June weather was unseasonably wet, with sweeping rainstorms for over a week, swelling the river and swamping the banks. Beatrice heard that houses were flooded and thus some of the poorest, scraping a living along the riverside, were worse off than ever. Out of work and now, out of house and home. The rain also meant an end to the excuse of walks for Beatrice, and with it, no opportunity to meet up with Owen. They had an agreement to meet at midday at the brickmaster's house every Tuesday, Thursday and Sunday, when they could manage it. But with the awful weather, Beatrice had missed three of these days and was pining for Owen so deeply, it felt like an insatiable hunger. She found herself seeking out food from the kitchens more often than ever, to fill her churning stomach.

She felt like a prisoner. At Southover, the day's proceedings were timed like military manoeuvres, under Queenie's strict regime. As much as Beatrice loved her great-grandmother, with no escape to soften it she felt disagreeably frustrated and took it out on her mother, griping at her over cards or at the breakfast table, when yet again the day promised nothing but rain. Her failure to deliver what Owen had asked of her was breaking her heart and her worry for the plight of the brickworkers only grew. But she could tell nobody here, which made it worse. Since she'd seen him last, she had tried on four different occasions to engage Queenie in a debate about the strike, trying to ease her way in through asking Queenie how it was going for her, for the Kings and the masters in general. But every time she tried to open a conversation about it, Queenie snapped it like a twig. She would not discuss it with her. Beatrice wondered if it was down to the fact that Beatrice had made it very clear how she felt about the brickworkers. Her dressed-up visit to the yard still remained a secret between the two of them and every time Queenie looked at her during these brief forays into the subject, Beatrice saw the accusatory stare of betrayal in Queenie's eyes. She wondered if her great-grandmother blamed her, too, for the meeting with Adam Jones not ending well. Thus, their discussions would end before they had really started. The feeling that they had joined forces to solve the crisis together had waned as the strike had progressed and relations between masters and workers had deteriorated further. Beatrice got the sense that battle lines were being drawn.

One Sunday morning, at breakfast, Beatrice took another slice of bacon, avoiding the smoked fish her mother was so fond of. Chewing away thoughtfully and staring over her mother's shoulder at the window beyond, she saw the first patch of blue sky she'd seen in days. Her dance lesson was due that day, which recently she'd been taken to in the carriage, due to the bad weather.

'Maman, look!' she said, pointing to the break in the clouds. 'I can walk today, yes? There is no rain.'

'Oh yes, so it is, *chérie*. Do walk if you prefer. I shall meet you there afterwards.'

'No, Maman!' she said urgently, then continued with a false brightness in her voice, 'I mean to say that last week Madame and I arranged that we would go for a stroll together after my lesson, as she had no more pupils after mine today.'

'Splendid,' replied her mother. 'Though it is worrying to hear that her day is not filled with lessons. I do hope Madame has enough pupils to make her way.'

'Indeed,' murmured Beatrice, thinking of how useful these weekly lessons had been to her and Owen. She had learnt very little about dancing, but had bought her freedom with the one regular chance she had to escape the house.

'And it's not long now until we shall be looking for an opportunity for you to have your first ball. You'll be coming out! Just think of all the excitement! Meeting the sons of all the masters in the area. I wonder who you'll fall in love with, my darling.'

'I wonder,' echoed Beatrice and hastily jammed her last piece of bacon into her mouth, before asking to leave the table.

After breakfast, she left by the front door, tying her bonnet ribbons as she hurried down the steps and onto the gravel. But the moment she'd left the house, she felt a drop of rain on her hand. She looked up to the sky, to see a dark mass of clouds above, but beyond it was more blue sky. So she hoped the rain would not last long. She decided to turn about and fetch her umbrella, just in case, then remembered that she had left it in the carriage under the seat the last time they'd been out. She crossed the driveway and walked around to the back of the house, where the stables and the coach-house were. There was a boy loitering near the horses but the coachman or grooms were not about, so she went in without having to speak to anyone about it. She opened the carriage door and found her umbrella, stowed under the seat and still damp. She grasped it, then shut the door, glancing outside to see the rain falling more heavily. She tutted and held out the umbrella before her. It was a pretty thing, with a mother-of-pearl handle and a pale pink canopy. She pushed it open and shook it out, drops of old rain flying off it in arcs.

'Oh no, miss!' came a cry.

She lifted her umbrella to reveal the stable boy had appeared in the doorway, staring at her, mouth open.

'What is it?' she said, annoyed but also a little alarmed.

'You mun open no numbrella indoors. It be the worstest bad luck.'

'Well, I'm not really indoors. The coach-house doors are open, see?'

The boy was shaking his head in horror. 'You mun never risk it. You'll be dead before the year be out.'

'Oh, what rot!' she scoffed and flourished her umbrella towards the boy, who fled. 'Superstitious nonsense.' Her umbrella was her friend today, allowing her to walk to her destination with some protection.

She walked out into the rain, her umbrella doing its job well. A movement in the corner of her eye caught her attention. Thinking it might be that superstitious boy again, she prepared to shoo him off, when she saw it wasn't him, but two other children. They were sneaking across the yard towards the back of the kitchen. There was no other way to describe it, as they were on barefooted tiptoe with their shoulders hunched and arms curved out, pattering along until they disappeared behind the kitchen wall. They did not work at Southover, that was for sure, as they were dressed in rags and as Beatrice had already spotted, they had no shoes on. Whatever were they doing here? She found herself sneaking along the wall too, to follow their route and peek around the corner of the building. But a spoke of her umbrella scraped against the wall as she came round and the two children looked up anxiously, ready to run, a boy and a girl. They were standing over a mound of rotting matter, old vegetable peelings and skins of fruit and other kitchen scraps. They both had what looked like potato skins in their hands and protruding from their mouths as they chewed voraciously.

The moment they saw her and clocked her rich clothes, they bolted.

'No, please!' cried Beatrice, as they ran. 'Please come back. I'll give you meat!'

They stopped dead in their tracks. The girl said something to the boy, but the noise of the rain obscured it from Beatrice. She called again, 'I mean it. I shall find you some bacon. Would you like that?'

The girl came forward nodding, while the boy hung back a little. As they approached, she saw more clearly how thin their arms were, how drawn their faces. They had those same young-old faces she had seen at the brickyard, children grown ancient before their time. They were shivering in the rain.

'Here,' she said and held out the umbrella to the girl, who was closer. The child stared at it, held out her hand and took it warily. Beatrice supposed she'd never held such a thing in her life. She grasped it awkwardly with both hands and held it high above her head. The boy came up and nestled under it, close against the girl. Beatrice looked down at their bare feet, so white they stood out like baked cod against the russet tiles of the yard floor. She glanced behind her at the coach-house and beckoned to the children, who watched her move over to the door and gesture through it. Another word or two passed between them and they decided to follow. Once inside the coach-house, the girl still held the umbrella up and Beatrice reached out, taking it gently from her.

The act of closing down the umbrella and placing it against the wall seemed to fascinate the two, as they gaped at Beatrice's every move.

'Wait here,' she said. 'I will fetch you something good to eat.'

The girl nodded. Beatrice went over to the kitchen and opened the door. Cook was there and two kitchen maids. Cook's face went from surprise to disapproval in a second.

'There inna anything for you here, miss,' said Cook.

'Oh, but it's not for me!' she cried, then realised that she hadn't meant to say anything about the children to anyone.

Cook narrowed her eyes and replied, 'Arr, of course it inna. It be for the fairies.'

Beatrice took a step forward confidentially and said, 'Please, Mrs Guest.' Cook look impressed that the daughter of the house had remembered her name, but Beatrice had learnt from Queenie that it was always wise to know the name of every servant. 'Please. I need a little food. It doesn't have to be anything fancy.'

Cook looked more amenable, but was still torn. The two maids watched with interest. 'Miss, you know I love to feed you up but your mother has made it most plain that I am not to give you food outside of reg'lar meal times. I canna go against Mrs Ashford, I canna.'

'Listen, please. There were two children outside eating potato peelings.'

'There wasna! Little ratlins!' cried Cook and went to go towards the door, presumably to chase them off.

'No, please, Mrs Guest. They were starving. They had only rags to wear, no shoes. Their faces were sunken. I have them waiting in the coach-house. I could not square it with my conscience if I did not give them some meat before they go.'

The maids looked at each other with raised eyebrows, but Cook was not moved. 'If you give 'em a scrap, they'll be back in their hordes tomorrow. There's a thousand like 'em all along the river and through town and the next town and the town after that. Feeding one or two wonna ever cure that.'

'You're right. I cannot cure poverty and misfortune. I have not the power. But I can do this one small thing to improve the lot of two children we have on our very doorstep. Can we not offer them a hand of kindness, this one time?'

Cook shook her head but gave in. 'Just a scrinch, mind. Girls, help Miss Beatrice.'

She was given a lump of cheese, a couple of cold rashers of bacon left from the breakfast plates and a hunk of hard bread from a stale loaf Cook had been saving to make breadcrumbs, all wrapped up in a cloth. Cook tutted throughout the procedure. 'Dunna give 'em my cloth!' she called to Beatrice as she left the kitchen. 'I want that back.'

Beatrice went back to the coach-house, half expecting them to have gone, as if she had imagined the whole thing. But there they were, standing in the exact same spot she'd left them, shivering and holding on to one another for more warmth. At the sight of food, all decorum left them and they threw down the umbrella and fell upon her hands, shoving the bacon into their chomping mouths first. Then they ate cheese, which the girl grabbed first and the boy grasped a chunk of before it disappeared behind her teeth. Then they ripped the bread apart and ate that noisily too. It was all gone so quickly, Beatrice felt ashamed she had not brought more.

'Have you no parents?' she said, softly, so not to frighten them.

'Yes,' said the girl, still finding crumbs about her mouth or down her front to pick at. The boy was crouched down and dabbing his fingers on the ground, securing more crumbs and licking his filthy fingers to get at them.

'You do have parents? Or you don't?'

'We've parents,' said the boy, not looking up from his work on the floor.

'What do they do? Do they work?'

The girl nodded. 'They be brickies.'

The boy stood up and smoothed back his wet hair. 'They be at your yard. Or they would be, if it wonna filled with Irishmen.'

The girl said, 'Shush!' and pushed the boy hard on the arm. She turned back to Beatrice and said, 'Thank'ee for the bait.'

'Come back tomorrow,' said Beatrice. 'Come every morning and I shall give you food.'

'Yes'm,' said the girl, but the boy grabbed her hand and ran off, dragging her with him. The little girl kept looking round at Beatrice, before the two of them disappeared into the woods behind the house.

Beatrice stood still for a moment. She looked up at the sky to see that the dark clouds were passing and the rain was almost gone. She knew that the sight of those waifs devouring that food would never leave her. She had used the word 'starving' before, to complain to her mother that she needed a snack, because she was a growing girl and nobody knew how constantly hungry she was. She now knew what it looked like to starve, to actually be starving. And her past words sickened her.

She returned Cook's cloth, then retrieved her umbrella, just in case, and walked out onto the yard. At that moment, the two kitchen maids appeared from around the corner and one lifted her chin and shouted, 'Louise!' The other one followed suit. Beatrice stepped back, so she was out of eyeshot and heard them gossiping about Benjamina, saying such things as 'We're always looking for that damned dog. Why does she let it run wild? It inna our job to look after it like a mollycoddled babby', and so on. Beatrice smirked as she listened, then their voices lessened as they disappeared behind the coach-house wall, but she could still hear them shouting the dog's name over and over as they went.

She stepped out and was ready to leave, at last, eager to get on and reach the old brickmaster's house. The thought of seeing Owen again, of touching him, made her cheeks go hot and she gasped at the strength of it. But someone was shouting behind her. It was the high, piercing voices of the kitchen maids. She so wanted to walk onwards, ignore whatever it was, some domestic disaster in which she had no interest. But their voices were shrill and she could not help but turn round and listen. One of the maids appeared and spotted her, her hand over her mouth.

Beatrice called across the yard, 'Whatever is it?'

'Oh Lord!' cried the girl and pointed behind her.

Beatrice walked quickly towards her. 'What? What is it?'

'Dead,' she said, her mouth gaping. 'She be dead as a doornail.'

'Who is?' said Beatrice, horrified to hear what was coming next.

But the maid was off, running into the kitchen. Beatrice raced off around the corner, in the direction the girl had come from. There was the other maid, staring at something on the ground. Beatrice ran up behind her, to see her step aside. There, on the ground, limp and pathetic, was Benjamina's little dog, Louise. Its veined eyes were wide open and its tongue stuck out, thick and dark.

The maid said, 'Oh, we shall be blamed! She will say it is our fault, all our fault. But how can we watch for a dog with all our chores to do? Oh, what will become of us!'

'Do calm yourself,' reassured Beatrice, staring at the poor dead dog, so grateful it wasn't the brickie girl, her first terrifying thought. 'I will take the dog. I will say I found her.' She put on a brave face and leant down to pick it up. The body was stiff and hard to the touch. She stood up straight, the body across her hands. As she stared at it, she realised the last thing anyone who loved this animal would want to see was its red eyes popping and its black tongue. She passed it to the maid, who took it with disgust.

'Find a sack for it and hide it, for the moment. I shall tell Mrs King.'

As she walked back towards the house, she knew she would not be seeing Owen today. She knew too that something terrible had happened here, beyond the death of a beloved pet. The animal had no blood upon it and no bite marks. That dog had been strangled.

Chapter 13

A week had passed since Louise's death. Beatrice had not been allowed out of the house at all since. That horrible day, Beatrice had told Queenie first, who looked dazed and then distinctly off-colour at the news, but soon recovered and said she would inform Benjamina. Since her arrival at Southover, Beatrice had seen that there was no love lost between Queenie and her daughter-in-law, but now she saw that Queenie was disgusted by what had happened to the little dog and was not looking forward to telling its doting owner. Beatrice went to her mother afterwards in her bedroom and told her what had happened. Maman was shocked to the core that 'such a cruel thing could be done to such an innocent'. At that moment, Beatrice thought of the two famished urchins that had devoured her food and she felt the phrase applied equally to them. Surely children were worth more than dogs. But the fact remained that her mother was right, the dog was innocent and had been deliberately killed to cause upset and fear.

Their talk was interrupted as they both heard a cry from the room across the hall, an inhuman wail that hollowed out the house. The strangeness of it left them both quiet and shaking their heads. Benjamina had not appeared from her room since, apart from the afternoon they had found Louise, where a solemn burial took place in the pet graveyard, alongside the bones of previous King dogs. Benjamina had insisted that no words were to be spoken, so she, Queenie, Margaret and Beatrice had watched the small wooden box the gardener had knocked together lowered into its resting place. Cyril was nowhere to be seen, Beatrice suspecting he had no time for the concept of dog funerals. Benjamina's face was unreadable, blank and pale. The little grave was marked with a posy of flowers, yet Queenie said Benjamina had ordered a gravestone with the inscription 'My beloved Louise, taken too soon by vengeful Death'.

The atmosphere in the house was stifling. The rains of the previous week had given way to muggy, cloudy heat that made the enforced curfew even more oppressive. Sometimes, to escape the house, Beatrice would take a turn around the gardens with her mother. They would talk of when Maman was a child and would tread the same walk. Maman told her how Benjamina had always had a little dog for company, but had loved this one the most. Sometimes, they would see Benjamina sitting at her window, staring out. Her large eyes in the white face were unsettling to look at and Beatrice would turn away. She was filled with guilt and confusion. It felt as if her family had been attacked and yet her loyalties lay more with Owen than the Kings. Her feelings were swirling so violently, she felt nauseous with the puzzle of it all. The worst of it was that she had nobody to talk to about it. She could not reveal the truth about her and Owen to anyone. And even with him, she could not discuss the strike properly, as he was wholly partisan, as anyone in his position would be. She guessed that Owen's people, the strikers, had killed the dog. Everyone said it was so. It was a sickening, despicable thing to do. But she also knew that some of the strikers' children were starving. She had seen it with her own eyes. She would screw her eyes up to rid herself of the sight, squeezing her mother's arm more tightly.

'I know it is a distressing time,' her mother said on one such garden stroll. 'But it will pass. There were similar times when I was a child, dark times. But they passed. The fire of people's anger burns less brightly, cools and dies. It will turn to ashes and be swept away, you'll see. All will be well.'

'I do not think it will be well, Maman.'

'Have a little faith. You are young and time passes slowly for you. See it from my perspective and this is simply another bridge to cross. But we will get to the other side.'

Beatrice nodded, but was not convinced. Her hopes for a life for her and Owen beyond it all seemed further out of reach as every day of the strike passed, with no resolution. But her love for him burned brighter with each passing moment. The life she wanted and the life occurring around her were moving in opposite directions, pulled by forces beyond her reach. Maman was watching her and there was a moment where their eyes met and her mother stopped walking and looked at her; above her head the treetops of the woods beyond waved lazily in the thick air. 'You know that you can speak with me about anything. You've always known that, haven't you, Bea?'

'Yes, Maman,' she said and forced a smile. 'I know that.'

Her mother stared at her a while longer, waiting for Beatrice to say something. But Beatrice changed the subject and asked Maman if she would like to go inside and cheer themselves up by playing a duet on the pianoforte. Maman smiled her consent but looked concerned. There was nothing Beatrice would like more than to pour her heart out to Maman. She had always told her mother everything. But this was beyond anything she could share. She knew loving Owen would be met with not only disapproval, but now – with Louise's strangling – she was loving the enemy, pure and simple.

But then a thought occurred to her, something that had come from her lessons with Maman's pupils. Their lessons had revolved around the teaching of the English language. But sometimes, with the older pupils, talk strayed into other subjects, such as English customs, manners and habits, as well as English history, inevitably including the many wars between England and France across the centuries. Beatrice always felt that sitting there, discussing and learning with these French children and she herself, being a child of an English mother, were great proof that society was moving in the right direction, that talking, getting to know each other, was the way forward for any civilisation. And the only way to prevent such wars happening again was through knowledge first and then its offspring, understanding.

'Maman, may I play duets with you another day? I have not spent much time with Great-grandmother in recent days and I feel remiss.'

Maman smiled at her and cupped her cheek in her hand. 'What a good, kind girl you are. Run along, then. Take a pack of cards. How she loves to play cards!'

Beatrice left her full of fizzing energy, bolting up the stairs and arriving at Queenie's door, breathing hard from the exertion. She calmed herself, then knocked lightly on the door.

'Enter,' came Queenie's voice and in she went.

Queenie was sitting up in bed, awake and rested from her after-lunch nap. She had been distant these past weeks, but her gladness to see her favourite was obvious and she reached out her hand to Beatrice, who rushed across the room to take it and give it a peck.

'How *are* you?' she asked Queenie, earnestly.

'I am quite well, my dear. And how are you? All of this must be very upsetting for you. I am sorry for it.'

'I am quite well too, Queenie. Please don't worry on my account.'

'But I do, my sweet. You came here to Southover to take your place in English society and have the joy and excitement of coming out. And I worry it has been ruined by all this trouble.'

'It is the trouble I wish to talk with you about.'

Queenie looked disagreeable and took her hand away, putting it firmly on her lap and looking straight ahead. 'I fear it will cause us to fall out with one another and I do not wish to do that,' she said.

'I think that we can strive to discuss important matters without resorting to anger, don't you? And I must tell you something I know, that I have seen with my own eyes. Children are starving. I have seen brickworkers' children eating potato peel, ravenously hungry. We cannot allow this strike to continue any longer while children are starving.'

'Where did you see them?'

'Here, at Southover. They were foraging from the heap of scraps outside the kitchen.' She omitted the part where she gave them food, assuming Queenie would disapprove.

'Yes and the very same ragamuffins most likely harmed poor Louise!' snapped Queenie.

'Impossible!' cried Beatrice. 'They were too skinny and underfed to have the strength. They were shaking and shivering. No, these children were closer to their own death. So, we must protect them from this fate. We must come up with a way to end the strike as soon as we can.'

Queenie let out an exasperated sigh and closed her eyes. 'You see everything in black and white. You have no idea of the complexity of the situation.'

'Teach me, then. Explain it to me. I am eager to learn.'

Queenie opened her eyes and gave Beatrice a long hard stare, then seemed to soften. 'My hands are tied. I cannot offer better terms, as I have signed an agreement with the other brickmasters. And even if I did, my weakness would be seized upon by these union types and then we would have strike after strike, on any occasion where there was something they didn't like. There would never be an end to it. Thus, I cannot end the strike. The workers we brought down from Liverpool have gone. They could not withstand the pressure from the other brickworkers hurling insults – and in some cases, real brickbats! – day in, day out. So now the yard is closed again and we are losing sales and goodwill with our clients. If the strike continues beyond the weekend, then I have decided that we will close the brickworks for good.'

Beatrice listened intently to every word. It was clear to her now that there was no way on earth that Queenie – and those she did business with – would ever budge. All of this gave her plan more credence. 'Then, I have a solution for you.'

'Really, my dear?' said Queenie, sounding tired of the whole thing and distinctly sarcastic.

'Yes. I have told you that I had a friendship with a brickworker named Owen. Now, hear me out, please.

Owen's family are related to Adam Jones, did you know that?'

Queenie narrowed her eyes. 'No, I did not. But how do you know of it, child?'

Beatrice hadn't thought that far ahead. But her mind skipped and found a solution swiftly. 'I hear things. The servants gossiping. I've heard them talking about it. Owen's father is Adam Jones's cousin or his first wife's cousin or something. Anyway, they are staying with Owen's family, in their house, since they left their home.'

'All very fascinating, my dear, I am sure. But what of it?'

'I have an acquaintanceship with Owen, as you know. And yes, I am well aware you disapprove. But listen, what if I were to use this friendship to visit Owen, at his home, and speak to Mr Adam Jones. Perhaps, I can persuade Mr Jones to change his mind or at least to speak with you again. It is worth a try, is it not?'

'It is out of the question!' said Queenie, eyes agog. 'How could you imagine I would agree to such a thing?'

'But why?' cried Beatrice, irritated. 'You and I went to visit the Joneses at their house. How would this be any different?'

'Yes and remember how badly that went,' said Queenie.

'But things have changed since then.'

'Yes, for the worse! These people are monsters! How could I agree to send my great-granddaughter into that den of wolves?'

Beatrice hung her head and took strength from a deep breath.

'They are not animals, Queenie. They are people. They are fighting for a better way of living. And the Kings are fighting for their business, I see that. But whatever they have done, we have done. Whenever the strike comes to an end, whatever the outcome, the damage has been done and crimes committed on both sides.'

'And what crimes, pray, have we committed? As far as I am aware, we have not burnt down anyone's sheds or murdered anyone's dog.'

'Yes, but our family has done its fair share of wrongs. The conditions at the brickyard. Allowing children to work at these damaging jobs, watching their lives drain out of them, when they should be growing and learning and laughing. It is so wrong. Think too of the desperation of the people now there is no money coming in. Children are starving. It would break anyone's heart to see them, if that heart were not made of stone.'

'You need to see both sides if you are ever to understand the nature of profit and loss. One must be hard-hearted to make a business flourish.'

'Maman said to me that people's anger would burn out and all that would be left was a pile of ashes. But I think there would be a solid lump of hatred left in those ashes, hard as rock. We must find a way to reach out and join the two sides. There must be a shift on both sides. Surely that will be better for everyone, the business included. People make this business work. Surely we must appeal to them as people, for that is what they are.'

'People who would murder a dog?'

'And what of people who would let a child starve?'

'These workers chose to go on strike. We Kings did not want it. Nobody forced them to do it. They are letting their own children starve!'

'How can you say that?' said Beatrice with exasperation. 'What parent would ever choose such a thing? Their conditions at work and their poverty at home have forced them into a life with no choice. Are you so blinded by profit you cannot see that?'

Both Queenie and Beatrice sat with their chins jutting out, their eyes defiant. They had reached an impasse.

'We are very alike,' said Queenie, the ghost of a smile about her lips. 'As chalk and cheese as we may seem.'

'Let me go and talk to Owen and his family. Adam Jones will probably be there if I go at teatime.'

'But what would you say to them? What could you say? Everything that can be said has been said, with no progress.'

'At the very least, I can take him the fact that you are about to close down the brickworks if the strike does not end. That gives him one last chance to change his mind and those of his workers. They won't listen to you or the other masters and certainly not

Uncle Cyril. But I am a girl, softer in their eyes, not so threatening. They may dismiss me at first, but I can speak well. I believe I can make them hear me and make them listen.'

'You certainly have that gift,' said Queenie and considered her for several moments, looking at her face, her hair, her hands, then her eyes, as if taking in all that Beatrice was to her. *She'll never agree*, thought Beatrice. *She won't let me risk it, not me.* Then Queenie breathed in sharply as if coming to a sudden decision. 'Do it then.'

'Truly?' gasped Beatrice, genuinely surprised.

'It might just work. And it might get us out of this mess. If you can change my mind, you can change anybody's.'

'Ha ha!' laughed Beatrice. 'I will do my best!'

'But my dear, you must take someone with you. It's out of the question that you be without a chaperone in such a place.'

Maman would immediately see that Beatrice was sweet on Owen. She had that ability, to read Beatrice's face like a book. 'I cannot go with my mother.'

'Yes, it is probably wise to keep her out of this. She would not approve of the whole enterprise. We must keep it from her. Well, there's nothing for it but to take Jenkins. She will keep you on the straight and narrow. Go tomorrow. I'll say Jenkins is taking you on a nature walk, teaching you about the flora and fauna of Shropshire.'

Beatrice grasped Queenie's hands and kissed them. 'Thank you!'

'Thank *you*, my dear. Your initiative and passion to help may just be our saviour in this unholy chaos. I have never met a child so selfless.'

The following morning, after a restless night bedevilled with nervous excitement, she heard an unfamiliar knock on the door, a staccato pattern. The sun was up, but the house was quiet. Beatrice dragged herself from her bed, went to her door and opened it to see Jenkins standing there, fully dressed.

'Chop, chop, Miss Beatrice. I'll send Dinah up to see to you. Choose your dress carefully. Nothing too fancy. We'll be walking a way and then visiting in a place that doesn't expect a crinoline. Keep it simple today, hmm?'

'Oh, yes, I see. Of course. Thank you,' stuttered Beatrice, half asleep but also a little afraid of Jenkins. She was the most senior female in the house, save Queenie herself, and had such an imperious manner, she demanded respect and awe from everyone beneath her. Beatrice included herself in the latter group. But then Jenkins did a funny thing, she winked at Beatrice, very deliberately, with an amused expression on her face. Then she turned and bustled off. Perhaps Jenkins was not so very fierce after all. At the very least, she seemed to be enjoying this subterfuge. Beatrice shut the door and turned with excitement back to her room. She went straight to her wardrobe to pick a suitable gown for the day. Not too showy and flouncy for the Malones and the Joneses of this world, but again pretty enough to hug her figure in all the right places, so that she looked her very best to see her darling again. It was a delicate balance, finding the perfect dress, and one she waited impatiently for Dinah to come up and assist her with, as she flicked through her choices, dismissing each one with mounting nerves.

After breakfast, the morning was spent twitchily, playing cards with Queenie for a while, playing duets with her mother too. Cyril came in and out, usually reading a magazine of some amusing sort. Benjamina stayed in her room, as usual. Lunch came and went, her mother and Queenie retiring to their rooms for a rest, to appear again at around three o'clock. Shortly after, Queenie announced to all that Jenkins would take Beatrice for a nature walk and they would take a picnic tea prepared by Cook. Jenkins knew the way, leading them through the woods, carrying their picnic in a basket. 'Nearly there now,' said Jenkins. 'When we arrive, I'll knock on the door and I'll introduce you. Any idea what you're going to say?'

'Some idea,' said Beatrice and gulped. She'd thought about it all night and all morning, but now all her speeches had flown out of her mind, like crows at the sound of a gunshot. The alarm of nearing Owen's cottage had unsettled her. She slowed her step.

Jenkins turned to her and said, 'Changing your mind? You don't have to do this, you know.'

Beatrice looked nervously at Jenkins and tried to smile. She could end all this right then and there, turn around and go home, where it was safe. But the image of the two hungry children floated before her. 'I know I don't have to. But I will do it. Someone must do something.'

'Good girl,' said Jenkins and on they marched.

The woodland path broadened and led them nearer to the river, which moved along swiftly on this humid day, still high from the recent rains. Beatrice could see the watermark halfway up tree trunks, with a couple of huts on the opposite bank submerged to the window ledges. Someone's home or livelihood lost. They were passing by some cottages now, safe on higher ground above the river. People were out and about, tending to livestock or smoking a pipe, watching the well-dressed pair pass by, no doubt wondering what on earth their business was here. A woman called for her chickens, 'Chook, chook!', then stopped and gaped at Beatrice, as a flurry of hens pecked about her own feet. Beatrice looked straight ahead, chin up. She wanted to appear like someone who knew exactly what she was doing. Inside, her heart was pounding.

'It's the third cottage along, over there,' said Jenkins, who approached the front door and rapped confidently upon it. The door opened.

There stood Owen. His curious glance changed to amazement as his eyes fell on Beatrice. She smiled, so widely, she forgot for moment that she did not like the shape of her teeth very much. How exquisite it was to see him with her own eyes instead of in her mind's eye. How she wanted to reach out and touch him. She had to pull herself together now.

'Mr Malone,' she began.

Owen was still staring at Beatrice, struck dumb. At that moment, a sound tore through them. It was a woman screaming. It came from within the cottage. Owen flinched as if struck, then stepped forwards, pulling the door to behind him.

'We cannot see anyone now,' he said. 'There is a baby coming.'

'Is it Martha Jones?' said Beatrice.

'Yes,' said Owen.

'Is the midwife there? Mrs Lunt?' said Jenkins.

'Yes, she's here,' replied Owen. 'But it inna going well.'

'How so?' said Jenkins.

'Martha's been at it for hours and hours now, since last night. The baby is stuck.' Owen pushed a hand through his hair and Beatrice saw his hand was shaking.

Jenkins said, 'Let me go in. I've seen more births than most. My mother was a midwife. Let me talk to Lunt.'

Owen stepped back, exhausted and in no fit state to argue. Jenkins put her basket on the ground next to the front door and went inside. Beatrice lost sight of her as the door swung back towards them, leaving it open only a crack. Beatrice turned to Owen.

'Are you well?' she whispered to him. How she wanted to reach over and touch his face. He looked older than when she last had seen him.

Owen glanced over her shoulder, chastened by the neighbours' inquisitive loitering behind them. 'Miss Ashford,' he said, a little louder. 'On any normal occasion, we would be honoured by such a visit. But today we are . . . we are . . .'

'Indisposed?' she tried.

'Yes, that,' he said. 'And I am sorry to say that now inna a good time.'

'Owen, let me help. What can I do? Can I fetch someone to help?'

Owen looked back at the door behind him, staring at the gap as if it had all the answers. 'The midwife . . .' he murmured.

Then the door opened. It was Jenkins. 'The woman needs a doctor.'

'We canna afford any doctor!' cried Owen.

'I can,' said Beatrice.

Owen looked desperately back into the house. They all heard another cry from a room to the side, the anguished cry of a woman in pain. Beatrice spotted three people inside, all talking in low voices, their faces drawn and worried. One of them was Adam Jones, whose arms were up, his hands at his scalp as if he were about to literally tear his hair out.

'No time to argue,' said Beatrice. 'We are going to fetch the doctor. Come, Jenkins.'

She did not look at Owen again before turning away. Jenkins led the way, down onto the river path, which they hurried along towards the bridge.

'What is happening with Martha?' Beatrice asked, breathlessly.

'I canna talk 'n' run!' snapped Jenkins. They went on, side-stepping passers-by who gawped at them. Under the bridge, up the steps and into the town. Across the square, around the back and along the street. Number ten, the brass plaque outside announcing the occupant's illustrious profession: Doctor Spencer Fitzpatrick, Physician.

Jenkins banged on the door with her fist, breathing hard. Beatrice was gasping, too, unaccustomed as she was to hurrying anywhere. The door opened and there stood a woman in a frilly mobcap, a hard look on her face, obviously used to fielding urgent enquiries to the doctor within. Her expression changed when she saw who had knocked upon her door.

'Why, Rose. Whatever is it? Trouble at the big house?'

Beatrice was almost startled out of her panic to hear someone call Jenkins by her first name.

'No, but we need Spencer now. Now, I tell you. Two lives are in danger.'

The woman at the door nodded and turned away swiftly. They waited, listening to the sounds of her footsteps receding and knocking on an inner door. A muted conversation, more footsteps and there appeared a man, receding grey hair swept to the side, which he was smoothing by the act of spitting in his palm and pressing it down hastily.

'Rose Jenkins,' he said. 'I can see in your face there's an emergency of some sort.'

'Indeed, Spencer. A woman and baby will die without you, sure as eggs is eggs. The Kings will pay, but these are poor folk. Will you come?'

'Anything for you, Rose,' said the doctor, turning to the woman who had answered the door to retrieve his physician's bag, coat and pearl-grey top hat.

'You have forceps?' said Jenkins.

'Yes, yes,' said the doctor.

Jenkins led the way, Fitzpatrick followed, glancing at Beatrice as he went down the steps, touching his hat briefly. She nodded and said, 'How do you do?'

'Charmed!' he said. 'And you are?'

'She's the Ashford girl, the King heir,' barked Jenkins as they went down the street.

'What on earth is she doing here?' he said.

'Enough of that and listen,' said Jenkins. They walked hurriedly together, Beatrice tagging along behind, trying to listen to everything, but missing the odd word or phrase here and there as they went. 'The baby is back to back . . . hours on end . . . Lunt has felt the bones in the skull . . . bad presentation . . . baby is stuck . . . mother in distress . . . Martha Jones, down at the Malones' cottage.'

Beatrice did not understand everything she was hearing, but it all sounded bad. They had rushed as quickly as they could, but she felt a sharp fear as they went along the riverside that it would be too late when they got there. Nobody was talking now, just striding forward, dodging obstacles, heads down. Three people on a mission to save two lives. This was not how Beatrice had imagined this day would turn out.

They came upon the cottage at last. As they approached, Beatrice watched with surprise as the doctor opened the door without a knock and walked straight in. Jenkins went after and though Beatrice felt nervous about entering without invitation, she followed Jenkins inside.

It was a one-storey house with one main room and one other off to the side. This room contained a large kitchen table and stove, a fireplace with chairs around it and in the corner a bed with a ragged rug beside it. Owen stood before the fireplace, staring at her, arms folded about himself, as if for comfort. His blonde hair stood up on end, clearly the victim of lack of sleep, and worried fingers trailing through it. Beatrice was about to go to him, say something to him, though she knew not what, when raised voices snatched her attention. The doctor had not yet reached the other room, where she could hear the mother-to-be moaning. A short, fat woman had appeared at its door, an apron and cap on. *That must be the midwife*, she thought. There were three other people by the kitchen table – Adam Jones sat slumped in a chair, looking as if the wind had been punched out of him. There was also another man and a woman, standing beside him. Those must be Owen's parents, the Malones. One of them was shouting.

'It's out of the question,' Owen's mother was saying. 'No doctors here.' Fitzgerald was trying to reason with her, but she was having none of it. 'There is no way on earth that people like us can afford you, sir. So please leave.'

Jenkins said, 'We've told you, Mrs Malone. We shall meet the doctor's bill.'

'Who, you? On a maid's pay?' she scoffed.

'Not me, the Kings will pay. Miss Beatrice here has assured it.'

All eyes turned on her. Beatrice saw Adam Jones, who looked at her blearily, a man who had clearly had no sleep, squinting at her, perhaps recognising her from that disastrous visit to his old cottage. But he seemed to have no strength to have an opinion on the subject. Next to him stood Owen's father, tall with thick, muscled arms, a kind face topped with fair hair, curious, looking her over with intelligent eyes. Then there was Mrs Malone, wavy red hair pulled back into a messy bun at her neck, scored through with a grey streak at her temple. She stared at Beatrice as she might at someone who had brought a dead rat into her house, disgusted and determined to get rid of the intruder.

Owen's mother spoke in a low guttural tone. 'We shall never take King money,' she said, spitting out the words as if they were a bitter herb in her mouth.

Jenkins said, 'Your husband and your son take King money every week.'

'Against my better judgment!' cried Mrs Malone.

Now Fitzgerald stepped forward. 'There is no time to be lost. Let me by to help this woman.'

Jenkins reached out and touched Mrs Malone's arm and said quietly, 'Please, Anny.'

Anny? Beatrice thought. She remembered that name. Her mother had had a friend called Anny when she was young. It had ended badly. Could this be the same one? It was a common enough name. And the woman must be about her mother's age. Surely it could not be. Could it?

Jenkins added, 'Let bygones be bygones, just this once.'

Anny Malone was still staring venomously at Beatrice, who felt acutely uncomfortable under her harsh scrutiny. Beatrice looked over at Owen, who was gazing at her too, but how different his expression was to his mother's. It was full of love and longing. She took strength from it. 'Please, Mrs Malone,' said Beatrice. 'Let us help Mrs Jones.'

'That's right,' said someone. It was Adam Jones, aroused from his stupor, standing up from his slump in the chair. 'It's my wife and my decision. I'll take it. I'll do anything for Martha. Go through, Doctor. Save my wife and child.'

'I shall do my best,' said Fitzgerald, walking onwards to the side room. 'Though we may be too late.'

The midwife said, 'Bleeding just started.'

Beatrice heard the doctor mutter, 'Oh Lord, the placenta, is it?'

The midwife went in first, followed by the doctor, who was backed up by Jenkins. Adam Jones turned and went in too, but was told forcefully to wait outside. The door was shut on him and he went back to his chair and resumed his collapsed position, staring into space.

Anny Malone turned away from them all and went over to the stove. She poured a jug of water into a kettle and placed it over the fire to boil.

'Miss King,' said Mr Malone, his face kindly yet embarrassed.

Beatrice said, softly, 'It's Miss Ashford, actually.' She hoped this would help the atmosphere. She wanted to reassure them that she was not actually a King, if that helped. 'My father was Jake Ashford, the artist.'

She heard Anny take a sharp intake of breath, then shake her head and stare pointedly at the ceiling. *What have I done now?* thought Beatrice, hopelessly.

'Would you like . . .?' Mr Malone began, then trailed off, looking about him, perhaps for something to offer her, though it seemed he could find nothing appropriate.

'I'm making tea,' snapped Anny Malone, but would not look around at anyone.

'Oh, the basket!' said Beatrice. 'We have a basket outside with a picnic in it, that we haven't yet consumed on our walk. Please, let us share it with you all.'

'We have no need of your vittles,' retorted Anny.

'But it would be my pleasure,' said Beatrice, looking at Mr Malone for support, who shifted awkwardly from foot to foot.

'I'll take Miss Ashford outside,' said a familiar voice to her right. It was Owen, whose hair seemed neater now. He must have smoothed it down when she wasn't looking. 'It is a warm day and there'll be a welcome breeze out there, I'm sure.'

Mr Malone nodded, then glanced round at his wife and frowned as she stood facing the wall. 'Good idea, son.'

A cry came from the other room and everyone froze. Owen moved forward and ushered Beatrice outside, shutting the front door behind him. They were alone at last, except they weren't alone at all. A little group of neighbours had gathered nearby, watching the house.

'Any news on Martha?' said one woman, a baby sleeping with its mouth open on her arm.

'Nothing yet,' said Owen.

'We be praying for 'er,' said the woman, now staring with unashamed interest at Beatrice.

'Thank'ee,' said Owen and nodded. He glanced at Beatrice and gestured towards the river. They walked across the yard and along the path a little. Beatrice could feel many eyes burning into their backs. The house was still in sight and there was an overturned log there, ready to sit on with a view of the river beyond. Though she was worried for Martha, it was still nice to be next to Owen. She sat down and Owen sat beside her. To be so close to him and yet to be unable to touch him was exquisite torture.

'We are being watched,' he said quietly.

'I'm well aware,' she answered.

'But they canna hear us here, if we speak softly.'

'Good,' she said.

She was afraid to look at him, but she could not resist. All this time she had longed to look upon him and she risked it. He was watching the river, sitting bolt upright, stiff and awkward. He glanced at her and his eyes softened, his head tipped back a little and shoulders slumped, as if the sight of her had instantly melted the ice in him. 'It is a wonder to see you,' he said, breathlessly.

'For me too,' she whispered. They smiled meekly at each other and inspected each other's faces, drinking it all in. She heard voices nearby and a couple of pipe-smoking men passed by, eyeing them with amused curiosity. Both she and Owen stiffened their stance again and looked forward at the river.

'Your mother doesn't like me,' she said.

'Dunna take it personally. She dunna like any of the Kings.'

'She seemed even more annoyed when I told her I was an Ashford.'

'Well, I dunna know why that should be. Listen, why did you come today? How did you manage it? I was that shocked to see you, I thought I was dreaming!'

She laughed.

'And who was that old battle-axe you were with?'

'Oh, she's no battle-axe. She's my great-grandmother's maid. She's rather wonderful, actually.'

'She seemed to know my mother. She called her Anny.'

'Yes, I noticed that. Owen, my mother said she had a friendship with someone called Anny when they were children. She said it went wrong somehow, but she wouldn't say any more about it. Was it your mother?'

'I dunna have a clue,' he said, shaking his head. 'I dunna know much about those days. All I know is that Mother was falsely accused by the Kings of stealing and sent to the gaol for a time, but she came out later. My nana and also Father nursed her back to health and they fell in love, married soon after. Also, my mother's father died at the King ironworks. Some say it was an accident, others say it was negligence. That's all I know. I know naught of friendship between the two families, only dislike. Only hatred, to be honest with you. And it inna very likely, is it? Best of friends, Miss King and Miss Woodvine? That's what her name was back then, before she met Father.'

'Well, we're not very likely either, are we? And yet, here we are. Side by side, on a log.'

They glanced at each other and laughed, breaking any vestige of awkwardness that remained.

'Why *did* you come, Bea?'

'I came to try to end the strike. I knew Adam Jones was staying with you and I hoped I could talk to him, try to come to terms. Queenie has told me she cannot budge an inch, that her hands are tied by an agreement with the other brickmasters. She said they'll have to close the brickworks on Monday if there is no resolution. I had hoped to persuade Mr Jones to call off the strike and get everybody to go back to work.'

'I see,' said Owen and looked back at the river thoughtfully. Despite being a little way from the cottage, a piercing cry came from it that they could hear clearly. They turned to look, as did everybody nearby, stopped in their tracks, then came a shaking of heads and going on about their business.

'I do hope that quack can help our Martha,' said Owen.

'I'm certain he will,' said Beatrice.

They sat silently for a while, listening to the flow and splash of the river beyond, watching the swallows dive down to it, hunting for bugs in the dense summer air. The afternoon was waning and evening was on its way. The door of the house opened and out came Mr Malone. He was carrying two cups and saucers, balanced on what looked like a wooden chopping board. Owen jumped up and ran over to him. Beatrice heard him say something about not having a tray. She stood up and walked over to meet them.

'Thank you,' she said, taking the cup and saucer gratefully. All her exertions had left her feeling parched.

'Where will you put it?' said Mr Malone, worried about etiquette of which he had no knowledge.

'I shall hold it and drink it. It won't last long, I assure you. I am quite in need of refreshment,' Beatrice said pleasantly. Mr Malone grinned at her and Owen took his tea, smiling approvingly, perhaps at the tea, or perhaps at her attempts to put his father at ease. 'Mr Malone, the basket down there, by the door – it is full of good things to eat. Please do share it amongst your family. It would be my honour to help at a time like this.'

'Thank'ee, miss,' he said, gently. 'You have helped us beyond measure already. But please, do eat your picnic yourself. You must be famished. The hour is getting on. I am wondering if Owen should be sent to fetch someone from your home to take you back there.'

'With all respect, I do not want to leave until I know the outcome.'

'Any news?' Owen said.

'Miss Jenkins just told Adam that the doctor is going to try delivering the baby with forceps. There was some bleeding. There is a lot of noise but no further news.'

Another cry came from the room, a screeching rasping kind of cry that was unearthly. Beatrice thought, *At least Martha is still alive. That is something.*

'Take Miss Ashford back to your seat and do have summat to eat. We shall call you when there is any news.'

But then, a call came from behind him. 'Mr Jones!' It was Jenkins's voice. Mr Malone turned quickly back into the room. Owen put his cup and saucer roughly down on the ground, the tea sloshing over the side and Beatrice did the same, then followed him inside. Jenkins was standing at the door to the other room, her bonnet off, her white hair half unpinned from its usual tight bun, greasy strands hanging limply down. Suddenly, a high-pitched shriek came from behind her, the unmistakeable sound of a newborn baby. 'It's a girl!'

Adam jumped up from his chair and said fearfully, 'Martha?'

Jenkins replied, 'She will be fine. She is weak now. She will need plenty of rest for many days. Lots of looking after. But the forceps did the trick and now the baby is out, Martha has a good chance of a full recovery.'

Adam whooped and clapped his hands, suddenly alive after looking like a half-dead man since the moment Beatrice had arrived.

Mr Malone clapped his hands too. 'Sebunctious tidings!' he cried.

Anny Malone had her hands over her face, tears streaming over her fingers. She shook her head with relief and sank down into a chair. Mr Malone went straight to her and crouched down beside her, putting an arm about her and whispering reassurance. Beatrice turned to Owen, who had tears in his beautiful eyes. Without a thought, they threw their arms about each other and hugged and hugged, the feel of his body so strong and warm and comforting, joy and relief coursing through them both. They were laughing and crying at the same time. When they finally released each other, they saw that everybody was looking at them, shocked. But too happy to let the break in decorum spoil the mood, the moment passed and Adam rushed in to see his wife and child. Beatrice remembered the basket and went outside to get it. She brought it over to the kitchen table and started unloading its goodies, tongue sandwiches, fresh tomatoes, chunks of cheese wrapped in wax paper, fruit scones and a punnet of raspberries.

'Please, everybody must help themselves,' she said.

She expected Anny Malone to complain, but she seemed too exhausted by the day's events to move, let alone speak.

'That is very kind of you, miss,' said Mr Malone, warmly. He patted Anny on the shoulder, who looked up briefly and nodded, the slightest of nods, but a definite acceptance of Beatrice's gift. 'It all looks delicious,' added Mr Malone, feasting his eyes.

'But I'd much rather have one of your fidget pies, Mrs Malone,' said Beatrice.

Anny raised her head at Beatrice, looking her in the eye for the first time. 'How on earth do you know about those?'

'Owen gave me a pie once. That's how we met.'

'You two . . .? You know each other?'

Owen looked a bit queasy but forced a crooked smile. 'I sold her a pie. Once.'

'Well, I tried to buy it, but you were so generous, you gave it to me. And then we became friends,' said Beatrice.

There was a heavy moment of silence as this fact landed in the midst of them all. But the spell was broken when in came Adam Jones, proudly carrying his newborn daughter wrapped in a chequered blanket. His eyes were dead tired, but his smile beamed.

'Here she is, the one that's caused all the mischief. Meet Hettie Jones.'

Every person in the room made a sound, a soft, breathy, marvelling sound reserved only for the arrival of tiny new things. Beatrice felt her eyes fill with unexpected tears. She blinked them away to look in awe at the baby, its little face screwed up with distaste at its new world, miniature fists curled by either cheek. Beatrice glanced at Owen, who was crying too. He looked at her and smiled, a laugh of relief and wonder catching in his throat, causing a tear to roll down his cheek as he gazed back at her, lovingly.

In her whole life, Beatrice had never felt such pure and utter bliss.

Chapter 14

The girl had gone now, thank heavens, gone off with the doctor and the old hag's maid. When Anny first saw the girl, she had the most awful shock. Those eyes. They were Jake Ashford's eyes. To see them again, after all these years. After staying up all night by Martha's side, then bleary with lack of sleep and wracked with worry, to see those eyes again, it nearly toppled her. The girl looked so much like Jake, it was hard to find any of her mother in her. But as Anny had looked more, in secret glimpses, she saw that she had Margaret King's mouth and chin. She had spent so many hours with Margaret when they were young – Peggy, as she called her then – she knew that face as well as her own. The eyes of Jake Ashford – she had gazed at them so much, she'd know them again anywhere. And then, when she was carted off to prison, she had dreamt of them often enough. Until she had heard of his betrayal with Peggy. The double betrayal was almost too much to bear, her best friend running off with the man she'd thought to marry and coming so soon after the death of her dear father. Her only consolation was that they had left the country and Anny wouldn't have to watch Peggy and Jake parading around Ironbridge, rubbing Anny's face in her own defeat. There was a stretch of sea between them and Anny had hoped that she would never have to lay eyes on them again.

But then gossip told her that Margaret was back, all these years later, with a daughter in tow, the artist Ashford's daughter. Rumour had it that Ashford had died of the pox, years back. A lucky escape for Anny, she had thought. But it was not so simple to recover from your first love. She had not seen Peggy and her girl about town, thankfully. She did not wish to. She did not trust herself not to walk over to Peggy and slap her across the face.

It sickened her to see that girl here, in her own home, proof positive of the betrayal of two of her most beloved people in the world, back then. And to discover that somehow, in some ridiculous twist of fate, the girl was already friends with her own dear son? But it looked like so much more than that. The way they'd thrown their arms about each other when the baby came. She had watched the two of them through the window when they sat on the thinking log by the river. She saw them talking, smiling and laughing. They were so easy together, as if they had spent a lot of time in each other's company. There was something rotten going on there.

After the unwelcome visitors had gone, Martha was sleeping. The baby was asleep too, after its first feed, wrapped up in a blanket and lodged in the top drawer of the bedroom dresser. Adam, Owen and Peter were sitting at the table, finishing off the last scraps of supper in a worried silence. Owen had just told them all the news the girl had brought, that the Kings were to shut the brickworks the day after tomorrow if the strike didn't end. Adam had been deep in thought ever since, staring at the tabletop.

Anny did not know what Adam would do about all that. It was a weighty matter to be sure, but more pressing to her at this moment was what on earth was going on between her son and that girl. She knew she should hold her tongue, that there were more vital things to deal with. But every time she looked at Owen, she wanted to scream. She stood now, watching him, wringing a cloth angrily about in her hands.

'I never thought I'd see the day when I was glad to see a King!' mused Peter.

'Me neither!' said Adam and shook his head. 'The girl brought terrible news about the strike. And heaven knows what I shall do about it. But thank God for 'em, too. As Martha and the littl'un would be dead now without 'em, I'm sure of that.'

Owen was nodding at this. 'Strange that they sent the girl to deliver such important news,' said Anny, staring at her son. He glanced up, saw her eye on him and looked away. Anny went on, 'Why would they do that, do you think?'

'I've met her before, the girl,' said Adam. 'She came with the old hag when they threw us out. Maybe they thought we'd be nicer to a girl.'

Owen was still not looking at her.

'And what were the two of you talking about all that time outside, eh, son?'

He still would not look at her. 'This and that. She couldna stay in here, with all that business going on in there. We passed the time of day.'

His nonchalant tone infuriated her. 'Don't you lie to me, lad. I'll put you across my knee! You aren't too old for it.'

'Now then, Anny,' started Adam, glancing sidelong at Owen. That look meant something, she was sure.

'And what do you know about it? Are you two in cahoots, or something?'

Owen said, 'The girl and me. We are acquainted, is all. I sold her a pie once, that's all.'

'Leave the boy alone,' said Adam. That was the last straw.

'Don't you tell me how to speak to my son, Adam Jones,' she snapped. 'Something is going on here and I want to know what. Owen, what is it between you and this girl, eh? Spit it out!'

Owen looked sick as a dog. But it was Adam who spoke again.

'Dunna torture the lad. I told him to do it. He's been on strike business.'

'What?' said Anny, exchanging a confused glance with her husband Peter, who obviously had no knowledge of any of this either.

Owen was staring at Adam now, who carried on, 'I told him to do it. Since the girl was sweet on him after this pie business, I told him he should cultivate it. Find out what he can from her. Ask her for information. He's been at it for weeks. He's been spying for us. So, now you know, all of yer. Now you know. She's fallen hook, line and sinker for him.'

Peter said, 'Is this true, lad?' His voice was flat and tired, tinged with disappointment.

Owen nodded but said nothing.

'So, leave him alone. He's a hero for the cause,' said Adam, standing up and pushing his chair back, striding over to the room where Martha rested, going in and shutting the door behind him, as if that put an end to it. A heavy silence hung in the air, thoughts racing, words forming.

'I'm going out,' said Owen, standing up and pushing his chair back, just the same way Adam had done it.

'No, you are not!' cried Anny.

Owen looked at her then. 'Yes, Mother. I am.' They'd had their little rows in the past, mother and son. But never had he looked at her with such defiance. Then, as she glared at him, his face softened. 'Dunna fret, both of yer. It inna a bad thing. We are friends, is all.'

'Didn't look like friends to me,' said Anny. 'All that hugging and longing looks. Adam said she'd fallen for you. Have you fallen for her?'

'No, of course not, Mother. I'm no fool. She is a means to an end, that is all. Try to have some faith in me, eh? I've been doing all I can to end this strike and if that meant I had to pretend to befriend a daft little rich girl, then I did it and gladly.'

Anny reached out and grasped at his shoulders. 'Don't lie to my face, son. You're in love with her. It's as plain as day.'

'For God's sake, leave me alone!' he shouted, stepping back roughly from her grip. She stumbled forward and his eyes switched to concern. He reached out to her, looking at her belly. But she backed off, crossing her arms and glaring at him. His eyes fell and he let out a long sigh.

Anny turned to her husband, who was not even watching, picking at the last morsels on the wooden board before him.

'And what do you make of all this, Peter Malone? Our son, whoring himself to the Kings for the good of the workers?'

Peter met her eye and said coldly, 'You told me once that anything was justified when it came to the strike. Why do you think I want no part of it? Now you see the results of that loyalty to . . . to *anarchy*. Everybody turns liar and cheat in the end. Nobody wins.'

His gaze fell again to the table and he went back to dabbing uselessly at the crumbs.

'Try not to take on so, Mother,' said Owen, fetching his cap. 'Dunna you think we've got bigger problems to worry about? I'm off down the tavern.'

'Owen,' she tried one last time. 'If you love that girl, if you love a King, why . . . it will kill me, son.'

'Enough of this now. Dunna get yourself in a terrible state. Think of the babby. We are friends, that is all. It's nothing for you to fret about. Anyway, with the threat of the yard closing, it'll all be over soon. Everything will.'

He left. Peter stood up too and started to clear away the feast. Seeing that girl place all that luxurious food on her own kitchen table had made Anny want to smash it all up with a brickbat. It was just like the girl's mother had done, all those years ago, at their second meeting in the forest, when Peggy had brought a picnic. She had devoured it then, noticing how Peggy ate little, but she herself was hungry, always hungry and had taken King food and loved it. That's what the Kings did, giving you things, winning you over with money and things and lies. It was all poison to her now. To think of the years wasted on that friendship, the long talks, the visits, the letters they hid in the fairy tree – the old lime tree with the hollow in its trunk.

The memory of it gave her an idea.

First, she'd need a snack. There were only plums in the bowl. No pies these days, as she could not afford the ingredients to make them, as nobody could afford to buy them. Two or three plums would have to do. Then, she needed paper and pencil. She found some in the drawer beside the bed. She wrote quickly, not as neat as her hand had been in younger days, when she had delighted in writing. She hardly ever wrote now, had no use for it any more. She wrote a note, with instructions on it. It was not a request. It was an order. She folded it up tightly.

Her husband was washing the dishes, an uncomfortable silence between them. Anny slipped outside. She saw a neighbour's child, a likely boy who was usually up for an errand with food as payment. She called him over and told him what she needed him to do and handed him the fruit, which he took with hungry eyes, licking his lips. It was evening now, but still light. It wouldn't take him too long to get up there and back. She said not to come and tell her anything afterwards, just to go home. She couldn't risk the others overhearing. She would crawl into bed beside Martha soon and try to sleep.

That night, the baby woke them up regularly, as babies do. Martha was still weak, so Anny fetched little Hettie. She cooed and shushed her for a moment, hoping she'd fall back into her infant dreaming. It was so good to hold a babe in her arms again, a small, warm package of life. Her own child was growing lustily inside her body and the excitement of that fact overcame her, after the fear she'd suffered these past hours when she thought Martha and the child would die. It terrified her to think of Peter and Owen, alone with her gone, or with a new baby to bring up without her. But all had turned out all right in the end, thanks to that blasted girl and the doctor her money had bought, but still. How Anny had longed for a daughter, all these years of trying and nothing to show for it but blood. Maybe she was carrying a girl now, who knew? She watched Hettie's dear face chronicle its babyish thoughts and fears, before her fists balled up again and she cried out for milk. Anny took her to Martha to feed. The men slept soundly in the next room, as she climbed into bed beside Martha and fell back into slumber, listening to the sound of Martha's voice humming a lullaby.

In her fits of restless sleep, Anny was visited by a dream Jake Ashford, young and dark-eyed, a gypsy air about him, as he always had. She told him in the dream, *You are dead and gone*. He gazed at her and said, in a ghostly whisper, *It is all dust and ashes without you*. In the morning, she found it difficult to look her husband Peter in the eye.

She dressed quickly and quietly, speaking to Peter in low tones so as not to wake the other sleepers in the house.

'I'm going for a walk in the woods to clear my head.'

'You should be resting, love,' he said, with a worried face.

'No, I need to stretch my legs and get a bit of peace. I'll be back soon.'

Owen and Adam were still fast asleep when she left. Adam had fretted till the early hours about what to do about the strike, but had come to no answer before he took to his bed. Owen had come home late, curled up in his place on the floor and slept like a log. Now he looked innocent as a babe, lying on his back with his mouth open.

Yesterday he had assured her they were just friends, him and the girl. But Anny would not be fooled so easily. She knew young love when she saw it. The very idea disgusted her. Fate was laughing at her, that was clear. Well, she had defied fate before and she would do it again. All this must be stopped. The boy must be told.

But she knew what children were like. The minute you tell them not to do something, they want to do it more than ever. If she shouted again at Owen, laid down the law with him, he would be more determined than ever to see the girl. That's how their minds worked, your children. You had to be cleverer than that, sneakier. You had to let them think they'd got away with things, sometimes. She had another notion in mind. She would seek out support for her plan, from the unlikeliest of quarters.

She made her way slowly to the fairy tree, enjoying the peace and freedom of a woodland walk, away from home, its responsibility and strain, its surplus of people, bursting the seams of their tiny home. Five adults and now a new baby was enough to tear at anyone's nerves. She liked Martha and Adam, and had offered herself to have them when that forsaken bastard Cyril had evicted them.

But now, to discover that Adam had led her son astray, into this nasty business, left a bad taste in her mouth. Using Owen like that, making him fool a girl into loving him, even a King. It didn't sit right with her. Anny had always got on well with Adam and could see that he and her son were thick as thieves, which she'd supported, as Owen was showing his full commitment to the cause. Peter had disappointed them all, with his lack of support for the strike. He had gone along with the union rules, but would not take part in any of the protests, preferring to stay at home and garden or clean than stand at the barricade and harry the scabs. But his defiance of these expectations was carried out so quietly yet firmly, that she couldn't help but admire his resolve. He had always made it clear to her that the strike was not in their interests and he would take no part in it, beyond stopping work as his comrades had done. And as things were turning out, Peter had been right, hadn't he? The strike dragged on, the masters wouldn't budge and along the river children were growing thinner by the day. The whole thing had turned sour and hopeless. It was always thus, the masters stamping on the workers, like earwigs.

She'd said that to Jake Ashford twenty years or so ago. And it was still true.

As she walked, she recalled the route she used to take every day from her parents' old house up the hill through the trees to the office where she had worked for Mr Brotherton, the Kings' estate manager. Proud and happy she'd been, taking that joyous walk each day. Cyril King, with his wiles and his threats and his disgusting designs on her had ruined it, then shattered her life with his tricks and his lies. She saw him sometimes these days, loafing about town, going into the taverns for daytime drinking. He was so wrapped up in his own selfishness, he never noticed her, a downtrodden, tired, middle-aged woman, her once fiery red hair he had so admired now faded to a russet brown lined with grey. He never noticed the woman whose life he nearly destroyed; the woman whose father was struck down in his prime by the furnace explosion that took him and other good men; the woman whose mother died soon after in penury, despite Anny's attempts to save her from the fever that took her one hot summer night. The Kings had paid each family recompense eventually, but too late for her. The money came two days after her mother died, when who knows, perhaps it could have been used to pay a doctor to save her – but it was too late.

These painful, bitter memories swirled about her head like midges in the summer heat. At least here, beneath the swaying trees, it was cooler and it was quiet. She took comfort from the swish of branches, the soft rattle of leaves, the calls of birds above and the endless flow of the river beyond. She was so weary, she considered sitting down right here and now and sleeping on the forest floor. But there was business to be done.

She steeled herself for the meeting she had arranged. She expected to get there first, as rich people always had a leisured attitude towards time, being able to buy it so easily. But as the spot where the lime tree stood came into view, Anny looked ahead to see a woman in fine clothes standing beside it, her back to her, a fashionable bonnet covering her hair and face. Anny knew that willowy, fine figure anywhere. It turned about to look at her. It was Margaret King, all grown up and middle-aged, like her. It was Peggy.

'Hello Anny,' she said, quite softly. There was no hatred in those eyes, just a kind of weary acceptance that, somehow, this meeting was inevitable.

'This is not a social call,' said Anny. 'I do not want to be here at all. And for the life of me, I cannot fathom why our lives seem to be so knotted together. However much I want to escape from the grip of the Kings, I always seem caught by you people, like a fly in your web.'

Margaret seemed at a loss for words. They stared at each other, both taking in the sight of their old friend. She said simply, 'How are you, Anny? I see . . . you are expecting?'

Margaret nodded towards Anny's bump, quite large and obvious these days. But Anny would not be swayed into an exchange of small talk. 'Like I said, this is not social. I have no interest in you or your kin. But something has come to my attention and it needs sorting. Your daughter and my son.'

'You have a son? How lovely. Wait . . . my daughter?'

This lack of knowledge of her family was either a prideful lie or typical of the Kings' ignorance of anyone beyond their narrow circle. 'Yes, I have a son. Owen. And he is sweet on your daughter. And she is sweet on him.' She certainly had no intention of telling Margaret the whole truth, about the subterfuge and the spying. But she did not want her son to be wrapped up in any of this anymore. And despite what Adam and Owen claimed, she knew what she had seen with her own eyes. Their children were deeply in love with each other.

Margaret frowned, uncomprehending. 'But how can this be? How can they have met?'

'Something to do with pies. But that's not important. The fact is they were at my house together yesterday, with Jenkins. They brought a doctor to help our friend have her baby. All much appreciated, I'm sure.'

'Jenkins? Yesterday?'

Had Margaret lost her reason in the past decades? She looked dazed, as if she'd bashed her head. 'Oh, do keep up!' Anny snapped.

'But they were going on a nature walk, Beatrice and Jenkins. They came home late, as they lost track of time.'

'Well, the girl's been lying to you. For quite a time, I reckon. I watched them yesterday, your lass and my lad. This was no chance meeting. They've been close for quite a while, I'd say. They were all over each other, as much as prudence would allow. I know first love when I see it. And they've got it, all right. They've got it bad.'

Margaret's thoughts flitted across her face. Anny guessed she was analysing many things that had been said to her, now putting a whole new slant on all of them.

'You have certainly surprised me, Anny. I thought I was here to talk about the strike.'

'Why would I want to talk with you about that? You are in no position to affect a thing.'

'I have the ear of my grandmother,' she retorted, some conceit in her voice. 'If there were a message you wanted me to relay, from the workers, I would be happy to deliver it. It's a nasty business, this strike.'

'I have nothing to do with any of that. I employ myself and run my own businesses. But while your family eats meals of many courses in your fine dining room, there are children hereabouts who are starving for want of a few pennies. A strike is the only way people like you would listen.'

Margaret glared at Anny, who raised her chin in defiance. Anny was finding this whole encounter increasingly satisfying. She heard her voice quavering, aware that there was twenty years' worth of resentment building up behind the wall of her self-control, ready to flood at the slightest provocation. But that was not her business today and she must get back to that.

'Listen, I could rail at you all day for the crimes your family have committed. A whole week of it would not be enough to list it all. But that is not why I have come. We must stop this foolishness between our children. I am certain you are as disgusted at the idea as me.'

'Nothing good could come of such a liaison,' said Margaret, imperiously, looking and sounding more like her grandmother than ever. Gone was the sweetness of her youth. Anny saw only a tired, aging woman, who had fallen back into her old ways of luxury.

'I ask for your help to end it, now. Speak to your daughter and warn her off. I will do the same with Owen. Lie to her, if you must.'

'I think there have been enough secrets and lies, don't you? I shall be telling her some choice facts. She knows nothing of our pasts, of what really happened. Does Owen?'

Anny wanted to scream that it was none of her damned business what her son did or did not know. Even hearing a King mention her son's name made her want to vomit. But, inwardly, she had to admit that it was time to tell the true story of their past. Only the truth could make them understand. Margaret was right about that, but she wasn't going to give a King the satisfaction.

'Tell her whatever you deem fit. This cannot be allowed to continue. Are we in agreement?'

Margaret nodded firmly. Anny had made her point. There was nothing left to say. She turned to walk away, her legs weak, her hands trembling. It must be because of her lack of sleep the last two nights. Yes, that was it.

'Anny? About Jake . . .'

Anny stopped dead and turned back. Her face must have looked like thunder, for at the sight of it Margaret flinched. 'I do not wish to speak to you about that, not now or ever.' Her voice shook with emotion. This would be the crack in the dam through which the torrent would soon come.

'He turned out badly. I left him.'

'I said speak no more!' shouted Anny, her rage boiling over now. She dug her fingers into her palms to stop herself marching over to this damned woman and strangling her.

'He died of syphilis.'

So the rumours were true. But to hear her speak of that man was more than Anny could bear. 'I am glad of it. You both received your just desserts.'

'I know you hate me. You have that right. Except there is much of which you are wholly ignorant. Did you know it was I who saved you from prison? Yes, that's right. I approached my grandmother and father with the help of our maid Lucy. Remember her? She saw Cyril commit his crime against you, placing that money in your bag. She and I joined forces to blackmail my father into dropping the charges against you. She was too afraid to speak alone, but I persuaded her. Without me, you'd still be rotting in that cell.'

Anny's head felt light and the ground seemed to swell beneath her. What was this? Margaret had saved her?

'I knew nothing of that,' she muttered.

'Well, now you know.'

'I suppose I must thank you for that, at least,' said Anny, though it was hard to say.

'You are welcome. But that is not all. There is more you need to hear. The truth is we were both led in a merry dance by Jake Ashford, you and I. He was lying to us both. He was a drunk, violent liar. Yes, I ran away with him, seeming to have taken the grand prize from you. But it was a poisoned chalice and he led me a sorry life, before I left him, fat with child as you are now. I went out onto the streets of Paris alone and never saw him again. I had to make a life for myself and my daughter, with no man to love and protect us and none of the King money to keep us safe. And I did it, through sheer hard work and determination. You are the one who found a good man, by all accounts. You have a home, a son and another child on the way. The truth is I envy you all of that. If it were ever a competition between us, be assured that you won. You won, Anny.'

Anny stared at Margaret. She had given this woman such a high pedestal of hate for so many years, she had loomed large in her imagination as a mighty villain. But now, these revelations and the sight of her standing there, looking far older than her years, diminished her old foe into something far smaller and more human. But it was not so easy to erase years of loathing in only a moment.

'You still took him from me. Worse, you left me. When I needed you most.' Anny's eyes were filling with tears and she cursed her weakness. She must not cry in front of Margaret King.

'He was a liar and a womaniser,' said Margaret softly. 'And he hit me. It was a lucky escape for you. Think of all you have now. And be satisfied.' And with that Margaret turned and began the walk back up the hill

For a moment Anny stood frozen in place, then overcome with emotion she sank to the forest floor and the tears came flooding out. She sobbed, rubbing her quivering hands over the mound of her belly to soothe herself.

'Shh,' she told herself, as if pacifying the babe inside her, not herself. 'Dunna fret.'

She stayed seated, sniffling and rubbing her eyes till she saw stars. She felt like a mad woman, grovelling on the ground like this. She thought she had pushed all of this deep down, the misery, the envy, the anger at Margaret King. Now it was bubbling up again violently, threatening to overcome her. And it was mixed with confusion, that her dearest friend Peggy had helped her, had released her from hell. It had been hard to carry hate for all those years, but somehow it seemed harder now to release it. She felt as if her mind would capsize and her body would be dashed against the rocks. But no, she would not allow that to happen. Everyone needed her. She was the iron backbone of her family. Everyone relied on her to be strong. When your sleep was stolen, this is what happened. She remembered it now from when Owen was a baby. You felt as if you were losing your mind. She was just tired, that was all. There would be no rest at home, not with the house full of needy folk. Anny pushed herself up from the ground and staggered over to a broad tree, which she leant against with one hand. She slid down and sat beneath it, her back up against its trunk, one arm cradling her bump, the other resting on the forest floor. It was comfortable there. *Just for a moment*, she thought. *Just a little rest*. She closed her eyes and listened to the lulling whisper of the woodland.

Chapter 15

When Margaret had left her daughter that morning, she had been playing cards again with Queenie. This was something Margaret had done regularly with her grandmother years ago, yet there the resemblance ended. When she had played Old Maid with Queenie, they had largely sat in companionable silence, their thoughts wandering and their interest directed at the game itself, which both of them had loved. But watching Beatrice play with Queenie was utterly different; they chattered and gossiped all the time, making each other giggle like schoolgirls. Margaret hated to admit it to herself, but she was envious of her daughter, jealous of the intimacy she had established with Queenie so quickly. Beatrice found it easy to make friends with anyone. It was something of which Margaret had always felt proud. She loved the way that people loved her daughter so easily and Beatrice loved them back, giving her love away like surplus bonbons to all and sundry. Yet she always felt that Beatrice's truest love had been reserved alone for her, her mother. It was her privilege and her joy to have this person who adored her above all others. But since returning to Ironbridge, Margaret felt she was losing that special position. Beatrice was withdrawing from her, in subtle ways, she had thought. Until now, until this revelation from Anny. Now she knew that there was nothing subtle about it. Beatrice had given her heart away to someone else. And not just anyone. Anny Woodvine's son.

During the walk back from the fairy tree, she'd considered her feelings at seeing Anny again. She was still beautiful, her hair darker now but just as glorious. Her crowning glory, she'd told Anny once. How she had been jealous of Anny's red hair, often feeling her blonde locks were too similar to Cyril's to be attractive. She was shocked to see Anny's pregnancy, telling herself how fortunate she herself was not to be married and having another child at their age. But if truth be known, when she'd seen Anny's bump, a shiver of envy had taken her.

Yet as she approached Southover from the woods, saw it loom above her and thought of the life of ease it now afforded her, she felt a spurt of happiness at it. One could blame oneself forever for the woes of others. But she had paid for it, twenty years of working alone, raising her daughter alone. Anny might be angry with her still, but Margaret knew she had more than paid her dues in her life. Now it was her turn to be happy. First, she must ensure her daughter did not throw away her life for nothing. She did not want Beatrice to make the same mistakes she had made, all those years ago, forsaking everything for first love. Knowing Anny, she was sure that her son would be a fine young man. But the idea that Beatrice might be with such a man, of his sort . . . that was ridiculous. And it must be quashed. Of that, she and Anny were in perfect agreement.

On entering the house, she heard no talking emanating from the drawing room, so went upstairs to Beatrice's room. Before knocking on the door, she heard chattering from inside there instead. She opened the door. Sitting on her bed was Beatrice, whilst beside her sat her maid, Dinah. Heaven knew what they were talking about. They both whipped round at the sight of her. Dinah scrambled up from the bed and rushed behind Margaret to the open door, a quick nod of the head, then out onto the landing, disappearing down the servants' staircase at great speed.

'You frightened her!' cried Beatrice, mock-alarm on her face, but still laughing.

Margaret closed the door and sat down beside her daughter, who immediately gathered something was up and composed herself.

'*Chérie*, you know how much I love you.'

'Yes, Maman, of course!' said Beatrice and hugged her. Margaret took the hug stiffly. She would not be put off.

'And everything I do and say is for your own good.'

Beatrice's eyes were now wary. The knowledge that her daughter had been lying to her, for months, made Margaret falter.

'What is it? You look sad.'

'I am saddened, I'll be honest with you. I have discovered something today. I know that you have been keeping something from me and it saddens me that you did not feel able to share the truth with me. I thought we were the best of friends.'

'Oh, we are! We are!' she cried and went to hug her mother again, who gently pushed her back this time, much to Beatrice's surprise.

'I know about Owen.'

Beatrice's face fell. She looked away sharply, showing her mother the back of her head. Margaret had dealt with tantrums before with her daughter, arguments that so often were like summer storms that passed by quickly, followed by the sun coming out again. They had been a team and never had a serious disagreement about anything. She supposed there had to come a time when Beatrice would begin to draw away from her and make her own life. She thought back to herself at Beatrice's age. If she shouted at Beatrice, she would receive only resistance. She had to be shrewder than that, if she wished to win her over.

'Tell me about him.'

Beatrice turned back to her, clearly surprised. She had tears in her eyes, which gripped Margaret's heart. But she had to stay strong.

'Maman, he is a good, kind person. He is intelligent and thoughtful. And full of . . . I don't know how to explain it. He is full of love! It brims over in him!'

Her eyes were shining now. *She's head over heels*, thought Margaret. This was going to be more difficult than she'd imagined.

'How did you meet? How did all this come about?'

'He gave me a pie, one of his mother's. He was selling them at Madame's house. We started talking. And we got on so well, as if we'd known each other forever! Quite extraordinary really.'

'*Chérie*, why didn't you tell me about him?'

Beatrice looked down at her hands. 'Because . . . you wouldn't understand.'

'Is that the only reason? Remember I eloped with your father. You know that. I think you knew I would understand that part of it, about falling in love.'

'That is true . . .' said Beatrice, biting her lip.

'So, what was the real reason you didn't tell me?'

'I . . . because of . . . well, I didn't think you'd approve of him. Because of his . . . class.'

'He is a brickmaker. The enemy, as far as your great-grandmother is concerned.'

'Yes,' she said, perking up. 'But the strike and all that didn't come about till later. And we were friends by then, close friends. We didn't . . . fall in love till after that. And then, it all seemed hopeless. And it's been terrible ever since. We haven't been able to see each other or talk or anything. And I have missed him so much. We have both missed each other. It's been like torture. And I know we are from different sides, from different classes, from different . . . everything. But love, love does not choose sides. Love is all that matters in the world, isn't it, Maman? Love conquers all!'

Beatrice's eyes were glistening with emotion and usually Margaret would take her in her arms to comfort her. But not yet.

'And I know another phrase about love. Love is blind. You are blinded by your desire for this boy. There are many truths that you are unwilling to see. It goes beyond your class, your stations in life, beyond even the brickworks and the strike. Firstly, there is the matter of money.'

'But we have plenty now!' cried Beatrice, cheerfully.

'No, we do not. I have virtually nothing. The comforts we enjoy here are courtesy of your great-grandmother. But Queenie will never endorse this relationship with this boy.'

'Then, we will go back to France. The three of us. Things are much easier there, much more understanding of love and freedom, surely.'

'I cannot afford to take us back to France! I have not a penny to pay for it and not the energy to earn it when we get there.'

'Then Queenie will help us. She adores me!'

'It is true that Queenie is fonder of you than anyone I've known, excepting Jenkins perhaps. But there is no way on earth she will ever consent to paying for us to leave her, to go back to France and fund our lives there, just so you can be with a brickmaker's son. Could you really imagine that would happen?'

'She'd do anything for me.'

'Oh child, not this! We are here in England to stay. We must make the best of this and do what Queenie wants, which is also what I want for you, too. That is, that you should make a good marriage and eventually, take over the family business with your husband. That is what we have planned and what you must do. That is how we will secure your future.'

Beatrice stared at her, her lips turned down, her cheeks reddening, as if her face had just been slapped.

'But I don't want any of that. And money doesn't matter to me.'

'Money isn't everything, but it keeps a roof over your head, your belly full. You are young and naïve. You don't understand what it is like to worry about money every moment of your life and compare it with this life, which is safe and secure.'

'But I do understand that perfectly. I lived alongside you all those years in France, watching you count every *sou*. I do know the difference. And I am prepared to give that up for Owen.'

Margaret could not contain her 'wise mother' tone any longer and heard herself raise her voice with frustration, before she could stop it. 'You'd live with a brickworker, in a filthy hovel?'

Beatrice looked narrowly at her then and stood up, walked to the window, her resolute back to her mother. Margaret regretted raising her voice but it was necessary. Beatrice had always been precocious in her speech, learning to talk early and easily. And this quality caused her mother to forget sometimes how very young and naïve she really was.

Beatrice's voice was small when she said, 'I had not thought much on how we would live. But I did have a little cottage in the forest in mind. With roses about the windows. And perhaps a goat to milk and make cheese.'

It was worse than she thought, this ridiculous vision of woodland harmony, like something from a fairy tale.

'That is not how it would be. Brickworkers earn a pittance!'

Beatrice turned angrily to her mother then and said, 'And whose fault is that?'

'Not mine, I assure you! *Chérie*, you must see that the very idea of you, Beatrice Ashford, heir to the King fortune, living with a brickmaker, is madness. It will never happen.'

'Only because of people like you, and Great-grandmother, who cannot see beyond your own prejudice. And imagine yourself superior to everyone who has not money and position.'

'That is not true. You and I lived on meagre earnings and amongst very mixed society in Paris, all of your life till now. I gave up this comfortable existence for love. This is not about snobbery, not on my part. This is about reality, the world in which we live.'

'I don't care for a world that does not accept our love. We shall make our own way!' cried Beatrice, her fist clenched with determination. Margaret could see the fire in her eyes and knew that no amount of reasoning would dim it. In fact, she understood Beatrice's resolve only too well. She remembered her own passion for Jake and how nothing could sway it. If her daughter loved this boy even half as much as she herself had loved Jake Ashford, then she pitied Bea with all of her heart. But gone was the time for sympathy. Now was the time for some harsh medicine.

'Beatrice, please sit down beside me.'

'I will not sit down!'

'Please, *chérie*. I have some truths to tell you, things you know nothing about. They will not be easy for you to hear. But hear them you must.'

Beatrice looked concerned, her resolve deflating a little. Then she sat herself on the end of her bed, her arms folded, her face turned away from her mother.

Margaret began, 'I will tell you what you know: your father and I eloped from Ironbridge. We were madly in love. We came to Paris to make a life for ourselves. But there is something you do not know. Something

I shielded you from, to protect you. Please, let me explain. Listen to the whole story and hopefully then you will understand why I did what I did. When I met your father, I had a best friend. Her name was Anny Woodvine.'

Beatrice turned to look at her. 'Woodvine? Anny Woodvine?'

'Yes, that was her name then. She has since married.'

'And her name is now Malone!' said Beatrice. 'I knew it!'

This wrongfooted Margaret. Had she discovered it from Owen? Or Queenie even? 'Yes, but how . . . ?'

'Owen told me what happened to his mother, that she was accused of theft and was in prison for a time. You said about a friend called Anny. I wondered if it could be her, but Owen said he couldn't imagine it, that the Kings and the Woodvines hated each other.'

'I see. Well, there is much more to it than that.'

'Tell me.'

'Anny was my best friend for many years. We kept it a secret at first, as we knew nobody would approve. But then we both met Jake Ashford, your father. Anny and I both fell in love with him. We were rivals then, though I hated the thought of it. I was torn between my best friend and the man I loved. But it was more complex even than that. Uncle Cyril was in love with Anny. He wanted to marry her. But she hated him. We all did then. He wanted to force her to love him. After she rejected him, he framed her for theft. She was sent to prison and later released when I persuaded Queenie and my father to drop the charges.'

'Was she not grateful to you? You saved her! Were you not reconciled?' Margaret could see Beatrice's mind working, that if there was reconciliation between the families, perhaps all was not lost.

'No, we were never reconciled. Because I left with Jake, and Anny had loved him. What I did not know was that he had played us both, that he had made her fall in love with him too, to make me jealous. That he was only after my fortune and when I refused to go back to Ironbridge for him to claim it, he beat me.'

Beatrice was frowning now, pulling back slightly from her mother, as Margaret leant forward to drive home the point of her story. Her voice had changed, as her old bitterness from the past was seeping into her throat.

'*Chérie*, this next part of the story will be very hard for you to hear. But now is the time to tell you and you must hear it. Your father beat me and told me he had never loved me. He drank all the time and he had . . . been with other women. He had not only romanced Anny, but had been with others. He told me all this the night before I left him, with you in my belly. I knew it was not safe to raise you with such a man. I packed my things and left, never to see him again. I never heard from him. A friend heard of his death, around four years later.'

Beatrice was slowly shaking her head, a look of disgust on her face. 'Why would you tell me such lies?'

'They are not lies. The story I told you as a child of your father and me, that was the lie. I told it to you to protect you. You were too young to understand it. And I did not want you to grow up hating the memory of your father or thinking that all men were like this. I wanted you to grow up with sweetness and light and beauty and love. I wanted you to feel that the world was full of possibility, not ruined by betrayal.'

'You lied to me, for years, all my life,' said Beatrice, her voice a dry whisper.

'I did. But I have explained my reasons why and I stand by them.'

'My father was alive, until I was four years old. He was alive when I was a child. I could have met him.'

'I know, *chérie*. I know. It's a hard fact to comprehend. But I was protecting you from him. If he could treat me so badly, I was determined he would not do the same to his child.'

'But it should have been my choice, not yours, if I wanted to know my father. It should have been his choice, not yours, if he wanted to know his child.'

'It sounds so simple, when you put it like that. But you were an infant and I had to protect you. As for him, he had lost all rights to you when he beat me and betrayed me. I protected you from all this so that you could grow up surrounded by love and light, not bitterness or regret.

I tell you now so that you will not make the same mistake I did.'

Beatrice's eyes were filling with tears now. She turned her head quickly to her mother and a fat tear sprang from her cheek and landed on Margaret's hand. 'You are saying that I was a mistake?'

'No! Never, *chérie*!' Margaret reached out and grasped Beatrice's hand and kissed it. 'You are the one good thing I have done in my life. No, my mistake was to rush blindly into love, to believe that love justified anything, that love would conquer all. That was my greatest blunder. It was proven cruelly wrong, in every way it could be. And I cannot allow you – my darling, my heart and soul, my life! – to commit the same foolish error.'

Beatrice wrenched her hand away and sat slumped, staring at the floor.

'Owen is not like that. He is not like . . . Jake Ashford.'

Margaret's heart broke, as she heard her daughter call him by his name, instead of her own name for him, Papa. She was beginning already to come to terms with the loss of the father she thought she'd had, to the man she now knew he really was. *Should I have told her? Should I have perpetuated the fantasy?* Margaret agonised. *But she had to understand. I am only being cruel to be kind.*

Margaret put her hand on Beatrice's shoulder, who flinched at her touch. '*Chérie*, he may not be. If he is like his mother, he may well be a good person, through and through. He may never have told you a single lie. But consider too that he has far more to gain than you in this relationship. You are a prize, a rich heiress, the daughter of the house of his enemies, not only the enemy of his family but of all his confederates at the brickworks. His intentions may not be . . . honourable. He may have told you all sorts of lies to make you love him.'

'He does not lie. I would know if he had,' Beatrice said breathily.

'It is very easy to be lied to and believe it, when one wants to believe it.'

'Yes, it surely is,' she said sarcastically and shot a look of loathing at her mother.

It was like an arrow to her heart. Her daughter had never looked at her so coldly. Margaret swallowed her feelings and continued, 'But whatever Owen's motives, surely you can see now, that it is impossible. There is too much water under the bridge between the Kings and the Woodvines. We are enemies and always will be. Nothing you can say or do will ever change that. And if you defy it, and run away together, one day you will find that you have thrown away your life for a man you barely know. And heaven help you then, for all will be lost.'

Beatrice put her hands over her face and cried into them. Margaret took her daughter in her arms and held her as she sobbed. 'My darling, *ma petite chérie*. I am so sorry. So sorry.'

She let her cry it out for a while, holding her throughout. Then Beatrice pulled away, wiping her face with a handkerchief her mother had given her. She blew her nose noisily and passed it back.

'Thank you, Maman,' Beatrice said quietly, staring at her shoes. Then she turned, smiled stiffly at her mother and said, 'Thank you for telling me the truth. I can see now that you are right, about everything.'

Margaret smiled back at her daughter, but the turnaround seemed too quick, the consent too ready. 'It is a lot to digest. It will take time for you to comprehend it all.'

'I don't need to think about it. I have learnt my lesson. I will stop seeing Owen Malone.'

Still, there was that stiff smile on her daughter's tear-stained face. *If only I could read her mind*, she thought, and not for the first time.

Chapter 16

'Your mother's been gone for hours,' said Peter, coming into the house from the garden, where he had been working on their patch of land.

'Maybe she went to chapel,' said Owen, sitting despondently at the table, feeling lazy and moody that sultry afternoon.

'Even so, it's a long time past that now. Will you go into the woods and shout for her? Have a look around for her? I've got chores around here to finish.'

'All right,' said Owen, but felt his father was fussing a bit. Mother could look after herself. His father must have seen his reluctance, as he added, 'She's in a delicate condition. Better to be safe than sorry.'

What an idiot he'd been to forget that for a moment. 'Course, yes. I'll go. I'll find her, dunna fret.'

As he left the house, Adam appeared, approaching from the path to town. He had been to talk with some other strikers about the latest news, that the Kings would close the yard tomorrow if the strike did not end. He'd asked Owen to go with him but Owen had said no, for once. He'd said he was tired. The truth was his mind was filled with confusion and he could not face a long conversation with Adam that morning about the strike or about anything really, especially not about Beatrice. Owen nodded at him and called out, 'Going to look for Mother.'

Adam nodded back, his face clouding with some concern.

Owen hurried off. He took the path worn by years of working people's feet taking their shortcut through the trees. Where had his mother gone for all this time? Perhaps it was just thinking time she wanted. Was it planning time? Or had she been to see someone about . . . things? She had the ability to read his mind from his face. She guessed about him and Beatrice at first glance; he saw it in that first look she gave him, when the girl had come in and smiled right at him.

He continued on, mulling over his thoughts. He raised his head and immediately saw something that shocked him so much he stopped walking and stood motionless. There, beneath a tree, was a figure. It was a woman hunched over, her lower back against the trunk. It was his mother. He broke into a clumsy run and sprinted up to her. He stopped dead for a moment, staring down at her form in shock. Was she breathing? He fell to his knees and said, 'Mother! Mother!' and stroked her hair.

A small groan came from her and he felt faint with gratitude.

'Mother? Are you well?'

A longer groan came and she started to uncurl like a fern frond, stretching out her arms. He looked at her dress for any sign of injury or blood. But there was none. She opened up her eyes blearily and looked about, startled. Then she focused on him.

'Oh, my son!' she said and smiled. 'Oh, I must've fallen asleep here.'

'Oh, Mother! We didna know where you'd be. You've been gone hours. Why are you sleeping here?'

'Hours, is it? Well, I must've needed the rest. Things lately . . . well, you know, they've been so busy at home. No rest, no peace. It's been taxing to say the least.'

'It has indeed. I'm just so glad to see you are all right and all is well,' he said, nodding at her bump. She smiled at it and ran a hand over it.

'Yes, all is well. Here, son, help me up. We shall take a leisurely stroll home and I shall rest on your arm like you were a proper gentleman.'

He did as she asked. It was good to feel her lean on him. She worked so hard and had always been his support. It felt right that he should be the one to do the same for her now. The shock of seeing her on the ground like that and fearing the worst had brought a tear to his eye, reminding him how much he loved and needed her. And with a pang, how much he regretted keeping the truth from her. He would not hide from her any longer. He owed her that and much more.

'Mother, can I speak to you about summat, in confidence?'

'Course you can, son. About any old thing. You know that.'

'It's about Beatrice Ashford,' he said and glanced round to gauge her reaction.

'I thought it might be,' she replied with a rueful smile. He took courage from that. At least it was not anger. 'I could see you two were singing out of the same book. A mother knows these things.'

'It started as we said, with her wanting a pie. Then Adam said it was useful and I should cultivate it. I did so and would report back to Adam anything I'd learnt. But then I . . . I started to . . .' Here he hesitated, not knowing how to frame it, how to explain such emotions to his mother, when he could barely articulate them to himself.

'Tell me how she made you feel,' she said, reading his mind, as ever.

He thought for a moment, picturing her standing before the old brickmaster's house, a shaft of sunlight beaming down on her through a gap in the treetops. 'Like the bright centre of the world,' he said. 'I knew she felt it too. We knew it was madness. But we couldna help ourselves. We . . . we have fallen in love. Completely and totally in love.'

They walked in silence for a time, listening to the sounds of the woodland around them and the dull crunch of their steps on the leaf litter underfoot.

‘What are your plans for this girl?’ she said.

He frowned and his head ached again. The thought of her had acted as a momentary painkiller, but the troubles ahead brought the soreness back with a thump. ‘We anna thought that far ahead. I suppose we’ve been living moment to moment, if you know what I mean, Mother.’

‘I do know exactly what you mean,’ she said and sighed. ‘As hard as it is to believe, I was once a young girl in love.’ He imagined his parents as young folk and smiled at the thought of them courting.

‘Owen, I have some tales to tell you now and you must listen well. It concerns our past, all of us. Me, your father, your girl and her mother. When you’ve heard it, you will see that whatever future you have half imagined for you and this girl . . . well, suffice to say, son, you will feel differently than you do at this moment. I am sorry for it, but it must be done.’

He expected a tale of woe about the prison, the Kings and their dastardly ways. He prepared himself to give a speech in defence of letting bygones be bygones, of mending the old feud. He would explain that the strike would come to an end soon and Beatrice had done all she could to help their side, that she was the bright future of the Kings and one day, who knew, perhaps society would accept their love and they would forge a new path together. But nothing had prepared him for what his mother was about to say. She stopped walking and looked away from him, staring down the incline they walked beside, down into the edges of the river, which lapped languidly against its banks.

'My first love was Beatrice's father, the artist Jake Ashford. He promised himself to me, said I should wait for him until he had made his fortune. I loved him with all of my heart, with my very soul. I imagined a great future for us, him painting his great scenes of industry, me a clerical worker in a fine office in Shrewsbury, maybe a lawyer's office or something illustrious like that. My future stretched before me like a shining path, just waiting for me to take my first step on it, arm in arm with Jake. But Cyril King had his eye on me, wanted me for himself. He found out about Jake and was madly jealous. He attacked me here, in these woods, trying to force himself upon me. He wanted to marry me and I rejected him most forcefully. I told him I'd rather die. He took me at my word. In revenge, he made it seem I had stolen money and I was sent to prison, as you know. Margaret King, Beatrice's mother, was my best friend. We had been secret friends for years. She came to the prison and swore she'd help me. The next time I saw her there, she told me my father was dead in an accident. But I knew he was killed by Ralph King cutting corners with the safety at the furnace to save money. My father was the dearest man in all the world to me. His death nearly ended me.'

His mother's head drooped forwards and she covered her face with her hands. He took a step towards her, but she lifted it again, wiping her eyes and shaking off her emotion, determined to continue.

'And that wasn't all Margaret delivered to me. She said too to forget Jake Ashford, that he would not be visiting me in gaol and that it would be better for everyone if I put him out of mind. I guessed why – she wanted him herself. I cursed her and her forsaken family. Then she betrayed me with Jake and they ran away together to the continent. Eventually, I was released from that hell-hole and made my way home, very ill and weak.' She paused, thinking about what she had just learnt from Margaret. But that was neither here nor there in terms of what Owen needed to know. Anny took a breath and continued, 'You may think you know that part of the story, but you do not know the details, the truth of what it was to live through that terrible time. I nearly died in that place. It was the site of the lowest degradation and brutality you can only imaginc. It brokc my body and it nearly broke my mind. Your father and his mother saved me. They nursed me back to health, in my body and in my mind. We married soon after. Then you came along. You know the rest, because you lived it. My life began again when yours did. I became a whole person again when you came into the world.'

He watched her staring into the flowing water below. Every ounce of devotion he owed to her surged in his chest and threatened to burst its banks. 'I didna know . . .' he began, clenching his fists with a rage that was brewing there too.

She turned to him, her face pale and eyes wide and white. 'I did not want to taint you with it. I wanted to escape those dark days of my youth and start afresh with you, my boy. You were all new, my perfect, pure, untouched, unblemished baby. I would not let the memory of the Kings' betrayal stain our life together. But the poison they poured into me flowed in my blood forever more. Surely, it slowed to a trickle as life went on and our happiness grew and grew, despite our poverty. But when the Kings took over the brickworks, the venom resurfaced in me and would not let me breathe freely. I felt choked by it more and more each day. Again, the Kings were directing my destiny and those of the people I loved. It was unbearable to me. Now you know the cause of many an argument with your dear father. He understood my hatred of the Kings, of course he did. He knew how I had been wronged. He saved me and made me anew. I loved him for that and for everything else that is in him. He is the great love of my life.'

His mother took a step forward and held out her hands to him. He took them and she squeezed them tightly, looking searchingly into his eyes.

'Do you understand now what I said to you yesterday? That if you love that girl, it will kill me?'

Her eyes were brimming, her face looked years older, drawn and thin. How could a son tell that face, those eyes, that he would willingly break her heart? Maybe another son could, another man, a lesser one. But Owen Malone – with his soft poetic heart he inherited from his father – could not.

When they returned to the cottage, Owen's father and Adam were waiting for them at the door, puffing on their clay pipes. Peter's face relaxed the moment he saw them. He popped his pipe in the corner of his mouth and came over to Anny, putting his arm around her, asking after her. She wouldn't have any fuss and went straight inside, the others following. Sufficient explanations were given and his mother was helped to sit at the table and tea was made and bread was sliced and spread with butter and jam, to put some colour back in his mother's cheeks. Martha was up and about, looking wan but much improved on the previous day. Baby Hettie slept on her arm and they all drank the tea down and were comfortable together, for the first time in a while. But inside, Owen's mind was aflame with a cauldron of emotions, new truths and old lies thickening the unholy brew. It was a great effort of will just to appear normal.

'We've been talking since you've been gone, Anny,' said Owen's father. 'Things need to change around these parts.'

'Oh, not more change, Peter,' sighed Anny with a smile. 'My head is spinning already.'

'Change for the better this time,' he replied. 'You've been doing far too much around here and taking too much onto yerself. You need more rest, with the babby on the way. Owen and I will be helping you more around the place. And Adam has summat to say on the matter too.'

All eyes were on Adam, who nursed a mug of tea in his large scarred hands and stared at the table top.

'I have decided that the strike must come to an end.'

The news fell upon silence. Nobody gasped, nobody said a word.

Adam went on, 'With this news come from the King girl that the works is to be closed tomorrow otherwise, I've been talking to the others and folk are telling me they canna afford to lose the works altogether. There is no appetite left amongst the workers for resistance. What's more, I've heard today that two more brickworks have gone back to work, Cooper and Colley's works and Heighway brick and tile too. That was the last straw for most folk. Most everyone I spoke with said the same, that it was time to go back. For myself, with a wife and child to support, I have no choice. And we've lived under your roof and relied on your kindness for too long.'

Anny spoke up, 'You know you're welcome as long as you need it, Adam.'

'I know that. But you need your home and your rest, and now the babby is here, we need our space too. We shall go back to our house, still empty I understand it, and take the old hag on her word and have our home again.'

Owen saw Martha nodding thoughtfully at this.

Adam continued, 'We must take the cut in pay and go back to work. I have called a meeting for four o'clock this afternoon, then I shall walk up to the big house this evening and tell 'em myself.'

A shocked silence followed, interrupted only by the drowsy grizzling of baby Hettie, unaware of the gravity of the situation. Owen imagined that each person around the table had their own differing reactions to the news, but nobody had the will to voice them or the vigour to dispute. The whole thing had staggered on for too long, now dropping by the wayside in a defeated heap. There was dejection in the room, but also a sense of relief. The strike was over and they had lost. Back to work it was, on far worse terms than before, but at least the strike was over.

The silence was broken by a small sound that came from Adam's throat. A stifled sob, that brought his fist up to his mouth. Owen could see that Adam was fighting back emotion, determined not to let it overcome him. He cleared his throat, sat up straight and set his face firm. 'It has been a fight for good, a fight worth fighting. They know now we are united, that we will speak for ourselves and not be trod upon like creatures of the dust. I may have failed this time . . .'

Adam stopped, swallowing down his feelings.

'That inna true,' said Owen firmly. 'You anna failed anyone.'

'Yes, I bloody have,' snapped Adam, then contained himself once more. 'But despite my failings, our cause was righteous. And I say, let this be the first of many, the stirrings of working people against the tyranny of masters. We have lost this battle, but the war will be long. One day, working people will be heard.'

'I'll drink to that,' said Peter. The two men looked at each other, so often at odds these past weeks, and a passing understanding was exchanged and they nodded.

Owen went with Adam to the union meeting. There were far fewer people there than previous ones and a similar air of defeat. A few mouthy ones grumbled against it, but Owen noted that everyone looked simply exhausted with it all, a mirror of those around his own kitchen table. People shuffled away after, saying little. Such was the lot of the working man and woman, their rounded shoulders seemed to express. There had been light and hope and much talking and jostling in their community for a while, but now it was time to return to real life. Adam had gone off to Southover to tell them the news, insisting he do it alone. Owen guessed he wanted no witnesses to his shame.

The next day they were all up early, his mother preparing as hearty a meal as she could for the three men, with the meagre provisions they had left, some eggs from the chickens out back, some porridge with milk from a neighbour's goat. There would be money coming in at the end of the week, less than ever, but at least it would be something and they could afford to get some meat. His mother said that she and Martha would pack up their things and get some boys to help them take their bits and pieces back to their old house. His father and Adam said they'd do the heavy bits when they came home. The three of them trudged the walk to work in silence, heavy feet and heavy hearts.

As they approached the yard, Owen watched as their fellow brickies traipsed in beside them, as if the whole place was a weak magnet, drawing them in slowly but surely, unwilling and gloomy. Clothes were more ragged and filthy than ever, the children shoeless of course, as they ever were. The adults looked similarly dishevelled. There was a meeting with Troon and everyone gathered to listen to his instructions. Owen could see that there were far fewer workers than before the strike. Some had moved away, looking for other work in neighbouring counties. Some had gone into the workhouse. Some had starved, some had succumbed to illness. It was a ragged congregation, appearing more fit for admittance to a hospital than a long day's labour.

Troon was assigning new roles for many, now that the workforce was depleted. As well as being his father's assistant brickburner, Owen would now need to help out at the pug mill, checking the equipment and keeping it running smoothly, as well as loading the clay into the machine, where the wheels and knives inside it sliced and mixed it to produce the right consistency. It was a step down for him to be doing that job and also extra work, on top of his existing duties at the kilns. Troon said that now pay had gone down by thruppence per thousand bricks, everyone would want to work harder to make up the shortfall, as well as make back what they'd lost during the strike. So, there it was, more work, for less pay, for longer hours. The faces of everyone around him registered the miserable truth of their situation. There they were again, worse off than ever. There were a few daggered looks thrown at Adam, who kept his head down. He had been their hero and saviour once. But people always looked for someone to blame, when things were wrecked and ruined.

Days passed in echoes of each other, long, shattering days of toil, lacking definition between one and the next. Owen worked and slept, worked and slept. He dreamt of Beatrice. He would wake up shaking and sweating, as if weaning himself off some dreadful addiction. He developed a cough and his mother wrapped warm poultices about his throat each night, which he threw off in the July heat. At the end of the first week back, everyone arrived again at work with eager anticipation of the pay that would be handed out later, this promise buoying up their flagging vitality, helping them to push through this last day before their one day of rest on the morrow.

Owen left his father at the kiln to check on proceedings at the pug mill. It was a huge contraption, towering above them, a barrel-shaped machine topped with a wide horizontal wheel which had a diameter about the length of a tall man. This was driven by a cog wheel that in turn was driven by a steam engine beyond. The hopper was below the wheel, where the clay was fed in, made malleable by the rotating knives inside. At the base, the reduced clay came out, ready to be taken by children over to the moulding tables. An engineer called Tinsley was in charge there, a bully of a man who liked to give the young'uns a clip round the ear for little or no excuse. Owen hated him and so was even more depressed to have been assigned to the pug mill. Brain was working in here now too. Good old Brain, just turned thirteen and taller by far than Tinsley, who was a wiry little man, bitterly resenting anyone that towered over him and punishing them for it. But Brain was immune to such hostility. He looked cheerful and happy to be back, full of gusto, despite his family nearly ending up in the workhouse these past weeks, saved only by a few pennies from the union fund and the ending of the strike. He seemed more like a jovial dog than ever, his hair long at the back, stiff and straggly with sweat and clay. Owen thought the pug mill was not the best place for Brain, being of such a simple turn, that labouring at digging up clay suited his mind better than all this machinery. But he was very glad to have a friendly face around.

Brain turned when he saw Owen coming in and called over, 'Ow bist, Owen? Ow bist, me owd butty? Pay day today!'

'Shut yer trap, yer drearing great lump,' snarled Tinsley. 'Oil that pinion wheel like I told yer. No time for socialisationing.' After Tinsley spat out that last mouthful of a word, annoyed that Owen had witnessed it, he stomped away, pushing Owen's shoulder roughly with his own as he passed. Owen was knocked off one foot and swayed to steady himself, turning to Brain to have a laugh with him about miserable old Tinsley.

In the moment he looked at Brain, reaching up under the moving wheel to oil it, Owen shouted, 'No, Brain! From above!'

But there was no time for Brain to listen, to hear that it was mortally dangerous to oil the wheel from below. There was no time because Brain's hands were already caught in the cogs and in one terrifyingly swift moment, his whole frame was jerked upwards, pulled in up to the armpits, his arms mangled in the wheel and his body thrown against the wall behind the machine. The force of it jammed him between the wall and the end of the pinion shaft.

Owen ran to him, screaming, 'Stop the machine!' The wheel was blocked, straining to go about its circular journey. Brain's face was white as a china plate, a thin line of bright red blood trickling from the side of his mouth. He uttered a high, wheezy whine. Thank God, he was still alive. Owen kicked over a barrow and jumped atop it, so that he could stand face to face with him.

'Brain,' whispered Owen, his hand hovering by Brain's face, afraid to touch it. 'Brain, we're gonna get yer out.' He looked wildly about the equipment, trying to fathom how to extricate Brain from the mess of it.

'Owen,' he murmured. His eyes were closed, tight shut, as if he were hiding from something. His lips were open, a row of crooked teeth visible, lined with red.

'Dunna speak,' said Owen.

'Owen, me owd mate,' Brain whispered, a bubble of blood appearing on his lower lip then bursting.

'Hush, Brain. We'll soon have yer out.'

'I didna know.'

Owen stroked his cheek now with the tips of two fingers. 'I know, Brain. I know. It inna your doing. It inna your fault. Hush, hush now.' Then, he jerked his head round and shouted, his voice cracking, 'Turn that bastard machine off!'

The wheels at once loosened and Owen grasped at Brain's back, afraid he would fall. Men were running in, swearing and gasping. Two came up behind Brain and took his weight. Owen felt a hand patting him firmly on his shoulder but could not turn his head from Brain, whose eyes were beginning to open a sliver, at the touch of men at his back.

'Owen,' said a familiar voice and he twisted his head to see his father's face. 'Come down, lad. They need to move the wheel a bit to free him. Come down out the way.'

But Owen could not move, frozen there. Peter took his shoulders firmly and guided him down off the barrow. Owen felt his legs give away, his arms flailing. Then his father caught him, saying, 'Now then, son', and dragged him up to lean against him, steering him away from the mill and out into the fresher air. Owen felt his feet stumbling beneath him, glad of the strength of his father's arms about him.

'He didna know what he were doing,' he cried. 'Tinsley never showed him properly. He'd never worked the pug mill before. He shouldna been in there at all.'

His father was hushing him now, as he himself had hushed Brain moments before. Owen suddenly felt a fool, for collapsing like that, when Brain was the one who was injured, not him. He pushed his father away and stood up on shaking legs, forcing himself to stand tall. He turned from him and marched back to the scene of the accident, to find that they had managed to get Brain out, who was now lying on the ground, someone's coat over his front, covering up his grievous injuries. Troon was there now and Adam. They were talking about getting the doctor and a boy was sent off running.

Troon said, 'It's hopeless, though. Look at him, mon.'

'Doctor can sew him up. He can . . . he can . . .' Adam said, gesturing vaguely towards Brain, 'Take off the arms. He'll be a cripple but . . .' His voice trailed off.

Owen looked down at Brain and saw Royce was there now, sitting on his haunches, his arms resting on his knees. He was staring grimly at his friend. He reached out a hand, then withdrew it, his hands joining together, wringing shakily. He dropped down to his knees and sat there, watching his friend's grey face. Owen stood observing them both, his arms hanging loosely by his side, his ears registering sounds around him of complaint and pity, the cries of women weeping and children sobbing, the voice of Tinsley defending himself and men arguing with him. Everyone knew that no amount of talk would bring Brain back and no doctor could save him now. Time washed over Owen, irrelevant, meaningless, as unstoppable and uncaring as a flowing river over a drowning man's head. All he could do was stand there and watch Brain die.

Chapter 17

Beatrice had never played card games before she came to England. Now she was addicted to Old Maid, played sometimes in fours with her mother, her great-grandmother and her step-grandmother, and it occurred to her that around the table, all the women playing, in one way or another, had something in common with the maid of the title. Three of them were widows, with no man propping them up. And the fourth, herself, was most definitely a maid, though she did not intend to remain one for long. The object of the game was to make a pile of pairs and avoid being the one left with the singular queen. But she was torn about this and, though loving to win, she also felt special if she was the one left holding the Old Maid. She thought the queens painted on the playing cards were beautiful and also mysterious. They had the allure of power about them, women in high places who could rule over others. She wondered if this was why Queenie loved the game too. Mostly it was played by just the two of them, sometimes for an hour or two or more. They never tired of it. For Beatrice in the days during the strike, it had served as a distraction from the constant frustration of being separated from Owen and worry about how everything would turn out for their families.

Now the strike was over and the brickies had been back at work for six days, Beatrice had been allowed out of the house again, if she wished to go. But the freedom she had longed for seemed a cruel trick on her now. She had kept to the house this past week, citing the heat or tiredness or a headache. The truth was that her mind was in turmoil. Her mother's revelations about the past had hit her hard, a cruel and unexpected slap in the face. The romantic vision she had grown up with of her parents' elopement to Paris had been shattered and in its place was a tawdry story of her father – the drunk, the womaniser and the wife beater. Such news might turn a girl against men for life, but all it did was serve to highlight Owen's qualities more than ever, as she knew in her heart that he was none of these things and would never be a man like that. He was good, through and through, and despite her protestations to her mother, inside she yearned for him desperately.

The story of his mother and her mother affected her deeply too. She understood her mother's motives in all of it, and sympathised with her. But she was ashamed to admit to herself that it was Anny who she empathised with. Such terrible things had been done to her by this family, it sickened Beatrice to be a part of it, though she loved her mother and her great-grandmother dearly. The wrongs that had been committed hung over her like a black cloud. She marvelled how the Kings could carry on so easily after destroying someone's life like that. It left her feeling conflicted about Queenie. How could she reconcile the great-grandmother she loved with the woman who had stood back and let a life be destroyed? It made her feel proud of her mother's flight to France, for at least she had the decency to go away and make her own life, away from the Kings and all that they stood for.

The atmosphere at home was cheerier for those around her. Benjamina had emerged from her room, perfectly turned out each day, seeming much more like her old self and talking about procuring a new puppy. Queenie was visibly happier, relieved that the strike business was finally over and done with and things could get back to normal. Cyril was restless, it had to be said. He'd seemed to enjoy the intrigues of the strike and now it was over and familiar routines had resumed, he was bored and fidgety. Beatrice's mother seemed content in a quiet way, yet Beatrice noticed her watching her from time to time, no doubt wondering if what Beatrice kept saying to her was true, that she was over Owen and never thought of him. Nothing could be further from the truth. Yet, on the surface, peace had been restored at Southover and everyone seemed better for it.

But then Troon came, on the Saturday afternoon, just before teatime. Beatrice and Queenie were in the midst of an Old Maid marathon, when Busby came and told his mistress that Mr Troon was here to see her. Beatrice saw Queenie's face fall at the news.

'Oh, will I never be free from these brickmakers? I've half a mind to close the place if this is how it's going to carry on.'

'Queenie!' said Beatrice, shocked to hear it after everything everyone had been through. 'You don't mean that!'

Queenie scowled and shook her head. 'Of course not, dear. But it's tempting.' She sighed and said to Busby, 'Show him in here, Busby. I am comfortable and do not wish to disturb our game.' Busby nodded and withdrew. Queenie went on, 'And anyway, Bea, it'll be useful for you to start taking an interest in the business. Maybe you'll take it over in the future, if I have my way.' She said this last with a twinkle in her eye.

'I don't know what I want for my future, really,' sighed Beatrice. 'But do you really think I have it in me to run all . . . this?' she said with a flourish of her hand.

'I do not *think* it,' said Queenie. 'I *know* it. You have the right kind of mind for it. You are confident too and easy with people. They relax in your company. You have a clear sense of what is right, which is what this company needs going forward, I believe, as long as you temper that with business sense. This can be taught, if you are willing to learn. The overseers like Brotherton can deal with all the administration. But you, my dear, with a good husband by your side, would make a fine heir to my role. It is what I hope for.'

Beatrice smiled at her great-grandmother and nodded her interest, but nothing like her assent as yet. Could she do what Queenie had done, step into her shoes? Queenie was formidable and Beatrice did not feel she would ever be so impressive. Or could she? She imagined herself, making decisions, holding meetings, reading reports. It was vastly preferable to a future of indolence, such as Benjamina had. Thoughts of the power it would afford her crept into her mind too as she pondered it all, when the door opened and Busby returned and after him, Mr Troon.

Troon's face was disturbing to look at. He had dark shadows under his tired eyes. He looked like a man with nothing good to say. Beatrice saw Queenie noted it too. They both placed their cards on the table.

'What is it, Troon?' said Queenie, her voice tinged with apprehension.

'I am sorry to report . . . an accident at the yard. A very serious accident.'

'Not Owen Malone?' cried Beatrice.

'No, miss,' said Troon, looking at her quizzically. Beatrice's heart had been clamped in terror at the news, but now she could rule out the worst of it, at least.

'What's happened, Troon?' said Queenie, with some irritation.

'It's a death, madam. A lad got his arms caught up in the workings of the pug mill. The doctor was sent for but the lad died at the scene. Nothing could be done for him.'

Queenie grimaced and said, 'A regrettable incident,' with a suitably sombre tone. 'Where is . . . the body now?'

'Doctor arranged for it to be taken by cart to his dwelling for examination. Said he would need to establish cause of death, for the coroner.'

'Of course. Was anyone else hurt?'

'No, madam. The workers are shocked and saddened, as you can imagine.'

'Was any equipment damaged? And is the brickworks up and running again?'

Beatrice stared at Queenie, incredulous of what she was hearing. A boy had died, in the most gruesome and unnatural way. And Queenie wanted to know if the business was still running. If this was what it took to be in her place, then Beatrice wanted none of it.

'Yes, all is in hand.'

'Very good. We shall speak again on Monday. Arrange for Brotherton to be informed and he should bring me the boy's details. I shall write to his parents. Thank you, Troon.' Queenie turned away from him, signalling that the audience was over.

'Madam, miss,' he nodded gravely at them both.

'Mr Troon,' called Beatrice as he began to turn away.

'Yes, miss?'

'How old was he?'

'Just turned thirteen, miss.'

'What was his name?'

'Brain. Harold Brain. But everyone called him Brain. He wasna too bright, you see. His brain . . . well, the Lord hadna finished him, if you take my meaning. So we all thought it funny, his name being Brain. He thought it were funny too. Never took offence, mind. So that's what we all called him. Brain.'

'Harold Brain,' murmured Beatrice.

'Yes, miss. And curious you should mention Owen Malone, for they were friends, in actual fact. And Owen was there when it happened. Saw the whole thing and stayed with him till help came. He'll be needed by the coroner, no doubt, as a witness.'

'That'll do, Troon,' said Queenie, quietly. He nodded again and left them, trudging across the floor and closing the door with care.

Beatrice stared at her great-grandmother, who picked up her cards again and studied them.

'This is terrible,' said Beatrice.

'Yes,' said Queenie, rearranging her hand of cards, pointedly not looking at Beatrice.

'It is *frightful*.' Her mind was filled with the image of Owen, seeing it all, staying with Harold Brain, talking to him. How the poor boy must have suffered . . . What did arms look like when they were 'caught up in workings'? It was ghastly and unthinkable. The agony of it. The horror Owen must have seen.

'We must do something,' insisted Beatrice, willing Queenie to look up from her cards.

'We will be doing something. I shall send my condolences to the parents.'

'A letter they probably can't read!' scoffed Beatrice.

Queenie looked sharply up at her. 'It is the way it is done. I cannot become too involved with it until the inquest is heard. This has happened at *my* brickworks. We must hear the evidence and then make our decisions about what is to be done. There is a matter of blame, of fault. It is not as simple as a tragedy.'

'But it *is* a tragedy!' cried Beatrice. 'A boy is dead. Killed by a machine. His arms, they must be . . . mangled. The pain! It must have been . . .' She could not find the words. Nothing seemed adequate.

'And this is what you must learn as the first rule of business. Never become emotionally embroiled in such things. Someone has to remain objective, until the evidence is gathered and the hearing has been held.'

'Do you have no softer feelings for these people? Can you find no kindness in your heart, as I do?'

'Twice I have followed your lead in such things and where has it got me? I visited the Joneses and was sent away with a flea in my ear. I paid the doctor's fee for them at your request and have I received a word of thanks or even acknowledgement? No, I have not. Nothing. These people do not understand kindness. And all that softness does is lead to weakness.'

'I don't understand you,' said Beatrice, coldly.

Queenie looked down at her cards, reordering them yet again. 'One day, you will understand. If you run this business, you will.'

Beatrice was gathering her words wildly, ready for a verbal attack. But she was interrupted by the entrance of a maid bringing the tea things.

'Time for afternoon tea,' said Queenie, sounding grateful. She placed her cards on the table.

Beatrice said nothing, turned away from her great-grandmother and looked out of the window. As tea was served, Beatrice stared at the green mass of trees beyond the drive, still as a painting in the breezeless day. She could leave, right now. She could go into the conservatory, out of the glass door and run into the woods, follow the river and go straight to Owen's house. But he would not be there, only Anny Malone would be there. And she would have no time for Beatrice, for Anny hated her, surely. She could run the other way then, down the driveway and into town, along the road and up the hill towards the brickworks, go find Owen there and . . . and what? How welcome would a King be there? They wouldn't care that her name was Ashford. She would be one of *them*, that was all. It didn't matter whose fault it was, the accident. The boy had been killed by King equipment. Owen might even hate her for that. The thought appalled her. If only she could go to him, right away. If only she could see his face, this instant, and know if he still loved her.

The door opened and in came Cyril, making a beeline for the cakes on the table.

'Don't mind if I do!' he said and stuffed one in his mouth, the crumbs cascading down his front and onto the carpet. Beatrice glared at him. Did he know what had happened? She shot a look at Queenie, who turned to him to speak.

'There is more bad news from the brickworks, I'm afraid to say.'

'What now?' said Cyril.

'A boy has died, caught up in the workings of the pug mill.'

Cyril grimaced. Beatrice watched his face. It was suitably sombre, but did not show what Beatrice would call suitable emotion.

'It is all in hand,' Queenie continued. 'But there will be an inquest and some unpleasantness, I daresay.'

'The workers will be itching for a fight again, no doubt,' replied Cyril, his tone a mixture of flippancy and tedium.

Beatrice glared at Queenie again, who gave her great-granddaughter a sympathetic look. Queenie had reacted coldly towards the news, but at least she wasn't dismissive of it, as Cyril was.

'It is a tragic thing, the death of a child,' said Queenie pointedly to Cyril. 'It would behove you to remember that, when dealing with any of our workers regarding this business.'

Cyril sighed and threw himself down on the settee in a dramatic pose. 'I know that, of course. Ghastly business. But I'm sick of it all. Sick of the brick business. And I'm sick of Ironbridge and all its petty squabbles.' He sat up straight and looked Queenie in the eye. 'And it's made up my mind, actually, Queenie. You remember the fellow I know from Liverpool? The one who got us all the scabs. James Melton.'

'Of course,' said Queenie. 'We are indebted to him for that. Do you wish him to visit?'

'No, I do not. I wish to visit *him* and then accompany him on a bit of a jolly. Listen, this new-fangled thing in the iron industry that's being talked about. The Bessemer process? It's a new way of making iron, turns it into steel. Well, it's the latest thing and it's driving forward the iron industry into the future. I'm sick of all this brickworks nonsense. I know the iron industry has been on its last legs round here for a while, but this new process sounds just the ticket to me. Melton has invited me to travel with him to America. We'll be inspecting the industries of Pennsylvania, the coal and steel industries. He is going to go in a month or so. I wasn't sure I could be bothered, but I'm sick of it here. I need to get away from all this provincialism.'

Queenie took a sip of her tea and replaced the cup neatly on its saucer, placing both carefully on the table before her. She was clearly mulling over Cyril's words as she did so.

'Cyril, you should go to America. It will be good for all of us. You'll bring back new knowledge and improve the business. It'll give you something useful to do and, the Lord knows, there is a first time for everything on that account.'

'Jolly good!' said Cyril and bounced up from the settee. 'I'll make the arrangements forthwith! Let me know if you need any assistance with this death business.' He grasped another cake and left the room, trailing crumbs as he went.

'I wonder where your mother and Benjamina are? Lounging around upstairs, no doubt,' said Queenie and took another bite of cake. 'They are missing out on a good sponge.' Queenie glanced up at Beatrice, then looked quickly away again. 'And we do need to inform them of the sad news.'

Beatrice felt nauseous. The lack of feeling towards the boy who'd died was sickening her and she could not bear to pretend any longer. Yet she did not have the strength to argue about it either. She stood up and said to Queenie, 'I feel somewhat ill. Please tell Maman that I shall retire to my room for the rest of the day. Please do not call me for dinner.'

Queenie looked concerned and said, 'Dearest, do not let Cyril upset you. It's just his way. And do not concern yourself too much with this latest problem. I do assure you that once the inquest has settled things, I will look out for the boy's family. All will be well.'

Beatrice could see Queenie was trying to be kind, but she had lost some faith in her great-grandmother, particularly her ability to make anything 'well' for her workers.

'Yes, I'm sure you're right,' she said, turning to leave the room. But Queenie hadn't finished with her.

'And soon, my dear, we shall launch you onto the social scene. There is a ball, I hear, in a fortnight's time, organised by Mr and Mrs Elkin. You remember meeting them at your grandfather's wake? They adored you. I think it should be the occasion of your coming out. We can order a dress from London. That will be something for you to look forward to, shall it not?'

'Yes, of course. Thank you,' murmured Beatrice and left the room. She began to climb the stairs slowly, but then the tears came and she took the last few swiftly, hurrying to her room to weep in private.

She cried herself to sleep, taking a fitful nap, fraught with nightmares. Her dreams were a swirl of misery, leaping from one dark thing to the next. She pictured the boy and his accident, the crushing of his arms, the blood and gore horrific. She imagined Owen, sitting beside him, watching him die. She should be with him, comforting him. She tried to reach him in the dream, but could not walk towards him, her legs strangely bound. She woke up damp with sweat, her mouth as dry as cotton. She knew in that moment that she would never be able to obey her mother's wishes. Whatever she had said to her about trying to forget Owen, she knew it was folly. She loved him. She wanted to take her place beside him, for the rest of their lives. The boy's death was a brutal reminder that life was short. She did not want to waste hers in regret. But how could such a fate be achieved?

Then she remembered Queenie's words from earlier, that one day Beatrice would take over the business. What had seemed a daunting responsibility, suddenly began to whisper possibilities to her, that if she was clever and bided her time, one fine day, she would take over from Queenie, run the business and promote Owen Malone to a position of power and prestige. They could see each other in secret, then when the time was right, they could marry and run the business together. With her common touch and the business knowledge gained from Queenie, and his industrial knowledge and understanding of the workforce, they would make the ideal team. Only that morning, it had seemed ridiculous, an impossible dream. But now, hope filled her heart. Her stomach grumbled and she realised how hungry she was. Perhaps she would go down for dinner, after all. She would need to eat to keep her strength up. She had plans to make. Her first must be to figure out a way to see her beloved Owen again.

Chapter 18

Beer was so comforting. It was liquid but it had body to it, a bit like soup, Owen mused. He downed the dregs and thought about getting another. A couple of days had passed since Brain's death and they'd arranged a hasty funeral. Most of the other mourners had gone home now. Brain's mother had cried all the way through the church service and family members had taken her home before the burial. She wasn't fit to stay. The brickies had clubbed together to pay for a headstone but the stonemason said it wasn't enough and nobody had any more to spare. Brain was buried in a pauper's grave. There were already a few bodies in there, the uppermost being very small, a baby of indeterminate age. The air was foul about the hole and nobody stayed long. It was best his mother didn't see where her son had gone to rest. Nobody let her see his body on the day of his death either. No mother should see their child like that.

Owen ordered another beer. His father had warned him not to stay too long and drink too much. His mother had said to leave him be, let him work it out his own way. His father had looked annoyed, like he knew that something had been going on between mother and son that hadn't included him. But just before they left, his mother had whispered in his ear not to get too drunk, as he'd regret it in the morning and the shifts were longer now and he'd need his wits about him. He was ignoring their advice, as was often the case these days. His father plodded on with work without question, which infuriated Owen, but he had not the energy to argue with him. And what would be the point anyway? Nothing would change.

As for Owen's mother, she was struggling with the pregnancy and looked so tired all the time, he had not the heart to discuss anything with her about the old truths she'd told him. He did not want to upset her by bringing all that up again. He just wanted his mother to be well.

Brain's mother relied on her son's meagre earnings as she was herself a widow and not of a hale and hearty constitution. Owen wondered what would happen to her now. He hoped there might be a relative somewhere to take her in, though he had not heard of one. Imagine having Brain as your comfort, he thought. Such a jolly soul. And then imagine losing him and having nothing and nowhere to go. Harold, his name was. Owen had learnt that at the church service in his memory. Harold Brain, the vicar had said, and Owen realised he'd never known Brain's first name, everyone calling him Brain from the day he started at the brick-works aged six. *Harold Brain*, thought Owen. *Harold. Did his mother call him Harry*, he wondered? *Or Hal?*

He closed his eyes and wished a man could wipe his thoughts clean, like a slate at school. Well, a few more of these beers and he could effectively do that, for a short time anyway. But the moment his eyes were shut, he saw Beatrice. He imagined her standing before him, her face a picture of concern, her hands reaching towards him, to comfort him. She put her arms about him and kissed him. The relief of feeling her again, the want of her was like an unquenchable thirst. The misery of Brain's death would never leave him completely, but it would be soothed by her presence, her touch, her love.

He snapped open his eyes. It was late, gone ten at night. She'd be in her bed now. A thought came to him and he shoved it away. He took another deep draught of beer. He ought to be getting home. But the thought came back, of walking the other way from the tavern, of going along the river path, then up through the trees, up to the house on the hill. If he could see her one more time, just one more time, then that would be enough. Then he could say goodbye and leave her forever. Just one more time would do it. That was all he wanted, wasn't it? Then he could give her up for good, as his mother wanted.

But he knew he was lying to himself. One more time would never be enough. It would only make it worse. It would only serve to sharpen his longing. He shook his head to rid it of the stupid notion. He finished off the dregs and did not order more. He was going to remain relatively sober tonight and he was going to walk straight home, as his father wanted. He would not be going to see Beatrice that night. He would be going straight home instead. Indeed, he would. He turned and set off, walking at a fair pace.

It was a warm, sticky night. The air was heavy with it. There had been cloudy skies all day and they had not dispersed, trapping the heat between heaven and earth. He stopped before his destination and stared at it. He leant against an oak tree and gazed at the King house across the lawn. Then, a yellow square of light appeared, flickering invitingly. The rest of the house was obscure and silent. He nearly turned away, went back along the dark whispering woodland path home, to where his parents would be waiting, hoping he did not come home too drunk this time. He remembered he would stink of beer and suddenly regretted it, imagining what Beatrice would think if he came to her smelling like a brewery. But he was not going to see Beatrice, of course, so it did not matter. How would he find her anyway? He had no idea which room was hers or how to get to her. The whole thing had been a fool's errand. He should turn and go home, this instant.

That is what he told himself as he stared at the lamplit window. Then, a figure appeared. Long, flowing hair, a white nightgown, pale as a spirit. But this was no spectre, this was flesh and blood, warm and real. It was Beatrice, leaning on her windowsill. He stepped over the lumpen roots of the oak tree and marched across the lawn. She saw him and her face lit up with a glorious smile. She beckoned and he broke into a trot, arriving beneath her window and gazing up at her.

'I cannot believe you are here!' she spoke in a hoarse whisper, her face lit up with delight.

'Nor I,' he said and grinned.

'I couldn't sleep. So I came to the window. And there you were! Am I dreaming? Can you be real?'

'You are not. And yes, I can. I am real. I am here, to see you!'

'Oh, my love!' she said and his heart lurched. 'But how shall we do this?' She peered behind her then turned back to him, biting her bottom lip. 'I might be able to sneak through the house . . .'

'No,' he said, looking about him. 'I shall come to you.'

'But how?'

Below her window was an ancient and sturdy wisteria. It clung to a trellis that was nailed to the brick. He could climb up the trellis and step onto the flat roof of the library beside it. Was it the beer that gave him courage or his need for her? Was it foolhardy? No, he decided. It had reason to it, if the trellis held. The angle between the flat roof and her window was sharp, but there was a ledge beneath her window that he could put a foot on and grab the gable. He wouldn't be relying on her to pull him in, but he thought he could make that ledge. He reached out and grasped the trellis, giving it a good yank to check its strength. It was firmly attached to the wall and he believed it would take his weight. He began to climb, the wisteria blossoms tickling his face as he ascended, filling his nostrils with a musky scent that was quite overpowering. He had to focus to keep his grip.

He reached the flat roof and climbed onto it. Her windowsill was more or less level with the roof. But the gap between the ledge and himself looked much wider now he was there. She reached out her hands towards him, but he shook his head. If he could reach the gable first, he could then get one foot on the ledge and pull the rest of himself over. There was nothing for it but to try. He leant out, glancing down at the ground that now seemed far below. He did not fancy landing on that gravel on his back. *Better not look down then*, he thought. He leant out, eased his hands along the bricks, then grabbed the gable, getting a firm grip on it before trying to hop a foot onto the ledge. It missed its spot at first and he pushed himself back onto the roof. But he had a better idea of where things were this time and he reached out again. Gable, ledge and his foot was there. He pulled his body up and hung onto the gable, his feet wedged safely on the ledge. He felt her hands on his legs and nearly let go, her touch affected him so. But he kept his wits about him and eased his way down, whispering 'Move back!' so that he could throw his feet inside and land on her floor.

Once inside, they both paused at the noise of his heavy boots landing on her carpet. No sounds came, nobody was the wiser. He was breathing hard from his exertions. He needed a moment to recover. He stood, his hands on his thighs, and stared at her. She was almost too beautiful to touch, but that did not stop him. All thoughts of the smell of beer and all commitments he made to never see her again were long gone, as he stepped forward and put his arms around her, drew her to him and they kissed, open-mouthed, deep, wet and glorious. He had never bedded a girl before, but he was certain in that moment that he would know exactly what to do. Her bed was beside them and he thought of it there, ready to take them, if she wanted him to. He wanted to. He wanted to very much.

Beatrice pulled away, buried her face in his shoulder and a little sob caught in her throat.

Owen whispered to her, 'Are you well?'

'I am well,' she said and smiled up at him. 'I am overcome.'

He kissed her again and ran his hands up and down her body, feeling her for the first time with only a thin layer of fabric between his hands and her flesh. His own body felt as if it would burst into flame, his whole being filled with an urgency to act that strained in every muscle. Would she let him? He would never force himself on her, on any girl. Would she invite him?

She stopped and took his hand. She sat down on the bed and he sat down beside her. But now she was kissing his hand lightly and smiling at him, squeezing his hand like a friend.

'Owen, I believe you can read minds.'

He hoped he could and he hoped also that she wanted the same thing as he did.

'Can I?'

'Yes, for I have been wracking my brain these last days, trying to think of a way to contact you safely and you managed it yourself.'

He did not want to talk. He wanted to kiss her again and pull her to him, lay her down and lie atop her. But there she was, talking.

'I thought of writing you a letter, but where would I send it? Your mother might see it and would guess it was from me, I thought. I could not think of a way around it. But you came to me!'

'I did.'

'I'm so glad you did. I'm over the moon!' she cried and squeezed his hand tightly. But then her face clouded. 'But I know I must not be so selfish as to be happy, when there are such sad things in the world around us. Owen, I heard about the accident at the yard. I heard about Harold Brain.'

'Yes,' muttered Owen and looked down, away from her face. He did not want to think about Harold Brain at this moment. Yet a series of gruesome images assaulted him and he looked back at her face to rid himself of the memories.

'I'm so sorry for it. So sorry.'

'That's all right. It's not your fault.'

There was a moment of silence between them, laden with questions. If the Kings were to blame, as they surely were, could she be included in that guilt?

'Troon told me you were with him at the end. That was so good of you. You are such a good man.'

'No choice. I was there when it happened. I saw the whole thing.'

'Oh, how terrible for you! Do you wish to speak of it? I will listen to anything you have to say. I am not a squeamish, silly girl.'

'I'd rather not,' he said, his desire ebbing as sombre thoughts filled his mind. The touch of her hand was comforting though and he squeezed it.

'I understand. Let us speak of other things. I have a plan, something that might sound mad at first, but it could change things around here, change them for the better. Please bear with me.'

He did not want to talk about anything, truth be told. He just wanted to rid his head of bad memories. But the night was long and maybe once he had heard this plan and discussed it sufficiently, he could stop her mouth with kisses and then . . . She was explaining something about becoming the mistress of the King business, taking over from the old hag and running it.

That she'd make sure he was well provided for and that one day, when they were older and he was promoted, they would marry.

'Marry?' he said.

'Yes, marry. If . . .' Now she looked uncertain and looked at him with large brown cow eyes. 'Don't . . . you want to marry me, Owen?'

He had wanted to see her. He had wanted to kiss her and take her to bed. He had not thought beyond that, not for a long time now.

'Of course I do,' he said. 'It's just that . . . it never seemed possible.'

'But with my plan in place, it is just that. It is possible now.'

'But what of the past? My mother told me things. If you dunna know them, I am afraid to tell you. But you mun know.'

'I know it all, Owen. Everything. My mother told me too. Terrible things. My father beat her. Your mother loved my father. The prison, Uncle Cyril, all of it. It is awful. But it has nothing to do with us.'

Owen dropped her hand that still held his. 'It has *everything* to do with us.'

'No, no. It does not. Don't you see? The past is past. We cannot let their mistakes haunt us. We are new and . . . and we shall be free.'

'You are wrong, Bea. Life does not work that way. The past is everything. It holds us and colours us. We cannot escape it. It lives in our bones and our blood.' She smiled at him, curiously. 'What are you thinking about, at this moment?' he said, as he realised, he never had a clue what she was going to say next, let alone what was going on behind that beautiful face.

'I was thinking that I love the way you speak.'

'Thank you, Miss Ashford,' he said and made a complimentary nod.

'You're welcome, Mr Malone,' she said. 'Being here with you, it is the most delicious treat to sit and listen to you speak! Better than ice cream, better even than *croissants aux amandes*, warm and fresh from the oven, spread with melting butter and *confiture d'abricot*!' He had no idea what that meant, but he did not care, watching her talk, drinking in the miracle of her face, her lips moving, her eyes deep and dark in the dim lamplight. 'We must keep talking, keep being honest with each other, share our innermost thoughts and feelings. If we always stay true to each other, we will weather this. Time will pass, our positions in life will change and society will change. And one day, one fine day, Mr Malone, you and I shall be together. Do you believe it?'

'I believe anything that comes from those lips,' he said, still transfixed by them.

'No, no, Owen,' she giggled. 'I am serious now. It will take time, much time. We can meet in secret along the way but we must both have patience. If we bide our time, one day, we shall marry and be together always. Do you trust me?'

'Yes, I trust you.' He did not have the heart to ask the same of her. Everything he was to her was based on a lie. Would she still feel the same if she knew he'd first courted her to use her an unwitting spy?

'Then, we shall say good night now. And you will come again soon.'

So tonight was done then. She thought they had a future together. But for him, it was just this one night only. The future beyond that was tangled up with the past, but this one night was theirs alone. But she did not know that, she thought it was the first of many to come. She was wrong and he could not tell her why.

'I dunna know when I can come again. My mother's babby will come soon.'

'Yes, of course! How lovely.'

'Yes, it is. But it means more work too and more help needed at home. And the yard since the strike, well . . . we have to work harder now.'

She looked down, perhaps with guilt.

'I am so sorry for that. I did what I could, for you and for everyone. But I failed.'

'It is not your fault. You did your best. It means much that you tried.'

'Thank you. I know times are hard. But promise me you will come to me here, at night, as often as you can. I cannot live without you, Owen.'

'Soon. I will come again soon,' he lied, knowing that he would have to make a choice, between his family and her, and it would be an impossible choice. 'I wish it were different, but wishing does not make it so.'

'It did tonight. I wished you to come and there you were, leaning against the oak tree. I know we will be fine. Everything will be fine.'

He grimaced then sought to cover it with a smile.

'What is it, Owen? Something is wrong.'

He turned away, afraid his face would tell more tales on him. 'Everything, of course. Everything is wrong.'

'But we love each other,' she said simply and reached out for him, drew him to her and held him close. It was not desire that held him there but comfort, pure and simple. The feel of her soft, warm body was a kind of luxury and he wished he could lie down and sleep with it, truly sleep, listening to her breathe until dawn came and woke him.

When she pulled away from him, he felt as if part of his soul had been wrenched and detached. She kept it and he had lost it. He looked at her, longingly.

'Your face . . .' he began, gazing at it. Words failed him. The beauty of it. 'Ducklings . . .' he began.

'Ducklings?' she whispered, quizzically.

'When ducklings are born, down by the river, they come out of the egg and they follow the first thing they see. It's usually their mother but you can make them follow you. They bond with it and love it, fall for it head over heels. They'll follow it anywhere. They fall in love, with just one look. That is how it was with me and with you. When I first saw you, your face appearing at the window of your coach, across the filthy yard. A pale face, lustrous hair, eyes like a tawny owl, round and dark. I saw you and I loved you.'

'You loved me?' she gasped, tears starting in her eyes.

'I love you,' he said.

'Oh, Owen! And I love you,' she said, placing her hand on his cheek. They kissed again and desire rose in him once more. She sensed it and pulled away. He wanted to pull her back to him, but he would not, unless she gave him some sign. 'We must . . . take care.'

He knew what she meant. 'Yes,' he replied, sharply disappointed but in agreement, in theory at least. 'We cannot afford to . . . complicate matters.'

'Indeed not, for then our plans will come to naught. A child now . . . would ruin everything. We must have patience.'

'It will be a trial,' he said, gazing at the creamy skin where her neck met her shoulder, imagining the curves and contours below it, beneath the thin cotton of her nightdress.

'We cannot meet in public now. But Owen, it is a hot summer and I leave my window open every night. Every single night. Come whenever you can. We shall talk further and make our plans. We have all the time in the world. We have the rest of our lives together.'

She smiled at him and kissed his hand, then led him to the window. Descending from her room was not as straightforward as its opposite. Clambering from the windowsill to the flat roof was a leap of faith and he was glad he had long legs to make the jump. He managed it, though a little winded, and climbed down the wisteria, his legs shaking, from the climb or from his feelings, he could not tell. He waved to her as she smiled down at him. Her long hair was hanging down about her face, the light from the window catching it, its ends glowing like embers.

He looked about him and went across the lawn, reached the trees and turned back. She was still there, one last wave between them, and he disappeared from her view into the woods. He stopped and took a glance back, saw her light go out and watched the window frame disappear into darkness. Then, he heard something behind him. It was the noise of bodies moving through the trees. Ready for fight or flight, he turned and clenched his fists. Who would be out at night in a forest, except lovers or thieves?

It was Royce and another bloke, Bolton, from the brickworks. He was a big lad. He dug out the clay and had thick arms and a broad neck. Royce's bulldog, Owen guessed. The sight of them there, so close to Beatrice's house, sickened him. They caught sight of him too and all three stopped, dead still, eyeing each other in the gloom of the woods.

'What the bloody hell are you doing here?' said Owen.

'Same question to you, mon,' said Royce, taking a step towards Owen, followed by Bolton. They stood in a shaft of moonlight and Owen could see them clearly now. Bolton's huge fists were curling and uncurling.

'Just walking,' said Owen. 'Couldna sleep. And you?'

'Just walking? Right past the King house, by some lucky chance?' sneered Royce.

'What business is it of yours, anyway?' said Owen, keeping an eye on Bolton's fists.

'King business is my business.'

'How do you figure that?'

'We're gunna do over the King house.'

'Do what?' frowned Owen.

'We're gunna pilfer some stuff to sell for money for Brain's mother. Not tonight, but soon. When they're all out.'

Owen shook his head and sighed. 'No, you inna.'

'We are, by God. They've got it coming to them, them Kings.'

'Big talk for a ratlin such as you,' said Owen, eyeing Royce's short frame up and down.

Royce lurched forwards, grabbed Owen's sleeve and said, 'We're gunna do it, Malone. And you're gunna help us.'

'Ha!' Owen gave a hollow laugh and wrenched his arm away. "Dunna be soft in the head. Just leave it. You inna robbing the Kings and I inna helping you.'

Royce said, 'You dunna think I can do it. Well, I've made my mark already. It was me killed the King bitch's dog.'

Owen scoffed, 'That was stupid. Why take it out on a creature? You just made things worse, you fool.'

Royce said, 'Dunna you care what happened to Brain?'

'Course I do,' Owen spat.

'Then prove it. We need a way in to the King house. We canna force our way in and be heard.'

'Then do it, if you mun. What's it to do with me?'

'We need you to find out from the King girl how to get in.'

'What do you know about that?'

'I know enough. I listen and watch. I know you were seeing her and she paid to save Jones's wife at your own house. I know things.'

'You dunna know a thing,' said Owen, the mention of Beatrice making his stomach lurch. 'Strike's over and all that business be done and over with.'

'Nothing be done and over with,' growled Royce. 'We want revenge on them Kings and by God we mun have it.'

'You're all talk,' said Owen with disgust and turned to walk away.

'Traitor.'

Owen stopped. He turned back. It had been Bolton's voice.

‘What did you call me?’ said Owen, his whole body tensing. Bolton was a head taller than Owen, but he didn’t care. He’d give this one a good larruping if he ever called him such a thing again. He stepped towards Bolton and saw his blank face and small black eyes in the moonlight.

Royce said, ‘Now then, lads. Let us not fight amongst ourselves. We are all on the same side.’

Owen said, ‘If he calls me that again, I’ll kill him.’

‘Well,’ said Royce, patting Owen’s shoulder. ‘Prove you inna. Help us.’

‘Make me,’ said Owen and squared up to Royce, inches from his face now.

How he wanted to punch Royce. But it would do no good. Together he and Bolton would thrash him black and blue and then he’d have all that to explain to his parents. He turned and left them. He thought they’d follow but didn’t hear them. He stumbled through the forest, tripping often in the darkness and cursing everything. When he came closer to the river, the moon shone on it and lightened the last part of his journey. He came within sight of home and saw the thinking log. He threw himself down on it and hung his head with the shame and the muddle of it all.

He looked up and watched the moonlight dappling across the ever-moving river. Eternal things, moons and rivers. They had lived forever and would live forever more. Maybe he could learn something from them. Maybe he could step out of the tangle of his own time and see things as they do, across long swathes of time. Beatrice could do it, could look ahead, could see change coming. He looked back at his house. Soon, the new baby would come. His mother was hefty with it now. She would be caught up in a brand new life. She might see things differently. Maybe it wasn't so hopeless, after all. Maybe Beatrice would take over the Kings' business and make things better. Maybe they would . . . marry one day? Was it possible? Just a couple of hours ago, it seemed as likely as reaching up and bagging the moon. But the way Beatrice explained it, it could happen. All they needed was time. And for things to heal. Perhaps then, anything was possible.

But one thing was for sure. If the King house was burgled by brickworkers, then all of their plans, however unlikely, would come to naught. And all of their lives would be worse for it. He had to stop Royce. But how? And who would help him?

Chapter 19

Ten days since she'd kissed Owen in her bedroom, Beatrice leant on her windowsill gazing at the woods, the trees barely moving in the heat of the summer evening, shadowy and eerie in the twilight. She'd done this every night that week, hoping and waiting, waiting and hoping. But he had not come back. In a minute, she would be called downstairs to meet the others before they all took the carriage to the Broseley town hall for the Elkins' party, her first ball of the season. Maman had helped her pick out a fine dress from the latest Paris fashions and they'd had it made in Shrewsbury and sent over this morning. It was utterly stunning. On any other night, at any other time in her life, she would have been overcome with delight to be sitting here, perched on the corner of her dressing table chair, her taffeta skirts about her. She stood up and twirled before her mirror. Her shoulders were bare, each sleeve gathered into a posy of silk rosebuds. The skirt was bell-shaped, sewn in four layers, with each layer accentuated by a line of ruffles, again formed from the same silken buds. The dress alternated pure white and soft pink. Her hair was gathered at the neck in two chignons, with a loop over each ear. It was a beautiful dress and she was delighted with it. But as she stared at herself in the mirror, all she could think was that Owen would never see her in it. What was the point of getting all dressed up, if Owen were not there to behold her? Everyone else in the world, every other word of flattery – all of it was hollow and held no music for her, unless it was from Owen. The poetry of his words had won her, as well as his blue-sky eyes and corn-yellow hair, golden in the lamplight. His strong arms about her felt like safety, yet the eagerness in his body felt like danger, a delicious danger she wished to throw herself into, like deep, inviting waters. She loved the way he looked, but she loved him for himself too, his kind soul, his humanity.

The call came. Dinah appeared at the door, all a-flutter at Miss Beatrice's beauty that night.

'Ooh, miss! You look so fine, all drawed out!' she had said earlier. This meant dressed up, Beatrice discovered.

Beatrice went carefully downstairs, her broad skirt skimming each step. The three King women and Cyril looked up at her, each face registering its preference. Margaret, proud; Queenie, approving; Benjamina, envious; Cyril, bored. He was staying at home, having said at breakfast that he'd 'rather stab a fork in his eye than spend an evening with those tedious Elkinses.' The four women were shown out to the landau by Busby. It was lucky that the other women did not go in for crinolines, as there would be only room for one in the carriage, and that was Beatrice's huge concoction. The coachman set off and they trundled down the gravel drive, the breeze from their momentum welcome in the stifling heatwave of the past few days. The weather had grown hotter and hotter, the wind dropping to nothing, as if the whole world held its breath, waiting for rain and relief. Out onto the tree-lined road, the coach picked up speed as it travelled towards town. All four women were lost in their own thoughts. To stop herself pining for Owen, Beatrice looked at them all, her mother beside her, whilst her step-grandmother and great-grandmother sat opposite, their backs to forward travel. Maman was lost in peaceful contemplation. Beatrice could only assume she was happy that her daughter was coming out at last. Benjamina sat in perfect composure, smiling complacently, as usual. But when she looked at Queenie, her great-grandmother's face gave her a start. She was staring at something behind the carriage, tilting her head this way and that, as if to catch sight of something that had been seen on the side of the road. Her eyes were wide and her arm moved unsteadily forwards, her hand forming a trembling point, as she stared fearfully behind Beatrice.

'Queenie,' said Beatrice. 'What is it?'

'Oh!' cried Queenie, shocking Benjamina, who turned abruptly to look. 'Oh, no!' she shouted, her voice strident and loud.

'Grandmother!' called Maman, reaching forward.

But Queenie's hands were about her face, shielding her from whatever she'd seen. And then she cried out again, a scream of horror that pierced the still night air. All in a rush, the horse behind where Queenie sat squealed with terror, long and loud, its back legs buckling and the landau throwing them all forward. The other horse neighed with alarm and the carriage tipped to the left, swerving towards the trees at the side of the road, whereupon the coachman yanked back on the horses and yelled something. The carriage finally came to a stop when its back end smashed into a tree trunk, leaving them listing at an awkward angle.

All four women were gasping and uttering sounds of distress. Maman turned to Beatrice and said, 'Are you well?'

'Yes,' she uttered breathlessly. 'I am well.'

She saw the coachman take a swift look behind him, to see that nobody was injured. He then jumped down and went straight to the horses, checking them both far more carefully than he had the humans in his charge.

'Queenie, are you well?' said Beatrice, reaching across and taking her hand, which was shaking and flailing about, as if swatting away bees.

'You stupid old woman!' shouted Benjamina, pushing Beatrice's hand aside and clambering over them both to reach the landau door. She shoved it open and stepped down into the road, went around the back of the landau and looked at the place it had struck the tree. 'The wheel is split in two. Ruined. We won't be going anywhere fast tonight.'

'Grandmother,' said Maman, reaching out to her too. Queenie was shaking her head from side to side.

'I saw her. I saw her,' Queenie muttered.

'Saw who?' Beatrice said.

'I've never seen her out here. She was pointing, back at the house. Pointing. With her long, white bony finger. Pointing to the house!'

Beatrice and her mother glanced at each other in confusion.

'Ellis,' called Benjamina, now walking around to the coachman, who was doing his best to calm the horses, who snorted and shook their heads, their back feet kicking at the landau once or twice. He spoke to them soothingly and they eased a little, the snorting changing to a blowing sound and eventually a gentle nicker.

Beatrice took his lead and spoke to Queenie, softly reassuring her. 'There, there. She's gone now, whoever she was. Whoever frightened you.'

'Yes,' murmured Queenie. 'Yes, she has gone now.' Her face crumpled and she hid it in her hands, shooing the others away who tried to comfort her. It was shocking to see her great-grandmother like that. Beatrice had only ever seen her in complete control, the very model of restraint. Whatever had come over her? It was baffling. Seeing that Queenie was shaking, Beatrice took off her wrap and hung it around Queenie's shoulders, then sat side by side with her great-grandmother, one arm around her to offer silent comfort.

Beatrice heard Benjamina and Ellis discussing the situation, formulating a plan. Benjamina came round to them, while Ellis continued to soothe the horses.

'Now then,' said Benjamina to them, pointedly ignoring Queenie's trembling body. 'This is what's to be done. Ellis will run back to the house and bring down the barouche and some extra men. Someone will take us on to the ball and men will organise what needs to be done with the landau. If they can fix it in the road, they will. If not, they shall arrange for a cart to bring it home and someone will lead the horses back. All understood?'

Maman said, 'A good plan in theory. But Grandmother is not fit to go out, Benjamina. Surely you can see that.'

'Quite right,' said Benjamina, looking at Queenie with annoyance. 'She must be taken home. Ellis, bring the barouche for us and Cyril's cabriolet for Mrs King senior.'

Ellis nodded, then said, 'I oughta unhitch the horses from the carriage, just in case they take it in their heads to bolt. Better it be just the two of 'em running down the lane, than dragging a broken landau along with 'em.'

'Yes, indeed, Ellis. Good thinking,' said Benjamina.

Once he had disconnected the horses from the carriage, he said to Benjamina, 'Someone needs to stay with

’em and keep ’em calm. They’re proper jittery and we dunna want ’em to bolt if we can help it.’

‘I’ll stay with them,’ said Benjamina, commandingly.

Ellis took one last look at the horses and went off up the lane, breaking into a run after a few steps. Beatrice watched all this skittishly, trying to concentrate on Queenie’s distress, but wanting to see what was occurring about her. She saw Benjamina standing to the side of the horses, holding herself in as elegant a pose as she could on the side of a road after a traffic accident. She ignored the horses completely, who shuffled nervously.

While they waited, Queenie spoke no further, only whimpering from time to time, as Beatrice and her mother stroked her hands or patted her arms. Queenie sat with her head down, her hands over her eyes. Beatrice wanted to ask a thousand questions, but she could see it would only whip up Queenie again. The evening had started with her despondency at the window and now, with this latest twist, it had led to a moment of terror and now a gnawing worry. The only thing she knew for sure was that she did not want to go to the ball any more, if she ever had. She did not want to face anyone, be forced to smile or speak small talk. She did not want to be anywhere but home.

‘Maman,’ she spoke quietly, so as not to disturb Queenie.

‘Yes?’

'I don't want to go to the ball.'

'Oh, *chérie*,' sighed her mother. 'Do not let this spoil things. I will stay with Queenie and look after her. You should go, with Benjamina.'

She looked at Queenie; her trembling had lessened, but she was still shaken. She couldn't imagine leaving Queenie like this, and all so she could spend an entire evening with the sons of brickmasters.

Her mother read her mind and smiled gently, adding, 'Yet if you felt too shaken by the accident to go on . . .'

Beatrice smiled wanly back and squeezed her mother's arm. 'You always understand me, Maman.'

A sound of clattering wheels approached and they turned to see two carriages coming down the lane, the larger barouche in front, the smaller cabriolet behind. As they came closer and eased to a stop, Beatrice was surprised to see Uncle Cyril clamber down from the cabriolet, dressed up in his finest dinner attire. Before him gathered a group of men from the house, stable lads and a couple of footmen, Ellis leading them forwards to the scene of the accident. But pushing past them all and making a beeline for Queenie was Jenkins, dear Jenkins. When she reached Queenie, she put her hand on Queenie's arm and said, 'I am here.'

Queenie came alive and said 'Jenkins!' in a pitiful voice.

Jenkins looked up at Beatrice and her mother, at which Margaret said, 'We shall alight, so that you can sit with Grandmother.'

Jenkins nodded, then Beatrice and her mother climbed down from the landau. Beatrice saw Jenkins get in beside Queenie and put her arm tenderly around her shoulders, whispering in her ear and taking her hand.

Meanwhile, Cyril had marched over towards Beatrice and the others, eyeing up the side of the landau with astonished amusement.

'What a damnable mess!' he cried, clearly enjoying the drama.

'What are you doing here?' snapped Benjamina.

'Now, now,' he said, grinning. 'Is that any way to speak to your knight in shining armour? I am here to rescue you ladies and take you on to the ball myself.'

'But you had no intention of going to the ball before,' said Benjamina.

Cyril replied, 'Oh, come on, old girl. It'll be a last hurrah for me before I go off to America in a couple of weeks. Ladies, will you join us?'

Beatrice's mother replied, 'We three will return home. Your grandmother is in shock and needs to rest. I fear the same could be said of the two of us as well. None of us feel in a fit state to proceed to the dinner. We would all rather return home immediately. Ellis, can we take the barouche with you back home?'

'Of course, ma'am,' said Ellis.

'Well, if that's what you wish. Beatrice too? It is your first ball, my dear,' said Benjamina, languidly. Beatrice sensed that she said it because it was the right thing to say, not because she had any desire for Beatrice to accompany them.

'I feel rather shaken by all this myself. I'd rather go home, if you don't mind,' said Beatrice, politely.

'Come, come, then Benjamina,' said Cyril, cheerfully. 'We shall take my nifty little cabriolet. Let us climb aboard my steed. Nice and cosy for me and Mrs K.'

Benjamina shrugged, then took his hand and went to the two-wheeled carriage. Jenkins helped Queenie descend from the landau. She was much more composed now, looking more like the Queenie they knew. She had not spoken a word though. Cyril and Benjamina took off smartly in the cabriolet, while Beatrice and the others climbed into the barouche. Ellis took the reins and directed them round in a gentle circle; the last thing Beatrice glimpsed of the scene was the stable boy she'd once talked to about her umbrella, staring at the broken wheel of the landau, slapping his thigh and laughing.

They advanced at a slow pace up the lane towards home, Beatrice imagining Ellis felt it was better to take it as easily as possible for the three shaken lady passengers. The accident had been a shock for all of them. But just as alarming for Beatrice was Queenie, to see her in such a dishevelled state, shaking and gibbering like that. Beatrice would never forget her face, white as a sheet and slack-jawed, looking for all the world as if she'd just seen a ghost. She watched her closely now, reassuring herself that Queenie would be alright.

When they reached home, Jenkins took Queenie slowly upstairs, whispering to her as they went, about who knew what. Beatrice followed her mother upstairs too, suddenly weary, her dress feeling heavy and tight. She found Dinah waiting for her. Her maid fussed over her and seemed almost relieved to have something to do when Bea suggested she might like a snack. Dinah assured her she would bring some very good supper for her to eat from a tray in bed and went off to sort it, after helping Beatrice off with her dress and underclothes, and into her nightdress.

Once in bed and waiting expectantly for her plate of goodies, there was a small tap on the door. She licked her lips ready for food, to see instead her mother, now in her own nightdress and dressing gown, her hair in a long plait over her shoulder. She closed the door and came to sit beside Beatrice, taking her hand and kissing it.

'Are you all right, *chérie*?'

'Yes, Maman. Truly, I am quite well. It was rather exciting, in a way! But Queenie. What on earth was wrong with Queenie? Is she unwell?'

'I don't know. I really don't know,' said Maman, looking concerned. 'I'm sure she'll recover. She's safe with Jenkins now. It's strange. I've seen her confused before. I've seen her angry. But I've never seen her scared like that before. Never.'

'It was so odd. Who do you think she saw?'

'I really have no idea. I very much doubt she will enlighten us. Though if she were to share her thoughts with anyone other than her beloved Jenkins, it would be you, *chérie*.'

'Her face was quite a sight. White as a sheet. I've never seen her like that. I know she's quite old, but she never seems it. She always seems so strong. I wish I knew what had frightened her like that. Perhaps I'll ask her tomorrow or when she has recovered.'

'Perhaps. I would not push her for answers though. She is such a private person.'

'You're right. She's a difficult person to get to know. But I do love her.'

'I know you do. Now . . .'

'Not as much as I love you, though, Maman!' And she reached out and hugged her mother, who squeezed her back affectionately.

'I know that, silly! You and I are two of a kind, always have been. A perfect pair, since I first felt you move, fluttering away in my tummy like a butterfly. And now, here you are. A beautiful young woman. I was so proud of you, watching you come down the stairs in your gown tonight, *chérie*. You truly are a stunning young woman. I am sorry you had to miss out on your first event. Once Queenie is better, we shall sit down with her and properly plan for your season. A series of balls and so forth, to launch you properly.'

'You make me sound like a ship, Maman!' She laughed with her mother, but she was thinking how a season, and balls, and dances, and small talk with local young men, was the last thing on earth she wanted. Would it be the right time to tell her mother that now? Right now? Perhaps she could spill her heart to her mother. She hated keeping things from her.

As ever, her mother watched her face and detected something in it, which Beatrice had sought to hide. 'But you are worried about something. Is it what happened tonight? Really, don't concern yourself too much. Queenie has always been a bit unusual and I'm sure she will recover fully. I remember her saying some very peculiar things when I was a child. But that was twenty years ago and nothing terrible has happened to her since, so you mustn't worry too much.'

'All right, Maman.'

But immediately, Maman knew that was not it. She sighed and took Beatrice's hand again, lacing their fingers together.

'If you are fretting about coming out, about meeting these young men . . .'

'A little,' said Beatrice, looking down at their hands, knitted together. She did not want her mother to see her eyes, as she feared they would betray her thoughts, filled with the image of only one particular young man.

'*Chérie*, I am so proud of you, for moving on and accepting the way things are. After . . . that boy.'

Beatrice could not look at her. She felt her mother's hand under her chin, lifting her face towards her. Beatrice felt her eyes fill and saw her mother's sympathy as a tear rolled down her cheek and onto her mother's palm. Maman took her in her arms again and held her. Beatrice fought to suppress her emotions. She missed Owen so much and pined for him dreadfully. She had lied to her mother too and did not want her to see her guilt. All of this, as well as tonight's misfortune, made the tears flow.

'I know first love is powerful,' said her mother, stroking her hair. 'Believe me, I truly do know. But these things pass. It seems they are solid as rock and will last forever. But instead, they are sand, washed away by the tide.'

'Yes, Maman,' she whispered to her mother, who drew back and wiped her tears away with her sleeve.

'Now then, perhaps a new plan of action might be in order.'

'What kind of plan?'

'If you do not feel ready to enter the social season here in Shropshire, perhaps you might prefer a change of scene.'

Beatrice thought only of Owen, that any time spent away from Ironbridge meant another week or fortnight or more where she could not see him.

'I'm very happy here, Maman.'

'I know that, but I think a break from this place might do you good. Get away, meet new people, see new sights. I'm wondering if you and I should join Cyril on his trip to America.'

'What? I thought you disliked Cyril. I know I do!'

'Yes, but he would merely be a means to an end. He would be our chaperone as we travel, yet upon arrival, we could go out for trips alone, the two of us. Visit places of interest, see the countryside. Imagine all the fascinating places that must be there. It would be good to broaden our horizons. What do you think?'

America was across the ocean! She would be away for months! It was out of the question.

'It is a very long way to America. And I do hate the sea.'

'I know but you are young and strong. You will cope. Think on it, *chérie*. It could be an adventure for us. And it would be good to get you away from . . . memories.'

Then came a knock on the door.

'That'll be Dinah with my meal,' said Beatrice, saved by the tray of food that her maid now carried in.

Her mother stood up, leant down and kissed her cheek.

'Think about it,' she said, smiling.

'I shall, Maman,' she said, reaching eagerly for her tray. Dinah had done her proud. Thick slices of ham, cheese, cucumber and buttered bread sat on a plate beside a bowl of cherry pie with cream for dessert. Dinah left a glass of warm milk on her bedside table.

'Goodnight, my beauty,' said Maman, lingering by the door.

'Night,' mumbled Beatrice as she bit down onto the bread, her stomach grumbling. Before Maman turned to go, Beatrice saw her framed in the doorway for a moment, her hair streaked with grey, her face wrinkled with smiles, yet also fatigue. The trip to America would be too much for her mother, she was sure. She needed to stay here and have an easy life. Maman was only trying to get her away so she didn't mope around about Owen. Beatrice would just have to act more carefully, convincing her mother that she had no need of being spirited away in order to forget her first love. She would have to be convincing. Perhaps she should even agree to meet a young man or two, just to put Maman off the scent. She resolved to start doing just that tomorrow. Yes, she'd have another talk about it all with her mother, tomorrow.

Taking a slice of ham and placing it on the bread, she took another large bite, then looked around at her open window. She prayed Owen would come to her, late tonight, so they could discuss more plans. She was sorely tempted to suggest they elope, to escape this American proposal. But she knew how badly elopement had turned out for her mother and really, she knew in her heart of hearts that though she loved Owen completely, she did not want to be poor and without her family. She liked food too much and the other comforts, and she loved the idea that she and Owen could change Ironbridge for the better. So, she would stay and stick to her plan. Her love for Owen was eternal and thus they would have to be patient, as she had told him. She polished off her supper, took a swig of the milk beside her bed and placed the tray on the floor. She turned down her lamp but left it dimly burning in the hope that Owen would see it and come to her. She snuggled down in bed, shoving off the covers as it was infernally hot in there. She lay still and waited, her eyelids drooping, though she fought to keep them open. Her last thoughts were about her mother, that whatever happened, whatever choices she and Owen made, her mother would still love her. Maman had always loved her more than anything in the world and Maman always would. The drama of the evening had worn her out and the heat lay on her like a heavy blanket. Within minutes, she was fast asleep.

Jenkins had only left her when she was sure Queenie was asleep. But Queenie had been feigning sleep, so that she might be left alone. It was horrid to be in distress and not be able to tell anyone – particularly her dearest ones – why she was in such a state. It was the ghost of Betsy Blaize she'd seen, standing beside the road as the carriage advanced, pointing back at the King house. Its white face had gaped open blackly again, as it had once before. It was a ghastly sight, enough to curdle blood. She had broken down in front of everyone, which was unforgiveable. But one would have to be made of stone not to in the face of such horror. The visitations were escalating and becoming more extreme. Either Queenie was losing her mind – something of which she would brook no serious contemplation – or the ghost was becoming more insistent in her demands. But Queenie had done all she could on that account. She had visited the Joneses at home and tried to make them stay. They had refused but now were back in their home, kept empty for them on Queenie's orders. She had been told by Jenkins and Beatrice of the need for a doctor to help at Martha Jones's childbed, and she had paid for the doctor and received no thanks. Surely this was enough; she had secured the safe passage of Blaize's descendants! What more could be asked of her? In fact, she had been convinced that was what the visits had been about. That the whole business had led to that moment, when, through Beatrice, she had been able to save Blaize's daughter and grandchild. Once the doctor's bill had been paid, she had been sure she would never see the ghost again. She had safeguarded Blaize's legacy. Why would she see her again now?

Queenie said aloud, 'Again, I say, I have paid my debts.'

Not all of them, came a ghostly reply.

Queenie's eyes snapped open and she shivered. A white light shone into the room through her open curtains, the window also left open to receive respite from the heat. It was silver like moonlight, yet bright like sunshine. She knew that unearthly light. She had felt braver the last time she saw it shining through her window, had been belligerent even with the ghost. But now, after seeing it beside the road, she feared it more than ever and trembled at the sight of that dazzling harbinger casting her room into stark white relief.

Come, said the voice. *Come outside.*

'I will not,' whispered Queenie, terrified yet with an ounce of defiance remaining.

Come to your husband's grave.

Queenie gazed at the light, tempted to stay safe in bed, but if she didn't nip this in the bud, it could go on forever. Steeling her spine, she pulled back the covers. She was Queenie King, she backed down from no one, man or ghost. Her feet were bare and made no sound on the floor as she approached the door and saw the key left in it, turned it to the right and opened the back door, stepping out into the night, the sky still coloured with the failing light, the woodlands about the house grey and obscure. There, across the gravel and beyond the low wooden fence, low enough to step over, were the neat rows of family graves, beyond them the collection of little gravestones to mark the dead family pets. Standing amidst them all was Blaize. Her white hair flowed like winter water and her eyes beamed blue, gazing into Queenie's soul.

She walked across the gravel, feeling the stones dig sharply into her bare feet, but she felt she had no choice but to proceed. She stepped over the low fence and approached Ralph King senior's grave. Betsy Blaize's spirit stood silently beside it.

You know what you did, said the spirit.

Queenie did not argue. She knew exactly what Blaize was referring to. Many times over the years the scene had entered her mind and each time it came she had shooed it away, unwilling to relive it. But as she closed her eyes to escape the sight of the ghost, the scene from her past replayed itself complete in her mind's eye.

She saw herself in a fine dress, a dark red gown with silver beading, one of her favourites from her fifties, when she still wore rich colours. Queenie recalled crossing the hallway, then seeing something amiss at the foot of the servants' staircase. There was a tray on the step, beside it a pile of broken glass and a puddle of liquor, which smelt like her husband's best whisky. She looked about for some explanation, but could see none. She walked onwards with displeasure, along the corridor to her husband's study, ready to complain to him of the state of the housekeeping these days at Southover, that it would not do, and that he must support her in beginning a new regime of discipline in the house. She recalled so perfectly her indignation at this latest outrage. Queenie had shown more interest in the business lately and the house had suffered. But why should it be only her that was responsible for the tenor of servants in the house? She went to see her husband with her grievances. She opened his study door quietly, wondering if at this time of the afternoon he was taking a nap on his chaise longue, which he sometimes did when his work tired him. She went in softly, peering around the door to see if he were at his desk – no – then looked around to the day bed and saw him there.

He was lying face down on it. He was moving around, his trousers were shoved down so she could see his naked backside and underneath him, squirming and small, was a tiny figure, looking like a doll beneath his tall, oversized frame. Her husband's head moved to one side, burying itself in the figure's neck, and Queenie saw the large eyes of the new maid, Betsy Blaize, her little face white with terror, her eyes blinking wildly until they found Queenie, staring at her from the doorway, and they stared back. Queenie had hired the child herself. She was twelve years old. Her lips were moving. They mouthed, 'Help me.' The man on top of her began moving more vigorously. 'Help me,' said the girl again, staring straight at Queenie now, as she stood more than two decades older, remembering it in perfect detail. Ralph's large hand came into view and clamped itself over the girl's mouth. Queenie saw her younger self step backwards in horror, standing in the corridor outside her husband's study. She turned round swiftly as a footman came along and stopped, standing to the side and bowing, waiting for her to move on. She quickly brought the door to, then closed it very gently, turning the handle to close it securely. She said some angry words to the footman, pointed down the corridor and he hurried off. She stood there alone, her hands trembling, as she brought them up to her mouth and covered it, her eyes staring downwards, her head shaking slowly from side to side.

Queenie now felt the tears streaming from her eyes, so much so that the image in her mind seemed to blur and vanish. Now, she could not see anything except her misery and shame. She dropped to her knees, grovelling at the feet of Betsy Blaize's spirit.

You knew, came its words. *You knew.*

'I'm sorry, I'm sorry, I'm sorry!' cried Queenie.

I asked you for help.

'I know, I know.'

Why did you do nothing? Why did you not help me?

'I could not, I could not!' she said, tearing at her nightdress in her distress. Queenie looked up, wiping the tears from her eyes, frozen again by the blue scrutiny of the ghost. 'I had no power. I was my husband's possession, just as you were. We are both women.'

I was not a woman. I did not choose to marry. I was a child. A man forced himself into me, over and over, in your house, under your watch. You knew it was happening. For three long years, you knew. And you did nothing.

'I am sorry. I can only say I am sorry, a thousand times.'

It is not enough! cried the ghost, her voice magnified, so that it sounded like a wind, a hundred winds roaring, a whirlwind of sound.

'Tell me,' cried Queenie, shaking like a leaf in a storm. 'Tell me what I must do.'

You must pay.

'Tell me the price! I will pay anything! Tell me, I beg of you. Tell me what I must do!'

You . . . must . . . suffer.

Queenie stared at Blaize, whose whiteness grew in intensity until she could bear to look upon it no more. She covered her eyes and buried her head in her arms, curling up on the brittle grass, dry from the heatwave. She hid her face there until she could hear no more, see nothing but the inside of her eyelids and feel nothing but the sticky night air on her bare legs and feet. That was the last sensation she experienced, before a blackness took her and she passed out, deeper than sleep, darker than night.

Chapter 20

'I'm off out now,' said Owen, pulling on his cap. He did not need his coat, as it was still as warm as an afternoon out there, despite being well past nine o'clock at night.

'Don't stay out too late, mind,' said his mother, resting by the cold fireplace, her belly a high mound.

'I wonna be too long,' he said and smiled at her.

'Mind you're not. This little'un needs her big brother around.'

'A girl now, is it?' said Owen, smiling at her.

'Wishful thinking,' she said. 'Less trouble than you boys, always getting into scrapes.'

'No scrapes, Mother. I promise,' he lied.

'Good lad,' she said and looked away, running her hands over her bump. She looked sleepy but content.

His father was outside next door, chatting with a neighbour, puffing on his clay pipe. He saw Owen leave and raised his hand in brief farewell. Owen nodded at him, then turned away and walked down the path to town. He was a little late for meeting Adam at the tavern. Adam had been the only one he could talk to about Royce's plan. He'd gone to his house a couple of days before, seen Martha and baby Hettie and cradled the baby in his arm nervously for a minute or two. Then he'd motioned Adam outside for a private chat. He didn't tell him about his feelings for Beatrice, only explaining the damage Royce's plans would do to the brickworks. He believed the Kings would close down the works if there were any more trouble. Adam was convinced and said he would talk to Royce and warn him off. But just yesterday, he'd seen Royce again with Bolton in town. They were talking together in the tavern, heads down, looking like conspirators if ever he'd seen one. Owen talked again to Adam and they agreed, Royce couldn't be trusted. Adam had heard from a servant at the King house that most if not all of the Kings were going to a ball that night in Broseley. It would be the perfect opportunity for Royce and his cronies to burgle the house. So, Adam arranged with Owen that they'd meet in the tavern, then go along to the King house and keep an eye on it. They'd make sure nobody did anything stupid. Owen never liked lying to his parents, but it was necessary. Adam would know what to do and the two of them would be able to talk Royce and Bolton down, if it came to that. Adam was handy in a fight and he himself was sure he could beat Royce to a pulp if necessary. He had the fuel for it.

Adam must have grown tired of waiting in the tavern, as Owen came across him on the path from town.

They turned about and walked the other way, along the river and up through the woodland towards Southover. They talked a little on the way, about conditions at work, the longer hours causing such fatigue in everyone that more and more mistakes were being made each day. They knew it was pointless discussing it, that nothing would change, but they liked to hear themselves moan about it. It rid their heads of it, at any rate. As they approached the King house, Owen was surprised to see lamps burning in quite a few windows, despite the fact that most of the family were out at the ball. He guessed they were there waiting for the family's return, which Adam had told Owen was supposed to be well past eleven that night, so they had a couple of hours to wait. They had guessed that Royce and company would not risk breaking in while it was still light, so left it till now to come. All seemed quiet, to Owen's relief. They stopped by the oak tree he'd stood by before, watching the house in silence for a while. Owen stared for a long time at Beatrice's open window, wishing she were there, wishing his father's cousin was not beside him, wishing he could sprint across the lawns and leap into her room in one bound and kiss her. Then, they heard a noise.

It was the stealthy movement of feet through the undergrowth, many feet not just two or four. Adam and Owen swapped glances, then melted back into the shadows behind the oaks. Adam saw Royce first and silently pointed him out to Owen. Royce had appeared from behind a copse of trees at the southern side of Southover. Bolton was there, too, but then they saw there were three others. Owen cursed himself for not coming more prepared.

'Five of 'em,' whispered Adam and grimaced.

'What shall we do?' whispered Owen.

'We need to end this, now,' said Adam, and Owen nodded. They stepped out onto the grass and marched towards them.

'Oi!' called Adam. All five men froze. They were picking up something from the ground, clutching something in their hands. Bottles. Were they ginger beer bottles? They looked just like it, just as Owen had drunk from many a time. Ginger beer? But there was a stink of fish. None of it made sense.

Royce sneered, 'Look what we have here! Jones and his lapdog Malone.'

'What're you doing, Royce?' said Adam. Royce looked momentarily nervous. That was the effect their union leader still had on the workers. But it was only a moment and soon he was squaring up to Adam, flanked by Bolton and his other henchmen, all much taller than him and twice as broad.

Royce turned to his men and said, 'Put the bottles down, lads. Nice and careful. We have another job to do first.' All the men lined up their bottles on the ground, pushing them into the soil. It was then Owen saw that each bottle was filled with a thick liquid and had an oily rag stuffed in its neck. He knew that smell. It was whale oil.

'I said, what the hell are you doing?'

'What needs doing. You couldna get what we needed. So we're taking it into our own hands.'

'Taking what?' said Owen. 'This wonna get you higher pay. It wonna get you nothing.'

'It'll get us satisfaction,' said Royce.

'And vengeance,' added Bolton.

'It speaks!' sneered Owen.

Bolton squared up to Owen. 'Say that again, Malone.'

'Come on, lads. This is a nasty kind of mischief that wonna do anyone any good,' said Adam.

'Dunna stop us, mon,' Royce said. 'Or we shall stop you, permanent like.'

Adam raised his voice now. 'Stop this, Royce. It's gone too far. There are innocent servants in there, mon.'

'No, they inna! They work for the Kings. And anyway, most of 'em are out tonight. It's the King house we want to burn to the ground.'

In the shock of the moment, nobody spoke, but Owen had heard enough. He let his fist fly and punched Royce in the side, winding him and making him drop to his knees. It was a moment of sweet satisfaction. But the next thing he knew, a fist was making friends with his head and a wallop had come from the left into his ear. He staggered to the side, then righted himself just in time to see Bolton coming at him. He ducked then punched Bolton in the stomach, taking advantage of his momentary recovery to try and hit him on the head, but he missed and someone pushed him hard. He struck out and hit someone, though his view was obscured by wrestling bodies. He scrambled up and hit the first person he saw, before someone grabbed his arms and pulled him away, throwing him to the ground. Before he could get up, someone had kicked him in the back. The pain was bad and he covered his head, afraid of being kicked there too. Another kick came to his legs and sent him curling up. He tried to look out to see how many had him on the ground, and if he could grab their legs. He caught sight of Adam being punched in the side of the head by a big bloke, who shouted 'Traitor!' at Adam as he fell straight over like a skittle, out cold. Then a blow landed on Owen's eye and he clutched at it, feeling something warm and wet. He tried to open his eyes only to discover one was blinded by blood. The other opened to see the world at the skewed angle of a man on his back, looking up at the dark tops of trees. He twisted his head to see four pairs of legs walking over to the house. He tried to drag himself upwards to go after them, but a searing pain in his back stopped him and he collapsed on the ground again. He watched Royce use a rock to smash a glass panel in a door, then four men went into the house carefully and quietly, carrying their bottles, shutting the door behind them. Two legs appeared in his line of vision, grasped the unconscious Adam and threw his head back against the ground, just in case. The last thing he saw was Bolton's face leering at him, grasping him by the scruff of the neck.

'See this fist?' whispered Bolton, brandishing it at him. 'It speaks!'

He punched Owen in the face and that was that.

Margaret was dreaming of Paris. She was turning the key in their front door, walking in to the little house in Montmartre and shutting it behind her. She could smell horse manure from the street outside, sweetened by the scent of baking bread. She could hear her neighbours chatting in melodious French. She saw her daughter, beautiful brown hair tumbling down her back in waves, sitting at the piano beside a pupil playing halting scales in a major key. Beatrice turned to smile at her. She had brought flowers home with her and found a vase on the windowsill, filled it with the flowers and water from a jug. She placed the vase on the table, where primers in English language were splayed open, layered with papers and pencils. It was evening and the sun was streaming through the window creating a yellow square on the table, criss-crossed by the shadows of the window leads. Her little world, her little life. Happiness.

But as she stared at the golden light on the table, it began to glow brightly. Brighter and brighter still, until it hurt her eyes to look at it. She put up her hand to shield herself and saw she could not find her hand before her face. Her head was surrounded by webs of grey, as if she'd fallen into a spider's web. She swiped at it to no avail, unable to see anything now but the dark grey and the blinding flash of light behind it. She fought to open her eyes and heard someone coughing. They were coughing fit to burst their lungs and she looked around wildly to find who it was.

When Margaret awoke, she heard the sound was coming from her own throat. She was choking. Finally, her eyes could open and she knew she was not in the world of dreams any longer. She was surrounded by smoke. She tried to call out, but only a hoarse scratch came. She realised her breathing was quick and shallow. She listened to it and tried to take a deeper breath, but that brought on the coughing again. She tried to sit up, but it made the coughing worse. She reached over to the bedside table and used it to pull herself out of bed and onto the floor, where she banged her arm and knee as she fell. She crawled under the bed, as there was not so much smoke there. It had been worse higher up in the room. She tried to call out again, but she had no voice.

'*Chérie*,' she uttered, a husky sound. She could see the door from under the bed and knew she had to get to it. Yet from here, she could see a line of bright light flickering at its base and it frightened her. She would have to get to the window instead. She pulled herself out from under the bed and there came the coughing again, wracking her chest until she felt nothing but a deathly exhaustion. She tried again to call out.

'Bea . . .'

It was a whisper now. She heard herself saying it aloud in her head, calling it along the street in Paris, where Bea would run off with her friends and look for snacks.

'Bea, ma *chérie* . . .'

But nobody came.

Beatrice woke with a start. She was coughing and the room was hazy, grey wafts of smoke circling around the dim lamp, its fingers reaching into each corner. She was slick with sweat. There was a sound surrounding her, a roaring sound, as if wind were blowing through her brain.

Fire, she thought. *The house is on fire.* She tumbled out of bed and ran to the door, went to touch the door handle, but it was hot. It hurt her hand and she cried out. She did not want to open that door. Yet beyond it would be her Maman and Queenie. They would never have left without coming for her first. She must go to them. But the scalding handle and the flames that lay beyond it trapped her in her room, cutting her off from Queenie, Maman and who knew who else. She turned and stumbled to the window. The sight she saw was terrifying. Below to her right was the conservatory, filled with flames. To her left was the flat roof of the library. It was not on fire as yet. That would be her escape route. She called out, hoping someone, anyone might have got out. Most of the servants had the night off, but she knew Dinah and Jenkins were somewhere in the house.

'Help!' she cried and coughed afterwards. Nobody replied.

She looked feverishly at the flat roof. It had looked so easy when Owen had jumped on to it. But he was taller and fitter than her.

'Help me!' she shouted again, louder this time, the coughing worse. Her throat ached but she had no choice; she had to try to raise help. 'Maman! Help me!'

It was no good. Nobody was going to come. Where was everyone? Were they hurt? Trapped? She couldn't think on that now. She had to get out. She stared at the flat roof, trying to work out how far she would need to jump and what would happen if she missed it. There was the drop and gravel below. It would hurt. She might break her legs, or her back, or her neck. But if she stayed . . .

She lifted up her nightdress and clambered onto the windowsill, sitting on it, her legs dangling. At least it was less smoky out here. She coughed and coughed, feeling light-headed and weak. She forced herself to concentrate. She couldn't sit here forever. She levered herself up, holding onto the top of the window frame and putting one foot, then the other on the sill. As she turned herself around slowly, her legs shaking, she saw the smoke rushing in under the door to her room now, the roaring sound louder than ever. Soon the door would burn down, she was sure of that. She held on to the gable and craned her neck round to look at the roof. It looked impossibly far away. How on earth had Owen done it? She pictured herself over and over again, making the leap and failing, falling to the ground and breaking her neck. Her legs were rigid and she could not make them move. Fear had frozen her.

Then, a sound came.

'Bea! Dunna move!'

It was Owen's voice. How she'd wanted to hear it. It must be her mind creating it, wishful thinking. She clutched onto the gable more tightly. Thick white smoke was billowing from her room now in two streams, divided by her body. She could not see and she began to cough horribly.

'Bea! Bea! I'm coming! Dunna move!'

It was Owen's voice, near and clear now. Was it really him? She could not open her eyes. She could not move her legs. She felt weak from the coughing, tried to open her eyes but was blinded by the smoke. Her grip loosened. She felt she would fall. She turned her head to try to look towards the flat roof, knowing it was now or never. Through the swelling smoke, she thought she saw someone, two arms reaching, shouting something at her again.

Was it really him? How was he here? How did he know she needed him? Or was she imagining it? So many times she had sat at her windowsill and conjured him with her mind, pictured him so clearly appearing from behind the oak tree and coming to her across the lawn. Was he real now? Or simply a mirage, created by her panic and the swirling smoke?

He had heard her before he saw her. He had come to with an aching head, and aching back, aching everywhere. He'd been badly beaten up and felt like a cracked plate, held in place by stillness but as soon as he moved, he feared he would break into pieces. But there it was again, that voice, calling. He forced his eyes to open and looked up into the canopy. There was a thickness to the air, beyond the heat, something tangible and there was a stink of bonfires. He turned his head with care, aware of a soreness in his neck, to see the King house was ablaze. It was so shocking to see, spectacular in its way, the white smoke pouring out from windows, flames engulfing the room the men had gone in by. They'd done it. They'd set the house on fire. But then he heard the sound again, a plaintive call. Someone was calling. It was Beatrice's voice. Bea!

Owen's body moved without his volition. He had jumped up and nearly tripped over Adam, out cold on the ground. He shook Adam by the shoulders and said his name. Adam groaned. Then he heard the voice calling again and knew he had to leave Adam and go. He started running towards the side of the house where her bedroom was, without even registering the pain all over his body. He lurched forward, his focus only on that one thing – her voice. He skirted the burning conservatory at a distance and came upon her room, seeing the flat roof he'd climbed first, then looking upwards. There she was! Clinging onto her window and trapped there.

He called to her, told her to stay still. He could climb up there and get her. The smoke was thick here. She would succumb to it soon and fall. He threw himself at the wisteria that was singed, embers of petals drifting on the air with the hot smoke. He climbed rapidly, grasping with desperate precision, never missing a grip or a foothold. Within seconds it seemed, he was up on the flat roof.

'I am here!' he shouted at Bea. 'Jump, Bea. I shall catch you. Jump!'

Her face was buried in her sleeves. She seemed too frightened to move.

'Bea, trust me! Trust me, you wonna fall. Open your eyes, Bea and look at me.'

She heard him and started to turn her head. She opened her eyes and squinted at him, the smoke thick around them. Both of them were coughing, he holding his arm across his mouth.

'Jump, Bea!'

'I can't!' she cried. 'I'll fall!'

'I'm here. I shall catch you. Trust me. I know you trust me, Bea. Come on, my sweetheart. Come to me.' He reached out towards her.

She didn't look down, she didn't say another word. She let her right hand drop and she leapt towards him, launching herself from the windowsill, her arms flailing. He made contact and held on tight, pushing himself backwards to take her weight. They tumbled down onto the roof and landed in a heap, the pain of his back searing through him, but the relief of having her in his arms swept through him.

'Come on!' he cried, scrambling up and helping her. She was coughing again. He had to get her off the roof and away from the smoke. It was smoke that killed folk, he knew, before the flames even touched you. 'I shall climb first and you shall come after. That way, if you fall I shall be below you. Come now.'

He reached over to the trellis and held on with two feet and one hand. He beckoned to her with his free hand. Her eyes were wide now, terrified. He feared she would freeze again but she moved and grasped the trellis. He hoped it would take the weight of both of them. He began to climb downwards as she did, making a move that echoed hers, always one step ahead, beneath her, his right arm on her at all times, in case she fell backwards. Then, the ground came and they were on it. No time for happy reunions. He grasped her hand and ran her away from the building to the safety of the trees. He had done it. He had saved her. They held on to each other and she wept, coughing and sobbing and saying his name. He held her and let her cry, thanking the Lord, the stars and everything that she was safe.

'Thank you, thank you,' she said and looked at him, kissing him messily. 'How are you here?'

'How are *you* here?' he said, unable to answer her question easily. 'You're supposed to be at the dinner with your mother.'

'Maman!' she cried and wrenched herself away from him. She was running toward the house.

'No, Bea!' he shouted after her. She was running around the house to the left, heading past the conservatory that was an inferno now, keeping her distance but not slowing or stopping. 'Come back!' he shouted again.

He could hear her screaming as he came around and saw her pointing up at the window above the conservatory. It must her mother's room.

'Maman is in there! I must go in.'

'No, are you mad?' he shouted above the roar and crackle of the fire and caught up with her, holding her back. Now he saw there were people on this side, servants standing at a distance from the house, some running to and fro from the stables that were not yet ablaze, bringing buckets of water and throwing them uselessly towards the conservatory, the heat being too great to get near enough. The grooms were leading the horses the other way to safety down the driveway, the poor, terrified beasts pulling frantically at their reins. More onlookers were gathering around the perimeter of the grounds, pointing and staring. Nothing and nobody could save the house now.

Beatrice wrenched herself away from him and ran over towards the huddle of servants, throwing questions at them and pointing towards the house. People were shaking their heads.

Owen caught up with her. 'Bea, come with me, away from the house,' he said, desperate now to keep her back, she was so rash and unpredictable in her movements. He half expected her to run wildly into the burning house itself.

'My mother is in there!' she cried, feverishly. 'I saw her go to bed. Nobody has seen her since. Nobody has seen Queenie either!'

'They may've come out a different way. Stay here and I'll go around the outside of the whole house, see if they're somewhere else.'

'I'll go that way, you go this way,' she said, nodding.

'No! No, you are weakened by the smoke. You must stay here.'

'He's right, miss Beatrice,' said a female voice. It was a maid, young and short, her face smeared with grime from the smoke. 'You mun stay here with us.'

'But Dinah,' replied Beatrice, 'my mother and great-grandmother may be in there. Where is Jenkins?'

Owen said, 'Keep her here,' and nodded at the maid, who nodded firmly back. He ran off, skirting the house at a safe distance. Around the other side were a few other servants gathered, while at the edge of the woods more crowds of locals were gathering. He could not see anyone in nightclothes or otherwise looking well-dressed, until he saw a frail old thing in a nightgown standing by the graveyard, her arms in the air, her mouth open wide as she cried out at the sight of the burning house. She was being comforted by another woman in a nightdress, who was grasping at her flailing hands. He recognised her, it was Jenkins. And there was old Mrs King with her. He had no time to think on them more, as he had to get back to Beatrice. He came around the other side of the house to see he had skirted its entire perimeter and was coming back to where Dinah and Beatrice had been. But Beatrice was not there. The maid was shouting and running forward.

As he came about, he saw a white flash disappear into the front door of the house. It was Beatrice's nightdress, he knew that, and without a thought he followed her in. The hallway was flanked by a searing wall of flame on the right-hand side. He could see Beatrice heading for the main staircase, where flames licked the bannisters, yet there was a path upwards. He could hear the roar and creak of a house about to cave in on itself and madly rushed forwards, grabbed at Beatrice and caught the edge of her nightdress. She screamed and fell forward, onto the first steps of the staircase. He held on tight, yanking her towards him and forcing her up and into his arms. Her eyes were wild and she screamed, 'Maman! Queenie!'

He was not about to argue and manhandled her across the hallway.

She screamed, 'I can't leave them!' and pulled away from him again. He reached out and grasped her, shoving her hard in the direction of the front door. He saw her lose her footing and stumble forwards out of the door and sprawl onto the gravel. Safe, at last. Bea was safe at last. Someone rushed forward to attend to her. Owen took a breath and stumbled forwards towards the open door, and fresh air and freedom. But a great splintering sound came from above and he looked up to see the ceiling rippling with flames and a huge fissure appearing across it. The next moment the ceiling opened up like a cracked eggshell, beams, joists, plaster and all, splitting and subsiding, and down it all came upon him.

Chapter 21

Beatrice had been in this room before, she recalled, as she looked around the drawing room of the old brickmaster's house. It was only a few weeks past, but it seemed like years, like a lifetime ago. In a way, it was, as the old Beatrice who had stood in this room had been another person. She had stood beside this window, surrounded by space and floating dust, a few sticks of furniture about covered in sheets. She had stood here with her young man and she had run from the room, smiling, determined to change their futures for the better. She had been a young fool, innocent of the world and its wanton violence.

A new Beatrice had been born – a hard, flinty version of the girl she had once been – the night she lost Owen and Maman.

Just to think of her brought on tears. The loss of Owen had been like a knife in her guts, a sudden, painful tear in the fabric of her existence. But the loss of her mother was broader, deeper and all-consuming. It felt as if the Biblical flood had come again, but instead of water, Beatrice's world had been drowned in darkness, a thick, drenching sadness that felt as if it would never clear. There was a hollow in the centre of herself she felt would never be filled. In the days after the fire she had wept like a person who had lost all reason. She was cosseted by maids and Jenkins was often by her side. She was given draughts to drink from the doctor that only served to haunt her sleep with nightmares. In those chaotic days, she was hardly aware of what was happening around her, but she recalled being taken to a hotel and thence to this house, filling daily with new things to make it habitable. She saw very little of Queenie, who had taken to her bed. She saw more of Benjamina, taking over the new arrangements with a kind of delighted panache that sickened Beatrice. How could anyone in this family enjoy themselves after the disaster that had befallen them all? Cyril was around too, grimly assisting Benjamina, but loudly complaining about their new situation and the vengeance that justice would pour out upon the heads of those responsible. He talked loudly too of his imminent trip to America, his plans unchanged by the tragedy. It was clear he couldn't wait to get away. All this passed by Beatrice as a kind of waking dream, something from which she could not escape.

Today was the first day she had been fully dressed and downstairs. She sat now in a narrow, firm armchair, its florid pattern bright with newness. She was alone, looking out of the window in a stupor for an hour or more now. She did not feel ill any more. She had stopped taking the doctor's concoctions as they made her feel worse. She felt clear-headed and clear-eyed, apart from the tears that sprang there each time she thought of those she had lost. She turned from the window and looked behind her at the sitting room. Just there, she had stood, Owen beside her. He had kissed her there, right there. Oh, the visceral pain of imagining his mouth, his lips! Another stab in the guts. She allowed herself the painful pleasure of picturing him there, his hair yellow like butter, his eyes blue like a summer sky. So handsome, so young. An image leapt into her mind of how his body must have been after the burning. And then her mother's. Thus was her mind swept with sweet, sad memories and harsh, violent images of death these past weeks. She stared at the room and knew in that moment that she could not stay there. Not in that room, that house or even that town. Every day would be painful, every minute would be torture, walking through the site of her abandonment, by every bright hope and tender love she had valued most highly. If she stayed in Ironbridge, she would be haunted, every second that passed, every breath she took. She knew it in her bones. She could not stay there and she would not. It was the first decision she had made since becoming an orphan – and in her eyes – a widow. They may not have been married in law, but in her heart her future husband was gone forever, her hopes and dreams along with him. Now, she had to make a new life. And it would not be here.

She stood and walked across the room, every step stirring up memories like the dust that floated about them the day she and Owen had come here to be alone. She went out into the hallway, its rich tapestry of tiles assaulting her with more memories she wished to escape. She ascended the staircase and approached Queenie's door. She knocked briefly twice then opened the door and went in. Jenkins appeared at the door opposite, the entrance to her own room, just off Queenie's, where Jenkins could keep a sharp eye on her.

'Miss Beatrice,' said Jenkins in a hushed voice, glancing cautiously at the bed in which her mistress rested.

'I have come to speak with her,' said Beatrice.

'I am not certain she's strong enough yet,' said Jenkins. 'Another day, perhaps?'

'Is that you, Bea?' came a voice, throaty and dry, unused to conversation these past weeks. Beatrice looked to see Queenie's head turned towards her, eyes wide open.

Beatrice ignored Jenkins and went to Queenie's bed. She sat down beside her great-grandmother's prone body. Not for the first time, she thought of how the old woman was now in her late seventies and it seemed so unfair that an elderly life should continue when such young lives had been cut short. She hated to think of it that way, she chided herself for it, but the thought still came to her, that Queenie seemed to live forever, while others perished along the way. But of course, she was glad that there was one person left in the world who understood her, who loved her, as Queenie did. And Queenie remembered Maman and loved her too, in her own way. It should be enough, to keep her there, Queenie's love. But as Beatrice took her hand and patted it, and attempted to turn up the corners of her mouth to smile at Queenie, she knew that even her great-grandmother's love was not enough to sustain her. She saw only hints of Maman in those eyes, those cheekbones. And it haunted her, just like the house.

'How are you today?' said Beatrice.

'I am feeling stronger, now that I have seen you.' Queenie's face wore a complex expression, a mixture of pity, compassion and desperation.

'Good,' said Beatrice and looked away. 'I am glad you are stronger. Queenie, there is something I must tell you.'

'No more revelations,' groaned Queenie. 'I may be regaining my health, but I have not the strength to hear more revelations of secrets and so forth. I really do not have the strength for it, my dear. Can't you see that?'

'Nothing like that,' said Beatrice, with patience. 'It is hard to say, though. But it must be said. I cannot stay here.'

'What do you mean, my love?'

Hearing the word 'love' made Beatrice pause. She had always had her mother's love and now that it was gone, she had but one person left in the world who truly adored her. But it was not enough to dent the hard shell she had grown since the fire. It would not stop her from what she felt she must do.

'I mean that I must go away. I wish to accompany Uncle Cyril on his trip to America.'

'But no!' Queenie sputtered. Jenkins must have been waiting nearby, as she came through the doorway and approached the bed, shooting Beatrice a testy glance, before taking Queenie's hand and saying, 'Hush now. Don't upset yourself.'

'Leave us, Jenkins!' snapped Queenie. Beatrice saw in that moment that Queenie had not lost her steely nature entirely. Jenkins was used to such rough handling and simply lifted her hands with forbearance and left the room, closing the door behind her. 'Now, Bea, listen to me.'

Queenie pushed herself up in bed and Beatrice went to help her, but was waved away by a dismissive hand. 'A terrible thing has happened. An awful, irreversible thing. You have lost your mother. She was the centre of your world, I know that. It will take much time to heal and you will always grieve for her, I know that too. I have lost someone I loved more than myself and I still think of her now, my dear sister. The loss will never leave you, it is true.'

Beatrice could feel the need to weep rise in her, but she forced it down. She had to remain hard now, if she had a hope of getting through this conference with her plans intact.

'Yes,' she simply said.

'But that is no reason to run away. One must face it and cope with it. Take all the time you need to grieve.

And after that period has passed, once we both feel stronger and more able to face up to matters, as we will, then it will be time to make plans and go out into the world again. And we will have many plans, I can assure you. Life will go on. Until then, the best place for you is here.'

'I cannot stay here,' said Beatrice, calm yet firm. 'I am telling you this with a clear head. This is not the grief talking. It is my survival. If I stay here, I will go mad.'

'Child, do not say that word!' Queenie cried. Beatrice saw true fear in her eyes.

'But I mean it. I surely will. This place is haunted.'

'What?' gasped Queenie. Her hands began to shake and Beatrice took one and stroked it as she went on.

'This house, this town. Everywhere I could go, I would see Maman in my memories. If I went back to Paris, it would be the same. And if I stay here, in this house, everywhere I look in this house I see him in my recollections.'

'See who?'

'Owen Malone.'

'The boy who saved you from the fire? Well, yes, that was a sad loss after he had been so brave to help you. But why on earth . . . ?'

'We were friends, I told you that. But it was more. We were in love.'

Queenie snatched her hand away. 'What nonsense is this?'

'It was not nonsense. We loved each other. We hoped to marry one day.'

'Over my dead body!' cried Queenie.

Beatrice suddenly felt very tired. She had no fight in her for one of their arguments about class and wealth and all that business. She saw the world through a different lens than her great-grandmother and she had not the interest or desire to educate this old woman in its use.

'It hardly matters now, does it? Now that he is dead.'

There was a silence between them. Beatrice imagined that Queenie's head was filling with feverish thoughts, while her own remained clean and clear as a glass of cool water.

'My sweet child, I am sorry to hear that you have lost not one but two people who were . . . dear to you. But let me say again that the answer to this is to cleave to those you have left, those who love you more than life itself. To me, Beatrice. Stay with me.'

'No,' said Beatrice, hearing the iron tone in her voice and surprised by it. 'I will not be staying. I will be going to America in three days. I will ask my maid Dinah if she is willing to come with me. And hopefully, if she agrees, we will travel on the ship with Cyril.'

'But you've never liked Cyril!' cried Queenie, seeming to pluck at any argument now to prevent her.

'That is true. But he is simply a means to an end. Someone to accompany me. A reason to be in America and not here, for a while at least, until I have blown all the cobwebs away and feel ready to return, rejuvenated. It is what I want and what I need. I am old enough to make my own decisions now. I am an orphan and a grown woman. This is what I have chosen and it is what I will do.'

Queenie turned her head away, but Beatrice carried on. 'I am sorry to sound so harsh, but I needed to make you understand. I am telling you in no uncertain terms that I cannot stay here.'

'So you have said.' Queenie's voice was cold.

'Great-grandmother.' There was no reply. 'Queenie, please. Look at me.'

Queenie turned and Beatrice saw the face she had known so well in their arguments of the past, which now seemed like a lifetime ago. Queenie's chin jutted out and her mouth was set in a hard line.

'We are very alike,' said Beatrice and smiled faintly at her. 'We are stubborn women. But we are strong. And we will prevail. We will survive this. And I will come back to you, renewed. But for now, I cannot stay here with you and you cannot come with me. I will go and you will agree it. Because you love me, as I love you.'

Beatrice saw her great-grandmother's eyes fill with tears and spill over, running down the rivulets of her face and into her white halo of hair. But Queenie shook them away and took Beatrice's hands, patting them firmly and nodding her head.

'Go then, if you must. Obstinate child. And make sure that when you return, you are ready to be the woman I need you to be. My legacy. My future.'

Queenie was up and about. She had felt stronger that March morning than she had in months. Jenkins came in to find her seated in a stiff new wing-backed chair by the window of her bedroom, looking out upon the budding woodland surrounding the old brickmaster's house. Everything in the house was new and uncomfortable. Benjamina had seen to it all. Since the fire, Benjamina had been trying to poke her nose into the King business, making a hash of it at every turn. So she instructed her daughter-in-law to take charge of the renovation of the old brickmaster's house, to keep her busy and away from the business. In just over seven months, Benjamina had managed to organise the redecoration of almost every room, excepting the kitchen and servants' quarters. Queenie surmised that Benjamina had decided that those particular rooms could wait a while, could wait till doomsday if needs be, as she didn't care a damn for them or their lowly inhabitants. Queenie disapproved of this and knew she ought to take Benjamina to task for it, but she had not had the energy for anything but existing these past months. When Beatrice and Cyril had gone to America, Queenie left the business in the hands of Brotherton and his foremen. She had gone into a kind of stupor, staying in her bed for days on end. It was similar to her mourning period after her husband's death, but this was worse, much worse. She still could not believe that her granddaughter was dead and gone and that her great-granddaughter had left her.

Jenkins came in. Dear Jenkins, her mainstay, her saviour. Queenie had been found by Jenkins on the night of the fire, on the ground by her husband's grave. Jenkins knew that Queenie had wandered there before and came straight to her when the fire had started. They had sat together, Queenie sobbing and shaking, clutching onto Jenkins as they watched the house burn. Only later could Jenkins persuade her to stand and approach the ruins and the terrible truth of what had been lost there.

Jenkins came over to her, capable and calm as ever, holding a letter.

Queenie said with anticipation, 'From the child?'

Jenkins shook her head and passed it over, then left her mistress alone to read in peace. It was not the letter Queenie wanted from Beatrice, but something else she had waited upon and was glad to see. It was from her solicitor. Weeks before, she had instructed her solicitor to act for her, sending a letter to the judge appointed in the case of arson and sedition upon the house of Southover. She was sure that the majority of the brickworkers charged had been fully involved. But there was one worker there who had been sentenced to hanging and Queenie did not want that to come to pass. She wrote to the judge, informing him that a certain Adam Jones had been an honourable man. Although he had been the head of the brickworks strike, he was a good man with a wife and child, who had always acted within the law. It was said that he had been found unconscious some way from the scene of the arson, where he had clearly taken a beating. The other arsonists had said Jones had led the attack on the house and that it was his idea to set the fire. Despite the other men implicating him in their testimonies, Jones had always maintained his innocence and that he had been there to try to stop the crime, along with Owen Malone, who was unfortunately killed in the fire. Thus, Jones's only reliable witness to his case was already dead. Jones had been convicted and sentenced to hang along with the others. Queenie explained that the evidence lay in his favour, that she had respect for him and his word, that in all their dealings he had always acted responsibly and truthfully. In short, she believed him. The letter from her solicitor which she now read informed her that the judge had commuted his sentence to transportation. He was to be sent to Australia for seven years. The others were all hanged. Queenie had read the news with satisfaction. She had saved the life of Martha's husband and the father of her child. Surely, the ghost of Blaize would be pleased with her on that account.

She had seen Blaize every day since the fire and no longer was the spirit doomed to roam outside. Blaize would now appear in her room, on the stairs, in the hallway and, most distressingly, behind Queenie in her mirror. This always made her jump fearfully and nearly gave her away to Jenkins, who assumed it was all down to the shock of the fire and everything – and everyone – that had been lost. Queenie was careful to maintain Jenkins's ignorance of her haunting. Queenie did not want any sort of word getting about to Benjamina that she was seeing things. Benjamina was on the rise these days. She could use this knowledge to finally carry out the threat the King men had made to Queenie before, of sending her to the asylum. So, whenever Queenie saw Blaize, she did her best not to flinch, not to gasp, not to cry out. She had to force herself to become accustomed to this fearful visitor and make her peace with its presence. At least the ghost's appearance had softened somewhat in these recent weeks. Blaize's spirit now did not shine so brightly, looking more like the girl she had in life, though deathly pale with those spectral blue eyes. She did not speak, just stared at Queenie, watching her closely, looking for signs of something.

'You are checking to see that your curse has come to pass,' she said to the ghost one day. 'To see that I suffer.'

Blaize had made no response, either from her mouth or within Queenie's mind. Blaize simply watched her, scrutinising her. In a strange way, her presence was oddly comforting. Queenie was aching from grief and loneliness, with the loss of Margaret and the absence of Beatrice. She had slept most of the first fortnight or so, missing Margaret's funeral, attended only by Beatrice,

Cyril, Benjamina and a few local people. She had heard from her sickbed the daily noise of Beatrice's inconsolable sobbing, assaulting the peace of the old brickmaster's house like an unattended baby. And then Beatrice had left her, gone across the ocean. Queenie was distraught about it, feeling the distance like a rent in her heart. Jenkins reminded her that Beatrice had promised to write. One letter had come from Beatrice, but it was brief and cold. It told Queenie only that the ship had arrived safely and that she would write again with news of their activities and an address in New York to which letters could be sent. But that was months ago and Queenie had only heard once from Cyril since, a short missive with the New York address. And nothing more from Beatrice. Had they had some misadventure? Were they ill or dead even? Nobody knew. America was a world away. Queenie longed for word, simply a sentence to let her know Beatrice was alive and well. But the days stretched on and nothing came.

Queenie called for Jenkins and said, 'I am feeling better today.'

'I can see that. You've colour back in your old cheeks.'

'I wish to write to Beatrice. Bring me my writing instruments and lay them out at my dressing table. I shall write it here.'

'Is that a good idea? You know how upset you get when you think about the child.'

'She is not "the child",' snapped Queenie.

'But you always call her that!' cried Jenkins, annoyed.

'She is . . . Beatrice.' Saying her name aloud was indeed difficult, and Jenkins could see this. She reached out a hand and placed it on Queenie's shoulder, who shrugged it off. 'And I wish to write to her. Now, get on with you and fetch my writing implements forthwith.'

Jenkins smiled at her and said, 'You *are* feeling better.'

As she waited for Jenkins to return, she pondered, what did she wish to say to Bea in this letter? What could she say to persuade the girl to come back, that her place was not across the blasted ocean, but here by her side? Somebody needed to unseat Benjamina and take this house and business in hand. In time, she knew she herself would grow stronger, but she needed help. Jenkins was not enough. She needed her strongest ally, her dearest one, her Beatrice. How could she say all this without sounding desperate? She had not begged for anything in five decades and she was not about to show that weakness now. At that moment, she glanced upwards and there was the spirit, behind her in the mirror, staring at her coldly. It made her jump, as ever, and she put her hand to her heart.

'Have I not suffered enough?' she muttered, dropping her eyes to the dressing table, unwilling to look upon the spirit yet again. 'Will you never leave me?'

I will, came the reply, inside her own head.

Queenie stopped and looked up. She turned around and Blaize stood close to her. It was the first time it had spoken to her since the fire.

'You will leave me, one day?'

Yes, came that inner voice again.

'When? When will you leave me?'

At the bright, good time, when sunlight will conquer moonlight.

'What does that mean? What do you mean?'

Blaize leant forward, her eyes hypnotic, her face so close now to Queenie's own. *The child will cross the bridge. The child will make one house from two. The child is the answer.*

Queenie gazed at the spirit, as she had never been this close to its beautiful face. She saw that it was transparent and subtly moving, as if its waterfall of white hair was wafted by warm air. She felt as if she could fall into its blue eyes and never stop falling. She wanted to touch it and reached out her hand, but the image of Blaize began to fade, subtly erasing itself until only a hint of its blue eyes remained and then they too had vanished.

The door opened behind the spot where Queenie had just a moment before looked upon the spirit of her dead maid. Jenkins came in and walked through the very spot Blaize had stood, oblivious to the fact. She placed the writing materials on the dressing table, then turned to look upon Queenie.

Jenkins frowned at her. 'Is this all too much? Do you wish for your bed again? You look a bit peaky, old girl.'

'No, I am well,' said Queenie, distractedly. 'I must write. Leave me now.'

'Very well,' said Jenkins and went, waiting at the door for a moment, at which Queenie gestured for her to go, so she did.

She filled out the necessaries at the top of the paper, then wrote, 'Dear Beatrice.' She thought about what she would say next. She would have to be clever in the way she framed it. She could not simply tell her great-granddaughter that a ghost had said Beatrice should come home and solve everything. Surely that is what the ghost meant, wasn't it? The child? What other child was there? Yes, Beatrice was the answer. Queenie just needed to word it with care, call up that prodigious vocabulary of hers and put it down in finely crafted sentences. She must persuade the child that her holiday in the New World was over and now it was time for her to come home.

It was the first warm day they'd had in months. Spring flowers were blooming along the fringes of the woods near Anny's house. It was a good day to sit outside and feel the sun on your face. She had spent the winter in the house, nursing her baby and speaking rarely. Peter tried to talk to her, tried to comfort her. But she only had eyes for her little one. It had been a cold winter, snow piling up against the door. Money had come from the Kings in reparation, swiftly this time, within weeks of the fire. Anny had sent it back without a word. They now only had Peter's wage coming in, as Anny was not fit to work, drained from the baby's needs and exhausted from grief. They lived as simply as they could. Peter hadn't pressured her, not for a moment, but she knew that come the spring, she'd have to start working again, making pies and taking in washing and sewing. Her little boy was seven months now and eating well. He was bonny and bright.

'He's a proper boster!' said Martha, as she came up the incline from the river path, carrying her daughter in her arms. Hettie was ten months now and toddling. She put her down and Anny reached out to her. Hettie came stumbling towards her, giggling, and those bright green eyes like her mother's bright with intent, losing interest in forward motion and staring instead at her clever feet. She stumbled and fell forward, Anny catching her, whirling her up and placing her down beside her boy on the blanket she'd spread out for them.

'He really is,' said Anny, proudly, looking at her healthy, chunky boy. Evan was delighted to see his best of friends, Hettie Jones. He rolled over from his tummy and pushed himself up onto all fours. He was crawling now, but to his constant bewilderment, could only crawl backwards and looked at Hettie in confusion as she seemed to retreat from him ever further. She toddled after him and leant down, gave him a clumsy hug, then slumped down on to her bottom. Anny picked up Evan and placed him on his bottom too, then passed them both a hunk of bread to chew on, which they did, with studied attention.

'I'll fetch you a chair,' said Anny.

'No, I'll do it. You stay there,' said Martha and went into the cottage, coming back out with a kitchen chair and placing it beside her.

'Nice to see you,' said Anny, watching the children.

'First decent weather we've had in a while,' said Martha. 'Nice to get out.'

They sat in companionable silence. They had lived together and spent so many days together, they were like sisters now. Their children were like siblings too. They had both suffered and comforted each other in the dark times. Brighter times were ahead.

'I had news today, Anny. I wanted to tell you. But I didna wanna upset you. I know you dunna like to talk about . . . that night.'

Anny frowned and reached forward, picking up the bread Evan had dropped and putting it back in his chubby hand.

'You're right. I dunna wanna talk about any of it.'

'But there is news. Good news. The best news. Can I tell you, Anny?'

Anny looked at Martha. Her green eyes were shining with emotion. Good news, she'd said. The best news. The only kind of news Anny was interested in would be that time had sent itself backwards, that the moment her son had turned to her and said, 'I'm off out', she had grabbed him and forced him to stay home. That all the Kings would have died in that fire and her Owen would have slept through the whole thing and woken up in the morning. His heart would have hurt at the loss of that girl, but it would have mended. And she would have him here, playing with his little brother on the blanket, instead of six feet under in his cold grave.

Anny said nothing. Martha would tell her anyway.

'A letter came. I couldna read it but a man on my street knew his letters and read it for me. Adam is not gonna be hanged, Anny. He is to be transported instead. Mrs King senior wrote for him and spoke up for him. He'll be going to Australia. But he wonna be hanged.'

Anny did not look at Martha. She could hear her voice crack with feeling. Martha would feel gratitude, no doubt, to God maybe, to Mrs King Senior, to providence and luck and everything. Her husband was saved.

'That is good news,' said Anny and nodded.

'I had lost all hope,' said Martha, her voice shaking now. 'I canna believe it.'

'Good,' said Anny. 'Good news.' She reached out a hand and placed it on Martha's lap. Martha took her hand and squeezed it.

'They said it'll be seven years away. Seven years. Hettie will be eight. But it's better than nothing. It's better than hanging. Anything is better than death.'

Anny felt her throat tighten. She gulped hard, to stop herself from choking. Martha glanced at her in horror at what she'd said.

'Oh, Anny!' she cried. 'Anny, I didna mean . . . I'm so sorry, Anny.'

'No,' said Anny and squeezed Martha's hand. 'Dunna tread round me on eggshells. I am all right. And this is good news. Very good news. I'm glad for you. Truly, I am.'

She had nothing else to say and could not look at Martha. She meant it, really she did. It was just so hard to be thankful for anything, now Owen was dead. It was so hard to hear gratitude to anyone or anything. It was hard to breathe, in and out, in and out. Sometimes the grief came over her like summer floods, warm and deadly, stifling her. She would gasp in it and writhe, dreaming of him and waking cruelly, with him gone and never to come back. Peter would hold her and she would push him away. And though his grief was terrible – wracked him with nightmares and hours of staring, wordless, at Owen's carved chess pieces, which he would turn over and over in trembling hands – she could not comfort him. He could not comfort her either, not for a moment. They barely looked at each other for weeks on end. She somehow blamed him, though she knew it was not his fault, none of it. He was Owen's father, though, and should've protected him somehow. She blamed herself too, for not taking Owen in hand enough, for assuming he'd listened to her properly when she told him to give up that girl. She blamed Adam Jones too, for leading him unto that place of death, secretly, and letting him run to the girl while he slept on the grass.

Surely she hated the Kings and blamed them for the fire that destroyed their home, stoking the hatred in their workers. But if truth be known, nobody was solely to blame. And others had lost terribly too. Margaret had not deserved to die. She had set Anny free from prison, after all. Anny felt with a guilty pang that even she herself shouldered more than a small part of the blame for what had happened to her own son. If she and Margaret had let go of their feud, if Anny in particular had cured her own hatred of Margaret and the other Kings, then their children might not have resorted to secrecy and lies. And perhaps Owen might still be alive. Even Owen played his part – if he had not been so brave, had not run in to a burning house to save a life, he would be with her now. His heroism was a glimmer of goodness in this tragedy, but that didn't lessen the pain.

Jenkins had come to tell her, the next day. When Anny saw her face at the door, she knew a terrible thing had come to pass. She screamed at her when the news was spoken, flew at her in a rage and had to be held back by Peter. A sharp pain came inside and she fell to the floor. The shock had shaken her so badly, she started to bleed and was taken to her bed. They all thought she'd lose the baby, grief piled on grief. But the bleeding abated, the bedrest did its work and she recovered. Anny's littl'un came quickly, on a wild and windy October evening. Peter held her on the bed as the babe came out of her, bawling away like anything. A boy. They called him Evan, a plain, solid name. He came into the world with a mother and father who adored him, and a dead brother who he would never know and who would not look upon him or hold him or marvel at the boy that would be his only brother in the world. With a brother or sister, a person need never be alone again, thought Anny, forever saddened that she'd never had one of her own, an only child to her parents, both dead and buried. But now baby Evan's brother was gone. And he was alone in the world. But what a delight he was for Anny and Peter and how they held him tight and fretted over his every moment. They began to look at each other again, their eyes shining, their new life drawing them back to each other a little more each day, step by step.

Hettie had finished her bread and Evan lost interest in his as soon as he saw Hettie stand up. Martha stood and reached over to her daughter, holding her hands to steady her. Evan gazed at his friend with unashamed adoration. Hettie took two steps towards Evan and sat down with a thump beside him. They watched each other for a moment, their serious mouths turning into smiles. Hettie reached out and put her arms about him, squeezed him clumsily and patted him on the back. They both giggled and patted each other, patting and patting. Never had patting been so hilarious. They could not stop laughing and could not stop patting.

Martha was watching Anny's face, her own a picture of concern. Martha reached out and touched Anny's cheek tenderly. The tears rolled down their faces. They did not need to speak their feelings. There was both too much to say and nothing to say.

The little ones were still laughing, both sitting on their bottoms again, patting each other's legs and arms and faces. Anny and Martha looked at them and wiped their tears away, the laughter infectious, as they chuckled at their children.

'They are proper sweethearts,' said Martha. 'Maybe they'll marry one day.'

Anny gazed at her beautiful son. He could not find a sweeter girl than Hettie, a nicer mother-in-law than Martha. But no, that was not what Anny had planned for her son. Wherever his heart might lead him, she would not make the same mistake again. She would raise him to want more from life than this, than the work of his father and his dead brother, than the grind of daily servitude. She would raise him to turn his back on this godforsaken place ruled over by the cursed Kings and make a new life somewhere else, somewhere new, somewhere far away and safe from the secrets of Ironbridge.

Epilogue

7th July 1859

112 Summer Street
Brooklyn
New York City
New York State
The United States of America

Dear Queenie,

I hope this letter finds you well. I have missed our chats so much and our card-playing contests! The evenings feel lonely without you to keep me company. It is a strange new world here in America, but also one that is full of interest and excitement. I miss Ironbridge and I miss you very much, dear Queenie. Yet despite this, I am learning to see this new land as an opportunity for me to start again and its very newness allows me to do that, to move on and to put the past behind me. Grief is a terrible thing and, though I know the losses I've suffered will never leave me, I believe I heal a little more each day.

It was so good to receive your letter and to hear news from Ironbridge. It was almost as if we were once again seated around the card table, sharing gossip, with Maman just steps away, playing at the piano. I wish we could turn back the clock and all be together once more. Sadly, time does not move in reverse.

And I'm afraid this is the reason I must disappoint you. Your request for me to return to you and take my place beside you, running the business, is a kind and generous offer, and one that I do not take lightly, I promise you. But I feel as if returning to Ironbridge would be like trying to travel back in time, to capture something that is lost to us now. This is something I cannot do.

Maman brought me to Ironbridge to give me a better life and you, Queenie, offered me the same idea, a life of comfort and prospects. I love you both for only wanting the best for me, but wealth and comfort isn't enough to sustain the soul. I was in need of friendship and companionship. I was in need of a soulmate with whom I could share my feelings. I found it in Owen Malone. It is hard to write his name without weeping. But you see, I have no regrets about my feelings for him. I truly loved Owen. Not a fleeting, girlish desire. I loved him and wanted a future with him. But that was not to be.

I know you may now be recoiling in horror from such a statement. I know what you feel, and what my mother felt, about relationships between the classes. But I have to disagree with you, then and now. For I believe that class is something we make, we construct out of our own false ideas of what is right and proper. But that is all it is: a construct. Class is something we build to protect ourselves, to tell ourselves that those who have and those who have not are a different breed. This makes us feel better about being rich and allows us to dismiss the rights of those who are not. I now believe with all of my heart that this is wrong. You will say it is the French in me, the influence of that revolutionary nation in my upbringing. You will say I am like my mother once was, young and foolish. My mother felt she was proven wrong. But I disagree. I believe that the class system we live by has robbed us all of those we love. The treatment of the brickworkers, the strike and its aftermath, the crimes committed on both sides, the separation of classes into masters and servants. All of this creates a society of conflict, envy and hatred. And it has directly led to the deaths of those we love. Anny Malone has lost her son Owen. I have lost my mother and you your granddaughter. And now, I fear, I must tell you that you will lose me, now and for the foreseeable future, at least.

Here, in America, I see a different way of life. To be sure, there are the rich and the poor, and the gap between them is just as wide as in England. But there is a different idea about it here, a different way of looking at it. If you speak to people here about their lives, there is hope for change. There is an idea of what can be if one works hard and believes. In England I saw some of that spirit in the brickworkers when they went on strike. Yes, they were opposed to you and I sympathise with you on that count. I know how hard it was for you to run that business fairly and in a way that made a profit. But the wrongs that were perpetrated against those workers were unacceptable; they were crimes in their own way and had to be paid for. You lost those you love and your house. They lost their hope. I see hope for improvement all around me here, not only between the workers and the masters but between men and women and people of all races. For America is a mixture of all types and shapes and sizes and colours, more so even than Paris, and a thousand times more than Ironbridge.

You see, there are people here who are fighting for change. I am living in New York with Dinah – remember Dinah, my maid? She is my maid no longer and we live together as friends. She is a fine artist – did you ever know that about her? One day, she drew a map for me to the very house you live in now and it was a work of art. I love to write and she loves to draw. Some friends we met on our ship to New York were in the newspaper business. On our arrival, Dinah and I were invited to stay with them. Uncle Cyril has gone to Pennsylvania with his companion James Melton, yet I decided to stay here at the comfortable home of our journalist companions, who have made Dinah and me so comfortable and welcome. Encouraged by them, Dinah began sketching scenes from the streets hereabouts and I wrote descriptions to go with them, a visitor's views of American life. We now have these published in a New York journal called *Street and Smith's New York Weekly*. It is a charming publication, full of fascinating facts and amusing anecdotes. Dinah and I are now members of the profession of journalists! Yes, we are paid for our work and we love it. Just yesterday, we met a man at a gathering who was once a slave here in America. He spoke of the rights of negroes and the rights of women too. He publishes his own newspaper and his name is Frederick Douglass. The sub-heading of his paper reads thus: *Right is of no Sex — Truth is of no Colour — God is the Father of us all, and we are all Brethren.* To read these words moved me very much. I said to Dinah afterwards that there would only be one thing I would add to it and that is this: Equality is of no Class. Just as there are movements here to unite all people, whatever colour or sex they happen to be, I believe in the movement to unite people of all classes. I believe that mankind will not progress if we continue in our current unequal and unfair distinctions between rich and poor.

All of this must sound like heresy to you, I am sure. But it sounds like music to me. Times are changing here. There is talk of war. Many do not agree with me. Many agree with you. Others hate and will kill for their beliefs. I hope it does not come to war. But if it does, I know *what side I will be on. And sadly, it will not be the same side as you, dear Queenie, or of any King. I am not a King. I am an Ashford. Though I love you, I cannot come to you. Though I wish you well, I will not live your life. I love you very much, Queenie, but I cannot accept the life that you live. There is a portion of my heart that will always be with you, that makes me yearn to return to you. But I know that ultimately I would be unhappy and that I would make you unhappy too. It would never work. It is a hard choice I make, but I must make it.*

I will write to you often and share my new life here with you on paper. I wish to make my living through words and will use words to conjure up my life here for you. I hope you will do the same and keep in touch with news from Ironbridge. It will always be a special place for me and I am so very fond of it. Some of the best people I have ever met are Ironbridge folk. But it was never my home. It could have been, if events had not turned out as they did. Instead, I spent a few heady months there, ending in unimaginable loss. I am afraid that it has become the seat of my pain and I cannot bear to live there again.

Thank you for offering to make me the sole recipient of the King fortune. But I tell you now, I do not want your money. I do not want any part of the King way of life. I will never take a penny of that money. Once, a lifetime ago, I spoke with Owen Malone about brickmaking. He told me, 'There is blood in those bricks.' Now that you know about Owen and my love for him, you will understand that I believe there is blood in that money. I want none of it. If you make me your heir, I will give it all away. Thus, please do not give me your money. Find someone else deserving who wants and needs it more than me. Assist those you have wronged. If you want to make it right, you need to do something to modify both your business and yourself. I believe you have it in you, Queenie. I have seen the goodness in you.

As I write this letter, I realise that today is the 7th July and is Hettie Jones's birthday. Exactly one year ago, I stood in Anny and Peter Malone's cottage and heard that child come into the world. My Owen was still with us. It was one of the most precious moments of my life. If you wish to contribute in any way to my happiness, then do not offer me money. Instead, help that child and others like her. Small alterations in your own life can lead to huge changes in the lives of others; you can bridge the divide. Improve the lot in life of the poor, in Ironbridge, in Shropshire, in England and the whole of society.

I will live my life here from now on. I wish you all the very best with yours.

Love and hope always,
from your great-granddaughter,

Bea

Acknowledgements

Tony Mugridge, expert artisan brickmaker, for teaching me how to make a brick by hand and giving me access to his incredibly detailed knowledge of nineteenth century brick and tile manufacture. Thanks also to Fliss Burke, for making me feel so welcome.

Shroppiemon, for offering dialect advice at any hour, reading the final draft, and tagging me in a huge range of useful posts on the marvellous Memories of Shropshire page on Facebook.

Stephen Dewhirst of the Broseley Local History Society, for extensive help with brickmaking resources, including contemporary newspaper reports, as well as reading the final draft and his helpful comments.

Jim Dale of BBC Radio Shropshire for the fascinating and fun interview on brickmaking at Tony's house.

Joanne Smith, Museum Registrar for The Ironbridge Gorge Museum Trust, for help with brickmaking resources, including the Blists Hill brickmaking materials and suggestions of clayworker books.

Karen Young at the Shropshire Archives, for help with items on brickmaking in the archives.

Chris Blanchett of Buckland Books (now retired), for directing me to the British Brick Society.

Mike Moore of Moore Books, for help with brickmaking titles.

Becca Burnton, Jessica Ryn, Jean Fullerton and Theresa Therrien for invaluable help with midwifery and obstetrics questions.

Jayne McDermott, Lin Keska and Claire Powick Hainsworth for information regarding the Benthall Waterwheel, posted in Shropshire Tales, History and Memories on Facebook.

Early readers of this book: Sue White, Lucy Adams, Lynn Downing, Pauline Lancaster and Louisa Treger for your quick reading and wonderful support, as ever.

Megan Prince of the Ironbridge Bookshop, young and talented bookseller extraordinaire, for marvellous support for the books and perfect bookselling at events and beyond. Thank you for looking after me so well at the events too, Meg.

The Ironbridge Festival of Imagination, for asking me to take part in events at the bookshop and at the Meadow Inn, including Simon Fletcher for organising the super Country Voices event.

The Friends of the Ironbridge Gorge Museum Trust, for inviting me to talk to them about the research for the Ironbridge Saga. Particular thanks to Geraldine King, Judy

Mondon, David De Haan and Glyn Bowen. Special thanks to the audience, who made me feel so welcome and asked excellent questions, as well as giving me such useful information and advice about coal mining for the next book.

All of the Facebook Shropshire groups for continued support of the Ironbridge Saga, as well as advice on all things Shropshire, from bricks to coal to wimberries. Particular thanks to administrators Lin Keska, Marcus Keane, Chris Hughes and Margaret Ann Roberts.

Tara Loder, my wonderful editor, who always goes above and beyond and is such an expert on character and plotting; these books would not be the same without her magnificent input.

Everyone at Bonnier Books, with special thanks to Claire Johnson-Creek, Katie Lumsden, Ellen Turner and Sahina Bibi.

My excellent agent Laura Macdougall, who continues to support me and my career at every turn with such brilliance.

My writing friends in the author community, particularly those in the Prime Writers and on Facebook, who provide companionship, advice, support and laughs.

Bookbloggers and readers, who have shared their appreciation of the Ironbridge Saga, online and beyond. A huge thank you to all of you – too numerous to mention individually – for reading and talking about the books, attending events and coming up to talk to me, as well as for so many kind messages.

Colin and Poppy, for listening to me go on and on about Shropshire stuff and word counts and edits, and not falling asleep as I do so. Mostly, for understanding the writer's life and always supporting me through it.

My lovely family and dear friends, for being there always, through hard times and easy times.

MEMORY LANE

Welcome to the world of *Mollie Walton*!

Keep reading for more from Mollie Walton, to discover a recipe that features in this novel and to find out more about Mollie Walton's inspiration for the book . . .

We'd also like to introduce you to MEMORY LANE, our special community for the very best of saga writing from authors you know and love, and new ones we simply can't wait for you to meet. Read on and join our club!

MEMORY LANE

www.MemoryLane.club

MEMORY LANE

Dear Reader,

Thanks so much for reading the second instalment in the Ironbridge Saga. I first had the idea for the saga when standing on the iron bridge itself and I've returned to the area many times since, not only for research but also for the love of it. Continuing the story of the Woodvines and the Kings was a wonderful experience for me, as I'd missed their company since finishing *The Daughters of Ironbridge*. I wanted to know what they were getting up to next! As with the first book, the research I needed to do was extensive. While iron was the main industry of *The Daughters of Ironbridge*, brickmaking became the focus of the second book. Since discovering the wonderful Shropshire groups on Facebook, I started by asking for advice there and was immediately recommended by several people to talk to Tony Mugridge. Tony is an artisan brickmaker and all-round expert on the history of brickmaking. Well, not only was Tony able to start me off in my research with various ideas, he also invited me to come to his workshop and make a brick myself. Of course, I agreed!

I visited his house in Madeley and met him and his partner Felicity Burke. They were both so kind and welcoming. Once in Tony's workshop, he showed me the lump of clay we were about to transform into a brick. He gave me a brick mould and showed me how to throw the clay into it, then beat it into the mould with a brickbat. It's like a short, stubby cricket bat and you could certainly do some damage with it. Once the brick was flattened down, he showed me how to slice off the top with a tool that looked a little like a mixture between a cheese-cutter and a bow for arrows. Lastly, we whacked the mould to release the brick and there it was, in all its glory: my very first brick! I was proud of it, as it actually looked brick-like. It took us several minutes to do it. But then Tony told me that a brickmaker in the nineteenth century would have had to produce around a thousand of these a day. A thousand!

At that moment, it truly came home to me what back-breaking work being a brickmaker was. Not only that, but also conditions at the brickyards were awful. The work was long and arduous, for very little pay. Small children were employed to carry the lumps of clay. The masters could drop wages and lengthen hours, whilst workers went on strike to improve conditions, sometimes with but often without success. It was then I knew that I'd chosen the right industry for this story. It was full of natural drama. Also, the topic was something that everybody had experience of; all of us have lived and worked in buildings made from bricks at some point in our lives. Furthermore, it is a subject of which many of us may be quite ignorant – that is, the actual process it takes to make a brick, from digging the clay, to moulding the brick, to firing it in the kilns, then transporting it around the country. It's so vital yet so often we think nothing of it when we see a house. I wanted to celebrate the hard work of those people who created the bricks that have built houses in which we still live and work today, still standing firm due to their expertise.

My experiences working with this expert artisan brickmaker was another in a line of wonderful meetings I've had with local people in the writing of these books. Having come to the Ironbridge area four years ago for the first time, to visit my brother and his wife, I've had a lot of contact with Shropshire folk, particularly through the Facebook groups that celebrate all things Shropshire. What I've learnt is that Shropshire folk are truly special. Their generosity is exceptional and their love for their county is second to none. I feel honoured to have met and corresponded with such a wide range of Shropshire locals in the writing of these books. I will be forever grateful for their kindness and warmth.

I hope that my stories have helped in some small part to throw a spotlight on this beautiful part of the world. If you have never visited, I urge you to do so! And if you do, when you walk across the iron bridge, perhaps spare a thought for the countless poor folk who lived near it and worked all their lives to create the Industrial Revolution, the fruits of which we enjoy today. Without them, there would be no iron, no coal, no bricks and all the rest. We owe them so much and it's an honour to tell their stories.

Glossary of Shropshire Dialect Terms

All drawed out: all dressed up
Anna: haven't
Arr: yes
Bait: food, a meal
Blackleg: a worker who goes back to their job despite the strike
Chunnering: talking too much
Boster: healthy, chunky baby
Butties: mates
Canna: can't
Cwtch: a cuddle or a hug
Danker me!: I'll be damned!
Darter: daughter
Didna: didn't
Drearing: loitering
Dunna: don't
From off: from outside the local area
Gunna: going to
Hadna: had not
Hasna: has not
Inna: isn't
Larruping: beating someone up
Mon: man, often used as a term of address to males
Mun: must
Nowt: nothing

Ow bist: how are you?
Owd: old
Ratlin: runt of the litter
Roadster: tramp
Scab: an outsider brought in to replace striking workers
Scrinch: a morsel
Sebunctious: something particularly special or good
Shanna: shall not
Shoulda: should have
Shouldna: should not/should not have
Singing out of the same book: courting
Summat: something
The Lord hasna finished him: historical term for intellectual disability
Unket: lonely
Wanna: want to
Wasna: wasn't
Werrit: worry
Wonna: won't
Wouldna: would not/would not have
Yer: you

MEMORY LANE

Wimberry Pie

Also known as Mucky Mouth Pie, wimberry pie is a kind of fruit pie that Anny makes for her customers, alongside her savoury fidget pies. Wimberries are traditional Shropshire fruit, picked on the hills and harvested in the late summertime. These berries go by many regional names around Britain, including wimberries, whinberries, windberries, bilberries, blaeberries, hurtleberries, fraughans, black-heart berries and myrtle berries. If you can't find wimberries, you can use blueberries, raspberries or blackberries in this recipe instead. You can also replace half of the wimberries with apples, if you prefer.

You will need:

For the shortcrust pastry:
6oz plain flour, and extra for dusting
3oz butter, diced
2–3 tbsp cold water

For the filling:
2 tbsp honey
½ tsp cinnamon
1 tbsp lemon juice
3 tbsp demerara sugar
5oz wimberries

Method:

1. Preheat the oven to 200°C/180°C/gas mark 6.
2. Sieve the flour into a large bowl, then add the diced butter. Rub it in between your fingertips, until the mixture resembles breadcrumbs.
3. Add the water, and mix together until it forms a smooth dough.
4. Knead this on a floured surface, then divide the pastry in two.
5. Roll out the first section into a circle about 1cm thick, and wide enough to line a pie dish or pastry tin. Press lightly into the dish, and trim off the edges.
6. In a separate bowl, mix together the honey, cinnamon, lemon juice and 2 tbsp of demerara sugar, then carefully stir in the wimberries.
7. Pour this mixture into the pastry case.
8. Roll the second section of pastry out into another circle, and lay on top to form the lid.
9. Brush the edges with water, and press them down to meet the pastry case below. Trim off the edges, then cut a small hole in the centre of the lid.
10. Bake for 25–30 minutes until the pastry has lightly browned.
11. Remove from the oven and sprinkle with the remaining demerara sugar.
12. Enjoy!